If it's not magic, she ⟨barcode: D1488582⟩ **it?**

She had no answer.

Giving in to impulse, Annja held the sword in both hands high over her head. Almost immediately, lightning reached down and touched the tip in a pyrotechnic blaze of sparks. For a moment the blade glowed cobalt-blue.

Annja dropped the sword, grateful she hadn't been electrocuted.

When she inspected the sword, it was unmarked. If anything, the blade seemed cleaner, stronger. Energy clung to the weapon. She felt it thrumming inside her.

Soaked and awed, Annja stood for a moment in the center of the city and knew that no one saw her. She was invisible in the night. No one knew what she held. She didn't even know herself. She breathed deeply, smelling the salt from the Atlantic and knew she'd somehow stumbled upon one of the greatest mysteries in history.

"Why me?" she shouted into the storm.

There was no answer, only the rolling thunder and lightning.

The
LEGEND

**...THE ENGLISH COMMANDER TOOK
JOAN'S SWORD AND RAISED IT HIGH.**

The broadsword, plain and unadorned,
gleamed in the firelight. He put the tip against
the ground and his foot at the center of the blade.
The broadsword shattered, fragments falling
into the mud. The crowd surged forward,
peasant and soldier, and snatched the shards
from the trampled mud. The commander tossed
the hilt deep into the crowd.
Smoke almost obscured Joan, but she continued
praying till the end, until finally the flames climbed
her body and she sagged against the restraints.

Joan of Arc died that fateful day in France,
but her legend and sword are reborn....

ROGUE ANGEL

Alex Archer

RENAISSANCE

A GOLD EAGLE BOOK FROM

W⊕RLDWIDE®

TORONTO • NEW YORK • LONDON
AMSTERDAM • PARIS • SYDNEY • HAMBURG
STOCKHOLM • ATHENS • TOKYO • MILAN
MADRID • WARSAW • BUDAPEST • AUCKLAND

First edition May 2008

ISBN-13: 978-0-373-62140-8
ISBN-10:   0-373-62140-X

CONTENTS

DESTINY

PROLOGUE

Rouen, France
30 May 1431

Out of breath, feeling as though the hounds of Hell pursued him, Roux whipped his horse mercilessly. The beast barely kept its feet on the muddy road. Bloody slaver covered its muzzle, streaking its neck and chest.

Straw-thatched houses lined the road, interrupted by the occasional stone building. He guided the horse between them, yanking the bridle hard and causing the animal to stumble.

"They're going to kill her," Durand Lassois had reported only a few days earlier. The big warrior had tears running down his scarred face and trickling through his black beard. "It's the damned English, Roux. They're trying her as a heretic. They're going to convict her and burn her at the stake. There's nothing we can do."

Roux hadn't believed it. The girl was marked for important things. She was a guardian of innocents, a true power to be reckoned with in the mortal world. The English were greedy bastards and fools besides.

He still didn't believe the girl would be killed now. He'd sensed the strength within her. Seventeen years old and she'd led men into battle at the besieged city of Orléans two years ago.

That had been the beginning of a string of victories that had lifted the English yoke from French necks. Her efforts, her conviction and her leadership brought the crown to the dauphin and allowed him to be crowned Charles VII.

Hypnotized by the power and a chance to negotiate peace, the new king had failed to act quickly and lost the tide of the war. The girl had been wounded during the attack on Paris. The French army never regained its momentum. She was captured during the attempt to lift the siege at Compiegne in May of last year. For the ensuing twelve months, the English at Rouen had held her.

Another half-dozen turns and traffic choked the roads leading to the market. Oxen-pulled carts, horses and asses stood in disarray. French peasants who had buried their hatred of the English in fear for their lives and armored English soldiers who pursued French maidens shared the road.

Roux jerked the reins and brought his horse to a stop. The flashing hooves threw mud over bystanders as the exhausted animal sagged to its rear haunches. Roux vaulted from the horse and landed in the mud.

Garin brought his mount to a similar sliding halt inches shy of colliding with Roux. The younger man's dismount was not nearly so elegant. His foot caught in a stirrup and he tumbled into the mud. When he rose, he was covered. He cursed in German as he tried to brush the muck from him.

Four inches over six feet in height, Roux's apprentice drew immediate attention because of his size. His straight black hair hung to his broad shoulders. Handsome features and his square-cut jaw, devoid of a beard because he was vain about his looks, drew a second glance from every female in the crowd. Magnetic black eyes held challenge and ferocity.

Gathering his riding cloak about him, Roux strode through the crowd. Grudgingly, people parted before him. He carried himself like a lord, though he was no such thing.

He looked like an old man, with white hair and a white goatee. His skin was fair, red from the sun and the wind during the long ride. Though not of the best quality, his clothing—pants, blouse and knee-high boots—showed signs of being well kept. At his side, he carried a saber with a worn handle.

Garin trailed Roux, swaggering through the crowd. He wore a

long broadsword scabbarded down his back so the hilt jutted up over his right shoulder.

Only a moment later, Roux stood at the front of the crowd.

The English had tied the maiden to a pillar in the marketplace. She stood atop a pile of wood and more logs were piled up to her calves. Her executioner had also outfitted her with faggots, small bundles of sticks and straw that were tied to her calves, thighs, hands, torso and hair.

Her death was intended to be cruel and painful.

Sickness twisted Roux's stomach. Steeling himself, he watched with grim expectation.

She will not burn, he told himself. She will not die.

This is not her destiny.

Still, for all that was in him to believe, he doubted. The young woman had always been stronger in her convictions. Her faith was one of the things that had drawn him to her. That, and the raw, un-bridled power that clung to her. Roux had never been able to with-stand the pull of that force.

As she faced death, clad in the same male clothing she'd worn so proudly in battle, she stood solemn and unshaken.

She didn't come here to die, Roux told himself. She's going to be all right.

"We can't just stand here and let them kill her," Garin said softly at his side.

"What do you propose, apprentice?" Roux demanded. "Should we rush in, you and I, and slay all the English warriors and free her?"

"No. We can't do that. They would only kill us." Garin's answer was immediate.

Pierre Cauchon, the presiding judge, stepped forward and read out the charges. Stern and dogmatic, he accused the warrior maiden of heresy and of being opposed to the church. He went on to add that she was a bloodthirsty killer and demon possessed besides. No mention was made of his own part in the bloody Cabochien Revolt in 1413 or his defense of the assassination of the duke of Orléans in 1407.

At the bailiff's command, soldiers lit fires along the pyre. Flames eagerly leaped up and twisted through the jumble of wood. The stench of smoke filled the air.

The young woman cried out, but not for help. She asked only that her friends hold up a crucifix so that she could look upon it. Two men did. In a strong, brave voice, the maid prayed to her Savior, asking for the aid of the saints.

You can't just let her die, Roux thought. Not like this. She's meant for more than this. His promise to her and to himself haunted him.

Unable to stand anymore, Roux surged forward. "Enough!" he cried, and he put all the long years of command he'd learned into his voice.

Heads turned in his direction. Several townspeople drew back from him fearfully as the English soldiers converged on him with drawn swords and maces.

Roux drew his saber with a rasp of metal. "Set her free!" he thundered. "By God, you'll set her free or you'll know the fiery pits of Hell yourselves for judging her so harshly!"

Before he could take another step, something crashed into the back of Roux's skull. The English soldiers took away his saber and kicked him dozens of times, breaking his ribs and the fingers of his right hand. They stopped short of killing him.

While Roux was being beaten, the English commander took the maiden warrior's famed sword and raised it high. The broadsword, plain and unadorned, gleamed in the firelight. He put the tip against the ground and his foot at the center of the blade.

The broadsword shattered, falling into fragments in the mud.

Peasant and soldier pushed forward and snatched the shards from the trampled mud. The commander tossed the hilt deep into the crowd.

Smoke obscured almost everything by then, but Roux still saw her. She continued praying until the end, until finally the flames climbed her body and she sagged against the restraints.

Roux wept, barely hanging on to consciousness.

"Did you see it?" an English soldier shouted suddenly. The frantic note in his voice drew the attention of his comrades away from Roux. "Did you see the dove? A white dove left her body at the moment she died!"

Consternation filled the crowd. They drew back from the blazing pyre. The French separated from the English. In that moment, Roux couldn't hold on any longer. He sunk into familiar inky blackness.

1

Lozère, France
Present Day

She was being followed.

Annja Creed knew that from experience. She'd been followed before. Stalked, actually. On two occasions—once in Venice and once outside Berlin—the experience had ended in violence.

"Wait," Annja told her young guide.

Avery Moreau, seventeen years old and French, his hair a thick black shock and his demeanor sulky, stopped. Thin and lanky, dressed in his American jeans, red pullover and gray Nike hoodie, he didn't look as if he'd be particularly helpful in a physical encounter.

"What's wrong?" he asked.

"I want to look at this." Annja stood in front of the shop window and gazed with interest.

The young man glanced at the window, then back at her. "You're thinking about going fishing?"

For the first time, Annja took her attention from the reflection of the two men following her and really looked at the shop window. Pierre's Rods And Flies was written in French.

It was funnier, Annja supposed, in English. Kind of an unintentional double entendre. But it was a bad cover to stop and check out the guys following her.

"In case I stay up on the mountain," Annja said.

"You're going to stay in the mountains?"

Actually, Annja wasn't planning on that. She had a day hike in mind. But she was getting a later start than she'd have liked. Finding provisions and supplies in Lozère was proving more difficult than she had expected.

"I'm not planning to," Annja replied, "but I've learned to be ready for anything."

The two men following her were in their early twenties, no more than two or three years younger than she was. They looked like hard guys off the street, dressed in leather jackets and jeans. Attitude rolled off them in waves. An old woman carrying a bag of groceries crossed the street to avoid them.

They weren't, Annja decided, the kind of guys who normally hung out in a small tourist town like Lozère. Metropolitan arenas seemed to be their more likely hunting grounds. They looked like the kind of men a single woman in a strange place would do better to avoid.

She wasn't afraid, though. At five feet ten inches, athletic and full-figured, and in shape from running, climbing, and martial arts, she knew she could take care of herself. Her chestnut-colored hair was tied back. Wraparound sunglasses hid her amber-green eyes.

However, she was worried about the young man with her. Avery Moreau didn't look as if he'd had to fight thieves in his short lifetime.

What are you doing here? Annja wondered. Why would anyone be following me?

"What will you do with fishing gear?" Avery asked.

"If I get trapped in the mountains," Annja explained, "by a storm or by bears—" She looked at him. "You did say there were bears, didn't you?"

He shook his head. "Wolves. I said there were wolves."

Annja nodded. "Right. Wolves, then."

The two men weren't going away. They stood across the street and tried to look inconspicuous. It didn't work. They might as well have been standing there with fireworks going off and wearing Scottish kilts in a Marilyn Monroe pose.

Who are you? Annja wondered.

She'd been in France for two days. She was rooming at a bed and breakfast outside of Lozère. So far, no one had bothered her.

But that was before she'd come into town and started asking questions about La Bête. The creature was one of French legend and its mystery had never been solved. She'd come to Lozère in an attempt to solve it.

And to get paid by *Chasing History's Monsters*, the cable show she did occasional pieces for to subsidize legitimate work in her field. It was strange how archaeologists could get paid more for something that remained mysterious, riddled with myth, and might never have been factual at all than for an honest look at history.

During the past two days, however, the local populace had learned that "the insane American woman"—they didn't know how well she spoke French or how acute her hearing was—was seeking the legendary monster.

"Well?" Avery prompted. He acted surly, as if he had something else he'd rather be doing.

"What?" Annja asked.

"Did you want me to take you to your car?" Avery had arranged to rent a truck that Annja would drive up into the Cévennes Mountains.

"In a moment." Annja nodded toward the shop. "Let's go inside."

She led the way, opening the door and causing the little bell over it to tinkle. Avery followed glumly.

Inside, the shop had a wooden floor and a simple demeanor. Shelves built into the walls held lures, line, reels and other fishing gear. Racks in the center of the room held up waterproof pants, vests and shirts. Farther back, displays of rubber boots, waders, seines and other equipment filled the floor.

"May I help you, miss?" a tiny old man behind the scarred counter asked. He polished his glasses on his shirt, then blinked at her and waited.

"Yes," Annja replied in French. "I'm looking for a tent pole."

"You don't have a tent," Avery said.

The old man pointed to one of the back corners.

Annja spotted a bin containing wooden dowels an inch in

diameter and four feet long. They were treated and varnished, improving their strength against wear and the elements.

Retreating to the back of the shop, Annja took one of the rods from the bin. She spun it experimentally for a moment, moving it from one hand to the other, and found the dowel acceptable.

She returned to the counter. "This is great. I'll take it."

The old man rang up the price.

Annja paid and thanked him, then asked, "Is there a back way out of here?"

"Mademoiselle?" The old man's gaze told her he didn't think he'd heard her right.

"A back way." Annja pointed to the rear of the store. "A way out into the alley?"

"Yes, but why would you want to—?"

Annja laid a hundred euros on the counter. "Please," she said.

The old man pointed with one hand and picked up the money with the other.

Annja grabbed Avery by the arm, guiding her guide for the moment.

"What are you doing?" he protested, pushing her hand away.

"Trying to keep you from getting hurt," she answered.

"Hurt?" Avery brushed at his hoodie, smoothing the lines.

"Didn't you see the two guys across the street?" Annja threaded her way through the displays at the back of the shop.

A small metal door let out into the alley. She opened the door and went through.

"No," Avery said defensively.

Gazing back, Annja saw that the two men were in motion, heading for the shop. "The two guys who were following us?" she persisted.

Avery shook his head.

He's just a kid, Annja reminded herself. He's probably never seen a mugging in his life. She took a quick breath.

"Okay," she said, "there were two guys following us for the last three blocks." It might have been longer than that. She wasn't sure. She was still jetlagged from the long trip from New York.

"Oh," Avery said, sounding confused.

The alley was narrow and the walls of the two adjacent buildings were crooked. Stones jutted out in a random pattern.

"I want you to go to the car," Annja said.

"Aren't you coming?" Avery looked worried.

"In a second." Annja slid her backpack from her shoulders and handed it to him.

The bag carried her cameras, journals, maps and pocket PC. Replacing those items would cost a few thousand dollars, but she figured they were safer in Avery's hands than hers for the next few minutes.

"Take this to the car. I'll be there shortly." Annja put a hand on his thin shoulder and gave him a gentle push. "Please, I want you to be safe."

Clasping the backpack to his chest, Avery looked uncertain.

"I'll be there," Annja told him. "In a minute. Now go."

Reluctantly, the young man left. In a handful of steps he was out of sight behind the twisting alley walls.

Threading her tent pole through her belt, Annja turned toward the back wall of the fishing shop. An accomplished rock climber, she skillfully scaled the wall and came to a rest atop the doorway. Turning around so that she faced the alley was difficult, but she managed.

She took the tent pole in both hands and waited.

HENRI FOULARD GAZED around the fishing shop. He didn't see the American woman anywhere. Growing anxious, he trotted to the back of the shop and looked through the displays.

"She's not here," Jean said.

"I see that," Foulard snapped. At that moment, the cell phone in his pocket rang. He answered it at once. "Yes."

"Do you have the woman?" Corvin Lesauvage's tone was calm and controlled. He always sounded that way. But to the trained ear, his words held a dangerous edge.

"Not yet," Foulard answered. His head swiveled, searching desperately for the woman.

"I want to talk to her."

"I know. You will." Foulard pushed through a rack of jackets.

"If she knows something about La Bête that I do not know, I must be made aware of it."

"Soon," Foulard promised.

"Do not disappoint me."

Foulard could not imagine anything in the world that he would want to do less. Lesauvage was a violent man with an unforgiving nature. People who crossed him died. Foulard had helped bury some of them in shallow graves. Others he had chopped into pieces and fed to the fish in the Seine.

The phone clicked dead.

Replacing the device in his pocket, Foulard turned to the old man whose owlish eyes were narrow with disapproval. Foulard knew the old man was not as annoyed as he was.

"Where's the woman?" Foulard demanded.

The old man gripped the lapels of his vest. "You need to leave my shop."

Foulard crossed to the man in three angry steps.

Reaching beneath the counter, the old man took out a phone. "I will call the police."

Without pause, Foulard slapped the phone from the old man's hand, then grabbed a fistful of his vest and yanked him close. Effortlessly, Foulard slipped the 9 mm pistol from beneath his windbreaker and put the muzzle against the old man's forehead.

"The woman," Foulard repeated in a deadly voice.

Trembling, the old man pointed to the rear of the shop.

Rounding the counter, Foulard stomped the phone to pieces. "Don't call the police. I'm cutting you a break by letting you live. Understand?"

The old man nodded.

Foulard shoved him back against the shelves. The old man stayed there.

"She spotted us," Jean said.

"You think?" Foulard shook his head and started for the back door. He kept his pistol in his hands.

"It's hard to stay hidden in a town this small," Jean said as he drew his own pistol. He held it like a familiar pet, with love and confidence.

"Lesauvage wants the woman alive," Foulard reminded him, knowing how his cohort loved to kill.

"Maybe he won't want to keep her that way for long," Jean said hopefully.

"She's just a television person," Foulard said. "A historian. She won't be any trouble. Don't break her."

Jean grinned cruelly. "Maybe we can just scare her a little."

Foulard grinned at the thought. "Maybe."

Together, they passed through the back door.

Foulard stood at the doorway.

Two paths lay before him. He didn't know which direction the woman went. Avery Moreau should have left him a clue. The boy knew what he was supposed to do.

"Should we split up?" Jean asked.

Foulard didn't want to do that. He didn't like the possibilities that existed when Jean was out of his sight.

Then a cell phone chirped.

At first, Foulard believed that his employer was calling back. Lesauvage could be an impatient man and a demanding taskmaster. Then, his hand on the phone in his pocket, he discovered that the device wasn't ringing and didn't even sound like his phone.

The noise came from above.

He looked up and his pistol followed his eyes.

AVERY PRESSED HIMSELF against the alley wall. Even though he hadn't been running, his lungs constricted and his own breathing sounded loud to his ears. His heartbeat was a snare drum in his heaving chest.

He felt bad at having left the woman. Of course he had known the two men were there. He had contacted them to let them know she was seeking to uncover the mysteries of La Bête.

Corvin Lesauvage, the man Avery had gone to with his own problems only weeks ago, was interested in La Bête. Everyone in Lozère knew that. In fact, most who lived around the Cévennes Mountains knew of Lesauvage's interests.

When he'd first offered his services to Annja Creed, Avery had mentioned that she should meet Lesauvage, that he was something of an authority on the subject. She had declined, saying she wanted to form her own opinions before she talked to anyone who might influence her views.

Avery grew afraid for the woman. He knew the kind of men who followed her. Lesauvage maintained two kinds of businesses. The two men on the woman's trail were of the dangerous kind.

Squeezing his eyes shut, willing himself not to cry, Avery thought of his father. Surely his father was cold in his grave now. The funeral had been two—no, three—weeks ago. He'd lost all sense of time. It was June now.

Pressing tight against the wall, Avery waited. He concentrated on the fact that what he was doing would help him get revenge for his father's murder. The policeman who had killed Gerard Moreau would not bask in his glory much longer. He would freeze in a grave during winter. Avery had sworn that.

A cell phone chirped down the alley. It was her phone. He breathed a sigh of relief to know she was still there. He'd been worried she'd figured out he'd led the men to her. More than anything, he couldn't fail Lesauvage.

Then a gunshot shattered the quiet locked in the narrow alley.

OKAY, ANNJA THOUGHT grimly as she listened to the strident ring of her cell phone in her pocket, the element of surprise is surprisingly gone.

The two men whirled to look up at her. Both of them held pistols and looked ready to use them.

With the tent pole in both hands, Annja leaped, propelling herself upward and out.

One of the men fired, and the bullet tore through the space she would have occupied if she'd thrown herself directly at them. The steel-jacketed round fragmented against the stone wall and left a white scar.

Annja flipped through the air and landed gracefully in the alley, now to the men's backs.

"No shooting!" one of the men bellowed.

With her feet spread apart, knees bent to remain low, Annja swiveled her makeshift *bo* stick from her left hand to the right and hit the shooter in the side of the face. His sunglasses shattered and blood sprayed from the impact. He squealed in pain.

Moving quickly to her left, using the stumbling man as a barrier to prevent his companion from aiming at her, Annja gripped the stick in both hands again. This was so not a good idea, she told herself.

She wasn't by nature a violent person, but she immediately resented anyone who tried to take advantage of or intimidate her.

That was one of the reasons she'd taken every martial-arts class she could in New Orleans as she'd grown up.

Plus, Sister Mary Annabelle at the orphanage—eighty years old and still spry—was a firm believer in a sound mind and a sound body. Sister Mary Annabelle had never missed a single tai chi class. She was an embarrassment to the other nuns, but she didn't care and Annja had loved the old woman for it.

Annja went on the attack at once. Outrunning a pistol in the twisting confines of the alley was out of the question.

Her phone rang again, sounding inordinately loud in the alley even after the thunderous peal of the gunshot. She wondered if anyone had called the police.

She stepped forward, her mind working rapidly as it always did. She wasn't scared. During her experiences as an archaeologist working in countries far from home, she'd encountered a number of potentially threatening situations caused by weather, ancient traps, geology and men.

Being scared wouldn't help anything.

Striding forward, her left hand over the top of the stick and her right hand under it, Annja slid her right hand down, leaving her right knuckle over the top of the stick as it came over and down, and struck.

The stick slammed against the man's forearm. Something cracked. He released his pistol and screamed. Annja cut off the scream with her next blow, an up strike that caught him under the jaw and dropped him to his knees.

Whirling, knowing the first man she'd attacked was regaining his balance, Annja took another grip on the stick. Stepping forward, she slammed the blunt end of the stick into the man's stomach, doubling him over.

Unbelievably, he brought his pistol up and squeezed the trigger. Two shots ricocheted from the wall behind Annja, missing her by inches.

Dodging again to the left, Annja spun the stick and swung at his gun hand, aiming for the thumb and wrist. Bones broke like dry branches cracking in a campfire.

Staying on the attack, Annja whirled again. She hit the man across the back, aiming for his kidneys. Then she struck him across the backs of his knees, dropping him to the ground.

Even then, doubtless blossoming with pain, he tried to face her. Annja drove the blunt end of the stick against his forehead. He was unconscious before he sprawled on the ground. Blood dripped from the half-moon wound on his forehead.

The other man reached for his dropped pistol.

Annja drove the end of the stick forward, catching the man in the side of the neck and knocking him aside. She kicked the pistol away.

Over the past few years, she'd learned how to use pistols, but she didn't want to touch either of theirs. There was no telling how many crimes were attached to them, and she didn't want to confuse the issue with her fingerprints in case they were all taken into custody.

Before the man could get up again, Annja pinned him to the ground with the stick against the base of his throat. "No," she said.

The man grabbed the stick in both hands and wrenched it away. She kicked him in the face with her hiking boot. The black La Sportiva with Gore-Tex lining had plenty of tread. For hiking slippery slopes and kicking butt, Annja thought, they just can't be beat.

The tread ripped at the man's face, opening a cut over his right eye. Annja put the end of the stick against his throat again, almost making him gag.

"Do that again," Annja said in an even voice, "and you'll regret it."

The man held his hands up beside his head in surrender. Blood trickled into his eye, forcing him to squint.

Holding the stick in place, Annja carefully stretched to search the unconscious man. She found money, two clips for the pistol, but no identification.

"Who are you?" Annja asked the pinned man.

The man growled a curse at her.

Annja pressed the stick against his throat and made him retch. She let him up enough to turn over and vomit.

"Bad mistake," she said.

A siren wailed in the distance, growing closer.

Annja decided she didn't want to be around to answer questions from the Lozère police. As an American, even one with a proper passport, things could become tense. She wasn't on a dig site with administration backing her.

She tapped the man hard on the back of the head with the pole. "Don't let me see you again."

The man cursed at her again, but he remained on the ground.

Annja held on to her stick and jogged down the alley. Her mind whirled and the adrenaline rush started to fade and leave her with the quaking aftermath. Her legs felt rubbery.

This wasn't supposed to happen. She was in Lozère hunting an old monster story. According to plan, she'd be in and out with a few details that would satisfy the young crowd who watched *Chasing History's Monsters*, and a paycheck would soon—she hoped—follow.

Was this a mugging? She wondered. Maybe the two men had heard about her or simply were intrigued enough about the backpack to come after her.

But she got the feeling something more was going on. She just didn't know what.

Get out of town, she told herself. Get to the mountains and see if you can find enough to do the story. Once you finish, you can get back to Brooklyn and edit it, get paid and maybe get to North Africa for Poulson's dig.

Poulson's dig site was interesting to her. The team was looking for one of Hannibal's campsites when he marched across with his elephants. Annja had never been to Africa. She'd always wanted to go. But Poulson's team was privately funded and he didn't have the budget to pay her way.

Still, he'd invited her. If she could make it on her own.

That was why she was here in Lozère chasing after a monster she didn't truly believe existed.

She kept running, telling herself that another day or two and she would be clear of France, and whatever problems the two men had brought with them.

2

The rental Avery had arranged turned out to be an old Renault pickup truck. If Annja had been a layman, maybe she'd have mistakenly called it ancient. But she was a trained archaeologist and she knew what *ancient* meant.

The man who'd rented it to her had seemed somewhat reluctant, but that had lifted once she'd put the money in his hand and promised to get the vehicle back in one piece.

For the money she'd handed over, Annja thought perhaps the man would replace the truck with a better one. But there weren't many vehicles to be had in town that the owners would allow to be driven where she was going.

At least the old truck looked high enough to clear the rough terrain.

After thanking Avery for his help and a final goodbye, Annja climbed behind the steering wheel, stepped on the starter and engaged the transmission with a clank. She headed toward the Cévennes Mountains.

Once out of town, following the dirt road leading up into the mountains, Annja took out her cell phone. It was equipped with a satellite receiver, offering her a link in most parts of the world. Still, the service was expensive and she didn't use it any more than she had to.

Caller ID showed the number that had called her while she'd been in the alley. She recognized the number at once.

Steering one-handed, trying to avoid most of the rough spots, Annja punched the speed-dial function and pulled up the number.

The phone rang three times before it was answered.

"Doug Morrell." His voice was crisp and cheerful. He sounded every bit of his twenty-two years of age.

"Hello, Doug," she said. "It's Annja. I'm returning your call."

Doug Morrell was a friend and one of her favorite production people at *Chasing History's Monsters*. He lived in Brooklyn, not far from her, and was a frequent guest and dining companion. He was young and trendy, never interested in going out into the field for stories as Annja did.

"I was just looking over the piece you're working on," Doug said. He affected a very bad French accent. "The Beast of Gévaudan."

"What about it?"

"French werewolf thing, right?"

"They don't know what it was," Annja countered.

"Looking over it today, after Kristie did the werewolf of Cologne, I'm thinking maybe this isn't the story we want to pursue. I mean, two stories set in France about werewolves might not be where our viewers want to go."

Annja sighed and avoided an angry response. Evidently lycanthropy wasn't as popular as vampirism because *Chasing History's Monsters* had done a weeklong series on those. And neither history nor geography was something Doug had an interest in.

"Peter Stubb, the so-called Werewolf of Cologne, was German, not French," Annja said.

"French, German—" Doug's tone suggested an uncaring shrug "—I'm not seeing a whole lot of difference here," he admitted. "Europe tends to blur together for me. I think it does for most of our fans."

That was the difference between a big-name show and one that was syndicated, Annja supposed. The networks had audiences. Cable programs had fans. But she could live with that. This check was going to get her to North Africa.

"Europe shouldn't blur together," Annja said. "The histories of each country are hugely different."

"If you say so." Doug didn't sound at all convinced. "My problem is I don't especially feel good about sticking two hairy guys on as my leads so close together."

"Then save the La Bête piece," Annja said as she became aware of the sound of high-pitched engines. Her wraparound sunglasses barely blunted the hot glare of the early-afternoon sun. Just let me do my job and give me my airfare, she almost said aloud.

"If I save the La Bête piece, I've got a hole I need to fill," Doug said.

"The pieces *are* different," Annja said. "Peter Stubb was more than likely a serial killer. He claimed victims for twenty-five years between 1564 and 1589. Supposedly he had a magic belt given to him by the devil that allowed him to change into a wolf."

Doug was no longer surprised by the amount of knowledge and esoteric facts Annja had at her command. He partnered with her at the sports bars to play trivia games on the closed-circuit televisions. He knew all the pop-culture references and sports, and she had the history and science. They split the literature category. Together, they seldom lost and in most of Brooklyn's pubs no one would wager against them.

"There's no mention of a magic belt in Kristie's story," Doug said.

Annja wasn't surprised. Kristie Chatham wasn't noted for research, just a killer bod and scanty clothing while prowling for legends. For her, history never went past her last drink and her last lover.

"There was a magic belt," Annja said.

"I believe you," Doug said. "But at this point we'll probably have to roll without it. Should send some of the audience members into a proper outrage and juice up the Internet activity regarding the show again."

Annja counted to ten. "The show's integrity is important to me. To the work I do." Archaeology was what she lived for. Nothing had ever drawn her like that.

"Don't worry about it," Doug said. "When the viewers start trashing Kristie's validity, I'll just have George rerelease video clips of her outtakes in Cancun while she was pursuing the legend of the flesh-eating college students turned zombies during the 1977 spring break. Her bikini top fell off three times during that show. It's not the same when we mask that here in the States, but a lot of guys download the European versions of the show."

Annja tried not to think about Kristie's top falling off. The woman grated on her nerves. What was even more grating was that Kristie Chatham was the fan-favorite of all the hosts of *Chasing History's Monsters*.

"The ratings really rise during those episodes," Doug continued. "Not to say that ratings don't rise whenever you're on. They do. You're one hot babe yourself, Annja."

"Thanks loads," Annja said dryly.

"I mean, chestnut hair and those amber eyes—"

"They're green."

"*You* think they're green," Doug amended. "I'll split it with you. We'll call them hazel. Anyway, you've got all that professorial-speak that Kristie doesn't have."

"It's called a college education."

"Whatever."

"She still has the breakaway bikini."

Doug hesitated for a moment. "Do you want to try that?"

"No," Annja said forcefully.

"I didn't think so. Anyway, I think we'll be okay. Maybe I can sandwich a reedited version of the zombie piece between the German werewolf and your French one."

"La Bête was never proved to be a werewolf," Annja said, skewing the conversation back to her field of expertise. "Between 1764 and 1767, the Beast of Gévaudan killed sixty-eight children, fifteen women and six men."

"Good. Really." Doug sounded excited. "That's a great body count. Works out to an average of thirty-three people a year. People love the number thirty-three. Always something mystical about it."

Annja ignored his comment because they were friends. She didn't bother to correct his math, either. Counting 1764, La Bête had killed for *four* years. "The creature was also reputed to be intelligent. It was an ambush predator and often avoided capture by leading horsemen into bogs around here. It also outran hunting dogs."

"This wasn't included in your outline."

"You said you don't like to read."

"Well, I don't," Doug admitted grudgingly. "But maybe you could put interesting details like this into your proposal."

"There's only so much you can do with half a page," Annja pointed out. "Double-spaced."

"Yeah, but you need to learn the right things to include. Body count. That's always a biggie."

When I get back, Annja promised herself, I'm going to finish that résumé. There has to be another cable show out there that's interested in archaeology. She knew she'd miss Doug, though.

"At any rate," Annja said, "no one ever found out what the creature was. It was supposed to be six feet tall at the shoulder."

"Is that big?"

"For a wolf, yes."

"I thought you said it wasn't a wolf."

"I said no one knew what it was."

"So it's not a wolf, not a *were*wolf. What the hell is it?"

"Exactly," Annja agreed.

"A mystery," Doug said with forced enthusiasm. "Mysteries are good. But only if you have answers for them. Do you?"

"Not yet. That's why I'm headed into the Cévennes Mountains right now."

"This creature was supposed to be up in those mountains?" Doug asked.

"Yes. According to some people, La Bête is still around. Every now and again a hiker goes missing and is never seen or heard from again."

"Cool. Sounds better already. How soon are you going to have this together?"

"Soon," Annja promised, hoping that some kind of breakthrough would take place. At the moment, she had a lot of interesting research but nothing fresh.

And she didn't have Kristie Chatham's breakaway top. Nor the desire to stoop so low. She said goodbye, then closed the phone and concentrated on her driving.

Glancing up at the mountains, Annja couldn't help thinking it would be better for her ratings if she actually ran into La Bête. Probably not better for her, though.

"THE WOMAN GOT away." Foulard sat in a small café across from the fishing shop. He held his beer against his aching jaw. The swelling made it hard to talk.

"How?" Lesauvage wasn't happy.

"She ambushed us." Foulard still couldn't believe the woman had leaped from above the door and taken them down so easily. It was embarrassing.

Lesauvage cursed. "Do you know where she's going?"

Foulard looked across the table at Avery Moreau. The young man was scowling. He sat with arms folded over his chest and blew out an angry breath now and again.

Foulard just barely resisted the impulse to reach over and slap the young man. It would have been a mistake. The police were still canvassing the neighborhood.

"The boy—" Foulard called Avery that on purpose, watching the young man tighten his jaw angrily "—says she is headed up into the mountains."

"Why?"

"That's where La Bête was known to roam." Foulard didn't believe in the great beast. But he believed in Lesauvage and the magic the man possessed. Foulard had seen it, had felt its power, and had seen men die because of it.

Lesauvage was quiet for a moment. "She knows something," he mused quietly, "something that I do not."

"The boy insists that she didn't."

"Then why go up into the mountains?"

Foulard cursed silently. He knew what was coming. "I don't know."

"Then," Lesauvage replied, "I suggest that you find out. Quickly. Take Jean—"

"Jean is out of it," Foulard said. "The police have him."

"How?"

"The woman knocked him out. I couldn't wake him before I had to flee. I was fortunate they didn't get me." Foulard rolled his beer over his aching jaw. "She fights very well. You didn't tell us that." He meant it almost as an accusation, suggesting that Lesauvage hadn't known, either. But he wasn't that brave.

"I didn't think she could fight better than you," Lesauvage said. "And I heard there were shots fired."

Wisely, Foulard refrained from speaking. He'd already failed. Lesauvage appeared willing to let him live. That was good.

"Find her," Lesauvage ordered. "Go up into the mountains and find her. I want to know what she knows."

"All right."

"Can you get someone to help you?"

"Yes."

Lesauvage hung up.

Pocketing the phone, Foulard leaned back and sipped the beer. Then he reached into his jacket and took out a vial of pain pills. They were one of the benefits of working for Lesauvage.

He shook out two, chewed them up and ignored the bitter taste. His tongue numbed immediately and he knew the relief from the pounding in his head would come soon.

Turning his attention to Avery Moreau, Foulard asked, "Do you know which campsite she'll be using?"

Arrogantly, Avery replied, "I helped her choose it."

"Then you know." Foulard stood. He felt as if the floor moved under him. Pain cascaded through this throbbing head. He stoked his anger at the woman. She would pay. "Come with me."

"What about Richelieu?"

It took Foulard a moment to realize whom the boy was talking about. "The policeman?"

Avery's blue eyes looked watery with unshed tears. "My father's murderer," he said.

Waving the statement away, Foulard said, "Richelieu will be dealt with."

"When?"

"In time. When the time is right." Foulard finished the beer and set it aside. "Now come on."

"Lesauvage promised—"

Reaching down, Foulard cupped the boy's soft face in his big, callused hand. "Do not trifle with me, boy. And do not say his name in public so carelessly. I've seen him bury men for less."

Fear squirmed through the watery blue eyes.

"He keeps his promises," Foulard said. "In his own time. He has promised that your father's killer will pay for his crimes. The man will." He paused. "In time. Now, you and I have other business to tend to. Let's be about it."

Avery jerked his head out of Foulard's grip and reluctantly got to his feet.

Across the street, the Lozère police were loading Jean's unconscious body into the back of an ambulance. The old shopkeeper waved his arms as he told his story. Foulard thought briefly that he should have killed the man. Perhaps he might come back and do that.

For the moment, though, his attention was directed solely at the woman.

A SNAKE LAY SUNNING on the narrow ledge that Annja had spent the past hour climbing up to. She had been hoping to take a moment to relax there. Climbing freestyle was demanding. Her fingers and toes ached with effort.

The snake pushed itself back, poised to strike.

Great, Annja thought. Climbing back down was possible, but she was tired. Risking a poisonous snake bite was about the same as trying to negotiate the seventy-foot descent without taking a break.

She decided to deal with the snake.

Moving slowly, she pulled herself almost eye to eye with the snake. It drew back a little farther, almost out of room. Freezing, not wanting to startle the creature any more than she already had, she hung by her fingertips.

Easy, she told herself, breathing out softly through her mouth and inhaling through her nose.

The snake coiled tightly, its head low and its jaws distended to deliver a strike that would send poison through her system.

At a little over twenty inches long, it was full-grown. A string of black splotches from its flared head to the tip of its tail mottled the grayish-green scales and told Annja what kind of venomous adder she faced.

Ursini's vipers were known to have an irritable nature, to be very territorial and struck quickly when approached.

Their venom was hemotoxic, designed to break down the blood

of their prey. Few human deaths were attributed to Ursini's vipers in the area, but Annja felt certain a lone climber miles from help in the mountains would be a probable candidate.

The ledge Annja clung to extended six feet to her left.

Okay, she mentally projected at the snake, not wanting to speak because the vibrations of her voice might spook the nervous viper, there's enough room for both of us.

Moving slowly, she shuffled her left hand over a few inches. The snake tightened its coil. She stopped, clinging by her fingertips. If she'd been wearing gloves she might have felt more comfortable taking the risk of movement. But at present only a thin layer of climbing chalk covered her hands.

She stared at the snake, feeling angry as it kept her at bay. She didn't like being afraid of anything. She was, of course, but she didn't like it. That something so small could impede her was irritating. If she'd worn a harness and had belayed herself to a cam, getting around the snake would have been a piece of cake.

But she hadn't.

"Bonjour," a voice suddenly called from above.

Gazing upward briefly, Annja spotted an old man hunkered down in a squatting position thirty feet up and to the right of her position.

He was in his sixties or seventies, leathery with age. Sweat-stained khaki hiking shorts and a gray T-shirt hung from his skinny frame. His white hair hung past his thin shoulders and his beard was too long to be neat and too short to be intended. He looked as if he hadn't taken care of himself lately. He held a long walking staff in his right hand.

"Bonjour," Annja responded quietly.

"Not a good spot to be in," the old man observed.

"For me or the snake?" Annja asked.

The man's face creased as he laughed. "Clinging by your fingernails and you've still got wit." He shook his head. "You seldom find that in a woman."

"You aren't exactly enlightened, are you?" Annja shifted her grip slightly, trying to find a degree of comfort. There wasn't one.

"No," the old man agreed. He paused. "You could, of course, climb back down."

"I hate retreating."

"So does the snake."

"I suppose asking for help is out of the question?"

The old man spread his hands. "How? If I try to traverse the distance, should I be that skilled, I would doubtless send debris down. It might be enough to trigger a strike."

Annja knew that was true.

"It is poisonous, you know. It's not just the sting of a bite you'll have to contend with."

"I know." Back and shoulders aching, Annja watched the snake. "I have a satellite phone. If I fall or get bitten, maybe you could call for help."

"I'd be happy to."

Annja held up a hand, letting go of her fear and focusing on the snake. Its wedge-shaped head followed her hand. Then, getting the reptile's rhythm, she flicked her hand.

The viper launched itself like an arrow from a bow.

Without thinking, Annja let go the ledge with her left elbow and swung from her right, crunching her fingers up tightly to grip and hoping that it was enough to keep her from falling.

The snake missed her but its effort had caused it to hang over the ledge. Before the viper could recover, Annja swung back toward it.

Trying not to think of what would happen if she missed or her right hand slipped from the ledge, she gripped the snake just behind its head. The cool, slickly alien feel of the scales slid against her palm.

Move! she told herself as she felt the snake writhing in her grip. Skidding across the rough cliff surface, feeling her fingers give just a fraction of an inch, she whip-cracked the snake away from the mountain.

Airborne, the snake twisted and knotted itself as it plummeted toward the verdant growth of the forest far below.

Flailing with her left hand, Annja managed to secure a fresh grip just as her right hand pulled free of the ledge. She recovered quickly and let her body go limp against the cliff side. Her flesh pressed against the uneven surface and helped distribute her weight.

"Well done," the old man called. He applauded. "That took real nerve. I'm impressed."

"That's me," Annja agreed. She blew out a tense breath. "Impressive."

She hoisted herself up with her arms, hoping the viper had been alone and hadn't been among friends. Even with the ledge, she tucked herself into a roll and luxuriated on her back.

The old man peered down at her. "Are you all right?"

"I'm fine. Just resting. I'll be up in a minute."

Taking out a pipe, the old man lit up. The breeze pulled the smoke away. "Take your time," he invited. "Take your time."

Annja lay back and waited for her breathing to calm and the lactic acid buildup in her limbs to ease. You should go home, she told herself. Just pack up and go. Things are getting way too weird.

For some reason, though, she knew she couldn't turn and go back any more than she could have retreated from the snake. As she'd begun her ascent on the mountain, she'd felt a compulsion to continue her quest.

That was dumb, she'd thought. There was no way she was going to uncover the secret of La Bête after three hundred years when no one else had been able to.

But something was drawing her up the mountain.

3

A dull roaring sounded in the distance.

Recognizing the noise, Annja sat up on the cliff's edge and peered out into the forest that broke across the foothills of the mountains like an ocean of leaves.

Six Enduro motorcycles bobbed and slid through the forest. The riders wore brightly colored leathers and gleaming helmets.

"Are you expecting company?" the old man asked from the ledge above.

"No."

"Perhaps they just came out here for the view," the old man suggested. "Or maybe they brought their own entertainment."

Meaning booze or drugs? Annja thought that was possible. But she didn't mean to get caught standing on a ledge if that wasn't the truth.

"Are you coming on up, then?" he asked politely.

"Yes."

"Good." The old man took a handkerchief from his pocket and wiped his face. "It's rather warmer up here than I'd thought it would be."

Annja stood, balancing precariously on the narrow ledge. She reached into her pack and took out a bottle of water. After drinking as much as she could, she replaced the bottle in her pack and started climbing again.

"There's a rock to your left." The old man pointed to the outcropping with his staff.

She curled her hand around the rock and heaved.

"There you go," he congratulated.

Listening to his speech, Annja wondered at his accent. He spoke English, but she believed that was because he knew she was American. But his French accent wasn't something she was familiar with.

Moments later, Annja gained the top of the ridgeline. The motorcycle engines had died and the silence seemed heavy.

"Thanks," Annja said.

The old man shrugged. "It was nothing. You climb well," he said.

"Thank you."

"But you shouldn't climb alone."

Looking around innocently, Annja asked, "Where's your partner?"

He shrugged. "I'm an old man. No one will miss me if I fall off the mountainside." He started up the ridgeline.

Having no other destination in mind at the moment, Annja followed. The compulsion that she only halfway believed in seemed to be pulling her in that direction anyway.

"What brings you up here?" the old man asked.

"La Bête," Annja answered.

Halting, he peered over his shoulder. "Surely you're joking."

"No."

"La Bête is a myth," the old man stated. "Probably a story made up by a serial killer."

"You would know about serial killers?"

"I would." He didn't elaborate. Instead, he turned and continued up the ridgeline.

"What are you doing up here?" she asked.

"Searching for something that was lost."

"You lost something up here?"

"No." The old man swung around a boulder and kept going up. "It was lost a long time ago. Hundreds of years ago."

"What was it?"

"Nothing you'd be interested in, my dear."

"I'm an archaeologist. I like old things." Annja instantly regretted her words when the old man turned around. If he was an old pervert, she'd just given him the perfect opportunity for an off-color remark.

"You?" he asked as if in disbelief. "An archaeologist?"

"Yes," Annja declared. "Me."

The old man blew a raspberry. "You're a child. What would you know about anything of antiquity?"

"I know that old men who think they know everything *don't* know everything," she said. "Otherwise *children* like me wouldn't be discovering new things."

"Learning about them from a book is one thing," the old man said. "But to truly appreciate them, you have to live among them."

"I try," Annja said. "I've been on several dig sites."

"Good for you. In another forty or fifty years, provided you don't die of a snakebite or a long fall, perhaps you will have learned something."

A tremor passed through the ground.

Annja froze at once, not certain if she'd truly felt it.

The old man turned around to face her. His face knitted in concern. Irritably, he tapped his staff against the ground. "Did you feel that?" he asked.

"Yes," Annja said. "It's probably nothing to worry about."

"It felt like an earthquake. This isn't earthquake country."

"Earthquakes take place around the world all the time. Humans just aren't sensitive enough to feel all of them," Annja said.

The ground quivered again, more vigorously this time.

"Well," the old man said, "I certainly felt that." He kept walking forward. "Maybe we should think about getting down."

Annja stayed where she was. Whatever was pulling at her was stronger than ever. It lay in the direction opposite the way the old man had chosen. Before she knew it, she was headed toward the pull.

"Where are you going?" the old man asked.

"I want to check something out." Annja walked along the ridge-line, climbing again. A small trail she hadn't noticed before ran between bushes and small trees.

A game trail.

Despite the tremors, Annja went on.

FOULARD'S MOOD HADN'T lifted. A burning need for some kind of revenge filled him. The woman, Annja Creed, had to be delivered alive to Lesauvage, but she didn't have to be unbroken.

He parked his motorcycle beside a new SUV. The five men with him parked nearby.

They dismounted as one, used to working together. Jean had been one of them, one of Lesauvage's chosen few.

Drawing his 9 mm handgun, Foulard took the lead. The other men fell in behind.

They went quickly. Over the past few years, they had learned the Cévennes Mountains. Lesauvage had sent them all into the area at one time or another. Foulard had been several times.

None of them had ever found anything.

Foulard truly didn't believe the woman had found anything, either. He hoped she hadn't. Once Lesauvage saw that she knew nothing, he would quickly give her to them.

Eagerly, Foulard jogged up the trail. His face and arms still hurt, but the pain pills had taken off the edge.

When the first tremor passed through him, Foulard thought it was the drugs in his system. Then a cascade of rocks rushed from farther up the grade and nearly knocked him from his feet.

"What the hell is that?" one of the men behind him yelled.

"Earthquake," another said.

"We don't want to be on top of this mountain if it's about to come down."

Foulard spun toward them. "We were sent here to get the woman," he said. "I won't go back to Lesauvage without her."

The men just stared at him.

The ground quivered again.

"I'll kill any man who leaves me," Foulard promised.

They all looked at him. They knew he would.

Another tremor passed through the earth, unleashing more debris that sledded down the mountainside.

"All right," Croteau said. He was the oldest and largest of them. "We'll go with you. But make it quick."

Turning, Foulard kept his balance through another jarring session, then started to run.

THE GAME TRAIL LOOKED old and, judging from the bits and pieces of it Annja saw along the mountainside, it went all the way to the top.

The ground heaved this time, actually rising up and slamming back down beneath Annja's feet. She dropped to all fours, afraid of being flung from the mountainside.

"This way," the old man shouted. "Come back from there before you get yourself killed."

This is insane, Annja thought. She felt the earth quivering beneath her like a frightened animal.

"Don't be foolish," the old man said.

Frustrated, Annja took out her Global Positioning System device. She took a reading.

Twenty-four satellites bracketed the earth. Every reading taken by the device acquired signals from at least twelve of them. When she returned to the mountains, she'd be within inches of the exact spot where she now stood.

Returning the GPS locater to her pack, she turned and started back down the mountain. The compulsion within her surged to a fever pitch with a suddenness and intensity that drove her to her knees in an intense attack of vertigo.

"Are you all right?" the old man asked.

She wasn't. But she couldn't speak to tell him that.

Without warning, she was no longer on the mountaintop. She stood in the middle of a blazing fire. Pain threatened to consume her.

Her whole life she'd suffered from nightmares about fire but, for the first time, it was happening while she was awake.

"Girl!" the old man bellowed.

"Girl!" he roared again. Panic strained his features. Some other look was there, as well. Perhaps it was understanding.

Annja didn't know. The nightmare abated. She focused on the old man.

Forced to use his staff to aid with his balance across the heaving earth, he came toward her. He held out his hand. "Come to me. Come to me now!"

Feeling drained and totally mystified, Annja tried to walk toward him. Then the ground opened up at her feet. In a heartbeat, the earth shifted and yawned till a chasm twenty feet across formed. Rocks and grass and debris disappeared into the earthen maw.

Barely staying on her feet, Annja backed away. She didn't want to try leaping down into the crevasse. During a quake, the earth could close back together just as quickly as it opened up. If the earth caught her, it would crush her.

"I can't reach you," she said.

The old man pointed, leaning on his staff as another quake shuddered through the earth. "There's a trail. Back that way. Just head down."

Turning, Annja gazed down the other side of the mountain. Here and there, just glimpses, she thought she saw a trail.

"Do you see it?" the old man called.

The earth heaved again, shifting violently enough that Annja almost lost her footing. "Yes!"

"Go!" the old man called. "Not much farther down, you'll find a campsite. I have a truck there. I will meet you." With more agility and speed than Annja would have believed possible, he started down the crest where he stood.

Annja didn't know what the old man was doing in the mountains. There were a number of hiking trails. Even famed author Robert Louis Stevenson, though in ill health, had been compelled by his curiosity about the Beast of Gévaudan to try his luck at solving the mystery in the mountains. The trail Stevenson had taken was clearly marked for tourists interested in the countryside, the legend or the author of *Dr. Jekyll and Mr. Hyde.*

The mountain shook again and Annja started running. Never in her research had she heard of any earthquakes in the area.

She followed the narrow path across worn stone that led through boulders and cracks along the mountainside. As she ran, the ground trembled and heaved. Several times she tripped and fell against the rock walls. Her backpack and the pouch containing the climbing chalk thudded against her.

"There she is!" The young male voice ripped across the sound of falling rock.

Going to ground immediately, Annja peered around.

Farther down the slope, one of the motorcycle riders, still wearing his riding leathers, peered up at her. For a moment she thought perhaps he was coming to help her.

Then she saw the small, black semiautomatic pistol in his hand and the bruises on his face. It was the man from the alley.

She turned and fled, racing back up the mountain.

The earth shook even more violently than before. A horrendous crack sounded nearby. Nearly knocked from her feet, aware that hundreds of pounds of rock and debris were skidding toward her, she pulled up short and tried to alter her course.

The ground opened up and swallowed her.

4

Out of control, Annja threw her hands out instinctively in an effort to catch hold of the sides of the fissure. Stone whipped by her fingertips, but she managed to somewhat slow her descent from a fall to a slide something short of maximum velocity.

Not a fissure, she told herself, her brain buzzing at furious speed the way it always did when she was in trouble. This is a sinkhole.

She felt the roughly circular contours of the shaft around her as she stretched to fill it. A sinkhole was a natural formation of a cave that finally hollowed out to the point it nearly reached the surface. As a nation, France was probably more honeycombed with caves and cave systems than any other country in the world.

The Cévennes Mountains held many volcanic caves, created by lava after it had cooled and the volcanoes had subsided. Along the coast, sea caves formed by waves had provided hidden harbors in the golden age of piracy. Limestone caves in the interior were made by erosion. There were even many caves made by the passage of glaciers across the land millions of years ago. Cro-Magnons had lived in caves at Pech-Merle and Lascaux, leaving behind cave paintings millions of years old.

Annja wasn't surprised to find a new cave in the mountains. In fact, in scaling the cliff she'd been hoping to find some sign of one. Le Bête had taken up refuge somewhere all those years ago.

However, she hadn't expected to *plummet* into her discovery.

In a hail of flying stones, she hit the ground hard. The impact drove the breath from her lungs. Blackness ate at the edge of her conscious mind, but she struggled through it and remained alert.

It's not the fall that kills you, she reminded herself. It's the sudden stop at the end.

She covered her head with her arms as more debris rained down around her. Several pieces of stone hammered her back and legs hard enough to promise bruises for a few days.

Then everything was quiet.

You're alive, she told herself. Get moving.

She pushed herself up. Nothing felt broken. That was always a good sign.

When her lungs finally started working again, dust coated her tongue. Reaching into her backpack, knowing by touch and years of experience where the contents were, she took out a bandanna, wet it with the water bottle and tied the material around her nose and mouth. The water-soaked cloth would keep her from suffering respiratory problems caused by inhaling too much dust.

Wet cloth won't protect you from carbon dioxide buildup or poison gas, she reminded herself. Carbon dioxide wasn't a natural byproduct of a cave the way coal gas was, but if humans or animals had frequented it, the gas could have filled the chamber. She hoped the opening created by the sinkhole would help.

Echoes sounded around her, indicating that the cave was large or long.

Fishing out one of the two halogen flashlights she habitually carried, she turned it on. Then she took off her sunglasses and stored them in the backpack, marveling that they hadn't broken during the fall.

The flashlight beam cut through the darkness but was obscured by the swirling dust that filled the cave. The chamber was at least thirty feet across and almost that high.

The sinkhole was at the back of the cave. At least, it was in the area she decided to refer to as the back of the cave. Almost four feet across, it snaked up but the twists and turns were so severe that no outside light penetrated the chamber.

Going back up is going to be a problem, Annja realized. If it's possible at all. She carried rope in her backpack. Over the years spent at dig sites, she'd learned that rope was an indispensable tool. She never went anywhere without it. But she wasn't sure it could help her now.

Bats fluttered from the stalactites. She swept the flashlight beam after them.

Okay, Annja thought, if you guys are in here, there's got to be another entrance.

Unless the sinkhole that had opened up had originally been some small holes that had allowed the bats to enter and exit. She didn't want to think about that possibility.

The air was thick and stank from being closed up. More than that, it smelled like an animal's den. That was good news and bad news. If the cave did provide a home to an animal, the chances were good that another entrance was large enough to allow her passage. The bad news was that wolves were in the area, as well as bears. Large predators weren't going to be welcome. Especially not in their den.

A swift examination of the chamber revealed a passage. She went to it, finding she had to hunch down to pass through and that the floor was canted. At least the structure looked sound. No cracks or fissures showed in the strata. If there was another tremor, she felt reasonably certain the rock would stay intact and not come down on top of her.

The passage went on for fifteen or twenty feet, then jogged left and opened into another chamber nearly twice the size of the one she'd fallen into.

When she passed the flashlight beam over the wall to her right, drawings stood out against the stone. Seeing what they were, guessing that no one in hundreds or thousands or millions of years had seen them, all thoughts of anything else—the earth tremors, the motorcyclists, the old man—were gone.

Playing the flashlight beam over the rough rock surface, Annja made out mastodons, handprints, figures of people, fires, aurochs— ancestors of modern cattle—and other images of Cro-Magnon life.

Excitement flared through her. During her career, she'd seen cave paintings. She'd even seen similar paintings at Lascaux after the cave had been closed to the public.

But she had never found something like this.

Hypnotized by the images, she took a credit-card-sized digital camera from her backpack. With the low light, she didn't know if the images would turn out, but whatever the camera captured would surely be enough to get funding for a dig site.

The Cro-Magnon painters had used animal fat and minerals to make colors. Black had been a favorite and easy to make. All that was required was charred bone ground into a fine powder mixed with animal fat.

She walked along the wall, taking image after image. Only a little farther on, the scenes on the wall were marred. Long, deep scratches ran through them, as if they'd been dug into the stone by great, dull claws. The claw marks were seven and eight feet high, so close together it looked as if an animal had been in a frenzy.

An animal marking its territory? she wondered. Or the desperation of an animal trapped inside this cave?

In that moment, Annja remembered she'd traveled to the Cévennes looking for La Bête. Then she tripped and nearly fell. Something furry brushed against her ankle.

For one moment she thought she felt it move. Stepping back quickly, she swung the flashlight around, prepared to use it as a weapon.

The light beam fell in a bright ellipse over a scene straight out of a nightmare. The half-eaten and mummified corpse of a sheep lay on the floor amid a pile of bones.

Tracking the bone debris, Annja shone her beam over the stack of skulls that had been arranged in an irregular notch in the chamber. At least seventy or eighty skulls filled the area.

Was this a place of worship? Annja wondered. Or an altar celebrating past triumphs?

She tried to imagine Cro-Magnon men sitting in the cave bragging about their success as fierce hunters. Except that the sheep's body was anachronistic. None of the sheep's forebears had looked like that in Cro-Magnon times. This sheep was small and compact, bred for meat and wool, not far removed from the sheep Annja had seen on farms she'd passed on her way to the mountain range.

Looking closely, she noticed that several of the skulls were human.

Used to handling human remains on dig sites, she had no fear of the dead. She set down the flashlight to illuminate the scene.

Upon further inspection, she discovered that several of the ribs, and arm and leg bones were likely human, as well. Shreds of clothing that looked hundreds of years old clung to some of the bones. Boots stood and lay amid the clutter.

A cold chill ran down her spine. Whatever had lived in the cave had preyed on humans.

Shifting the light, heart beating a little faster, Annja spotted the great body stretched out on the floor. For a very tense moment, she'd thought the animal was lying there waiting to pounce. She froze.

The light played over the mummified lips pulled back in a savage snarl that exposed huge yellow teeth. The eye sockets were hollow, long empty and dry. In that moment, the animal musk she'd smelled seemed even more intense.

Death had stripped the fantastic creature of much of its bulk, but it was still easy to see how huge it had been in life. The head was as big as a buffalo's but more bearlike in shape. Its body was thick and broad and the limbs were huge. It was unlike anything Annja had ever seen before.

Making herself move despite the fear and astonishment she felt, Annja took pictures of the creature with the digital camera. Maybe she'd made two incredible discoveries in the same day.

Finished with the camera, she hurriedly took out a small drawing pad and a mechanical pencil from her backpack. If the camera failed to capture images, she could at least draw them.

On closer inspection, Annja saw a broad-bladed spear shoved through the beast's chest. Beneath the corpse of the impossible animal was a human corpse.

Decomposition hadn't settled in. Locked in the steady climate of the cave environment, kept bug-free by depth and ecology, the dead man had mummified as the beast had. His hands, the flesh so dehydrated it was almost like onionskin over the bones, still held tightly to the spear. Man and beast, locked in savage combat, had killed each other.

Kneeling beside the dead man and beast, she reached out her empty hand.

Something gleamed at the dead man's throat.

Taking a surgical glove from her backpack, Annja plucked the gleaming object from the corpse. It had partially sunk into the dead man's chest. A leather thong tied the object around the corpse's neck.

After freeing the gleaming object, Annja held it up so her flashlight beam could easily illuminate it. A jagged piece of metal, no more than two inches to a side, dangled from the leather thong.

The piece looked like an ill-made coin, hammered out on some smith's anvil in a hurry. One side held an image of a wolf standing in front of a mountain. The wolf was disproportioned, though the oddities seemed intentional, and it appeared as though the wolf had been hanged. The obverse was stamped with a symbol she couldn't quite make out.

Annja remained kneeling. She was checking the image when a flashlight beam whipped across her face.

Instinctively, she dodged away, remembering the motorcyclists and the old man she'd seen outside. She tucked the drawing pad, pencils and charm into her backpack as she scooped up her flashlight and switched it off.

"Where the hell did she go?" someone demanded in French.

Shadows created by the glow of the flashlight trailed the beam into the chamber.

Annja stayed low as the light sprayed around the room. She barely escaped it before reaching the pile of skulls. Once there, she flattened herself against the wall.

Light played over leather-clad bodies that stepped into the chamber.

Evidently the motorcyclists had made their way down the sinkhole. They'd come along the passage Annja had found. She'd been so absorbed by her discoveries that she'd forgotten all about them and hadn't noticed them. Silently, she cursed herself.

"She can't have just vanished," another man said.

In the soft glow of the reflected light from the flashlight, all six of them stood revealed. All of them held pistols.

"If we lose her, Lesauvage is going to kill us." The speaker's voice was tight with fear.

"We haven't lost her," someone stated calmly. "We came in that hole after her. There's no other way out."

"You don't know that, Foulard."

Another man gave a startled curse. "What the hell's lying there?"

Foulard aimed his flashlight at the creature's huge mummified body.

"The Beast of Gévaudan!" someone said. "It must be! Look at it!

My grandfather told me stories about this thing!" His voice dropped and took on a note of awe. "I never believed him. Thought it was all crap old men told kids to scare the hell out of them."

Hidden by the shadow of the skulls, Annja's mind raced. They came here looking for me.

"Forget about that damned thing," Foulard commanded. "Spread out. Find the woman. Lesauvage wants to speak with her. I don't want to go back and tell him we lost her."

He directed his flashlight at the cavern's ceiling, providing a weak cone of illumination from above.

Thankfully, the light didn't quite reach the cavern floor. Annja sank down low. Her free hand plucked up one of the human skulls. Her fingers slipped easily through the empty eyeholes to secure her hold. It wasn't much as weapons went, but she hoped to improve her standing.

5

Annja leaned forward, skull in one hand and flashlight in the other, hunkered down in a squatting position.

The six men spread out. Foulard took his own path, but the other five stayed close enough to take comfort in the presence of the light.

"Do you think that really is the Beast of Gévaudan?" one of them asked.

"I don't know, but I heard the creature was a werewolf," another said. "He was supposed to be a guy, Count Vargo, who got cursed by a band of gypsies after he raped one of their daughters."

That was not a werewolf, Annja thought fiercely as she remembered how the great beast looked. It's some kind of mutated species. She pressed against the wall, profiling herself into it.

One of the men came close to her. Annja waited as long as she could, knowing their eyes were adjusting to the darkness. His body language, that sudden shift to square up with her, gave away the fact that he had seen her.

She rose, uncoiling as the viper had done earlier, and swung the skull with all her strength. The aged bone shattered against the man's face, driving him backward.

"There!" one of the men yelled. "Over by Croteau!"

Foulard swung the flashlight in Annja's direction.

Scuttling quickly, flinging away the remnants of the skull, she slid low along the unconscious man. Her partially numbed fingers found the 9 mm pistol lying on the cave floor. She fumbled it into her grip as the flashlight splashed over her and blinded her.

"She has Croteau's gun!"

"Kill her!" Foulard yelled. His pistol barked and spit flame that lit up the angry terror on his face. She recognized the bruises on his face and knew he was the man from the alley.

The wind from the bullet cut the air by Annja's left cheek. If she hadn't already been moving to her right, it would have crashed through her head.

"Lesauvage wants her alive!" someone yelled. "Stop shooting!"

Firing on the fly, Annja put two rounds in Foulard's immediate vicinity. Someone yelped. She'd taken one man out of play.

Annja tried to get her bearings. Maybe they'd used a rope to get down through the sinkhole, and maybe that rope was still there, just waiting. All she had to do was reach it.

Instead, still suffering from partial blindness caused by the bright flashlight beam, she ran into one of the other men in the gloom, unaware that he'd been there. He caught her gun wrist and shoved his own pistol into her cheek below her left eye.

"Move and I'll kill you!" the man shouted.

Immediately, Annja drew her knee up into the man's groin, twisted her head to the left and snapped backward. The pistol barked and the superheated barrel painfully kissed her lips with bruising force.

The detonation temporarily robbed her of her hearing, rendering her partially deaf in addition to the blindness. The man also stripped her borrowed pistol from her fist.

Before her would-be captor recovered, she butted her forehead into his face, breaking his nose and splitting his lips, causing him to stagger back.

Foulard fired again. His bullets ripped into the man who'd held Annja. Crying out in pain, the man dropped to the floor.

Annja was in motion at once, knowing that the bullets had been meant for her. She bent, trying to find one of the lost pistols. Her backpack spilled and something metallic slid free, dropping onto the dust-covered floor.

She skidded to a halt and reached for the necklace. Before she could close her hand on it, Foulard fired three more shots.

Two of the rounds thudded into the dead man and the third struck the metal charm, sending it skidding across the cave floor.

As Annja spun to look at the man, to attempt to read his next move, another figure stepped into the light pool created by Foulard's flashlight.

Savagely, the old man with the walking stick rammed the bottom of his thick staff into the back of Foulard's skull. Crying out in pain, Foulard sagged to the cave floor.

Moving quickly, the old man surprised the remaining men and came out of the darkness. He swung the staff, taking each man's feet from beneath him, then driving the end of his weapon into each man's chest hard enough to take away his breath.

The old man looked at Annja. "Come on, then. It wouldn't do to stay around until they get a second wind."

Despite the fact that an earthquake had occurred and the men had pistols and didn't seem afraid to use them, the old man acted perfectly calm. As if this was something he did every day.

Fisting the charm, Annja stood. The metal caught the glow of the light for an instant, twirling in her grip.

"What is that?" the old man demanded. "What did you find?"

Foulard roared a foul curse and pointed the pistol at them.

"Which way?" Annja yelled. The old man hadn't come from the passageway that led to the sinkhole.

"Here." The old man turned and ran as bullets struck the cave walls.

Almost immediately, the earth quaked again.

Thrusting her arms out in front of her, not understanding how the old man appeared able to see so well in the darkness, Annja located the opening in the wall by feel just in time to keep her face from smashing into it.

For a moment, until they left the glow of the flashlight behind them, the old man was a dimly visible patch of gray ahead of her. Then they twisted around a bend in the tunnel and he vanished.

"Watch your head," he advised.

Annja put a hand over her head in time to ward off the passageway's low ceiling. The rough impact bruised her forearm. How can he see down here?

"Who are those men?" Annja asked.

"I don't know. They were after you."

"What are you doing here?"

"At present, saving you. Unless you want to go back there and get acquainted with those highwaymen."

Highwaymen was an odd description. Annja thought about that for a moment, but swiftly geared her mind back to self-preservation as a flashlight beam cut through the darkness behind them. Foulard and his companions had evidently rallied.

"Left," the old man called.

Annja didn't respond at once and crashed into the bend of the passageway.

"Aren't you listening?" the old man snapped.

"Yes." Annja recovered and flicked on her flashlight.

The old man stood around the bend. He didn't protect his eyes from the sudden light that sent painful splinters through Annja's.

Satisfied that she was intact, the old man turned and ran with improbable speed. He carried his staff close to his body as if it were an appendage.

Annja followed through the next turn, then the opening of another chamber dawned before them. Low-level light from outside filled the chamber, coming from an entrance in the mountainside.

"I have a truck," the old man said. "Farther down the mountain. Try to keep up."

Try to keep up? Annja couldn't believe he'd said that. Who is this guy? she wondered.

Then he was outside the cave, sprinting down the steep, trembling mountainside as surefootedly as a mountain goat. Annja was hard-pressed to keep up, but she knew despite his boasting that she could have outrun him. If she'd known which way to go.

They ran, crashing through brush and avoiding trees and boulders that were in their way. An elegant light blue Mercedes SUV sat parked beneath the heavy boughs of a towering Scotch pine only a short distance ahead.

"There," the old man said.

"I see it," Annja acknowledged. She ran to the passenger side as the old man headed to the driver's side.

The Mercedes's alarm system squawked as he pressed the keyless entry on the fob he'd fished from a pocket.

"Belt yourself in." The old man started the engine and pulled the SUV into gear. He didn't bother backing up, just pushed through the brush and came around in a tight circle to get back onto a narrow road that wound through the thick forest. Splashes of sunlight whipped across the dusty windshield.

Annja fumbled with the seat belt and got it strapped just as she heard motorcycle engines roar to life. As she glanced over her shoulder through the back window, the old man put his foot down harder on the accelerator.

"Did you manage to get one of their guns?" he asked.

"No."

"You had one," he accused.

"They took it back." Anger surged in Annja at his tone. Despite the fact that they were running for their lives, the old man's rudeness bothered her on some baseline level. Like fingernails on a chalkboard.

"You should have shot them," he said.

"I tried."

Shaking his head, barely navigating a sudden turn that sent them skidding out of control for a moment, he reached under his seat and pulled free a rack. Restraining straps held two pistols and a cut-down shotgun securely in place.

"Do you always go this well prepared while hiking?" Annja couldn't help asking.

"Yes. It usually saves me from embarrassing situations like running for my life down a mountainside."

Annja couldn't argue the point.

Behind them, two motorcycles roared in pursuit, quickly closing the distance. Bullets crashed through the back glass and broken shards ricocheted inside the SUV. The old man pulled fiercely on the steering wheel again.

"Can you shoot?" he demanded.

Without responding, Annja freed one of the pistols. It was a .40-caliber Heckler & Koch. She racked the slide.

"It's already loaded," the old man said.

A fat round spun through the air. Annja dropped the magazine from the pistol, and replaced the bullet. She popped the magazine back into place with her palm.

"It would be pretty foolish to carry around an unloaded weapon, now, wouldn't it?" he asked sarcastically.

Another fusillade of bullets hammered the SUV.

"Perhaps," the old man said in exasperation, "you could try shooting *back* at them."

"I was just listening to that last-minute pep talk," Annja replied.

Hunched over the steering wheel, holding on with both fists, the old man grinned at her. "You do have a certain amount of spunk. I like that."

Annja didn't care what he liked. Despite the fact that he'd helped save her life, the old man annoyed her in ways she'd never before encountered, at a level that she hadn't believed possible.

Twisting in the seat, Annja rested her right hand in her left and took aim with both eyes open. The British ex-SAS officer who had taught her to shoot had ground that into her on the indoor and outdoor firing ranges. A shooter was never supposed to limit vision, not even on a scoped weapon.

The motorcycles had closed to within thirty yards and were coming closer, fishtailing and lunging as they pursued their prey. Annja couldn't help thinking of the hunters who had chased La Bête all those years ago. Surely they had pursued it through these same woods.

But they'd never found the lair, had they? Despite her concern over her present situation, Annja couldn't help feeling a little joyful triumph mixed in.

She squeezed the trigger, blasting through a 3-round salvo. One of the bullets hit the lead motorcycle's handlebars and jarred the wheel. The rider quickly recovered and opened fire again.

"You missed!" the old man roared.

"I see that," Annja replied. "I kind of got that when he didn't fall off the motorcycle."

Bullets bounced off the SUV's exterior again, sounding like hail.

"Hold steady," Annja instructed, taking aim again.

"On this pathetic excuse for a road? Ha!" The old man jerked hard left, following the twists and turns.

Annja fired again, deliberately aiming toward the center of the lead rider's chest. She kept up the rate of fire, hoping to get lucky or at least give their pursuers something to think about.

One of the bullets struck the motorcycle's front tire. Rubber shredded and the motorcycle went out of control, lunging suddenly into the forest and smashing against a boulder the size of an earthmover. The gas tank ignited and exploded, blowing the rider free.

Her weapon empty, Annja reached for the second pistol. More rounds hammered the Mercedes.

The old man cursed, but his words were in Latin. And very descriptive.

"Latin?" Annja asked in surprise.

"I find the language more…native to my tongue," the old man said. He followed another turn and the road flared out straight for a hundred yards. "Hold on."

Annja didn't have time to brace herself on such short notice. The seat belt bit into her chest as it clamped down when the old man jammed his foot on the brakes. She whipped her head around, watching as the last motorcycle following them down the mountainside tried to stop.

The man's efforts only succeeded in locking up his brakes and sending him into an out-of-control skid. He hit the back of the SUV and flipped over the top, landing on the hood of the Mercedes. He lay there for a moment, then weakly, tried to bring up the pistol he'd somehow managed to hang on to.

Annja lifted her own weapon, but the old man shoved the transmission into reverse and spilled the man from the hood before she could fire. Then the old man shifted back into a forward gear, floored the accelerator and ran him down as he tried to get to his feet.

A dull thud sounded as the man struck the front of the SUV. A moment later the Mercedes rocked back and forth as it crunched over the man's body.

In disbelief, Annja whipped her head around and looked back. The man lay twisted and broken in the path.

"That was cruel," she said.

"You're right," the old man agreed. "Shooting him would have been much more merciful. After all, for reasons unknown to me, he was willing to kill me to get you. However, I didn't see that we were going to be successful in persuading him to stand still long enough for you to shoot him several times. He'd probably have preferred blowing up against the side of a boulder like his friend."

"I don't know who they were," Annja said. "We could go back and check for identification."

"Men like that, assassins, rarely carry identification," the old man said, continuing to gain speed. "Feel free to jump out and go back. I won't have hurt feelings. It wouldn't be the first time I've saved someone's life only to have them squander it foolishly against the very person or thing I saved them from. Do you know if the other men in the cave are dead?"

"No," Annja replied.

"Well, I suppose you might consider the possibility that they're still indisposed is worth the risk. I, however, don't."

"Your attitude leaves a lot to be desired." Annja settled back in the seat, loosening the belt.

The old man shook his head and laughed. "You're hardly the grateful sort yourself." He shoved out his hand.

She took it, surprised at the strength she felt in his grip. Then it felt as if she'd grabbed hold of a branding iron.

The old man took his hand back and the strange sensation ended.

"Are you all right?" Concern touched his blue eyes beneath the thick white eyebrows.

"Yes," Annja replied, annoyed that he would think she wasn't.

"Good." He paused and looked back at the road. "My name is Roux," he said, as if it would explain everything.

TWO HOURS LATER, Annja sat waiting quietly in the Lozère police station. She was pointedly ignored.

"I think you've disrupted their day," Roux said. "Now there will be paperwork generated, reports to file."

"This is ridiculous," Annja said.

"You're an American." Roux sat in a chair against the wall. He held a deck of cards and shuffled them one-handed. "They aren't particularly fond of Americans. Especially ones that claim to have been shot at."

"There are bullet holes in your vehicle."

Roux frowned and paused midshuffle. "Yes. That is regrettable. I don't get overly attached to vehicles, but I did like that one."

Annja shifted in the hard chair she'd been shown to. "Don't you want to know who was shooting at us?"

The old man grinned. "In my life, I've found that if someone truly wishes to harm you and you survive the attempt, you usually get a chance to get to know them again." He paused and looked at her. "You truly don't know who tried to kill you?"

"No."

"Pity."

"Back at the cave, one of the men mentioned someone named Lesauvage," Annja said.

Roux took a moment to reflect. Then he shook his head. "I don't know anyone named Lesauvage."

Working quickly, he shuffled, cut the deck and dealt out four hands on the chair between them. When he turned the cards over, she saw that he'd dealt out four royal flushes.

"Are you certain you won't play?" he asked.

"After seeing that?" Annja nodded. "I'm certain."

Smiling a little, like a small boy who has performed a good trick, Roux said, "Not even if I promise not to cheat?"

"No."

"You can trust me."

Annja looked at him.

"I believe in the game," Roux said. "Cheating…cheapens the sport."

"Sure."

Roux shrugged. "Let's play a couple hands. I'll put up a thousand dollars against the trinket you found in that cave."

"No."

"We could be here for hours." Roux shuffled the cards hopefully.

"Mademoiselle Creed."

Glancing up, Annja saw a handsome man in a black three-piece suit standing in front of her. His dark hair was combed carefully back and he had a boyish smile.

"I'm Annja Creed," she said.

The man looked around. No one else sat in the waiting room.

"I'd rather gathered that you were." He held out his hand. "I am Inspector Richelieu."

"Like the cardinal," Annja said, taking his hand and standing.

"In name only," the inspector said.

Since Cardinal Richelieu had been responsible for thousands of people being beheaded on the guillotine, Annja realized her faux pas.

"Sorry," she said. "I haven't met anyone with that name before. I meant no insult."

"I assure you, *mademoiselle,* no insult was taken." Richelieu pointed to the rear of the room. "If you would care to join me, I will take your statement in my office."

6

Brother Gaspar of the Brotherhood of the Silent Rain sat at his desk and contemplated his future. It was not a pleasant task. Thankfully, there was not much of it left. Surely no more than three or four more thousand mornings and as many evenings.

He wore a black robe against the chill that filled the room. The years had drawn him lean and spare. Beneath his cowl, his head was shaved and his skin was sallow from seldom seeing the light of day. He got out at night. All of his order did, but they couldn't be seen during the day because it raised too many questions among the townsfolk.

As leader of the Brotherhood of the Silent Rain, he did not truly have a future. His mission was to protect and unlock the past. If he succeeded in the first, no one would ever know the monstrous predations his order had allowed to take place three hundred years ago.

But if he succeeded in the second and unlocked the past, made everything right again, his whole life would change. He looked forward to that possibility.

Even at sixty-eight years old, he believed he had a few good years left. It wasn't that he looked forward to getting out into the world. He had renounced all of that when he took his vows. But he had read all the books and manuscripts in his small post.

He longed for the true manuscripts, the ones he had seen as a child in Rome, where he'd been trained in the secrets he had to keep. The documents that told of secret histories and covered holders of power who weren't known to the general masses.

He sighed and his gentle breath nearly extinguished the guttering candles that illuminated the stone cave. The monastery, hidden from sight, was located deep inside the Cévennes Mountains. It wasn't a true edifice built by the hand of men in service to the church. Rather, it was an aberration within the earth that earlier monks had discovered and elaborated on.

On good days, Brother Gaspar thought of the monastery as a gift from God, made expressly for his order. On bad days, he thought of it as a prison.

He sat at his desk and wrote his weekly letter to Bishop Taglio, who guided his moves and provided counsel when needed. Although written with handmade ink, in elegant calligraphy, on paper made by the order, the letter was merely perfunctory. It was merely a chore that occupied his head and his hands for a short time.

After thirty-seven years, since he had taken on the mantle of the leader of the order, Brother Gaspar had begun to have difficulty finding ways to express the situation. *Everything is fine and going according to plan. We are still searching for that which was lost.*

He kept the references deliberately vague. Enemies didn't quite abound these days as they had three hundred years ago, but they were still out there.

In fact, even a few treasure hunters had joined the pack. Corvin Lesauvage had snooped around for years. Over the past few the man had become extremely aggressive in his search. He had killed two monks who had fallen into his hands, torturing them needlessly because they didn't know anything to assuage his curiosity.

Only Brother Gaspar knew that, and he shuddered to think about falling into Lesauvage's hands. Of course, he would not. He would die before that happened.

His fellow monks had orders to kill him the instant he fell into someone else's custody. Since he never went anywhere alone, and seldom ventured outside the monastery walls, he didn't think he would ever be at risk.

Only the imminent disclosure of the secrets he protected would bring him forth. God willing, he would find the truth of those secrets himself. But, as they had remained hidden for three hundred years, there was little chance of that.

"Master."

Startled, Brother Gaspar looked up from his broad table and the letter he had been writing. "Yes. Come forward that I may see you."

Brother Napier stepped from the shadows. He wore hiking clothes, tattoos and piercings, and looked like any young man who prowled the Parisian streets.

"Yes, Brother Napier," Brother Gaspar inquired.

"I did not mean to bother you while you were at your letter," the younger monk stated.

Brother Gaspar put his pen in the inkwell with slow deliberation. "But you have."

"For good reason, master."

"What is it?"

"The woman has found something."

"The American?"

"Yes, master. She found La Bête's cave."

Angry and frightened, Brother Gaspar surged to his feet. He leaned on the desk and his arms trembled. "It can't be."

Kneeling in supplication, Brother Napier held up his hands. Sheets of papers containing images rested on them. "It is true, master. I saw the cave myself. But only for a short time. The earth closed back over it." He looked at Brother Gaspar. "I saw it, master. I saw the Beast of Gévaudan. The stories were *true*."

Of course they were, the older monk thought. Otherwise we would not all be trapped here.

Rounding the desk, Brother Gaspar took the papers from the young monk's hands. He stared at the pictures. They showed the young American woman on the mountaintop and apparently running for her life. Other pictures showed motorcycles chasing an SUV.

"You saw La Bête?" Brother Gaspar asked.

"Yes."

"Was it—" he hesitated "—alive?"

"No. It was dead. Very dead. A warrior killed it."

"A warrior?" Excitement flared through Brother Gaspar. The old stories were true. The knowledge offered validation for all the years he had spent at the monastery. "How do you know a warrior killed it?"

"Because he was still there."

"The warrior?"

"Yes, master."

"He was dead, as well?" Brother Gaspar doubted the man could have been in any other shape, but just knowing the story was true and knowing all the arcane things connected with it, he felt compelled to ask.

"Yes, master. It looked as though he and La Bête had fought and killed each other."

Brother Gaspar felt the air in the cave grow thicker than normal. "Did you examine La Bête's body or that of the warrior?" he asked.

"I did. But only for a short time. The cavern was shaking. The earthquake was still going on. Luckily, I got out before the cavern closed."

"It closed?"

"Yes, master."

"You could find this place again?"

The young monk nodded. "But it would do no good, master. The earth has sealed the cave tightly." He paused. "Perhaps a quake another day will reveal it again."

"We will watch for this, then," Brother Gaspar said. His hand caressed his throat. "When you looked at the warrior, did you see anything?"

"You mean the necklace?"

Brother Gaspar's heart beat sped up. "Yes," he replied in a hoarse whisper.

The necklace was the greatest secret of them all.

"The American woman carried a necklace from the cave," the young monk said.

"You followed her?" Brother Gaspar asked.

"As far as I could," the young monk agreed. "She was pursued."

"By who?"

"Lesauvage's men."

That announcement poured ice water into the old monk's veins. "How did they get there?"

"They followed the woman. I only happened to be in the mountains when I saw her with the old man."

"What old man?" Brother Gaspar was alarmed.

"I do not know, master."

Brother Gaspar went through the sheets of pictures. "Is he in these?"

"Sadly, no. I thought I took his picture, but when I developed the images, I found I had not."

Brother Gaspar, whose life had been so carefully ordered for so very long, felt very unsettled. He didn't like the fact that Lesauvage's men had been so close to the discovery of La Bête or that his monks had merely been lucky.

When he had found out about the American television person, he had dismissed her at once. *Chasing History's Monsters* was pure entertainment and a complete waste of time. No one doing research for such a show presented any threat to uncovering his secrets. Or so he had believed.

"Who has the necklace now?" Brother Gaspar asked.

"The woman, I think." Brother Napier looked flustered. "Lesauvage's men gave pursuit, but the American woman and the old man shot back at them and escaped."

"Where is the American woman?"

"She was staying in Lozère. I don't know where."

Lamenting that he hadn't given more thought to the threat the woman might have posed, Brother Gaspar sighed. "Find her. Find out if she still has the necklace."

"And if she does, master?"

"Take it from her and bring it to me."

"Of course." Brother Napier bowed and backed out of the room.

Resentfully, Brother Gaspar glared at the table. His nearly completed letter sat there.

It would have to be rewritten, of course. And he would have to call the bishop. Perhaps, Brother Gaspar thought, he would soon be free of his prison.

7

Inspector Richelieu's office was neat and compact. Not the kind of office Annja expected of a working policeman. She'd seen cop's offices before. None of them were this pristine.

She wondered if maybe Richelieu was gay or lived with his mother. Or perhaps he was a control freak. A personality trait like that was a real relationship killer.

Not that Annja was looking for a relationship. But the inspector did have nice eyes and nice hands. Her mind wandered for a moment.

"Have a seat," Richelieu invited, waving to the chair across from his tiny metal desk.

Annja sat. In the too neat office, she felt dirty and grimy. Outside in the main office with the other policemen, she'd felt that she belonged. Now she wanted a hot bath and a change of clothing. And food. She suddenly realized she was starving.

"I gave a statement to one of the officers," Annja said.

"I know." Richelieu sat on the other side of the desk. "I read it. Both versions."

While waiting for something—anything—to happen, Annja had written up her statement herself in addition to the one the policeman had taken. She hadn't trusted his eye for detail. Or his ear.

"Your penmanship and your French are exquisite," Richelieu commented.

"Thanks," Annja said, "but I wasn't here for a grade."

Richelieu smiled. "I've also been investigating the supposed site of the chase down the mountain."

"Supposed?" Annja echoed.

"Yes." The inspector looked concerned for a moment. "Would you prefer to speak in English? I'm quite good at it and perhaps it would be easier."

"French is fine," Annja said.

"I thought perhaps you hadn't understood."

"I understood perfectly." Annja put an edge to her words. Getting dismissed out of hand in the field of archaeology because she was a woman was something she'd had to deal with often. She didn't take it lightly. "There was no 'supposed' chase site. It was there. Along with two or three dead men."

Richelieu waited a moment, then shook his head. "No dead men."

Annja thought about that. "Perhaps Lesauvage had the bodies picked up."

"Why would he do that?"

"I don't know," Annja replied. "I came here to you to find out why he would send men looking for me in the first place."

"Do you know that he sent the men?"

"I overheard one of the men say that they were working for Lesauvage."

"But you don't know that they, in fact, did."

"Why would they say they were if they weren't?"

The inspector looked amused and perplexed. "I'm quite sure I wouldn't know."

"I could ask Lesauvage," Annja said.

"I thought you didn't know him."

"Maybe you could introduce us," Annja suggested with a smile. The inspector wasn't the only one who could play games. He was just the only one at the moment with some reason to.

A sour smile pulled at Richelieu's lips. He pulled at his left ear. "You're intimating that I have some kind of personal relationship with Lesauvage?"

Returning his gaze full measure, Annja asked, "Are you sure

speaking French works for you? Maybe English translates more plainly."

Richelieu scowled. "I didn't come here to listen to disparaging remarks directed at me, Miss Creed."

"I didn't come here to cool my heels for three hours, then get patted on the head and sent away."

Opening the slim notebook computer on his desk, Richelieu opened a file that displayed several pictures. "We investigated the site. I took these pictures. I found expended cartridges, bullets in the trees and scorch marks." He paused. "No bodies. No motorcycles."

"Then Lesauvage picked them up."

"Why?"

"So he wouldn't be implicated."

Closing the computer, Richelieu looked at her. "I was hoping to establish the veracity of your claim, Miss Creed. I did find damage done out in the forest—which is federally protected, I might add, and something you might be called upon to answer for—but nothing that you and your friend couldn't have done yourselves."

"We didn't intentionally damage the forest," Annja said. She was annoyed. Truthfully, she hadn't expected much in the way of help from the police. This man, Lesauvage, appeared to have a large organization at his beck and call. Assuming he had inroads with the local police was no great leap of imagination.

"So you say," the inspector said.

"I *do* say."

"I will note your disavowal in my reports."

"Why would we do something like that?" Annja asked, exasperated.

Richelieu spread his hands. "You're a television personality, Miss Creed. Here in Lozère chasing a monster that's three hundred years old. Perhaps you thought tales of a running gun battle through the forest would, perhaps, *spice up* your tale. For your viewers. I am told that you people in television will do anything to improve your ratings."

"I wouldn't do that," Annja said angrily.

"Perhaps not. But there were no bodies out there. Nor was there a giant crevasse leading to an underground cave containing the remains of La Bête."

"The earthquake must have closed it back up."

Richelieu nodded. "Amazing, isn't it, that nature herself would align against you?"

"What about the bullet holes in the old man's SUV?"

"A lover's quarrel?"

Frowning, Annja said, "Me? And that old man? Please."

Richelieu laughed. "Perhaps it was over business. Perhaps you were both shooting at game and hit the truck instead."

"No."

"Your report here could be just to falsify an insurance claim."

"That's not what happened."

"But you are on the show with the woman with the...*problematic* apparel."

Terrific, Annja thought. Maybe poltergeists could get chased away from historic manors, but she'd be haunted by Kristie Chatham's bodacious ta-tas forever.

"I have never had a problem with my apparel," Annja pointed out.

"I have made a note of that, as well."

Annja reached into her pack and took out her digital camera. She switched it on and brought up the pictures she'd shot inside the cave. In spite of the darkness, the images had turned out well.

"This is La Bête," Annja said.

Taking the camera, Richelieu consulted the images, punching through them one by one. He handed the camera back. "Anyone with Photoshop could make these."

"And take the time to put them on a camera?" Annja couldn't believe it.

"It would," the inspector said as inoffensively as he could, "make your story seem more legitimate. When *The Blair Witch Project* appeared in theaters, many people believed the video footage was part of an actual paranormal investigation. And Orson Welles anchoring *The War of the Worlds* in news reports on the radio in 1938 was also deliberate, causing mass hysteria throughout your country. Media people know best how to present anything they wish to."

"Those are real pictures," Annja stated.

"If you insist."

Angrily, Annja put the camera away. "Who is Lesauvage?"

"A figment of your overactive imagination," Richelieu said.

Without a word, Annja got up to leave.

"Or…" Richelieu let the word dangle like a fishing lure.

Annja waited. Mysteries always kept her hanging well past the point she should leave.

"Or he's a man named Corvin Lesauvage," Richelieu said. "If it is this man, he's very dangerous. He's a known criminal, though that's never been successfully proved. Witnesses have a tendency to…disappear. Likewise, so do past business associates."

"Can you help me with him?"

"Can you offer me any proof that he's truly after you, Miss Creed?"

Annja thought for a moment. "There was a man who was knocked unconscious in an alley earlier this morning. In the downtown area."

More interested now, Richelieu leaned forward. "Do you know something about that?"

Ignoring the question, Annja asked, "Did he work for Corvin Lesauvage?"

"We don't know."

"Then I suggest you ask him."

Richelieu frowned. "We can't."

"Why not?"

"He was killed. Less than an hour after we took him into custody."

Annja thought about that. Evidently there was something at stake here that she didn't know about. "Did Lesauvage do it?"

"We don't know who did it."

Meaning you don't know if it was done by an inmate or a police officer, Annja thought.

"There was a local boy with me this morning," Annja said. "His name is Avery Moreau. I hired him to set up my trip, arrange for things."

Richelieu nodded. "I know Avery. He's a sad case."

"Why?"

"His father died quite suddenly a few weeks ago."

"I don't understand," Annja said.

"His father was shot to death."

"By Lesauvage?" Annja asked, thinking maybe the men had been after Avery more than her.

"No," Richelieu said. "By me."

Annja didn't know what to say to that, so she said nothing. She wondered if perhaps Richelieu was warning her.

"Gerard Moreau, Avery's father, was a small-time burglar," Richelieu said. "He'd been in and out of jail for years. That is a matter of record and was covered in the media. It was only a matter of time before we put him away for good or a homeowner shot him. As it happened, I shot him while investigating the report of a burglary. He hadn't made it out of the house and came at me with a weapon." The inspector leaned back in his chair. "Needless to say, Avery Moreau has been less than cooperative."

Thinking about things for a moment, Annja said, "Let's say for a moment that you believe me about the chase down the mountain."

Richelieu smiled. "Let's."

"Why would Lesauvage recover the bodies of the dead men?"

"To avoid being implicated."

"Which is what I said."

"You did. It's a conclusion that fits the facts as you present them. We're entertaining that for the moment."

"Why would Lesauvage risk sending men after me in the first place?"

"You know, Miss Creed," Richelieu said with a smile, "as I read your reports and listened to you now, I have asked myself that several times. I'm open to your suggestion."

Annja had no idea what was going on. The weight of the charm rested heavily in her pocket. She hadn't told the inspector about it. If she had, he would have taken it away. Countries were funny about things that might be national treasures.

"I don't know," Annja finally said. "But I intend to find out."

OUT IN THE MAIN ROOM, Roux was playing poker with some policemen. He looked up as Annja stepped from the inspector's office.

Annja walked past him.

"Gentlemen, it's been a pleasure, but I'm afraid I have to go now," Roux said as he gathered the pile of money he'd won. He winked at the policemen and fell into step with Annja. "Are we going somewhere?"

"No."

"Humph," Roux said. "Our friend the inspector didn't believe your story?"

"Someone removed the bodies," she said. "The quake closed the cave again."

"Pity. It would have been an exciting episode for your show."

She whirled on him. "You know about *Chasing History's Monsters*?"

"I must confess," Roux admitted, "I'm something of a fan, I'm afraid. Not quite as stimulating as *Survivor*, but well worth the investment of time. I particularly like...I can't remember her name. The girl with the clothing problems." He smiled a little.

"You would," Annja said, disgusted.

Look at the fire in her, Roux thought. Simply amazing.

"I'm a man of simple pleasures," Roux said.

"Mr. Roux," Inspector Richelieu called out.

Roux turned to face the man. "Yes, Inspector?"

"Would you like to make a statement?"

Grinning, Roux shook his head. "No. Thank you." When he turned around, he discovered that Annja had left him. She was making her way out the door. He hurried to catch up.

Night had fallen while they were inside the police station. Shadows draped the streets.

"You'll have a hard time finding a cab at this time of night," Roux said.

She ignored him, arms folded over her breasts and facing the street.

"Probably," Roux went on, "walking back to wherever you're staying wouldn't be the wisest thing you could do."

She still didn't respond.

"I could give you a ride," Roux suggested. More than anything, he wanted a look at the metal charm she had found in the cave. If it was what he thought it was, his long search might at last be over. "I at least owe you that after what we've been through."

She looked at him then. "You didn't try to tell them about the men who chased us."

"No."

"Why?"

"I knew they wouldn't listen."

She continued to glare at him.

"Corvin Lesauvage," Roux said, "is a very connected man in this area. A very dangerous man."

"Tell me about him."

"Over dinner," Roux countered. "I know a little bistro not far from here that has some of the best wines you could hope for."

She looked at him askance.

"You won't regret it," Roux said.

8

The bistro did carry a very fine selection of wines. Roux insisted on their sampling a variety during dinner. The meal was superb. Annja devoured filet mignon, steamed vegetables, baked potatoes smothered in cheese, salads and rolls as big as her fist and so fresh from the oven they almost burned her fingers.

She hadn't eaten since breakfast, so she didn't strive for modesty. She ate with gusto, and Roux complimented her on her appetite.

As it turned out, Roux didn't know much about Corvin Lesauvage. All he had was a collection of vague rumors. Lesauvage was a murderer several times over. He ran drugs. He peddled archaeological forgeries. If an illegal dollar was made in the Lozère area, ten percent of it belonged to Corvin Lesauvage because he brokered the deal, allowed it to take place or kept quiet about it.

The bistro was quiet and dark. French love songs played softly in the background. A wall of trickling water backlit by aquamarine lights kept the shadows at bay. The wait staff proved almost undetectable.

Warmed by the wine, exhausted by her exertions, Annja found herself relaxing perhaps a little more than she should have. But her curiosity about Roux was rampant.

"Are you French?" she asked after they had finished discovering how little he knew about Lesauvage.

"As French as can be," Roux promised. He refilled her glass, then his own.

"Yet you speak Latin fluently."

Roux gestured magnanimously. "Doesn't everyone?"

"No. What do you do, Mr. Roux?"

"Please," he said, turning up a hand, "just call me Roux. It's a name that's suited me long enough."

"The question's still on the table," Annja pointed out.

"So it is." He sipped his wine. "Truthfully? I do whatever pleases me. If fortune smiles on me, there's a reason to get up in the morning. If I'm truly blessed, there are several reasons."

"Then you must be independently wealthy," Annja said, half in jest.

"Yes," he admitted. "Very. I've had plenty of time to amass a fortune. It's not hard if you live long enough and don't try to be greedy."

"Where do you live?"

"In Paris." Roux smiled. "I've always loved Paris. Even after it's gotten as gaudy and overpopulated and dirty as it has. You open the window in the morning there, you can almost feel the magic in the air."

"How did you make your fortune?"

"Slowly. Investments, mostly. I've been very lucky where investments are concerned. I've always been able to take the long view, I suppose."

Annja eyed him over her glass. "How old are you?"

"Far, far older than I look, I assure you." His blue eyes twinkled merrily.

Santa Claus should have eyes like that, Annja couldn't help thinking.

"You are quite aggressive in your investigative approach," he said gently.

"I've been accused of that before." Annja leaned forward, studying him. "I've made my peace with it. As an archaeologist, you're trained to ask questions. Of the situation. Of the people around you. Of yourself."

"I see."

"What were you doing up in the mountains this afternoon?"

"Taking a constitutional."

Annja smiled. Despite the abrasive nature the old man brought out in her, there was something about him that she liked. He was as openly secretive as the nuns at the orphanage where she'd grown up.

"I don't believe you," she told him.

"I take no offense," he told her. "I wouldn't believe me, either."

"You were looking for something."

Roux shrugged.

"But you're not going to tell me what it is," Annja said.

"Let me ask you something." Roux leaned in close to her and spoke conspiratorially. "You found something in that cave this afternoon, didn't you?"

Annja picked at a bit of leftover bread and used the time to think. "I found La Bête."

"A creature that you believe was once La Bête."

"I showed you the pictures."

"I saw it, too," Roux reminded her.

"You don't believe it was La Bête?" Annja asked.

"Perhaps." Roux lifted his shoulders and dropped them. "The light was uncertain. Things were happening very quickly in there."

"What do you think it was?"

"A fabrication, perhaps."

"It was real." Annja had no doubt about that.

"There's something else I'm interested in," the old man replied. "Something you haven't told me. I saw you in that cave. You had something in your hand."

"A human skull," she replied.

"That isn't all."

The charm was still in Annja's pocket. She'd had it out only once. That was back in the police station bathroom. She'd been afraid the police were going to take charm away from her so she'd made a rubbing of both sides in her journal.

"I saw you with something else in your hand," he said. "Something shiny. Something metallic. It looked old." He paused. "If you found it in the cave, I would think it was very old."

"Not when compared to the Mesozoic period."

Roux laughed. The sound was easy and pleasant.

Annja found herself laughing with him, but thought it was as much because of the wine as of the humor in the situation. She didn't trust him. She was certain his presence in the mountains was no accident.

"Touché," he replied. He sipped more wine. "Still, you have me intrigued, Miss Creed."

She looked at him. "I don't trust you. But don't take that personally. I don't trust most people."

"In your current state of affairs, with a criminal figure pursuing you for some unknown, nefarious reason, I wouldn't be the trusting sort, either."

"I was taught by the best to be slightly paranoid."

Roux lifted his eyebrows. "The Central Intelligence Agency?"

"Worse than that," Annja said. "Catholic nuns."

Roux grinned. "Ah, that explains it."

"The paranoia?"

"The fact that you don't come bursting out of your shirts on the television program." Roux looked at her appraisingly. "You're certainly equipped."

Annja stared at him. "Are you coming on to me?"

"Would it be appropriate?"

"No."

Roux tapped the table with his hand. "Then that settles it. I was *not* coming on to you. It's the wine, the candlelight in your hair and the sparkle in those marvelous green eyes. A moment in a beautiful restaurant after a delightful repast."

"I think," Annja said, "that you probably hit on anything that has a heartbeat and stays in one place long enough."

Leaning back in his chair, Roux laughed uproariously. He drew the unwelcome attention of several other diners. Finally, he regained control of himself. "I do like you, Miss Creed. I find you...refreshing."

Annja sipped her wine and considered her options. So far, the origins of the charm had stumped her. She looked at the old man. "I'm going to trust you. A little."

"In what capacity?"

"Something professional."

Anticipation gleamed in his bright blue eyes. "Whatever you found in the cave?"

"Yes. How experienced are you in antiquities?"

Roux shrugged. "I've made more than a few fortunes dabbling in such luxuries. There are a great many forgeries out there, you know."

Annja did know. She had dealt with several of them. In addition to everything else she did, she also consulted on museum acquisitions and for private buyers. Her certificate of authenticity marked many of them.

"This isn't a forgery." She took the piece of metal from her pocket and placed it on the table between them.

A look of pleasant surprise filled Roux's face. "You didn't give it to the inspector?"

"No."

"Why?"

"He didn't possess an archaeologist's mind-set."

"I see." Roux gestured to the medallion. "May I?"

"As long as I can watch you, sure." Annja leaned in and watched carefully.

"You carried this unprotected in your pocket?" His voice carried recrimination.

"I wasn't able to properly store it."

"Perhaps something in your backpack."

"Perhaps the police could have gone through my things."

"Yes. Of course." Roux pushed the medallion around, studying the image stamped onto it.

As he touched the charm, the fiery vision that had filled Annja's head during the earthquake returned to her in full Technicolor.

"Are you all right?" He was looking at her.

"Yes," she said, though she didn't honestly know.

"Do you know what this is?" Roux asked.

"A talisman of some sort. Probably for good luck." Annja described how she had found it tied around the dead man's neck.

"Not very lucky," Roux said.

"He killed the Beast of Gévaudan."

"Even if this nameless warrior had received the glory due him, fame is a poor consolation prize."

"I don't think he was interested in prizes."

"You believe he was slaying a monster."

"Yes," Annja replied. Despite her experience disproving myths, she had always believed in slaying monsters.

"Do you know what this symbol is?" Roux asked.

Moving the flickering candle flame closer to the charm, Annja shook her head. "I've never seen it before."

"Nor have I." Roux reached into his pocket and took out a Leatherman Multitool. He held the charm in his fingers and aimed the point at the grimy buildup surrounding the image of the wolf and the mountain.

"Wait a minute," Annja said.

"Trust me. I'll be careful. I know what I'm doing."

Breathing slowly, Annja watched. She didn't think the old man could hurt the charm, but she didn't like having it out of her possession.

Roux worked gently. The grime fell away in tiny flakes. Beneath it, the metal proved as lustrous and shiny as the day it had been forged.

Given the conditions of the cave, Annja had expected a fair amount of preservation. Ships had spent hundreds of years in caves and were found remarkably intact, as if the pirates who had hidden there had only left days ago instead of centuries.

"Beautiful," Roux whispered when he had finished. He turned the piece of metal in his fingers, catching the candlelight again and again.

Annja silently agreed. "Have you ever seen anything like this?"

"A good-luck charm? Of course I have."

"Not just a good-luck charm," Annja said, "but one like this."

Roux shook his head. "It's a charm. I believe that. Since you found it around the dead man's neck, I'd say it was made to defend him—"

"—against the Beast of Gévaudan," Annja finished. "I got that. But the mark on the obverse looks like it was struck by a die. The wolf and the mountain appeared to have been carved."

"So you believe this to be a unique piece rather than one of many?" Roux asked.

"I do," Annja agreed. "You can see the die mark wasn't struck quite cleanly and two of the edges are slightly blunted."

Peering more closely at the charm, Roux said, "You have very good eyes." He studied the image for a moment. "And, you're exactly right." He looked up at her.

"Have you seen such a die mark before?" Annja asked.

"No."

Studying the old man, Annja tried to figure out if he was lying to her. If he was, she decided, he was very good at it. "I was hoping you had."

"Never. I would be very interested to learn what you find out about it." Roux studied her. "Tell me, in your archaeological travels, have you ever had cause to research the history of Joan of Arc?"

"I'm familiar with her stories, but I've spent no real time with them," Annja said.

"Pity. She was a very tragic figure."

For just a moment, Annja remembered the visions she had experienced. Joan of Arc had burned at the stake not far from where Annja now sat. Had her subconscious summoned that image during the quake?

"She was a very brave young woman," Roux said. "Foolish, certainly, but brave nonetheless. She should not be forgotten."

What are you trying to tell me? Annja wondered.

"One thing you should start doing immediately is taking better care of this charm." Roux said. "After all, it could prove to be a significant find if you discover its history." Roux took a handkerchief from his pocket and dropped the charm into the center of it. Picking up the ends of the handkerchief, he folded the charm inside. Then he handed the makeshift package to Annja with a smile. "There. That should better protect it until you can put it in a proper storage container."

Annja closed her hand over the handkerchief and felt the hard outline of the disk inside. She put the handkerchief into her shorts pocket and closed the Velcro tab.

"Thank you," she said.

Roux looked around, then tapped the table and said, "I'll be back in just a moment. Too much wine."

Comfortable and almost sleepy, Annja settled back in her chair and relaxed. Thoughts of the cozy bed at the bed-and-breakfast where she was staying danced in her head. She tried to marshal her thoughts and figure out her next course of action.

Identification of the charm was paramount. Doug Morrell would love the story and not hesitate at all over the digital pictures she had taken of La Bête. The television producer wasn't like some police inspectors Annja had met.

Thinking of Inspector Richelieu reminded Annja of Corvin

Lesauvage. It didn't make sense to think that a well-organized crime figure would send a team after her for the camera equipment and whatever cash she carried.

But that wasn't what they were after, was it? The man had wanted her. Lesauvage had wanted to talk to her.

She started to feel frightened.

Suddenly she realized how much time had passed since Roux had quit the table. He had been gone a long time. Too long.

Glancing around the bistro, Annja discovered that the server and the manager were watching her. She stood and looked outside. Sure enough, the bullet-scarred SUV was no longer parked at the curb.

"Mademoiselle?"

Annja turned and found the young brunette server standing at the table.

"Is something the matter, *mademoiselle?"* the young woman asked.

"I don't suppose he paid the bill before he ducked out, did he?" Annja asked.

"No, *mademoiselle."*

Annja sighed and took out the cash she carried. "How much is it?" The server told her.

"That much?" Annja was surprised. She put her money back and reached for her credit card.

The waitress nodded contritely, obviously still hopeful of a large tip.

"He was supposed to be independently wealthy," Annja said. "Several times over."

"Yes, *mademoiselle."* The server took Annja's credit card and retreated.

Then Annja remembered how Roux had effortlessly shuffled and cut the deck of cards one-handed at the police station. A sick feeling twisted in her stomach.

She removed the folded handkerchief from her pocket. The disk shape was still there, but the panic within her grew as she opened the cloth package.

Inside the folds she found a two-euro coin. It was two-toned, brass and silvery, bright and shiny new.

Just the right size to make her think Roux had handed her the charm. Not only had he stuck her with the bistro tab, but he had also stolen her find.

Carefully, she folded the coin back in the handkerchief, noting that it was monogrammed with a crimson *R*. If she got lucky, he'd left her with more than he'd intended.

9

"You're getting back quite late, Mademoiselle Creed."

"I am, François. I'm sorry. I should have called." Annja stood in the doorway of the bed-and-breakfast. She'd come in feeling inept and foolish, and angry with the local police because they didn't know Roux and hadn't even bothered to ask his name. No one had even taken down his license plate. She'd wasted an hour and a half discovering that.

She hated feeling guilty on top of it.

The clock on the mantel above the fireplace showed that it was almost eleven p.m.

François Lambert was a retired carpenter who had thought ahead. While building homes for others, François had also built for his own retirement years. The bed-and-breakfast was located a few miles north of Lozère, far enough out of the town to afford privacy and a good view of the Cévennes Mountains.

One of the things that Annja loved most about her vocation was the endless possibility of meeting people. They hailed from all walks of life, and were driven by all kinds of dreams and desires.

Over seventy years old, François was long and lanky, a whipcord man used to a life filled with hard work. He had a headful of white hair brushed back and touching his collar. His white mustache looked elegant and aristocratic. He wore slacks and a white shirt.

François waved away her apology. "I was worried about you, that's all. Lozère can be dangerous sometimes when it is dark." He studied her. "But you are all right, yes?"

"I am. Thank you."

He took a pack of cigarettes from his pocket and shook one out. He lit up with a lighter. "I heard the police were involved."

Small towns, Annja thought, you have to love them. She did, too. They were usually quaint and exotic and moved to their own rhythm.

But gossip spread as aggressively as running bamboo.

"I was attacked," Annja said. "Up in the mountains."

François shook his leonine head. "A beautiful woman such as yourself shouldn't be out alone. I told you that."

"I know. I promise I'll be more careful in the future." Annja started up the stairs.

"Were you injured?"

"No. I was lucky."

"I heard Corvin Lesauvage was involved."

Annja froze halfway up the stairs. "Do you know anything about him?"

A pensive frown tightened her host's lined face. "Very little. I'm told that is the best thing to know about him. Lesauvage is a bad man."

"Inspector Richelieu told me that, as well."

"You went to him for help?" François looked concerned.

"He was assigned to the investigation."

"He is not a good man, either, that one. He tends to take care of things his way."

Annja hesitated a moment. "I was told he shot Avery Moreau's father."

"Yes." François looked sad. "It is a bad way for a boy to lose his father. Avery, he struggles with right and wrong, you see. At least when his father was around, knowing that his father was a thief, he had an idea of what he didn't want to be when he grew up."

"You didn't mention this when I hired him to help me," Annja said.

François's face colored a little. "If I had, would you have hired him?"

Annja answered honestly. "I don't know."

"I was only looking out for the boy. Someone needs to. But I should have told you."

"This," she said, wanting to let the old man off the hook, "had nothing to do with that."

"I hope not."

"I'm sure it doesn't."

François nodded. "Camille wanted to know if you would be joining us for breakfast."

"Yes," Annja said. "I've got a lot to do tomorrow. There is one thing you could help me with."

"If I may," he agreed.

She asked for some rosin from his violin kit and was quickly supplied with a small portion in a coffee cup. After thanking François, Annja said good night and went up to the room she'd rented.

She had a lot to do tonight. She didn't intend to let Roux get away with what he'd done.

ANNJA'S RENTED ROOM WAS small and cozy. Camille Lambert had filled it with sensible curtains and linens. But the bed, desk, chair and trunk all spoke of François's knowing hands.

She opened the windows and stood for just a moment as the night breeze filled the room. She took a deep breath and let go of the anger and frustration she felt. Those emotions were good motivators, but they wouldn't sustain her during a project.

No, for that she'd always relied on curiosity.

This time, there were a number of things to be curious about. Why was a man like Lesauvage interested in her? Why had Roux stolen the charm she'd found in La Bête's lair? Could the hidden cave in the Cévennes Mountains be found again? What did the designs on the charm mean?

And who was Roux?

Annja started with that.

Although the house was wired with electricity, power outages sometimes occurred. The Lamberts had shown her where the candles were kept for emergencies.

She took one of the candles, placed it in a holder on the desk and lit it. Then she held one of her metal notebooks a few inches over the flame. In a short time, a considerable amount of lampblack covered the metal surface.

Using a thin-bladed knife she generally used on dig sites, Annja scraped most of the lampblack into the coffee cup with the rosin. When she was satisfied she had enough of the black residue, she used the knife handle to grind the lampblack into the rosin. The mixture quickly turned dark gray.

She spread Roux's handkerchief on the desk. Using one of the fine brushes from her kit, she dumped some powder onto the euro coin.

Gently, she blew away the powder. When she could remove no more in this manner, she employed the brush, using deft strokes like those she would use on a fragile piece of pottery to reveal the images she was after.

A fingerprint stood out on the coin.

Annja smiled. Roux hadn't been as clever as he'd believed.

Working with meticulous care, which was a necessary skill in archaeology, she trapped the fingerprint on clear tape. She mounted her discovery on a plain white index card.

Taking a brief respite from the backbreaking labor, Annja straightened and placed her notebook computer on the desk. She hooked it to her satellite phone, then used the Web service to log on to the Internet.

Moving mechanically, she brought up alt.archaeology and alt.archaeology.esoterica, her favorite Usenet newsgroups. The former was a format for archaeology and history professors, students and enthusiasts to meet and share ideas. The latter held discourse on more inventive matters.

If she needed hard information, Annja resorted to alt.archaeology. But if she needed something more along the lines for guesswork, she would generally post to alt.archaeology.esoterica.

Since she had no idea where to begin with the images of the charm, she elected to post to both.

Taking her digital camera from her backpack, she changed lenses and switched the function over to manual instead of automatic. She also used a flash separate from the camera rather than mounted on it.

Working quickly, confidently, she took pictures of the rubbings of the charm she'd made in her journal. Then she took pictures of the fingerprint from the coin.

Opening a new topic on the alt.archaeology newsgroup, Annja quickly wrote a short note.

I'm seeking information about the following images found on a charm/talisman/coin? Not sure which. I saw it in France recently, at a small town called Lozère. It caught my attention and now I can't get it out of my mind. Can anyone help? Is it just a tourist geegaw?

She framed her request like that to detract immediate attention. She knew if she sounded like a newbie other wanna-be experts wouldn't leave her alone and would try to impress her. Hopefully only someone who knew something about the images would bother to respond.

She attached the images of the charm's rubbings and sent the postings to both newsgroups.

Going to her e-mail service, she opened her account, ignored the latest rash of spam and picked a name from her address book.

Bart McGilley was a Brooklyn cop she occasionally dated when she was home. He was a nice guy, on his way to making detective at the precinct. They had a good time whenever they were together. Thankfully, he shared an interest in some of the city's more historical settings and museums.

She typed a quick note.

Hey Bart,
I'm in France doing a workup on a piece for *Monsters*. I'm keeping my blouse together, so I'm having to make this good. Points of interest, rather than interesting points.

I ran into a guy who swiped something from me. Nothing big. But I thought if I could give the police his name, it might help.

I know it's a big favor to ask, but could you run this print?
Best,
Annja

She attached the image of the fingerprint and sent it. She also took a moment to send the pictures of La Bête and the cave to Doug Morrell. Then she retreated to her bathroom.

One of the finest things François Lambert had done in creating his retirement business was to add a soaker tub to each guest bathroom. It wasn't something that many bed-and-breakfasts in the area had. But it was one of the selling points that had caught Annja's attention.

Once the tub was filled, she eased in and turned on the jets. In seconds, the heat and the turbulence worked to wash away the stress and tension of the day.

CONTROLLING THE EXCITEMENT that filled him, Roux drove toward the iron gates of his estate outside Paris. The land was wooded and hilly. The large stone manor house and outbuildings couldn't easily be seen even by helicopter.

At a touch of a button on the steering wheel, the iron gates separated and rolled back quietly. An armed guard stepped out from the gatehouse holding an assault rifle.

"Mr. Roux," the man said.

Roux knew another man waited for confirmation inside the bulletproof and bombproof gatehouse. Not only was his landscape well tended, but so was his security. He paid dearly for it and never begrudged the price.

"Yes," Roux said, turning his head so he could be clearly illuminated by the guard's flashlight.

The guard swept the SUV with his beam. "Ran into some trouble?"

"A little," Roux admitted. There was no way to conceal the bullet holes from a trained eye.

"Anything we should know about?"

The guard was American. He was direct and thorough. Those were qualities that Roux loved about the Americans. Of course, they balanced that with obstinacy and contrariness.

"I don't think this will follow me home," Roux said. "But it wouldn't hurt to be a trifle more vigilant for a few days."

"Yes, sir."

Roux drove through. The gates closed behind him. For the first time since he'd left Lozère, he felt safe.

His headlights carved through the night as he followed the winding road to the main house, which butted up against a tall hillside. The location helped hide the house, but also allowed a greater depth than anyone knew of. Another electronic device opened the long door of the five-car garage bay.

He pulled the SUV inside and parked next to a new metallic-red-and-silver Jaguar XKE and a baby-blue vintage Shelby Cobra. He loved cars. That was one of his weaknesses.

Poker and women were others. Of course, he never bothered to make a list.

Henshaw, his majordomo and a British-trained butler, met him at the door to the house.

"Good evening, sir." Henshaw was tall and thin, thirty-eight but acting at least forty years older.

"Good evening, Henshaw."

Roux's good-natured greeting must have taken the man by surprise. Henshaw's eyebrows climbed.

"There's been a problem with the SUV?" Henshaw asked. In his capacity during the past six years, he was well aware of some of the problems Roux dealt with.

"Yes." Roux tossed the man the keys. "Take it. Dispose of it. Destroy all of the paperwork that ever tied me to such a vehicle."

Henshaw caught the keys effortlessly. He wasn't surprised by the request. He'd done it before. "Of course, sir. Will there be anything else?"

"A drink. Cognac, I think. The Napoleon."

"A celebration, sir?"

"Yes. In the study, if you please."

"Of course, sir."

Roux walked through the house, across the marble floor of the great room with its sweeping staircase and private elevator, to his personal study.

The study was huge, very nearly the largest room in the house. It was two stories tall, filled with shelves of books and artifacts, scrolls and pottery, statues and paintings. Even a sarcophagus, canopic jars and the stuffed and mounted corpse of an American West gunslinger that had been so gaudy he just hadn't been able to resist acquiring it.

At the back of the room, Roux took out his key chain and pressed a sequence of buttons on the fob.

Immediately, the back wall separated into sections and slid back to reveal a huge vault. It was built into the hillside. The only access was through the heavy vault door.

As Roux pressed more buttons, the vault's door tumblers clacked and turned. When it finished, the door slid open on great hinges.

Lights flared on. Shelves held money and gems and bearer's bonds. Roux didn't care much for banks. He'd found them greedy and unscrupulous, and entirely too curious about where his wealth had come from.

He had other such hiding places around the globe. When he'd told the young American woman he was independently wealthy, he hadn't been lying.

A sealed case five feet long occupied a pedestal at the back of the vault. He pressed his hand against the handprint scanner. Ten seconds later, the locks clicked open.

The excitement thrummed within him as he flipped open the lid. He gazed down at the weapon protected within the case.

The hilt was plain and unadorned. The blade, when it had been whole, had been nearly four feet long. Now it lay in pieces but appeared almost intact.

Over the years, Roux had scoured the world in search of the fragments. He couldn't believe how far and wide the pieces had been scattered.

Or how quickly. After the sword was shattered, they had seemed to disappear overnight.

Only a small piece, no bigger than a large coin, remained to be found.

Surprised at the way his fingers trembled, Roux took from his pocket the charm the young American woman had found in the cave. He still wondered about the way she had found it. In all the times he had visited the Cévennes Mountains, he had never known an earthquake to take place.

Hesitantly, almost reverently, Roux held the charm in his fingers and positioned it the best way to fit with the sword. He dropped it onto the velvet bedding.

Nothing happened.

Roux noticed he wasn't breathing and thought it might be better if he were. He frowned.

Looking at the piece, he had no doubt that it was the one he'd been seeking. But why wasn't anything happening?

"Bollocks," Roux snarled. "After five-hundred-plus years, *something* should bloody well happen."

Steeling himself, he nudged the missing piece in closer to its mates. Still, nothing happened.

"Oh, *bollocks!*" Roux roared, unable to restrain himself. He glared at the broken sword and wondered what the hell was wrong.

"Sir."

Turning, Roux stared at Henshaw standing in the study. He held the brandy and a snifter.

Angrily, Roux stormed out of the vault. He thumbed the remote control and heard the vault hiss shut behind him. A heartbeat later, the wall reassembled.

"Something wrong?" Henshaw inquired politely.

"Yes," Roux growled as he snatched the brandy and snifter from Henshaw's hands.

He dropped into the large leather chair behind the ornate mahogany desk and poured a copious amount of brandy into the snifter. Then he drank it like water. It wasn't the most refined way to enjoy two-hundred-year-old brandy.

"Will you need anything else, sir?" Henshaw asked.

"A miracle, obviously," Roux grumbled. He filled the snifter again.

"I'm afraid I'm short of miracles, sir."

"I know," Roux stated sourly. "But once, I tell you, the world was fairly littered with them." He shook his head, thinking of the twisting flames that had consumed the young woman to whom he'd promised fealty. "So many people believed in them. And died because of them." He sighed. "I was stupid to believe. It's my own fault. I'm just lucky it hasn't gotten *me* killed."

10

The strident ring of Garin Braden's cell phone woke him from a narcotic-and-sex-induced slumber. It was something he'd almost grown used to. He peeled the arms and legs of two young women off him and reached for the bed's remote control.

Fumbling, Garin pressed buttons from memory and caused the bed to swivel around to the nightstand that held his cell phone. Cupping the tiny device in one of his huge, scarred hands, Garin stared blearily at the buttons and hoped for the best.

"Hello?" He didn't know who would call him at—he looked at the clock across the room and couldn't make out the hand placement—at whatever time it was.

"Are you awake?" the scurrilous voice at the other end of the connection demanded.

Garin was now. He knew the voice immediately. It belonged to a man he'd hoped would never contact him again.

Instantly, feeling as if deluged by ice water, the narcotic haze enveloping Garin's thinking and senses evaporated. He shoved himself up from the bed and looked back at the twisted and intertwined limbs of the women he'd convinced to share his bed last night.

He stood to his full six feet four inches, shook his long black hair and blinked his magnetic black eyes. He gazed at his reflection in the mirror. A goatee framed his mouth and he knew he looked like his father.

Scars covered his body from fights he'd had over the years. One of the scars was over his heart and had nearly killed him in Los Angeles. He'd stayed there too long and had almost been staked as a vampire.

It was amusing to him now, but at the time it caused quite an uproar. He gazed at the women again. At the moment, he couldn't even recall where he'd met them. The occurrence wasn't too uncommon.

"I'm awake," Garin finally said.

"You don't sound awake," Roux argued.

Stealthily, Garin crossed the room and checked the elaborate panel that relayed all the information about his security system. Everything was intact. No one had breached the perimeters.

No one was caught, Garin reminded himself. Even in this age of marvels, nothing was infallible.

The bedroom was large, filled with electronic entertainment equipment. The pedestal under the bed contained several items for adult entertainment. And a large supply of batteries and lotions.

"I'm awake," Garin said again. He slapped a hand against a section of the wall near the bed.

A panel flipped around and exposed a dozen handguns—revolvers and semiautomatics—and three assault rifles. There was even an assortment of grenades. He picked up a Smith & Wesson revolver and quietly rolled the hammer back with his thumb.

One of the women turned over on the round bed, and Garin was so startled he nearly shot her through the head.

"Why are you calling me, Roux?" Garin asked. "The last time we talked, you swore that you'd kill me."

"I was angry with you."

Garin prowled around the room. If Roux wanted to invade his penthouse, Garin was certain the old man could do it. When they were partners all those years ago, Garin had seen Roux do some amazing things.

Shortly after that, the friendship was lost. Only a few years passed before the old man swore to kill him. That had been over four hundred years ago.

"Aren't you still angry with me?" Garin walked to the brocaded curtains covering the floor-to-ceiling windows that peered out over downtown Munich.

It was late. Or early morning. Colorful neon lit up the city. A jet roared through the night, the red-and-white lights blinking slowly.

"I am," Roux admitted. "But not enough to kill you. At the moment."

Garin stayed behind the curtains. It wouldn't have been hard to set up with a sniper rifle on one of the other buildings and shoot him.

"That's good," Garin said. "How did you get this number?"

"I read it in tea leaves."

Garin said nothing. He didn't believe it, but he supposed if that were possible, Roux was the one who could do it. Remaining as calm as he could, he fumbled in the dark for the pants he'd worn earlier, then pulled them on.

"Are you all right?" Garin asked. It felt strange asking that. On several occasions, some of them not so long ago, he'd hoped the old man would die.

In fact, he'd even sent two assassination teams after Roux to accomplish that very thing. Garin had never heard again from the mercenaries he'd hired.

"I'm fine," Roux said.

"You're drinking," Garin accused.

"A little." Roux slurred his words slightly.

"Not just a little. You're drunk."

"Not drunk enough." His voice somehow managed to carry the scowl over the phone connection. "I don't think I'll ever be drunk enough."

Garin paced the room with the pistol in his hand. Talking to Roux was impossible.

"What's happened?" Garin asked. He was surprised that he still wanted to know. But then, Roux was the only man in the world who really knew him.

"I found the *sword,* Garin. All of it. All the pieces. Every last one of them."

"You're sure?" Garin asked, not wanting to believe it.

"It's taken me over five hundred years to find them all."

A sinking feeling filled Garin's stomach. He tried to detect something different in his physical well-being, then felt comfortable that nothing had changed. But that wasn't true. Something had changed. The sword—her sword—had been found.

"You found the sword?" Garin sat in one of the overstuffed chairs in front of the floor-to-ceiling window. He edged the curtain open with the pistol barrel.

"I said I did, didn't I?"

"Yes." Garin didn't have to ask why Roux had called him with the news. Even though they were enemies these days, there was no one else in the world Roux could tell about the sword. "What happened?"

Roux paused, then whispered hoarsely, "Nothing. Nothing at all."

"Something was supposed to happen, right?" Garin asked.

"I don't know."

"Have we *changed?*"

"Nothing happened, Garin. The sword is just lying there. Still in pieces."

"Maybe you've missed one."

"No."

Garin stood and walked into the next room where the wet bar was. Chrome-and-glass furniture, looking somehow fragile and dangerous at the same time, filled the room. He put the pistol on the bar and fixed himself a tall drink. Roux's announcement had taken the edge off his buzz.

"Maybe the sword can never be put back together," Garin suggested.

"I know it can be."

Garin didn't argue with that. He had always been sure of it himself. "You're missing something," Garin said.

"Don't you think I bloody well know that?" Roux snapped.

"Yes." Garin sighed and took a long drink.

"That's why I called you."

That would be the only reason the old man called, Garin thought. "Tell me what happened."

He listened as Roux told him of the discovery of the last piece of the sword.

"The woman—the American—she was the one who found the last piece of the sword?" Garin asked when he'd finished.

"It was by accident," Roux insisted.

"Roux," Garin said in exasperation, "the earth *opened* up for her. Don't you find something significant about that?"

"I was there, too."

Garin sighed. He'd forgotten about the old man's ego.

"Who's to say the earth didn't open up for *me*?" Roux demanded.

"The sword didn't fix itself," Garin pointed out.

"Maybe it's not supposed to," Roux said suddenly. "Maybe *I'm* supposed to fix it. It's possible that it simply has to be forged once again."

Before Garin could suggest that perhaps being around a forge after drinking as much as Roux had wasn't a good idea, the old man hung up.

Garin's immediate impulse was to call back. He checked the caller ID. It was blocked. He left the phone on the bar.

He sat and drank. By dawn he'd thought up and discarded a hundred plans. But he knew he really had only two options.

One involved killing Roux, which would not have been the most intelligent thing he could do, given that the pieces of the sword had all been found and he didn't know what would happen next.

The other involved finding the American woman.

Neither option appealed to him. Both included the possibility that his life would change. At present, he was worth millions, owned companies and parts of corporations and did whatever he pleased.

He'd come a long way for a German knight's bastard son who had once been apprenticed to an old man who claimed to be a wizard.

It had taken all of five hundred years.

He finished his drink, picked up the gun again and went to take a shower.

Shortly after dawn, Garin was in his car and flying down the autobahn. He just hoped Roux wasn't setting a trap. The old man had never seemed to take any of the assassination attempts personally, but a person never truly knew.

Annja woke feeling refreshed but sore. A quick check of her e-mail and the newsgroups showed that Bart McGilley hadn't responded but there were twenty-seven hits on alt.archaeology.esoterica.

Nineteen of them asked for personal information, as if her age, sex and location had anything to do with the charm's images. Four solicited further information, but Annja didn't have any and suspected the authors just wanted to open a dialogue. Sometimes it felt as if alt.archaeology.esoterica were a lonely-hearts club for geeks. Two offered to do further research—for a price.

But Zoodio@stuffyourmomdidnttellyou.net wrote:

Don't know about the image of the wolf and mountain, but the other side—the stylized rain—

Curious, Annja looked at the images of the charm. She hadn't thought of the die mark as rain. She'd thought of braille at first, but the coin had been too old to use braille. That language for the blind hadn't even been invented at the time the charm disappeared in La Bête's cave.

Looking at it again, she decided it could be rain. She wished she still had the charm itself, and she faulted herself for getting taken in by the old man.

Annja returned to the Web site posting.

—the stylized rain—looks like something from one of the monasteries in that area. I'm fairly familiar with the Catholic orders here. Do you know the time period?

Annja sighed. She hadn't expected to have all the answers overnight, but it would have been nice. She dashed off a quick reply.

Zoodio,
Thanks for the help. No, I'm afraid I don't know the time period. At least four-hundred-plus years. The disk was worn as a charm. To ward off evil, I think. Kind of fits with the religious motif. If that gives you a clue, please let me know. I'm stumped.

After a quick shower, she dressed and packed the notebook computer in her research backpack. She decided to take the field pack with her, but doubted she'd get up into the mountains again.

Then she went downstairs to see if François could give her a lift into town. Otherwise she was in for a long walk.

"No, ANNJA, I got the pictures," Doug Morrell said. "They were great. I just need more."

Annja made her way through the dusty shelves of the old bookstore she'd discovered on her first day in Lozère. When dealing with fairly recent history, it was amazing what finds were often made in old bookstores, pawnshops and at garage sales. If the city, town or village was large enough to support such enterprises.

People wrote books, journals and papers that were often shuffled around, loaned, borrowed or sold at estate auctions that ended up in those businesses. Colleges and students sold off old books that somehow stayed in circulation for a hundred years or more.

Over the past decade, though, many of those finds ended up on Amazon.com or eBay. Genealogy centers took up a lot of old documents, as well.

"There are no more pictures," Annja said. She ran a forefinger over multicolored spines that were more than four and five times her age.

Roland's Bookstore was a treasure trove. She'd already purchased seventeen books and shipped them back to her apartment in Brooklyn. Where she was going to put them in the overflowing mass that she laughingly called her library, she had no clue.

"There have to be more pictures," Doug whined.

"Nope."

"If you're holding out for more money—"

"That's not it."

Doug was silent for a moment. "You don't want more money?"

"More money would be nice," Annja said, "but it won't get you more pictures."

"You should have taken more pictures."

"Did you read my e-mail?"

"Yes."

"The part about how I was chased out of the cave by guys with guns?"

"Maybe."

"You didn't."

"I think I did, Annja," Doug said defensively. "I mean, I remember it now. I was just blown away by these pictures."

"I was nearly blown away by the guys."

"Why?"

"I don't know." Annja turned the corner and went down the next aisle. She usually read books written by religious groups. Amid the doctrine and self-righteousness and finger-pointing, nuggets of history and details about people's lives resided.

"Were you somewhere you weren't supposed to be?"

"I was in the Cévennes Mountains. They're open to the public."

"Those guys just didn't want you there?" Doug asked.

"I don't know."

Doug let out a low breath. "Generally when people chase you, there's a reason."

Annja smiled at that. "Have you been chased before, Doug?"

"I'm just saying."

"Maybe they wanted the gear I was carrying."

"You said the ground opened up and dropped you into this cave."

"Yes."

"Then it closed after you left."

"Right." Annja found a blue clothbound book placed backward on the shelf. When she extracted the volume and turned it around, she found the book had a Latin title. She translated it as if she were reading English.

The Destruction of the Brotherhood of the Silent Rain.

She flipped the book open and stared at the plate inset on the first page. It was a match to the image on the back of the charm.

"Do you think if you packed a few explosives back up into those mountains," Doug began, "that you could—?"

"Doug!" she interrupted.

He paused.

"No," Annja said.

"No?" The producer sounded as petulant as a child.

"No explosives. No more pictures. That's what we have. It's more than anyone else has *ever* had."

"You don't understand, Annja. You've got the makings of a great story here. A body count. An unidentified monster. Thugs chasing you. An earthquake."

And a mysterious missing charm, Annja thought. She hadn't told him about that.

Quickly, she flipped through the book. It appeared to be a history of a monastery that had fallen onto hard times and been disbanded. She knew the chances were good that it wouldn't help her, but gathering information meant taking in more than she needed in hopes of getting what she needed.

"How much longer do you think you'll need for the piece?" Doug asked.

"A few more days."

"The deadline looms."

"I know." Annja understood deadlines. Even in archaeology there were deadlines. Teams had to be in and out of dig sites during their agreed-upon times.

"If you need anything else, let me know."

"Sure."

"Maybe Kyle and the art department can touch up these pictures—"

Annja counted to ten, slowly. "Doug."

"Yes," he said contritely.

"If you touch those pictures—"

"They need to be enhanced."

"If anyone touches those pictures—"

"Just a little tweaking. I promise. You won't even know we did anything."

"Doug!"

Doug sighed in surrender.

"I'm going to call your mother and tell her about Amy Zuckerman," Annja threatened.

"You wouldn't."

"Do you remember the lagoon-creature piece I did a few months ago?"

Doug was silent.

"You took a perfectly interesting piece about a legendary swamp monster—"

"The mangrove coast of Florida isn't that interesting," Doug argued. "I had to switch the location to Barbados."

"You turned it into a freak fest. You stood me up in front of a digitally created, shambling pile of muck with eight-inch fangs—"

"The fangs were too much, weren't they? I told Kyle that the fangs were too big. I mean, who's going to believe a seven-foot-tall mud monster with eight-inch fangs? I wouldn't. I'll tell you that," Doug said.

"You told people the footage was shot somewhere it wasn't." Annja hadn't seen the finished piece until it aired. Then the phone calls started coming in. She still hadn't lived down the fallout from that. If it weren't for the big checks that *Chasing History's Monsters* cut, or the fact that she couldn't get them anywhere else, she wouldn't continue her association with them.

"We got a lot of favorable comments about that show," Doug said defensively.

"I'm a respected archaeologist," Annja said. "I work hard at that. I'm not some wannabe video-game heroine."

"You'll always be respectable to me," Doug promised.

"Not when you stand me up in front of digital monsters that don't have shadows."

"That was an oversight. All the monsters we do now have shadows."

"Amy Zuckerman," Annja stated. "You burn me, that's the price tag for the damage."

"That's low, Annja. Truly low." Doug took in a deep breath. "Amy was a mistake. A tragic mistake."

"Your mother would never forgive you," Annja agreed.

"You know, it's conversations like this that remind me I should never drink with friends."

"At least friends put you in cabs and send you home," Annja said. "They don't roll you and leave you lying with your pants around your ankles in a rain-filled alley."

Doug sighed. "Okay. We'll do it your way. I have to tell you, I think you're making a mistake, but—"

"Bye, Doug. I'll talk to you later." Annja broke the connection and zipped the phone into her jacket pocket. She continued scanning the shelves.

The small bell above the entrance rang as someone opened the door.

"Ah," Roland greeted from the front counter, "Good morning, Mr. Lesauvage."

Cautiously, Annja peered around the bookshelf and tried to stay in the shadows.

12

Corvin Lesauvage was around six feet tall. He was broad and blocky, and looked like he could easily handle himself in a physical confrontation. Sandy-colored hair, cut short, framed his face. He looked freshly shaved, his jaw gleaming. Dark green eyes that held a reptilian cast gazed around the shop. His pearl-gray suit was Italian. So were the black loafers.

"Good morning, Roland," Lesauvage said. His voice was low and rumbling.

"I haven't any more books for you, sir." Roland was a gray ghost of a man. Life had pared him down to skin and bone long ago. But he was attentive, intelligent and quick. He barely topped five feet.

"I knew that," Lesauvage said. "If you'd found any, you'd have sent them along."

"Yes, sir. I would have."

"I came today only to browse." Lesauvage studied the stacks, but his cold eyes never found Annja in the shadows. "Is anyone else about?" he asked.

"A guest, Mr. Lesauvage." Roland never called the prospective buyers who entered his establishment customers. Always *guests.* "Just the one. Shouldn't be any bother to you," he assured Lesauvage.

"Who?"

"A young American woman."

Lesauvage smiled. "Good. I was hoping to catch her here."

Annja looked around the shop. There was no other way out. The bookshop butted up against a launderette in the back and was sandwiched between a cobbler and a candy store. The only door was at the front.

And at present, Lesauvage stood blocking the way.

"Have you met Miss Creed?" Roland asked. "She's a television celebrity."

"So I'm told. Unfortunately, I haven't had the pleasure," Lesauvage said. "Yet." He raised his voice. "Miss Creed?"

Annja debated calling the police. But after the report last night and their lack of interest, she doubted the effort would prove worthwhile.

She reached into her backpack and took out the spring-loaded stun baton she'd brought with her. The weapon was legal to carry as long as she packed it in luggage checked at the airport.

Sliding the baton into one of the deep pockets of her hiking shorts, Annja stepped around the bookcase so she could be seen. "Mr. Lesauvage," she said.

Roland blinked behind his thick glasses. "Do you know each other?" He looked at Lesauvage. "I thought you said—"

"We've got mutual acquaintances," Annja said.

Lesauvage smiled. "Yes. We did."

For just a moment, Annja thought about Avery Moreau and worried that something had happened to the young man. Surely if something had, it would have been in the news.

"What can I do for you, Mr. Lesauvage?" Annja asked.

"Actually, I thought perhaps there might be something I could do for you."

"Nothing that I can think of."

Lesauvage flashed her a charming smile. If he hadn't sent men to kidnap her and possibly kill her, Annja thought he would have been a handsome man with intriguing potential. But now she knew he was as deadly as the Ursini's viper.

"I suggest that perhaps you haven't thought hard enough," Lesauvage said.

Roland, obviously unaware of the subtext that passed between them, said, "I hadn't mentioned Mr. Lesauvage as someone you might talk to, Miss Creed. Though maybe I should have. He's one of the more educated men in the area when it comes to history and mythology."

"Really." Annja tried to sound properly impressed. But she never took her eyes from the dangerous man.

"Oh, yes. He's interested in La Bête, too. And he's been research- ing the Wild Hunt—"

Lesauvage cut the old man off. "I think that's enough, Mr. Roland. There's no need to bore her with my idiosyncrasies."

Annja wondered why Lesauvage was interested in the Irish myth that had its roots in the days of the Vikings. She considered her own knowledge of the Wild Hunt.

According to Scandinavian myth, the leader of the Norse gods, Odin, was believed to ride his eight-legged horse, Sleipnir, across the sky in pursuit of quarry. Annja's quick mind juxtaposed the tale of the Wild Hunt and La Bête, finding similarities.

Except that she was in Lozère hunting La Bête, and Lesauvage, who was keenly interested in the Wild Hunt according to Roland, was hunting her. As an archaeologist, Annja knew coincidences happened all the time. But she was sure this was no coincidence.

"I don't think your interests are boring," Annja said. "To the contrary, I find the idea of the Wild Hunt suddenly quite enlightening."

Lesauvage frowned. It was obvious he'd rather she not know of his obsession. "Perhaps we could talk elsewhere," he said.

"Do you have somewhere safe in mind?" Annja countered.

"There's a coffee shop across the street," Lesauvage suggested. "Or, if you're unwilling, I'm sure Mr. Roland would put us up for a brief conference."

Annja thought about the veiled threat in Lesauvage's words and hated the man for them. Roland would obviously be an immedi- ate casualty.

"All right," she said.

DURING THE WALK across the street from Roland's bookstore, after she had paid for her purchase, Annja had been aware of the sleek gray Mercedes limousine that followed Lesauvage like a pet dog. Three men sat inside.

Annja wondered if Lesauvage had matched the color of his suit to the car.

The server guided Annja to a table in the rear. Lesauvage followed.

As she sat across from him, Annja took the baton from her pocket and placed it on the seat beside her, within quick, easy reach.

"You're being overly cautious," the man told her.

"After being shot at by your people yesterday?" Annja shook her head. "Overly cautious, in fact, sensible, would have been climbing onto the first plane out of France."

"But you couldn't do that."

"I can." Annja had no illusions about her courage. There was a fine line between bravery and stupidity. She knew what it looked like and made a habit of never crossing it.

"But you haven't."

Annja didn't say anything because there was nothing to say.

"You're here for a story," he said. "About La Bête."

"Yes."

"How did you find that cave yesterday?" he asked. "I've had men up in those mountains for years."

"There was an earthquake. I fell in."

"You're joking."

"No."

The server brought two steaming cups of espresso.

"I sent those men back up in the mountains last night and this morning," Lesauvage said. "During all the confusion—"

"During their attempts to kill me," Annja stated flatly.

"I ordered them only to restrain you and bring you to me."

"Kidnapping is a big crime," Annja pointed out. "Huge."

A feral gleam lit Lesauvage's eyes. "Let us cut to the chase, Miss Creed."

Annja waited.

"You have something I want. Something that you found in that cave."

"What do you think I found?" Annja countered.

"A coin," Lesauvage said. "About this big." He circled his forefinger and thumb, gapping them about the size of a euro. "On one side is the image of a wolf hanging in front of a mountain. On the other is a die mark."

"The symbol of the Brotherhood of the Silent Rain," Annja said.

"Yes," Lesauvage admitted reluctantly. He pursed his lips unhappily. "You know more about this than I'd believed."

Elation filled Annja. She had confirmed a piece of the puzzle. She decided not to ask about the monastery. She'd consult her new book later.

"Knowledge, Miss Creed," Lesauvage said in a dead, still voice, "is not always a good thing."

But it's the things that you don't know about that kill you quickest, Annja thought. She chose to ignore the threat inherent in his words.

"Why do you have an interest in the Wild Hunt?" Annja asked.

"I want the coin you found," Lesauvage said. "I was told you found it around the dead warrior's neck. He wore it on a leather strap."

"Most people believe the Wild Hunt is an Irish myth," Annja said. "Or British. Depends on your bias. They're supposed to be a group of ghostly hunters who go galloping across the sky on their horses. They blow their hunting horns and their hounds bay." She grinned, noting the man's discomfort. "It's supposed to be a really spooky experience." She shrugged. "If you believe in that kind of thing."

Sitting back in his chair, Lesauvage regarded her from under hooded lids. "You don't believe in it?"

"No," Annja replied. "It's an old tale. A good one to scare kids when you want them inside the house after dark. According to the legend, if you witnessed the Wild Hunt, you would either become their prey or one of them."

"Yes."

"I hadn't thought about it until this morning," Annja said, "but the legend of La Bête might have something to do with the myth of the Wild Hunt."

Lesauvage remained silent.

"Did you know that several people in history claimed to have taken part in the Wild Hunt?" Annja asked. She remembered the drunken arguments Professor Sparhawk had had with an undergraduate during the Hadrian's Wall dig in England. It had continued over the three months of the dig a few summers ago.

Shifting uncomfortably, Lesauvage crossed his arms and glared at her as if she were merely an annoyance.

"Primitive peoples among the Gauls and Germans used it to combat the encroachment of civilization," Annja said. "The Harii warriors painted themselves black to attack their enemies in the night. They pretended they had special powers granted by the gods they worshiped. Whipped everyone there into a frenzy."

"You're wasting time," Lesauvage interrupted.

Annja ignored him. "Others took part in it, too. There are documented cases showing involvement by St. Guthlac and Hereward the Wake. In the twelfth century, one of the monks who wrote the *Peterborough Chronicle* gave a treatise on a gathering of warriors under the Wild Hunt banner during the appointment of an abbot. The monks and the local knights later disbanded the warriors."

"I want the coin," Lesauvage repeated. "Or things could get dire."

"I hadn't thought about La Bête being part of the Wild Hunt," Annja mused. "Not until you came calling this afternoon." She studied him. "Why are you so interested in the Wild Hunt? And why did you send your men after me? Unless you figured La Bête was part of something you were interested in."

"You're playing with things that don't concern you, woman." Menace dripped in Lesauvage's words.

Annja closed her hand over the baton.

"Now I want that damned coin."

"I don't have it," Annja said. She didn't want to make herself a target. She had the rubbings. For the moment, they would have to serve to help unlock the mystery before her.

"You're lying," Lesauvage snarled. His face grew dark with suffused blood.

"No," Annja said, "I'm not. The old man I met in the mountains has it."

"What old man?"

"Didn't your men tell you about him?"

Lesauvage stared daggers at her.

"His name is Roux."

"What's the rest of his name?"

"That's all I know."

Lesauvage cursed, drawing the attention of nearby patrons. Even the English and German tourists who didn't speak French understood the potential for violence. They got up with their families and started to sidle away.

"We're done here." Annja said, grabbing her pack and sliding out of the booth.

Lesauvage reached for her with a big hand.

Pressing the button on the side of the baton, Annja released the extended length, giving her almost two feet of stainless steel to work with. She slapped Lesauvage's wrist away, causing him to yelp in surprised pain. Shoving the baton forward with an underhanded strike like she would deliver with an épée, Annja caught him with the end between the eyes and batted his head back. Before he could recover, she was on her feet.

With the baton still in her fist, her heart thumping rapidly, Annja strode toward the front door. Just before she reached it, two men dressed in black robes blocked the way.

They were young and hard-looking. When they lowered their cowls, she saw that their heads were shaved smooth. Tattoos at their throats repeated the same design that had been struck on the back of the charm.

"Miss Creed," one of them said in flawless English, "you must come with us." He reached for her.

Annja struck at the man with her baton. The other man shifted then, revealing what he hid beneath his robe. The short blade caught the light as it came up to intercept the baton.

Metal shrieked against metal.

Annja disengaged at once, stepping back to give herself more room. Glancing at the coffee shop's rear entrance, she saw that two more black-robed men were entering there. Outside the big windows that lined the side wall, four more black-robed men stood waiting.

Things did not look good. Annja hadn't been this outnumbered in a long time. Well, yesterday seemed like a long time ago.

She tightened her grip on her baton and looked at Lesauvage.

The man sat at the table cradling his hand. He grinned at her. "They're not after me."

The black-robed warriors closed in on her.

GARIN BRADEN WAITED in the black Mercedes while Avery Moreau dashed inside the bookstore to find out if the woman was still there.

After arriving in Lozère, Garin had experienced no trouble in picking up Annja Creed's trail. Within an hour, a private-investigations firm he owned had located the bed-and-breakfast where she was staying. Over the years, he'd found the investment in the detective agency had helped with a number of things, including blackmail and corporate espionage.

Camille Lambert had been glad to help Annja Creed's television producer find her. Apparently the old woman was quite taken with her guest.

She'd also given Avery Moreau's phone number to Garin and suggested hiring him to help track down the woman.

They'd already been to the museum and the library, two places the young man said the woman liked to haunt while she was in town. Now they were at Roland's Bookstore.

The cold air-conditioning cycled around Garin. A German industrial metal group played on the stereo, filling the big luxury car with sound.

He wondered what Roux was up to. If all the pieces of the sword were truly gathered, why had nothing changed?

The only conjecture Garin had come up with was that the woman was important to everything they were dealing with. After all, she was the one who had fallen into the bowels of the mountain and discovered the last piece of the sword.

Roux liked to look for hidden meanings and allegories and secrets. When serving as the old man's apprentice, Garin had discovered that not everything was filled with plots and portents. Sometimes things were as simple as they looked.

Like the fact that the woman was somehow mixed up with the sword.

Garin knew that Roux would take forever to get around to that line of logic. Roux's ego wouldn't let him arrive at that conclusion. Presumably, they both had forever to wait, but Garin didn't like waiting. Even after five hundred years, he was impatient.

If the sword—if *Joan's* sword, he corrected himself—was going to be a threat to him, he wanted to know now.

The young man ran back out of the bookstore.

Garin rolled the electric window down with a button.

"She's not inside," Avery said. "Roland said he thought she went over to the coffee shop." He pointed—and froze.

Following the direction of the boy's arm, Garin looked. He saw the men dressed in black robes surrounding the coffee shop and guessed at once that this wasn't a normal occurrence. Through the windows, he spotted Annja Creed backing away from the men closing in on her.

Without a word, Garin dropped the transmission into reverse. The powerful engine roared. Whipping the steering wheel and throwing an arm over the seat as he stared backward, he backed the Mercedes around in a tire-eating ninety-degree turn. He narrowly missed a farm truck and two small cars in the other lanes. Horns blared and angry voices followed him.

He reached under his jacket for the S&W .500 Magnum and backed into the coffee shop's parking lot, slamming into three of the black-robed warriors and sending them flying.

13

The chaos in the parking lot drew the attention of everyone inside the coffee shop.

Annja stared in disbelief as three men skidded across the concrete. One of them slammed into a parked car, setting off the alarm, and crumpled into a heap. Another slid under a car that had been backing out. The third man lay under the heavy luxury car.

A fourth man stayed on his feet. He pulled a semiautomatic pistol from somewhere inside his robe.

A huge man with the blackest hair Annja had ever seen—black as sin, she'd heard someone describe a color like that—pushed out on the driver's side. Dressed in black, from his gloves to his long coat to his wraparound sunglasses, he looked like the specter of death in a medieval painting. He held what looked like, and in the next split second, sounded like a small cannon.

The man pointed the pistol at the black-robed man without even looking in his direction and pulled the trigger. The muzzle-flash ballooned from the barrel.

The black-robed man jerked backward, fell and lay still. His pistol skittered across the pavement.

Calmly the big man aimed the pistol at the coffee-shop windows. Everyone inside the shop hit the floor amid curses and cries for help.

Even Corvin Lesauvage was on the floor.

Guess this guy doesn't work for him, Annja thought. She crouched near one of the tables, but knew she couldn't stay there. The black-robed men at either entrance were duckwalking toward her.

The big man outside shot the large plate-glass window twice. The glass fell in sheets and shattered into thousands of pieces against the floor.

"Annja Creed!" he yelled in a deep voice. He spoke in English. "I've come to help you!"

Annja backed away from the nearest black-robed man. She stared at the livid tattoo on his neck. Without warning, he lunged at her.

She dodged back, falling to her left hand and sweeping the baton back with her right. The metal end caught her opponent along his jaw and broke his forward movement. She thought she broke his jaw, as well.

Then the man behind him pulled a pistol from his robe and aimed at her. "Come with us," the man demanded in accented English, "or I will kill you."

Annja believed him.

Before she could reply, before she could even figure out how she was going to react, the black-robed man's head emptied in a crimson rush and he pirouetted sideways. Then the massive boom of the big man's pistol filled the coffee shop again.

The lesser of two evils, Annja decided. These guys have promised to kill you, and getting kidnapped by them doesn't seem too appealing.

She pushed to her feet and ran for the broken window. The backpack's weight with the computer slowed her a little, but she gained a tabletop in one lithe leap. Shadows moved around her as she leaped through the broken window and cleared the hedges before the parking lot.

The big man took aim again.

For a moment, Annja feared she'd made the wrong choice. But when he fired, she wasn't the target.

"The door's unlocked," he said conversationally, as if he wasn't killing people and was only out for a walk. He broke open the massive handgun and spilled empty brass onto the ground with audible tinkling. Taking a speed-loader from his pocket, he refilled the cylinder and snapped the weapon closed.

Annja's hand found the car's door latch. She opened the door and clambered into the plush leather seat. Bullets hit the window as she tried to close the door, causing it to shiver under the impacts. She expected to feel shredded glass and metal tear through her.

That didn't happen.

When she looked back at the window, all she saw were faint hairline cracks.

"Bulletproof glass," the stranger said as he dropped into the driver's seat. He grinned at her and she saw her reflection in the black lenses of his wraparound sunglasses. "I never go anywhere without it."

Several other bullets caromed from the car without doing any appreciable damage.

The big man grinned at the men running out of the coffee shop toward them. "Idiots."

"They could shoot out the tires," Annja pointed out.

"Let them try," he growled. "They're run-flats. They would have to blow them off the car to get them to fail."

"If we wait, maybe they'll roll in a tank," Annja said, only half-joking.

He smiled at her. "You've got a sense of humor. I like that." Then he put the car into gear, shoved his foot down on the accelerator and sent them screaming out onto the street.

TWELVE ANXIOUS MINUTES later, with no sign of pursuit visible through the rear window, Annja turned to the driver. "Who are you?"

"Garin," he said, offering a hand. The pistol was tucked between his legs. "Garin Braden. At your service."

Caught off guard, Annja took his hand. Before she knew what he was doing, he folded her fingers inward and kissed the back of her hand.

"Enchanté," he said, then released her hand.

"Me, too," Annja whispered. She didn't know how to react. "Do you always go around rescuing people from—" she didn't know what to call the black-robed men "—other *strange* people who want to abduct or kill them for unknown reasons?"

"Not always." Garin drove confidently.

"How did you happen to be there?" she asked.

"Actually, I was looking for you."

Annja took a fresh grip on her baton. If Garin noticed he obviously didn't feel threatened. "Why?"

"Aren't you glad I was?"

"For the moment," she said.

He laughed then, and the noise was filled with savage glee. "I have no reason to wish you harm, Annja Creed."

"Then what do you wish?"

Looking at her, he asked, "Would you like to get back the charm Roux took from you?"

"Yes," she answered without hesitation.

"Then we'll go get it." Garin paused. "If that's what you want to do."

Annja considered her options briefly. She didn't want to remain in Lozère with Lesauvage and the black-robed warriors hunting her.

Getting to the airport and getting out of the country was out of the question. Inspector Richelieu probably had a warrant out for her arrest by now.

Leaving without understanding at least part of the reasons why everything was happening also didn't appeal to her.

"Well?" Garin asked.

"All right. Where are the old man and my charm?"

"In Paris. That's where he's lived practically forever." Garin kept his foot heavy on the accelerator.

THREE HOURS LATER they stopped for fuel at a truck stop.

Annja tried to open the door but it remained locked. When she looked for the door release, she saw that it had been removed. Feeling a little uneasy, she turned to Garin.

Without a word he pressed the release switch and the lock sprang free. He got out of the car with a lithe movement for such a tall man.

Outside the car, Annja looked around. Dozens of cars and trucks filled the service area. People milled about, making selections and chatting briefly. Most of them complained about the high price of fuel or confirmed directions to their destinations.

If she ran, Annja doubted Garin could stop her.

"They have a restaurant," Garin said as he opened the gas tank and shoved the nozzle inside. "If you're hungry."

Annja realized she was famished. She'd skipped the breakfast table Camille Lambert had laid out, then worked through lunch in Lozère searching for books.

For the first time she realized that most of her possessions, including most of her cash, was at the bed-and-breakfast. Using her credit cards meant leaving an electronic trail. She was sure it wasn't safe to do that.

"I'm hungry," Annja admitted. "Though I have to tell you, if you intend to walk away from the check on me, I'm coming after you."

"What?" Garin appeared confused.

"Nothing." Annja waved the question away. "How do you know the old man?"

"Roux?"

"Yes."

Garin shrugged as he settled back against the Mercedes and watched the digital readout on the gas pump flicker. "I knew him a long time ago."

"You don't look that old." Annja thought maybe he was in his early thirties.

"I'm older than I look. So is Roux."

Annja let the statement pass without comment. "Why did Roux take the charm?"

"He thought it belonged to something else he's been looking for."

The gas pump sounded as it shut off.

"Does it?" Annja asked.

Garin removed the nozzle from the gas tank. "I don't know. Maybe."

"What was he looking for?"

"You'll have to see." Garin hung up the hose and tossed her the keys. "Pull the car around to the restaurant side. I'll pay for the gas and join you there."

Keys in hand, Annja watched him walk away. There was nothing keeping her from taking the car and going. She had a full tank of gas. Paris was two and a half hours away. She could go to Paris and board a plane for New York.

If there's not a warrant out for your arrest, she told herself.

She didn't like the idea of running, though. And there was the matter of the charm and the black-robed men to consider. The book she'd found at Roland's had been quite helpful. She'd read most of it over the past three hours.

But it had also deepened the mystery. She knew what the Brotherhood of the Silent Rain had been, but not what had destroyed it.

Or driven it underground, she thought, remembering the tattoos at the throats of the black-garbed men.

In the end, she slid behind the wheel and started the engine. She drove to the parking lot by the restaurant and parked.

Garin Braden had never once turned around to check to see if she'd driven off. His confidence was almost insulting.

AFTER HE PAID for the fuel with cash, because he didn't want to be traced in case someone in Lozère had managed to identify the car, Garin purchased a phone card and retreated to the bank of pay phones in the back.

He consulted his PDA and retrieved the phone number he was looking for. Then he dialed.

The phone rang twice and was picked up by a man with a British accent. "Lord Roux's residence."

The announcement caught Garin by surprise. He hadn't talked to Roux in years before last night. "*Lord* Roux, is it? When did the old bastard get titled?" he asked.

"Excuse me?" The man at the other end of the connection sounded offended.

"Let me talk to Roux," Garin demanded.

"Lord Roux is not—"

"He'll talk to me," Garin growled. "Tell him Garin is on the line."

"Garin," the voice repeated. The way he said it told Garin that he had at least been briefed on the importance of the name if not why it was important. "Hold on, please."

Glancing up at the clock over the exit doors, Garin knew he didn't have long before the woman started getting suspicious about the length of time he'd been gone. Annja Creed was very alert, very much aware of things that were going on around her. She was no one's fool.

More than that, she was a beautiful woman. During the three-hour trip, while she'd evaded most of his attempts at conversation and kept her nose in her book, he'd wondered what she would be like in bed. Those thoughts had made the past three hours even more grueling because he didn't feel safe acting on impulses he normally didn't restrain. For the first time in a long time, Garin felt nervous.

"Garin," Roux said.

"Yes," Garin replied. He sighed, angry with all the troubling notions spinning around in his head. Here was the source of all his discontent.

"How did you get this number?"

"You gave it to me last night," Garin said because he'd always hated the old man's pomposity.

"I did not. Last night—"

"You were drunk," Garin interrupted.

"Not that drunk."

"We could argue the point." Garin had put his private detectives to work looking for the number upon his departure from Munich. It hadn't been easy to find.

"What do you want?" Roux demanded.

"Maybe, this time, I have something you want."

Roux was silent at the other end of the line. Then he said, "You have the woman."

Garin silently cursed. Of course Roux would figure out why he was calling. The man was keenly intelligent. "Yes."

"Is she alive?"

"For now."

"Why did you take her?"

"Because of the sword," Garin replied.

"It's not like you to be curious."

"I'm not. I'm scared."

Roux laughed. "I thought you had gone out and conquered the world, Garin. You with all your untold millions and women and fine living."

"I wouldn't say you've avoided wealth."

"No, but I live my life differently than you. I still enjoy taking risks. Throwing the dice and seeing what happens."

"I take risks, as well."

"Carefully calculated, carefully measured ones."

Garin knew it was true. Even the gunplay in Lozère was measured. He'd gone into it feeling supremely confident that he could get the woman. Or at the very least emerge from the encounter relatively unscathed.

The sword was another matter entirely.

"You have her with you now?" Roux asked.

"Yes."

"Where are you?"

"About two and a half hours from you."

"Good. Bring her here. I'll be waiting."

The phone clicked dead in Garin's ear. Trembling with anger and frustration, he cradled the handset. He took a deep breath. For those last few seconds of that phone call, he'd felt like that awkward nine-year-old child Roux had taken in trade for services rendered all those years ago.

I'm not that child anymore, Garin reminded himself. I'm my own man. A very dangerous man. If my father were to know me now, he would fear me.

But that hadn't been the case when he was a child. He'd been the son of a serving wench. Unacknowledged by his father. An object of scorn for his father's wife. An embarrassment to his blood mother. And a target for villainies perpetrated by his half brothers and half sisters.

Roux had taken Garin away from all that. But the old man had not done him a kindness by dragging him out across the harsh lands they traveled. He had used him as a vassal, to wait on him hand and foot.

Taking another breath, Garin calmed himself. Then he walked to the adjoining restaurant. Roux would see that he had changed. Even if Garin had to kill the old man to prove it.

14

Seated in a booth by the window overlooking the restaurant parking lot and the Mercedes, Annja glanced up at Garin's approach. She took in the man's dark mood at once and felt a little threatened.

"Something wrong?" she asked.

"No," he lied, then sat in the booth across from her.

"Oh," Annja said in a way that let him know she was fully aware that he was lying. She'd learned that from the nuns at the orphanage. The soft vocal carried a deadly punch of guilt that usually demolished the weaker kids. Annja had always continued stoically until she knew for certain she'd been caught. She'd been punished quite often for exploring New Orleans after lights-out.

"I've got a long history with the man we're going to see," Garin said.

Maybe he'd been raised on guilt, too, Annja thought. "What kind of history?" Annja asked.

"We don't exactly get on."

"I'm not surprised. He comes across as very arrogant and selfish."

"Those," Garin said with a grin, "are his redeeming qualities."

Annja decided she liked him a little then. Not enough to trust him, but enough to explore working together. Saving her life—or at least saving her from capture—back at the coffee shop in Lozère had been a mercenary action. She just didn't know what the price tag was yet.

"You called him?" Annja asked.

To his credit, Garin hesitated only a moment. "Yes. To let him know we're coming."

"He's okay with that?"

"Yes."

Annja leaned back in the booth and thought about Roux. "Going to his house doesn't exactly make me feel all warm and fuzzy."

Garin bared his white teeth in a predator's smile. "It's not exactly a trip to grandma's house. But you don't have a lot of choices, either."

"I think I do."

"Really?" Garin leaned back as well. "Do you know who is trying to kill you?"

"A man named Corvin Lesauvage and the monks of the Brotherhood of the Silent Rain."

Garin's eyes flicked to the book on the table. "You've been reading about them."

"You," Annja said distinctly, "can read Latin."

Garin shrugged. "One of several languages."

"You share that with Roux."

"I should. He taught me."

"What kind of work do you do, Mr. Braden?"

"Me?" Garin held a hand to his chest and smiled brilliantly. "Why, I am a criminal."

Somehow, Annja wasn't terribly surprised. From the way he'd moved back at the coffee shop, she might have guessed that he was in the military. She nodded.

"You knew that?" Garin asked in the silence that followed his declaration.

"I'd thought you were a soldier—"

"I've been a soldier many times," Garin said. "The tools change, but the practice and methodology remain much the same."

"But I realized a soldier would have stayed in Lozère and straightened things out with the law-enforcement people."

"The police and I, we're of a different...persuasion." Garin waved at a passing server. "Staying in Lozère was not an option. I could not protect you there."

"Or take me to Roux."

"Exactly."

The server took their order. Garin ordered for them both, which Annja found somewhat old-fashioned and pleasant. He was, she admitted upon reflection, an oddity. He had undoubtedly killed men only a short time ago and evidently gave no further thought to it.

Then she frowned at her own line of thinking. She'd more or less done the same thing herself yesterday. Or at least tried to. She didn't know if she'd actually killed anyone. Roux certainly had.

For a moment she felt stung by the guilt the sisters at the orphanage had worked so hard to foster in her. Then she pushed it out of her mind. If she'd learned one thing in those gray walls filled with rules and recriminations, it was to take care of herself. She'd learned the hard way that no one else would.

"Do the monks work for Lesauvage?" Garin asked when he'd finished speaking to the server.

"No." From Lesauvage's reaction to the situation, Annja was firmly convinced of that.

"Then they're working independently." Garin picked up a package of crackers, tore them open and started eating. "Who is Lesauvage?"

"A criminal."

"I've never heard of him. What does he want?"

"The charm your friend Roux stole from me."

Garin frowned. "Roux is not my friend." He shifted. "Why does Lesauvage want the charm?"

"I don't know. Does Roux?"

"If he does, he hasn't told me. What about the monks? What do they want?"

"During their attempt to abduct me, they didn't say."

Garin pointed at the book on the table. "Did that offer any clue?"

"No. According to the authors, who were monks, the brotherhood was a peaceful group. Big on vineyards and cheeses."

"Must have been very profitable being a monk back in those days. Or at least a good time."

The server returned with two glasses of wine and placed them on the table.

Garin hoisted his glass and offered a toast. *"Salut."*

"Salut," Annja said, meeting his glass with hers. "Why does Roux want the charm?"

Garin hesitated.

"If you start holding out on me, I'll have to reconsider my options," Annja said.

A look of seriousness darkened Garin's face. "Have you studied Joan of Arc?"

"Roux asked me that, too," Annja said.

"What did he say about her?"

"Nothing really. He moved the conversation on to the charm."

"Did he? Interesting. Obviously he didn't want you to know what he's working on."

"What are you talking about?" Annja asked.

"Roux believes the charm was part of Joan of Arc's sword."

Annja was stunned. She remembered the histories and the stories. The young woman had been burned at the stake, labeled a heretic by the church. Some tales claimed that her sword had magic powers, some that it had been shattered the day she was burned at the stake.

"Does Roux have other pieces of the sword?" she asked.

"With the acquisition of the piece you found, Roux thinks he has them all. That's why we're going to his house. That's why I'm risking my life taking you there and trusting that he will at least set aside our differences."

"Why?" Annja asked.

"Because I am convinced you have something to do with the sword."

"But I've never even had any real interest in Joan of Arc." The story was one Annja had read as a girl in the orphanage. She'd been fascinated by Joan's heroism and bravery, of course, but the whole "called by God" thing had left her skeptical.

"The earth," Garin stated, "opened up and let you find the final piece of the sword. Even after it had been hidden from sight for hundreds of years."

"That was an earthquake." Annja was beginning to feel that she was stepping into a side dimension and leaving the real world behind.

"It was a miracle," Garin said.

She looked at him, wondering if he was deliberately baiting her. "Do you really believe that?"

Pausing a moment, Garin shook his head. "I don't know. And I've got more reason to believe it than I'm willing to go into at this moment. For the rest of the story, we'll have to talk to Roux."

"Even if that charm was part of Joan of Arc's sword, that doesn't mean it was the last piece."

"Roux says it is."

"Do you believe him?"

"In this, of all things, I do."

"Then how do I fit in?"

"I don't know. I know only that you must. As ego deflating as it is for him, Roux has had to face that, as well. That doesn't mean he accepts it."

The server returned, carrying a massive tray piled high with food.

"Let's eat," Garin suggested. "At the moment, there's nothing more to tell."

Despite the confusion that spun within her, Annja hadn't lost her appetite. There was more to Garin's story. He was holding something back that he considered important. She was convinced of that. But she was also convinced that he wouldn't tell her any more of it at the moment.

As she ate, she kept watch outside the building. Part of her kept expecting to see local police roll up at any moment.

Night filtered the sky, turning the bright haze to ochre and finally black by the time they finished the meal. Then they were on the road again. The answers, at least some of them, lay only a few hours into the future.

15

"Put this on."

Avery Moreau accepted the robe fashioned from wolf pelts. It was heavy and itchy against his bare skin. He wrinkled his nose in ill-disguised disgust. And it smelled like wet dog even more this time than the last.

Without a word, he pulled the robe on and stood waiting in the small room lit by the single naked bulb. The air felt thin and tasted metallic. He struggled to catch his breath but couldn't quite seem to.

Where he had expected to feel only anticipation at this moment, he now felt dread. He hadn't succeeded in his assignment. Surely Lesauvage wasn't going to initiate him now.

But here he stood, clad in the furs of the Wild Hunt, called to one of the secret meetings.

Marcel stood before him, already wearing the wolf's-head helmet that masked his features. He was big and blocky, one of the older boys whom Avery had grown up in fear of. Like most of Corvin Lesauvage's recruits, Marcel had been a bully all his life and had developed a taste for violence.

Avery had never truly felt that way. He'd been violent over the years. Growing up as the son of a known thief would do that to someone. If his father had been a successful bank robber or knocked over armored cars on a regular basis, perhaps things

would have been different. There might even have been money
in the house.

But Gerard Moreau hadn't done those things. He'd barely stolen
enough to keep his family fed and a roof over their heads most of the
time. He'd been too lazy to work at an hourly wage, which wouldn't
have fed them, either, and too unskilled to find a job that would.

Gerard Moreau had been trapped by circumstance into the life
that he had. Until the night Inspector Edouard Richelieu shot and
killed him in cold blood. The act had been nothing less than pre-
meditated murder.

That night, Avery had been with his father. Posted as a lookout, Avery
had to keep watch and make sure no one approached from outside.

No one had approached from outside the house. The police inspector had been inside the house. Richelieu had been entertaining
Etienne Pettit's wife that evening, unbeknownst to anyone in Lozère.

Pettit was a powerful man in the town, and not one who would
have put up with being cuckolded in his own home by a police inspector who lived with his mother. If Pettit had found out about his
wife's infidelities, the man would have divorced his wife and left her
with nothing. And he would have broken Inspector Richelieu, had
him tossed out of the police department onto the street.

That was why Richelieu had shot Gerard Moreau six times. The
police inspector loved his job because it validated him in ways that
Avery didn't understand but knew existed.

When he closed his eyes, Avery could still see his father fleeing
for his life through the window to the backyard. He'd slipped and
fallen in dog feces, and tried to get back to his feet.

Then Richelieu, totally nude, stood in the window with his pistol
in his fist and opened fire. The rolling thunder had driven Gerard
Moreau to the ground and ripped the life from him in bloody handfuls.

Avery had hidden. He'd been too afraid to act, and too inexperi-
enced to know what to do if he had tried. He'd held himself and cried
silent tears. In the end, he'd had to clap a hand over his mouth in
order to keep from crying out.

Later, Richelieu told everyone that he had been the first to respond
to the burglar alarm at the Pettit house. After he'd dressed, he'd obviously told Isabelle Pettit to set off the alarm.

No one asked why Richelieu felt compelled to shoot a fleeing suspect six times in the back. The police inspector had simply stated that it had been dark, which was the truth, and he claimed not to have known who the burglar was.

Everyone knew that Gerard Moreau never carried a weapon. He'd always stolen what he could, laid out his time in jail, and lived a mostly quiet life.

Gerard Moreau had tried to stop his son from becoming a thief. In the end, though, there hadn't been any other way for Avery to get the kinds of clothes he needed to wear or any of a thousand things it took to be a teenager in today's world.

When he'd seen he couldn't curb his son's ways, Gerard Moreau decided to properly train Avery in the ways of a burglar. He'd claimed that as his father, he could do no less than offer him the trade that he had employed to sustain his family.

That night at the Pettit house had been the first—and last—time father and son had worked a job together.

Knowing that his voice would never be heard—if it was, his tale would only land him in jail and would not bring his father's murderer any closer to justice—Avery ran that night. Later, when the policemen came calling at his door, he'd acted surprised about his father's death. Even if they'd suspected anything, his grief was real and they'd left him alone with it.

Three days after he'd been shot and killed, Gerard Moreau had been laid to rest in a pauper's grave in the church cemetery. And Avery had sworn revenge.

The only way he could conceive to get it, though, was through Corvin Lesauvage and his secret society. Avery had known about them through some of the other guys his age who had become part of Lesauvage's gang. Pack, they called themselves. They were part of what Lesauvage termed the Wild Hunt. And Lesauvage had a magic potion that could make men invincible.

"Are you ready?" Marcel asked.

Not trusting his voice, Avery nodded.

Turning, Marcel knocked on the wall of the basement beneath the big house Lesauvage owned. Gears ground within the wall, then a section of it pulled back and away to reveal a doorway.

"Praise be to the name of the Hunter," Marcel intoned as he stepped through the doorway.

"Praise be to the name of the Hunter," Avery echoed as he followed Marcel. He didn't know who the Hunter was.

But Lesauvage and his pack took their mysticism seriously.

Another young man dressed in wolfs' hides stood in the middle of the narrow, twisting flight of stairs that led down into the bedrock. He held two flaming torches. He passed one to Marcel.

In silence, they marched down the stairs. The wavering torchlight made footing tricky. Several times Avery made a misstep that could have sent him plunging down the stairs. He didn't think anyone waiting down there would have bothered to carry him back up.

The pack waited at the bottom. There were at least thirty of them standing together, each of them with a torch.

The first time Avery had come here, he'd been scared to death. There were caves all throughout the area, but he hadn't expected to walk around in one under a house near the center of town. According to the tales he'd heard, the cave had once served as a smuggler's den for pirate goods hauled up from the southern coast of France and bound for Paris.

Bats hung among the stalactites. Several of the corresponding stalagmites had been removed. Avery thought the cave smelled like death. It also smelled like wet dog and bat guano.

Marcel put a hand against Avery's chest and stopped him. Then Marcel and the other pack member went to join the group.

Avery felt the fear returning. Being set apart from peers had always been a bad thing. Either as punishment or as a reward, getting singled out nearly always resulted in negative consequences. He'd learned that in school. It was one of those lessons that stayed with a person the rest of his life.

"Avery Moreau." The deep voice echoed within the vast cavern.

"Yes." Avery had to try twice to get his voice to work. He raised a hand to shield his eyes from the light. Even squinting didn't help against the bright torchlight.

"You failed me."

Fear gripped Avery's heart then and he stood—barely—trembling. "I did everything I could. I led you to the woman. I told you where she would be in the mountains."

"Annja Creed escaped, and she took something that belonged to me." Lesauvage, dressed in hides and wearing a helmet that sported huge deer antlers, stepped forward from the pack. His helmet came complete with snarling deer features that were stained muddy scarlet. His light-colored eyes glittered.

"That wasn't my fault," Avery said. "I didn't do it."

"You bear the blame for this," Lesauvage accused. "You brought the outsider to the woman."

What about the other guys? Avery wanted to ask. What about those men dressed in black? It's not my fault they showed up!

"Look," he said desperately, "that wasn't my fault. I'll do anything you want me to."

Lesauvage stepped toward him.

Avery backed away.

"You failed us," Lesauvage said again. "But you can still serve us." He drew a long-bladed knife from the sleeve of the robe he wore under the wolf hides.

At a gesture from their leader, the pack descended upon Avery. Working quickly, as if they'd done this sort of thing countless times, they bound his hands and feet and draped him over a rounded stalagmite in the center of the cave.

One of them brought out a goat, yanking the poor creature savagely. Lesauvage stepped over to the goat and dragged his knife along its throat.

Blood spewed out. One of the pack members held a stainless-steel pot under the flow. But the dying creature fought and kicked, spattering the stone floor with its lifeblood. Finally, it grew still.

Chanting and cheering, two of the pack members seized the goat and heaved the animal into the shadowy crevasse. There was no thump of arrival. No one had ever measured the waiting fall.

Another pack member passed out tin cups and each person took a portion of the blood. Lesauvage passed among them, dropping powder into the steaming liquid. They stirred the brew with their fingers and drank it down.

Howling like madmen, their faces red with goat's blood, the pack danced with savage abandon as the drugs worked into their systems.

Avery had seen a sacrifice only once before. It had been two weeks ago, after his father had been murdered and before the American woman—Annja Creed—had arrived to search for La Bête. It had scared him then. Tied up as he was on the rock, potentially their next sacrifice, he was now even more frightened.

Lesauvage gestured to Avery.

Immediately four members, including Marcel, descended upon him like carrion feeders. They forced open his jaws and poured down a cup of goat's blood and drugs, howling in his ears the whole time.

At first, Avery thought he was going to drown. He tried not to drink, tried to turn his head away, but they held him firmly. He swallowed, gagging as he almost inhaled it. Once he'd drawn a full breath, they filled his mouth again.

Over and over, the salty taste of the blood coated the inside of his mouth. He thought he was going to be sick. I didn't want this! I only wanted justice for my father!

Finally they left him alone and returned to chanting and singing. They whirled and slammed into each other, laughing when they knocked each other down.

And the drugs hit Avery's system like surf smashing across a reef barrier, gliding through in a diffused spray that hit everything. The fear inside him evaporated. Energy filled him.

Lesauvage came and stood over Avery. The knife in the man's hand dripped blood.

"You can still serve us," Lesauvage told him.

Avery thought the way the man's voice echoed and rolled and changed timbres was amusing. So amusing, in fact, that he was laughing out loud before he knew it.

Then Lesauvage leaned in close to Avery. Light exploded all around, glinting from the crimson-streaked edge of the knife.

"Now!" Lesauvage shouted. "Now you will serve us!"

Avery watched as the blade rose and fell. He didn't know whether to laugh or to scream.

16

"Are you nervous?" Annja asked as Garin slowly approached the huge house built into the hillside.

"A little." Garin shrugged. "Roux and I never part on good terms. Not since—" He paused. "Not for a very long time."

"The last time I saw him, he walked out on a dinner tab on me." Annja gazed up at the house. She didn't know where they were. Garin had taken a number of turns after they'd left the highway. All she knew was that they were somewhere south of Paris.

"A dinner tab?" Garin chuckled.

"It was nothing to laugh about. My credit card took a serious hit over that."

"The last time I saw Roux," Garin said, "he tried to kill me."

Annja stared at him.

"I attempted to blow up his car first," Garin explained as if it was nothing. "With him in it. So I suppose he was entitled." He shrugged. "He was dazed at the time, or maybe he would have got me. I truly didn't expect him to survive."

"Then why isn't he meeting you at the gate with a rocket launcher?" Annja asked while wondering once again what rabbit hole she had fallen down.

"Because I've got you and he's interested in talking to you. Right now. Perhaps getting out of the house will be more...risky."

"Oh." Annja thought maybe she should have opted for the airport and a chance at escape.

But she would have left behind the mystery and she didn't like unfinished business.

"Maybe Roux has gotten over your attempt to kill him," Annja suggested.

"I doubt it. He can be rather unforgiving."

She thought about Lesauvage and the Brotherhood of the Silent Rain. She didn't feel very forgiving toward them.

Garin eased to a stop at the gatehouse. His gun rested in his lap. He dropped his right hand over it.

"How long has it been?" Annja asked. "Since you tried to blow him up, I mean?"

"Twenty years. In Rio de Janeiro."

"Twenty years ago?"

"Yes." Garin's attention was on the armed guard approaching the car.

Annja thought he had to be joking. But as he thumbed down the window, he was tense as piano wire. It wasn't a joke. *But twenty years?*

"You hold your age well," she commented dryly.

"You," Garin assured her, "have no idea." He raised his voice and spoke to the guard. "Stay back from the car."

The guard started to lift his assault rifle.

"If you raise that rifle," Garin said, showing the man the big pistol, "I'm going to kill you."

The guard froze. "Mr. Roux," he said in a calm voice.

"Yes," Roux's unmistakable voice came over the radio.

"Your guest is armed."

"Of course he is. I wouldn't expect him any other way. Let him pass. I'll deal with him."

"Yes, sir." The guard waved to his counterpart inside the gatehouse.

Garin smiled but never moved the pistol from the center of the man's chest. "Thank you." The gates separated and he rolled forward, following the ornate drive to the big house.

"A lot of testosterone in the air tonight," Annja commented. She had to work to make herself sound calm. She was anything but.

"There is a lot," Garin said, "that you don't know."

ROUX STOOD outside the house, defiant and confident, as if he were a general in control of a battlefield instead of a lion trapped in his den. He wore a dark suit that made him look like a wealthy business-man. His hair and beard were carefully combed.

A young man in butler's livery opened Annja's car door. He said, "Welcome, miss," in a British accent sharp as a paper cut.

Annja stepped out, still wearing the blouse and shorts she had worn for her research trip through Lozère that morning and after-noon. She felt extremely underdressed.

Garin's black clothes suited the night and the surroundings. He slipped the big pistol under his jacket.

"Miss Creed," Roux greeted her with a smile, as if they had just been introduced and none of the previous day's weirdness had occurred between them. "Welcome to my home."

Annja tried not to appear awestruck.

The home was huge. Palatially huge. Ivy clung to the stone walls and almost pulled the house into the trees that surrounded it, soft-ening the straight lines and absorbing the colors. The effect was clearly deliberate.

The butler stood by Roux and his eyes never left Garin. In response, Garin bared his teeth in a shark's merciless grin.

"You have a new lapdog," Garin said.

"Do not," Roux growled in warning, "trifle with Henshaw. If you do, one of you will surely be dead. I will not suffer his loss willingly."

Roux even talked differently in his home, Annja realized. He's really buying into the whole lord-of-the-manor thing.

"An Englishman?" Garin snorted derisively. "After everything we've been through, you trust your life to an Englishman?"

"I do," Roux said. "I've found few others worth trusting."

Garin folded his arms and said nothing.

Roux turned his attention to Annja. "You must be tired."

"No," Annja replied.

"Hungry?"

"No," she said. She returned his bright blue gaze full measure. "Eating with you is too expensive."

Roux laughed in honest delight. "I did hope you had enough to cover the bill."

"Thanks," Annja said. "Tons." She held out her hand. "You owe me for your half of the bill."

Amused, Roux snaked a hand into his pocket and pulled out a thick sheaf of bills. He pressed several into her hand.

Annja counted out enough to cover his half of the bill, then gave the rest back.

He frowned a little. "I'm sure the tab was more than that."

"It was," Annja said. "I only took half. Plus half the tip."

"I would have paid for it all."

"No," she told him. "I don't want to owe you anything."

Roux put the money way. "There's still the bit about me saving your life in the cave."

"Really?" Annja smiled sweetly. She spoke without turning around, but she could see the man in her peripheral vision. "Garin?"

"Yes," he replied.

"Do you want to kill Mr. Roux right now?"

"Nothing," the big man said, "would make me happier."

"Please don't."

Garin's smile broadened. "If you insist."

"I do." Looking directly at Roux, Annja nodded. "We're even. I just saved your life."

A displeased look filled Roux's patrician features. "You're going to be trouble," he declared.

"I find I'm liking her more and more all the time," Garin said.

"If nothing else, this should be interesting," Roux announced.

"I want to see the charm," Annja said.

Roux ushered them into his house.

If THE HOUSE HAD APPEARED wondrous and magical on the outside, it was even more so on the inside.

Annja gave up trying to act unimpressed. Paintings, ceramic works of art, stained glass, weapons, books and other pieces that should have been in museums instead of a man's home adorned the spacious rooms. Most of them had private lighting.

If Roux wasn't already wealthy, he would be if he sold off his collections. And a crook besides. Several of the pieces Annja saw were on lists of stolen items or had been banned from being removed from their country of origin.

The trip back to his personal office took time. Garin—obviously no lover of antiquities—looked bored as he trailed along after them, but Roux took obvious delight in showing off his acquisitions. He even offered brief anecdotes or histories regarding them.

Annja didn't know how long it took to get to the sword, but she was convinced it was a trip she'd never forget.

"The sword, the sword," Garin said when he could no longer hold his tongue. "Come on, Roux. You and I have waited for over five hundred years. Let's not wait any longer."

Five hundred years? Annja thought, realizing only then what he'd said. She figured it was only an exaggeration meant to stress a point.

Roux's office offered an even more enticing obstacle course that cried out for Annja's attention. Evidently he kept his favorite—and unique—items from his collections there.

Finally, though, with much prodding from Garin, and a promise of physical violence that almost triggered an assault from Henshaw, they reached Roux's vault room.

The huge door swiveled open. Roux disappeared inside the vault and returned carrying a case. He placed the case on the huge mahogany desk and opened it.

Something deeply moving attracted Annja's attention even more strongly than all the priceless objects she'd passed to reach this point. She stared at the pieces that had once made up the sword blade. Some of them were only thin needles of steel. Others looked as if they'd burned black in a fire. None of them would ever fit together again.

Yet she knew they all belonged together.

Somehow, on a level that she truly didn't understand, Annja knew that all the pieces were there. And that they had at last come home.

Unbidden, she stepped forward and reached out her right hand. Heat radiated against her palm.

"The pieces are hot," she said.

Standing beside her, Roux stretched out a hand. "I don't feel anything," he said.

Annja shook her head. "These pieces are giving off heat. I can feel it." She studied the pieces, finding the charm she had discovered in La Bête's lair.

It lay with the wolf and mountain side up. Bending down, the switched on the desk light and peered at the image.

"What do you know about the charm, Roux?" she asked.

The old man shrugged. "Nothing. I only knew when I saw it that it was part of this sword."

"Joan of Arc's sword?"

Roux turned on Garin. "You told her?"

The younger man looked impassive. "Does it matter?"

"You're a fool," Roux snapped. "You've always been a fool."

"And it's taken you over five hundred years to find the pieces of this sword," Garin returned. "*If* you've found them. I'd say that's pretty ineffectual. Perhaps recruiting people to help would have moved things along more quickly."

Annja moved her hand slowly over the sword fragments.

Roux, Garin and Henshaw all drew closer.

"Is this really her sword?" Annja asked. She moved her hand faster. "Joan of Arc's?" The heat was back, more intense than before.

"Yes," Roux said hoarsely.

"How do you know?"

"Because I saw her carry it."

Annja looked at him. "That was more than five hundred years ago."

"Yes," Roux agreed seriously. "It was. I saw the soldiers break Joan's sword. I watched her burn at the stake." Sadness filled his face. "There was nothing I could do."

Numb with disbelief, but hearing the echo of truth in the old man's words, Annja tried to speak and couldn't. She tried again. "That's impossible," she whispered.

The old man shook his head. "No. There are things you don't know yet. Impossible things happen." He paused, studying the pieces. "I'm gazing at my latest reminder of that."

Annja held her hand still. The pieces seemed to quiver below her palm. Before she knew she was doing it, she shoved both hands closer.

Her fingers curled around the leather-wrapped hilt.

An explosion of rainbow-colored light filled the case and overflowed into Roux's den. The shadow of something flew overhead on wings of driven snow. A single musical note thrummed.

For one brief second, Annja lifted the sword from the case. In that second, she was amazed to see that the sword's blade was whole. The rainbow-colored light reflected on the highly polished metal.

Images of other lights were caught in the blade's surface. A hundred pinpoints of flaming arrows sailed into the sky. Small houses burned to the ground. Running men in armor and covered with flaming oil died in their tracks, their faces twisted by screams of agony that thankfully went unheard.

At that moment, more than anything, Annja wanted to protect the sword. She didn't want Roux or Garin to take it from her. She had the strangest thought that it had been away too long already.

The sword vanished. The weight dissipated from her hands. She was left holding air.

"Where did it go?" Roux roared in her ear. "What did you do with the sword?" He grabbed Annja roughly by the shoulders and spun her around to face him. "What the hell did you do?"

At first, Annja didn't even recognize he was speaking in Latin. She reacted instinctively, clasping her hands together and driving her single fist up between them to break his hold on her. Still moving, she swung her doubled fists into the side of his head.

Roux spilled onto the Persian rug under the ornate desk where the empty case now sat.

The sword was gone.

17

Garin and Henshaw froze. Annja knew if either of them had so much as flinched, someone—perhaps both—would have died.

Getting to his feet with as much aplomb and dignity as he could muster under the circumstances, Roux cursed and worked his jaw experimentally, a bad combination as it turned out.

Annja dropped into fighting stance, both hands held clenched in fists before her. "I didn't do anything to the sword," she told the old man. "It disappeared. I lifted it from the case—"

"The pieces disappeared as soon as you touched the hilt," Roux snarled. "I saw that happen."

"Pieces?" Annja echoed. "It wasn't pieces that disappeared. I drew the sword out of that case. It was whole."

Roux searched her face with his harsh, angry gaze. "Poppycock. The sword was still in pieces."

He's insane, Annja thought. *That's the only explanation.* And Garin, too. Both of them as mad as hatters. And they've given you something—a chemical—something that soaks in through the skin. Or maybe the room has something in the air. You didn't see what you thought you saw. Something like that can't have happened.

She told herself that, but didn't completely believe it. She'd been under the influence of hallucinogens strong enough to give her waking dreams and walking nightmares before.

Once, in Italy, she'd come in contact with a leftover psychotropic drug used by one of Venice's Medici family members that had still been strong enough to send her to the hospital for two days.

In England, she'd been around Rastafarians who had helped with packing the supplies on a dig site who had smoked joints so strong she had a contact high that lasted for hours. She'd never used recreational drugs. But she knew what kinds of effects to look for.

There were none of those now.

"Think about it, Roux," Garin insisted. "If she took the sword pieces, where are they? She has no pockets large enough to store them. We were all watching her."

Roux cursed more as he searched the case and came up empty again.

"The sword wasn't in pieces when it disappeared," Annja told them. "Aren't you listening?"

"It was in pieces," Roux growled. "I saw them."

"I took the sword from the case—"

"Those pieces disappeared while they were still inside the case," Roux snapped. "I watched them."

"Then you didn't see what happened." Annja blew out her breath angrily. "The sword was whole."

Roux turned to Henshaw. "What did you see?"

"The sword was fragmented when it disappeared, Mr. Roux," Henshaw said. "Just as it was when you first showed it to me. Never in one piece."

"There you have it," Roux declared angrily. "All of us saw the sword in pieces."

"No," Annja said. "You didn't see it properly."

"You're imagining things." Roux sank into the huge chair behind the big desk. He regarded her intently. "Tell us what happened."

"I reached into the case for the sword—"

"Why?" Garin asked.

"Because I wanted to feel the weight of the haft," Annja answered. She didn't feel comfortable talking about the compulsion that had moved her to action. "As I touched the sword hilt, the pieces fit themselves together."

"By themselves?" Roux asked dubiously.

"I didn't move them."

"She didn't have time to fit the pieces together," Garin said. "You, on the other hand, have had time. And I'll bet nothing like this happened while you were trying to put those pieces together."

After a moment, Roux growled irritably, "No."

"*Something* happened to the sword fragments," Garin said.

"It was whole," Annja said again. She could still see the sword in her mind's eye. It felt as if she could almost touch it.

But neither of the men was listening to her.

"Five hundred years, Garin." Roux leaned forward and put his head in his hands. "*Over* five hundred years. I searched everywhere for that sword, for those pieces. Now they're all gone."

Garin's voice was gentle and kind. He didn't sound like someone who had tried to kill Roux.

Of course, Annja decided, he didn't sound insane, either, and he had to be. Both of them had to be.

Roux stared at the empty case.

"Once I had them all together, *something* should have happened," Roux complained bitterly.

"It disappeared," Garin said. He looked relieved.

"It wasn't supposed to do that," Roux argued.

"You said you didn't know what it would do."

"Wait." Annja held her hands up and stepped between them. "Time out."

They gave her their attention.

"*Who* told you to find the sword?" For the moment, Annja decided to go along with their delusion or outright lie that they had seen Joan of Arc carry the sword.

"I don't know," Roux said.

The old man shrugged. "Joan was one of God's chosen. A champion of light and good. It was my duty."

Annja breathed deeply and tried not to freak. The situation was getting even crazier.

An alarm erupted, dispelling the heavy silence that fell over the room.

Immediately, a section of the wall to the left of the computer desk split apart and revealed sixteen security monitors in four rows. Ghostly gray images sprinted across the landscaping outside the big house.

"Intruders," Roux said.

The intruders wore familiar black robes and carried swords that flashed in the pale moonlight. They also came armed with assault rifles and pistols.

A security guard took up a position beside the house and fired at the monks. Almost immediately, a monk with an assault rifle chopped him down, then turned and came toward the house.

The new arrivals began targeting the security cameras. One by one, the monitors inside Roux's study went dark.

Galvanized into action, the old man ran for the vault. "Who the hell are they?" he shouted.

"Monks," Garin replied.

"Monks?" Roux took an H&K MP-5 submachine pistol from the vault, shoved a full magazine into it and released the receiver to set the first round under the firing pin.

Annja was familiar with the weapon from the training she'd received.

"Some kind of warrior monks from the looks of them," Garin added. "Like the Jesuits. With better firepower."

"What are monks doing attacking my home?" Roux asked.

"In Lozère, they were looking for the woman," Garin said. After a brief glance at Roux's armory, he took down a Mossberg semiautomatic shotgun with a pistol grip and smiled like a boy on Christmas morning. He shoved boxes of shells into his jacket pockets.

Roux turned his gaze on Annja, who stood panicked and confused.

"Do you prefer a short gun or long gun, Miss Creed?" Henshaw asked. He had two rifles slung over his shoulders and was buckling a pistol around his waist.

"Pistols," Annja said, thinking that they would be more useful in the closed-in areas of the big house.

Henshaw handed her a SIG-Sauer .40-caliber semiautomatic with a black matte finish.

"I thought I saw another one in there," Annja said.

For the first time that night, Henshaw smiled. "Bless your heart, dear lady." He handed her a second pistol, then outfitted her with a bulletproof vest with pockets for extra magazines.

Roux buckled himself into a Kevlar vest, as well. "I don't suppose they're here to negotiate?" he asked rhetorically.

The lights went out. For a moment blackness filled the room. Then emergency generators kicked to life and some light returned.

Roux clapped on a Kevlar helmet. "What the bloody hell do these monks want?"

"Their mark was on the back of the charm," Annja said. "What do you think the chances are?"

"I think I should have paid more attention to that damned charm. Giving it back to them before was merely out of the question. Now that option appears gone for good."

"This house is pretty well fortified," Garin said as he saw to his own protection.

"Thank you," Roux said. "I tried to see that it was well-appointed."

"Do you think they can get through the front door?"

A sudden explosion shuddered through the house with a deafening roar.

Roux touched a hidden button on his desk. The dark monitors, powered by generator, came back on. This time the views were from inside the house.

On one of the screens, a dozen monks poured through the shattered remains of the elegant front door. They opened fire at once.

"Yes," Roux declared. "I believe they can." He picked up the submachine pistol.

"Do you have an escape route?" Garin asked.

"I recall having escaped from your assassins on a number of occasions."

Garin scowled. "This isn't a good time to revisit past transgressions."

"Then you'll warn me before you transgress again?" Roux asked.

Garin remained silent.

"I didn't think so," Roux said. "Henshaw?"

"Yes, sir." The butler stood only a short distance away, always positioned so that Garin couldn't take him and his master out at one time with a single shotgun blast.

"You know what to do if this bastard shoots me," Roux said.

"He won't live to see the outcome, sir."

"Right." Roux smiled. He took the lead with Garin at his heels as if they'd done it for years.

At the wall beside the security monitors, the old man pushed against an inset decorative piece. A section of the wall yawned open and revealed a narrow stairwell lit by fluorescent tubes.

"Where does it go?" Garin asked.

"All the way up to the third floor. Once there, we can escape onto the hillside. I've got a jeep waiting there that should serve as an escape vehicle." Roux stepped into the stairwell and started up the steps.

Garin followed immediately, having to turn slightly because he was so broad.

Two monks dashed into the study and raised their rifles.

Calmly, Henshaw pulled the heavy British assault rifle to his shoulder and fired twice, seemingly without even taking the time to aim. Each round struck a monk in the head, splattering the priceless antiques behind them with gore.

Before the dead men could fall, Henshaw had a hand in the middle of Annja's back. "Off you go, Miss Creed. Step lively, if you please." He sounded as pleasant as if they were out for an evening stroll.

Annja went, stumbling over the first couple steps, then running for all she was worth. The door closed behind them. Her breath sounded loud in her ears as she rapidly caught up with Garin. Gunshots sounded behind her, muffled by the door, and she knew the Brotherhood of the Silent Rain was tearing up Roux's study.

All of this over a charm? Annja couldn't believe it. The charm was hiding something, but she had no clue what.

THE TUNNEL ENDED against the sloped side of the roof. Roux sprung some catches and shoved the hatch open.

Through the opening, Annja stood on the roof and gazed around. The pistols felt heavy in her hands. Cooled by the breeze skating along the trees behind the house, she surveyed the area. Shouts echoed from inside the tunnel as their pursuers followed.

"Here." Roux ran toward the tree line where the house butted into the hill. There, barely lit by the moon, a trail whipsawed across the granite bones of the land. "Another two hundred yards and we'll reach the jeep."

At that moment, shadows separated from the trees and became black-robed monks.

Garin swore coarsely. "These guys are everywhere!" The shotgun came to his shoulder and he started firing at once, going forward after Roux all the same.

Annja fired, as well, but she didn't know if she hit anything or just added to the general confusion. Bullets pocked the rooftop, tearing shingles away at her feet.

Another round hit her, slamming into her high on the shoulder. The Kevlar vest did its job and didn't allow the bullet to penetrate, but the blunt trauma knocked her down all the same.

She fought her way back to her feet, stayed low and moved forward. When her second pistol fired dry, she whirled behind a tree, shoved the first one up under her arm to free her hand and reloaded the second. She was reloading the first when a monk leaped out of the shadows in front of her.

His face was dark and impassive. "We have come only for the charm," he said in a quiet, deadly voice. "That's all. You may live."

"I don't have it," Annja said as she brought the pistols up.

He leaped at her, his sword held high for a killing stroke.

Crossing the pistol barrels over her head, hoping she wasn't about to lose her fingers, Annja blocked the descending blade. When she was certain the sword had stopped short of splitting her skull and lopping her hands off, she snap-kicked the man in the groin, then again in the chest to knock him back from her.

Before Annja could get away, two more monks surrounded her. They didn't intend to use swords, though. They held pistols.

"Move and you die," one of them warned.

Annja froze.

"Drop the pistols."

She did, but her mind was flying, looking for any escape route.

One of the monks spun suddenly, his face coming apart in crimson ruin. The bark of the gunshot followed almost immediately.

The surviving monks turned to face the new threat. Muzzle-flashes ripped at the night and lit their hard-planed faces.

Garin fired the shotgun again, aiming at the nearest target. The monk moved just ahead of the lethal hail of pellets that tore bark from the tree behind him.

While the attention was off her, Annja stooped and scooped up the pistols. Just as she lifted them, a monk rushed Garin from the rear, following his sword.

"Behind you!" Annja pointed the pistols toward the monk, but Garin swung around into her line of fire.

The sword sliced through Garin's black leather jacket. Coins and the keys to his car glittered in the moonlight as they spilled out. Catching the man on the end of the shotgun's barrel, Garin loosed a savage yell and fired.

Trapped against the body with nowhere for the expanding gases to go, the shotgun recoil was magnified. Caught while turning on the soft loam, Garin went down under the monk's body. Carried by the forward momentum he'd built up, almost ripped in half by the shotgun blast, the dead man wrapped his arms around Garin's upper body.

Shouting curses, Garin rolled out from under the corpse and pushed himself to his feet. Gunshots slapped against his chest. Another cut the side of his face and blood wept freely. He pulled the shotgun to his shoulder and tried to fire, but it was empty.

He looked at Annja. "Run!" Then he sped up the mountainside as fast as he could go.

Annja tried to follow. Before she went more than ten feet, the arriving monks turned on her. The escape route was cut off. She didn't know if Garin was going to make it before he was overtaken.

Metal glinted on the ground only a few feet away. Even as she recognized what the object was, she was firing both pistols, chasing the monks back into hiding. It was a brief respite at best.

When both SIG-Sauers blasted empty, she dropped the pistol from her left hand and scooped up Garin's keys amid the scattered change lying on the ground. Then she turned and ran back down the mountain. Garin's car, almost as heavily armored as a tank, still sat out in front of the main house. If she could reach the car, she thought she had a chance.

18

"Stop her but do not kill her!"

As she ran, Annja knew the command gave her a slight edge over the monks pursuing her. She didn't try running back onto the roof of the house. Monks were already taking up perimeter positions atop it.

Instead, Annja ran for the side of the house. When she was past the house's edge, she put the car fob between her teeth, shifted the pistol to her left hand and used her right to drag against the house. Her fingers clutched and tore at ivy as she began the steep descent.

She ran faster and faster, gaining speed as gravity reached for her and she raced to keep up the pace by lengthening her stride. But in the end she didn't have a stride long enough to remain in control.

Somewhere past the second story, Annja's foot slipped on a rock, her hand tore through the clinging ivy and she grabbed a handful of air.

She fell.

Tumbling end over end, unable to control either her speed or her direction, Annja gathered a collection of bruises and scrapes. She landed with a force that left her breathless.

Get up! she willed herself. Somehow, her body obeyed, pushing, shoving, working even though she felt as if she'd been broken into pieces. Incredibly, her knees came up and she was driving her feet hard against the ground.

Bullets slammed into the house beside her and into the ground. A man stepped out of the darkness ahead of her. She brought her pistol up automatically and fired for the center of his body. The bullets hit him and drove him back.

She was around the house and running for all she was worth. Shadows closed in around her. She couldn't help wondering how many members belonged to the Silent Rain monastery.

She thought of the sword in her hand. The look and feel of it, the weight, it was almost there. As if she could reach out and touch it.

Everyone around her seemed to be moving in slow motion. But she moved at full speed.

Bullets thudded into the ground where she'd been. She moved more quickly than the monks could compensate. When she saw Garin's Mercedes, monks flanked it, standing at either end. One stood on the hood of the car and raised an assault rifle.

She didn't hesitate; there was nowhere else to go. Pointing the pistol, never breaking stride, she found she'd fired it dry. Knowing that if she turned away she would only be an easier target, she ran straight toward the monk and leaped, sliding across the car's hood and knocking her opponent from his feet as he fired over her head.

Landing on the other side of the car in a confusing tangle of arms and legs, she fought free and stood. The man standing at the rear of the car tried to turn but he was too slow. She swung the empty pistol at the base of his skull and knocked him out.

As the man fell, she stepped forward and delivered a roundhouse kick to the monk in front of the car. Her foot caught him in the chest and knocked him backward several feet.

Annja was too scared to be amazed. Adrenaline, she told herself. She'd never kicked anyone that hard in her life.

She slid behind the wheel, keyed the ignition and heard the powerful engine roar to life, and shoved it into gear. The rear wheels spun and caught traction, then she was hurtling forward.

The front gates were still locked. Annja mentally crossed her fingers and hoped that the armored car was sufficient for the task. As she drove into the gate, she ducked her head behind her arms and hung on to the steering wheel.

For a moment, it sounded as if the world were coming to an end.

An ugly image of her trapped and burning in the car filled her head. Fire had always been one of her greatest fears.

The car shuddered and jerked. Then, miraculously, it powered through the broken, sagging tangle of gates. Sparks flared around her as the car rode roughshod over the gates. She was on the other side, fighting the sudden fishtailing as the car lunged briefly out of control.

She cut the wheels just short of the trees at the side of the road and managed to keep the Mercedes pointed in the right direction. One of the headlights was broken—she could tell that from the monocular view of the road—but she could see well enough with the other.

She hoped Garin, Roux and Henshaw had made it to safety, but she had no intention of trying to find them. She'd had enough craziness for now.

Switching on the car's GPS program, she quickly punched in directions to Paris. She was catching the first flight to New York she could find.

Annja bought a change of clothes—a pink I Love Paris sweatshirt and black sweatpants—a black cap she tucked her hair into and black wraparound sunglasses at a truck stop outside Paris. They were tourist clothes, overpriced and gaudy. It wasn't much of a disguise, but wearing her own clothes was out of the question. Somewhere along the way she'd gotten someone's blood on them. She left them in the trash in the bathroom.

She abandoned the car and caught a ride with a driver making a delivery to the airport, wanting to conserve her cash in case she had to run again.

As Europe's second-busiest airport, Charles de Gaulle International was busy even at one o'clock in the morning. The driver was kind enough to drop her at Terminal 1, where most of the international flights booked.

Annja cringed a little when she paid full price for the ticket, but went ahead and splurged for a first-class seat. After the events of the past two days, she didn't want people piled on top of her.

Especially not when the persons around her could be black-garbed monks in disguise.

You're being paranoid, she chided herself. But, after a moment's reflection, she decided she was all right with that. A temporary case of paranoia beat a permanent case of dead.

ANNJA DOZED fitfully on the plane. No matter what she did to relax, true sleep avoided her. Finally, she gave up and spent time with her journals and notebook computer. Thankfully she'd left them in Garin's car when they got to the mansion. She didn't know if she'd ever again see the materials she'd left at the bed-and-breakfast.

She opened the computer and pulled up the jpegs she'd made of the sketches she'd done of the charm. She moved the images side by side and examined them.

"Would you like something to drink, miss?"

Startled, Annja looked up at the flight attendant. The question the man had asked slowly penetrated her fatigue and concentration.

"Yes, please," Annja replied. "Do you have any herbal tea?"

"I do. I'll get it for you."

The flight attendant returned a moment later with a cup filled with hot water and a single-serving packet of mint tea.

"Are you an artist?" the flight attendant asked.

"No," Annja answered, plopping the tea bag into the cup. "I'm an archaeologist."

"Oh. I thought maybe you were working on a video game."

"Why?"

The flight attendant shrugged. He was in his late thirties, calm and professional in appearance. "Because of the coin, I suppose. Seems like a lot of games kids today play have to do with coins. At least, that's the way it is with my kids. I've got three of them." He smiled. "I guess maybe I'm just used to looking for hidden clues in the coins."

"Hidden clues?"

"Sure. You know. Maybe it's a coin, but there are clues hidden in it. Secret messages, that sort of thing."

Annja's mind started working. She stared at the side of the charm that held the wolf and the mountain. Is there a clue embedded in here? Or is this just a charm? Why would that warrior wear it when he fought La Bête? Another thought suddenly struck her. Why was the warrior alone?

"I'll leave you alone with your work," the flight attendant said. "Have a good flight."

"Thank you," Annja said, but her mind was already hard at work, separating the image of the wolf and the mountain into their parts.

The obverse was the stylized sign of the Brotherhood of the Silent Rain. But she didn't know how stylized it was. Perhaps something had been added there, as well. She peered more closely, pumping up the magnification.

A moment later, she saw it. Behind three of the straight lines in the die mark of the Brotherhood of the Silent Rain, she saw a shadowy figure she hadn't seen before.

WHEN SHE REACHED New York City, the first thing Annja did was look to find out if she was going to be picked up by the police. Since the NYPD SWAT team wasn't waiting to cuff her when she stepped off the plane, she hoped that was a good sign.

Still, she didn't want to go home without knowing what to expect.

She hailed a cab in front of LaGuardia International and took it to Manhattan to an all-night cyber café. Since she lived in Brooklyn, she felt reasonably certain Manhattan would be safe.

Settled into a booth, her laptop plugged into the hard-line connection rather than the wireless so there would be no disruption of service—or less of it at any rate—she opened her e-mail. A brief glance showed she'd acquired a tremendous amount of spam, as usual, and had a few messages from friends and acquaintances, but nothing that couldn't keep.

There was a note from NYPD Detective Sergeant Bart McGilley that just read, Call me about those prints.

Annja didn't know if he was going to protest being asked to look them up or if he'd gotten a hit. Or maybe he was just the bait to bring her in. That gave her pause for a moment.

She decided to put off the call for a few minutes. At least until she had time to eat the food she'd ordered with the computer time.

She was surprised to find that once her mind started working she didn't feel the need for sleep. She didn't know where she was getting the extra energy from, but she was grateful.

She opened the alt.archaeology site and found a few comments expressing interest in the images she'd posted, but nothing helpful.

The alt.archaeology.esoterica board netted three replies to her question regarding the images.

The first was from kimer@thetreasuresinthepast.com.

Saw your pictures. Loved them. What you're looking at is some kind of coin minted for the Brotherhood of the Silent Rain. Wasn't used for money, but it's made of silver, Right?

If it is, then it's legitimate. There were also copper ones, and there are rumors of gold ones, too, though I've never talked to anyone who's seen one.

I've been researching European Monastic cults for my thesis. The brotherhood was disbanded three or four hundred years ago for some kind of sacrificial practice.

Sorry. Don't know any more than that. If you find out anything, I'd love to know more. Always curious.

The sandwich arrived, piled high with veggies and meat, with a bag of chips and a dill pickle spear on the side. A bottle of raspberry iced tea completed the meal.

As she ate one-handed, Annja worked through the other entries.

You've probably already found out that the stylized rain on the back of the coin represents the Brotherhood of the Silent Rain. They were one of the longest-lived monasteries in the Lozère/Mende area. Back when it was more commonly called Gévaudan.

That made the tie to La Bête more accessible, Annja thought. Since she didn't truly believe in coincidences, she looked for the connection.

Anyway, what you might not know is that it's still around. That coin you found was only minted for a few years. Maybe a dozen or twenty. Like everything else the monks did, they smithed the coins themselves. Had a forge and everything. What you've got there is a real find. I've got one of them myself. I've included pics.

Why would a basically self-supporting monastery mint its own coins? Annja asked herself.

Not only that, but the charm hadn't been minted of silver. Whoever forged it made it from the metal of the sword.

From Joan of Arc's sword. Annja still couldn't get around the thought of that.

Setting her sandwich to the side for a moment, Annja opened the attachments. The poster had done a great job with the pictures. They were clear and clean.

Judging from the pictures, the coin the poster owned was very similar to the one Annja had found in the cave. But that one looked like silver, even carried a dark patina that had never touched the one that Annja had found.

However, the coin in the pictures only had the image of the mountain, not the wolf. And there was no shadowy figure trapped behind three lines in the die mark.

She sighed and returned her attention to her sandwich. The mystery had deepened again. She loved archaeology for its challenges, stories and puzzles. But she hated the frustration that sometimes came with all of those.

The third message was from Zoodio, the original responder to her posting.

Hey. Hope you've had some luck with your enigma. I've had a bit, but it appears contradictory and confusing.

Welcome to archaeology, Annja thought wryly.

The coin you've got is different than the ones minted at the monastery. And minting for a monastery is weird anyway. I understand they took gold for the Vatican and all that. Had to fund the additional churches somehow. But they marked ingots with the papal seal. Most of the time, though, the church never bothered to melt down and recast anything that came through the offerings.

I noticed differences on your coin, though. I mean, the images I pulled up and got from friends are different. But I didn't find any that looked like the one you've got.

Taking a moment, Annja opened the images Zoodio had embedded in the message. Sifting through them, she found they were similar to the ones she'd gotten from the previous poster.

To start with, the coin you found doesn't appear to be made out of silver. Some other material?

Also, yours has differences. Did you notice the shadowy figure behind the stylized rain? I didn't at first. Had to look at it again, but I think it's there.

Excitement thrummed through Annja. She clicked on the embedded picture and it opened in a new window.

The image was one of those she had posted, but Zoodio had used a red marker to circle the shadowy figure, then colored it in yellow highlighter to make it stand out more.

This really caught my eye. I love stuff that doesn't make sense. I mean, eventually it will, but not at that precise moment, you know?

So I started looking. Turns out that the original Silent Rain monastery was attacked and burned down in 1767.

Shifting in her seat, noticing that it had started to rain outside, Annja felt another thrill of excitement. Zoodio hadn't been looking for a connection between the Brotherhood of the Silent Rain and La Bête, but she had suspected it was there because of Lesauvage's interests.

Of course, the monks showing up hadn't daunted that conclusion.

La Bête had claimed its final victim, at least according to most of the records, in 1767, over three hundred years ago. And the monastery burned down that same year. Annja smiled at her rain-dappled image in the window. That can't be a coincidence, she thought. She was feeling energized. I do love secrets that have been hidden for hundreds of years.

She pondered the sword and how it had vanished. That was a whole other kind of secret.

During the flight back to the United States, she had come to the conclusion that Garin and Roux had somehow tricked her. She didn't

know how, and she didn't know why, but there was no other explanation for the sword's disappearance that made any sense at all.

She shivered slightly and returned her focus to the computer.

Turns out that the monastery was self-contained. They didn't
take just anyone who wanted in.

Not only that, these guys are supposed to be like the
Jesuits. Warlike, you know? Trained in the sword and the
pistol. Supposed to be masters of the blade and crack shots
and all that rot.

Well…Annja thought, maybe they weren't as good as their reputation. Or maybe the latest generation has gotten rusty.

Then again, Roux, Garin and Henshaw weren't your average man
on the street. The monks had walked into a hornet's nest.

The brotherhood wasn't well liked by the rest of the church.
Too independent, too self-involved. Instead of reaching out
to the community, the brotherhood sort of withdrew from it.

From the accounts I read, they didn't want to be contam-
inated by outsiders.

Then where did they get recruits? Annja wondered. She opened
her journal and started making notes. As questions arose, she entered
those, as well.

Later, she'd timeline it and start combing through the facts and
suppositions she had and try to find the answers she needed. She'd
learned to work through an outline, make certain the bones were
there regarding an event she was researching, then flesh it out once
she knew what she was looking for.

In a way they became the perfect prison.

Shortly before the monastery was destroyed, the pope or
one of the high church members ordered a prisoner moved
there. The Silent Rain monks were supposed to keep the
prisoner until they were told to set him or her free. Rumor
exists that the prisoner was a woman.

Annja found the possibility intriguing. Why would a woman be locked up in a monastery? Normally a woman would have been sent to an abbey. Or simply imprisoned.

But the story of Joan of Arc, how she'd been imprisoned and later killed at the hands of brutal men, echoed in Annja's head. Written history had a way of being more kind and gentle than what an archaeologist actually found broken and bashed at the bottom of a sacrificial well or buried in an unmarked shallow grave.

While working on dig sites throughout Europe, and even in the American Southwest, Annja had seen several murder victims. Those people had never been important enough in history's selective vision to rate even a footnote most of the time. People were lost throughout history. It was a sad truth, but it was a truth.

Whoever it was, the story goes that an armed force descended on the monastery to free the prisoner. During the battle, the monastery burned to the ground. The fields were sown with salt so nothing would grow there for years.

And, supposedly, everyone at the monastery was killed. No one knows what happened to the prisoner.

But there's also a story that a few local knights, unhappy with how the church was speaking out against their hunting parties, decided they'd had enough and razed the monastery for that reason.

Don't know.

But I found the shadowy image (if it's there and not just a figment of my imagination!) really interesting.

I hope you'll let me know what you find out.

Annja closed down the notebook computer and gazed out the window. There were so many unanswered questions.

A few minutes later, she flagged down a taxi and gave her address in Brooklyn. The sound of the tires splashing through the rain-filled streets lulled her. Her eyelids dropped. She laid her head back on the seat and let her mind roam. So many images were at war for her attention. The find at the cave. La Bête. Lesauvage, so smooth and so dangerous. Avery Moreau, whose father had been

killed by Inspector Richelieu. The Brotherhood of the Silent Rain.
Roux. Garin.

And the sword.

In her mind's eye, she pictured the sword as it had been, broken
into fragments. She could clearly see the piece that had been stamped
by the Silent Rain monastery.

In her memory, she reached for it again. Incredibly, the pieces all
fit together and the sword was once more whole. She reached for
the sword, felt the rough leather wrapped around the hilt and the cold
metal against her flesh.

When she closed her hand around the sword, she felt as if she was
connected to it, as if it was part of her, as if she could pull it out of
the case again.

She played the memory slowly, feeling the solid weight of the
sword. Slowly, unable to stop herself from attempting the task even
though she knew it was going to disrupt the memory, she withdrew
the sword from the case.

It came, perfectly balanced for her grip.

"What the hell are you doing, lady?"

Annja's eyes snapped open. In disbelief, she saw the sword in her
hand, stretched across the back of the taxi. It obstructed the driver's
view through the back window. He looked terrified.

She was holding the sword!

19

Cursing loudly, the taxi driver cut across two lanes on Broadway. Thankfully traffic was light at the early-morning hour, but horns still blared in protest. His tires hit the curb in front of a closed electronics store.

Still under full steam, the driver leaped out of the taxi. He reached under the seat for an L-shaped tire tool that looked as if it could have been used on the kill floor in a slaughterhouse.

He jerked Annja's door open. "You!" he snarled, gesturing with the tire tool. "You get outta my cab!"

He was thin and anemic looking, with wild red hair tied back in a bun, wearing an ill-fitting green bowling shirt and khaki pants. He waved the tire tool menacingly.

For the moment, though, Annja ignored him. Somewhere during the confusion, the sword had disappeared. But it was here, she thought. I saw it. I felt it. *It was here.*

"C'mon!" the driver yelled. "Get outta there! What the hell do you think you were doin' waving that sword around like that? Like I wasn't gonna notice a sword!"

Dazed, Annja got out of the taxi. "You saw the sword?"

"Sure, I did!" the driver shouted. "Six feet long if it was an inch! And it—" He stopped suddenly. In disbelief, he stared at Annja, who stood there with her backpack slung over her shoulder.

Then he motioned her away from the taxi. "Back up. Get outta there already."

Annja complied.

The driver's antics had drawn a small crowd.

The cabbie looked all over the back seat of the taxi. Then he dropped to his hands and knees and peered under the car. He even dragged his hands through the shadows as if doubting what his eyes revealed.

He clambered back to his feet. "All right," he demanded, "what did you do with it?"

"Nothing," Annja replied.

"You had a sword back there, lady. Biggest pig sticker I ever seen outside of *Braveheart*." The taxi driver glared at her.

"I don't have a sword," Annja said.

"I saw what I saw, lady."

Realizing the futility of the argument, Annja dropped twenty dollars on the seat, then turned and left, walking out into the street and hailing another cab immediately. She rode home quietly, trying not to think of anything, but wondering about everything.

To THE CASUAL OBSERVER, Annja's neighborhood was run-down. She liked to think of it as lived-in, a piece of Brooklyn history.

Sandwiched amid the tall apartment buildings, the delis, the shops, the pizza parlors and the small grocery stores, her building was one of the oldest. Only four floors high, the top two floors were divided into lofts instead of apartments. An artist, a photographer, a sculptor and a yoga instructor lived there.

The ground floor was occupied by shops, including a small gallery that showcased local artists. A violin maker, a dentist, a private investigator, a fortune-teller and music teachers occupied offices on the second floor.

A freight elevator ran up all four stories, but Annja didn't take it. The residents had a tacit understanding that no one used the elevator at night because of the terrible noise it made. Annja had also found that she could generally just about pace the elevator as it rose.

She took the stairs in the dimly lit stairwell. In the years that she'd lived there, she'd never had any trouble. Vagrants and thieves tended to stay away from the building because so many people lived above the shops and kept watch.

Her door was plain, scarred wood under a thick varnish coat, marked only by the designation 4A. She liked to think of it as 4-Annja, and that was how she'd felt when she'd first seen the loft space.

She worked through the five locks securing the door, then went inside.

A feeling of safety like she'd never known descended upon her as soon as she closed the door. For a moment, she stood with her back to the door, as if she could hold out the rest of the world.

As far back as she could remember, she had shared her space. Though she'd been so young when her parents were killed that she couldn't really remember living with them. In the orphanage, there had been bunk beds stacked everywhere, and nuns constantly moving among them. Privacy had been nonexistent. As she'd grown older, her roommates had dropped down to four, but there was still no privacy.

In college, she'd shared a dorm room the first year, then settled into an apartment off campus with a revolving cast of roommates until graduation because none of them could afford to live on their own. The first few years after she'd graduated had been much the same. Only she'd been on digs—sharing campsites—ten months out of the year.

But then she'd sold her first book, a personal narrative detailing her experiences excavating a battlefield north of Hadrian's Wall in Britain. The rumor was that the legendary King Arthur had fought there. At least, the man the stories had been built on was believed to have fought there.

Professor Heinlein hadn't found any trace of King Arthur or his Knights of the Round Table, but he had discovered the murders of a band of Roman soldiers. In the official records, the unit had been lost while on maneuvers. From the evidence Annja had helped to unearth, the commander of the Roman centurions had killed them because they'd discovered his dealings with the Picts.

It appeared that the Roman commander had managed quite a thriving business in black market goods. Most wars inevitably produced such a trade, and there were always men ready to make a profit from it.

During the dig, though, Annja and the others reconstructed what had happened. The intrigue—digging for bones, then going through fragments of old Roman documents to re-create the circumstances—had captured her attention. Everyone on the dig team had been excited by what they were finding and by the murders.

She'd kept a journal simply to keep track of everything they were figuring out, detailing the dig with interconnected pieces on what must have happened during that action all those years ago, interspersing colorful bits of history and infusing the story with life. A British journalist had taken an interest in her writing, and read everything she'd written. He'd made a lot of suggestions and pointed out the possibility of a book.

Annja had worked on the journal, with an eye toward possible publication, at the site and when she'd returned to New York. Two years later, after the manuscript had found a publisher and come out as a book, it was enough of a success to allow Annja to make the down payment on the loft. Reviewers had said she'd made archaeology appealing for the masses and kicked in a bit of a murder mystery on the side.

After that, she'd continued getting dig site offers because the book served as a great introductory letter and résumé. She'd also made some appearances on the late-night talk-show circuit and had a chance to show that she was good in front of a camera.

She became a favorite of David Letterman, who worked hard to keep her off balance and flirt with her at the same time. Her minor celebrity status eventually landed her on *Chasing History's Monsters*.

Annja looked around the loft. The big room had a fourteen-foot ceiling. Shelves filled the walls and sagged under the weight of books, rocks, artifacts and other finds. Her desk sat overflowing with open books, sketchpads and faxes. File folders, although everything was in order about them, stood stacked in haphazard piles. A sea of technology washed up around the desk: scanners, digital cameras, audio equipment, GPS devices, projectors and other items that she found useful. Despite her love of history, she loved technology, too.

She'd had every intention of cracking the notebook computer open and working on what she'd found out about the coin and the Brotherhood of the Silent Rain. But it felt so good to be home.

Instead, she barely made it through a shower and into an oversize T-shirt before she collapsed into bed.

Her thoughts were of the sword. Had she really held it? Had the taxi driver really seen it? Was she losing her mind…?

THE ANNOYING SOUND of a ringing phone penetrated the haze of sleep.

"Good morning," Annja said. Without opening her eyes, she rolled over in bed and struggled to think clearly. She felt as if she'd been on cold medicine.

"Don't you mean 'Good afternoon'?" the caller asked. NYPD Homicide Detective Bart McGilley always sounded way too chipper, Annja thought grumpily as the words slowly registered.

She opened her eyes and looked at the skylight. From the hard, direct shadow on the varnished floor, she knew it had to be around noon.

Glancing over at the bedside clock, she saw the time was 12:03.

"Sorry." Annja pushed herself up from bed. She never slept this late. "You woke me. It's taking me a minute to catch up with myself."

"When did you get in yesterday?"

"You mean what time did I get in this morning?"

"Ouch. That's harsh. You must have slept hard."

Annja sat on the edge of the bed. "Why?"

"I called three times already."

"I didn't hear the phone ring."

"Lots of fun in France?" Bart sounded a little envious. He'd told her more than once he could find his way around New York City blindfolded. Seeing something new would have been welcome.

"Hardly." Annja yawned and suddenly realized she was ravenous. "Did you find out something about those prints I sent you?"

"I did. We need to talk."

"We are talking." Annja heard the hesitation in his voice. It wasn't something she usually heard in Bart McGilley.

"Face-to-face," he told her.

"Is it that bad?" Annja stood and walked to the window. She moved the curtain aside and peered out. She loved the view from the building. The streets were filled with pedestrians and cars.

"Are these fingerprints new?" he asked.

"Would that make a difference?"

"It would make it weird. Bad may follow. I've noticed that with you. You archaeologists sometimes lead strange lives."

You, Annja thought, remembering the Brotherhood of the Silent Rain and the disappearing sword, don't know the half of it.

"Besides," Bart added, "I've missed talking to you."

"I need to get dressed," she told him.

"I could come over and help."

Annja smiled at that. The thought was a pleasant one that she'd entertained before. Bart McGilley had great eyes and great hands.

The problem was, he was the marrying kind. He couldn't deal with a relationship where all things were equal. Getting involved with him would mean a regular struggle choosing between relationship and career.

And Annja couldn't leave archaeology. There were too many wonders out there just waiting to be discovered. She could share her life, but she couldn't give it up. Finding a guy who could meet her halfway was going to be hard, and she wasn't even sure she wanted to look.

"I appreciate the offer," Annja said, "but I'm sure you have better things to do."

Bart sighed. "I don't know about better, but I know the captain's kicking tail for me to move some files off my desk."

"So we'll meet for lunch," Annja said. "I'll buy. Where to you want to meet?"

"Tito's?"

Tito's was one of their favorite Cuban restaurants. It also wasn't far from her loft.

"Tito's sounds great. Are you in the neighborhood?"

"If you hadn't answered the phone this time, the next thing you'd have heard was me knocking on the door."

"See you there in twenty minutes?"

"If you show up in twenty minutes, I'll be the guy with the surprised look."

ANNJA ARRIVED at the restaurant in twenty-seven minutes. She dressed in jeans, a fitted T-shirt, a leather jacket against the cool breeze and carried a backpack containing her computer and accessories.

She also turned the head of every male in the restaurant. After everything she'd been through the past few days, she indulged a moment of self-gratification.

Tito's carried the flavor of Cuba in the fare and the surroundings. The smoky scent of fajitas swirled in the air. Spices stung her nose. Lime-green seats and yellow tables filled the hardwood floor. The drinks came crowded with fruit and a little umbrella.

"Annja!" Standing behind the counter, Maria Ruiz waved excitedly. Plump and gray-haired, she was in her sixties, the mother of Tito, and the chef who made the kitchen turn on a dime. Nothing escaped Maria's sight. She wore a short-sleeved floral shirt under her apron.

"Maria," Annja said warmly, and stepped into the short woman's strong embrace.

"It has been too long since you've been with us," Maria said, releasing her and stepping back.

"I've been out of the country," Annja replied in Spanish.

"Then you should come and bring pictures," Maria said. "Show me where you have been. I always enjoy your adventures so much."

"Thank you. When I get everything ready, I'd love to."

Maria wiped her hands on her apron. "Let me know when. I'll make a special dessert."

Annja smiled. "I'll look forward to that." And I'll have to go to the gym for a week afterward. Still, she loved Maria's attentions, even if she had to pay for it in extra workouts.

"Do you need a table?" Maria asked.

"Actually, I'm meeting someone."

Maria's eyebrows climbed.

"I'm meeting Bart," Annja said, laughing.

"He's a good-looking man," Maria observed.

"Yes," Annja agreed, "but I think he already knows that."

Maria waved her comment away. "You could do much worse."

"I know."

Shaking her finger in warning, Maria added, "You're not getting any younger."

Chagrined, Annja smiled and shook her head. If Maria had her way, she'd already have her married off.

"He's here already. Come with me." Maria led the way through the packed restaurant, calling out instructions to the busboys, urging them to greater speed. She also dressed down a couple of waitresses who were lingering with male customers.

Bart sat at a table in the back that offered a view of the street. He was six feet two inches tall, with dark hair clipped short, a square jaw that was freshly shaved and wearing a dark blue suit with a gold tie firmly knotted at his neck. He stood as Maria guided Annja to the table.

"You look like a million bucks." Bart pulled out a chair.

"You see?" Maria pinched Bart's cheek. She spoke English so he could understand. "You see why I like this one? Always he knows the right thing to say."

Annja put her backpack on the chair next to her.

Embarrassed and off balance, Bart sat across from her.

"Have you ordered?" Maria asked.

Bart shook his head. "I was waiting for Annja."

Maria threw her hands up. "Don't you worry. I'll prepare your meals. I'll make sure you get plenty." She turned and walked away.

Bart shook his head and grinned. "This is a big city. How do you get to know these people so well?" he asked.

"I like them," Annja said.

"Then you like a lot of people. It seems like everywhere we go, you know somebody." Bart didn't sound jealous.

"I've met a lot of people."

"But you're an absentee resident. Gone as much as you're here."

"I grew up in an orphanage," Annja said. "I learned to meet people quickly. You never knew how long they were going to be around."

Bart leaned back in his chair. "I didn't know that."

Annja smiled. "It's not something I talk about."

"I mean, I figured you had a family somewhere."

"No."

He shook his head. "How long have I known you?"

"Two years."

Smiling, he said, "Two years, four months."

Annja was surprised he'd kept track. It made her feel a little uncomfortable. She didn't timeline her life other than when she was on a dig site. In her daily life, she just… flowed. Got from point A to point B, with an eye toward a multitude of possible point Cs.

"I'll take your word for it," she told him.

"It's been that long. And in all that time, I didn't know you were adopted."

"I was never adopted," Annja said. For just an instant, the old pain twitched in her heart. "I grew up at the orphanage, went to college and got on with my life."

Bart looked uncomfortable. "Hey, I'm sorry. I didn't mean to get into this."

"It's no big deal," Annja said. But she remembered that it used to be. She'd walled all that off a long time ago and simply got on with living. Just as the nuns had counseled her to do.

Gazing into her eyes, Bart said, "It's just that you have this way about you. Like with that woman—"

"You mean Maria?"

"See? I didn't even know her name."

"That's because she's never been a homicide suspect," Annja said.

Bart gave her a wry look. "No. That's not it. You're just... someone people are lucky to get to know."

"Thank you." Annja felt embarrassed and wondered if the meeting was going to suddenly get sticky and if Bart wanted to explore the possibilities of a relationship.

"I was telling my girlfriend about you. That maybe we should try to fix you up with somebody we knew."

Annja didn't think she'd heard right. "Girlfriend?" She suddenly felt let down in ways she hadn't even imagined.

"Yeah. Girlfriend."

Hesitating, Annja said, "How long have you had a girlfriend?"

"We've dated off and on for the last few years," Bart said. "It's hard to maintain a steady relationship when you're a cop. But a week ago, we got engaged."

"You asked her to marry you?" Annja was reeling.

He grinned and looked a little embarrassed. "Actually, she asked me. In front of the guys at the gym."

"Gutsy."

"Yeah. She's some piece of work."

"So what did you say?"

Bart shrugged. "I told her I'd think about it."

"You did not."

"No," he agreed, "I didn't. I said I would." He shifted in his seat. "I'd like to ask you a favor if I could."

"You can. I seem to ask you for favors from time to time." Annja didn't like the little ember of jealousy inside her. She knew she didn't want commitment at this point in her life, but she'd liked the idea of having Bart kind of waiting in the wings. She didn't like how casually that had just been taken off the table. Or how she'd made the wrong assumptions about his feelings for her. She felt foolish.

"I'd like something special for a wedding ring," Bart said. "Something that has…a history to it. You know. Something that has—"

"Permanence," Annja said, understanding exactly what he was looking for.

Bart nodded and smiled happily. "Yeah. Permanence. I want to give her something that didn't just come off an assembly line."

"I can do that. How much time do I have?"

Spreading his hands, Bart shrugged. "A few months. A year. We haven't exactly set a date yet."

"What does she do?"

He gazed at her through suspicious, narrowed eyes. "Are you curious about the kind of woman that would go out with me? Or choose to marry me?"

"I figured I'd be checking a psych ward."

Bart snorted.

"Actually," Annja went on, "I was thinking it might be nice to get her something that might tie in to her profession. Give her a duality. A bonding of her life with you as well as the life she's chosen."

"I like that," Bart said seriously.

"Good. So what does she do?"

"She's a doctor. In Manhattan."

"A doctor is good," Annja said. "What kind of doctor?"

"She works in the ER. She patched me up three years ago when I was shot."

"You never told me you'd been shot," Annja said.

"I didn't die. Nothing to tell. But I got to know Ruth."

"Ruth. That's a good, strong name."

"She's a strong lady."

"So the offer you made earlier about coming up to my loft and helping me dress—"

"Whoa," Bart protested, throwing his hands up. "In the first place, I knew you would never say yes."

Feeling mischievous, Annja said, without cracking a smile, "And if I did?"

"You wouldn't."

She decided to let him off the hook. "You're right."

"So what about you?" he asked. "Do you have a special guy stashed someplace?"

"No."

"Then you should let Ruth and me fix you up."

"I'm not looking for a relationship," Annja said. "I have my work."

"And that's why I knew you wouldn't let me come up." Bart smiled. "Speaking of work, yours, as I might have mentioned, has taken on a decidedly weird twist."

"How?" Annja asked.

"Those fingerprints you asked me to run? They're connected to a homicide that took place sixty-three years ago."

Surprise stopped Annja in her tracks for a moment. "A homicide?"

"Yeah. They belong to the prime suspect."

20

"Sixty-three years ago," Bart McGilley went on, "a woman was found dead in a hotel room in Los Angeles. She worked for MGM studios. Bought set pieces. Stuff they used in the backgrounds to make a scene more real."

"Anyway, from the way everything looks, this woman, Doris Cooper, age twenty-eight and an L.A. resident, was murdered for one of the things she bought."

"What was it?" Annja felt a sudden chill.

Bart shrugged. "Nobody knows. Nobody knew what she'd bought that day. The detectives working the case didn't follow up all that well. During the heyday of the movies back then, the death of a set designer only got a splash of ink, not a river of it."

"She was a nobody," Annja said, knowing the sad truth of how things had gone.

"Right."

Annja wondered if Roux was the type to kill a woman in cold blood. It didn't take her long to reach the conclusion that he was—if he was properly motivated. She was doubly glad that she hadn't followed Roux and Garin. Their talking about having lived five hundred years was already weird enough without also thinking of them as murderers.

"Those fingerprints popped up on a computer search?" Annja asked.

"At Interpol," Bart replied. "They're called friction ridges in cop speak, by the way. Back in the day, so the story goes, the L.A. investigators thought maybe the guy was from out of the country. On account of how Doris Cooper bought a lot of things from overseas. So they sent the friction ridges over to Interpol. After you sent them to me, I sent them on, thinking maybe you were looking for an international guy."

"Interpol happened to have the fingerprints of a sixty-three-year-old murder suspect?"

Bart blew out his breath. "Interpol has a lot of information. That's why they're a clearinghouse for international crimes. They've gone almost totally digital. Searchable databases. You get a professional out there in the world doing bad stuff, they've got a way to catch them. This case was one of those they'd archived."

"There's no doubt about the prints?"

Bart shook his head. "I had one of our forensics guys match them up for me. When I saw what I saw, that these friction ridges belonged to the suspect on a sixty-three-year-old murder, I knew I wanted a professional pair of eyes on that ten-card."

"Was there a name attached to the friction ridges?"

"No."

Two of Maria's cooks arrived with steaming plates of food. They placed them on the table in quick order and departed.

Annja's curiosity didn't get in the way of her appetite. Laying a tortilla on her plate, she quickly loaded it with meat, tomatoes, peppers, onions, lettuce and cheese.

"So this guy you printed," Bart said, "he was what? Eighty or ninety?"

He didn't look it, Annja thought. She would have guessed Roux was in his early sixties, but no more. During the shoot-out with the Brotherhood of the Silent Rain, he hadn't moved like even a sixtysomething-year-old man.

"I found the fingerprints on a coin," Annja said truthfully. She didn't want to mention that the coin was of recent vintage.

"So you thought you'd send them along to me?" Bart shook his head. "You had more reason than that."

Annja looked at her friend, thought about him getting married and realized that she truly hoped things didn't change between them. She knew one of the things that would change their relationship, though, was a lie.

"I was given the coin by a man in France," she told him. "He swapped it, while I wasn't looking, for a charm I'd found."

"Was the charm valuable?"

"Maybe. It was made out of hammered steel, not gold or silver. Not even copper. I haven't even found a historical significance yet." Annja couldn't tell him that it had been part of a sword that Roux had claimed once belonged to Joan of Arc.

Bart took a small notebook from inside his jacket. "Did you get his name?"

"Roux," she answered. "I'm not even sure of the spelling."

He wrote anyway. "No address?"

Annja thought of the big house butted up against the hill outside Paris. She'd never seen an address and Garin had never mentioned one.

"No," she said. "No address."

Bart sighed and closed the notebook. "I can ask Interpol to look up records on this guy. Maybe we'll get a hit on something."

"Sure," Annja said. Curiosity nagged at her. Roux was wanted in connection with a sixty-three-year-old murder. She wondered what other information the old man was hiding. She was glad that she was out of France and far away from him.

ANNJA SPENT the afternoon putting together the video on La Bête. She used the software on her desktop computer, loading up the video footage of Lozère, the books she'd cribbed for pictures and drawings of what the Beast of Gévaudan might have looked like, and the digital pictures she'd taken of the creature in the cave.

Using the green screen setup in one corner of the loft, she filmed different intros for the segment, a couple of closings, and completed the voice-overs. When she had it all together, it was late and she was tired.

She watched the completed video and timed it. *Chasing History's Monsters* generally only allowed nine to ten minutes per segment, allowing for setup by the host and the ensuing commercials.

So far, she was three minutes over but knew with work she could cut that down.

Okay, she told herself, all work and no play makes Annja a dull woman.

After grabbing a quick shower and a change of clothes, she packed her gym bag and headed out of the loft.

EDDIE'S GYM WAS an old-school workout place. Boxers exercised and trained there, smashing the heavy bag then each other in the ring. It had concrete floors, unfinished walls, and trendy exercise machines had never taken up residence there. Free weights clanked and thundered as lifters worked in rotation with their spotters.

It was a place where men went to sweat and burn out the anger and frustration of the day. Young fighters learned the intricacies of the fighting craft and the statesmanship necessary to sweep the ring and move up on a fight card. No one tanned there, and hot water in the showers was a random thing.

There really was an Eddie and he and another old ex-boxer had each been Golden Gloves and fought professionally for a time. They owned the place outright and didn't suffer poseurs or wannabes with no skill.

Training wasn't part of what a membership bought. That was given to those deserving few who caught the eye of Eddie and his cronies.

Occasionally, young men who had seen *Fight Club* too many times came into the club and tried to prove they were as tough as Brad Pitt or Edward Norton. The regulars, never very tolerant, quickly sent the newbies packing with split lips and black eyes.

Eddie's was all about survival of the fittest. Annja liked to go there because it felt real, not like one of the upscale fitness clubs that were more about the right kind of clothing and the favorite smoothie flavor of the week.

When she'd first started working out there, she'd had trouble with some of the men. Eddie hadn't wanted her around because he didn't want the complication.

But she'd stood her ground and won the old man over with her knowledge of boxing. The knowledge was a newly acquired thing because she'd liked the gym, had wanted to work out there and did her homework. She also worked out at a couple of martial-arts dojos, but she preferred the atmosphere at Eddie's. She was a regular now and had nothing to prove.

"Girl," Eddie said as he held the heavy bag for her, "you musta been eatin' your Wheaties. You're pounding the hell outta this bag more than ever before."

Annja hit the bag one last time, snapping and turning the punch as Eddie had taught her.

"You're just getting weak," Annja chided playfully.

"The hell I am!" Eddie roared.

Annja grinned at him and mopped sweat from her face with a towel hung over a nearby chair. She wore black sweatpants and a sleeveless red shirt that advertised Eddie's Gym across it in bold yellow letters. Boxing shoes and gloves completed her ensemble.

Eddie claimed he was sixty, but Annja knew he was lying away ten years. The ex-boxer was black as coal, skinny as a rake, but still carried the broad shoulders that had framed him as a light heavyweight. Gray stubble covered his jaw and upper lip. His dark eyes were warm and liquid. Boxing had gnarled his ears and left dark scars under his eyes. When he grinned, which was often, he showed a lot of gold caps. He wore gray sweatpants, one of his red shirts and a dark navy hoodie. He kept his head shaved.

"Don't tell me you just dissed me in my own place of business!" Eddie shouted.

"You're the one who said he was having trouble hanging on to the bag," Annja reminded him. He sounded mad, but she knew it was all an act. Eddie was loud and proud, but she liked him and knew that the feeling was reciprocated.

"Girl, you're hittin' harder than I ever seen you hit. What have you been doin'?"

"Archaeology." Annja shrugged.

Eddie waved that away. He looked at her. "You don't look no different."

"I'm not." Annja mopped her arms. "Maybe you're just having an off day."

"I told people I had an off day when I fought Cassius Clay. The truth of the matter was that man hit me so hard I couldn't count to two." Eddie picked up a towel and wiped down, as well. "But something's different about you."

Annja shrugged. "I just feel good, Eddie. That's all."

"Humph," he said, looking at her through narrowed eyes. "Usually when you come back from one of your trips, it takes you a little while to get back to peak conditioning."

"I do my roadwork and keep my legs strong wherever I go," she replied. But she knew what he was talking about. Tonight's workout had seemed almost…easy.

She'd done plenty of jump rope, the speed bag and the heavy bag, a serious weight rotation with more weight and more reps than she'd ever put up before. Something was different. Because even after all of that she felt as if she could do it all again.

EDDIE STOOD by his office with his arms folded and stared at the young black man in headgear beating on a guy who couldn't seem to hold his own against his opponent. Annja had noticed the guy, watching the sadistic way he'd beaten the other fighter.

"Who's the new fighter?" she asked.

Eddie shook his head. "Trouble."

"Does he have another name?" Annja watched as the fighter knocked his opponent down again.

Three men about the fighter's age all clapped and cheered the fighter's latest triumph.

"Name's Keshawn. He says he's a businessman." Eddie didn't sound ready to give the young man an endorsement.

Annja took in the tattoos marking the fighter's arms and legs. "He looks like a banger," she said.

"He is," Eddie agreed. "Knew him when he was little. Had a heart then. It all turned bad now. He keeps doin' what he's doin', he'll be dead or locked away in a couple years."

This time the other guy in the ring couldn't get to his feet. Keshawn's hangers-on cracked up, cheered and threw invective at the man.

Keshawn turned to Eddie and spit out his mouthpiece. "Hey, old man!" he yelled. "You sure you ain't got nobody that'll spar with me? Just a couple rounds? I promise I won't hurt 'em much." Arrogance and challenge radiated in him like an electric current.

The other boxers working the rotations didn't respond.

"Anybody?" Keshawn gazed around the club. "I got a thousand dollars says nobody here can put me outta this ring."

"It time for you to go, boy," Eddie said. "Your ring time is up."

Keshawn beat his chest with his gloves. "I'll fight anybody who wants this ring."

Eddie walked toward the ring. "That ain't my agreement with you, boy. You paid for time, you took your time. Now you haul your ass outta my place."

A cocky grin twisted Keshawn's lips. "You best stop callin' me 'boy,' old man. I might start takin' it personal."

Annja stepped behind Eddie, staying slightly to his right.

"Go on," Eddie growled. "Get outta here."

Releasing his hold on the ring ropes, Keshawn skipped out to the middle of the ring and took up a fighting stance. "You want this ring, old man?" He waved one of his gloves in invitation. "Come take it from me."

Eddie cursed the younger man soundly, not holding back in any way. "You best come on down outta there."

"You best not come up in here after me," Keshawn warned. He was over six feet, at least two hundred pounds and cut by steroids. His hair was blocked and he wore a pencil-thin mustache. He grinned and slammed his gloves together. "You'll get yourself hurt, old man."

Eddie started to climb up into the ring.

Annja caught the old man's arm. "Call the police. You don't need to go in there."

"This is my place, Annja," he told her fiercely. "I don't stand up for what's mine, I might as well pack up and go sit in an old folks' home." He shrugged out of her grip and slid between the ropes.

Keshawn smiled more broadly and started skipping, showing off his footwork. "You think you got somethin' for me, old man?"

Annja caught hold of the ropes and stood at the ring's edge. The confrontation had drawn the attention of the rest of the club's regulars. No one appeared ready to intercede, though. Annja hoped someone had called the police, but she didn't want to leave long enough to go to her locker for her cell phone.

Slowly, hands at his sides, Eddie walked toward the younger man. "I told you to get outta here, boy. I meant what I said."

Keshawn danced away from Eddie. "They say you used to be somethin' to see, old man. Were you really? Were you a good boxer?"

Eddie moved so fast that even Annja, who had been expecting it, almost didn't see it. He fired a jab straight into Keshawn's face, slipping past the headgear and popping the younger man in the nose.

Surprised, Keshawn staggered back. He cursed virulently. Holding a glove to his nose, he snorted bloody mucus onto the canvas. Crimson ran down his face. "You're gonna pay for that, old man."

"I told you to get out," Eddie said. Although his opponent was taller and bigger and at least forty years younger, there was no fear in the old boxer. "You best listen to your elders. Somethin' you shoulda learned at your granny's knee."

Without a word, Keshawn attacked. For a minute, no more, Eddie withstood the flurry of blows, tucking his elbows in and keeping his curled fists up beside his head to protect his face. He even managed a few punches of his own, but Keshawn blocked them or shook them off, in the full grip of rage.

In seconds, Keshawn had the old boxer penned in the corner and was beating and kicking him.

Annja used her teeth to unlace her gloves, then shook them off. Other gym members started to move in, but Keshawn's hangers-on held them back.

Annja rolled under the ropes and onto the canvas before anyone could stop her. Coming up behind Keshawn, she kicked the gang-banger's legs out from under him and pulled him away from Eddie.

"You shouldn't a done that," Eddie whispered, barely able to hang on to the ropes. "Should've stayed outta this, Annja."

Annja didn't say anything. There had been no choice. She turned as she sensed Keshawn moving behind her.

"Don't know who you are, white girl," the big man said, "but this sure ain't any business of yours."

"Somebody's called the cops by now," Annja said, lifting her hands to defend herself. "If you stay here, you're just going to get arrested."

Fear wriggled inside her. She felt it. She breathed in and out, concentrating on that, keeping herself ready. Reading his body language, she knew exactly when he was going to throw the first punch.

21

Keshawn threw a jab with his left hand.

Twisting, Annja dodged the blow, letting it fly past her head to the left. At the same time, she brought her right hand up and slammed the Y between her thumb and her forefinger into the base of her attacker's throat.

As he stumbled back. Annja rolled her hips, drew her right hand back and swiveled. She drove her left foot into Keshawn's face so hard that she forced him back several feet.

Stunned, he landed hard, off balance, and rolled over to his knees. He looked at her in shock and rage, blood dripping down his chin. Leaping to his feet, he launched himself at her.

Annja dodged away, planting both hands in the middle of his back and shoving him into the ropes. He was tangled for a moment, cursing loudly and promising her that she was going to die.

Annja believed he meant it. She saw that Keshawn's friends were still struggling with other gym members.

He stood again, then came at her more slowly, trying to keep his hands up and use his size and reach, getting more canny now that his confidence was eroding. He threw punch after punch. Annja easily dodged them or blocked them, giving ground and drawing him to the middle of the ring. He breathed like a bellows.

Incredibly, even after her workout, Annja still felt fast and strong.

Her breathing was regular, her mind calm. Eddie had been right. She *had* changed. She didn't know where the extra energy was coming from. She guessed anger and adrenaline had kicked in powerfully.

Annja stopped giving ground. Keshawn came at her with another flurry of blows. She stood still, moving her arms just enough to block everything he threw at her. Then—when he was tiring, gasping for breath—she struck back.

The right fist swept forward. Her first two knuckles slid through his defense and between the slits of his headgear. More blood gushed from his nose.

She lifted a knee into his crotch hard enough to raise him from the mat. Before he could fall, she swept her leg out and knocked the unsteady man's feet out from under him. He hit the mat hard.

Sirens wailed just outside the gym.

"You're done," Annja said in a slow, controlled voice. She felt much cooler than she would ever have imagined.

ANNJA WATCHED as EMTs worked on Eddie Watts. Most of his injuries were superficial. He bled from his nose, split lips and a cut over his right eye. His left eye was swollen shut.

Uniformed police officers had taken Keshawn and his friends into custody. Detectives stood questioning witnesses.

"Are you sure you're okay?" Annja asked as she held Eddie's callused hand.

"I'll be fine, girl. When I came outta that fight with Cassius Clay, I looked worse than this." Eddie gave her a lopsided grin. "Don't know what you been doin', Annja, but what you just did?" He shook his head gingerly. "That was something special. Ain't ever seen nobody do that before."

Annja didn't know what to say. She couldn't believe everything that had happened. Over the years, she'd had to fight on occasion. Even in the past few days, she'd had to fight against the Brother-hood of the Silent Rain.

But this time *was* different. She had changed.

HOURS LATER, after the police had finally released her and she'd checked on Eddie in the hospital, finding that the old boxer's daughter was with him, Annja returned home.

She took a shower so hot that it steamed up the bathroom, leaving fog on the glass walls and the mirror. Scrubbed and feeling clean again, she sat on the floor in the center of the loft with the lights out. She pulled herself into a lotus position, back straight, and breathed deeply.

Working slowly, knowing it would take time, Annja gradually relaxed her body. She breathed in and out, slowing her heartbeat, centering herself the way she had been taught.

She stared at the dark wall, then imagined a single dot on it. She focused on the dot until the city ceased to exist around her.

Something had changed about her, and she sought it out. In Eddie's Gym, she'd moved with greater speed and more strength than she'd ever possessed. Where had that come from?

Something had unlocked the speed and strength inside her. It wasn't just adrenaline. She'd been afraid before. She'd felt pumped from fear. But she'd never been that strong or that fast. The source was something else.

The image of the sword appeared in her mind.

Earlier that day, after she'd returned from lunch with Bart McGilley, she'd sat in her loft and tried to reach the sword the way she had in the back of the taxi. Nothing had happened.

Now she saw the sword perfectly. It was whole, resting once more in the case.

Slowly, Annja reached in for the sword, closed her hand around the hilt and drew it out. When she opened her eyes, the sword was in her hand.

It was real.

She stood slowly, afraid that it would disappear at any moment as it had in the taxi the night before.

Taking a two-handed grip, Annja started moving through one of the forms she'd been taught in martial arts. Her interest in swords had started early, before she was even a teenager. She'd learned forms for the blade in several disciplines.

In the quiet of the loft, in the darkness of the night with the moon angled in through the window, Annja danced with the blade. In no time at all, it felt as if she'd always known it, and that it was a part of her.

THE RINGING PHONE WOKE Annja. She blinked her eyes open and glanced at the clock beside the bed. It was 9:17 a.m. Caller ID showed it was Bart, calling from his personal cell phone.

"Hello?" she said, her voice thick.

"Sorry," Bart said. "I guess I woke you."

"Yeah, again." Annja sat up and reached for the sword. It was gone. She'd laid it beside the bed before succumbing to fatigue in the wee hours.

"I heard you had a late night and a little excitement," the policeman said. "I told you before that Eddie's Gym is a rough place."

"I like Eddie. He's a good guy," Annja replied.

"He is a good guy," Bart agreed. "But his place is in a bad neighborhood."

Annja pushed up out of bed and walked over to the window. She raised the blinds and peered out. The city was alive and moving. "I live in a bad neighborhood."

"I know. Anyway, I wasn't calling to gripe at you. I just wanted to know if you were okay."

"I am," she said. "Thanks for caring." *Where does the sword go?* she wondered, distracted.

"I heard Eddie's going to be okay."

"He will be."

"Good. Do you need anything?"

"No."

"So what are your plans?"

"I'm going to stay in all day and work on my segment for the show."

"Fantastic," Bart said. "The way your luck has been running lately, maybe it's in your better interests to keep a low profile for a while."

Annja smiled a little. "I resent that."

"Yeah, well, sue me. Right now, you seem to be quite accident prone."

"No more than normal," she said, laughing.

"Stay in, Annja," Bart said. "Stay safe. If you need anything, call me."

"I will. You, too." Annja broke the connection.

She put the phone away and looked for the sword again. It made no sense. She wondered again if she was losing her mind.

Had the sword really belonged to Joan of Arc? She had no way of knowing. But she wanted to make sure she wasn't hallucinating. She didn't believe in magic. But every culture she'd studied had very deep and abiding beliefs in the supernatural and incredible powers.

Taking a deep breath, she visualized the sword hanging in the air before her. She reached for it. When she closed her hand around the hilt, she felt it. It was real.

Walking over to the bed, she put the sword down and drew her hand back. The sword remained where it was. She sat down in the floor and watched it. Twenty minutes later, it was still there.

Deciding to experiment, she closed her eyes and wished the sword was not there, that it would return to where it came from.

When she opened her eyes, the sword was gone. Panic swelled within her. She couldn't help wondering if she'd wished it away and broken whatever mysterious force bound them.

Stay calm, she advised herself. Breathing easily, shaping the sword in her mind, she reached for it.

She held it in her hand once again.

It was the most frightening yet wonderful thing she had ever seen.

FRUSTRATED, her back aching, Annja straightened up from her desk. Judging from the darkness outside her windows, it was evening—or night.

She'd worked without stopping since that morning, except for phone calls to different museums and libraries to gain access to information that wasn't open to the general public. Instead of working on the La Bête piece, she'd researched Joan of Arc.

Surprisingly, she didn't really find much more than what she'd remembered from childhood. There was little mention of the sword other than it was commonly believed at the time that it held magical powers. And there were stories that it had been shattered. But as far as she could tell, no fragments from the warrior maid's weapon had ever been authenticated.

Giving up for the time being, totally stumped as to what to do next, she went to the bed and picked up the sword. She was ready to experiment some more.

Annja dropped the sword back onto the bed.

Leaving the loft, she made her way up to the rooftop. Lightning ran thick veins across the sky, heated yellow blazing against the indigo of swirling clouds. The wind rushed through her hair and cooled her. She breathed in, wondering if what she proposed would work.

Closing her eyes, she imagined the sword and reached for it. She felt the cool of the metal and the roughness of the leather in her hand. When she opened her eyes again, she held the sword.

Thunder rolled, pealing all around her and echoing between the buildings. A light rain started, cooling the city and washing the air free of dust and pollution for the moment.

Filled with childish glee, still not quite believing what she had proved over and over again, Annja whirled the sword. The blade glinted and caught lightning flashes. In seconds, her clothing was sodden and stuck to her, but she didn't even think of going inside.

The bizarre reality of her situation struck her hard. She was holding Joan of Arc's sword! And somehow it was bound to her!

On top of the building, with the sounds of modern life echoing through the concrete caverns of the city, Annja went through the sword forms again. This time she elaborated, bringing in different styles. Her feet moved mechanically, bringing her body in line with the sword.

No matter how she moved, the sword felt as if it were part of her. When she was finished with the forms, breathing hard and drenched by the rain, she closed her eyes and placed the sword away from her.

She felt the weight of the sword evaporate from her hand. When she opened her eyes, the weapon was gone. Another breath, eyes still open, and she reached out for the sword. In a flash, the sword was in her hand.

Despite her familiarity with the process now, she still felt amazed. If it's not magic, she asked herself, what is it? She had no answer.

Giving in to impulse, Annja held the sword in both hands high over her head. Almost immediately, lightning reached down and touched the tip in a pyrotechnic blaze of sparks. For a moment, the blade glowed cobalt-blue.

Annja dropped the sword, grateful she hadn't been electrocuted.

When she inspected the sword, it was unmarked. If anything, the blade seemed cleaner, stronger. Energy clung to the weapon. She felt it thrumming inside her.

Soaked and awed, Annja stood for a moment in the center of the city and knew that no one saw her. She was invisible in the night. No one knew what she held. She didn't even know herself. She breathed deeply, smelling the salt from the Atlantic, and knew she'd somehow stumbled upon one of the greatest mysteries in history.

"Why me?" she shouted into the storm.

There was no answer, only the rolling thunder and lightning.

OF COURSE THE IDEA CAME to her in the middle of the night. That was when her subconscious mind posed a potential answer to one of the riddles that faced her.

She sat up in bed and found the sword lying on the floor. I've got to protect this sword, she told herself.

Though after the blade had been hit by lightning and hadn't been harmed or allowed her to come to harm, she didn't think much could destroy it.

The sword was destroyed once, she reminded herself. Roux had told her that. She had seen the pieces. But why was it back now?

Slowly, she visualized the pieces in the case at Roux's house. She drew her fingers along the sword's spine, trying to link to whatever force tied her to the weapon.

Part of the sword had been the charm she'd found on the warrior who died bringing down La Bête. Somewhere inside that sword, the mark that had been struck on both sides of that piece of fractured metal still existed.

In her mind's eye, she lifted the image of the wolf and the mountain to the surface of the blade. On the other side of the weapon, she brought up the die mark of the Brotherhood of the Silent Rain.

Thunder cannonaded outside, close enough to make the windows rattle.

Annja focused on the sword. She traced her fingers along the blade. This time she felt the impressions of the images.

Opening her eyes, she looked down. In the darkness she couldn't see the images she felt. Then lightning blazed and lit up her loft for a moment.

There, revealed in the blue-white light, the image of the wolf and the mountain stood out in the smooth grain of the steel. When she turned the blade over, the die mark of the Brotherhood of the Silent Rain was there.

She grabbed one of the digital cameras she used for close-up work. She took several shots of the images.

When she was satisfied that she had all that she needed, she stared at the imperfections on the blade. She ran her fingers over them again, feeling how deeply they bit into the metal.

The sight of them, the feel of them, was almost unbearable.

She willed the sword away, back into wherever it went when it was not with her. It faded from her hands like early-morning fog cut by direct sunlight.

Taking a deep breath, she reached into that otherwhere and drew the sword back. Light gleamed along the blade. The marks had disappeared.

A quick check of the images on the digital camera revealed that the shots she'd taken still existed. She put the sword on the bed and turned her full attention to the camera images.

Was the sword weak while it was shattered? Annja wondered. *Or had it allowed itself to be marked? And if it had allowed itself to be marked, why?*

She set to work.

22

Using the software on her computer, Annja blew up the images of the wolf and the mountain. After they were magnified, she saw there were other images, as well. The detail of the work was amazing.

The shadowy figure behind the bars was better revealed. Although manlike in appearance, the figure was a grotesquerie, ill shaped and huge, judging from the figure of the man standing behind him.

With her naked eye, Annja had barely been able to make out the second figure. Once the image was blown up, she couldn't miss him. He wore the armor of a French knight. A shield bearing his heraldry stood next to him.

Annja blew up the image more, concentrating on the shield.

The shield was divided in the English tradition rather than the French. That surprised Annja. The common armchair historian assumed that all heraldry was the same, based on the divisions of the shield that English heraldry was noted for. But the French, Italians, Swedish and Spanish—as well as a few others—marked their heraldry differently.

This one was marked *party per bend sinister*—diagonally from upper right to lower left. The upper half showed the image of a wolf with its tongue sticking out. The animal didn't have much detail, but Annja got a definite sense of malevolence from the creature. The lower half of the shield was done in ermines, a variation of the field that represented fur. Ermines were traditionally black on white.

The design was unique. If it hadn't disappeared in history, there would likely be some documentation on it.

Annja cut the shield out of the image with the software, cleaned up the lines as much as she could and saved it.

Logging onto alt.archaeology, she sent a brief request for identification to the members. She also sent an e-mail to a professor she knew at Cambridge who specialized in British heraldry. She also followed up with a posting to alt.archaeology.esoterica.

What was a British knight doing at a French monastery of an order of monks that had been destroyed?

Annja returned to the image.

The shadowy, misshapen figure had another drawing under it. Annja almost missed the discovery. The image had been cut into the metal but it was almost as if it had been scored there only to have the craftsman change his mind later.

Or maybe he was told not to include it, Annja thought.

She magnified the image and worked on it, bringing it into sharper relief with a drawing tool. In seconds, she knew what she was looking at. A lozenge.

Annja sat back in her chair and stared at the image, blown away by the possibilities facing her. The shadowy figure wasn't a man. It was a woman.

The lozenge was heraldry to represent female members of a noble family. Designed in an offset diamond shape that was taller than it was wide, a lozenge identified the woman by the family, as well as personal achievements.

This particular lozenge only had two images on it. A wolf salient, in midleap, occupied the top of the diamond shape. At the bottom was a stag dexter, shown simply standing. A crescent moon hung in the background with a star above and a star below.

Annja repeated her efforts with the postings, sending off the new image, as well.

Back aching from the constant effort, Annja decided to take a break. She quickly dressed and went out into the rainy night, surprised to find that dawn was already apparent the eastern sky.

ANNJA HEADED for the small Italian grocery store several blocks from her loft. The Puerto Rican bodega she favored was closer, but it wasn't open at such an early hour. She didn't mind as she wanted to stretch her legs.

She loved being in the middle of the city as it woke around her. Voices cracked sharply. Cars passed by in the street, horns already honking impatiently.

Stopping by the newsstand, she picked up a handful of magazines—*Time, Newsweek, Scientific American, People, Entertainment, Ellery Queen Mystery Magazine,* and *Magazine of Fantasy* and *Science Fiction.*

She liked to keep up with current events. The entertainment and fiction magazines were guilty pleasures. If she hadn't been able to occasionally borrow from fictional lives in the orphanage, she sometimes wondered if she'd have made it out with the curiosity about the world and the past that she now had.

At the grocery store, she passed a pleasant few minutes with the owner, who loved to talk about her children, and bought a small melon, eggs, fresh basil, a small block of Parmesan cheese and garlic bread. She also picked up a gallon of orange juice.

Back at the loft, Annja let herself in through all five locks. She was startled but not entirely surprised to find Garin seated at her desk. Her eyes immediately strayed to the bed, but the sword was nowhere to be seen.

"You're looking for the sword?" Garin seemed amused. He wore a black turtleneck, jeans and heavy black boots. A leather jacket hung on the back of the chair.

"How did you get in?" Annja demanded. She stood in the open door, ready to flee immediately.

"I let myself in," he said. "I did knock first."

Suspicion formed in Annja's mind. She had the definite sense that he'd waited for her to leave, then broke in.

"You weren't here," Garin said.

"Odd that I happened to miss you," Annja said.

Garin smiled. "Serendipity. You can never properly factor that into anything."

"You could have waited for me to get back," Annja pointed out.

"And stood out in the hallway so that your neighbors would gossip about you?" Garin shook his head. "I couldn't do that."

Deciding that she didn't have anything to fear from the man—at least for the moment—Annja walked into the kitchen area and placed the groceries on the counter.

"Breakfast?" Garin asked.

"Yes." Annja took a big skillet from the wall.

"We could order in. I noticed there are some places nearby that deliver," Garin said.

"I've eaten restaurant food for days," Annja replied. "Here and in France. I want to cook." She put the skillet on the burner to warm, then cracked eggs into a bowl.

Glancing over her shoulder, Annja saw that he looked amused. She resented his presence in her home, the fact that he had broken in, and she was distrustful of him. Still, she couldn't just pretend he wasn't there when she was about to eat.

"Have you eaten?" she asked.

"No. I just got in from LaGuardia." Garin sat at the desk. "But that's all right. You go ahead."

"Nonsense. There's enough for both of us. More than enough."

"That's very kind of you. Can I help?"

Annja chopped the basil and Garin grated the Parmesan. She mixed both with the eggs, then poured olive oil into the skillet. "Have you really lived over five hundred years?" she asked, suddenly aware of feeling comfortably domestic with this mysterious stranger.

Garin smiled. "You find that hard to believe?"

Annja didn't answer. She sliced the garlic bread and the melon.

"You know what happened to the sword, don't you?" Garin asked. "You've got it."

Annja poured the eggs into the skillet, then popped the bread into the toaster.

"Where is the sword?" Garin asked.

"It disappeared," Annja replied. "Somewhere outside Paris."

Grinning, he said, "I don't believe you."

"We share a trait for skepticism." Annja scrambled the eggs. "Would you care for some orange juice?"

Garin walked around the loft, gazing at all the things Annja had collected during her years as an archaeologist. "You have a nice home," he said softly.

Annja had deliberately left the bread knife close at hand. So far, Garin didn't appear to be armed. "Thank you," she said, watching him closely.

"I know you're lying about the sword," Garin said, looking at her.

The bread slices popped out of the toaster. She laid them on plates, buttered them. "That's not a polite thing to say to someone about to serve you breakfast."

"The sword was on the bed when I arrived," Garin told her.

For a moment, Annja felt panic race through her. She concentrated on the eggs, removing the skillet from the heat. *If he'd taken the sword, he wouldn't be here now.*

"It disappeared when I tried to touch it," Garin said.

"Maybe it was just a figment of your imagination," Annja said, flooded with relief.

Garin shook his head. "No. I've seen that sword before. And I've lived with its curse."

"What curse?" Annja asked.

Approaching her but staying out of arm's reach, Garin leaned a hip against the kitchen counter. "A story for a story," he told her. "It's the only fair way to do this."

Annja dished the scrambled eggs onto the garlic toast. She added slices of melon.

"Very pretty," Garin said.

"I prefer to think of it as nourishing." Annja handed him his plate.

Garin looked around. "I don't see a dining table."

"That's because I don't have one." Scooping up her own plate and orange juice, Annja walked to the window seat. She thought about the Mercedes Garin had driven in Lozère. "Probably isn't exactly the lifestyle you're used to," she said, feeling a little self-conscious.

"Not the lifestyle I now have," he agreed. "But this is a lot better than I started out with."

Annja folded herself onto one end of the window seat. "Where did you grow up?"

"One of the city-states in Germany. A backwoods place. Its name

is long forgotten now." Garin sat and ate his food. "I was the illegitimate son of a famous knight."

"How famous?"

Garin shook his head. "He's been forgotten now. But back then,
he was a name. Famous in battle and in tournaments. I was the only
mistake he'd ever made."

For a moment, Annja felt sorry for Garin. Parents and relatives
who simply hadn't wanted to deal with kids had dumped them at the
orphanage. It was an old story. Evidently it hadn't changed in
hundreds of years.

If Garin could be believed.

"I like to think that my father cared for me in some way," Garin
went on. "After all, he didn't give me to a peasant family as he could
have. Or let my mother kill me, as she'd tried on a couple of occasions."

Annja kept eating. There were horrible stories throughout all
histories. She wasn't inured to them, but she had learned to accept
that there were some things she couldn't do anything about.

"Instead," Garin went on, "my father gave me to a wizard."

"Roux?" That news startled Annja.

"Yes. At least that's what men like him were called in the old days.
Once upon a time, Roux's name was enough to strike terror in the
hearts of men. When he cursed someone, that person's life was
never the same again."

"But that could simply be the perception of the person cursed,"
Annja said. "Zombies created by voodoo have been found to be
living beings who are so steeped in their belief that their conscious
minds can't accept that after their burial and 'resurrection' they are
not zombies. They truly believe they are."

"What makes the sword disappear?" Garin asked, smiling.

"We weren't finished talking about you." Annja took another bite
of toast, then the melon, which was sweet and crisp.

"I was nine years old when I was given to Roux," Garin went on.
"I was twenty-one when he allied himself with the Maid."

"He allied himself with Joan of Arc?"

Garin nodded. "He felt he had to. So we traveled with her and
were part of her retinue."

"Fancy word," Annja teased, surprising herself.

"My vocabulary is vast. I also speak several languages."

"Joan of Arc," Annja reminded.

"Roux and I served with her. He was one of her counsels. When she was captured by the English, Roux stayed nearby."

"Why didn't he rescue her?"

"Because he believed God would."

"But that didn't happen?"

Garin shook his head. "We were…gone when the English decided to burn her at the stake. We arrived too late. Roux tried to stop them, but there were too many English. She died."

Annja turned pale. It was all too fantastic to be believed, yet she didn't feel any sense of danger—just curiosity. Who is this man? she wondered. What is going on?

"Are you all right?" Concern showed on Garin's handsome face.

"I am. Just tired."

He didn't appear convinced.

"What about the sword?" Annja asked.

Garin balanced his empty plate on his knee. "It was shattered. I watched them do it."

"The English?"

He nodded. "Afterward, Roux and I realized we were cursed."

Annja couldn't help herself. She smiled. Anyone could have read about the legendary sword. The details were open to interpretation or exaggeration, as all historical accounts were. Where will this elaborate hoax lead? she wondered.

Then she remembered how Bart McGilley had told her that the fingerprints—*friction ridges*—she'd pulled from the euro Roux had given her belonged to a suspect in a sixty-three-year-old homicide. She thought about the sword.

"Who cursed you?" she asked.

Garin hesitated, as if he were about to tell her an impossible thing. "I don't know what Roux thinks, but I believe we were cursed by God."

23

After Garin finished his story, Annja sat quietly and looked at him. The fear that he had felt all those years ago—and, in spite of herself, she did believe him about the five hundred years—still showed in his dark features.

"You helped Roux look for the sword?" Annja asked.

Garin shook his head. "No."

"Why?"

"I was angry after Joan's death and I had no idea there would be consequences if the pieces of the sword weren't found."

Annja had to admit the man had a point. "So when did you start to believe?"

"About twenty years later."

"When you didn't age?"

"No," Garin answered. "I aged. A little. It was when I saw Roux again and saw that he hadn't aged. I began to believe then. I'd thought he would be dead."

"So he has looked for pieces of the sword for over five hundred years?"

Garin nodded. "He has."

"And you didn't help?"

"No. I tried to stop him. I tried to tell him that as it stood, we could live forever. I was becoming wealthy beyond my grandest dreams."

"That was when you started trying to kill him."

Grinning, Garin asked, "Wouldn't you? If you were promised immortality by simply not doing a thing, wouldn't you take steps to make sure that thing didn't happen?"

Annja didn't know. She regarded Garin with renewed suspicion. "Why are you here now?"

"I'm still interested in what happens to the sword." Garin shrugged. "Now that it is whole again, does that mean I no longer have untold years ahead of me?"

"Noticed any gray hairs?" Annja asked.

He smiled at her. "Your humor is an acquired taste. When you were in Roux's face, I found you delightful. Now I feel that you have no tact."

"Good. But keep in mind that I fed breakfast to a man who broke into my home." Trying not to show her anxiety, Annja took her plate and Garin's to the sink.

"Tell me about the sword," Garin said.

Turning, Annja leaned a hip against the counter and crossed her arms over her breasts. "What do you want to know?"

"Mostly whether it can be broken again."

Annja shook her head. "Honesty's not always the best policy."

"I've *never* thought it was."

She grinned at that.

"If I had lied," he asked, "would you have known?"

"About this? Yes."

"I already know about the sword," Garin pointed out. "I could have left before you returned."

"After you happened to arrive while I was out."

"Of course."

Annja respected that. He could have done that. She reached out her right hand, reached out into that otherwhere and summoned the sword. She held it in her hand.

Garin's eyes widened as he got to his feet and came toward her. "Let me see it."

"No." Annja leveled the sword, aiming the point at his Adam's apple, intending to halt him in his tracks.

In a move that caught her totally by surprise, Garin tried to grab the blade in his left hand and slam his right forearm down to break it. Instead, his hand and arm swept through the sword as if it weren't there.

Annja reacted at once, throwing out a foot that caught Garin in the side and knocked him away. He scrambled to his feet and fisted the bread knife on the counter.

As Garin brought the bread knife around, Annja took a two-handed grip on the sword and slashed at the smaller blade wondering if it would pass harmlessly through. The bread knife snapped in two, leaving Garin with the hilt in his hand.

Annja planted the sword tip against his chest right over his heart. The material and flesh indented. Maybe Garin couldn't touch the sword, they both realized, but the sword could touch him.

"Are we done here?" Annja asked.

Garin swept his left arm against the blade to knock it away, but again his arm passed through. His effort left him facing Annja, his chest totally exposed to her retaliation.

Annja pressed the sword against his chest. "I've fed you breakfast," she said evenly. "I've overlooked the fact that you broke into my house. I'm even willing to forgive you for trying to break my sword."

"Your sword?"

"Mine," Annja responded without pause or doubt. The sword was hers. It had chosen her. That much was clear. "But if you ever make an enemy of me, if you ever try to kill me like you did Roux, I'll hunt you down and kill you."

"If I try," Garin promised, unwilling to back up another inch, "you'll never see me coming."

"Then it would be in my best interests to kill you now, wouldn't it?"

Garin stood stubbornly against the sword.

Annja pressed harder, watching the pain flicker through his features and hate darken his eyes. He stumbled back, then turned and walked away. She let him retreat without pursuit.

Garin wiped at the blood seeping through his shirt. "How much?" he demanded.

"For what?" Almost casually, as if she'd been doing it forever, Annja balanced the sword over her right shoulder.

"To break the sword."

Annja shook her head. "I'm not going to break this sword."

In truth, she didn't know what would happen if she tried. An image of the lightning bolt passing through it filled her mind.

She had a definite feeling that whatever happened if she tried to destroy the sword wouldn't be good. Also, she felt that she would be betraying the spirit of the sword. Joan of Arc had led people in a war against oppression with it.

"I could give you millions," Garin said. He waved to encompass the loft. "You wouldn't have to live like this."

"I happen to like the way I live." Annja watched the dark calculations take place in his eyes.

"You love knowledge," he said finally. "With the money I could give you, *would* give you, you could go anywhere in the world. Study anything you like. With the best experts money can buy. You could open up any door to the past you wanted to."

The idea was tempting. She believed Garin could provide that kind of money. She even believed he would.

"No," she said. As if to take the temptation out of his hands, she willed the sword away.

He came at her without warning, rushing at her low and grabbing her hips as he shoved her back against the stove. He fumbled for one of the knives in the wooden block by the sink. Grabbing a thick-bladed butcher's knife, he raised it to strike.

Freeing her right arm from Garin's grasp, Annja drove the heel of her palm into his nose. Blood spurted as the cartilage collapsed.

He yowled in pain and tried to hang on to her. His knife hand came down.

Annja twisted and avoided the knife. The blade thudded deep into the countertop. She reared up against him, forcing him back.

Shifting, she butted him aside with her hip, heel stamped his foot, head butted him under the chin, and brought an elbow strike into line with his jaw.

Garin stepped back, his black eyes glassy. He punched at her but she slapped his arm aside. Then he caught her with an incredibly fast left hand.

Annja dropped as if she'd been hit with a bag of wet cement. Her senses spun and for a moment she thought she was going to pass out.

Garin came after her immediately. On the ground, she knew from experience, his greater size and weight would take away every advantage her speed and strength gave her.

She rolled backward and flipped to her feet in the center of the loft. Annja only had to think of the sword for a split second and it was in her hand. Stepping back, right leg behind her left, hilt gripped firmly in both hands, she readied the sword.

Garin halted, completely out of running room.

All Annja had to do was swing. But he'd stopped his aggressions. *Will it be murder?* she wondered.

"Are you going to kill him, then?" a raspy voice suddenly asked.

Circling slowly, Annja maintained her grip on the sword. She turned just enough to see Roux standing in the doorway.

"Don't either of you respect a person's privacy?" Annja asked.

"I knocked. No one answered. Then I heard the sounds of a scuffle." Roux entered unbidden. "I thought it best if I investigated." He closed the door behind him.

Okay, Annja thought, at least I know he's not a vampire.

Roux took off his long jacket. He wore a casual tan suit. "Are you going to kill him?" he asked again as if the question was a typical greeting.

Garin watched her carefully. He kept his hands spread to the side, ready to move.

Annja continued to slowly circle, never crossing her feet, so she wouldn't trip. She stopped when Roux was behind Garin.

"I don't know yet," Annja admitted.

"My vote is no," Garin said.

"You tried to kill me," Annja said, "right after I told you that I would kill you if you tried."

"I really didn't think you meant it," he said.

"You would have killed me."

Garin was silent for a moment, then nodded. "Probably."

"Miss Creed," Roux said.

"Do you want to kill him?" Annja asked. Maybe that would be better. Although it would still be in her loft. She wondered if she could talk the old man into killing Garin somewhere else.

"No," Roux answered.

"Why not? He's tried to kill you, too."

"I've been like a father to him. It doesn't seem fitting."

"He's tried to *kill* you," Annja said in exasperation.

"Ours has been a…difficult relationship at best," Roux said. "That's the way it is between fathers and sons."

"I'm not your son," Garin snarled.

"You were as close as I ever had," Roux said. He looked around. "May I sit, Miss Creed?"

"Could I stop you?"

"Not if you intend to continue menacing Garin with the sword." Roux sat in the window seat. "Is that melon?"

"Yes."

"May I help myself?"

"Sure," Annja replied, not believing he'd actually asked. "I'm trying to keep the homicidal maniac from killing us."

"I'm not a homicidal maniac," Garin objected. "If you'd just let me destroy that sword—"

"Apparently you can't," Annja taunted. At the moment, after he'd tried to kill her twice, she didn't mind acting a little superior.

"—we could all walk out of here happier," Garin finished.

"I wouldn't be happier," Roux said. He looked for a plate, found one in the cabinet and put melon pieces on it. He returned to the window seat. "I spent five hundred years and more looking for the pieces of that sword. I don't care to repeat that experience any time soon."

"We're immortal, Roux," Garin growled.

"Not immortal," Roux replied. "If she'd cut your head off the day she met you, you'd have died."

"You know what I mean."

"I do." Roux ate the melon with obvious gusto. "This is quite good."

"Why are you here?" Annja asked.

"I thought maybe you might have come looking for me before now," Roux said. "I thought surely you would be curious about the sword. Since you didn't, I thought perhaps it was best if I came looking for you."

"Why?"

"Because of the sword, of course. I knew it couldn't have just disappeared. After you got away and the sword never showed up again, I knew it had gone with you."

"How?"

"As I said, it didn't turn up again at my house." Roux frowned. "Which, I might add, may never be the same again. Why did the Brotherhood of the Silent Rain attack my house?"

"They were after the charm I found in La Bête's lair," Annja said. "How did the sword come with me?"

"Magic. Arcane forces. Some psychic ability on a higher plane," Roux said. "Take your pick."

"Which do you choose?"

"I know why the sword came with you," the old man said.

"Why?" Annja asked.

"Destiny."

Annja was speechless.

"You were destined to hold that sword, Annja Creed," Roux said. "Otherwise you wouldn't have found the last missing piece or me. And, judging from the years I've spent searching for that final piece, no one else could have found it. If you'd found the piece but not me, you wouldn't have found the rest of the sword. Therefore it's destiny."

It was a lot to take in at one time. Annja had trouble dealing with the whole concept. But here she stood, with the sword pressed to the throat of the one man who wanted desperately to destroy it.

She tried to remember when she'd last felt that anything made sense.

She looked at Garin. "Sit over there by the desk."

"Sure." As though he'd just been invited to tea, Garin walked over to the desk and sat.

"We're all three bound by Joan's sword," Roux said. He held up a hand. "May I?"

"I don't think that's such a good idea," Annja said.

"From what I gather, Garin can't touch the sword."

"No."

"It would be interesting to find out if I can."

Annja hesitated.

Roux waved his hand impatiently. "If I didn't want to ask you, I'd simply shoot you and take it off your body."

"You don't have a pistol," Annja said.

Lifting his jacket, Roux revealed the small semiautomatic

leathered beneath his left arm. He dropped the jacket to hide the pistol again. "Please."

Reversing the sword with a flourish, Annja laid the blade over her arm and extended the hilt to him.

Roux took the sword easily. He examined it carefully. "This is truly exquisite. You can't see where any of the breaks were."

Tense, Annja waited. She didn't like the idea of anyone else holding the sword.

"Here you go, Miss Creed." Roux passed the sword back. "Do you want to tell me how you did that vanishing trick back at my house?"

Gripping the sword, Annja willed it away. The weapon faded from sight.

Roux grinned in wonder. "Splendid!"

Garin cursed. "You're a fool, old man. Now that the sword is whole again, we're no longer cursed to walk the earth after it. We're no longer immortal."

"Long-lived," Roux argued. "Not immortal. Long-lived. And that remains to be seen, doesn't it?" He looked at the kitchen area. "Do you have anything to drink?"

"Orange juice," Annja said. "Or tea."

"Juice, if you please."

Annja got a glass and filled it with orange juice. She took it to Roux. "What's your interest in this?"

"In the sword?"

She nodded.

"I don't know that I have one," Roux replied. "The sword is complete. I'm not sure what happens now. "

"I know about the curse."

"I suppose you do." Roux sipped his drink. "At any rate, it may well be that my part in this whole affair is over. I truly hope that it is. I have other pursuits I'd like to follow. I'm going to be playing in a Texas Hold 'em Tournament soon and I've qualified for a senior's tour in golf."

"Did you know you're listed as a suspect in Doris Cooper's murder?" Annja asked.

"No. Though it doesn't surprise me."

"Did you do it?"

"No."

"Did Garin?"

"I don't even know anyone named Doris Cooper," Garin protested.

"I don't know," Roux said. "Doris was a good person. Too trusting, perhaps, but a good person."

"Why didn't you try to clear your name?" Annja asked.

"Hollywood was a rat's nest in those days," Roux said. "If the Los Angeles Police Department was determined to pin the woman's murder on me—and I tell you right now that they were—they would have done it. I left the country as soon as I knew they were looking for me." He paused. "Do you want to talk about things that have no bearing on where you're going or what you're going to do? Or do you want to discuss the sword?"

Before Annja could answer, the phone rang. She considered letting the answering service pick up, but she decided she wanted a few minutes of diversion. Things were coming at her too quickly.

"Hello?"

"Miss Creed?" The voice was urbane, accented, and almost familiar.

"Yes," Annja said. "Who is this?"

"Corvin Lesauvage. We met briefly in Lozère."

"I remember you, Mr. Lesauvage," Annja replied. Her thoughts spun. Glancing at Roux and Garin, she saw that both of the men were listening with interest. "You were trying to have me abducted, as I recall."

"Yes, well, I've had to reconsider that. I still want that charm you found and I've had to find new leverage to achieve that goal."

"I don't have the charm," Annja said. "I told you that."

"Then you'll have to get it, Miss Creed," Lesauvage said. "Because if you don't, Avery Moreau will die and his death will be on your head."

24

For just a moment, the loft seemed to spin around Annja. She stood with effort, remembering the young man who had been her guide in Lozère.

"What are you talking about?" she asked.

"If I don't get that charm, Miss Creed," Corvin Lesauvage said, "I'm going to kill Avery Moreau. Do you have Internet access?" His voice oozed self-satisfaction.

"Yes."

"Log on, please, and go to this Internet address—LesauvageAntiquities.com."

Waving Garin away from the desk, Annja opened the Web page. It was attractive, neat and precise, with everything in place. The casual peruser knew immediately that Lesauvage Antiquities did business in appraisal and research, as well as purchases and sales of antiques. It was a nice cover for a man who was a drug runner, thief and murderer.

"The Web link I'm about to give you is masked," Lesauvage said. "You'll have to be quick."

Annja didn't say anything. Roux had gotten up and stood behind her, whether out of interest or to help protect her from any attempt Garin made, Annja didn't know.

"Click on appraisals, then hit the F12 key immediately," Lesauvage ordered.

Annja did.

The Web page cycled, then stopped. A window popped up and asked for an ID and password.

"Okay," Annja said.

"Good. The ID is 'Avery.' The password is 'Mort,'" Lesauvage said.

Mort was French for "death." Reluctantly, Annja entered the keystrokes.

Another window opened. This one filled with a video download that took forty-three seconds. When it finished, it opened and played.

There was no audio, but the video feed was clear enough. Avery Moreau, tied up and dressed in some garish costume, lay on a flat rock in a cave. Blood covered his face. There was too much blood for it to be his without some obvious sign of injury.

Wearing a similar costume but with a mounted-deer-head helmet, Lesauvage entered the camera's view. He raised a knife, then drove the blade down into Avery's left hand, all the way through to the rock beneath.

Avery jerked in pain and screamed. Even without the audio, Annja could hear his agony and fear.

Garin swore.

Thankfully, the video ended.

Annja was breathing deeply. "What do you want, Lesauvage?"

"As I told you, I only want the charm. Bring it to me and I will let Avery Moreau live. If you do not, I will kill him. Make your travel arrangements. Once you know when you will return to Lozère, let me know. I can be reached at this number at any time." He gave her the number and the phone clicked dead.

Annja cradled the handset.

"A threat?" Roux asked.

"Lesauvage is going to kill Avery Moreau if I don't bring the charm back."

"Well, that's a shame," the old man said, "but you can't be expected to save everyone."

"I'm not going to let him die," Annja said and immediately started looking on the computer for flight possibilities.

Roux stared at her. "You can't be serious. That man is a villain of the basest sort."

"I know the type," Annja said.

Garin grinned at her. "So you're going to rush off and play the savior."

"I'm not going to let Avery Moreau die." Annja backed up all her files on the charm, the heraldry and the Brotherhood of the Silent Rain onto an external hard drive.

"Lesauvage will kill you," Roux protested. "The sword will be lost again."

"One can only hope," Garin said.

"I'm not planning on dying," Annja said. She looked for her suitcase, then realized it was still at the Lamberts' bed-and-breakfast outside Lozère.

All right, then, I'm already packed. All I have to do is live long enough to collect my luggage.

"Don't be foolish," Roux said. "You don't even have the charm."

"I took pictures of it," Annja said. She brought them up on the computer.

"How did you do that? You didn't have time to photograph it like this in Lozère."

"I summoned it up on the sword," Annja explained as she stuffed gear into her backpack.

"It's still part of the sword?"

"I don't know. Maybe." Annja lifted the phone.

"Call the police in Lozère," Roux urged. "Let them know what is going on."

"Do you remember Police Inspector Richelieu?" Annja asked.

"Yes."

"He shot Avery Moreau's father."

"Whatever for?"

"Gerard Moreau was a thief. He broke into the house where Richelieu happened to be entertaining the wife."

"It wasn't the inspector's wife, was it?" Roux said.

"No." Annja dialed information and asked for the number to Air France.

"Excuse me," Garin said.

Annja looked at him.

"I've got a private plane. Actually, a Learjet, at LaGuardia."

"You'd let me use your jet?" Annja asked, surprised.

"If it's going to allow Lesauvage to kill you more quickly, certainly." Garin appeared quite earnest.

"You're going with us." Annja hung up the phone.

"Us?" Roux repeated.

"We're not finished talking about the sword, are we?" Annja asked the old man.

"Perhaps," Roux said.

"Fine," she told him. "Then you can stay here. If Garin and his pilot jump out of the plane somewhere over the Atlantic and I go down, you can hope you don't have to wait another five hundred years for the sword to wash up on some beach."

Roux grimaced. "If I was certain my part in all of this was finished, I wouldn't entertain this at all."

"Why am I going?" Garin asked.

"Because I don't trust you not to have someone fire a heat-seeking missile at us while we're en route. If you're along for the trip, I figure that's less likely to happen." Annja didn't know if Garin could actually get his hands on something like that, but she wouldn't put it past him.

"That's *your* reason to get me to go," Garin said. "*I* don't have a reason."

"If you go," Annja said, "maybe you'll get to see Lesauvage kill me."

Garin thought about that briefly. "Good point."

GARIN'S PRIVATE JET WAS outfitted like a bachelor pad with wings. It was divided into three sections. The cockpit was the most mundane thing about the aircraft. The living quarters and the bedroom shared equal space and came with a personal flight attendant.

Annja sat in one of the plush seats. Equipped with a wet bar and the latest in technological marvels, including a sixty-inch plasma television and a Bose surround sound system, in-flight entertainment was no problem. There was also a satellite link for phones and computers.

The bedroom, which Annja had not seen and had no intention of seeing, contained a king-size bed.

Garin and Roux had settled into their seats and started watching a televised poker championship.

Hooked up to the Internet, Annja continued her research into the

Brotherhood of the Silent Rain and the charm. Those were at the heart of the mystery before her.

There were new postings at alt.archaeology and alt.archaeology.esoterica.

Two were from Zoodio.

Hey! I traced that shield heraldry you posted. Interesting stuff.

From what I found out, the shield belonged to a British knight named Richard of Kirkland. He was thought to be a great-grandson of one of the English soldiers that burned Joan of Arc at the stake in France.

A chill passed through Annja. She hadn't expected the hit to be tied so closely to Joan.

Supposedly, the great-grandfather's luck turned sour after he got back from France. Devotees of Joan swear he was cursed.

Anyway, that curse seems to have passed down to his great-grandson, who somehow got himself titled along the way. He had a daughter in 1749 who was supposed to have horrible birth defects.

If you're not careful when you do your research, you'll find entries that list her as dead. She even has a gravesite in a private cemetery outside London. Her name was Carolyn. In 1764, Sir Richard of Kirkland took his daughter to the Brotherhood of The Silent Rain.

Why not an abbey? Annja wondered again.

Some reports say Carolyn died in 1767 when the monastery was destroyed. Hope this helps.

It did and it didn't, Annja ultimately decided. She skimmed through the list of sources he'd included. Many of them were on personal Web sites so she was able to check them out.

She saved the Web links to Favorites, then read the next posting by researchferret@secondlook.org.

Zoodio has it wrong. Sir Richard's daughter wasn't his daughter after all. She was his *wife's* illegitimate child.

While Sir Richard was off fighting in one of the wars, his wife was having an affair with one of the inbred members of the royal family. Which was why there were so many birth defects in the child.

The wife also tried to abort the child, and even the church got involved because of all the political unrest the baby would cause.

Despite everything everyone did, the baby went to term. When Sir Richard got home, knowing that he wasn't the father—can you imagine how pissed this guy was, out risking his life, and his wife's shacking up?—he probably had to be restrained from killing the baby and his wife.

The church, trying to cover its own ass, told Richard that a demon had fathered the child. They arranged for the baby girl, when she got to be fourteen, to go to the Silent Rain monastery. Can you say cop-out?

"Annja?"

Startled, she looked up and saw Roux standing there. "What?"

"Would you like something to eat?"

"Whatever you want to nuke in the microwave will be fine."

"No nuking," Roux responded. "There's a full galley."

"Do you think it's safe?" she asked. "I mean, he could poison the food."

Roux smiled gently at her. "I'll make sure that doesn't happen."

"All right."

"What would you like?"

"Surprise me."

Roux nodded. He started to turn away.

"Hey," Annja said.

The old man turned back around to her. "What?"

"You've really lived over five hundred years?"

He smiled and shook his head. "My dear girl, I've lived far longer than you can even imagine."

Whatever, Annja thought, thinking the comment was sheer brag-gadocio. "Did you know a knight named Sir Richard of Kirkland?"

"An English knight?"

Annja nodded.

"I knew of such a man, but I never knew him personally. He was—"

"English. I know. I got it. English was bad back then."

"Yes." Roux's blue eyes twinkled. "He was a tournament champion all over Europe. And he fought in a few skirmishes. There was something about a child that besmirched his reputation. A child born out of wedlock, I believe."

"A child the church contended was spawn of the devil," Annja said. "And she was locked up in the Silent Rain monastery."

"Truly?" Roux seemed amazed.

"Yes."

"Why wasn't she taken to an abbey? Several of the female children born in brothels were taken there."

"I don't know."

"If you find out—"

Annja nodded. She returned to her reading.

"I'll go and attend to our lunch," Roux said. "Then, at some point, you and I need to discuss what's going to happen with the sword."

Three spam entries followed the one by Researchferret. Then Zoodio had posted again.

I missed that one. Good catch.

Interesting. I looked at the data you sent to support what you posted, Researchferret. And I found something you missed.

According to the journals of Sister Mary Elizabeth of a local London abbey, the sisters took in a fourteen-year-old girl early in 1764.

Sir Richard's name isn't mentioned. Neither is the girl's. But it does say she's the illegitimate child of a tournament hero and thought to be the daughter of the devil.

Sounds familiar, huh?

Annja silently agreed.

Also truly weird are the murders that occurred in the abbey in 1764.

That instantly caught Annja's attention.

Early in 1764, January and February, two nuns, then a third, were beaten to death in the basement of the main building. The rumor was that an insane man had broken into the building and killed the nuns while looking for church silver or donations to pilfer.

However, Sister Mary Elizabeth notes that the strange girl the abbey had taken in murdered the nuns. According to her entries during those days and the days that followed, the girl had been restrained in the basement, had gotten loose, and had beaten the nuns to death *with her bare hands*.

Yikes!

This story gets creepier and stranger the more I look into it. More later.

Of course, that entry started a flurry of postings that included Jack the Ripper theories and led to the Loch Ness Monster before taking a detour through the twilight zone.

25

Roux brought Annja a plate while she was still sorting through the entries.

Reluctantly, Annja pushed the computer off to the side and flipped out the tray built into the seat. She surveyed the plate for the first time while she was spreading a linen napkin across her lap.

A small steak shared space with a baked potato and a salad. The steak was grilled.

"No poison, I assure you." Roux sat in the seat next to her and set up his own plate. He tucked a napkin into his shirt collar. "I trust you like steak?"

"Yes." Annja cut the meat and found it sliced easily.

"From the last time we shared a meal, I knew you had a robust appetite. Judging from the way most young people your age eat, missing meals when you get busy and such, I thought a solid meal was called for."

"This steak is grilled," Annja said in amazement. She'd never had a steak actually grilled in midflight.

"Garin has always been one for whatever is new and flashy," Roux admitted. "I found his galley is equipped with all manner of culinary accoutrements."

"And it has a grill, too." Annja poked fun at the old man's verbosity.

Roux got the joke and smiled. "Although not my native language, I find that English does have its charm. So does French."

That surprised Annja. "French isn't your native language?"

"No. Why? Do I sound like a native when I speak it?"

"Yes."

Knife and fork in hand, Roux attacked his steak. "What have you discovered about the charm?"

Briefly, Annja brought him up-to-date.

"What are you going to do?" Roux asked when she was finished.

"Find out the truth about what happened all those years ago," Annja said. "Discover who the prisoner was in the monastery and what happened to her. Why the monastery was destroyed. Why the monastery still exists even though it's been destroyed. Why the monks of that monastery want the charm. Why Corvin Lesauvage wants the charm."

"Don't forget, you want to save this young man, as well."

"Avery Moreau. I haven't forgotten."

"Quite a shopping list." Roux abandoned his plate and leaned back to digest his meal.

"It is," Annja admitted. "But it's what I do."

"Look for truths in the past?"

Put that simply, Annja had to admit her job sounded too altruistic. "I love learning about the people who lived in the past. Who they were. What they did. Why they did it. Where they lived. How they saw the world and their places in it."

"You only left out 'when.'"

Despite her tension, Annja smiled. "'When' is sometimes part of the mystery, too. Carbon dating is pretty exact, but you don't always have it, and the results can be off enough to seriously screw with a theory."

"You're a classically trained archaeologist?"

"I am, but I've also got degrees in anthropology and ethnography."

"Good. I know it's hard for a traditional archaeologist to find work inside the United States and in most parts of the world these days. The focus tends to be on culture rather than things."

"You know about archaeology?" Annja was surprised.

"I know a lot about a great many things. I was with Dr. Howard Carter while he was doing his exploration of the Valley of the Kings in Egypt."

"That was in the early 1900s." Annja still couldn't believe they were talking about a period a hundred years ago, or that Roux might actually have seen it.

"Yes. Though Howard didn't find the tomb of Tutankhamen until 1922." Roux smiled. "I was there. It was a most gratifying moment. The man who funded the search, Lord Carnarvon, had very nearly given up on Howard. But Howard, for the most part, remained certain he was about to find the tomb. And he did. It was most impressive. The world will very probably never see the like again."

"I hope that's not true," Annja said. "Egypt grabbed everyone's attention, especially the British after Napoleon's army found the first pyramids there during the war. But there are other things out there we can learn."

"You're probably right. The world has forgotten more than anyone alive today will ever know." Roux talked as if he were an authority on that line of thinking. He was silent for a moment.

"What about the sword?" Annja asked.

Roux looked at her. "What do you mean?"

"I mean, why me?"

"My dear girl," Roux said, "the sword *chose* you."

"FROM THE VERY FIRST TIME I met Joan," Roux said, "I knew she was destined for greatness." In his mind's eye, he could see her again, proudly riding the great warhorse and carrying the banner. He had never—or, at least, very seldom—met anyone like her. "When you've been alive as long as I have, you tend to recognize such things."

"You've never stated your age," Annja said.

Roux grinned. He discovered he liked dueling with the young woman seated next to him. Not only was she beautiful, but she possessed mental alacrity, as well.

However, she was still naive in many ways. He hoped to be able to occasionally use that to his advantage. He had served the command he had been given. Now his life was his to do as he pleased.

"Nor will I state my age," Roux said. "But I do forgive your impertinence in your not-so-subtle attempt to find out."

She smiled at him, rested her elbows on the chair's arms and steepled her slender fingers to rest her chin.

Looking at her, Roux knew she was going to break many men's hearts. She was too beautiful and too independent—too driven—not to.

And now she carried Joan's sword, and everything that such a calling brought with it. That taken into account, and the looming confrontation with Lesauvage and the Brotherhood of the Silent Rain, she might not live to see the end of the week.

"As I said," Roux returned to his story, "I met Joan and I was very much taken with her. I saw that she was going to be a...*force*. No other word can match what I saw in her."

"You were a fan," Annja said. Her tiger's eyes gleamed with humor.

"I was," Roux admitted. "I was quite taken with her. But it was the power invested in her that drew me the most. The company of others has seldom been a preoccupation for me."

"Except for the part about hearing your own voice, I've noticed."

Roux grimaced. "There used to be an appreciation for storytelling."

"There still is," Annja said. "But now it also includes brevity. Getting to the point. That kind of thing."

"I believe Joan was supposed to help the balance," Roux said.

"What balance?"

"The balance between good and evil."

Annja paused, thinking, her brows tightly knit. "With a big *G* and a big *E?*"

"Exactly. The cosmic balance. A turning point between order and chaos." Roux sighed and still felt hugely guilty even after more than five hundred years and the vexing job of finding all the sword pieces. "But the world was cheated of her presence far too early."

"Because you got back to her late."

Roux shifted uncomfortably in his seat. Across the room, Garin lounged on a full-sized sofa and enjoyed the conversation, smirking the whole time.

"I wasn't the one who threw her up on that bloody stake and roasted her alive," Roux snapped. His own guilt was one thing, but he bloody well wasn't going to have it shoved on him by someone else.

Annja was quiet for a moment. "No," she said finally, "I suppose you weren't."

"That's right."

"So what's supposed to happen now?" Annja asked.

Roux was quiet for a moment, knowing what he was about to say would have a lasting impact on the young woman. At least, it would as long as she lived.

"I believe that the inheritor of Joan's sword is going to have to live up to that same potential," Roux said. "You're going to be asked to intercede on the behalf of good. Or not, if you so choose."

That shocked her. He saw it in her eyes. She was silent and still for a moment.

"That's ridiculous," the young woman finally said.

"Is it?" Roux gazed at her. "Yet, here you are, racing to the rescue of some unknown young man who actually may have set you up to be kidnapped while we were in the mountains."

"I'm not going because of the sword."

"Then why are you going?"

"Because I don't want Avery Moreau to die."

"Why? You don't truly know him. He may already be dead. More than likely, he betrayed you to a vicious enemy. You'd be a fool to do anything to help him." Roux leaned back. "Furthermore, you could call and let the local police deal with the matter."

"The sword has nothing to do with this."

"Perhaps not. Perhaps by your very nature you're quixotic. I submit to you, Miss Creed, that is probably the very reason the sword chose you."

Annja was silent for a moment, blinking as if she was dazed. Then she said, "You can't be serious."

"Of course not," Roux said. "I'm just leading you on a wild-goose chase. And the sword can't really appear and disappear just because you want it to. And it didn't somehow re-form itself from pieces when you touched it. All those things are lies."

A troubled look flashed in her eyes. "It also drew a lightning strike from the sky."

Roux was intrigued. "When?"

"Last night. On top of my building."

"You left the sword lying on top of a building?"

"I was holding it at the time."

Roux's eyebrows lifted. "Lightning struck the sword while you were holding it?"

"Yes."

"And you were undamaged?"

Annja nodded.

"This is fascinating. May I see the sword again?"

She held out her hand, paused a moment, then drew the sword from thin air.

Roux accepted the weapon as she handed it to him. He examined the blade. "It's unmarked."

"I know. Doesn't make a lot of sense, does it?"

"Neither does the fact that it shows no sign of ever having been shattered." Roux held on to the sword, wondering what other properties might manifest. Then it faded from his grip. He looked at her. "You did that?"

Annja nodded. "I guess I did. I was feeling…uncomfortable with the way you were holding on to the sword."

So stealing the sword, should he ever decide to do that, was out of the question. Roux felt challenged. He couldn't help wondering what would happen to the sword if Annja Creed were suddenly dead.

Roux happened to glance over at Garin, who smiled broadly. Roux knew he had spent too many years with his apprentice; Garin knew exactly what was crossing his mind. The old man was just thankful the young woman didn't have the same expertise.

ANNJA STARED at the lozenge. The heraldry beside the shadowy figure on the obverse of the coin was key to unlocking the mystery. She felt certain of that.

The diamond-shaped image containing the leaping wolf, the stag at rest and the crescent moon with a star above and below, had to mean something.

She continued searching through the pages of heraldry. Patience was one of the first and best skills an archaeologist learned.

THE RING OF HER cell phone startled Annja out of a near doze. She fumbled to find the device and catch the call.

"Hello."

"May I speak to Ms. Annja Creed, please?" a crisp British voice asked.

"Graham," Annja said.

"Ah, Annja. I wasn't sure at all if it was you. You sound as though you're talking from the bottom of a well. Come to think of it, the last time I spoke with you, you *were* talking to me from the bottom of a well. Didn't you get out?"

Annja smiled. Professor Graham Smyth-Peabody was professor emeritus at Cambridge University. He was in his early eighties and taught only those classes he wanted to during times he wished. Tall and distinguished-looking, he was a frequent guest on talk shows when discussions of British royalty were the subject.

"I did get out of the well," Annja said. That had been in the Bavarian countryside pursuing the lost loot of a highwayman. She hadn't found that, but she still occasionally sifted through the information she had about the event.

"Have you found another, then?" Smyth-Peabody laughed at his own wit.

"Actually, I'm flying on a private plane," Annja said.

"Jet," Garin growled. He sat on the couch with a drink in his hand. His disposition hadn't improved.

"Your publisher must really like you," the professor said. He hesitated. "You're able to afford a private plane because of the book, right? You haven't suddenly decided to start losing your shirt like that other young woman on that dreadful program on the telly?"

"No," Annja said. "I manage to keep my shirts on."

"Jolly good. I understand why you do those pieces for that program, but you should keep your naughty bits to yourself."

Despite the tension and all the trouble waiting on her in Lozère, Annja had to laugh. The professor was in rare good form.

Papers rustled at the other end of the phone connection. "I've managed to identify the heraldry you e-mailed me," the professor said.

"You could have e-mailed me back."

"Of course, of course. But I shall own up to a bit of curiosity here. I've found something a bit incongruous."

Annja pushed out of her seat and paced the short length of the jet's living room. "The shield bears markings of Richard of Kirkland," Annja said.

"Yes, yes. Quite right. So you've identified that."

"It makes me feel better to hear you agree with the answer I've received."

"He was knighted in 1768."

The monastery outside Lozère was burned down in 1767. Experience had taught Annja not to overlook coincidence. "Why was he knighted?" she asked.

"According to the documentation I found, it was for special services to the crown."

"What services?"

"I'm afraid it doesn't say, my dear."

"You would think the conferring of a knighthood under George III would have been important enough to record."

"Indeed," Smyth-Peabody agreed. "Perhaps it even was. But you have to remember, George III wasn't called the mad king for vacuous reasons. The man had porphyria, a most debilitating affliction that ultimately ruined his health and rendered him mad as a hatter. And there was a lot going on during his reign. He undermined the Whig Party, including Pitt the Elder, fought the French for seven years, then turned around and fought you Americans, not once but twice, staved off another attack at political control by the Whigs under Pitt the Younger, and managed to fight Napoleon's efforts at world domination twice."

"Those campaigns were managed by the Duke of Wellington."

"Quite. But they were under George III's reign. Perhaps he wasn't aware of what was going on by that time, but his royal historians were kept busy nonetheless."

"Point taken." Annja sighed. History and archaeology were sometimes at odds with each other. Then when a research project brought in other branches of science, things became even more convoluted.

"You are aware he had a daughter?" Smyth-Peabody asked.

"Carolyn," Annja said.

"Yes. Do tell me there is something I've left to amaze you with?"

"I'll let you know when we get there. Tell me about Carolyn."

Smyth-Peabody cleared his throat. "Sir Richard's daughter was born to his wife while he was tending the king's holdings in the New World."

"Richard wasn't in France?"

"No. He was one of the king's primaries during engagements in King George's War. You Americans refer to it as—"

"The French and Indian War," Annja said. "From 1757 to 1763."

"Yes. A rather melodramatic name, don't you think?"

Annja's mind flew. "Did Richard see any action in France?"

"No. According to the texts I've been through, Richard spent his whole military career marshaling forces in America. Until his death in 1777 at the Battle of Brandywine Creek when General Howe's troops forced the Continental Congress from Philadelphia."

"Richard never served in France?"

"I never found mention of it. I didn't know that was an important detail. I suppose I can go back through the research."

"What about Richard's wife?"

"Victoria, yes. By all accounts, she was rather a handful. She was married at fourteen to Richard, who was twenty years her senior."

Annja wasn't surprised. Marriages were often arranged for officers in the British military. Poor working-class parents wanted to get rid of a mouth to feed and hoped that a daughter, who wasn't allowed to work, might find a good home.

"Evidently being married to Richard didn't agree with her," the professor continued.

"What makes you say that?"

"She *did* have the affair behind her husband's back. After she lost the baby, I'm sure things weren't any easier."

"The baby didn't die."

Smyth-Peabody was silent for a moment. "Are you quite sure?"

"Yes. I'll forward the documentation on to you."

"In everything that I read, the child died and was buried in a private cemetery on family land outside London."

"Was the cause of death mentioned?"

"I inferred there were massive birth defects. There was, in one of the resources I investigated, some reason to believe there were instances of inbreeding within Victoria's family. Perhaps even incest."

"Where did you get that?"

"From the newspapers. They were little more than gossip sheets at the time."

The jet hit a downdraft. For a few seconds, Annja felt weightless. Then her stomach flipped and gravity held her in place again.

"What about the lozenge?" Annja asked.

"It never existed. Or, I should say, it never existed in the form that you showed me." The professor paused and the computer keys clacked. "The wolf design?"

"Yes."

"That was one that Sir Richard had ordered designed for his wife. She was going to be given her own coat-of-arms on the birth of their first child. The lozenge was never struck."

"The stag was part of the design?"

"No. The stag belonged to Sir Henry of Falhout."

"Could he have been Carolyn's father?"

"He died in 1745 while at sea in a tragic accident. It would have been quite impossible."

"Did he have a son? The coat-of-arms would have descended to him."

"Sir Henry did have a son, but he was only eight at the time Carolyn was born."

"What about brothers?" Annja kept trying to make sense of the puzzle. The image of the lozenge wouldn't leave her thoughts. Someone had initially thought to put the inscription on the charm, then had decided—or been told—not to. It had to be important.

"Sir Henry did have two younger brothers. The youngest brother died while fighting the French in 1747."

"What about the other brother?"

"I've not found anything out about him. He seems to have disappeared," the professor said.

"No family fortune to care for?"

"Remember, dear girl," the professor said, "this is Britain. We had the law of primogeniture here. Only the eldest male issue shall inherit family estates. Once Sir Henry had a son to carry on the family name, the rest of the family got nothing."

"Then who would use his heraldry?"

"I don't know. I shall keep looking and endeavor to find out. But as it stands at the moment, I'm at a loss to explain it."

"Thanks, Graham," Annja said.

"Of course, dear girl. I am yours to command. I have only one request."

"Yes."

"Once you decipher this puzzle, come to England and share the story with me. It's been too long since I've seen you."

"I will," Annja said, and hoped she survived the encounter with Lesauvage to do that.

26

"Annja."

Waking with a start, Annja lifted her hands in front of her in a defensive move. She blinked, focused and saw Roux standing in front of her.

"What?" she asked. Her throat was dry.

"We're descending. We'll land in a few minutes."

Annja felt the shift in the jet then. "Thanks." She put her seat belt on again.

Roux looked guilty. "I feel bad for waking you. You've hardly been asleep at all."

"I'll be fine." Annja uncapped a bottle of water and drank. The truth was, she didn't know how much longer she could keep going. It seemed as if the past few days had all turned into one exhaustive blur.

"May I?" Roux gestured to the seat next to her.

"Sure."

Roux sat and belted himself in. "I plan on accompanying you." He paused. "Unless you have an objection."

Annja thought about it. She really didn't want to be on her own facing Lesauvage and possibly the Brotherhood of the Silent Rain.

"It's going to be dangerous," she warned.

Roux favored her with a small smile. "Now that you have the sword, I should wonder if you will ever know peace again."

Annja lay back in the seat. "I hope you're wrong."

"You could give up the sword." He regarded her with idle speculation.

For a quiet moment, Annja thought about it. She could give up the sword, simply lay it down and walk away. But she knew she wouldn't. That wasn't her way, and…the sword had felt entirely too right in her hand.

"No," she said. "I can't."

"I'M NOT GOING."

Standing at the door of the jet, the noise of the airport loud in her ears, Annja looked at Garin.

Hands clasped behind his head, he lounged, barefoot, on the sofa.

"I thought you couldn't wait to see me get killed," Annja said.

Mirthlessly, Garin grinned at her. "If I go with you, I might be tempted to help you. If I did, I wouldn't be helping myself, would I?" He shook his head. "No. I'll sit on the sidelines for this one, and wait to see how it turns out."

Without a word, Annja ducked through the door and went quickly down the steps to the tarmac. Roux followed her, carrying a slim, dark wood walking stick. He exchanged no words with Garin. After more than five hundred years of being mentor and student, then enemies, what was left to say?

A jet screamed through the air overhead. Annja looked up into the night and adjusted her backpack over her shoulder.

Eyes were watching her. She was sure of that. She wondered if she would ever see Garin again.

THREE MEN WAITED outside the gates, near the baggage-claim area. They were better dressed than the motorcycle riders but they were the same kind of stock.

"Miss Creed," one of them said.

Annja stopped. "Who are you?"

"Mr. Lesauvage sent a car for you."

"I prefer my own car," Annja said.

"Mr. Lesauvage," the man said more harshly, *"insists."*

"He can call me and arrange a meeting place." Annja stared at him. "I insist."

The man stepped forward and grabbed Annja's upper arm. She reacted without thinking, opening her fist and popping him in the throat.

Buckling, gasping for breath, the man staggered away. The second man reached for her, but she shifted, grabbed his arm and bent it behind him, then lifted his arm high between his shoulders and rammed him into the nearest wall. Senseless, he collapsed.

The third man took one step, then Roux swung the walking stick up between his legs. Mewling with pain and grabbing himself, the man dropped to the floor.

Roux adjusted his collar and tie. Frowning, he gazed at the rapid approach of the security people. "Well, so much for the quiet arrival."

IT TOOK almost an hour to straighten out the mess with airport security. In the end, one of Lesauvage's men claimed to have staggered drunkenly into Annja and caused the misunderstanding. Annja had supported that by saying she might have overreacted. The security chief let them go with a stern warning, and probably because he didn't want any further paperwork than he already had.

"Have you always been this way?" Roux asked while they stood at the car-rental desk.

Annja was quiet for a moment. Then she looked at him. "I grew up in an orphanage. You learn not to let people push you around in there. If circumstances were different, if I didn't already know that Lesauvage was slime, maybe I would handle this a different way."

The agent brought a set of keys to a Nissan Terrano 4X4. The cost was extra, but Annja wanted the off-road capability.

"But Lesauvage is a criminal," Annja went on, "and circumstances aren't different. I'm preparing for war."

Roux smiled and shook his head. "You remind me so much of her at times. So focused. So deliberate. So convinced of your own righteousness."

"Of who?" Annja signed the agreement and left the desk. She knew whom Roux meant, but for some reason she wanted him to say it. That way maybe he'd remember that he'd been too late last time and would put forth greater effort.

Roux fell into step beside her. "Of Joan."

For a moment, the image of the burning pyre filled Annja's head. "Joan's dead."

"I know," Roux said. "I was going to remind you of that."

ANNJA WAS KEYING the ignition when her cell phone rang. Fumbling it from her backpack, she answered.

"Miss Creed," Lesauvage said.

Annja paused with the Terrano in gear. All around her, people arrived and departed the busy airport even this late in the evening. All of them had places to go, were starting journeys or ending them.

And what are you doing? she wondered. Starting one or ending one? She didn't know.

"We'll meet outside Mende," Annja said with cold deliberation. She tried to sound as though she weren't about to throw up.

"I sent a car for you," Lesauvage stated.

"I declined. Move on to your next point." Annja couldn't believe how forceful she was being. Maybe it was from watching all those adventure movies with Sister Mary Annabelle when the other nuns were away. Or maybe it was just that in this situation a whole lot of dialogue wasn't needed.

"I could kill Avery Moreau," Lesauvage threatened.

"And I could get on the next plane out of here." Glancing back over her shoulder, Annja spotted the three men moving toward her. "Call your men off."

"We're going to do this my way," Lesauvage said.

"No," Annja said, "we're not." She broke the connection, tossed the phone onto the dashboard and looked at Roux. "Buckle up."

Without a word, the old man did. But a faint grin pulled his lips.

Annja shoved the transmission into reverse and backed toward Lesauvage's three men. Trapped in the ruby-and-white glow of her taillights, they tried to run. She managed to clip one of them with her rear bumper and send him sprawling into a parked car. The alarm roared to life and lights flashed.

The other two men ran to help their companion to his feet. They tried to run to their car, but public parking was a long way from rental parking.

Annja switched on her lights and merged with the departing traffic.
The phone rang again.

Grabbing the phone, Annja said, "Be polite."

"Where," Lesauvage asked, "do you want to meet?"

Annja named a kilometer marker a short distance from the city.
Then she hung up again.

For a short time, Roux let her drive in silence, long enough to get
onto the loop around Paris so they could head south. Finally he said,
"You realize, of course, that Lesauvage and his men will outnumber
you when you reach that destination."

"Yes." Annja made herself try to believe that she wasn't sleepy
and that driving was taking all of her attention.

"What do you plan to do?"

"I don't know," she replied, "exactly." She paused. "Yet. This is
still a work in progress."

"You're trusting that Lesauvage won't kill you."

"He won't." Annja thought that through. "He can't. He wants the
charm and whatever secrets it possesses."

"Once he has it, he may well kill you. Us."

Annja looked at him and smiled. "Are you worried about us? Or
you?"

"Both, actually." Roux regarded her. "I'm fascinated by you. I'd
like very much to see what you do with Joan's sword."

Me, too, Annja thought. Then she turned her attention back to her
driving. The rendezvous was hours away.

"IT APPEARS we have a tail," Roux announced when they were three
kilometers north of their destination.

"We've had one for the past half hour," Annja said.

"We'll not be arriving unannounced," Roux stated.

Annja looked at him. "I could let you out."

Roux gave her a crooked smile. "No. I've seen myself through
worse than Corvin Lesauvage."

"You mean Garin?"

Roux studied his hands. "I mean much worse than Lesauvage or
Garin." He wouldn't say any more.

Annja glanced in the rearview mirror again and watched the car holding steady at the same speed it had for the past thirty minutes. She still hadn't been able to tell how many men were in the car.

It didn't matter, though. There would be a lot more waiting with Lesauvage.

A roadside sign announced the rest stop she'd chosen was only two kilometers distant.

PULLING OFF the highway, Annja drove into the rest stop. The building was off to the right with a small park behind it. Security lights marked the parking area in front of the building and at the north side.

Lesauvage waited on the north side. A sleek black BMW looked like a predatory cat hunkered down between two stalwart Renault Alpines. Only a short distance behind them, a cargo van sat solid and silent. A dozen motorcycles were spread around the cars. They had the whole end of the parking area to themselves.

Annja's cell phone rang.

"Yes," she said.

"I see you, Miss Creed," Lesauvage announced. "Do come in. There is no need for further game play. You will not leave this area unless I allow it. And I will kill Avery Moreau just to show you that I mean what I say."

The tail car, flanked by two others, pulled in behind Annja. One came alongside on the left and blocked the exit lane. The other two remained behind her. Their lights shone through the Terrano's back glass.

Annja remained where she was. As she stared at the cars and motorcycles ahead of her, Lesauvage got out of the BMW and stood in front of the vehicles. He held his cell phone to his ear and smiled broadly. His sandy hair caught gold fire in the light.

"At this point, Miss Creed," Lesauvage said, "you truly have no choice."

Without replying, Annja closed the cell phone and shoved the device into her backpack. She drove the SUV toward the BMW.

Roux gripped the suicide handle above his head. "You purchased the optional insurance, didn't you?"

"I never go anywhere without it," Annja said as she put her foot down harder on the accelerator. She drove straight for the BMW. The cell phone shrilled for her attention but she ignored it.

Lesauvage turned abruptly and waved to the BMW's driver. The man engaged the transmission and squealed backward, sliding out of the protective custody of the two Renaults. In his haste, the driver ran over one of the motorcycles.

Annja braked and skidded to a halt between the two Renaults.

"Well," Roux said in a calm voice as he released his hold, "I'm sure we wouldn't have enjoyed a more welcome response before this anyway."

Quivering a little inside, knowing that she was laying her life—and Roux's—on the line, Annja nodded.

One of the men wearing motorcycle leathers ran and jumped onto the Terrano's hood. He landed in a kneeling position with a deadly machine pistol in his hands. Annja didn't recognize the weapon, but she knew it for what it was.

"Don't move!" he shouted in accented English. "Keep your hands on the steering wheel!"

Annja did.

"And you, old man," the thug went on, "you put your hands on the dash!"

"Impertinent twit," Roux growled.

For a moment fear ran rampant in Annja's stomach. She felt certain Roux was not going to do as he'd been ordered. Then, thankfully, he put his hands on the dash.

Lesauvage stepped to the Terrano's side and gazed into the vehicle with a hot-eyed glare. A tense moment passed. Annja returned the man's gaze without batting an eye.

"Get them out of the car," Lesauvage ordered.

MINUTES LATER, Annja sat on the floor in the back of the cargo van. Her hands were cuffed behind her. Roux sat near the double doors at the back. His hands were also cuffed. He sat impassively, watching the exchange between Annja and Lesauvage.

You have no business being here, Annja told herself again. The statement was now a litany that spawned over and over again in her head like a video-game monster.

But every time she looked at Avery Moreau, sitting shaking and frightened across from her, she knew she couldn't have stayed away.

"You did not bring the charm, Miss Creed." Corvin Lesauvage paced the carpeted rear deck of the van.

Annja made no reply.

"What did you hope to accomplish?" Lesauvage demanded.

"You would have killed Avery Moreau if I hadn't come," she said.

"Yes."

Avery looked up at Lesauvage. The young man held his injured hand cradled in his lap. Red streaks along his forearm showed the onset of infection. Even though Lesauvage had wounded him, Avery still looked surprised by the man's quick admission.

"So here I am," Annja said.

"What good are you?"

"I memorized the charm," Annja said. "I know what it looks like. Do you?"

Lesauvage drew back his hand to strike her. Annja didn't flinch, fully expecting to feel the weight of the blow.

"Don't," Roux said. There was something in the old man's voice that stayed Lesauvage's hand.

The criminal stepped away, fastening his gaze onto Roux. "You should have stayed out of this, old man."

"Perhaps," Roux replied. "But, then, you don't know who you're trifling with, do you?"

Annja watched Lesauvage. This wasn't like the final tense moments in a movie where the villain laid out his plans for conquest. In the movies, the script kept the villain from killing the captured heroes. Annja was desperately aware that there was no such script here.

Joan of Arc died at the hands of her enemies, Annja thought. For a moment she believed Lesauvage was going to kill Roux.

"What do you want?" Annja asked.

Visibly restraining himself, Lesauvage took a deep breath and turned to face her. The constant roar of the tires against the pavement filled the van. They were obviously headed for a destination, but Annja had no clue what that might be.

"How familiar are you with the Brotherhood of the Silent Rain, Miss Creed?" Lesauvage asked.

"I know they represented the church and were known for keeping to themselves," Annja said. "They worked on scholarly pieces for the church libraries and were self-sufficient. I know they also took a stand against the French noblemen who wanted to continue the Wild Hunt. I know their monastery was destroyed in 1767. I assume that was done by the same French noblemen they displeased."

"It was," Lesauvage said. "But that monastery was destroyed and the monks slain for more than mere interference."

Annja waited. She'd baited him. She could see that. He loved knowing more than she did and he couldn't hold that knowledge back.

"The Brotherhood of Silent Rain wasn't just against the Wild Hunt," Lesauvage said. "They also protested the search for the Beast of Gévaudan, saying that the creature was imagined and the poor people were killed by the noblemen only to justify the Wild Hunt."

"Why would they do that?" Annja asked.

"Because," Lesauvage said, "they were providing safe harbor for La Bête. The beast was living among them."

27

"How do you know La Bête was living at the monastery?" Annja asked.

Lesauvage showed her a grin, then lit a Gaulois cigarette and breathed out a plume of smoke. "You're not the only one who does research, Miss Creed."

"Not to be offensive," Annja stated evenly, not truly caring if the man took offense, "but you hardly seem the sort to crack a book."

"I didn't." Lesauvage stared at her coldly. "All my life I've been told that a knight named Benoit of Mende, nicknamed 'the Relentless' because he never gave up on anything he set his mind to, found out that the monks of the Brotherhood of the Silent Rain were providing shelter to La Bête. He blackmailed the monks into giving him a huge ransom."

"Instead of telling others who might help kill the beast?" Roux asked.

Lesauvage grinned. "Benoit was truly a man after my own heart. Always looking after himself."

"How did he find out the monastery was sheltering La Bête?"

"He was a master of the Wild Hunt. No beast—no man—was safe once Benoit took up the trail." Lesauvage's eyes gleamed with excitement at the telling. "He followed the creature back there in 1767. The following morning, he went to Father Roger, who was master of the monastery, and told him they would have to pay for his silence.

Reluctantly, the monks agreed. And they began to gather up the gold and silver Benoit exacted for his price. But he knew they would try to betray him. After all, everyone knows you can't trust the English."

"The English?" Annja repeated.

"Father Roger was English. He was banished to the Brotherhood of the Silent Rain years before for some transgression against the church."

"What transgression?"

Lesauvage shrugged. "Does it matter?"

Annja knew it did. Lesauvage was missing a large part of the story, but she thought she had it. "Go on."

"Thank you," the man said sarcastically. "At any rate, knowing he couldn't trust the English, Benoit arranged to accept delivery of the ransom. He and his men fled from the monastery that day. A sudden storm rose up and chased them down the mountain."

"What mountain?" Annja asked.

"Up in the Cévennes," Lesauvage said. "That's where we're going now. We'll see how well you remember the charm."

Annja didn't respond. "You're looking for the treasure."

"But of course. On his way down the mountainside, Benoit fully expected to be attacked by the monks. What he had not counted on was being pursued by La Bête. He thought to outmaneuver the monks, though. There are some old Roman ruins up in the Cévennes."

"Several of them are at Nîmes," Annja said.

"You know of them? Excellent. But there are several others. The Roman legions marched everywhere through France on their way to conquer the rest of the known world. They left garrisons, temples and buildings everywhere they went. Quite the builders, the Romans. Benoit chose to hide his treasure in those ruins."

"And you believe it's still there?" Annja shook her head.

"I do."

"That was 240 years ago."

Lesauvage glared at her. "The treasure was never found. Benoit and ten of his finest knights, accompanied by twenty peasants, raced down the mountain with La Bête on their heels. Benoit had counted on having the day to help him. Instead, the sky had turned dark and rain lashed the forest. The horses skidded and tumbled, hardly worth attempting to ride."

"On the ground, in full armor, the knights were sitting ducks for La Bête," Annja said.

"They had no chance," Lesauvage said. "La Bête was among them in minutes. Benoit said that he heard the screams of his men as they were slain."

"I guess he didn't stay to help them," Roux said dryly.

"Benoit was no hero," Lesauvage said. "He was a fighter. He stayed and fought only when he knew he was going to win. Against the rain, unhorsed and on the treacherous slopes of a forested mountain, he knew he could not win. His only victory lay in survival, being able to live to reclaim his fortune. So he ran."

As Annja listened to the man's words, she imagined what the battle must have been like. She'd seen La Bête's huge body in the cave. Trapped in their armor in the mud as they had been, instead of secure on horses, the knights had little chance.

"In the end, the knights were all slain," Lesauvage said.

"What happened to the peasants?" Annja figured she already knew, but she had to ask.

Lesauvage grinned. "After they'd helped hide the treasure in the ruins, Benoit and his men killed them. Well away from the hiding area, of course."

Roux growled a curse.

"Secrets, you see, are hard to keep when they're shared so broadly," Lesauvage said.

"I take it Benoit didn't die," Annja said.

"No," Lesauvage agreed. "Benoit didn't die. The storm that poured out its fury and took away his fighting terrain also offered him a means of escape. A stream runs at the foothills of the Cévennes near the ruins. With the arrival of the storm, the stream swelled and overflowed its banks, becoming a raging torrent."

Annja had been in mountains caving when flash floods had struck. She'd always been amazed at how much water was dumped during a sudden storm.

"Benoit shed his armor as he ran, knowing his only chance was the stream." Lesauvage flicked ash from his cigarette. "He reached a cliff overlooking the water. Before he could jump La Bête overtook him." Lesauvage smiled. "They fought. Benoit was armed with only a knife. He didn't fare well. But he wounded the beast enough that he was able to escape and leap into the stream. La Bête tried to follow, but couldn't swim."

"Why didn't Benoit recover his ransom later?" Annja asked.

"Unfortunately, Benoit was not only injured by La Bête, but also by the plunge into the river. He was in a coma for nine days. Everyone thought he was dead. Then, on the morning of the tenth day, he woke to find that he had suffered a spinal injury that robbed him of his legs and most of the use of his arms."

Annja waited, knowing Lesauvage was doling the story out as he wanted to.

"Condemned to his bed, Benoit still intended to have both his ransom and his vengeance against the monks," Lesauvage said. "He rallied the other knights who shared his interest in the Wild Hunt and told them that the monastery of the Brotherhood of the Silent Rain was giving shelter to La Bête."

"They believed him?" Annja asked.

Lesauvage shrugged. "Either way, they were going to be rid of the monks and their insistence that the Wild Hunt be stopped. They took up arms and destroyed the monastery, pulling it down stone by stone and burning what was left. For his revenge against the monster, Benoit struck a secret deal with the most renowned knight in all of Gévaudan at the time, Scarlet Didier, whose blood was made of ice water and whose thirst for action was unquenchable."

"He agreed to hunt La Bête?"

"When it wasn't found at the monastery, yes."

"Why?"

"For money, of course. Benoit had claimed a coin from the monastery. A piece of metal stamped with the Brotherhood of the Silent Rain's symbol. On the other side, Benoit crafted an image of a wolf and a mountain."

Annja waited.

"That image," Lesauvage said, "is a map to the treasure. Benoit gave the charm to Scarlet Didier and told him he would give him the secret of the map after he had killed La Bête and brought back the creature's head."

"Scarlet Didier didn't come back from that hunt," Annja said. She remembered the dead man holding on to the spear in the cave.

"No. After Didier went up into the mountains, he was never heard from again," Lesauvage said. "Three days after Didier left, Benoit had a relapse caused by an infection. He died a week later, never regaining consciousness."

"You expect that treasure to still be there after two hundred years?" Roux asked in a manner suggesting that Lesauvage was insane or a fool.

"It was never found," Lesauvage replied.

Roux snorted in open derision. "More than likely the monks took it back."

"The treasure was never found at the monastery," Lesauvage argued.

"Then it never existed." Roux's conviction was damning.

Lesauvage wheeled on the old man and struck him with his fist. Roux's head turned to the side. When the old man turned to face his tormentor, he glowered at him.

"No man," Roux said in a quiet, deadly voice that barely rose above the steady whir of the tires, "has ever laid a hand upon me without paying the price in blood. I will kill you."

Bending down, Lesauvage shoved his face close to Roux's. He raised his voice. "Marcel," he called.

One of the guards stepped forward.

"Tie that length of chain around the old man's leg," Lesauvage directed.

The big man knelt and carried out the order. The oily black chain left smudges on Roux's pants.

"Now open the cargo doors."

Marcel opened the cargo doors. The highway passed in a dizzying rush. Trees stood black and dark against the moon. One of the Renaults, flanked by motorcycles, followed closely.

"When I tell you to," Lesauvage said, "heave the old man out the cargo doors. If he somehow is missed by the car or survives the impact, we'll keep dragging him until there's nothing left of him."

The big guard nodded and seized Roux's bound feet. He dragged and pushed the old man to hang poised over the edge. Roux never said a word.

Horrified at the prospect of what was happening, Annja tried to break free of her bonds. The metal cuffs felt loose, but she could not break them.

She pictured the sword in her mind's eye and reached for it. But somehow she couldn't manage to take the hilt up into her bound arm. It was as if the sword were suddenly behind a glass wall.

Frustrated, Annja said, "If you hurt him, you might as well kill me."

Lesauvage threw up a hand, freezing his minion in place. "Are you that brave?" he asked.

"If you're going to kill him," Annja said, "I know you'll kill me. If I know you're going to kill me, why should I help you?"

"What do you propose?"

"Leave him alone," Annja suggested. "Once we get up into the mountains, I'll help you find the ransom Benoit hid."

"You'll help me anyway." Lesauvage leered. "I've got a taste for torture. Breaking you could be a delight."

Swallowing the fear that threatened to engulf her, Annja made herself stare back at Lesauvage. Don't let him see that you're afraid. He's like any other predator. Keep him off balance, she thought.

"Breaking me will take time," she promised. "And what do you do if you go too far? Do you want to lose time and take the chance on losing the information I have?"

Lesauvage stood. "Pull the old man back inside and close the door."

The guard did that. Immediately the road noise inside the van diminished.

"Now," Lesauvage said to Annja, "here's the deal you reaped. The first time I get the impression that you're lying to me, I'm going to kill all of you. And I'll take my time while I'm doing it." He paused. "Is that understood?"

Annja nodded, not trusting her voice.

"Good," Lesauvage said.

LITTLE MORE than an hour later, they were up in the Cévennes mountains. They left the BMW, Renaults and van at the base of the mountains.

Lesauvage checked the GPS locater he carried, then gave directions to his team. All of them were heavily armed. From his conversation over the cell phone, Annja knew that he had a helicopter standing by. Evidently Lesauvage planned to use the helicopter to transport the treasure and for a quick exit.

"Are you going to continue to be his captive?" Roux whispered. He stood beside her against the van.

"I don't have much choice," Annja said.

"You have the sword," Roux hissed.

"The sword isn't exactly available at the moment."

Roux glanced at her in consternation. "What do you mean?"

"I can't get to it." Annja flexed her hands behind her back. The cuffs held her arms in place. "I reach for it, the way I always have, only it won't come."

"But it's there?" Roux asked.

"It feels like it is."

Lesauvage returned, closing and pocketing his cell phone. At his command, one of the men placed Roux on the back of his motorcycle.

Annja was seated on another. Avery Moreau, looking feverish and exhausted, was placed on the back of a third.

Only a moment later, they were tearing across the night-darkened terrain, heading steadily up into the Cévennes Mountains.

THE MOTORCYCLE CARAVAN reached the ruins over an hour later. The long ride left Annja's legs in agony. She hadn't been on a motorcycle in a while and being handcuffed while riding kept her in an uncomfortable position.

Near the top of the mountain, they found the remains of an old Roman garrison. Judging from its position, the stronghold had once existed as a checkpoint along a trail that led over the mountain.

In its time, the garrison had probably looked formidable. Now it looked like the scattered blocks of a giant child. Forest growth had shot roots into the mortar, gained hold and was inexorably pulling the structure into its destructive grip. One day, if no move was made to preserve the garrison, it would crumble, devoured by vegetation.

Lesauvage and his men carried powerful flashlights. The driver in front of Annja helped her off the motorcycle but wasn't gentle about it. She stood on wobbly legs, but her strength quickly returned.

Roux and Avery appeared to have the same problem for a while longer.

"There is a cave inside the mountain," Lesauvage said.

Annja had already known there would be. The Romans had used every advantage the land they built upon would give them, then manufactured others. Having a cave meant having a place to store provisions, as well as retreat to.

"Hasn't the cave been explored?" Roux asked.

"Hundreds of times," Lesauvage answered, gazing at Annja in open speculation.

"Then you're on a fool's errand," Roux snapped.

"For your sake," Lesauvage said, "I hope not."

Like you're going to set us free, Annja thought derisively. But the idea of the cave captivated her thoughts. Even places that had been investigated for hundreds of years sometimes turned up surprises. Often secrets weren't revealed until the searcher knew what to look for.

She pictured the charm in her mind again. The hanged wolf stood out against the background of the mountain.

Why a wolf? she wondered. Why was it hanged?

"Miss Creed?" Lesauvage prompted.

"I'll need my hands," she said.

Lesauvage hesitated, then nodded at one of his men. Two others kept their weapons leveled at her. The cuff around one wrist was removed only long enough to bring her arms in front of her, then was once more secured.

But during that moment, Annja had reached out and touched the sword. It was there. She just couldn't take it from that otherwhere with her hands bound.

"I need a flashlight," Annja said.

Lesauvage handed her a flashlight. Lightning stabbed across the sky. The wind changed directions and rose in intensity. The temperature seemed to be dropping a few degrees.

Good thing you don't believe in omens, Annja told herself. She switched on the light and walked through the remnants of the checkpoint and into the cave beyond.

BROTHER GASPAR WOKE in the stone niche that served as his bed. He heard his name repeated, then looked over at the doorway where one of the young monks stood holding a single candle.

"What is it?" Gaspar asked, pushing himself into a sitting position.

"Lesauvage and the American woman have returned to the mountains." The yellow glow of the candle flame played over the young monk's tense features. "They're at the Roman checkpoint where Benoit was believed to have hidden the ransom he extorted from our order."

"Why?"

"I don't know."

For a moment, Gaspar sat wreathed in his blankets. The caves were always damp and chill. He had never questioned where God had chosen to assign him, but he sometimes longed for the day when he would know a warm bed at night.

"Get everyone ready," Gaspar said. "Let's go see what they found."

After the young monk left to wake the others, Gaspar wondered if all the secrets they had protected were on the verge of finally coming out. Over the years of its existence, the church had covered up many things. Men served God, and men were always made of flesh and blood. And flesh and blood were doomed to be forever weaker than faith.

28

Annja followed the narrow passage, having to duck twice. Not wide enough for two men to walk abreast, the passageway formed a bottleneck that would have been suicidal for an opposing force to attempt to breach.

Almost twenty feet in, the passageway opened into the first cave chamber.

Playing her flashlight beam around, Annja discovered the cave was a near rectangle thirty feet wide and about fifty feet long. The ceiling averaged about fifteen feet up, but dipped as low as five feet.

Her foot slipped over the edge of a hole and she barely caught herself.

"Careful, Miss Creed," Lesauvage admonished.

Pointing the flashlight down, Annja discovered she'd almost stepped into a hole nearly five feet in diameter and at least six feet deep.

"It's a trap," Lesauvage explained.

"I know." Annja shone her beam around and discovered that the pits made a checkerboard mosaic across the front of the cave entrance. Some of them were filled in with dirt, debris and rocks.

"Back in the days of the Roman soldiers," Lesauvage said, "I'm told stakes were placed in the traps to impale the unsuspecting. The stakes are long gone now, of course."

Annja stepped around the pits; stakes or not, they'd make a nasty fall.

At the back of the cave, she found three passageways. All of them led to smaller caves. She guessed they'd been used as storage areas and barracks.

Puzzled, she played the flashlight beam over the cave walls and ceiling again. Bats clung to stalactites that had been chipped and broken off at uniform height.

"What are you looking for?" Lesauvage asked.

"A way out," Annja answered. "It doesn't make sense that Roman soldiers would plan on falling back into a cave they couldn't escape from. There has to be a way out." She started testing the walls.

"People have looked for that treasure in the caves for years," Lesauvage said angrily. "If there had been a secret door in one of the walls or the ceiling, it would have been found."

Annja ignored the comment. Discoveries had been made in what were believed to be "explored" areas before. She just had to put her mind into finding the solution.

"Perhaps," Roux suggested, "the monks already reclaimed the treasure all those years ago. It could be they didn't tell anyone so the search would continue as an exercise in frustration. And to remind everyone that no one could steal from the church. The Vatican liked the idea of divine justice and curses overtaking thieves who robbed them." He stepped into the last cave with a flashlight and helped her look.

Annja wondered why Roux was helping, then decided maybe his own curiosity had prompted him to action.

"They could have," Annja agreed. "This wasn't the best hiding place for Benoit to attempt to stash the ransom."

"There was no other place for him to hide it in the time that he had," Lesauvage said. "It was this place—or no place."

"Perhaps he never got a treasure at all," Roux suggested. "The tale about the treasure could have been merely a way for him to get his vengeance."

"The knights all resented the Brotherhood of the Silent Rain," Lesauvage said. "They needed only the smallest excuse to tear down that monastery."

Annja went back to the second cave, ignoring the fact that Lesauvage's men held guns on her. Her mind worked to solve the problem she'd been presented. She was drawn more into that effort than in being afraid. Something chewed at the back of her mind and restlessly called attention to itself.

"Benoit swore that the charm held the answer to the hiding place," Lesauvage said.

Annja stumbled over a depression in the ground. Aiming the flashlight down, she saw a round hollow.

"Perhaps we should look outside," Roux said.

Lightning flashed, invading the caves for a moment. Almost immediately, thunder shook the earth. Loose rock tumbled from the ceiling and skidded down the walls.

"This isn't gonna cave in, is it?" Avery asked nervously.

Lesauvage sneered at the young man. "You wanted revenge for your father. Don't you realize you need a spine for that?" He cursed. "Instead, you came to me, imploring me to unleash my Wild Huntsmen on Inspector Richelieu."

Annja looked at the young man.

Tears ran down Avery's face and dripped from his scruffy chin. He spoke in French. "He killed my father! I saw him do it! It's not fair that everyone thinks he's a hero! My father wasn't even armed. He was just a thief, not a murderer." He wiped at his face with his bandaged hand. The handcuffs gleamed in the flashlight's beam.

Annja felt a surge of compassion for the young man. She'd never known her parents. She couldn't imagine what it would be like to watch a parent's murder.

"Stop your damned sniveling, child," Lesauvage commanded. "Otherwise I'll have you taken out and shot."

"No," Annja said.

Lesauvage turned on her. "I'm getting tired of your continued insistence on giving the orders around here, Miss Creed. You've not done as I've asked and brought the charm, and now you're wasting my time."

"I don't have the charm," Annja said. "I told you that. You choose not to believe me. I can't help that. I've offered you the best help that I can."

Smiling, Lesauvage pointed his pistol directly between Annja's eyes. "I won't kill you, Miss Creed. Not yet. But I am going to kill one of these two men if you don't have some degree of success." He paused. "Soon."

Unflinching, Annja stared across the barrel of the pistol. Lesauvage's men shifted uneasily behind him.

"Choose one of them," Lesauvage ordered. "Save one. I will kill the other."

"I need a shovel," Annja said.

Lesauvage blinked at her. "What?"

"I think I know what the charm referred to," she said.

"Tell me."

Annja pointed to the depressions in front of the smaller caves. "These were traps at one time."

Surveying the ground, Lesauvage nodded. "So?"

"I think at least one of them is more than that." Excitement filled Annja as she thought about the clue her subconscious mind had given her. "You and I have been speaking English. Avery spoke in French."

"How has that any bearing?"

"Because it made me think of what these traps were originally called. Have you heard of the word *loophole?*"

"As in a legal maneuver?" Lesauvage sounded impatient.

"As in the origin of the word," Annja said.

Lesauvage glared at her. "I don't care for a lesson in wordplay."

"You should. Two hundred and forty years ago, wordplay was everything in entertainment. Puzzles, limericks, jokes and brainteasers took the place of television and video games. When I work a dig site, I have to keep that in mind. Words can have several meanings, not just the superficial ones. The hanged wolf on the charm was a clue, and it was an icon. A picture of the word Benoit perhaps didn't know how to write."

"A loophole was an opening in a defensive wall on a structure or a cave in the forest," Roux said, smiling as if he knew where Annja was going. "A way a traveler might check for wolves lying in wait outside the wall. Or, as they were known in French, *loupes.*"

"That's right," Annja said. She gestured toward the trap. "Pits like these were used back in the days of Julius Caesar. He wrote about them in his *Commentaries on the Gallic Wars*. But do you know what they're called in French?"

Lesauvage shook his head.

"Trou de loup." ·

"Wolf trap," Lesauvage said.

"Yes. The charm had a picture of a hanged wolf on it," Annja said. "But maybe it wasn't a hanged wolf. I think it was a trapped wolf."

Lesauvage looked down at the *trou de loup* beneath Annja's feet. "Get her a shovel," he ordered. "Get them all shovels."

ANNJA DUG. The effort brought a warm burn to her arm, shoulder and back muscles. The chill of the cave left her.

The work went easily. Someone had filled in the wolf traps a long time ago, but the earth wasn't solidly packed. The shovel blade bit down deeply each time. Roux and Avery dug out the other two pits.

Annja reached the bottom of her pit first. Stakes had impaled a victim hundreds of years ago. Bones and a few scraps of fabric testified to that. She knew the time frame from the few Roman coins and a copper bracelet she dug up on the way to the bottom. The coins, bracelet and the bones were all that were left. The stakes had splintered long ago. When they had been placed all those centuries ago, the Romans had hammered the stakes into bedrock.

Lifting the shovel in both hands, Annja drove the blade down against the bedrock. Satisfied it was solid, she tossed the shovel out and climbed from the pit.

Lesauvage looked at her.

"It's solid," she replied.

"If you're wrong about all three," Lesauvage taunted, "at least you'll have your graves dug."

Annja ignored the comment. They had freed her from the handcuffs. In her mind she had reached out and touched the sword. It was there, waiting.

"How are you doing?" she asked Roux.

"Almost there." Grime stained Roux's face as he worked by lantern light. He turned another shovelful of dirt from the wolf trap. "You do realize that simply losing the treasure wasn't enough to keep the Brotherhood of the Silent Rain in hiding. They were, and still are, one supposes, being punished."

"I know. I have a theory about that, as well. They weren't ostracized by the church for their failure to protect the gold and silver they lost," Annja said.

"It was because of La Bête." Roux took a handkerchief from his pocket and wiped his face.

"Yes."

"Then they did give the beast shelter."

Annja nodded. "They did."

"But whatever on earth for?" Roux asked.

"The clue to that is in the lozenge," Annja said. "In the heraldry that was almost marked for the shadowy figure on the charm."

"Do you know who that figure was?"

"I think I do."

Lesauvage stepped forward and cursed. "Enough talk. More digging."

Annja tapped on Avery's shoulder. The young man's wounded hand had bled through the bandages and formed a crust of dirt.

"What?" Avery asked.

"Let me do it," Annja said.

He scowled at her. "I can do it." Stubbornly, he pushed the shovel back into the dirt.

"You'll be lucky if you don't bleed to death at the rate you're going," she pointed out.

"Go away."

Stepping forward, Lesauvage said, "Get out of there. You're digging too slowly."

Eyes tearing with emotion, looking scared and confused, Avery climbed from the hole. He threw the shovel back into the half-dug pit and started cursing.

Quick as a snake, Lesauvage slammed his pistol into the side of Avery's head. Dazed and hurting, the young man dropped to the ground. He rocked and mewled in pain, holding his head, bleeding down the side of his face. Crimson drops fell from his jawline to the stone floor of the cave.

Anger surged through Annja, but she knew she had to contain it for the moment. At the bottom of the wolf trap, she paused a moment and reached for the sword. The leather-bound hilt felt rough beneath her fingers.

Then she drew back her hand and started to dig. Now wasn't the time. But soon.

For a time only the sounds of the storm and the two shovels cleaving the earth existed. Thudding impacts competed with the rumbling that sounded as if it were on top of the mountain.

A moment later, Roux's shovel struck something hollow.

"Here," he called.

Annja vaulted out of the pit where she worked and crossed the cave. Roux tapped the shovel several times, causing the hollow thump each time.

Looking at Roux's pit, Annja immediately noticed the difference between it and the two she'd worked in. The ones she'd dug tapered like inverted cones. As she'd neared the bottom, the excavation had been harder because the earth had been previously unworked.

Roux's pit had obviously been completely dug out. He kept shoveling, working around a stone oval that fitted onto mortared stoneworks below.

"Is that a tunnel?" Lesauvage asked.

"Maybe," Annja answered. "It could also be a well. The Roman soldiers would have wanted a water source if they were besieged."

More of Lesauvage's men shone their beams into the hole Roux had made.

Within minutes, the old man had completely dug out around the oval. He leaned back against the wall. Perspiration soaked his clothing.

Fear swarmed inside Annja. They were nearing the point of no return. Soon, Lesauvage would no longer need them. If the treasure was revealed beneath, she was certain they'd be shot immediately.

"Get that cover off," Lesauvage ordered.

"I can't," Roux replied. "It's too heavy." He levered the shovel under the stone oval and demonstrated the difficulty he had in raising it only a couple inches.

"We need ropes," Annja said. She directed the flashlight up at the ceiling. There, almost hidden in the shadows, an iron ring was pounded into the ceiling. If it had been found in the past, it might have been mistaken for use with heavy supply loads.

"Get the ropes," Lesauvage ordered. He grinned at Annja. "Very good, Miss Creed."

MINUTES LATER, Annja had tied a harness around the stone oval, then connected that to a double-strand line running through the iron hook mounted in the ceiling. Lesauvage put a team of men on the rope. Together, they pulled and the stone lid slowly lifted from the hole. The sound of running water echoed inside the cave.

Anticipation fired every nerve of Annja's body.

When the lid was clear, Lesauvage walked to the edge of the wolf trap and aimed his flashlight beam. The yellow cone of illumination melted the darkness away.

"What's that sound?" Lesauvage asked.

"Running water," Annja said. "There's probably a stream or groundwater running down there. Like I said, the soldiers would have wanted a steady supply of freshwater."

"How far down?"

Holding her flashlight, Annja climbed down into the wolf pit. She shone the light around and spotted rusty iron handles covered with fungus set into the wall.

"Do you need a rope?" Lesauvage asked.

"No." Annja threw a leg over the edge of the pit and started down. Her boots rang against the iron handles. Three rungs down, one of them snapped off beneath her weight, nearly rusted through.

She almost fell, only hanging on with her hands.

The tunnel walls showed tool marks. Someone had cut through the solid rock into the shallow stream below. Cold air rushed up around Annja, chilling her.

She thought about the tunnel. The Romans, or whoever had constructed it, had known the stream was there. They hadn't drilled blindly through the rock in the hopes of hitting water.

They found it sometime before they decided to dig down to it, Annja realized. And if they found it before they dug down to it, there had to be another entrance.

That gave her hope. She finished the climb and dropped into the stream. The water came up to her calves, but her boots were tall enough to keep her feet dry.

She aimed the flashlight up the stream and down. The tunnel was almost eight feet across and barely five feet in height.

Upstream? Or downstream? She wasn't sure. Her flashlight didn't penetrate far enough to show her much.

A gleam of white suddenly caught her attention. Mired in the dirt and clay that coated the rock, scattered bones lay in disarray.

Enemies? Annja wondered. Or soldiers no one else cared enough to bury?

Amid the death, though, the dull gleam of metal reflected the flashlight beam. She knelt and dragged a hand through the running water, closing her hand on some of the smaller objects she touched.

When she lifted her hand, she held three gold coins and two silver ones. One of the gold ones bore the insignia of the Brotherhood of the Silent Rain.

"Miss Creed?" Lesauvage called.

"I'm here." Annja pocketed the coins and returned to the tunnel. When she looked up, Lesauvage was shining his light into her eyes.

"Well?" he asked.

"I'm coming up. Douse the light."

For a moment Lesauvage hesitated, obviously struggling with whether he wanted to obey.

"Please," Annja called up. "I can't see the rungs."

That near admission of helplessness salved Lesauvage's pride somewhat. "Of course." He moved the light away.

Annja glanced down, trying to will the spots from her vision. Then she noticed a single green leaf riding the stream.

Upstream, she thought, smiling. There's nowhere else that leaf could have come from. She felt certain another opening existed upstream. The storm's fury had probably torn leaves from the trees, and at least one of them had found its way into the cave.

She took hold of the rungs and climbed. At the top, she clambered out of the wolf trap.

"Well?" Lesauvage asked.

Roux and Avery stood near the wolf trap. The young man looked anxious. Roux wore an irritated look, like someone who'd been asked to stay on long after a party had lost its charm.

Annja looked at Roux and spoke in Latin, trusting that for all his hauteur, Lesauvage hadn't learned the spoken language. He might have learned to read bits and pieces, but surely not enough to speak it.

"We can escape down there," she told Roux. "Upstream. Take the boy."

Roux nodded, looking slightly less irritated.

Lesauvage pointed his pistol at Annja's head. "What the hell did you say?"

Without a word, Annja took the coins from her pocket and tossed them to the middle of the stone floor. Enough light existed to catch their golden gleam.

"The treasure's down there." Annja pictured the sword in her mind as she switched off her light and shoved it into her pants pocket. "It's in the stream. You're rich."

Drawn by greed, Lesauvage and his men looked at the coins, swiveling their flashlight beams.

"Now," Annja said in Latin.

Roux grabbed Avery and shoved him toward the hole. The boy yelped in fear and tried to get away, but the old man's strength proved too much for him. Avery disappeared, falling through the wolf trap with Roux on top of him.

Cursing, Lesauvage raised his pistol again. "Kill them!" he shouted.

Annja closed her hand around the sword and pulled.

29

As soon as the sword was in the cave with her, Annja's senses went into overdrive. It was like time slowed down and everyone was moving in slow motion.

She swung the sword, cutting through Lesauvage's pistol before he could fire, hitting the barrel and knocking the weapon off target. When he fired, the yellow-white muzzle-flash flamed in a spherical shape and the bullet ricocheted from the ceiling.

The other men had trouble aiming at her for fear of hitting Lesauvage. She stepped toward him as he tried to point his pistol at her again.

Planting her right foot, Annja pivoted and slammed her left foot into the center of Lesauvage's chest, knocking him back into his men. Machine pistol-chatter filled the cave with a deafening rattle that defied the sonorous cracks of thunder. Ricochets struck sparks from the wall, and two of Lesauvage's men went down with screams of pain.

Annja ran for the wolf trap and dropped to the bottom of the pit. Bullets cut the air over her head and slammed against the stone oval hanging from the ropes.

Reacting instinctively, as if the sword had been part of her for her whole life, Annja swept the blade from her hip and launched it at the double-stranded line.

The sword sailed straight and true through the rope. Stepping over the tunnel's edge, she dropped and landed in the stream below, bending her knees to take the shock.

Lying in the rush of water, Avery and Roux stared at her in surprise.

In the next instant, the ropes parted and the heavy stone oval slammed down onto the tunnel. The fit wasn't exact. Flashlight illumination leaked through the cracks. It was enough to show that Lesauvage's men were wasting no time about pursuit.

"The sword." Roux pushed himself to his feet.

Annja reached into the otherwhere for the weapon and was relieved to find it there. "I've got it," she said.

"Did you get any of their weapons?" Roux asked.

"No."

The old man cursed and shook his head. "At the very least you could have slain one of them and taken his weapons."

"Next time," Annja said. "If you want, you can wait for them down here. They'll probably get that tunnel opened again in a minute. You can get all the weapons you want."

Roux glared at her. "She was never a wiseass."

"I'm not Joan," Annja said. She turned her attention to Avery.

The young man looked as though he was in shock and about to pass out. He cradled his wounded hand in his good one.

"Can you run?" Annja asked.

"I…I think so."

"Upstream," Annja said. "There should be another way out." She took the lead, splashing through the water. She set the flashlight to wide angle.

Behind them they could hear Lesauvage's men wrestling to remove the heavy stone oval.

"What makes you think there's another way out?" Roux asked. "I trust you haven't been here before?"

"I saw a leaf float past me. It came from outside."

"It could have passed through an underwater opening. For all you know, this stream could run for miles underground."

"I hope not." Annja followed the slope up into the heart of the mountain.

The way got tricky and footing was treacherous. There were sinkholes along the way that plunged them up to their chests in near freezing water. They scrambled out and kept going. The rock ran smooth as time and fungus had made it slippery. Again and again, they fell with bruising impacts that left them shaken. They kept moving, certain that Lesauvage and his men would follow.

Annja tried to make sense of the direction they were heading, but she had to give up and acknowledge that they were lost. She listened, but she couldn't tell if they were being pursued.

Maybe not, she thought hopefully. With the treasure right there, Lesauvage wouldn't let anything else stand in his way.

She kept running.

CORVIN LESAUVAGE WAS in heaven. Hanging from the rungs set into the wall, he played his flashlight beam over the treasure that Benoit the Relentless had dumped into the Roman garrison's hiding place all those years ago.

It didn't matter to Lesauvage how Benoit had managed to find the place. Maybe he'd learned of it while searching for La Bête. Or perhaps one of his men had known about it.

The fact was that everyone who knew about it now was dead.

Except for Annja Creed, Avery Moreau and the hard-eyed old man who had accompanied her.

Lesauvage reconciled himself with the knowledge that they wouldn't get down off the mountain in the storm. He wouldn't allow that to happen. If they told the authorities about his ill-gotten gain, it could cause him no end of problems.

He stared at the gleaming precious metals in the glare of his flashlight a moment longer, then he climbed the rungs back up to the cave. His men awaited him.

"We hunt," he declared.

They all grinned and howled in eager anticipation. Quickly, they took up the old Celtic chant he'd taught them in the cave beneath his house. Then they took the special concoction of drugs he'd created, which he told them contained ancient magic. It was mostly speed with a mild hallucinogenic, enough to make them physically able to push themselves past the level of normal human endurance and never know any fear.

Within minutes, they were all high, edgy and ready to explode. Eager to kill.

"They're down there," Lesauvage said, feeling the drug's effects himself. He felt impossibly strong and invincible. Almost godlike. "I want them dead."

Dropping back through the wolf trap, Lesauvage lowered himself into the stream. He didn't know which way to go. Closing his eyes, he tried to sense his prey, but there were no signs of them.

He reached into the water and came up with a gold coin. He laughed a little, feeling the heavy weight of it in his hand. The coin had two sides. One was blank. The other held the symbol of the Brotherhood of the Silent Rain. He designated the insignia "heads" and flipped the coin.

The gold disc whirled in the air. Lesauvage slid a hand under it and looked down at the symbol lying in his palm.

It was heads.

"This way," he told his men. They headed upstream.

Baying and laughing, the Wild Hunt took up the chase.

BROTHER GASPAR STOOD back for a moment while two of the young monks entered the Roman garrison. Cold rain pelted him, a barrage of hostility fueled by nature. He fully expected an exchange of gunfire within the cave at any moment.

Instead, the two monks returned. They were armed with pistols, rifles and swords.

"There is something you should see," one of them said.

Brother Gaspar followed the monks into the cave. He saw the stone oval suspended over the wolf trap at once. Peering down into the hole while another monk pointed his flashlight, Brother Gaspar saw the water and the gold and silver below.

"Benoit's ransom," Brother Gaspar said. "I'd thought it lost forever." He looked up at the young monk. Then he noticed a dead man sprawled on the floor. "Who is that?"

"One of Lesauvage's men."

Brother Gaspar knew that Lesauvage and his men had not left. Their motorcycles were still parked outside. "What happened to him?"

"He was shot," the young monk said. He touched a spot between his own eyes. "He was dead when we got here."

"They're in the tunnel below." Brother Gaspar looked down at the water. "Where does it lead?"

The young monk shook his head. "We've tapped into an underground stream as a well. Perhaps it's another one."

"And perhaps this one leads to the one we use." Brother Gaspar realized that the monastery had been left virtually undefended. He turned from the wolf trap. "Take half of your men into the tunnel. Follow them. The others will return to the monastery with me." He hurried out into the storm, once again hating the secrets that bound him to his life in this horrible place.

The treasure had been found. Did that mean that Father Roger of Falhout's dreadful secret had been discovered, too?

Brother Gaspar lifted his robes and ran as fast as he was able. Nearly 240 years ago, some of the terrible secrets the Vatican had chosen to hide had spilled out. Over a hundred deaths had resulted because of that choice.

How many more lives would be sacrificed to keep the secret?

LIGHTNING FLARED overhead, exploding inside the cave like a light bulb shorting out.

Glancing up, shielding her eyes against the spots that danced in her vision, Annja saw a hole nearly a foot across at the roof of the cave they were in. The hole was almost twenty feet above them.

"There," Roux said, pointing.

"I see it," Annja replied.

Lightning strobed the sky again, igniting another flare that danced across the water swirling at their knees. The water level was rising, and that concerned her. A flash flood would drown them.

"We can't get up there," Roux said, slapping the slab of rock that framed the cave.

Judging from the walls, the cave had been carved by constantly flowing water thousands of years ago. The result was a smooth surface that couldn't be climbed.

"Then we keep going," Annja said. Heading upstream once again, she ran, knowing that Avery Moreau was growing steadily weaker and the flashlight beam was growing more dim.

LESS THAN FIFTEEN minutes later, Annja found the source of the water. A cistern had formed within the mountain. The hollow half bowl collected water in a natural reservoir, but with the current storm, it had exceeded capacity.

However, the thing that drew Annja's attention most was the light that bled through the cracks where the cistern had separated from the cave roof. A waterfall of glistening water poured into the lower cave.

"Light," Roux said.

"I see it." Warily, Annja drew her sword and moved closer.

The light source was stationary, not the flickering randomness of the lightning. And it was pale yellow, not flaring white.

Cautiously, she made her way up the pile of broken rock that had spilled over the cistern's side. Holding the sword in one hand, trying to avoid as much of the water as she could, Annja peered through the crack.

A room lay beyond. It was another cavern actually, but someone had built a low stone dam to help trap the water in the cistern. Plastic five-gallon water containers sat in neat rows beside the dam. Candles burned in sconces on the walls.

"What is it?" Roux asked.

"A room," Annja answered.

"Someone is living there?"

"Several someones from the look of things," Annja answered. The cold was eating into her now. She was beginning to feel as if warmth had never existed.

"Is there a way in?" Roux asked.

Annja tossed him the flashlight. He caught it before it hit the water.

Avery Moreau leaned against the wall nearby. He held his arms wrapped around himself. His teeth chattered and his breath blew out in gray fogs. "He's going to kill us, you know. Lesauvage. He won't let us escape because we know too much."

"Hang in there, Avery," Annja said.

Reluctantly, the young man nodded. He heard her, but he didn't share her hope.

Hefting a large stone block, Annja took a firm hold and swung it at the cistern's edge. The impact sounded like a cannon shot inside the cave.

The third time she slammed the stone into the cistern, the side cracked. Then sections of the cistern tumbled to the cave floor and the stream below. Water deluged Annja, knocking her from her feet.

Roux tramped through the sudden increase in the water level and pinned her with the flashlight beam. "Are you all right?"

"I'm fine." Annja pushed herself to her feet. She was soaked and the cold ate into her like acid.

The broken section of the cistern wall drained most of the water. Annja knew whoever had purposefully created the larger reservoir from the natural one wouldn't be happy with the damage she'd done.

Catching hold of the cistern's edge, she heaved herself up and in. Kneeling, she offered her hand to Avery and pulled him along, then did the same for Roux. She took a candle-powered lantern from a hook on the wall.

Stone steps, shaped from the bones of the mountain, led out of the cistern room. Annja was certain they followed the meanderings of a cave shaft—with occasional sculpting, as testified to by the tool marks on the walls—but there was function and design.

When she waved the lantern close to the steps, she found impressions worn deeply into them.

"Whoever lives here has been here for a long time," she observed.

"It's a monastery," Roux said. His voice echoed in the stairwell.

"What makes you so sure?"

"Can you imagine anyone else living like this? Cloistered. Underground. With only the rudimentary amenities. And you said you didn't know where the Brotherhood of the Silent Rain came from." Roux looked around. "I think you can safely say that you do now."

THREE TURNS LATER, Annja came upon a door to the right. She tried it and found it unlocked.

I guess there's no need to lock doors on a subterranean fortress no one knows about, Annja thought. She followed the door inside.

The cavern was long and quiet. Spiderwebs filled the open spaces of the roof. Rectangular openings in the walls occurred at regular intervals.

Annja held the lantern up high. Another doorway stood at the opposite end of the cave.

"What is this place?" Avery asked. His voice sounded brittle.

"A cemetery," Annja said.

The young man stopped in his tracks. "We shouldn't be in here, should we?"

"No," Annja agreed. "But we are. This could be the shortest route to an exit." She didn't really think so, but there were questions she needed answered. She walked to the closest wall and began examining the coffins.

All of them were crafted of flat stones mortared together in rectangular shapes left hollow for the bodies. Once the dead were interred, the lids were mortared on, as well.

Annja brushed at the thick dust that covered them, searching for identification marks. Near one end of the coffin she was examining, she found a name carved into one of the rocks:

Brother Gustave
1843-1912

"What are you looking for?" Roux joined her in the search, working on the other side.

"Father Roger." Annja moved on to the coffin above the first one she'd inspected.

Rats, no doubt drawn into the caves by the ready supply of food kept on hand by the monks, scattered across the top of the coffin. She didn't want to think about what the rodents would have done to the bodies if they'd gotten inside.

"Who was he?" Roux asked.

"He was head of the monastery in 1767 when it was destroyed." Annja read the next inscription, but it wasn't the one she was looking for, either.

Reluctantly, Avery joined in the search. He approached another wall of coffins tentatively.

"'Roger' isn't exactly a French name," Roux said.

"It's English." Annja went to the next stack and swept dust from it, as well. "He was once Roger of Falhout."

Roux looked at her then. "Wasn't he the man whose heraldry is represented on the lozenge?"

"No. That heraldry belonged to his brother, Sir Henry. And to Sir

Henry's father before him. Roger was Sir Henry's younger brother. One of them, anyway."

"But he wasn't entitled to the heraldry because of the law of primogeniture," Roux said, understanding.

Avery turned to them. "I don't know what that law is."

"Basically," Annja said, moving to the next coffin, "it's a law that keeps the family farm from being split up. Say a man has three sons. Like Sir Henry's father. The eldest son, Sir Henry, inherits all the family lands and titles. At the time, it took a lot of land to field a knight, and knights were the lifeblood of a king's army."

"That's not true anymore," Avery said.

"No, but it was when Father Roger was around." Annja frightened away another rat and read the next inscription. "Fathers had to have a system to keep brothers from fighting over the lands. So a simple method was devised. The first son inherited the land. The second son was given to the military. The third son was given to the church."

"And if there were more?"

"They were apprenticed to master craftsmen as best as could be done," Annja said.

"Roger was a third-born son," Roux said.

"Right," Annja agreed. "He was given to the church."

"Which wasn't without its own problems," Roux said. "England had fought the Roman influence for six hundred years before the Anglican Church was declared."

"Henry VIII closed the Roman Catholic abbeys and monasteries during his reign," Annja added, "and supported the Anglican Church. Father Roger, as evidenced by his presence here, was Roman Catholic."

"Why did they send him here?" Roux asked.

"As punishment."

"For what?"

"I think he fathered Carolyn. The girl who was born while Sir Richard of Kirkland was over in the New World fighting the French and the Indians."

"What makes you think that?"

"Why else would the Falhout family heraldry be on the lozenge?"

Roux had no answer.

30

"I think the Roman Catholic Church found out about Father Roger's indiscretion with Sir Richard of Kirkland's wife," Annja went on. "And once they did, I think the Vatican shipped Father Roger here before the affair caused any further problems in London."

"Such as Sir Richard coming home and killing him?" Roux suggested.

"Yes. King George III would have backed one of his knights in such a matter, and the Roman Catholic Church could have lost even more ground in England. They'd already lost a lot by that time."

"So it was better to hide the problem than to deal with it," Roux said.

"Hiding the problem *was* dealing with it. But I think they had more to hide than they'd originally believed." Annja moved to the next stone coffin. "They also had Carolyn to hide."

"The child?"

Annja nodded. "The daughter of Father Roger and Sir Richard's wife. Some of the reports I read suggest that she showed signs of inbreeding, but I believe that was a cover-up, an attempt to point the blame elsewhere. I think Carolyn's condition was caused by something worse than inbreeding."

"What?" Roux dusted off another coffin.

"Have you heard of Proteus Syndrome?"

"The disfigurement that created the Elephant Man?"

"Yes. Joseph Merrick's X-rays and CT scans were examined by a radiologist who determined that the disease was Proteus Syndrome."

Roux turned and faced her. "You think Carolyn had Proteus Syndrome?"

"Yes. More than that, I think she was La Bête." All the pieces came together in Annja's mind. She was certain she had most of it now. "I saw that creature in the cave where I found the charm. It looked almost human. At least, aspects of it did."

"But Proteus Syndrome is debilitating and life-threatening," Roux argued. "It creates massive tissue growth. Merrick's head was too misshapen and too heavy for his body. He died at twenty-seven, strangled by the weight of his own head."

"Does Proteus Syndrome always have to present negatively?" Annja asked. "Couldn't it sometimes be an unexpected change and growth that makes a person stronger?" She looked at Roux. "I saw all those pieces of this sword become one again. I think that's harder to believe than my suggestion about Proteus Syndrome."

"You believe the disease turned her into an animal?"

Annja took a deep breath. "We'll never know if it was her condition or the treatment she received as a result of it. That's an argument for the nature-versus-nurture people. Sir Richard disowned Carolyn and cast her from his house. Her mother never visited her in the abbey. And the nuns—" She shook her head, thinking about the afflicted child. Sometimes things hadn't been easy in the orphanage where she'd grown up, but the conditions had to have been a lot better than in the eighteenth century. "The nuns couldn't have known how to treat her or what to do."

"They would have believed she was demon spawn," Roux said quietly. He shrugged. "In those days, the church believed everything, and everyone, who was different was demon spawn."

Annja silently agreed.

"Carolyn killed the sisters in the abbey where she was first kept," Roux said. "You have to wonder what triggered that, but I'm afraid I could hazard a guess. The human mind has its breaking points."

Annja was surprised. She hadn't known the old man had been truly listening to her while she'd pursued the truth. "Yes. Then they faked her death and shipped her here."

"To be with her father."

"Yes."

"As further punishment?"

Shaking her head, Annja said, "I think Father Roger wouldn't allow any harm to come to his daughter. He forced the church to send her here."

"How did he do that?"

"I don't know. I only know that he must have. Otherwise she wouldn't have been here." Annja moved on to the next coffin. "Once here, Carolyn must have grown bigger, stronger *and* more intelligent. Or possibly she was always intelligent. Either way, she learned to escape from the monastery."

"She was La Bête," Roux said, understanding.

"I believe so. If you look at those pictures I took of the corpse in the cave where I found the charm, you can see the misshapen limbs and body. Proteus Syndrome didn't occur to me then, but it did later."

They kept searching.

"Here it is, then." Avery brushed layers of dust from a stone coffin. Joining him, Annja held her candle lantern closer to the inscription.

Father Roger
1713-1767
Cursed by God
Condemned by Believers

Below the inscription was a carving of the standing stag that matched the one on the charm. Annja placed the candle lantern on the coffin and brushed at the dust, exposing the top to see if there were any more inscriptions.

Emotions swirled within her. There was excitement, of course. There always was when she made a discovery. But it was bittersweet this time. She couldn't help thinking about the innocent child afflicted with a disease no one had understood or even known existed at the time.

"The grave diggers always get the last word," Roux said. "Not very generous, were they?"

"Or very forgiving," Annja agreed quietly.

"He was a sinner," a strong voice filled with accusation announced.

Annja spun, summoning the sword as she turned. Light splintered along the sharp blade.

A man in his sixties stood in the doorway. He was wearing monk's robes. A dozen more flanked him.

"I suppose," Roux whispered, "in retrospect we truly should have posted a lookout to keep watch."

"Next time," Annja promised.

"More than merely being a sinner, though," the old monk said, "Father Roger was an embarrassment to the Vatican. They had empowered him to act on their behalf in London. England had already stepped away from much of the Roman Catholic Church's auspices. News of Father Roger's perfidies would have made things even worse. You were wondering how he got his bestial child transferred here when by all rights she should have been taken out and euthanized."

"I was," Annja admitted.

The monk stepped into the mausoleum. The other monks followed. Light from their lanterns and flashlights filled the arched cavern.

"Father Roger wrote out a document detailing his transgressions," the monk stated. "He admitted to carrying on with a married woman and fathering a child by her." He shook his head. "It was more than the Vatican wished to deal with. Sir Richard of Kirkland, the cuckolded husband, and Sir Henry, Father Roger's brother, were landed gentry. Men who were important to the king."

"The Vatican didn't want to run the risk of the king's wrath," Annja said.

"That's correct. Neither of the knights knew the truth of the child's heritage. Sir Henry would not have accepted his brother's expulsion from the church. So the decision was made to bring Father Roger to the Brotherhood of the Silent Rain. He could have lived out the rest of his days making books. Instead, he saw to sowing the seeds of his own doom by blackmailing the church into bringing that dreadful creature here."

"Who are you?" Annja asked.

"I am Brother Gaspar," the old monk said. "One of the last of those who safeguard the secrets that nearly escaped our monastery all those years ago."

"Looking back on things," Annja said, "with over a hundred people dead, I'd say your 'secret' got out on a regular basis."

"Regrettable, but true," Brother Gaspar said. "If I had been leader of the order at that time, Father Roger's child would not have escaped."

"Would you have killed Carolyn?" Annja demanded.

The old monk's answer came without hesitation. "Yes."

"She was a child," Annja protested. "Children aren't born evil."

"By all accounts, she was a child of the devil allowed entrance into this world by the sin committed by her mother and father. She was a murderess and a monster." Fire glinted in the old monk's eyes. "Don't you dare try to tell me what she was. All of my order since that time have lived our lives in darkness here within this mountain because of her and her blasphemous father."

"Why did you stay here after the monastery was torn down?" That was the only part Annja hadn't been able to resolve.

"That's none of your business," Brother Gaspar snapped.

"Father Roger left his record," Roux announced. He looked at Annja. "That has to be the answer, of course. No one at the monastery would hear his confession. Or if they would, perhaps he thought it wouldn't matter. No one here worried about Father Roger's eternal soul. In their eyes he was already damned to hell."

"Is that it?" Annja asked. "Is that why you people have been stuck here?"

For a moment, she didn't think Brother Gaspar was going to answer.

"Unfortunately, that's true. One of the documents, his confession, was found at the time of his death. He died during the destruction of the monastery. It wasn't until later that the document was found among his papers."

"I don't see the problem," Annja said.

Brother Gaspar shook his head. "It was clearly marked as the second copy." He shrugged. "I think it was habit for Father Roger to number his copies. The monastery worked on books here. Handwritten and illuminated. We still do. It's a habit to number all versions."

"For all these years that the monastery has gone underground, you've been searching for the original copy?" Annja asked.

"Yes. We won't be permitted to leave this place until we have secured that copy. Or confirmed its destruction." Looking at her, Brother Gaspar lifted an eyebrow. "You have been so clever so far, Miss Creed. Finding the lost treasure. Finding this place when it has been secret for all these years. Figuring out the truth of La Bête. Locating the charm that Father Roger wore. I would have hoped you could divine where Father Roger's missing documents were."

"Father Roger wore the charm?"

"Before Benoit took it, yes." Brother Gaspar paused. "I'd heard Benoit took Father Roger's charm and fashioned it into a map of sorts."

"He did."

"No one at the monastery ever saw it. We thought it lost forever."

"It was around the neck of the man who killed La Bête. Carolyn."

"Was it?" That appeared to surprise the old monk. "You have been quite resourceful."

"I'm good at what I do," Annja said.

"On any other subject," Brother Gaspar said, "I would probably offer you accolades on your diligence and devotion to your craft. I would warn you about putting other pursuits ahead of God, but I would congratulate you." He paused. "Unfortunately, all I can show you for your endeavor is imprisonment."

"What?" Avery exploded. "We've done nothing wrong! The treasure is still where we found it! We only came here because we were trying to escape Lesauvage!"

"But you know too much," Brother Gaspar explained patiently. "I can't afford to let you leave."

At his signal, the monks lifted their weapons and took deliberate aim.

Annja looked over her shoulder at the other door. Three monks stood there with pistols and swords. Cowls shadowed their faces.

"Now," Brother Gaspar said, "your choice is to come willingly…or be shot and interred in this mausoleum. Which will it be?"

Avery looked at Annja. Fear widened his eyes.

"Easy," she said. "Roux?"

"I have him," Roux stated quietly.

"The sword, Miss Creed," Brother Gaspar commanded. "Throw it down, and any other weapons you might have, or we'll take them from your lifeless bodies."

After a momentary hesitation, Annja lowered the sword to the mausoleum floor and slid it across. The weapon stopped in the center of the room.

"Very good," Brother Gaspar said. "Now—"

Hoarse shouts cut off the old monk. Sharp bursts of gunfire followed. One of the monks standing out in the hallway twisted and went down, his face ripped to bloody shreds.

"Kill them!" Corvin Lesauvage shouted out in the hallway. "Kill them all!"

"Roux!" Annja yelled as she turned toward the other door. She reached for the sword and suddenly the intervening twenty feet were no longer there; the sword was in her hand.

Launching herself forward, Annja slashed the sword across two of the assault rifles. The impacts knocked the weapons from the hands of the men.

The third man aimed his weapon and pulled the trigger.

Annja went low, just under the stream of bullets that hammered the stone floor and threw splinters and fragments in all directions. She swept the man's feet out from under him in a baseball slide that tangled them both up for a moment. Before the man could recover, Annja slammed the sword hilt into the side of his head. His eyes turned glassy and he sagged into unconsciousness.

Rolling to her feet, Annja avoided one man's outstretched arms, then popped up with a forearm that caught him under the jawline. He flew back against the stone wall and collapsed.

The third man drew a long knife and sprang at her. Annja fisted his robe and fell backward, planting a foot into his stomach and tossing him back into the center of the mausoleum.

Rolling to her feet again, Annja saw Roux shove Avery Moreau out into the hallway, then bend down to slide a pistol from one of the monk's robes. After he tossed the weapon to Annja, he took another pistol and an assault rifle for himself. He palmed as many magazines as he could find for the weapons and shoved them into his pockets.

Annja headed into the hallway as Brother Gaspar and the monks fled their positions and flooded toward them. Bullets slapped the cave walls and ricocheted overhead, filling the air like an angry swarm of bees.

Roux knelt like a seasoned infantryman and aimed his assault rifle low. He fired mercilessly. Bullets chopped into the wave of fleeing monks, turning the middle of the mausoleum into a deadly no-man's-land. As flashlights and lanterns hit the ground, the illumination was extinguished and the room turned dark.

Peering around the corner of the doorway, Annja spotted Lesauvage and his men racing into the mausoleum. Most of the monks were down. Brother Gaspar lay draped over one of the stone coffins, dead or dying.

Lesauvage laughed like a madman and strode through the large room as if he were invincible. Bullets had smashed two of the coffins open and the withered bodies inside had spilled onto the blood-stained floor.

Roux withdrew. He released the magazine from the assault rifle and shoved another one into place.

"Go," he told Annja. "We can't stay here."

Annja turned. She realized then that she'd left her candle lantern on one of the coffins. Thankfully the hallway was lit. She held the pistol in her left hand and the sword in her right. She pushed her left hand against the small of Avery Moreau's back, urging him into motion.

"Run," she said. "As fast as you can."

The young man ran and Annja passed him, taking the lead. The hallway twisted and turned. She tried to keep a mental map going in her mind but quickly grew uncertain.

The footfalls of Lesauvage and his men thundered through the cave tunnels in pursuit.

THE DRUG COCKTAIL BLAZED hotly within Corvin Lesauvage. He strode through the mausoleum and looked at the dead monks lying around the cave.

A few of his men were down, as well. Two of them were dead. Another sat holding an arm across his midsection trying to keep his intestines from spilling out.

"Damn!" the young man said. "Look at this!" He gazed at his bloody guts shifting inside his embrace. "This can't be all me!" He threw his head back and howled with laughter, as if it were the funniest thing he'd ever seen. "Somebody help me!"

Lesauvage walked over to the man and gazed down at him coldly. "You're dying," he said.

"I know!" The man laughed again, but tears skidded down his face.

Taking deliberate aim, Lesauvage squeezed the trigger and put a round into the man's mouth. It took him nearly a minute to wheeze and choke to death on his blood. The death wasn't as merciful as Lesauvage had intended.

Still, it was finished.

"What did you do?" another man asked.

"He was dying," Lesauvage explained.

Several of the men were in the process of tearing open the stone coffins. Corpses littered the mausoleum.

Lesauvage fired a round into the ceiling. The detonation drew everyone's attention.

"They were monks!" Lesauvage roared. "They won't be buried with anything worth the time it takes to bust open those coffins!" He waved his pistol. "Find the woman! We don't need a witness to talk about what we've done here!"

Howling with gleeful anticipation, the Wild Hunt once more took up the chase, pounding through the doorway where Annja Creed had fled.

31

Annja's breath tore hotly through her lungs as she ran up the next flight of stairs. Halting at the top of the stairs, she took up a position by the opening, listened intently for a moment, then realized she couldn't hear anything over the sounds of the Wild Hunt closing in on them.

She whirled around the opening and dropped the pistol out before her. She held her sword arm braced under her gun wrist.

The next cave was a library. Books lined handmade shelves mixed with plastic modular shelves. Furniture consisted of large pillows and tent chairs. Candelabras heavy with partially burned candles and bowls of wax occupied tables in the cave.

Life as a monk of the Brotherhood of the Silent Rain hadn't been easy.

Curiosity pulled at Annja's attention. She couldn't help wondering what kind of books were on those shelves. Copies of books from around the world wouldn't have interested her as much as personal journals and collections of observations during the past few hundred years.

"Annja."

Roux's voice drew her from her reverie. She glanced behind her and found that Avery and Roux hadn't joined her. Turning back to the stairway carved in the sloping tunnel floor, she looked down and saw them huddled on the last landing. Men's laughter and threats cascaded around them like breakers from an approaching storm front.

"I can't…do it," Avery wheezed, shaking his head. He doubled over and retched. "I can't…breathe…can't run… no more."

Roux didn't look very good, either, but he was still moving.

"If you stay here, boy," the old man said. "They'll kill you."

"I…*can't!*" Avery doubled over and retched again.

The voices grew louder.

Running down the steps, Annja shoved the pistol into her waistband at her back, then grabbed Avery and threw him across her shoulders in a fireman's carry. She'd thought she'd barely be able to move with the extra weight. Instead, Avery felt light as a child.

"You can't carry him," Roux objected.

"I can't *leave* him," Annja responded. Holding her free arm over his arm and leg, she started up the steps. She expected her body to protest. Instead, it seemed to welcome the challenge.

She turned the corner at the library, then rushed through the doorway on the other side. Another flight of steps awaited her. She went up, hoping that the entrance to the monastery was in that direction.

She was just starting to breathe harder. She was surprised by the strength, stamina and speed that she had—even while carrying Avery Moreau. Where had it come from? The sword?

Or had the sword only awakened something within her?

Annja put the questions out of her mind and concentrated on escape. If she survived, maybe she could figure out what it all meant.

Like the Roman garrison cave, the entrance to the main chamber used by the Brotherhood of the Silent Rain was narrow. Once they reached it, she had to put Avery on his feet and shove him ahead of her.

A faux wall covered the opening. Latches held it in place.

Annja opened the door.

Beyond, the storm continued with renewed fury. Gray rain ghosted across the mountain in sheets as neatly as marching soldiers. Annja felt the chill of the rain even before she stepped out into it.

"Which way?" Avery asked, holding his arms across his body.

Roux played the flashlight around. The ground was stone. No path existed.

Of course there's no path, Annja thought. They'd have to be careful about their comings and goings. They couldn't afford to be seen.

"Down," Annja said.

Roux took the lead, making his way as fast as he dared. The yellow beam of the flashlight revealed the weakening batteries.

Avery followed, hunched over and moving more slowly.

We're not going to make it, Annja thought grimly. The certainty almost made her sick. She'd come all this way, solved most of the puzzles that were presented, and she was going to die inches short of the finish line.

Lightning flared, filling the sky with white-hot incandescence.

Below, not more than a hundred yards away, a road ran down the mountain. Even as Annja recognized it, she spotted five motorcycles speeding into view. Another blaze lit the night. Annja knew the men were after them.

At that moment, they saw Roux and Avery.

The motorcyclists pulled up short and unlimbered assault rifles, pulling them quickly to their shoulders.

"Roux!" Annja yelled.

The old man looked up and saw her standing on the mountainside. Then he saw the motorcycles. He reacted instantly, grabbing Avery and pulling him to ground behind a copse of trees and boulders.

The motorcycle riders howled like beasts. Rain and shadows turned their faces into those of snarling animals. They brought the rifles around in her direction.

Annja ran, hoping she could keep her footing, and plunged toward the brush to her right. Bullets ripped after her, tearing through the leaves and branches.

Knowing if she stopped she was only going to be pinned down, then attacked from above and below as Lesauvage and the rest of his men emerged from the monastery, Annja kept moving. She threw herself through the brush, heart hammering inside her chest. She knew she was moving fast; everything was in slow motion around her again.

She tripped over a loose rock and fell, sliding through the brush at least ten yards on the wet surface before she could roll to her feet. She steadied, whipping through branches and plants, skidding across loose rock.

One of the motorcycle riders pitched sideways, knocked down by rounds from Roux's rifle.

Ten yards out, almost running into a hail of gunfire from the other riders, Annja ran up onto a boulder, took two steps across it and launched herself into the air, hoping that the dark night and the rain would help hide her. She flipped, drawing the sword, then spreading her arms out to her sides to help maintain her balance while keeping her feet together.

Lightning blazed overhead and tore away the darkness.

Annja knew the men saw her as she fell toward them. Their faces filled with awe and fear.

"An angel!" one of them cried. "An angel with a sword!"

It was the drugs, Annja knew. They'd caused the man's hallucination and preyed on his fear.

She landed among them. She swept the sword out, cutting a diagonal slash through one man's weapon as he fired. The rifle blew up in his face and threw him backward.

Moving forward, Annja kicked the next motorcycle's handlebars, sending it crashing into the one beside it, taking down both riders.

The fourth man fired, missing Annja by inches as she whirled. She lashed out with the sword again, turning it so the flat of the blade caught the man along the temple and knocked him out.

I won't kill them, she told herself. Not unless I have to. Somehow that thought made a difference.

The fifth man dodged back, then dropped like a puppet with its strings cut. He hit the ground and rolled onto his back. A bullet from Roux's stolen rifle had torn out his throat. His chest jerked spasmodically twice, then he went slack.

Move, Annja told herself. Don't think about him. Deal with it later. Get everybody out safe now.

Annja grabbed the nearest motorcycle and pushed it upright. When she pulled in the clutch and touched the electronic ignition, the engine grumbled to life.

Roux ran toward her, dragging Avery after him.

"You could have gotten yourself killed with a damned fool stunt like that," the old man shouted.

"It worked," Annja replied. "There wasn't a lot of time. There still isn't." She pushed the motorcycle toward him. "Can you ride?"

"Yes. You live five hundred years, you learn a few things." Roux reloaded the assault rifle and slung it over his shoulder. Then he threw a leg over the motorcycle and climbed aboard. He glanced at Avery. "Can you ride, boy?"

"No." Avery looked like a drowned rat.

Roux sighed. "This mountain is going to be difficult at best. Carrying double is foolish." Then he shook his head. "I'm getting foolish in my dotage. Climb on, boy."

"Thank you." Avery climbed on back of the motorcycle.

"Get a good grip," Roux told him.

For just a moment, Annja couldn't help but think about Garin's story, about how his father had sent him off on horseback with Roux all those years ago. There was something paternal about Roux that she hadn't seen before.

"Here." Annja clapped a helmet on Avery's head that she'd taken from one of Lesauvage's riders.

Roux looked at her. "Can you ride one of these mechanical nightmares?"

Annja smiled at him, seeing the concern in those electric-blue eyes. "Yeah," she said. "I can. Probably better than you can."

Roux harrumphed his displeasure. "Well don't get overconfident and get yourself killed. There are still things we should talk about."

Lightning threw crooked white veins across the troubled sky. Movement along the ridge higher up caught Annja's attention.

Lesauvage and the survivors of his group fanned out along the mountainside.

"Go," Annja said.

Roux revved the motorcycle's engine and took off. Clutching him tightly, Avery hung on. Bullets raked the stones and the muddy earth where the motorcycle had been.

Taking advantage of the distraction Roux's escape afforded her, Annja retreated to another of the motorcycles. She righted it, started the engine and threw a leg over while it started forward. She stood on the pegs, cushioning the rough terrain and muscling the motorcycle to keep it upright in the mud and on the slick stone surfaces exposed between the earth and vegetation. She focused on Roux, spotting his headlight and following it along the trail.

Because he was riding double, Roux struggled with the motorcycle. Avery had no aptitude for riding. He swayed wrong or stayed straight up as Roux handled the motorcycle, creating even more difficulty.

Glancing over her shoulder, Annja saw that Lesauvage and two other men had recovered the three remaining motorcycles. They sped along in pursuit, closing the distance quickly.

We're not going to make it, Annja realized. Between the storm and Avery, we can't escape. She cursed herself for not disabling the other motorcycles, then realized that she'd only been thinking forward, not backward.

When Roux disappeared in front of her for just a moment, a desperate plan formed. Annja crested the hill Roux had just passed over, then switched off her motorcycle and ran it into the brush off the trail into the shadows. The droning engines of the pursuit motorcycles filled her ears.

She waited nervously. She breathed deep, blinking the rain from her eyes, concentrating on what she had to do. Reaching behind her, she removed the pistol from her waistband and waited.

The three motorcycles whipped by, never spotting her in the darkness.

Coolly, Annja lifted the pistol and fired at the last motorcycle's back tire, placing her shots just below the flaring ruby taillight. On the fifth or sixth shot, the rear tire blew.

Slewing out of control, the motorcycle went down in a skidding heap, shedding the rider and pieces of the fenders and body.

The pistol blew back empty. Out of ammunition, Annja tossed the weapon away. Then she pressed the electronic ignition and the engine roared to life as her headlight came on. She twisted the accelerator and let out the clutch so fast she almost lost the motorcycle.

She was speeding along the trail, standing on the pegs again as she slitted her eyes against the rain. Her face stung and her vision occasionally blurred, but she held the motorcycle to the course. She gained ground quickly, but knew she was going to arrive too late when she saw Roux lose the motorcycle. Roux and Avery tumbled across the ground, trying to get up even as Lesauvage and the remaining rider bore down on them.

Roux stood but appeared dazed. Avery didn't get up.

Lesauvage and the other rider roared past them and came around in tight turns, putting their motorcycles between Roux and the one he'd lost.

Roux fumbled for the assault rifle draped over his shoulder. Somehow he'd managed to hang on to it.

Lesauvage pulled his pistol from his shoulder holster and took aim. At that distance, there was no way he could miss.

"Lesauvage!" Annja screamed.

The other rider raised his assault rifle, bringing it up on a sling.

Annja hit the same rise that had dumped Roux and Avery. But she twisted the accelerator, gaining speed, then yanked back on the handlebars.

The motorcycle went airborne. Throwing her body sideways, Annja turned it with her, performing a tabletop aerial maneuver she'd seen on X Games.

Not wanting to be trapped under the weight of the motorcycle, Annja released it and kicked free of the pegs. The motorcycle rider dodged to one side as her bike crashed into his and they bounced away in a rolling mass that exploded into flames.

Annja landed hard on the ground. Out of breath, her lungs feeling paralyzed by the impact, she managed to push herself to her feet.

The motorcycle rider rose up on his knees, cursing foully. He pulled the assault rifle to his shoulder.

Without thinking, Annja summoned the sword and threw it.

Glittering in the sudden flare of lightning, the sword seemed to catch fire as it looped end over end. It struck the gunman full in the chest, driving him backward, his heart pierced by the blade.

For a moment, everything was frozen.

Lesauvage stared at the dead man in disbelief. Then he started laughing. "That was stupid!" he roared. "You threw away your weapon!"

From more than thirty feet away, Annja reached for the sword. It faded from sight where it still quivered in the dead man's chest.

The sword was in her hand.

The confidence drained from Lesauvage's features. He lifted his pistol and took a two-handed grip on it.

Annja rose, knowing it would do no good to run. He would only shoot her in the back. She held the sword in front of her, the blade bisecting her vision, her left foot in front of her right.

She thought about Joan of Arc dying on the pyre. Annja didn't want to die, but if she were going to and she couldn't die old and famous and in her bed with a man she loved, this was how she wanted it to happen, looking death in the eye.

"You brought a sword to a gun fight," Lesauvage sneered. He fired.

Annja saw the muzzle-flash rush from the pistol barrel. She even believed she saw the bullet streaking toward her, knowing there was no way it was going to miss her. She waited to feel it bite into her flesh.

But her hands moved instinctively, tracking the projectile. Incredibly, she saw sparks as the bullet hit the sword, felt the vibration race through her hands, then heard the bullet whiz within inches of her ear.

Annja was already moving toward Lesauvage instead of away from him. She threw herself into a flying kick, sailing above Lesauvage's next round, then lashing out with her left foot when she came within range.

The kick drove Lesauvage from his feet, knocking him backward. He lost the pistol before he slammed against the boulder behind him.

When Annja stood, she held the sword to Lesauvage's throat.

He stared at her over the blade as lightning blazed and burnished the steel. The sound of the rain drowned out everything but the hoarse rasp of their breathing.

"Kill him," Roux directed, limping up. Blood threaded down the side of his face, diluted by the rain.

"I can't," Annja said. She couldn't even imagine taking a man's life in cold blood.

"He would have killed you."

"He didn't."

"He tried to kill you."

Annja trembled slightly. "That wouldn't make killing him right."

Roux grinned and shook his head. "I hate moral complications. Wars and battle should be so much simpler." He bent down and picked up Lesauvage's pistol, taking time to wipe the mud from it. "You have to realize that you've made an enemy here."

"Like you did with Garin?"

"No, that's different," Roux said. "Garin made an enemy of me. If he had the chance to kill me, I truly think he would." He nodded toward Lesauvage. "This one, if he gets the chance, will kill you someday."

Annja lowered her sword and stepped back. She glared at Roux. "I'm not a murderer."

"There are," Roux said, "worse things to be." He shot Lesauvage between the eyes.

Lesauvage pitched forward onto his face. The back of his head was blown off.

"Thankfully," Roux continued as if he hadn't a care in the world, "I'm none of those things."

Annja wheeled on him, looking at him and realizing that she didn't know him, and certainly didn't know what he was capable of. She held her sword ready.

Roux tossed the pistol away and spread his arms, leaving his chest open to her attack. He smiled benignly. "Lesauvage still has other drug-crazed fools in the mountains tonight. Do you want to argue about this right now?"

Annja knew he was right. They still had to escape. "No," she said in a hard voice. "But we *will* talk about this at a later date."

"I look forward to it," Roux said. "There's a lot you're going to have to learn. If you want to survive your destiny."

Ignoring him, Annja turned back to the two surviving motorcycles. Avery Moreau sat huddled in a ball and looked consumed with fear.

She righted one of the motorcycles, threw a leg over, started it and looked back at the young man. "Come on. Let's get you safe."

Slowly, Avery climbed onto the motorcycle with her. He wrapped his mud-covered arms around her, shaking with terror as he held on.

Annja didn't wait to see if Roux could manage. Even though he was limping and banged up, she felt certain the old man could fend for himself. She accelerated and raced down the mountain, hoping to get out of the cold and the wet soon.

Epilogue

Annja Creed swam with an easy stroke. As soon as her feet touched the sandy bottom, she stood and walked out of the ocean. She was conscious of dozens of male spectators watching her, maybe wishing she'd gone topless instead of wearing the bright red bikini she had on, and for a moment she luxuriated in the harmless attention.

She crossed the beach, basking in the heat after the cool of the sea, knowing that her tan was unblemished by scratches or bruises. She had healed quickly from her minor injuries.

Annja thought the sword had somehow enhanced her, but Roux didn't believe that was true. He wished she knew who her parents were. But if anyone had ever known, all that information had been lost when New Orleans drowned during the hurricane in 2005.

Roux was sitting in a chaise longue near hers when she returned to her seat. A large, colorful umbrella shaded both chairs.

"Enjoying the afternoon?" Roux asked.

"Yes." Annja wrapped a towel around her waist and sat. "There's not much of it left."

"Ah, well," Roux said. "That only means the evening and all the nightlife won't be far behind."

"I'm not much for nightlife," Annja said. "I prefer quiet places and just a few people." She gazed at the crowd scattered along the oceanfront. "Personally, I could do with a more secluded beach."

"I know of several good ones," Roux said. "I'd be happy to take you there sometime."

Annja slipped on her sunglasses and regarded the old man warily. They had talked a little about Roux's murder of Corvin Lesauvage. At best, though, they'd agreed to disagree. Roux had ultimately decided that she didn't have to kill anyone she didn't want to kill, and he didn't have to spare anyone he didn't want to let live. Under the circumstances, and since Roux pointed out that he'd lived in such a manner for centuries, she had shelved the argument.

"Would you?" Annja asked.

"Well," Roux said, "not right away. I'm going to be playing poker soon. I'm not about to give that up." He took a cigar from his jacket and lit up. "Have you given any thought to staying for a while?"

"I have." For the past three days, while waiting anxiously to see how the events that had happened up in the Cévennes would touch her, Annja had slept, read and swam, hardly leaving the spacious hotel suite Roux had arranged for her.

"And?"

"I'll spend some time," Annja said.

"Splendid," Roux enthused.

"A short while."

"Good. Because I don't want you underfoot while I'm playing poker."

"Have you heard from Garin?" she asked.

"No, but I still check for traps routinely." Roux patted the arms of the chair. "And I suddenly realize this isn't really a good place to be if he's hired an assassin."

"Maybe Garin doesn't really want you dead as much as he claims."

"Truthfully," Roux said, "I think the sword being reassembled has him spooked. He probably wants it destroyed more than he wants me dead. At least for now. Until he discovers whether the sword's reemergence is going to have an effect on him. If it does, who else is he going to talk to about it?"

A server passed by and Roux ordered drinks. In short order, they were delivered.

"Thank you," Annja said, lifting her glass.

"My pleasure."

Annja sipped, enjoying the cool, clean taste of the fruit and alcohol. With the wind skating under the umbrella and the sand warm around her, the mountain seemed very far away.

"Did you arrange for an attorney for Avery Moreau?" she asked.

"I did. I understand Inspector Richelieu is about to be temporarily suspended while an investigation into the death of Avery's father is conducted."

"What about Avery?"

Roux shrugged. "I don't know. Even after all these years, I still find that I can't judge people well. They constantly surprise you."

Annja silently agreed with that. Life was full of surprises. She sipped her drink again and smiled. "I've been thinking about Father Roger's confession. The one that he threatened the Vatican with."

"And?"

"I think I know where it is."

Roux shook his head. "I'm quite certain it doesn't exist."

Annja sipped her drink again and remained silent.

After a while, Roux's curiosity got the better of him. "Enough with the mystery. Tell me what you think."

"Are you sure you want to hear? I mean, you do think you're right."

"Of course I do. But I'm willing to entertain a possibility of it being somewhere else."

"It's in Carolyn's grave."

"Where you found the last piece of the sword?" Roux asked.

"No," Annja said. "In the false grave she was given in England. In Sir Richard of Kirkland's holdings. Or whoever has them now. I think he hid the truth in a lie."

Roux smiled. "If he did, that was very clever."

"There's only one way to find out."

"Does it look like there's a bit of grave robbing in your future?"

"No," Annja replied. "I thought maybe you, using some of your money and influence, could arrange for an exhumation of Carolyn's grave in England."

"So you could broadcast it on that tawdry television show you do pieces for?"

"I thought about that, actually. I mean, I could propose a whole new possibility about who and what the Beast of Gévaudan was. It could be a good move."

"Yet you're undecided about doing it," Roux said.

"No, I'm decided. I'm not giving this story to *Chasing History's Monsters*. Though it is tempting to allow Father Roger his final jab at the Vatican."

"The man did break his faith with God and the church," Roux pointed out. "Not to mention disrupting a marriage."

"I think he was punished enough for that. So was Carolyn."

Roux nodded. "You're probably right." He smoked his cigar for a time and they sat in silence.

Annja sipped her drink and studied the foaming white curlers rushing in from the sea. "What am I supposed to do with the sword?" she asked.

"What do you mean? It's your sword now. You do with it whatever you wish to do with it," Roux stated.

"But shouldn't I do something special with it? Become—I don't know—*something?*"

Roux looked at her seriously. "Annja Creed, you are someone special. The sword only allows you to act on your natural gifts with more authority. You have a destiny ahead of you that no one in this world has ever had. You've not been given the sword to be another Joan of Arc. She did what she had to do." He paused. "You have to figure out what it is you're supposed to do like everyone else, one day at a time."

Annja looked at him and felt he was telling the truth. Roux had lied about things in the past and would again in the future, but she knew he wasn't lying now.

"Thank you," she said. She moved the umbrella and lay back in the warm sun. She thought about everything she should be doing—

all the cataloging of the things in her loft, the certificates of authenticity she had to do, the trip she wanted to take to North Africa, the next story she'd have to pitch to Doug Morrell—and somewhere in there, she dropped off to sleep.

Her destiny stretched out before her. There was no need to rush to meet it. It was waiting for her.

SOLOMON'S JAR

1

On long tanned legs Annja Creed ran through the hardwood forest. Rays from the sun hanging precariously above the great mountains slanted like pale gold lances at random between the boles. They caressed her sweaty face like velvet gloves as she ran through them.

Despite sweating in the heat, she breathed normally, dodging thicker stands of brush, crashing through the thinner ones. Late-season insects trilled around her and in sporadic spectral clouds tried to fly up her nose and into her mouth. The birds chattered and called to one another in the trees. The woods smelled of green growth and mostly dried decayed vegetation, not at all the way she imagined a true rain forest might smell, lower down in the Amazon basin proper. Up in the watershed of the Amazon's tributary the Río Marañón, in eastern Peru, the early autumn was drier and cooler, the growth far less dense.

Her heart raced as much as any person's might have after running at high speed for over two miles, up and down steep ridges. It had little to do with the exertion, though.

She ran for her life.

DAYLIGHT CAME LATE and evening early to the small Peruvian village of Chiriqui. The sun had rolled well past the zenith. Though shadows weren't yet very long, it wasn't far from vanishing behind the tree-furred ridge to the west when the blast of a diesel engine ripped the calm air.

Beyond the ridge loomed the mighty peaks of the Andes themselves, looking close enough to topple and crush the little village into its dusty hillside, their blue tinge hinting how far away they really stood. The hills were mostly covered in patchy grass, dry as the hot Southern Hemisphere summer ended. Stands of hardwood forest rose on some of the heights, interspersed with tough scrub.

Chickens flapped their wings in annoyance and fled squawking as a big blue Dodge Ram 2500, battered and sun faded, rolled into the small plaza in the midst of the collection of a couple of dozen huts. A tethered spider monkey shrilled obscenities and ran up a pole supporting a thatch awning as the vehicle clipped the edge of a kiosk and spilled colorful fruits bouncing across the tan hard-packed dirt. The owner remonstrated loudly as the vehicle stopped in a cloud of exhaust and dust.

Men began bailing out of the truck's extended bed. Men dressed in green-and-dust-colored camouflage who carried unmistakable broken-nosed Kalashnikovs and grenades clipped on their vests like green mango clusters.

They were gringos, unmistakably, who towered over the small brown villagers. The vehicle sported a powerful Soviet-era PKS machine gun mounted on a roll bar right behind the cab.

The people of Chiriqui knew better than to call attention to themselves when such visitors came to town.

"Gather 'round," the apparent leader commanded in clear but *norteamericano*-accented Spanish. He wore a short-sleeved camo blouse, a similarly patterned baseball cap atop his crewcut red head, and carried a black semiautomatic pistol in an open-top holster tied down his right thigh like a movie gunslinger.

Unlike people familiar with such things only from watching television from the comforts of their dens, the villagers knew well the difference between semi and full automatic.

The villagers stared, more as if their worst nightmares were coming true than from any lack of comprehension. Because, of course, that was exactly what was happening. The gringo soldiers with their hard faces grinning mean white grins spread out in pairs with rifles at the ready to enforce their leader's command.

IN THE RELATIVE COOL of her hut Annja Creed sat straining to read by the light coming in by dribs and drabs through gaps in the hard-wood-plank wall. A bare bulb hung by a frayed cord perilously low over her head at the table on which she had spread the ancient book. It was unlit. The people of the village of Chiriqui had already done more than enough for her; she had firmly but with effusive thanks refused their offers to burn up more of their scarce, precious fuel to run the generator to provide artificial illumination. She could smell hot earth outside, the thatch, the sun-dried and splitting planks of the walls. And most of all the familiar musty odor of an ancient volume.

"...*herb has most salubrious effects,*" she read, "*particularly with regards to ye falling sickness, the effects of which fit it serves to ameliorate most expeditiously...*"

That was how she would have translated it into English, anyway. The Jesuit Brother João da Concepção's seventeenth-century Portuguese gave her no problems; modern Portuguese had changed less in the intervening centuries than most languages. Even other Romance languages, which if translated literally tended to sound archaic and formal even at street level to English ears.

She knew her Romance languages. She knew the majors, Spanish, French, Italian and, of course, Portuguese. Plus she was rudely conversant in some of the minors, such as Catalan. Of the whole group she knew little of Romanian. She read and wrote Latin superbly; it had formed the core of her language study since she had learned it in the Catholic orphanage in New Orleans.

What gave her fits was Brother João's crabgrass handwriting. The ink had faded to a sort of faint burgundy hue on the water-warped pages of the ancient journal. In some places water spots or mold obscured the text entirely. In others the words faded entirely from visibility as of their own accord.

"This would probably be easier if I went outside in the direct sun," she said aloud. She had a tendency to talk to herself. It was one of several reasons—that she knew of—that the villagers called her *la gringa loca*, the Crazy White Lady. That she spoke Spanish and was willing to share her medical supplies or give impromptu English lessons to the local kids—or their elders—helped keep the inflection friendly when they said it, so all was well.

As for going out in the sun, she'd had about enough of it in the weeks she'd spent tramping the hills looking for the tome. It wasn't as hot there as it was down lower in the Selva, the great jungle of the Upper Amazon. But to compensate, the high-altitude sun was more intense, with less air to block the UV rays that punished her fair skin. And it was hot enough. Even in the shade of the hut she had to keep constantly on her guard to prevent sweat from running the line of her chestnut hair, tied back with a russet bandanna, and dripping off her nose onto the priceless pages.

"Anyway," she said, aloud again, "I'm just being impatient. I could just wait till I'm back at the hotel."

Having searched a month to find the book, she was eager to confirm its contents. However, she was still a day or two from any kind of reliably illuminated, not to mention air-conditioned, surroundings; she was meeting a farmer from up in the hills about sunset. He had agreed to give her a lift into the nearest town of consequence in his venerable pickup.

Annja's impatience was rewarded. It seemed that the hints she'd been pursuing had been correct. The long-dead friar had cataloged a wealth of herbs of the Upper Amazon and watershed, along with a remarkable accounting of their observable effects on various maladies so systematic that it prefigured the scientific method. She wondered if an early stint in China, with its extensive *materia medica* assembled over millennia, and its own tradition of systematic observation and trial and error, had influenced him.

Excitement thrilled through her veins as she carefully paged through the book, reading passages, looking at the pictures Brother João had drawn in almost obsessive detail. She knew nothing about botany, and even the mid-seventeenth century was straying beyond her actual scope of formal training, which was medieval and Renaissance Europe. But since she had taken on this new life, she'd found herself constantly expanding her horizons.

She was barely conscious of the outlaw-motorcycle rumble and snarl of the diesel truck pulling into the plaza. None of the villagers possessed a motor vehicle, but a few, mostly pickup trucks, wandered through Chiriqui almost every day.

"Senorita," a childish voice said, low and urgent behind her. She turned.

"What is it, Luis?" she asked the tiny figure who stood in the door, a tattered T-shirt hanging halfway down his bare brown legs. His eyes were great anthracite disks of concern beneath his thatch of untamed black hair.

"You must go," he said.

He looks so innocent, she thought, not overly concerned despite his apparent urgency. She knew how kids tended to dramatize.

"Why?" she asked.

His eyes grew bigger and his voice more grave. "Bad men come," he said.

From outside came the sudden, unmistakable clatter of automatic gunfire.

THE VILLAGERS CROWDED into the square and stared as one at the man who lay writhing on the slope across the stream, guts and pelvis pulped by a burst of steel-jacketed rifle bullets. The stink of burned propellant and lubricant stung the air.

"My, my," the intruders' leader said, wagging his head reprovingly. "You people are slow learners. Don't you know by now that when we come around you don't run, because you'll only die tired?"

For a moment there was no sound but the pinging of the truck as it cooled and the groans of the mortally injured man. "Don Pepe, front and center," the redheaded man in the ball cap commanded.

A burly black trooper rudely thrust an old man with a full head of white hair forward. Don Pepe was skinny and stooped, in his formerly purple-and-white-striped shirt, faded by sun and repeated washings to dusty gray, his stained khaki shorts and rubber sandals. Big dark splotches of sweat spread outward beneath the pits of his scrawny arms.

Don Pepe staggered a few steps. Then he straightened and approached the intruder with dignity.

"Why are you doing this?" he asked. "We paid our taxes. Both to the government and to Don Francisco."

"Don Francisco is the main *traficante* in the region," Luis said.

He stood beside Annja as she crouched in the shade of an awning behind a blue plastic barrel used to collect rainwater. "These are his enforcers."

Annja made gestures to silence Luis. The boy seemed unfazed by the throes of the man who'd been shot. Annja knew him as a villager who'd lived here his whole life; he was probably at least a semidistant cousin of the boy. *This isn't the first man he's seen shot*, she realized with a jolt. Maybe not even by these men.

She felt a flare of righteous fury. She suppressed a strong desire to rush in. The mercenaries were too many and too well-armed, and she knew well what her failure would cost her friends.

The tall man, his skin sunburned an uncomfortable pink, wagged a finger. "Ah, but that's not why we're here. You're harboring a spy—a journalist."

Don Pepe raised his head and stared the man in the eye. He did not speak.

"Not going to deny it, huh?"

"Tell him, Pepe!" a middle-aged woman screamed. "She's no journalist! She's an archaeologist."

A Latino soldier drove the steel-shod butt of his Kalashnikov into her belly. She staggered back and sat down hard in the dust, clutching herself and gasping for breath.

Annja went tense.

"Anybody else care to speak out of turn?" The red-haired man surveyed the crowd. The villagers shifted their weight and glared sullenly. But they said no more.

"Didn't think so. Now, Don Pepe, here. He's a man of the world. Aren't you, Pep? He knows all this archaeology noise is just a bunch of bullshit. Right?"

The old man shook his head. "It is true. She is no journalist."

The mercenary shrugged. "Doesn't matter. A spy's a spy. You know better than to shelter outsiders. So do yourselves a favor and give her up."

Don Pepe shook his white head. "No."

The other cocked his head to one side. "What's that, old man? I don't think I heard you correctly."

"I will not. We will not. She has done you no harm. She has come among us as a friend. She—"

The vicious crack of a 9 mm handgun cut him off. Don Pepe's head whipped back, but not before red blood and dirty white clots flew out the back of his ruptured skull. He fell.

The red-haired man tipped the barrel of his Beretta service side arm skyward. A tiny wisp of bluish smoke curled from the blue-black muzzle.

"So much for old Don Pepe. Anybody else care to step forward as a spokesperson—preferably somebody smart enough not to contradict me?" The echoes of the gunshot reverberated on and on, from the far hillside where the first man still lay dying in agony, from all around.

Behind the rain barrel, Annja backed away. "Where do you go?" Luis asked in alarm.

"To give them what they want," she said grimly.

"You can't! They'll kill—"

But she was gone.

"LOOKS TO ME as if there's gonna be a village massacre here, boys," the redhead told his men in English. "Those atrocity-loving leftist guerrillas. So sad."

"Even if they give the bitch up, boss?" a hatchet-faced trooper asked.

"Do you even need to ask? Examples need to be made here. Remember, we got to be back in time to secure the airfield by 1900. Got an extraspecial shipment headed out tonight on the Freedom Bird."

Then, returning to Spanish, the leader announced, "All right, people. Listen up, here. You have ten seconds to give up the spy. Or else the nice lady sitting there gets it in the belly. Understand?"

THE TROOPER WHO STOOD in the Ram's bed behind the mounted machine gun had blond hair shorn to a silver plush and ears that stuck straight out from the sides of his head beneath his crumpled camouflage boonie hat like open car doors. He couldn't possibly have been as young as he looked. Not and be old enough to have had the military training and the seasoning these men showed. Annja was still new to the game, still finding out—as she was to her horror today—just what it entailed. But she knew it took time to become a killer.

Her rage, her sense of mission, quieted the roiling in her gut. And the adrenaline song of fear in the pulse in her ears.

The boyish gunner had his attention focused wholly on the villagers.

So stealthily did Annja creep up in the dust behind the truck that he would have had a hard time hearing her even if he had been listening. But there was no way he would miss the shift in balance as she climbed up in the bed, no matter how carefully she moved.

So instead she simply crouched, then leaped like a panther, over the tailgate and in behind him. The corrugated soles of her ankle-high hiking boots still made little noise as she landed. The truck's rocking alerted him. He started to turn.

She caught him around the throat with one arm, his head with the other. He reached for the combat knife hanging from his belt. But the sleeper hold she put on him cut off blood flow to the brain and put him out almost instantly.

Annja held him for an endless half minute, just to be sure. Heart pounding, she feared one of the intruders would look around, or one of the villagers would spy her and give her away, deliberately or through simple reflex surprise. But the mercs and their captives had eyes only for one another, as the shadows of evening stole across the village.

Slowly she lowered the unconscious man to the bed.

The machine gun was fed by a belt from a box attached to its receiver. Annja stood up straight behind the weapon, grabbed the pistol grip, swung the butt around to her shoulder and boldly announced her presence.

"Here I am!"

"WHAT HAVE we here?" the leader of the intruders asked sarcastically, putting his hands on his hips. "You here to do the right thing and give yourself up, save these good people a lot of suffering and dying?"

Annja swiveled the barrel so it aimed straight at the freckled bridge of his nose. "Not a chance," she said. "Throw down your weapons and walk out of here, and it's you who'll be saving yourselves."

"I think not," he said. "I think I'll just start executing one of these little people every count of ten, say, until you decide to surrender." He raised his Beretta and aimed it at the head of a man who stood nearby.

Annja pulled the trigger.

Nothing happened.

Safety, she thought, with a gut slam of shock. She knew pistols and rifles fairly well. But next to nothing about machine guns.

She spun away as a trooper behind the leader whipped his AKM to his camo-clad shoulder and triggered a burst. The bullets cracked over her head. She dived over the tailgate as a grenade thumped in the bed.

The explosion drove the big Ram down hard on its suspension. As it flexed back up, the fuel tank went up with a loud whomp, sending an orange ball rolling into the sky, trailing a pillar of black smoke.

A figure reared up from the truck bed, all orange, waving wings of flame. Demonic screams issued from it.

"Billy!" shouted the trooper who'd thrown the grenade.

Frowning slightly, the leader raised a straight right arm, sighted down his handgun and squeezed off a single shot. The flame-shrouded head snapped back. The shrieking ceased. The figure settled back into its pyre.

"Spread out. Find the bitch," the redhead said coldly.

"What about these people?" asked the tall black trooper.

"The hell with them. I want her dead!"

THROUGH GATHERING EVENING, Annja ran.

Not so much for fear of her own life. To her own surprise she felt little concern for that. Rather, for her mission. The thought that her mentor might have labored half a millennium to find the sword, and to find a new champion, only to have his labors made futile by such men as these made her blood boil.

Her footfalls thudded in her ears, above the buzz of swarming insects and the swishing and piping cries of the birds that swooped between the trees in pursuit of them. She had no idea how many men hunted her through the hills. They seemed to operate in teams. Three times they had spotted her and opened fire with their false-flag Russian weapons. Fortunately her reflexes—or distance—had prevented her being tagged.

That and her knowledge of the terrain. She had spent the better part of a month tramping these hills, looking for buried treasure: the cache where Brother João had hidden his voluminous journal from the planters and the troops who hunted him to steal his secrets. She had found it not two days before beneath a cairn of stones half-buried in a hillside, using clues left by the friar after he made his escape to Goa, India.

She knew Chiriqui's intimate environs far better than her pursuers were likely to. And they didn't seem inclined to slow themselves down by dragging along a local to serve as a guide. Besides, she could see they were manifestly arrogant to the point of blindness, accustomed to believing themselves so superior to anyone else that they'd never think of dragooning help.

She paused in the shelter of an erosion-cut bank, trying to control her breathing with a yoga exercise. The sun had gone from sight, although the sky remained light, stained with peach toward the west. The hollows and low places were filled with a sort of lavender gloom that was almost tangible.

A deep ravine gashed the land just over the next ridge. Using such cover as scrub and rock outcrops offered, she climbed the slope, senses stretched tight as a guyline. She paused in the deep shade of the broad-leaved trees at the crest. A hill across from her still hid the sun. Below her the ravine was a slash in gloom crossed by a pale blur— a rope-and-plank footbridge common in the erstwhile Incan empire.

She drew a deep breath. Almost out of here, she thought. She walked down the slope.

A nasty crack sounded beside her left ear. She felt something sting her cheek. By uncomprehending reflex she turned to look back up the hill.

A yellow star appeared in the brush at the foot of the trees, not far from the point where she'd left them. It flickered. She heard more cracking sounds.

She turned and raced for the bridge. The short, steep slope gave no cover. The bridge gave less. But the only chance she saw was to make it across and lose herself in the night and far hills. Her pursuers might have night-vision equipment but she'd just have to chance it.

She zigged right and zagged left, running flat out. The grayed, splintery-dry planks were bouncing beneath her feet with a peculiar muted timbre as she darted out onto the bridge.

It had not occurred to her to wonder why these hardmen, who seemed to know their business had gotten a clear, close shot at her back—and missed.

But then a pair of men rose up from the bushes clustered on the far side and walked onto the bridge to meet her. Men in mottled brown-and-khaki camouflage. Each carried a rifle with an unmistakable Kalashnikov banana magazine slanted in patrol position before his waist.

Feeling sick, she grabbed the wooly guide rope with one hand and turned. Another pair of men strolled almost casually down the hill behind her, likewise holding their weapons muzzle down. Their crumpled boonie hats were pulled low, making their faces shadows.

"Might as well give it up here, miss," a man called from the bridge's far end in a New England accent. "Only way out is down. And it's a long step."

"What do you think you're doing?" a nervous voice asked from behind her.

"What do you think?" the New Englander called out with a nasty sneer. "The first white woman we see in weeks, and she's a babe with legs up to *here*. You want to let that go to waste?"

"Plenty of time to waste her later," the big merc added. "Sorry, lady. Nothing personal. Life's just a bitch sometimes, ain't she?"

Annja let her head hang forward with a loose strand of hair hanging before it like a banner from a defeated army. Her shoulders slumped. She sat back against the guide rope heedless of the way it swayed over emptiness.

"That's more like it, honey," the trooper said. "You've got a good sense of the inevitable."

He was close now. Holding his weapon warily in a gloved right hand, he reached for her with his left.

Her face hidden, she frowned in sudden concentration. She reached with her will into a pocket in space, into a different place, always near her but always infinitely far away.

Suddenly a sword was in her hand, a huge broadsword with an unadorned cross hilt. She swept it whistling before her.

The hand reaching for her pulled back. Blood shot out from the arm, more black than red in the twilight. It sprayed hot across her face.

The mercenary staggered back, shouting more in astonishment than pain. That would come later.

But he had no later.

Annja dropped to the planks, catching herself with her hands, her right still wrapped around the sword's hilt, ignoring the agonizing pressure on her knuckles. She could see the stream meandering more than three hundred feet below, visible between wide-spaced planks as a pale ribbon through shadow.

Gunfire rapped from the bridge's far end. The flash and vertical flare-spike from the muzzle brake lit the canyon like a spastic bonfire. The bridge bounced and boomed as men raced toward Annja.

She jumped to her feet. She looked at them for a heartbeat. The man in front faltered, allowing the one behind to blunder into him.

"A *sword?*" he asked, momentarily stunned.

His eyes read Annja's intent. He flung out a desperate hand. "No!"

The sword went up and down. Left and right. The guide ropes parted with ax-blow sounds, turning into muted twangs. Turning her upper torso sideways, Annja seized the hilt with both hands and slashed through both foot ropes with a single stroke.

The bridge parted. Its sundered halves fell into the ravine. So did all the men on it.

The merc in back on the west side might have managed to get a grip and conceivably climb to safety. But his partner panicked, turned and ran right into him as the boards fell away beneath his boots. The two fell in a screaming tangle of arms and legs and weapons.

Annja let the sword slip back into its space as she fell. She felt no fear, only thrill-ride exaltation. She had escaped. That was victory. Her right hand shot out and caught a plank. Splinters gouged her palm. She gripped with all her strength regardless.

The slam into the sheer bank broke her nose. But it did not break her grip. She hung on while bells and firecrackers went off behind her eyes.

Then, blood streaming over her lips and dripping from her chin, she began straining her eyes to pick out the best climb down to the safety of the streambed.

2

"Say, lady," a voice called through the rain. "Hey, pretty lady. Hey, there."

Annja paused. She was walking home from the little Puerto Rican bodega around the corner from her loft with a small bag of groceries. She wore a light jacket, a calf-length skirt in dark maroon and soft fawn-colored boots that came up almost to meet it, leaving just two fingers of skin bare. A long baguette of French bread stuck up from the brown paper sack, shielded from the patchy downpour by a black umbrella. She liked to get small amounts of groceries during the brief intervals she spent at home, to force herself to get out at least once a day. Otherwise she'd spend all her time cooped up with her artifacts and monographs, turning into a mushroom. Or so she feared.

She looked into the doorway framed by grimy gray stones from which the words had issued. The speaker looked anything but threatening.

Don't make too many assumptions, she warned herself.

A small man lay sprawled in the arched doorway with his legs before him like a rag doll's. He looked emaciated within a shabby overcoat, knit cap and a pair of ragged pants, smeared with patches of grime, that came up well above grubby, sockless ankles and well-holed deck shoes. All might have possessed color at one point. Now all, including his grime-coated skin and stubble beard, had gone to shades of gray

The closest thing to color he displayed was the yellowish brown of his teeth and the slightly lighter but similar shade of the whites of his mouse-colored eyes.

In a quick assessment, she reckoned she could take him. It was part of the calculus of life as a New Yorker. And even more of the life she had taken on.

"What can I do for you?" she asked.

"Need some change," the man muttered in a voice as colorless as his skin. "Got some change for me?"

"You're right," she said. "You do need change. But I can't give it to you."

The man cawed bitter laughter. "Shit, lady. I need a drink not a sermon." Spittle sprayed from his gray lips, fortunately falling well short of her.

"At least you're honest," she said. "I do want to help you."

The impatient traffic hissed through the rain behind her. "But if I give you money, am I helping to keep you here? Is that really kindness or compassion?"

He had cocked his head and was staring at her fixedly. She realized he was contemplating trying to threaten her or outright rush her: a nice middle-class twentysomething white girl with more education than sense.

I've got victim written all over me, she realized.

She had already stopped talking. Instead she turned and lowered her head to bear squarely on his face and hardened her eyes. She would not summon the sword unless he displayed a weapon. And maybe not then; even before her transformation she had known how to take care of herself and been surprisingly good at it.

But if he actually tried to coerce her she would react with force as ungentle as it was unarmed. She had always hated victimizers. Now as her life's destiny had begun to unfold she found herself growing almost pathological in her hatred for them.

Something in her manner melted his resolve, which had never so much as gelled. The readying tension flowed out of him. His head dropped and he muttered into a filthy scrap of muffler wrapped around his neck.

Annja realized he wasn't a victimizer, not really. Just another opportunist who had realized on the teetering brink of too late that the opportunity he thought he saw was the eager smile of the abyss. He was weak rather than committed to anything. Even evil.

In a way she found that sadder.

She struggled with her groceries, her hand fumbling in her pocket, then handed him the first bill she found. "In the end, I find myself fresh out of answers," she said. "So I guess I'll take the easiest course." And wonder who's really the weak opportunist, she thought.

He snatched it away with crack-nailed fingers swathed in what might have been the shredded gray remnants of woolen gloves, or bandages. The movement sent a wave of his smell rushing over her like a blast of tear gas. Eyes watering, trying not to choke audibly, she turned and walked away.

"Hey, what's this?" he screamed after her. "A lousy buck? Tight-ass bitch! Don't care about anybody except yourself."

HER LOFT HAD a window seat. She liked to half recline on it as she studied or read her e-mails. It gave her a cozy feeling, surrounded by her shelves of books and the artifacts, the potsherds, bone fragments and chipped flint blades, that seemed to accrue on every horizontal surface. Today the clouds masked the time of day and veils of rain periodically hid and revealed the distant harbor. Rain ran long quavering fingers down the sooted, fly-spotted glass.

She sipped coffee well dosed with cream and sugar. The way she'd loved it as a child at the Café du Monde. Which, of course, wasn't there anymore.

As active as she had always been, she had never had much need to watch her diet. And now that her activity levels had increased, her main problem was keeping *up* weight.

She frowned slightly as she finished downloading headers from her favorite newsgroups, alt.archaeology and its companion, alt.archaeology.esoterica. There enthusiasts, nuts, grad students and professional archaeologists, mostly anonymous, would splash happily together in the marshy outskirts of her chosen discipline.

She quickly surveyed the headers in alt.archaeology. To her annoyance a number were obvious spam. While she was in South America she hadn't been able to keep the filters up to date. She resented having to spend the time and effort to do so, but it was like weeding a garden: either you did it regularly or gave in altogether to the forces of entropy.

Part of living in the modern world, she told herself, as she added a few new exclusions. It helps to keep me appreciative of the Middle Ages. Not that she was naive or romantic enough to wish away little things such as air-conditioning and antibiotics, she thought with a laugh.

The spam du jour was real estate. Before that it had been small-cap stocks, and before that, the heyday of male enhancements. She had filtered all of them out. She manually deleted all the new spam she could identify as such, and also the vast majority of legitimate headers that failed to spark her interest.

The usual controversies were being trotted out, she saw: the coastal-migration theory of the human settlement of South America. The authenticity of the Vinland map. Nothing of terrific appeal to her. As usual the flames raged hot and furious.

She switched to alt.archaeology.esoterica. Though it dealt with the far fringes and beyond of archaeology—or what was accepted— the discourse was actually less vitriolic than the regular archaeology group. If only just.

There was the usual debate about pre-Columbian visits to the Americas from Europe and Asia, and a thread about the building of the Great Pyramid that people kept poking at sporadically like a hollow tooth. She opened a message at random:

I give you your Caral pyramids, built even before the Egyptian pyramids. But if there was contact between Peru and Egypt, why didn't the Caral people learn about ceramics, as well as megalithic civil engineering?

The next header down was something new and different. It caught her eye. "Solomon's Jar?"

She downloaded the thread and read.

I have come into possession of an antique brass jar, which I believe may be the jar in which King Solomon is said to have bound the demons after he used them to build his temple in Jerusalem. Can you tell me, please, how to authenticate? Also how much it might be worth?

The poster was shown as trees@schatwinkel.com.nl. Annja knew the suffix .nl meant the address was in the Netherlands.

The last question could have been asking what the worth of such a discovery would be to science. Somehow she doubted that was how it was meant. The responses—many—were the usual flames and derision such naive questions from obvious nonprofessionals engendered. About half of them were from the reflex skeptics who derided the idiocy of believing in demons, in a jar in which they were bound, and for that matter that any such person as King Solomon ever existed. The others were from believers of one degree or another abusing the debunkers.

"Hmm," she said aloud. Annja closed the cover of her notebook computer.

THE SWORD IN HER HAND, she flowed through the ritual motions.

Though it was a gray day outside, she left the overhead light off. She enjoyed a companionable semidarkness; unless she was reading or examining an artifact, she didn't care much for intense light.

Annja had changed into a gray sports bra and a matching pair of terry trunks that clung to her long, lithe form. Her feet were bare on the hardwood floor of her exercise space, which was separated from her living area by a fifteenth-century north German carved altar screen representing the Annunciation. Her steps echoed. Though it cost her dearly, she lived in that most enduring of Hollywood clichés, a New York loft apartment.

Still, it was worthwhile. She needed room both to keep her specimens and books, and to *move*. To work out.

It wasn't as if she was dependent on grants anymore. She had some royalties from her book. Although it was temporarily in abeyance she also had money in the bank from her work on the cable-television series, *Chasing History's Monsters*, from which she was taking an indefinite sabbatical as she sorted out the details of her new life. When she'd gotten back from South America she had found her answering machine jammed with pleas from the show's boy-wonder producer, Doug Morrell, to come back immediately if not sooner....

The sword made soft swishing sounds in the air. She turned, holding it blade up in her right hand. She had the first two fingers of her left hand extended and pressed against the inside of her right forearm.

The ritual had nothing to do with the sword as such, nor her mission—so far as she understood either. So far as she knew. Which, she had to admit, wasn't far.

SHE HAD MET Roux, the ageless man of mystery when the earth literally opened at her feet and swallowed her up.

It happened on a mountain in France, while hunting the legend of the Beast of Gévaudan for *Chasing History's Monsters*. Shortly thereafter she had fallen into a sinkhole that opened beneath her feet during an earthquake. In the caves where she landed she had found the skeleton of the beast herself, as well as the man who killed it—and a medallion that proved to be the final, missing piece of the sword of Joan of Arc, which had been broken by the English when she was burned as a witch at Rouen in the fifteenth century.

Roux, it turned out, had been there. He had been Joan's mentor.

The old man had stolen the medallion from Annja in a restaurant. She had tracked him down to his mansion near Paris with the help of billionaire industrialist Garin Braden, who claimed to have been Roux's apprentice—half a millennium before. And there, by some means of which she still had not the slightest comprehension, she had *healed* the ancient blade—made it whole again out of fragments by no more than the touch of her hand.

It had caused Roux to proclaim her the spiritual descendant of the martyred Joan, and her fated successor as champion of the good. It had also inspired Garin to try to kill her. Or at least to break the sword, fearing that its restoration would break the spell—Roux named it a curse—that had kept both men alive and unaging for centuries.

She was still sorting this all out in her mind, trying to integrate a lot of fundamentally dissonant facts.

Unexplained things happened. She knew that. That the parents she could not remember had died and left her in an orphanage in New Orleans had rubbed her nose in that truth at a very early age.

Earthquakes happened. The earth opened. But that didn't stop it all from being a little too coincidental—providential, one might say.

The fact she just happened to be dropped more or less on top of the final piece needed to restore the sword was just too neat for rational explanation. Thinking about that—she did that a lot these days, trying to find her bearings—made her wonder about what she had been accustomed to thinking of as "rational." Because in this case truth and rational explanation were divergent. They had wandered far down very different pathways indeed.

IN THE WEEKS since taking the sword as her own burden to bear, Annja had worked assiduously to learn to use the mystic weapon. Roux had her start conventional fencing, mostly for conditioning. Even with her impressive physical abilities, she needed training. And that training hurt, for she was using her muscles in unaccustomed ways and taxing them to their utmost.

But Roux expressed contempt for fighting with what he called "car aerials," although he admitted the épée approximated a useful weapon in size and balance, and that the cut-and-thrust of the saber mimicked actual combat, however faintly. He spurned the modern mythology of point-fighting as the be-all and end-all of sword combat.

So she went beyond modern, conventional fencing. She studied sixteenth- and seventeenth-century sword manuals by masters such as Vadi and Meyer—even published a paper on them. She sought out live-steel masters of reconstructed sword techniques from the Middle Ages and Renaissance and learned from them.

What she was doing now, though, was a form meant to be performed with a two-edged sword. It was convenient to do, kept her body fluid and mobile and perfected her balance. It helped familiarize her with the sword—and it with her. The form also helped to soothe her mind and spirit. That was something she put a premium on these days, even as she found it increasingly difficult to do so.

She especially liked the symbolism of the left hand, the empty hand. It was traditionally held with first two fingers extended, the latter two folded into the palm with the thumb across them: what was called the spirit sword.

She found it appropriate, somehow. And the slow motions were easy on her nose. It was still tender from having been broken when she did the face-plant against the cliff in Peru.

AFTER SHE HAD GONE for a run in the rain, then come back and spent twenty minutes stretching, she showered and occupied herself fixing dinner. Then she watched part of the DVD set that had arrived in the mail while she was away, the first season of *Ally McBeal.* She didn't really watch much television, and hated waiting from one episode to the next of a show. She much preferred being able to watch as many episodes as she cared to at a sitting. Besides, she'd always harbored a sneaking prejudice for artifacts of the past...even the very recent past.

Leaving the television turned on for a little bit of light and motion, but no sound, she settled herself back on the window seat to see what had developed in her newsgroups.

As the colored shadows played disregarded across her face, and outside the great light went down and the little lights came on in fairy profusion, she went back to alt.archaeology.esoterica. The post about Solomon's Jar had elicited a new slew of comments. She scanned the headers.

The majority remained abusive. As usual, she found that once the comments nested more than a couple of removes from the main thread they had little or nothing to do with the ostensible topic. So she concentrated on comments on the original post, and immediate replies to them.

One username caught her eye: seeker23@demon.co.uk, a British domain. She had seen the name before. Often. He was a quixotic defender of the borderlands of respectability, of the realm of the possible—who nonetheless spoke knowingly in the jargon of archaeology. And never once in screaming caps. Seeker23 even knew that *it's* isn't a possessive, a rare attainment anywhere on the Net.

She downloaded the comments he—or she, but the tone caused her to sense the poster was masculine—had posted. Mostly they were calm pleas for open minds. But one uncharacteristic sally made her sit up and open her eyes.

There are even rumors that the crew of a Greek fishing trawler who found the supposed jar were mysteriously slaughtered on board afterward. Such a massacre did take place, in Corfu a couple of months ago. It's possible, always, that was merely coincidence. But I hope Trees is exercising due caution.

That brought him a positive flame tsunami, of course. Annja paid no attention. She could have recited most of the contents of the negative responses aloud without ever reading them anyway.

She minimized her newsreader window and fired up Firefox. A Google search of news items brought a number of hits from the wire services. Six Slain In Fishing-Boat Massacre, she read. The crewmen had been found hacked to death as the boat lay tied at the dock in its home port on the island of Corfu.

Annja closed her computer and stared out the window. The rain had started up again. The hard little lights across the East River seemed somehow muted, as well as blurred by chill tentacles of rain that stretched across the windowpane, that ran down the glass like the fingertips of dying men....

Shuddering at the sound of unheard screams, the nape of her neck tingling, she opened the computer up again and went to a travel site to check flight times and prices to the Netherlands.

3

A string of Balinese brass bells tinkled musically to announce her as Annja pushed her way into the little shop in Amsterdam.

Inside was warm, dark and fusty after the late North Sea afternoon with its high, pallid sky and brisk spring breezes off the IJ estuary. She closed the door as gently as she could, not wanting more racket from the string of tiny bells, while contradictorily saying "Hello?" at normal conversational volume.

Great, she told herself. I try to sneak in while announcing myself out loud. She sighed. She had a lot left to get used to, it seemed.

No one answered. She looked around.

The bronze plaque outside had described the establishment as Trees's Schatwinkel. What trees had to do with it she wasn't sure; the somewhat skinny lime trees on the street hadn't struck her as anything to name a shop after. Her first impression was that it was like her own home, but more so. The walls were lined with shelves of books, some glassed in as if to indicate rarer and more expensive volumes. The muted glow, which became more apparent as her eyes accustomed themselves to indoors, came from lights on the sculpted and painted metal ceiling. They were turned to spill illumination down the bookcases, and a few discreetly spotlit displays. Tables of artifacts were crowded between the bookshelves, along with some glassed-in cases.

The street sounds were muted to a near subliminal murmur. The tiny shop had the sort of reflective quiet she always associated with such places, along with museums and cathedrals. Its smell struck her as unusual, though. Along with the usual dust and mildew one encountered in such places, however scrupulously kept up, and the smell of old paper and leather and paint, her nostrils detected incense and a particular if unidentifiable sweetish smell. There was something else that underlay it all, but she couldn't yet define it.

Along with the books the store was crammed with a variety of artifacts, from age-blackened icons hung in the niches between bookcases to various coins in glass display cases. In one case near Annja lay an exquisite wheel-lock pistol with an ebony stock intricately inlaid in silver; beside it lay a scrap of Egyptian papyrus inscribed with faded hieroglyphs. Annja couldn't read them; they were too far out of her own scope.

A quick survey told her most if not all of the merchandise on display had likely come from private collections—including the rather nice trilobite fossil resting on its own pedestal to the left of the cash register. None of it, at a guess, was extremely valuable, in part because of clouded provenance.

Perhaps more importantly, none of the artifacts looked to her like illicit antiquities. It was basically a curio shop, and the items for sale would range in price alongside high-end souvenirs or contemporary artworks in the modest little galleries that catered to tourists in the Old Town district of the city's center.

But then, she thought, if they are trafficking in illegal antiquities, they'd hardly have them out front in the display cases.

She was surprised that no one had emerged to the sound of the bells or her own cautious greeting. Perhaps the Dutch were unusually law-abiding, although she'd seen her share of panhandlers and tough, drawn street people working the canals and narrow streets. Still, she guessed the proprietors knew their own business.

In the back of the shop a door opened onto what was presumably a storeroom. A dingy yellow light spilled out into the small main shop. No doubt the clerk or proprietor was back there somewhere, most likely in the bathroom. In the meantime, Annja walked up to the cash register and looked around.

She saw nothing out of the ordinary. There were small items like chocolates wrapped in brightly colored foil for sale in baskets on the counter, and on the wall behind hung what she guessed were licenses and permits of various sorts, along with a number of small framed lithographs from various time periods. Half-tucked under a rubber mat meant to keep metallic objects from marring the glass counter-top a business card caught her eye.

She pulled it out with the tip of a finger. It was slightly yellowish off-white, like old ivory. One end was printed in dark green, with a stylized tree showing through in the color of the paper. In the same dark green was embossed The White Tree and below it, Metaphysical Inquiries and a UK address complete with phone number and e-mail.

She slipped it back where it had been.

She looked around. Still no sign of life in the place. Perhaps the staff had slipped out back into the alley for a smoke to abide by the stringent EU antismoking laws.

Annja slipped behind the counter. She wasn't sure what she was looking for; she only hoped she'd know if she found it.

Unconsciously she realized her nose was wrinkling. There was an unmistakably off smell mingling with all the others. The air was still and definitely beginning to cloy.

A phone with a digital display sat beside the register. The command buttons were unsurprisingly labeled in Dutch. They looked fairly conventional. She hit a sequence of keys she hoped would bring up the last number to have called the shop. A numeral string obediently appeared. Annja was surprised to see a New York area code.

Little bells rang as the front door suddenly swung open.

A young man entered the shop. For a moment the bright light from outside gave the impression he was surrounded by a nimbus of light. Then he stepped in and shut the door, and the illusion was gone.

He looked to be about Annja's height, five foot ten. Slim, he wore a white shirt with an open collar and the sleeves rolled up to midforearm and blue jeans. His hair was dark and curly and hung down around his ears. When he stepped forward with a smile she saw his complexion was pale, with very pink cheeks. His eyes were penetrant blue.

"Do you work here?" he asked in English as he came up to the counter. His accent was British.

"Oh, ah, no. I'm sorry. I was just making a phone call," Annja replied.

It was a clumsy evasion. She saw suspicion flicker in his eyes. They narrowed, and his smile slipped.

"Where's the proprietor?" he asked.

"I don't know, actually," she said. "I came in and there was nobody here."

"So you just went around behind the cash register?" His tone was challenging.

She shrugged. "I just got into town. I needed to call my hotel."

He leaned forward to peer over the counter. "You're wearing a cell phone at your waist."

Annja smiled sheepishly. "Battery's dead. Isn't that the way it always goes?"

"You came to an antiquities shop before you even checked into your hotel?"

"I'm really very fascinated by antiquities. It's like a hobby." She patted the backpack she was still wearing. "I travel light, anyway."

He scowled as he looked at the backpack. For a moment she thought he would demand she open it to prove she hadn't filled it with purloined goods.

"Oh, really," he said. "American, aren't you?"

"Yes. You can always tell, huh?" Maybe if I play stupid enough he'll get exasperated and go away, she thought. She felt a bit of a pang at the thought; it was too bad they were getting off on the wrong foot like this.

"What sort of antiquities, then?" he asked. "Americans aren't usually interested in the past."

"I guess I'm the exception that proves the rule. I like antiquities of all kinds."

"Like this figurine here?" he asked, tapping a finger on the glass above a four-inch tall statue of a bearded warrior with a conical helmet and staring eyes. "Viking, wouldn't you say?"

"Oh, no," she said. "Eleventh-century Friesian."

He looked at her. Uh-oh, she thought. I let my stupid slip, there.

"You do know your antiquities, don't you?" he murmured. "Have you really no idea where the owner of the shop is?"

She shook her head. "Like I said, I just came in—"

He held up a hand. "I know. To use the phone. Well, don't you *wonder* why no one's come out to ask what we're about, then?"

"They're out to lunch?"

He looked at her levelly for a moment. She could tell he was dying to remark that they weren't the only ones. She seemed to have recouped her airhead bona fides.

"I think I'll just have a look in the back room," he said.

"I'm not sure that's a good idea," she said, moving out from behind the counter. He glanced at her, more with curiosity than anything else. She realized she didn't have a very good pretext for preventing him. Indeed, she wasn't even sure what her reason was. But she didn't want him looking in the back room.

His slightly snubbed nose wrinkled. "Do you smell something odd?"

"Yes," she said. "A little bit…stale, I guess. Maybe a rat died in the baseboards."

"If you don't mind I'll have a look in the back, make sure nothing's wrong," he said, and stepped past her.

He froze in the entryway. "Oh, my God," he said.

THE PROPRIETOR HAD BEEN stout, middle-aged and female. She wore a skirt and practical shoes with white ankle socks. And that was about all Annja could tell. Because her face was a crumpled pudding of blood, her upper garment was soaked and her hair was dyed and soggy with the stuff. Blood was splashed in bright sprays and swatches on the cardboard boxes and crates to either side of the body. It was congealing in pools on the scuffed linoleum floor. There were even suspicious stains on the bare lightbulb hanging from the ceiling overhead.

The smell was blatant now that she knew what it was. It was a smell most archaeologists were quite unfamiliar with: they had few occasions to deal with fresh death. Annja knew it all too well. But the incense and other odors had masked it.

She pushed past the young man to kneel by the body. She touched a bit of blue-white neck between blood rivulets. The skin was cool and gummy, and there was no pulse, confirming what the smell, and the visual evidence, had told her already.

Something lay by Annja's left shoe. She looked down. It was a small oblong box with gaudy colors and unfamiliar writing. "Clove cigarettes!" she exclaimed. Some of the other kids at the orphanage had tried smoking them, to hide the vice from the nuns. It never worked. Nothing ever fooled the nuns. "That's what that spice smell was."

"Don't touch anything!" the young man said.

"I won't," she said, standing. The tips of her fingers felt strange where they had touched the dead skin, and she felt an urge to wash them. Maybe you never get used to this sort of thing, she thought.

"Shouldn't we call the authorities?" he asked. He was shaking.

"Not from here," she said, "unless you feel like answering a lot of questions for some very skeptical police officers. There's nothing we can do for her now."

"But we have to do something!"

"Really?" She cocked a brow at him. There didn't seem any point in keeping up the bubble-head act any longer.

With a musical ripple of sound the front door opened once again.

The young man went tense. Annja looked past him as three men entered the shop. The first was on the small side, at least a couple of inches shorter than she was, wearing a tan suit over a shirt with an open collar. He was trim and moved with unusual assurance and economy. His hair was cropped short and seemed to be light and receding. With him standing in the darker outer room it was impossible to tell more.

The two who came in behind him towered over him. One was lean, dark haired and unshaved, wearing a shiny suit coat over, of all things, a white T-shirt with horizontal blue stripes. The other was more like a granite slab. His suit fit as if he went to a tailor who specialized in circus chimps.

Annja's life experience had taught her enough to make the two big guys as cheap goons immediately. The smaller man was a different order of being entirely, she knew at once. Not any nicer, perhaps. But he wouldn't come cheap. Not at all.

"Excuse me," he said, coming forward. His English was excellent but strongly Russian accented. "Are you Trees, by any chance?"

Then he stopped. Intuition-flash told her he recognized the smell before he saw the body in its graceless supine sprawl on the linoleum.

He rapped out a command to his men. Annja didn't understand much Russian. But she didn't need to.

There was no mistaking the intent of the two henchmen as they advanced toward her and the youthful Englishman.

4

Annja kicked the moving block of concrete in the baggy crotch of his suit pants as he reached out a golem arm for her. Sometimes the old ways were best.

It was an easy move to block, as she knew perfectly well. But that old devil perception played the huge Russian false. Her appearance took him in—both their appearances, as middle-class young Westerners, students most likely, culturally conditioned to thoroughgoing helplessness in the face of threats of violence. He wasn't expecting the attractive young woman with the green-and-brown backpack to plant a boot in the old and dear.

The air exploded out of his huge chow-dog face and he staggered, bending over to clutch at his violated parts. The very hair in his ears seemed to stand up in anguish.

His leaner, darker partner cruised past him. His body language told Annja he'd sized her up as a basically helpless woman who'd gotten lucky. He wasn't going to mess with an open-handed bitch-slap, but he did feel confident enough to launch a fist in a looping haymaker.

Annja spun away from the blow, clockwise and kept turning into a spinning back kick that caught the man in his wide-open right rib cage. With a loud crack of bones snapping he was catapulted sideways into a pile of crates. All fell over with satisfactory crashing and banging.

The big goon, cursing in a strangled voice—she was fairly sure that's what he was doing, but *all* Russian sounded to her like swearing—reached inside his revival-tent-sized suit coat. She knew what that gesture meant.

Turning away, she snagged the ingenue young Englishman by the wrist with one hand. He resisted like a little boy trying to avoid a bath. It did him as much good. She caught a corner-eye flash of his sky-blue eyes going wide as he found himself towed irresistibly after the young woman.

She heard the dapper little Russian shout something. It may have been a command not to shoot, or the big guy, who wasn't having his best day at the moment, fumbled his piece getting it into action. Whichever way the shattering noise and searing pain as bullets sleeted into her back didn't happen.

It was a straight dash to the back door of the shop. Because Annja was moving faster, the young man came gangling after her in a sort of high-speed prolonged stumble, devoting more effort to not falling on his face than anything else. In racing flat-out for the door, she placed his body between potential gunfire and hers. It was not an ideal way to protect the innocent, but compromises sometimes had to be made.

As she approached the door she gave the Englishman's wrist a final yank to keep up his forward momentum. Then she jumped into the air, half-turning to deliver a flying side kick. She turned her hips so that her leg shot out straight behind her as if in a back kick. Under normal circumstances, especially with the momentum of a brisk sprint, she knew it would be perhaps the hardest blow a human body could deliver.

Annja felt the door resist. She feared it may have been bricked over on the outside. Or perhaps it was simply rusted in place by long disuse. For an instant of compressed perception she feared her shin bone would give way before the door did.

Then with a squeal of tormented metal and wood both jamb and hinges gave. The whole door exploded out into the alley in a whirlwind of dust and splinters. It landed with a thud and bounced. Annja belly flopped on top of it. Last of all came the young man, sprawling on top of her. The breath left her body in an ungraceful grunt.

At last the anticipated gunfire ripped the air. A snarling burst of fully automatic fire sounded high-pitched and rang in her ears. A handful of bullets cracked over their heads to splatter against a whitewashed brick wall opposite, and ricocheted with nasty whining moans down the alley. Clutching at random for a grip on the young man, she rolled the two of them violently to the right, to get them clear of the doorway's fatal funnel.

She had by chance seized an upper arm. Somewhat to her surprise it had a refreshingly wiry tone to it, despite his peaches-and-cream complexion and somewhat soft impression. She jumped upright, hauling him bodily to his feet with her.

"What on earth are you?" he started to say.

"Later," she said. Grabbing his wrist again like a mother with a recalcitrant child, she ran for the traffic crossing the alley mouth as another burst crashed through the doorway.

"UNCULTURED IDIOT!" Valeriy Korolin snarled, slapping the big man's sparsely furred head. "How often have I told you not to use that stupid Stechkin? No one can hit anything with a full-auto pistol. Why don't you use a Glock like a normal human being?"

"But it shoots real fast," the man replied.

"Augh! Can you miss fast enough to catch up? Anyway, I told you to grab them, not shoot them. How did you ever get out of the Panjsher alive?"

"My colonel always used to ask me that, too," the big man replied.

"Well, catch them, dammit! You too, Arkasha!"

The lean man with the striped T-shirt beneath his sports jacket rubbed a stubbled jaw. Several other men had come in through the front door. "How, Captain?" Arkasha asked.

"The old-fashioned way. Run after them, very fast. Chase them down. Lay hard hands on them. Bring them to me. Alive!"

The two men stood staring at him. "You are still here, why?" he asked, his voice low, sinuous and dangerous.

They fled.

ANNJA AND HER COMPANION had almost reached the end of the alley when another pair of burly men came running into it.

By this time the Englishman was running on his own. Annja wasn't sure whether he was actually following her or simply fleeing in the same direction. Either way served her purpose.

One of the Russians reached to grab her. In a move far more reminiscent of rough flag-football games at the orphanage than her extensive martial-arts training, Annja stiff-armed him. He flew back into his comrade, who in turn slammed back against the green brick corner above the gray stone footing of the building.

Annja risked a lightning glance toward the front door of the shop. Several more overt hardmen milled near the brass plaque of the curiosity shop.

"What in bloody hell is going on?" demanded her accidental companion, stumbling as he stared at the fallen pair. She towed him remorselessly into traffic. Somehow, amid squealing brakes and bleating horns, they made the other side.

"Russian *mafiya* convention, looks like," she said.

"And who are you?"

"Probably your best chance at living to see sunset. Come on."

From the corner of her eye she saw the man she had stiff-armed. He lay on his back, jerking feebly. More to the point, she saw his partner, still half-leaning against the wall, dive inside his own *Miami Vice* pastel sports coat with one hand. She yanked the Englishman around the corner as a burst of gunfire rattled off the pizzeria at the near end of the block, miraculously missing the plate-glass window. A flyer hit the sidewalk and ricocheted off into the high white sky with a lost-soul whine.

The tourists, locals and vendors on the street showed little reaction as Annja and her companion raced away. Either they think it's fireworks, or there's a lot more street violence in Amsterdam than I knew about, she thought.

In a moment they were among a thicker crowd. She slowed. The young man slowed with her. He was breathing hard and seemed aggrieved to see she was not.

"What are you?" he asked. "Some kind of CIA cowgirl?"

She laughed. "That's the last thing I am. I'm just a tourist with an interest in antiquities. You?"

"The same." She noticed he wasn't any more eager to volunteer his name than she was. It was far down on her list of priorities. "What now?" he asked.

She looked back. Several men shouldered purposefully along the street behind them. At least one had his hand ominously inside his coat. "We need to lose them," she said.

In front of them a bridge crossed one of the innumerable canals lacing Amsterdam. She had no idea which one; the street signs would have meant little to her even if she had been able to read Dutch. It was as much as she could do to know they were inside the Singelgracht, the canal that had once encircled the medieval city, and innermost of the major concentric canals radiating from the arm of the North Sea called the IJ.

Glancing right, she saw the street widen where the space between two parallel canals had been paved over. A crowd of people were gathered there. She heard tinny distorted techno music and voices expanded and garbled by loudspeakers.

"This way," she said. "We might lose them in the crush."

Her companion glanced back the way they had come. His color had risen high in his cheeks. He was really very pretty, she couldn't help noticing, although still very masculine. His was an appearance that put her in mind of the poets Shelley and Lord Byron—though without showing any signs of the latter's brooding and somewhat sinister nature. She had let his arm go by now. He continued to follow, probably because he had no idea what else to do.

He thinks I do, she thought. Silly rabbit.

"They're gaining," he grumbled. She looked back as if rubbernecking in approved tourist fashion. He was right. She could pick out at least half a dozen men, distinguished from the crowd not so much by their attire, which ranged from eighties casual to ill-tailored modern professional, as by their unidirectional purpose. They were like steel marbles rolling through custard, although they did restrain themselves from jostling the burghers and tourists too briskly and drawing further attention to themselves.

"Even they won't shoot in a crowd scene like this," she said, mostly because they hadn't. Not unless they're sure of their targets, she chose not to say. Why they had been shooting she found more than a bit mysterious. But she didn't plan on asking them.

Not unless she managed to get one alone for a brief and personal conversation.

The crowd on the wide paved common in front seemed to be protesting something. But the crowd looked like a group of hippies. As she and her reluctant escort worked their way among the protesters she could see the fronts of their signs. She couldn't read them. They were all in Dutch. They seemed emphatic. They were also very… illuminated, to borrow a term from medieval manuscripts: embellished with fancy borders and scripts, sometimes to the effect she wouldn't have been able to read them had they been written in English.

There was a platform erected up front, near the end of the commons. A skinny speaker with a rainbow afro that might have been a wig exhorted the crowd in Dutch, vying with the thumping blast of music that was so distorted she suspected it was being piped through an amp from somebody's iPod. Near the front, an eight-foot-tall black-and-white bipedal cow cavorted, waving its forehooves as if to emphasize the speaker's impassioned rhetoric.

"Excuse me," she said, inadvertently jostling a large man with a peace-sign bandanna and an almost white beard.

"Certainly," he said with a smile. His English was crisp despite his accent. That was something she'd noticed about the people of Amsterdam: most of them spoke English, and most were unfailingly polite. Even when protesting, it appeared.

"What are you demonstrating about?" she asked. Glancing back, she saw several of the Russians standing on the edge of the protest, looking around as if uncertain what to do. If they dived into this crowd the way they had driven through the pedestrians, however crowded together, they would attract way too much attention from the Dutch police standing around looking politely bored in their khaki uniform shirts and dark trousers. "Animal rights?"

"No," the man said. "I am sorry. We demonstrate here for higher government subsidies to artists. We are all artists here."

"And craftpersons!" said the woman who stood on the other side of him, a smallish intense woman with a great cloud of kinky white-streaked ginger hair and a severe face.

"Ah, yes," he said.

"But what about the person in the cow suit?" Annja asked.

"That's Thijs," her informant explained.

"Why a cow suit?"

He shrugged. "He does soft sculpture of animals. Last time he was a giraffe. It was truly something to see."

"Sorry I missed it," she said. "Thanks."

The latter was spoken as she moved on with as much purpose as she could muster without calling attention to herself. The Russians had split up and were working their way around both edges of the herd of subsidy seekers.

"What was that all about?" her companion demanded to know. Taken apparently by surprise when she started walking, he had darted a few yards to catch up, fortunately drawing little attention.

"Camouflage," Annja said. "Also curiosity. I'm a stranger in town."

She kept her face turned vaguely in the direction of the podium, where a mime had taken the stage and was mugging and making inexplicable circular motions in the air with gloved palms toward the crowd, to the evident annoyance of the speaker.

"Mimes," her companion said in distaste. "I hate mimes."

She flashed him a smile. "There's something else we have in common."

She kept her eyes moving briskly side to side. Trusting her peripheral vision to alert her if any *mafiya* goons overtook them on the crowd's fringe, she mainly scouted for their next escape route.

Ahead to the left, one of the ubiquitous tour boats, low slung with a glass top, had pulled in just short of the commons' end. The tourists were filing off up a brief stairway of stained white stone to street level. She got the impression this was a shopping stop; there seemed to be no ticket kiosk at the small stone pier.

From nowhere a hand gripped her bicep. Hard.

5

"A word with you in private, miss," a heavy voice said in her ear, in English with a Russian accent you could have knocked off in chunks with a chisel.

"Oh, I'm sorry," Annja said. "You say you're ill?"

She turned her hips clockwise, at the same time rolling her shoulder. It put the whole weight of her body at the gap between his thumb and gripping fingers. Even had he been anticipating the action, which clearly he hadn't, it was unlikely he could have kept his grip.

As soon as her arm came free she rotated back to face him. He was another tall and rangy sort in a weird, faintly pink sports jacket and dark blue shirt. His breath smelled of lavender pastilles, of all things. He smiled, but it was reminiscent of a shark's.

"Ill?" he said, trying to not too obviously snatch her arm again. "I don't have any idea—"

She twisted again, this time even harder. Her left hand, knotted into a fist, drove the knuckle of her forefinger into the Russian's right kidney with the force of a riot baton.

The air rushed out of him. The color drained out of his fair face, leaving him green beneath his indifferently barbered blond bangs. His knees buckled. She caught his right arm as people turned to stare.

"The poor man," she said to them. "I think he's got appendicitis."

Some warning sense within her tingled. She felt a hand grab her right shoulder even as she readied herself.

She spun back as if startled. Quicker than the eye could follow, she hoped, her right elbow stabbed into the solar plexus of the beefy man who had seized her. His blue-green eyes, slightly slanted, bugged out as he doubled over.

"Oh!" she exclaimed. "You poor man. Perhaps there's a food-poisoning epidemic?" She turned, peeled his loosening hand the rest of the way off her shoulder, twisted it in a discreet come-along and, with pressure on the elbow, drove him face first to the cobblestones. He hit hard—but to all the nearby onlookers, themselves conditioned heavily against violence, it looked like nothing so much as if he had collapsed on his own, and his weight had proven too much for a girl, even a tall, athletic one, to control.

"We'll go get help," she told the circle of pale surprised faces turned toward her. "Come on, Eric."

The protesters crowded in on the fallen pair. The man Annja had kidney punched sat on his knees, moaning. The other lay with a trickle of blood running down his stubbled slab cheek; he had either broken a tooth or bitten his tongue, and was in all events stunned. As the artists and craftspersons all pushed together, jostling and trying to outshout each other with knowledgeable-sounding advice, Annja grabbed the Englishman's wrists and they were off again, running ahead and to the left.

"Eric?" he demanded. He wasn't hanging back this time.

"Improvising!" she said.

She turned her head enough for her peripheral vision to register that at least two men pursued them along the left-hand edge of the crowd. The commotion she had caused with the pair she had dropped was serving as a strange attractor for much of the crowd now. Everybody else seemed to be looking that way, even the disgruntled orator and the mime.

"What are we going to do now?" the Englishman asked as they darted free of the crowd, heading for the stone steps, now vacated by the tour boat passengers, who had wandered off down a side street toward one of the local attractions.

"Commandeer a ride," she said.

"Commandeer? You mean steal?" He sounded outraged.

"Whatever. Would you rather get to know the *mafiya* up close and personal?"

Heavy footsteps drummed the pavement behind her. A large flock of pigeons took off in a panicky flight from the top of the canal wall.

"You go negotiate passage for us," Annja said, propelling him down the steps with a hand between the shoulders. The boat driver, a young man with dark blond hair hanging lank from beneath a billed cap, looked up, his mouth agape beneath the gold ring in his nose.

She turned. Two new Russians slowed to a heavy-breathing stop three yards away and began walking toward her with broad grins.

"You gave us a good run, miss," said the taller of the two, walking straight toward her. He had a gold incisor and a startling Aussie accent overlaying the Russian. "Now the show's over."

She punched him. Hard. She threw a good, straight right, putting her hips into it, driving with her legs, putting all the force she was capable of up the bones of her arm and through the last three knuckles of her fist into his face. She felt cartilage squash and blood squirt, as if she'd punched a fruit. The man sat down hard and fluids began to flow.

His partner was all over her from her right side, trying for a bear hug. She reached up, grabbed a handful of padded shoulder and, putting her right hip hard into his groin, cartwheeled him right over her shoulder. It could easily have been a death stroke, but she wasn't ready for that. Rather she pulled him in so that instead of smashing the back of his skull to pulp on the stone of the pier he slammed down on the top of his back. The air exploded out of him, and she thought she felt his shoulder pop free of the socket. What a shame, she thought with a grin.

The other guy was rubbing his face, trying to clear his eyes of tears and the scarlet sparks that the pain from his nose were doubtless still shooting through his forebrain. Her own nose panged in sympathy. She leaped down the six feet to the landing, flexing her legs to take the shock.

Her companion stood arguing with the tour boat pilot. Both turned to gape at her. She hopped onto the boat, said, "Sorry," to the young boatman and pushed him straight over the gunwales. He landed in the water, limbs flailing, and threw up a giant wave of stinking green water.

"Let's go," she said, revving the engine and grabbing the tiller.

The Brit stood still staring openmouthed at her. She got the boat's prow turned upstream, away from the pursuit, and accelerated. He windmilled his own arms. She had to grab the front of his shirt to keep him from flying over the stern.

She dragged him to a seated position. From behind a ripple of gunfire crashed as one of their pursuers opened up from the concrete railing. Bullets sent miniature geysers spouting white behind the churn of their propeller. Then they were through the round arch of the next bridge down.

Her companion was staring at her with eyes and hair wild. His shirttail had been pulled out of his jeans. His hands were plucking and pushing at it as if to tuck it in again, but he didn't seem to have good command over them.

"Are you quite sure you're not some covert government agent?" he shouted at her.

"Yep."

"You're daft!"

"Pretty much," Annja replied laughing.

Something cracked right above their heads.

THE SOUND WAS MORE like something breaking than a pop. It *was* something breaking, Annja knew instantly: the sound barrier. Someone had fired a high-velocity round at them.

She reached out, grabbed her companion by the shoulder and pitched him facedown to the deck before he could react. Then she looked back.

The Russians were living up to their reputation for dogged determination. Three of them had hijacked a canal boat of their own and were speeding in their quarry's wake. Two of them were standing up, risking a nasty high-speed spill into the murky waters of the canal, firing handguns at them.

She turned her eyes forward just in time to swerve through an archway of another bridge rather than accordion themselves on a piling. With her free hand Annja grabbed the young man by the collar and hauled him to a seated position. Ahead she could see the masts of sailboats and a long, low, rust-colored barge cruising slowly past the canal mouth.

She felt a sharp pang of yearning for her sword. She was aware, all too aware, it couldn't help her here. She couldn't slice bullets out of the air with it, and anyway, the middle of a densely populated city was not the place to pluck a sword from thin air and start waving it around. She knew that through her wit and will alone she would prevail or fail.

"What now?" the young man asked.

Good question. The last bridge was coming up fast. The Russians were closing, though still a good hundred yards back. Annja undid her belt, yanked it off, leaned over, did something fast and purposeful. Then she threw both arms around him.

"Take a deep breath," she said.

THE RUSSIANS DUCKED low as their boat flashed beneath the final bridge. Ahead of them their quarry wallowed and then began to turn right in the slow but heavy crosscurrent.

"We got them!" one of the men crouching in the bow shouted triumphantly.

His comrade, less intrepid, had gone all the way to his knees. "Wait!" he shouted over the whine of their engine. "Where did they go?"

The smaller boat rolled as it cruised out into the IJ. The standing man toppled and barely prevented himself from going into the estuary.

"It's empty!" he shouted.

The water flattened around them in a sudden downdraft. Above them they heard the sound of a helicopter rotor.

And from the quay behind they heard the distinctive, angry voice of their leader.

BOBBING TO THE SURFACE in the dark shadow of the archway, the young man shook his head like an angry terrier.

"You're daft!" he exclaimed. "You're mad. Barking bloody mad!"

Treading water beside him Annja looked out into the IJ. The pursuing boat had cut its engine and was drifting sideways as its impromptu crew put their hands in the air. A harbor patrol helicopter hovered above them.

"It worked, though," she told him.

She swam back to the upstream side of the bridge and climbed onto the small concrete pier. She reached out a hand to help her companion from the water. He shook her off angrily and sprang out. He was fairly fit, she realized—agile. Plus he'd mostly kept up with her, although unlike her he was breathing hard.

He followed her into a side street. "We've got to go to the authorities," he told her.

She shrugged. "Your call. It might take you longer than you like to answer to their satisfaction the questions they're going to ask. And our friends, there—" she bobbed her head back toward the canal, clearly indicating their erstwhile *mafiya* pursuers "—are known for having tentacles deep into police forces all over the world."

"But there are surveillance cameras everywhere!" he exclaimed, waving his hand toward one mounted on a metal post beneath a lantern with a crown surmounting it. It seemed to stare at them like an idiot eye.

"They've got them all over your country, too," she said, "and street crime's skyrocketing there."

He made an inarticulate noise compounded of frustration, disgust and reaction. He held up his hands before his dripping, anger-pink face and shook them. "Don't," he said, "follow me. We're done. Understand?"

"Have it your way," she said. She resisted the temptation to call, "You're welcome" after him as he stomped off down a side street. Instead she began looking around.

Something tells me, she thought, *I need to get out of Holland fast.*

THE LITTLE BOXY rental car was parked with its snub snout almost touching one of the three-foot metal stanchions that studded most of the sidewalks to protect pedestrians from vehicles and also to keep the drivers off the sidewalks. Valeriy Korolin stood before it, arms akimbo, glaring into the estuary with the tails of his sports coat flapping in a brisk breeze that smelled of fish, stale saltwater and diesel fumes.

"Now look what you fools have done," he said. "What possessed you to shoot at them? This is Amsterdam, not Tbilisi."

"But Captain," said one of the two men who'd piled from the car with him. "They killed the shopkeeper."

"Fool! Did you see any blood on them?"

"Well, no—"

Around them sirens blared. "Did you fail to notice," the captain said, voice razor edged with sarcasm, "that the interior of the store-room looked as if someone had set off a grenade in a can of red paint? Haven't you ever beaten anybody to death before, Gena?"

"Well, yes, comrade Captain. But—"

"It's not 'comrade' anymore, you buffoon. And quit calling me Captain!"

"This is the police!" a polite but brisk electronically amplified voice called out.

The car had been surrounded by Amsterdam police cars, white with red-and-blue hashmarks on their sides. Either presuming that anybody making such a commotion in Amsterdam must be a Yankee, or simply playing it safe since most Netherlanders and most tourists understood some English, the officer spoke that tongue. "Put your hands behind your heads."

"All right, all right," Korolin called. He turned to face the nervous pair of cops approaching behind drawn handguns. They held their weapons as if expecting they might suddenly turn and bite them, like vipers. "I am Colonel Sergei Arbatov, of the Russian Federal Security Bureau's Anti-Terrorism Task Force. You will find my iden-tification in my right inside coat pocket. Please permit me to speak to your superior at once!"

6

Still breathing easily after a brisk two-mile ride, mostly uphill, Annja swung off the bicycle before the gateway to the manor house. Red brick gateposts rose from pale granite bases. The gate had a black wrought-iron arch across it with a tree worked in the center and painted white. The gates themselves stood open. A brass plaque, on the near upright, kept polished to a bright yellow, read Ravenwood Manor—The White Tree Lodge.

The sun hung low over green hills to the west. The clouds, strung across the sky like clots of cream, had toward the horizon begun to take on evening tints of cream and gold below, pale blue and dove-gray above. The hills were fairly sharp for England, though their outlines were softened by grass and copses of trees. They stretched west from the ancient Cinque Ports town of Hythe, bounding the fabled Romney Marsh. The Kentish Channel coast had become heavily encrusted with urbanization, especially since the building of the underwater chunnel from Featherstone, and the green countryside of Kent as a whole had been reduced by the encroachment of suburbs and bedroom towns from London.

The hill rose in a gentle slope toward a big white house on the crest. An immaculately tended crushed-shell drive curved subtly up through an equally compulsively manicured lawn, as uniformly green as a carpet. Annja saw no formal garden around the three-story

Georgian house. Rather it stood amid a stand of trees, big ashes and vast, spreading oaks with massive, bent, cracked-bark trunks, themselves probably older than the nearly three centuries the house had stood. They masked several outbuildings, at least one of substantial size, which stood behind the great house on the back slope.

She took a drink of water from the bottle clipped to the bicycle frame. Then she swung a long, lithe leg over the seat and started pedaling up the hill. She felt no fatigue, only a bit warm, and that from exertion in the thin high-latitude sun more than ambient temperature, which had been on the cool side since she'd set out. Annja's rented bike was an ancient but well-repaired blue machine with a white fender on the front tire and no top strut on the frame, what was often called a "girl's bicycle" back home.

She wore khaki pants with some subtle cargo pockets, a cream-colored shirt with the sleeves unbuttoned and rolled up her tanned forearms. It was practical yet not disrespectfully slovenly to the people she meant to talk to.

It was an excellent disguise, she thought. She'd masqueraded as herself.

Crushed shell crackled beneath her tires as she rode up the sloped drive. She studied the house and its environs as she reflected on what her research had unearthed. A moldering stone wall encircled the structures behind it. The largest took shape as a half-ruined slump of stone, its walls almost obscured by ivy. It was an ancient abbey, built, according to legend, on a sacred site immeasurably more ancient, sacked and burned some said by Henry VIII's looters, and others by Cromwell's iron-clad iconoclasts. The manor itself had been destroyed during the English Civil War. When, decades later, a new noble master had built the current manor house atop the hill the ruin was left in place as a sort of garden ornament.

Not that the derelict abbey had remained unused. Legends spoke of unholy rituals—or orgies outright, depending on point of view—conducted between the once consecrated walls by the well-connected members of the scandalous Hellfire Club from nearby London. And the current proprietors likewise conducted rituals within its precincts. Annja had read all about it on their Web site.

The house was built of local limestone, with a sloping roof of gray slate. Though carefully pruned shrubberies huddled against its foundations like green sheep, its walls were kept clear of climbing vegetation, giving the manor an austere but not quite stark look.

Annja leaned her bike against the concrete footing. As she did she felt a curious chill, as if the sun had fallen behind a cloud on its way to the horizon. At the same time her nostrils wrinkled to a faint but unmistakable stink of decay. It was as if a breeze had blown over a recently opened grave. Just a random smell from the old graveyard out back, she told herself, though she had felt no actual motion of the air.

She put it from her mind and walked between stone lions weathered almost to outsized pug dogs to ring the bell. A medium-sized man with dark receding hair, middle-aged and trim in a butler's garb, greeted her. He accepted a business card embossed with the name of Amy Corbett, archaeological researcher and the name of a private North American institute—one that actually existed and would vouch for her identity thanks to *Chasing History's Monsters*.

The butler escorted her into a foyer. A spray of hothouse flowers in a white porcelain vase painted with climbing roses sat on an antique table on one side and a silver-framed oval mirror on the other. Bidding her to wait in tones more superior than deferential, he bowed and disappeared into the house's interior. Annja used the mirror to check herself and tucked a few vagrant wisps of hair back into the severely professional bun she'd tied at the back of her head.

"Ms. Corbett?" a cultured voice said. A cultured young masculine voice.

She turned. A painstakingly well-groomed young man stood there, her height or a little taller, her age or a little older, with round pink cheeks creased by a smile and dark hair slicked back sleek as a seal's fur. The pinkness of his cheeks reminded her of her nameless companion of her adventure in Amsterdam, but the resemblance ended there. He lacked the ivory whiteness of skin that had given such contrast to that young Englishman's complexion, to say nothing of a demeanor light-years from the mildly but boyishly disheveled affect the lad who fled with her through streets and canals had displayed. And though his smile seemed genuine, as most heterosexual males' tended to be when looking at her up close, his politeness was buffed to a polish so high and hard she couldn't see the character behind.

"I'm Reginald Smythe-George," he said. "So pleased to meet you. Please come with me."

He bowed slightly and gestured to a hallway opening to her left. He wore a dark suit whose exact shade she could not distinguish in the foyer's half light, subtly pinstriped, with a stand-up collar and four-in-hand tie. She had little knowledge of fashion much past the sixteenth century, but his outfit suggested late Victorian to her—or Carnaby Street in the sixties. He also wore a large silver medallion bearing an image of the tree that was on the front gate.

"Of the noted occultist family?" she asked. She started walking the indicated path.

He slid past smoothly, to open a white-painted door before her. "Indeed," he said. "I'm surprised you know of us. So many in your profession tend to…look down upon my distinguished forebears."

"I try to keep an open mind," she said. "Scientific objectivity is a powerful tool. But like fire, it's a capricious master."

He raised an eyebrow. "Indeed? You possess rare insight for one with so much of your career before you."

Points for a diplomatic way of calling me young, she thought, given his own age. She smiled a middle-candlepower smile at him—it never hurt to keep things cordial, without lighting any fires she might need an extinguisher to put out later—and entered a white sitting room. Or what she suspected might be a sitting room.

It had chairs and tables, in any event. A low fire crackled in a white marble fireplace. Something else practically screamed for her attention. She fixed it upon the young man's sleek, smiling visage.

"Sir Martin will see you shortly," her escort said, and went through the next door, which he quietly but firmly closed behind him.

She took stock of her surroundings. The room fell just short of sterile. It was painted and decorated in a variety of shades: off-white, ivory, cream, bone. The chairs were upholstered in a leather that was almost pale beige. Some touches of color decorated the room, largely hues of gold, including the ormolu clock on the mantel, the frame of a large painting and the painting itself, depicting a pure white tree standing amid a green sun-shot forest.

There was one more touch of yellow metal. It was the thing that had caught her attention on entering the room. A plain container of shiny brass, like a globe with a tall narrow funnel stuck in the top and curling thin handles, perhaps a foot high.

A jar.

It looked like an antique Mediterranean jar might look, dredged from the sea bottom, if the sea-salt deposits and verdigris were cleaned off. It was a procedure no responsible archaeologist could condone, for risk of damaging the artifact. But a collector might not be so scrupulous. Nor might someone with other than strictly scientific ends in mind.

She took it from the mantel to examine it. If cleaning it didn't hurt it, picking it up won't do much, she thought—except leave fingerprints she could readily wipe away. Provided it's even an ancient artifact in the first place.

It felt surprisingly heavy in her hand. She was far from expert on biblical-era artifacts. But within her limited scope of knowledge she could discern no reason it might not have dated from Old Testament times. The wide mouth was open.

It was, she saw, inscribed with symbols. The marks were thin, shallow, spidery; invisible from a few feet away. The symbols were unfamiliar to her: lines, curved, straight and angled; circles; odd compound geometric shapes.

Something about the vessel felt strange. Then she realized the strangeness wasn't a result of something the jar possessed, but what it lacked.

If King Solomon had had a jar, and had once bound demons in it, this was not that jar. She felt certain such a use would leave it charged in a way that even after millennia its very touch would send a thrill like electricity through her body. This object was inert as a hammer.

She turned it over. The lower curve was curiously dented. In the indentation she thought she could see small flecks of dried brownish residue. She smelled a faint, cloying stench.

Then once more she felt a chill, and seemed to smell an opened grave.

A footfall from outside the door alerted her someone was coming. She quickly replaced the jar and turned.

Reginald Smythe-George opened the door, entered with a quick smile for Annja, and stood aside. A tower-tall and spectrally thin man entered at stately stilting pace behind.

"Sir Martin," the young factotum said, "may I present Ms. Amy Corbett? Ms. Corbett, Sir Martin Camdessus Highsmith, *Adeptus Primus* of the White Tree Lodge."

She stepped forward, extending a hand. Sir Martin took it in a firm, dry grip and shook, once. His hair was white and looked as if each individual strand had been arranged by hand just before he entered. His face was a collection of knobs and flanges that looked almost harsh. He wore an immaculately tailored suit with the same color scheme as the room itself—jacket, trousers, shirt and old-time silk cravat all in shades of white and near-white.

The only discordant element in the whole image was his eyebrows. They were fierce white projections, untamable as flames, above eyes of a blue so pale they were almost a shade of white themselves.

"Pleased to make your acquaintance, Ms. Corbett," the master of the house said in a baritone voice that might have been toned by a tuning fork. "Please be seated."

He waited until she sat in one of the lesser chairs, then took what she had rightly guessed was his accustomed place in a cream-colored wingback.

"This is a very beautiful house, Sir Martin," she said. "Is it your family's?"

"Thank you. And no, Ms. Corbett. My esteemed ancestors frittered away the family fortune before the Great War—our estates were sold for taxes between the wars. This house is provided to the lodge through arrangement with the National Trust."

He cocked his head at her. "You are an archaeological researcher, then?" he asked.

She smiled and nodded. "Writing an article for *Archaeology Today* magazine. On spec, I'm afraid. With, ah, an interest in the history of the Western Hermetic tradition," she said.

"Indeed? I imagined it was the archaeological heritage of the site that drew you here."

"To be sure, that adds interest, Sir Martin. As I understand, the manor is built on the site of one of the earliest Anglo-Saxon hill forts and the attached abbey at what is supposed to be the juncture of several ley lines."

"You've done your homework, then," he said, nodding approvingly. "But what I think you will find most vital—and key to our whole endeavor here—are Neolithic artifacts discovered on the grounds that demonstrate that this site has been recognized as holy throughout the entirety of its human occupation."

His eyes had begun to shine.

"I'm afraid my primary knowledge is focused on the Middle Ages forward," she said, "although I was aware of Neolithic and Bronze Age discoveries."

"*Bronze* Age," he said as if mentioning something the dog did on the rug.

She raised an eyebrow at him. "My knowledge is incomplete and purely academic," she said, "but I thought it was cold iron that conflicted with magic."

"Iron. Bronze. This to them!" He dismissed all metals with a wave of a long, well-formed hand. "They are pollution in and of themselves."

"Do they not occur in nature, Sir Martin?"

"Of course. It is when they are plundered from the bosom of the good earth and elaborated in profane ceremonies that they become taints, poisoning the human spirit and poisoning all life."

"I had understood that Wiccans—"

"We see again that *knowledge* is not the same as *understanding*, Ms. Corbett. Therein lies one of the tangled roots of the modern malaise, prizing mere information while understanding nothing, or next to it!"

"I think I agree, Sir Martin, but I'm not sure I see your point," Annja said.

"If you will forgive my rudeness in contradicting you, you don't understand our lodge at all if you believe we are part of Wicca. To be sure some of their rituals have merit, and a certain naive power, for all that they were largely created from whole cloth in the nineteenth century."

"But it was my understanding—forgive me, my impression—that the lodge practiced a traditional Western form of nature worship."

"That much is certainly true. But that does not make us Wiccans, dear lady."

He leaned forward, and his passion seemed to glow from his eyes and radiate from his prominent teeth, which were themselves a shade of off-white, she couldn't help noticing.

"Leave aside the truth or falsity of the ancient worship of the Great Mother and the horned god," he said. "We subscribe to the *true* old religion," Sir Martin proclaimed.

"Don't the Wiccans make similar claims?" Annja asked.

He dismissed the notion with a wave of his hand. "I mean the religion of the dawn men. From before the druids, before the pyramids, before the great crime of agriculture. Ours is the primal religious ecstasy expressed by the cave painters of Lascaux. Our worship is devoted to the earth's very self—we do not profane and diminish the earth by personalizing it as a mere human. Especially now, when humans have covered much of the beautiful face of the planet with their concrete canker sores, and the waters with their muck and ooze."

He sat upright again with a half-rueful smile. "You must forgive my vehemence," he said.

"You certainly have the courage of your convictions, Sir Martin."

"Thank you, my dear. You are most kind."

"So the lodge believes that our modern technological civilization is a mistake?" she asked.

"A desecration," he said.

Then his near white eyes slid past her. She turned her head but slightly. Far enough for her peripheral vision to register the direction of his gaze. He was looking straight at the brass jar on the mantel.

He knows, she realized. Might as well be hanged for a sheep as for a lamb, she thought. She drew in a deep breath. Then she plunged in head first.

"Given your institute's focus on prehistoric native beliefs," she said, "I admit I find its interest in a relic such as the alleged jar in which King Solomon bound the demons to be quite curious."

He looked directly at her for a moment. It seemed that his expression hardened, and that his eyes went from silver to steel.

"So," he said—softly, as to himself. "The margin of error is small, so small, in this terrible modern world of ours. As you observed, Ms. Corbett, I am passionate in my convictions. Sometimes my passions overwhelm me. Especially when my dearest expectations are raised, only to be cruelly dashed."

He stood. "As to my interest—our interest—the earth's interest in the jar of Solomon, it would be pure waste to tell you now. No point, really."

Either his disdain for modern technology did not forbid him from carrying some kind of wireless communicator hidden on his person, or he possessed strong psychic powers. Annja did not discount the latter possibility as readily as she might have a year earlier. The door opened suddenly and two men, dressed in rough, soil-stained workman's garb that seemed itself to belong to an earlier century, stepped in.

"Mal, Dave," Sir Martin said. One newcomer was short and broad, with dark hair on his balding head and sticking from his prominent ears. The other was a huge, near shapeless mound of muscle. He was an albino with skin as chalky as the famous cliffs nearby and hair whiter than anything else in the white room. Both wore silver lodge medallions. The squat dark man carried a double-barreled shotgun under one arm.

"My Purdey, Dave?" Sir Martin inquired.

The squat man shrugged. "It'll do the job, won't it, Squire?"

"Ms. Corbett is leaving us," Sir Martin said. "Permanently, I fear. Reginald, I fear we need to clean up after my…indiscretions. See to it, won't you, there's a good lad?"

"Of course, Sir Martin," Reginald said coolly.

"Please take our guest into the back garden, kill her and bury her in the churchyard where none will be the wiser. And for nature's sake, do it quietly!"

THE HUGE ALBINO, Mal, picked up a shovel leaned against the moss-grown stone wall as they passed beneath a gateway arch at the back of the great white house. Annja didn't know whether it was intended to kill her or inter her. Probably both she guessed. The White Tree Lodge did not seem to disdain modern concepts of efficiency. She wondered, idly, how they justified their reliance on the techniques and technologies they so despised.

The derelict abbey reared to the right. Ivy practically encrusted the limestone walls, which had fallen in at the top. A passageway led between rosebushes just beginning to bud with spring. Beyond lay another arched gateway. Through it the granite-and-limestone headstones of the churchyard were visible, jumbled gray-and-white shapes in the thickening twilight.

"We really don't have to play it this way, gentlemen," Annja said when there were walls all around. Flying things fluttered about, shadows tracing oddly irregular paths, bats or swallows she could not tell. The sun no longer shone here this day. It felt as if it never had.

"Coo," said the short, squat Dave. "I fancy hearing what the bird has to offer. What about you, Mal?"

The albino grunted.

"Not a bit of it, lads," Reginald Smythe-George called out, coming along seven yards or so behind as if pulling rear guard. Maybe he didn't want to risk getting his expensive trousers splattered, Annja thought. "This is lodge business. No time for frivolity," he said.

"What's the point of belonging to a fertility cult," Dave groused, "if you can't enjoy a few rites o' fertility—if you know what I mean?"

Mal smiled.

"So this is the way it has to be?" Annja asked. She walked toward the churchyard with head down and shoulders slumped.

"That's right," Dave said, "and a damned dirty shame it is. But there it is. Just take it easy, now, and it'll go easy, if you know what I mean."

"Sure," she said, and spun.

Mal's bulk and slow, shambling motion conspired to suggest slow-wittedness. But there was nothing slow about his response. No sooner had Annja begun to turn than he raised the shovel in both hands. Even as she came around to face him the blade descended to split her head.

But her right hand was no longer empty. She hacked across her body right to left with the sword. She felt two moments of resistance.

Blood hosed her from the stumps of two thick, severed arms.

Mal's mouth opened and closed. His tongue looked red as blood in contrast to his colorless face. Or perhaps he had bitten it in shock. He made gobbling sounds, quick and bubbling with desperation as he stared at his massive wounds.

"Bloody hell!" Dave exclaimed. He brought up the Purdey.

Annja was on him. A backhand slash severed both barrels of the priceless double shotgun with a belling sound. Reflex made the man yank the now-sawn-off shotgun skyward. Reflex clenched his finger on both triggers. The barrels gouted pumpkin-sized flames into the dove-gray evening air.

Dave roared in surprise and pain as the unexpected recoil broke his trigger finger and possibly his wrist. He had not been gripping the gun properly when Annja amputated two-thirds of its barrel. The giant muzzle flames blossoming so close to his face had ignited the front of his curly hair.

His cry was cut short as Annja took the sword in both hands and raced past him to his right, swinging horizontally as she passed him. He froze. Blood gushed from his mouth and jetted from his chest. He fell to flagstones half-buried in the turf.

A flash snapped her eyes forward. Simultaneously Annja heard a *pop,* not particularly loud. Then another. Something plucked like fingers at a lock of her dark hair hanging by her left cheek.

Young Reginald Smythe-George had a tiny black pistol in his hand and was shooting at her from twenty feet away.

Her instructors had always told her to run away from a knife but charge a gun. Of course, they might not have been so cautious about the knives had they known she had a very large knife indeed, carried in the otherwhere where an act of will could bring it to her hand at need. But the advice for firearms remained sound. Fast as she was, she couldn't outrun bullets. Nor even appreciably dodge them.

She *could* try to dazzle the shooter with footwork, throw off his aim—which was lousy anyway—and perhaps even startle him too much to shoot. She ran two light steps toward him and threw herself into a cartwheel, neat as a high-school cheerleader.

She heard no shots, felt no slap or sting of impact. Her hair flying loose about her shoulders, she landed on her feet and flowed instantly into a lunge.

The sword entered Reginald's chest right between the wings of his natty coat.

For a moment they posed there, eyes locked on eyes. Smythe-George's were very surprised. He tried to say something, but it came out as a large slurp of blood that ran down his chin and made his wine-colored necktie darker. Then his eyes rolled back and he slumped over as life left him.

Annja turned her hips away as his knees gave way beneath him, pulling the blade from his body. Then she flicked her wrist, clearing the mystical blade and dewing the broad leaves of the ivy on the passage wall with blood.

"You gave me no choice," she said.

With a push of her will she put the sword away. She looked around. The western sky looked as if the blood she'd shed had stained it. The manor showed no light nor sign of life. If anyone had witnessed her reversal of circumstance, they were keeping mum about it.

Gathering herself, she climbed to the top of the six-foot side wall. Then she dropped down to the lawn outside. She hoped to have cycled most of the way back to the bike shop before Sir Martin thought to miss his lackeys.

7

Roux pushed his sunglasses halfway down his nose to look at Annja as she walked toward him along the Riviera beach. She wore a green tube top with a hint of blue, shorts in an explosion of colors, red, yellow, blue, white. With her lithe shape and panther poise, she could. Silver-framed sunglasses hid her eyes behind dark lenses. Her hair blew free in the brisk Mediterranean morning breeze.

"You certainly took your time," the old man said querulously.

He had a metal-and-yellow-plastic-mesh chaise longue unfolded on the sand beneath a green-and-white parasol. He wore a Panama hat with a red-and-black band, a bush jacket, Bermuda shorts and sandals. He sipped a tall iced drink through a straw.

Annja sat next to him on a towel he had spread out beside him in anticipation of her arrival. She drew her long legs up under her chin, and gazed out to sea, where the surreally long low shape of a super-tanker made its way west toward the Straits of Gibraltar.

"I thought I was here on time."

"I don't mean today, girl. I mean, what in the name of merciful God took you so long to think to come and visit me? You've left half of Europe in an uproar in your wake. You're more like a hurricane than a force of good."

A pair of adolescent girls emerged from the surf wearing nothing but bikini bottoms. They ran past, giggling in the self-consciousness of their scandalous near nudity. Annja shook her head.

"You disapprove?" Roux asked.

"I'm thinking about the sunburn." She shuddered.

"What about you?"

"What about me?"

"Will you remain covered?"

"Of course. I don't need that kind of sunburn." She tipped down her own shades and studied him. "Are you being a dirty old man?"

"Who knows? Perhaps I would disapprove."

They sat a moment in silence. Above them the sky was clear but for a few faint brush-strokes of cloud and a contrail making its way south across the sea. Gulls swarmed above the water like white scraps of paper borne on the breeze. The beach smelled of hot sand, salt water, seafood somewhat past its sell-by date, semirandom petroleum fractions. Roux smelled of sunscreen with aloe vera and coconut oil, old man's sweat and faintly of alcohol.

"What about Peru?" she asked.

"The manuscript has been duly sold to an Asian consortium that will ensure its discoveries are brought to the world at reasonable price, not coopted by either greedy governments or the Western pharmaceutical cartel." He sipped and smiled. "We realized a tidy sum on this transaction. Altogether a good thing; we certainly have expenses to defray."

"What about the people?" she asked impatiently.

"No further harm came to them." He shrugged. "For the most part drug barons cannot afford to act the way their counterparts do in the movies. They sacrifice too much of their support among the populace that way. They start to act like outlaws."

"What about those mercenaries? What happens to them?"

"Nothing."

"Nothing?" Annja was outraged.

"Nothing. Their operation is very highly connected in the United States."

Annja shook her head in disgust.

"You must learn to accept what is beyond your power to change, child," Roux said. "You cannot save the world."

"I thought that was my mission."

"Perhaps. But you must learn to prioritize. Nothing is more certain than that you cannot save it all at once."

At that she turned a frowning face out to sea. A few sails stood up above the water like white fins. The supertanker had almost dissolved into the haze. The seagulls cried like lost souls.

"Tell me," Roux said at length.

So she did. She held back nothing, from the first hint on the Usenet of the discovery of Solomon's Jar; to her adventures in Amsterdam and subsequent escape from the Netherlands into Germany posing as the relief driver for a friendly, and well-bribed, Belgian lesbian trucker; to her visit to Ravenwood Manor.

At the last Roux grunted. "Does the expression, 'leading with your chin' suggest anything to you?"

She tipped down her shades and grinned at him. "Apparently a course of action."

He nodded and looked at the water. His expression was dark. "I have lost one champion already," he said. "I don't want to mislay another and spend the next half millennium looking for *her* replacement. Try to learn a modicum of caution, if you please."

"It's on the to-do list. You know what puzzles me?" Annja asked, quickly changing the subject.

"Of course not. I make no pretense at clairvoyance," Roux said, perturbed.

"It's not important at all, but it keeps niggling at my attention. Who or what was 'trees'?" Annja asked.

"Terry."

"Huh?"

"Don't say 'huh,' young lady. It indicates muddy and undisciplined thinking," Roux scolded.

Fleetingly Annja wondered just how much her predecessor had personified lucid and disciplined thinking. Not much, from Annja's reading of history. She chose to say nothing because it was a tender subject for Roux and she had no desire to hurt him with flippancy. Also, because he took gloomy satisfaction in lecturing her about her forerunner and her unpleasant demise, and it always made Annja acutely uncomfortable to hear the facts surrounding Joan of Arc's destruction.

"I beg your pardon," Annja said precisely and formally.

"That's better. 'Trees' is short for 'Theresia,' which is cognate to your English 'Theresa.' Trees's Schatwinkel means, Terry's Treasure Shop," Roux stated.

"Oh. I didn't know you spoke Dutch."

"You'd be surprised what oddments one picks up in a few short centuries, my dear."

He sipped his drink down until his straw slurped noisily in the ice at the bottom of his plastic cup. "So, has the true jar been found? What do you say?"

Annja frowned. "I don't know if we have sufficient evidence to say one way or another."

"Evidence? Bah!" Roux produced a theatrically Gallic sniff. "You moderns, with your veneration of rationality."

"Not everybody feels that way," she said.

"You refer to the Paleolithic dreams of your friends in Kent? Those who would cast away all modernity and return us to squinting at graffiti scrawled on the walls of caves by smoky firelight are as superstitious as those who cannot imagine life before text messaging! What you fail to realize is that rational thought is a *tool*. It suits some uses and not others. It is no less—and certainly no more."

She smiled at him. "I presume you had a point?"

"Of course! Use your intuition. You knew at once that the jar you found on Highsmith's mantel was false. What do you feel about the real Solomon's Jar?"

She expected to have to scrunch her face up and squint and concentrate. Instead she found herself answering, "It has been found," without her own conscious volition.

Roux nodded his white-bearded chin. "Indeed."

"You knew?"

"Of course. Otherwise, why would the crew of the fishing trawler who found it be murdered? A random maniac would be too coincidental, *non?* And the fact that six men were butchered in a manner which inevitably must have proven as noisy as it was messy implies strongly the existence either of confederates or supernatural strength and speed."

She cocked a brow at him. "You think demons were involved?"

"Perhaps. Not in the way you think." He shook his head. "No.

Those men were murdered, most likely, by other men possessed of ample evidence that the true jar of Solomon had been found."

"Now you're using reason," Annja said.

"Of course. Did I not say it was a handy tool indeed—when appropriately used?"

He stood and began to fold his parasol. "I must be on my way. There's a world poker tour tournament commencing in Monte Carlo this evening, and I don't want to be late to put down my entry fee. I believe I've spotted a tell in Phil Ivey on the television."

"I'll never know how you square gambling with your service of the good."

"It's not important that you do so," he said. "Keep in mind that there are many paths to righteousness. And unrighteousness, as well. Your view of good will not always concur with that of others who may serve it as fully and diligently as you do yourself. That's another reason not to go looking for wrongs to right or, more precisely, not to go looking for witches to burn. You may find you have destroyed another great warrior for the cause."

Annja winced. She knew he would not use that particular metaphor lightly. He of all people.

"We will ourselves not always see eye to eye, my child," he told her, his voice gentler now. He folded up the chaise. "We may yet find ourselves at cross purposes, or even open opposition. And yet still fighting with true hearts for the same great cause."

"So you admit to working for good? I thought you were indifferent. Or undecided, maybe."

He ignored her. "The path of good is not supposed to be easy. That is the allure of the path of evil. Few who wreak great harm do so with any intention of working evil in the world. Most often their intent is exactly the opposite. And most who do lesser evils do so because it is the simplest and most expedient thing to do."

"So what's my next move?" Annja asked.

"Must I tell you everything?" Roux said dismissively.

"Well, if you aren't willing to forgo the pleasure of picking my performance apart after the fact—"

He sighed. "Don't imagine your powers shield you more than they do."

"I don't, by and large," she said. "Otherwise I wouldn't have run away so fast."

"I worry."

She reached up and briefly squeezed his hand. The flesh was re-silient, like any strong hand. Yet somehow she thought to feel in its dry grasp the strength of ages.

"Thank you," she said.

"As for whence to proceed from here," he said, "you are the ar-chaeologist. But I would be so bold as to suggest the source. I bid you good day."

He tipped his hat and walked off along the beach. His stride belied his years—the age he appeared, and vastly more his real age.

Seventeen hours later she was on an El Al Boeing 737 touching down outside Tel Aviv.

8

There was a riot going on at the Temple Mount.

Jerusalem was above all else a city of contradictions. Contrasts, between cultures, between faiths, between old and new, what had been celebrated or lamented into the ground centuries before were on studied display like trinkets in a tourist-trap window. The quaint biblical streets of the Old City, narrow and winding, were appropriately inconvenient. Mostly Annja found the place hot, dusty and tense. And that was before the riot.

Walking past a pair of Israeli soldiers standing in front of a coffee shop, their bulky battledress casting grotesque late-afternoon shadows down one of the broader streets, Annja found herself wondering why the Holy City didn't make more of an impression on her. Although biblical archaeology wasn't her field, the fabled jar of King Solomon would have held at least academic interest for her, if not more.

Perhaps it was the depressing present. From the evident hostility among rival Christian creeds and sects, to the division between Arab and Israeli, to the less known but virulent differences among the Israeli people themselves, the city that should have been a haven of spiritual peace was a hotbed of worldly strife.

Annja had little plan at the moment. She was fairly sure the jar wasn't where legend had it, the demons King Solomon had subsequently bound within it had built him a mighty temple. Yet Roux had suggested she seek the source for knowledge.

The disturbance—maybe she had been premature in characterizing it as a *riot,* but she could feel something coming on, like a thunderhead rising from just beyond the horizon—was packed into the plaza where the Moroccan quarter had once stood, hard up against the retaining wall built by King Herod to aggrandize the temple, and also to keep the sides of Mount Moriah from slumping into what was even then a substantial urban concentration. Its gray stone face, knobbled like a collection of knees, age pitted and sprouting random tufts of brush like hair on moles, was turned all orange and gold by the setting sun. The crowd's sullen mutter washed against it and broke back like storm surf. Cutting through the white noise came the stridency of an electronically amplified voice whose words Annja could not make out.

She had passed through the forty-foot stone walls Süleyman the Magnificent had surrounded the Old City with in the sixteenth century at the New Gate and made her way through the Christian quarter. She wore what she considered standard adventure tourist drag: white cotton blouse with long sleeves rolled up, khaki cargo pants with many invaluable pockets, sunglasses and Red Wing low-top hiking shoes, unfashionable but likewise indestructible. The clothes were of good quality and were far from being glamorous or provocative. Annja knew conservative religious elements, of all three major faiths with spiritual interests vested in the country, had a record of hassling or even attacking female tourists whose dress they considered scandalous. Her ensemble was designed to make her unremarkable, as inconspicuous as her height and willowy build and looks allowed. She had a bulky pack that could serve as a daypack or masquerade as a big utilitarian purse slung over one shoulder. A digital camera rode around her neck on a strap.

As she approached the Western Wall, she noticed that the tourists and idlers and even businesspeople suddenly began to thin from the streets like townsfolk in advance of a gunfight in a Western movie. She started seeing more Galil-toting soldiers, then riot police standing between the mob and the Wailing Wall itself. The riot squad wore dark blue helmets and bulky synthetic body armor that looked startlingly like the armor of the Roman legionnaires.

Then she spotted that most infallible sign of trouble brewing, more certain than circling vultures. Vans from the international news services were parked around the edge of the big plaza, with satellite antennae sprouting from their roofs.

She didn't read Hebrew, so many of the signs being waved by the protesters, most of whom wore yarmulkes, meant nothing to her. But there were plenty of signs written in English to clarify the situation.

This particular disturbance, she gathered, was being pitched by West Bank settlers resisting government attempts to remove them from their claims outside the country's acknowledged boundaries. Some of the antigovernment sentiments were astonishingly vitriolic, making her wonder what the signs she could not read might say. As she drew near she heard the cries of the protesters as they hurled insults at the riot cops and the soldiers who formed a loose cordon along the outside of the crowd.

The demonstrators were also throwing physical items that looked like bits of stone pried from the ancient walls and streets of Jerusalem itself. That tightened her brow and mouth and narrowed her eyes. She had to remind herself that more important issues lay at stake here than the preservation of random antiquities. But it ran altogether contrary to her archaeologist's instincts to think that anything could be more important.

Annja moved around outside the cordon of glumly businesslike soldiers. She still wasn't sure what she was doing here, what it was she expected to see. She felt an increasing sense of urgency, though. She was meant to be here; that much she knew.

The electronically amplified individual voice emanated from a podium erected hard by the wall itself. A tall man in a business suit with a yarmulke perched on an expensive-looking dark blond coiffure and some kind of cincture around his neck in lieu of a tie, urged the protesters to peace, love and moderation, in what Annja belatedly realized was English. Distortion and the setting's strangeness had conspired to prevent her from recognizing the calming words.

She frowned. She wasn't an avid follower of popular culture—at least, not more modern than five hundred years old or so. Still, she had the itching impression of having seen that rather handsome face, perhaps on the cover of a celebrity magazine on a table in a dentist's waiting room. She felt as if she *ought* to know who he was.

To her amazement the police and soldiers stoically endured the stones pelting off their helmets and riot shields as if they were rain-drops. Occasionally a demonstrator would turn and try to loft a rock up over the top of the wall toward the black dome of al-Aqsa Mosque, peeking over the wall's top. None of them had the range.

Some protesters turned their ire on a passing businessman—an Arab she guessed from his appearance and hunched, harried posture, though he wore a shabby tan Western-style suit. For a moment he just pulled his head farther down between his shoulders and tried to weather the abuse. Then something stung; he straightened, turned, spit something.

Instantly a pair of soldiers pounced on him and slammed him to the irregular gray flagstones with the metal butts of their rifles.

The mob surged outward, flowing around the other soldiers like water between tree boles. Whether they were themselves trying to attack other, largely Arab, passersby or simply started like a flock of pigeons by a sudden eruption of the violence that charged the air like electricity before lightning, Annja couldn't tell. The soldiers grabbed futilely at the protesters, or pushed them with their assault rifles. The mob largely ignored them, thrusting them rudely aside and flowing past, until a trooper managed to catch a handful of somebody's shirt.

Motivated, Annja guessed, by little more than the policeman's predator pounce reflex, the riot phalanx charged. They hit the mob from behind like a mobile wall. She noticed they used Roman tech-niques, too: jabbing with their short-sword-sized batons, then club-bing in lieu of hacking with the *gladii.*

Tentacles of the mob blew forth like debris from an explosion. One group blasted straight at her. It consisted mostly of unshaved young men who, in her flash impression, seemed more like middle-class kids dressing down than the proletarian types their work shirts and dungarees suggested. They spotted her and veered toward her, screeching in a combination of rage and triumph. Whether they took her for a possibly unsympathetic journalist or just felt like venting their feelings in some good old-fashioned foreigner bashing she couldn't tell. It didn't much matter. Annja turned and darted into the maze of narrow streets and alleys that veined the Old City.

Their cries pursued her. With the pedestrian traffic and obstructions littering her path she couldn't move very quickly. Indeed, because her pursuers had fewer compunctions about shoving people out of the way or simply running over them, they quickly gained on her.

When an age-bent man with a black hat, frock coat and snowy beard and earlocks opened a half-sprung screen door directly in her path, Annja's pursuers caught up. As she reared and stopped, without space even to dodge for fear of bowling the old man over, a hand roughly seized her right shoulder from behind.

It was almost a relief to be able to act rather than flee. As the man who held her pulled she did not resist, but rather clapped her left hand over his and turned the way he urged her. At the same time she peeled the hand off and twisted it painfully down against itself, then turned it to lock the man's elbow. Before he knew it her attacker was doubled over and immobilized.

Three more men closed in on her from behind. The lead attacker, who was skinny with a bluish white complexion emphasized by his white shirt and the blue-black hair spilling out from beneath his yarmulke, had arms spread as if to catch her in a bear hug. Sensing her first foe was controlled for the moment, Annja fired a high front snap kick straight at the point of the young man's chin. He was wide open and the kick came as quickly as a boxer's jab. His teeth clacked together, his eyes rolled up and he toppled, stunned, against a crumbling wall.

The first assailant was struggling and complaining in energetic Hebrew. Still keeping his wrist twisted and her forearm pressed against his arm Annja brought a knee up into his midsection. The breath burst from him. He doubled over even tighter.

The two still standing had fanned out left and right. They also wore white shirts, black pants and pasty complexions; one sported thick glasses. I'm beating up a bunch of nerds, she thought.

"We can call this off anytime," she told them.

They rolled their eyes wildly at each other. The one she'd kicked sat rubbing his jaw and weeping.

The two still on their feet issued inarticulate screams and charged. The one to Annja's left hugged the wall. She spun the man she was still holding and launched him into the man with a thrusting side kick. They went down in a tangle of limbs.

The last assailant closed, flailing punches. Annja ducked down behind raised forearms, fending off the flurry of swipes with motions of her elbows. The young man breathed like a bellows; his spittle sprayed Annja's face.

"Enough," she said. She quit blocking with her right, allowing a clumsy blow to glance off her lowered forehead. The hand she'd freed seized the front of the youth's shirt and yanked him toward her. She met him with a head butt to the bridge of the nose.

She heard cartilage crunch. She pushed the man away. He stumbled back several paces, sat down and stared at her. Blood cascaded from his broken nose and streamed into his lower jaw, which hung slack with astonishment. He gagged as he became aware of the taste of his own blood. Then he covered his face with both hands and began to wail.

Annja shook her head. She wasn't sure what had motivated the young men to attack her.

A furious shout brought her head up and around. Men crowded into sight around a dogleg in the claustrophobic lane behind her. Those she could see well enough in the thickening gray shadows and velvet gloom wore yarmulkes and protesters' armbands.

That ended their similarities to the quartet of fervent young students who lay moaning and disheveled in the gutter at Annja's feet. These men wore the same workmen's clothes. But these looked used. They were more filled out, too, especially in the area of chest, shoulders, and biceps—and bellies. Their hands were strong and work roughened. They gripped the tools of clubs and staffs and a length of metal pipe or two as if used to wielding hard things.

Burly as they were, they came fast. Annja turned and fled.

She vaulted a pile of crates. She paused long enough to scatter the pile across the narrow passage between stone walls irregular and grimed with not particularly graceful age. A couple of the lead pursuers duly tripped over them and sprawled hard on the cobblestones in sprays of splinters and curses in English and Hebrew. At least she assumed the Hebrew was cursing.

They swore louder as their mates trampled right over them, dogged in pursuit. Others smashed the crates to jagged slats.

Annja had long legs and a runner's wind. She should have left the mob in her dust with ease; though the deep-tanned look of some of them indicated they had the kind of endurance to labor all day in the hot Holy Land sun, that sort of thing didn't translate well into running either fast or far.

But with random loose stones underfoot, various cornices or piles of goods intruding in the inadequate right of way, and the constant intrusion of passersby who simply couldn't get out of the way fast enough, she could run little if any faster than her pursuers. Glancing over her shoulder, she saw one of them stiff-arm an elderly man face-first into a wall.

Anger kindled within her, a smolder fanning rapidly to a blaze. She longed to invoke the sword and dispense some well-earned justice. A dozen armed and burly men pursuing a single woman was not some semiharmless emotional venting but a lynch mob. Why they were after her she didn't know, but they obviously didn't intend to sit her down for an earnest discussion of internal Israeli politics if they caught her. She knew she had every right to take their lives if they raised their weapons against her. She formed her hand as if grasping a simple hilt, began to summon her will....

Annja stopped herself. She ducked left down an alley, tripped over the supporting slanting stanchion of a shabby gray-and-black-striped awning, fell, rolled and was up again barely slowed, her trousers streaked with dust and alley grime. Her leading pursuers went down with furious yells, tearing at the cloth that wrapped them up and barking their shins on the planks.

I can't, she grimly realized. The bruises she had given the angry students were one thing. In the current political climate if she left bodies bleeding in the ancient dust all hell would break loose.

Yet her mission was too vital to be brought to an end in an alley by a band of thugs, whatever their motivation. Roux had warned her to be cautious. Even after half a millennium the terrible death of his first protégée was like an incurable wound within him.

Maybe I can handle them unarmed she thought. She did have advantages, not least of which was that none of her pursuers could possibly suspect just how effective she could be at close combat, with or without a weapon in her hand. But for all her speed, strength and well-honed fighting skills, and even for the fact that such a number of them would inevitably get in one another's way, particularly in such tight confines, she well knew it would only take one lucky hit to put her down.

She started left down another alley. A knot of beefy men appeared at the far end like a cork stuffed in a bottle. They held clubs, too. "There's the bitch!" one shouted in pure New Jersey English.

Where did these thugs come from? she wondered. With a shock like a belly punch she realized this was no random outburst of violence. This attack was *directed*.

At her.

Annja turned and bolted out of the alley. A man loomed up to her right, both hands holding a length of white-painted pipe above a face beet-red from sun and blood pressure. She side kicked him in the midst of his well-filled work shirt. Air blew out of him in a furious shout, but his belly saved him from any serious harm. He did fly back into the faces of his nearest comrades, buying her a few shavings of a second to run again.

The street turned right before her. She darted around.

And found herself staring at the cracked khaki stucco of a blind wall.

She was trapped.

9

Annja looked up. A lot of the one-story buildings in the Old City had fairly low rooftops given that a millennium or two's accretion had raised the level of the streets. She could climb such. But it was hopeless. The three walls that hemmed her all rose at least two stories. A battered sheet-metal drain pipe ran down from the rooftop to her right. At least one of the clamps holding it in place had come entirely free of the crumbling wall, and the rest were being held in place only by paint or rust or habit for all she knew. Even if she could scramble up the pipe in time, there seemed no way it would ever support her weight. Muscle mass was dense. Especially hers.

Behind her she heard men's voices braying in unmistakable triumph. The thunder of pursuing boots dwindled. The thugs behind her had slowed to a walk.

They know I'm trapped, she thought. They're savoring the moment.

She eyed the rickety pipe again. If I can catch it high enough up… She braced herself to spring.

A doorway she hadn't even seen suddenly opened to her left. "This way, dearie," a voice hissed in English from the darkness within.

"Who are you?" Annja asked.

"Witness to your demise if you don't move *now*."

A voice called loudly from out of sight around the corner. The words weren't clear, but their import was.

Annja dodged through the door. It shut quietly behind, sealing off the last gray light of dusk.

FOR A MOMENT IT SEEMED she stood in hot, claustrophobic blackness. She felt panic thrill within her.

"Easy, dearie," the voice said. "Just breathe deeply. You're safe now—safe as you are anywhere, anyway. The door's locked. Also it's not so easy to see from outside, as you might have noticed."

Annja became aware of an orange glow rising before her. It became a brass oil lamp, reflecting the orange light of its own flame, being brought up to the level of her face. She sensed a shadowy form behind it, heard breathing.

"Come with me." The voice was American. It was that of a woman of mature years, she realized.

The lantern swung around. Butter-colored light glowed in the coarse weave of a hood covering the mysterious woman's head as she led off down a corridor. A moving arc of light traveled with them, revealing rough stone walls and a low ceiling. The passageway led down a ramp, sufficiently smooth from use to be slightly slippery, then up a set of steps.

Up and down the shrouded figure led her, right and left. Sometimes they passed open doorways, dark oblongs that signaled their presence by making the lamp-flame waver and brushing cool across Annja's cheek. Once or twice they came upon a side chamber illuminated from within, once by candles on tables and set in niches by the wall, a second by a low-wattage lamp beneath a heavy shade. In both, silent, dark figures huddled, reading or contemplating, Annja could not be sure.

Such directional sense as she may have possessed had long been destroyed by apparently random windings, and incipient strangeness, by the time her guide pushed open a door of age-blackened wood and led her into a small side chamber.

"Sit yourself down," the woman said from inside her cowl. She gestured toward a rude round wooden table flanked by two stools in the center of the room. It reminded Annja of nothing so much as a monk's cell.

When Annja hesitated the woman set the lamp down on one side of the table and said, "We have relatively little time here. Relatively, because it would take a lifetime or so to tell you all you need to know. And I'd have to learn most of it first. So let's get started with what I can give you, all right?"

She pushed the hood back. Big dark eyes gazed at Annja from a strong-featured, leanly handsome face. A mane of heavy dark hair, maybe black, and marked with a showy silver-white blaze above the right side of the forehead, framed it.

"I'm Tsipporah," the woman said. "I'm a student of kabbalah. I'll be your guide for this portion of your journey, so you might as well make yourself comfortable. And you are…?" She stuck out a hand.

"I'm Annja Creed. Pleased to meet you." She shook the offered hand, then blinked. "You acted as if you knew me."

"I know *what* you are," Tsipporah said. "It practically blazes from you. Be wary, child, because anyone you come across with any degree of real insight can spot you instantly. But my own understanding doesn't quite extend to names and personalities. Mostly I'm a keen spotter of the blindingly obvious. And while you might want to stand, I'm going to take a load off, if you don't mind."

Tsipporah sat. A beat later Annja emulated her. The room was almost claustrophobic, with pale-stuccoed walls and a low ceiling of dark planks. From the cool and earthy smell Annja knew she was underground. She realized the chamber must have been a first floor at some point, or perhaps higher. The street level had risen much farther over the years than she'd first appreciated.

"Excuse my ignorance of Jewish tradition," Annja said, "but I thought only men could study kabbalah. Or are you—?"

"One of the goofy followers of young Mark Peter up there?" The woman laughed. Picking up the lamp, she put the flame to a cigarette she'd produced from somewhere and puffed it alight. "I'm surprised you recognized him."

"It's hard to miss Mark Peter Stern in the media these days," Annja said. "Although it took hearing the name to jog it into my memory. He's the flavor-of-the-month guru for all kinds of celebrities, isn't he?" She shook her head. "Even somebody with as little interest in popular culture as I have can scarcely miss him. His face looks out at you from every other magazine cover in airport news-stands, as well as being all over television and the Internet."

Tsipporah nodded. "There are two traditional rules about studying kabbalah. One, that you must be at least forty years old. The other that you be a man. Neither was ordained by the Creator. One arises from sound sense, the other from fear. The first is wise—and as you probably gather, Stern certainly failed to honor it. He qualifies now, though you'd hardly know it to look at him. Meanwhile, I'm hardly the first to violate the latter prohibition, nor am I likely to be the last.

"But on to business. Time's an illusion, but it's a fleet one. You seek the jar, don't you?"

Annja hesitated. Roux had warned her almost compulsively about security—as if keeping secrets was anything alien to a kid raised in an orphanage by nuns. Yet Tsipporah seemed to know a lot about her already. Annja got no sense of evil or menace from the older woman—not that she regarded her danger sense as anywhere near infallible. And anyway, she thought, if she knows enough about me to even ask the question, what do I really give up by answering honestly?

"Yes," she said after processing her thoughts.

"All right." Tsipporah smiled as if her guest had passed a test. "Then you might benefit from the straight scoop, don't you think?"

Annja frowned. "With all due respect," she said, trying to match tone to content, "why are you helping me? I'm a foreigner and a total stranger."

"No stranger than anybody else in this town," the older woman said. "And as you probably guessed from my accent, I'm not exactly a local myself."

"New Jersey?" Annja guessed.

"Right the first time. You seem to have a bit of an accent in your own speech. Well hidden, but it's there." She cocked her head to one side. With her triangular chin and big dark eyes it made her look like a shrewd bird. "New Orleans?"

Annja nodded. "I didn't think any trace remained."

"I told you I'm very observant," Tsipporah said. "Anyway, about those demons. The story says that Solomon bound them and used them to build his temple overnight. Maybe it didn't happen literally that way. But take my word for it—there are demons out there. You probably have some idea about that already, although you still probably can't fully bring yourself to believe. King Solomon bound them to serve him. And serve him they did, in whatever particulars."

Annja felt her heartbeat pick up. The woman was reading her all too well, so far. "I don't want to…overstep any religious boundaries. But I thought Solomon was considered a holy man in Judaism, as well as Christianity."

Tsipporah held one hand out flat, palm down, and rocked it side to side. "You want to know why a righteous man would have traffic with demons, right?"

"Right."

"The short answer is because he could. Summoning and binding demons to your will is more of a gray area, morally and theologically speaking. It isn't intrinsically unrighteous."

"But aren't demons evil?" Annja asked.

"Absolutely. In ways I doubt you can begin to fathom. Although with a little time I suspect you'll know far more about them than you want, dearie."

"Then why isn't it evil to deal with them?"

"We're talking about binding and using them, not the other way around. Of course, there's always the risk of role reversal—gives the whole thing a certain spice. You might think of them, in the proper hands, as tools, morally neutral when under control. For our purposes, I think you can safely take it that King Solomon was indeed a righteous man. And an extremely powerful magician."

Annja shook her head. "Forgive me. It's a little hard to get my mind around the concept of magic and evil. Demonology, anyway. In a conventional, I guess, religious conception."

"Oh, it *is* evil—to conventionally religious eyes. Remember your illustrious predecessor was condemned for witchcraft. And she never even practiced."

Annja caught her breath. "How do you know about that?"

"Joan of Arc? Doesn't every schoolchild—"

"That she was my predecessor. How did you know?"

"I know the signs. I travel the *sephiroth*—the spheres, you might call them. Sometimes I have visions. Sometimes I just have hunches.

Sometimes I'm just a batty old lady who ought to take up a different hobby, like knitting."

Annja laughed. She couldn't help liking this peculiar woman, with her mixture of brashness and what seemed genuine humility. "I have a hard time seeing you knitting."

"Don't sell it short, sweetie. Keeps the fingers nimble and arthritis at bay." Tsipporah blew smoke at an angle up into the air. "To get back to my story, from which I so inconsiderately distracted myself, whatever the demons did for Solomon, when they were done with it— or he was done with them—he bound them in a brass jar. He then sealed it with lead, inscribing in it the sign of the five-pointed star—"

"Not six?" Annja interrupted.

"Nope. The good old pentagram."

"But I thought the six-pointed star was the shape of Solomon's seal, as well as the shield of David."

"That bit of confusion seems to have cropped up late in the nineteenth century. Probably for political and nationalistic reasons more than anything else—to kind of add throw weight to the six-pointed star as the symbol for Judaism. Good King Solomon sealed the demons in with lead, with the pentagram, and threw the jar into the Red Sea."

"The Red Sea? But supposedly the jar was just recently fished out of the Mediterranean."

Tsipporah wagged a finger back and forth before her. "Tch, tch. You're getting ahead of me. Legend says somebody fished the jar out of the Red Sea a long, long time ago. Treasure hunters, of all things, eager to use the demons to uncover riches."

"How'd that turn out?"

The other woman shrugged. "Don't know, truth to tell. Might not've turned out badly, if the people who uncorked the demons didn't get greedy and try to control them all, which is a very poor idea if you don't happen to be, say, King Solomon. Then again, anybody who'd let loose seventy-odd powerful demons on the world to get their hands on treasure is probably too greedy by definition, no? Anyway, I've never seen a good accounting for exactly what came next, not that I trusted, nor have I got any kind of insight into it. The key thing is, what with one thing and another, the jar, now emptied of demons but not power, got chucked into the Mediterranean. Where, in the fullness of time, it was discovered by some Greek fishermen who later came to very sticky ends."

Annja leaned forward. Her pulse spiked again. "So it's true? The real jar has been found?"

"What are we doing here, sweetie? You tell me. I'm not going to tell you to trust me. You do know never, ever to trust anybody who tells you to, right?"

Annja smirked.

"Good—thought so. But look at the circumstances. Here you are. Here I am. How did we happen to come together, anyway?" Tsipporah asked.

Annja looked at her for a moment. "All right," she asked, "how?"

"I don't know, exactly. I just know why. We were supposed to." She stubbed out her cigarette in a little flat tin that looked to Annja like a tuna can she'd picked up from the floor beneath the table. She immediately lit another.

Annja frowned slightly but resolved not to be a smoking prude. Lots of people smoked here anyway. Almost everybody, in fact.

"I might have hired those big, strapping men to chase you here," Tsipporah said through the smoke, "even if they are a bit sweaty for my tastes. But then how would I know those things I do about you? I didn't know your name before you came here. Didn't really know what you looked like, beyond some fairly broad outlines. But I knew you were good. And that you seek the jar."

Tsipporah smiled. "Put another way, it's destiny, sweetie. Get used to it. You'll find yourself being in the right place at the right time a lot. Or the wrong place at the worst possible time. All a matter of perspective."

"So what do you get out of this, anyway, Tsipporah?" Annja asked.

The older woman tipped her head back, let smoke trail toward the ceiling, laughed. "If more people remembered to ask that question the world would be a happier place. Let's just say that I regard myself, in my own small and studious way, as a servant of good."

"Does that mean God?" Annja asked

Tsipporah smiled a crooked smile. "The Creator is served in many ways, some of which would curl your hair. We all serve the Creator, dear. The worst no less than the best. Let's just say that you and I both choose to serve the good and leave off splitting those particular hairs. Fair?"

After a moment Annja nodded. "Fair." She didn't sound any more convinced than she felt.

"Let's also just say I enjoy a vicarious thrill as much as the next person," Tsipporah said. "You're embroiled in a mission that has three parts. It's of the mind, of the spirit and of the body. Let's just say I'm not up to the run-and-jump part these days. In fact, being a kabbalist is about as bookish a pastime as there is. Sedentary, you know. So I get a kick out of being involved, at whatever remove, in your adventures."

Annja smiled. It seemed to her a little silly that anyone else might envy her the indecision and inconvenience and the not infrequent terror that went with her new life.

"Speaking of kabbalists—I know that's kind of a clumsy segue— but that reminds me about Mark Stern. What's he doing up there, anyway, with his megaphone by the wall?"

"He's associated with the settlers' movement. The government wants to close down some of the settlements in occupied territory. Some of the residents object pretty vehemently." Tsipporah sighed. "There's a good reason I decided to immerse myself in the study of the Tree of Life, and put such worldly political concerns behind me."

With a sudden flash of insight, Annja said, "You were a political activist?"

"What else?' The older woman drew on her cigarette. "I'm still a devoted Marxist, of course."

"I didn't know they believed in kabbalah."

"Groucho's my favorite," Tsipporah went on laughing. "You probably figured that out already. Never really cared for Harpo, though."

10

"Mark Peter Stern positions himself as a voice of peace and reason between the government and the settlers," Tsipporah said. "Me, I'm not so sure."

"How good a kabbalist is he?" Annja asked.

Tsipporah compressed her lips to a line and sat back in her chair with her chin sunk toward her sternum. "Kabbalah is infinite," she said at last, "and to know who's *really* wise in its ways would therefore take infinite understanding, it seems to me. Not something I pretend to, egotistical as I am in my dotage. And then again, there are plenty of pious Jews rather more than Gentiles, I expect, who'd tell you there *is* no such thing as a good kabbalist."

She looked up sharply. "So I reckon what you really want me to tell you is how good a *man* Mark Stern is. Right?"

"All right. You caught me. But don't expect me to buy any of that 'dotage' nonsense from you," Annja said.

"Allow me my little conceits. One of the worst consequences of a culture that overvalues youth is that eventually it comes to over-value age. Big mistake—experience is a wonderful teacher, but she has some real schmucks for pupils. Also making a big deal of my age gives me license to spew random drive-by aphorisms like that. Anyway, before I disappoint you with my pop-psych assessment of the man, why do you ask?"

"Aside from the fact he happened to be in the same place at the same time as we were, functionally?"

"Right. There's no such thing as coincidence. But that doesn't imply everything is about us," Tsipporah said.

"I found a number for the Malkuth Foundation's New York offices on the caller ID of a murdered woman's phone," Annja said, "in a shop that may have had possession of the jar."

Tsipporah sat upright. "Tell me."

Annja did. She felt no more than the slightest tug of reluctance. She sensed no taint of evil in this woman or in this place. And even if she was wrong, it seemed unlikely she was telling her mysterious hostess anything she couldn't find out by some means of her own. *Or maybe I'm just rationalizing again*, she thought wryly.

"Hoo." Tsipporah let her breath slip out between pursed lips when Annja concluded. "That is quite the story. I'm caught up in more of an adventure than I even realized."

"I've been wondering, though," Annja said. "The jar on Highsmith's mantel. Was that the real jar?"

"What does your heart tell you?" Tsipporah asked.

Annja shook her head. "It told me it wasn't."

"In cases like this that's probably as good a test as any. A person in your position could feel the presence of power like that. Trust yourself."

"Not always as easy as it sounds," Annja said.

"Whoever promised you easy?"

"Something about the jar that was there puzzles me," Annja said. "Of course, I'm not sure it has any significance."

"Tell me," Tsipporah said. "Gratify my curiosity, if nothing else."

"It was covered with symbols. Small, crabbed, hard to read—at first I thought they were just scratch marks."

"What kind of symbols?"

"I'm not sure. I've never really seen anything like them before. Convoluted. The closest thing I can compare them to is symbols on an electronic-circuit diagram."

"Sigils," Tsipporah said.

"What are those?"

"Personal symbols for each demon that had been confined within the jar. Like seals—a king's signet ring, that sort of thing." She looked thoughtful in the wavering orange light. "That's highly significant. It may not have been the real jar—I'm sure it wasn't—but it sounds like an awfully good copy."

"Why would anybody make a copy of Solomon's Jar? For that matter, why would anybody want an empty jar badly enough to kill over it?" Annja asked, still unsure of what to believe.

"Because it has power. By use of the proper magics the demons might be forced to enter it again. Or it might be used to compel demons to obedience." She dipped her head briefly to the side. "It might even be destroyed—this being the preferred outcome of the demons themselves, I expect."

"Tsipporah," Annja said, "what are demons, anyway?"

"Bad. Powerful forces. Pretty much as advertised."

"Look, if there are demons, why don't we see them more?"

"I could give you the canned, expected answers about all the nasty things people do to each other," Tsipporah said, "except most of those are just that: we do them to each other. No demons need apply. A demon can get you to do nasty things. Things you'd never do on your own—that's what possession's all about. They can even boot you out of your own body for good and take over. That's what the Catholic Church calls *obsession*. But the bad urges that give rise to the bad things we do, demons don't cause them. They make use of them. They don't start the fire. But they do spray gas on it."

She took a hit from her cigarette. "And that's the reason you don't see them walking down the street. Under normal circumstances, at least. For various reasons—partly constraints imposed by the nature of reality, partly preference—they do the vast amount of their work indirectly. Influencing our thoughts and emotions. Their actions are almost exclusively in the realm of the psychological. Although to dismiss them as purely psychological phenomena is a very bad mistake indeed."

For a moment they sat in silence. The lamp flame flickered low. Annja realized she'd lost count of how many cigarettes Tsipporah had gone through. She was too caught up in what the older woman was telling her to be much bothered by the smoke, though it did make her throat scratchy.

"So what about Stern?" she asked at length. "Is he a charlatan?"

"That depends. By charlatan, do you mean someone who pretends to mystical powers he doesn't have? Or one who has no mystical powers, but pretends to?"

"I don't see the distinction, I'm afraid," Annja said.

"Then look again, sweetie. Stern has powers, make no mistake. Just not necessarily the ones he tells his followers he has. He may not even believe he really has any power, in which case he's the most deluded of all. What's most painfully apparent is that he doesn't really know what he's doing."

She ran a hand through her silver-streaked hair, then laughed. "But then, why should he be any different from anybody else, hey? And like all of us, he doesn't let the fact he doesn't know what he's doing slow him down."

Annja chewed her lower lip, trying to not let Tsipporah see the schoolgirlish gesture. She was thinking glumly about how much that aphorism applied to her.

I'm the champion of good, she thought, and I don't really know what that means. Nor what good actually is, for that matter. Am I the schmuck here?

"You seem troubled," Tsipporah said gently.

The words broke the surface tension of Annja's reverie. She realized her own head had drooped toward her chest. She lifted it and looked at Tsipporah. The vague glow of the lamp no doubt softened and flattered the older woman's features, but she looked agelessly beautiful and wise. Like some sort of archetype, Annja thought.

"Well—I don't know if I should talk to you about this," Annja said. "But I need to talk to somebody. And you seem, well, wise."

Tsipporah held up a weary hand, cigarette clipped between two fingers, and drew a zigzag in the air, like Zorro. "I'm just somebody who dragged you in off the street, sweetie. Don't impute more to me than I even pretend to claim for myself." She took a drag. "Bring wisdom into it, how wise are you to trust somebody you met like this? Huh?"

"Humor me, then. You're the closest thing to a sage I've come across in a while." Annja wasn't sure if Roux counted, or to what extent. She wasn't sure how wise it was to trust *him*, for that matter. The more so since he kept hinting she shouldn't, necessarily.

"I wonder if I am worthy. I have shed blood," Annja said.

"In defense of innocence?"

"Yes. And of myself as well."

The older woman laughed. "'If someone comes to kill you, kill him first,' as the great commentator Rashi interprets the Torah. That's the common right of all humans. Do you think you have fewer rights than the meanest goatherd when fighting for good?"

Annja looked at her through wide eyes. "Do you—" There's no tactful way to say this, she realized with a sinking heart "Do you believe in my mission, too?"

"You think I'd be here talking to you if I didn't?" Tsipporah rolled her eyes.

"But I thought—"

I'm not sure what I thought, Annja realized. In spite—or perhaps because—of the ferocious ministrations of the nuns at the orphanage in New Orleans, she did not think of herself as conventionally Christian at all, much less Catholic. To her amazement Roux had assured her, when she'd finally confessed the fact to him, that it didn't matter. She still wasn't sure she believed him....

"You thought Christians had a monopoly on the good, maybe?"

"No—God, no. I mean—that didn't come out right—I mean I'd never..."

Tsipporah reached out and took her hand with one hand and patted it with the other. "Ease up, dearie. I'm only messing with you. Of course you don't. Guess what? Neither do we, chosen people or not.

"Which do you think is more likely? That a given religion is bigger than the Creator, or that the Creator is bigger than any and all religions? Which vessel is the larger, do you reckon, my dear?"

"The Creator, I guess. I don't pretend to know for sure, though."

Tsipporah laughed again. "Right answer, dearie! If you could truly *know* the Creator, you'd *be* the Creator, yes? Who less could understand such a One? Not to mention such a Nothing."

She shook her head. "But enough of my goofy wordplay. We humans cannot really understand the Creator. But it falls to some of us to try, anyway. Some of us call ourselves kabbalists. I don't know which of us has the worse job, my child. Yours is the more athletic, in any event.

"But I do think you're right on track with that concern. You're called on to defend others, as well as yourself, of course. And that's righteous—being given a sword only you can wield is what I'd call pretty clear evidence of some kind of mandate."

Annja felt her eyes widen. "You know?"

Tsipporah patted her cheek. "Of course, dearie. Goes with the territory. And now the word of warning. You need to watch for any tendencies to, ah, freelance."

"Meaning?"

"If you go looking for dragons to slay, it's surprising what'll soon look like a dragon to you. Be always alert to the difference between righteousness and self-righteousness."

Annja smiled a bit tentatively. "I've been told that while saving the world is my job description, I need to prioritize."

"That's true. But it's only part of the truth," Tsipporah stated.

She leaned forward and caught Annja's hands in both of hers. "Listen to me on this. *Hear* me. Demons do their deadliest work through our virtues."

"How do you mean?"

"Even as the strong are more dangerous than the weak," Tsipporah said, "the best are more potentially destructive than the worst. Only those who consider themselves the most selfless are capable of conceiving a notion like cleansing the world by exterminating all the people of a certain race, just to pluck an example out of the air."

"Isn't selfishness wrong?"

"You already know better than that, girl," Tsipporah said, letting go and leaning back. "All things that live are selfish. Anyone who claims otherwise is lying right there—and don't you think it's worse if they don't *know* they're lying? The merely self-interested are far less destructive than the convinced selfless.

"And that's why Mark Peter Stern might be a very dangerous man, my dear. Not because he's a bad man. But because he's so good—and so invincibly *convinced* of it. Such a man is capable of anything. For the good, of course."

Annja felt a sinking sensation in her stomach. "What you're really warning me against," she said quietly, "is myself."

"Both, honey. That said, have faith in yourself." Tsipporah patted her cheek. "You just always have to guard against the temptation to cross the line from defender of the innocent to attacker of the wicked."

Annja sighed. Her burden seemed heavier than the weight of all the masonry above—than the weight of all the noble sanctuary, up there on that mount, that was so drenched in holiness that half the world's people seemed ready to kill each other over it.

"What do I do now?" she asked.

"Sweetie, you know how this mystic-guide shtick works. I can help you find out where you are, and clarify where you've been. I can drop a hint or two about the paths that lie open to you. But you have to choose. Only you."

Annja grimaced. "You can't even give me a *hint?*"

Tsipporah laughed. "I wish I had a mirror! Didn't your parents teach you not to make faces like that?"

"My parents died when I was small," Annja said in a level voice.

"I'm so sorry. I didn't mean—"

"It's okay. Not about my parents, of course. That'll never be okay. I thought I'd get used to it for a long time. But it's never happened. The best I can do is put it away and not think about it.

"But what you said—no harm done, Tsipporah. And as for making faces, the nuns at the orphanage where I was raised used to crack me on the knuckles with a ruler when I made them."

Tsipporah roared with laughter, surprisingly robust, ringing in the womb-like confines of the room. "So naturally you kept doing it! Ladies and gentlemen, we have a winner! Now that I know you, I feel a lot more optimistic about the cause of good than I have in years."

Annja smiled crookedly. "In spite of my problems with authority?"

"Because of them, dearie." She leaned forward across the table, until Annja feared she'd catch her hair on fire from the flickering lamp flame.

"I can tell you this much, the Jar of Solomon must be found. And seen into the proper hands."

Annja laughed. "Gee, thanks. And of course you can't tell me whose hands those are."

Tsipporah sat back. "Of course." She sighed. "Well. Time to be moving along. We each have our destinies." She rose and moved to a wall, made a gesture. Annja heard a slight click.

A light fixture mounted into the ceiling overhead came on. Annja had not noticed it in the gloom.

"A lightbulb?" she said, as scandalized as surprised. She blinked dazzled eyes. "There was an electric light here all along, and I've been sitting squinting in the dark for hours until I'm half blind?" Her voice rose rather higher than she'd intended at the end of the question.

"Of course," Tsipporah said. "This is a modern country, sweetheart. Of course there's electric light."

"Then why?" She could muster no more than a sputter.

Tsipporah laughed. "Because talking about esoteric matters goes much better with that sort of illumination." She gestured toward the oil lamp, whose flame, now guttering low, was scarcely to be seen in the light of what Annja, her eyes somewhat adjusted, realized as a pretty weak bulb. "Don't you have any sense of the mystic?" She shook her head. Her heavy mane swept around her shoulders. "You may be up on the latest fashions, but you need to cultivate a sense of *style*."

"You think I'm fashionable?" Annja asked, perplexed.

"Come on, rouse yourself and give me a hug," the older woman said. "Then I need to lead you out of here."

"Not by the most direct route, I'm guessing."

Tsipporah's smile was radiant. "Of course not! Now you're getting the idea."

11

The night air was cool. It smelled of dust, cooking spices, the inevitable diesel exhaust. Annja realized she had no idea what time it was. The streets of the Old City seemed deserted, or at least the narrow street outside the door Tsipporah held open for her.

"I can't tell you to go safely," the older woman said, "for I know you won't. I could bid you to walk always in the light—but I'm sure you shall. So I'll wish you all the joy it's possible for you to attain."

They embraced, kissing each other on the cheek. Annja wasn't sure whether the warmth she felt toward this woman was more like the feeling for the mother she'd scarcely known or the sister she'd never had. Lack of referents, she guessed.

"One final word about Mark Stern," Tsipporah said. "He's better at stirring up forces than he is at controlling them. And he's got poor judgment in associates."

Annja nodded. "Thank you. I'll keep that in mind. Will I see you again?"

"Unlikely, child." Tsipporah shook her star-blazed mane regretfully. "You will most likely not find this place again, either. You are fated to move through life forming few lasting connections, at least so long as you bear your burden. It is a harsh road for a woman to walk."

She smiled. "But I believe it will have its compensations."

THE OLD CITY SEEMED to have rolled up its sidewalks along with the vendors' rugs. By keeping the well-lit dome of al-Aqsa Mosque atop the Temple Mount at her back Annja knew she was heading west. It was her only reference point in the maze into which Tsipporah had released her.

She had picked her way down no more than three twists of narrow streets and shoulder-width alleys when she heard a growl of angry voices to her right. She moved toward the sound, telling herself she needed to make sure trouble wasn't about to erupt all over her from some unforeseen direction.

She came to a blind alley or small cul-de-sac. She saw six burly men in weathered work clothes with necks as large as their heads. Three of them held clubs, either batonlike sticks or metal pipes. Three held big-bladed weapons, more short swords than knives, at least two feet long with broad chopping blades. Annja thought of machetes, although she had no idea if they were that or some local equivalent. It wasn't exactly an exotic design.

Annja drew in a sharp breath.

They had her pale, black-haired Englishman backed against the steel-slat shutters covering the front of a tobacco shop.

"What you want with the jar?" one man said in guttural, heavily accented English. In the gleam of a streetlight the hair cropped close to his head showed hints of red. He wore some kind of dark band around his throat. It looked braided. He held one of the broad-bladed chopping weapons in a ham-sized fist while he prodded the notch of his captive's collarbone with a sausage-like finger. "Tell or it will go hard on you."

To Annja, standing unnoticed behind the men, whose attention was riveted to their prey, it looked as if things had already gone hard for her unnamed friend. His face, hanging down toward his open collar, was swollen and starting to discolor into one giant bruise. One eye was almost swollen shut; blood from a broken nose made a dark beard and mustache and had poured down to dye a messy bib on the front of his shirt.

He looked up. "I told you," he said. His lips were swollen and split. The words came out half whisper, half mumble. "I'm an archaeological researcher. Such a find would be of inestimable value—"

A beefy fist rammed into his belly from a man standing to the red-haired man's left. The young Englishman doubled over as the air was driven from his body. He gagged, coughed, then tried to straighten.

"He's not saying anything," another man said. "Let's do him. Let the filthy Arabs take the blame. Just another tourist cut up by savages."

"Who cares what he has to say?" said the man who had most recently punched the Englishman. His free hand held a club. "We just need to make sure he can't meddle anymore."

"Hear that, friend?" the red-haired man said, almost avuncular. "You're running out of options pretty quick now. But if you sing me a sweet enough song, who knows? Maybe you will live."

The young Briton tried to stand erect but could only manage a painful half-stoop. "Sorry to disappoint you," he said in a clearer voice. "But I can't carry a tune in a bucket. In good faith, though, I have to warn you—" he turned his head aside and spit blood at the cobblestones "—it's you lot who have the problem now."

And he lifted his head and looked right past them.

His captors stood staring at him a moment, postures redolent of suspicion, leaning forward like hungry dogs. Apparently none of them wanted to be first to fall for the old "look over there" gag. After a few heartbeats the central man, apparently the leader, slowly turned.

Standing three yards behind him, Annja smiled. His slitted eyes went wide.

She held the sword.

"Throw down your weapons and walk out of here," she told them in a ringing voice. She didn't particularly care if she attracted official attention, at least at this point in the proceedings. Search how they might, the police would never find her in possession of a weapon. Nor would they believe it if they saw it. "I will let you go unharmed."

All six goggled at the cross-hilted steel in her hand. They were having trouble believing, too. But it made an impression; she could see that. They had a sense of history in this part of the world, to understate grandly. The Crusaders' swords with their cruciform hilts were remembered with fear and respect by Muslim and Jew alike.

It had been a reluctant if flash decision to summon the sword before making her presence known. This way there was a chance to avoid bloodshed. These men were serious and their every attitude and action showed they were accustomed to doing violence. Annja knew merely being seen would never make them scuttle away like roaches, as it did many common-thug types. And if an unarmed and obviously American woman challenged them, they'd just laugh.

They did anyway, as she feared they would. "You may believe your actions to be righteous," she told them, words cracking like a whip, "but your actions are evil. Go now and save yourselves a lot of pain."

The Englishman called out something in Hebrew from behind them. The dark-haired man who had earlier gut punched him back-handed him with a casual swipe, not so much as turning his head. The black-furred back of his hand took the young man across the mouth and slammed him back into the shutters with a clanging impact.

"Nice try, girlie," the leader said. "But you have waded in much too deep. Throw that toy down before we take it away and spank you with it, hey?"

With impeccable pack-predator instincts his comrades had begun to move forward slowly. They fanned out so far as the street's width permitted, to take her from the sides. She held her face immobile. She knew there was a reason for the, "charge a gun, run away from a knife" adage.

She was about to teach it to them.

She made herself pull each breath deep down to the center of her body. Adrenaline flowed in her veins like an army of crazed jesters. Part of the mad chorus was due to fear. They were many, strong and seasoned fighters. And part came from anticipation.

"Touch me," she said, "and you will die."

"Listen—" the leader said. The man to his right, the man with the shock of dark hair who had struck the Englishman twice in Annja's sight, suddenly grabbed her right wrist. He pulled hard to yank her into a bear hug.

She didn't move. She had rooted, dropped her weight and sunk into poised relaxation. His slitted eyes went wide.

She turned toward him. The sword flashed. Its blade bit with an ax-on-wood sound.

It flashed between the wrist of the hand that held her and the man's arm, scarcely slowed.

The hand tightened spasmodically on her arm. Without the aid of the muscles of the arm it lacked strength. It was more a nervous jitter.

Blood squirted from between hand and stump. The man screamed as if only realizing a beat late what had befallen him. He staggered back, holding his truncated arm before his eyes, slipping into shock.

Annja sensed a rush of movement from her right. She continued her spin to her left, coming around as the man who had gotten around to her right side rushed in with a wild scream and an overhand cut of his machete. She caught his forearm with her left hand. It was like gripping a telephone pole. Using her hips, driving with her legs, she continued her turn, guiding his downward stroke as she did.

The wide blade of the machete bit with a crunch into the side of the recent amputee's head. His eyes rolled up. He fell like a bag of wet laundry, straight down.

The eyes stood out from the head of the man whose arm Annja had guided to deliver the death blow to his friend. Vomit slopped over his lower lip. Veins stood out on the side of his head in such shocking relief she half expected skyrocketing blood pressure to stroke him dead right there.

She felt no inclination to trust to chance. His gagging turned to a squeal of shock and anguish as she thrust the sword beneath his armpit through his torso.

She put a hiking shoe sole against the man's side and thrust kicked him into a man charging from her left with a raised club. She leaned forward as a machete whistled down past her back. Rising, she turned, holding the sword high. Her opponent's broad blade clacked on the cobbles behind her turning right heel. She slashed down at the wielder.

She felt impact. An instant of resistance.

He dropped to the street bleeding.

A pipe descended from close by. She ducked her head. The club glanced off the back of her skull. She tasted iron on her tongue and her stomach revolted.

But she kept her presence of mind—without which, she knew, she was lost. She cocked her left leg and thrust outward in a side kick, aiming by sheer body sense. Her shoe took a capacious paunch in the middle, sank deep into the flab that cushioned hard muscle. The attacker was driven back against the red-haired leader.

The final man to her left swung his club like a bat at her as she turned to face him. She slipped the home-run cut like a boxer, ducking her body to her right and down. The man used his own momentum to swing the four-foot baton over his head for an ax stroke to her head.

Taking the sword's hilt with both hands, she lunged toward him, slashing across her body. The sword took him under the armpit and opened his chest in a gush of blood. She followed through to clear her blade, then slashed back one-handed to strike the forearms of the pipe wielder she had kicked into his leader. He stared at the bleeding wounds as the club clattered on the cobblestones. He fell to his knees screaming in pain.

"Die, bitch!" The man with the cropped red hair launched a whirl-wind attack. He had no more skill than a standard street fighter, whose usual methods were stealth or pack hunting; he hacked at her with his machete as if trying to chop through a log. But he was a strong man, built like a bull, and his own veins were ballooned with the mad adrenaline dump of intolerable fury and fear.

Desperately Annja backpedaled, barely managing to interpose her blade for two glancing impacts that sent sparks dancing in yellow arcs across the narrow street. Had she not used both hands on the hilt he would have beaten down her guard despite her strength.

He cocked his heavy-bladed weapon over his right shoulder for his own two-handed strike. Screaming, he swung at her face.

A ringing clang sounded with an off-key end. He swung through, then raised his hands to stare in uncomprehending horror at the mir-ror-bright line where the sword had cut through his machete, a handspan from its hilt.

He raised his face to stare at her with eyes like eggs totally deflated with shock. "What are you?" he asked.

The boiled-egg eyes rolled up to watch the long, straight blade as it descended flat on the top of his head. Then, quite slowly at first, they rolled up and back. His body collapsed at Annja's feet.

Her friend the Englishman was on his knees vomiting. She glanced at the man whose hand she had amputated. He lay with one cheek in the midst of a lake of congealing blood, eyes staring.

She knelt and started to wipe her blade on the back of the unconscious red-haired man. Then she stopped. She'd seen enough forensic-science shows on television to know that her straight two-sided sword would leave a blood smear as distinctive as a fingerprint. One that could not possibly have come from any of the wide single-edged chopping weapons of her assailants.

I wonder if the blood and dirt would even go with the sword to wherever, she thought. Now seems like a pretty poor time to experiment.

The dead man's shirt had come out of his slacks. She used the hem to clean her blade. Then she willed it away.

Suddenly the full impact of what she had just done struck her. She had just spilled human lives into a blood lake on the ancient cobblestones of the Holy City. Her head turned. She had to exert all the will she had not to emulate the man she had rescued. The hot smell of his vomit made it all the harder.

She moved to the Englishman's side. She stepped gingerly, not wanting to slip and do a pratfall in congealing blood. Although it would be appropriate penance, somehow, she felt.

His spasms had blessedly passed. He had settled down so that his buttocks rested on his calves as he stared at the dead men. He looked at Annja with his eyes wide as the puffiness and incipient shiners would allow. Even in the dubious half light of the distant street lamps they were an amazing blue.

"Did you *have* to do that?" he demanded.

"Yes," she said. She knelt beside him. He flinched away from her touch. "Are you all right?" she asked.

"What the bloody hell do you think?" he flared. "Of course I'm not all right. Are you quite mad?"

"Probably." She reached down, grabbed a handful of his shirt and hauled him to his feet.

"Would you please stop doing that?" he demanded. Then he swayed. She kept him upright.

"Don't mean to make a habit of it," she said. "Now, come on. We need to get far away from here—and see if we can clean up a bit before anybody sees us."

12

"Bloody hell," the young man said, slopping coffee over the brim of his mug to stream down the back of his hand and drip between the metal meshwork of the tabletop. "I'm all over nerves, and this whole wretched town has never heard of decaf."

He looked indignantly at her. They had picked sidewalk tables well back from the dubious yellow puddle of light from the street lamp up the block, as well as the more substantial shine from the West Jerusalem coffee shop's front window. After slinking out through the crenellated Jaffa Gate and cleaning themselves in a fountain as best they could, they had by tacit agreement chosen to regroup—and discreetly probe each other's motivations. They looked, Annja thought and hoped, no more damply disheveled than any other pair of tourists who'd spent the day touring in the hot Mediterranean sun. At least in light this uncertain.

"I'm still afraid of trying to get back into my hotel," Annja confessed. "I must look like the last survivor from a slasher film."

Her companion barked a laugh. It had a hard and brittle clang to it, like the gleam in his eyes. "Don't bother yourself. This is Jerusalem, city of conflict holy and otherwise. Hoteliers have a couple millennia experience in seeing their guests straggle back in looking as if the cat dropped them off on the stoop. Besides, should a bellhop or concierge spot you and raise an eyebrow, your American dollar isn't yet so depreciated that throwing twenty of them his or her way won't induce the desired degree of amnesia." He hoisted his mug. "Bribery, the universal language."

"Good point," Annja said.

He looked up at the mug, sighed, lowered it gingerly to the table. "The only reason I'm as calm as I am is that I don't really believe what I saw," he said. "Did you have to kill them?"

"Yes," she said. "They would have killed both of us. Would you rather I'd let them?"

He shook his head. "Perhaps I'm not properly civilized, but I'm not so soft as all that. Before you got there they were talking to each other in Hebrew, and made altogether clear their intention to carve me up like a Christmas goose no matter what I said or did."

He smiled, or made a brave attempt anyway. She gave him full credit.

"They made the standard mistake," he said, "of believing the bloody tourist didn't know the local lingo. Especially one as tricky for a native English-speaker as Hebrew. Still, you didn't kill any of those Russians chasing us all over Amsterdam with guns. Even though they killed that poor shopkeeper."

"But they didn't," Annja said, shaking her head.

He halted with his mug to his mouth. "I beg your pardon?"

"The Russians didn't kill Trees. The antiques shop proprietor. They'd never have come back the way they did if they had."

"I rather thought of them like jackals returning to their spew—if you can forgive the coarseness of the simile." He sipped. "I thought they'd just decided to take us up and see what we knew."

"That much is correct, I'm pretty sure, as subsequent events showed. But while I can't pretend to know much about them, the impression that I get is that the *mafiya* are pretty professional. If they committed a murder they wouldn't risk exposure by traipsing blithely back to the scene of the crime—even if they own an assortment of Amsterdam police officials, as I kind of presume they do. That'd be pushing their luck. Besides, it was pretty apparent they were at least as surprised to see us as we were to see them. And every bit as surprised to find the shopkeeper had been murdered."

He shrugged. "I suppose you're more up on these criminal undertakings than I am."

She sighed inwardly at the dig. He was upset, on edge and mistrustful, despite the polite sheen dictated by his upbringing and some sense of gratitude for her saving of his bacon. She couldn't blame him, not by any stretch. But she couldn't help regretting it.

She was struggling to contain her emotions. Now that the adrenaline in her blood was beginning to break down she felt sandbagged by her own reaction to the violence in the cul-de-sac. She knew her actions had been justified. She did not regret the deaths of the men she had killed. Not as such. But she knew there would be family and friends to mourn them, and did regret the choices they had made that had led them to earn such an end.

She was also feeling, keenly, the truth of Tsipporah's prophesy about her going through life without lasting attachments. Her companion was an intelligent young man, obviously, quick-witted and not without charm, even under reasonably dire circumstances. Manifestly they shared some interests. And yes, he was easy on the eyes.

Even if she didn't know his name.

"I'm Annja Creed, by the way," she told him. Though she had entered Israel using a false identity provided by Roux, she felt she could trust this young man with that truth. It's important to trust your instincts, she told herself.

His chin had sunk to his chest, in reverie or just plain nervous exhaustion. He snapped it up and blinked at her owlishly. "Oh. Forgive me. I've quite forgotten my manners. It's a pleasure to meet you, Ms. Creed. I'm Aidan Pascoe."

"I'm not sure it really is a pleasure for you, under the circumstances," she said, "but points for saying so."

He laughed briefly. Then his brows drew together again and he leaned forward. "Where on earth," he said in conspiratorial tones, "did you get that sword?"

"I beg your pardon?" Annja had expected the question.

"The implement with which you dispatched my tormentors—and to give you your due, no avenging angel could have wielded it with more aplomb."

I suppose I should consider that a high professional compliment, she thought, considering.

"I'm sorry," she said, shaking her head. "I don't know what you're talking about."

His laugh was high-pitched. "Don't be stupid! You chopped those men to chutney. I'm no martial-arts expert, but I know you didn't do it with your bladelike hands. Anyway, I was there, if you'll recall."

"Of course. But you weren't in the best position to see what really happened, what with blood in your eyes and your head spinning. I picked up a slat of wood to have some sort of weapon when I confronted them—that was what you saw in my hand. Then when they attacked me with those machetes or whatever they were—" she shrugged "I didn't see I had much choice but take one away and defend myself with it."

"But I saw a *sword*," he persisted. "A cross-hilted broadsword. In your hands."

Annja smiled. "I think you said it yourself earlier. In your state I must have appeared like, well, a rescuing angel. Quite a misidentification, but understandable under the circumstances."

He shook his head and muttered under his breath. "Be bloody-minded, then."

Her smile got sweeter. "I just wouldn't want you to have any false notions. Now, why do you happen to be interested in the legendary jar of King Solomon?"

As a flying subject change, it was outstandingly clumsy, she knew. But its very ham-handedness served the purpose of bringing home to Aidan that the subject of the sword was not just closed, but sealed. And anyway, she needed to know.

A tightening of his somewhat full lips told her he saw through the ruse. Also that he had dimples.

"I'm an archaeologist," he said. "I read the subject and biblical antiquities at Oxford. Although the truth is I've a lifelong fascination, bordering upon obsession, for the fringe areas of archaeology. Indeed, I have actively crusaded to open the minds of my colleagues—albeit, in a cowardly way, making use of the anonymity of the Internet. Or perhaps, *pseudonymity*, should such a word exist."

"You're seeker23!" she exclaimed.

He performed a mock genuflection. "Guilty, *mademoiselle*."

"*Parlez-vous français?*" she asked.

"*Oui,*" he said with a nasal Parisian accent that made it almost *way*. "Bloody badly, as befits an Englishman."

He took a sip of coffee and studied her. "It seems to me I might have seen your name, once or twice."

"Sometimes I ask a question or two. I usually try to stay clear of the flame wars," she said.

"Wise of you." He took another drink, eyeing her with a slight pensive frown.

She leaned her elbows on the metal table, holding her mug in both hands. She had to adjust her weight to keep the off-balance table from tipping. She resisted the urge to improvise a shim; her tendency to want to fix things that were wrong could distract her at key moments.

"Tell me about yourself," she said. Lame! she thought. Growing up in the orphanage and then a career in research hadn't exactly prepared her to make small talk.

"As I said, I've long been fascinated with the way-out and wonderful," Pascoe said. "I've no particular fondness for biblical archaeology, however."

She cocked an eyebrow. "Really?"

He smiled self-deprecatingly, shaking his head. "My father was a solicitor in Weston-super-Mare," he said. "Not a highly remunerative job."

That surprised her. She knew a solicitor was a kind of lawyer.

"I've an uncle, though, who made a few bob in sum through trade." He pronounced the word *trade* with evident contempt. "He's rather a bug on the literal truth of the Bible. The Old Testament in particular—all the Sturm und Drang and bearded prophets and she-bears rending the wicked appeals to him more than parables of a gentle Christ, I'm afraid."

He shrugged. "He should have been a Yank, really."

"We're all fundamentalists, of course," Annja said with no effort to conceal her sarcasm.

"Sorry, sorry. It's not on to let my prejudices show. *Especially* to a woman who has made such a habit of saving my life the last week or so."

"At least this time I wasn't the one who put it in jeopardy."

"Have I not apologized for my intemperate remarks in Holland?

Something about being shot at and then dunked in a canal made me, shall we say, a trifle testy? Anyway, my uncle was willing to subsidize not just my advanced education but actual field researches. I see you cocking your brow skeptically at me. I'd be tempted to say it's rather fetching, but I'll refrain for fear of making myself a sexist pig."

She laughed. "Don't hold back for that. I have a pretty high sexual-harassment threshold."

"And some rather brisk penalties for crossing the line, I imagine."

She shrugged. "Accept as a ground rule that compliments are safe. So long as they're tasteful."

"Ah." He touched a fingertip to the side of his nose. "I've wanted to do that since childhood. Well, a nod is as good as a wink to a blind bat, say no more, as Monty Python said. In any event, I note your skepticism, and in fairness to the old gent—yes, and to myself, as well—I have to say that so far he has been quite scrupulous in accepting what I've been able to discover, whether it happens to harmonize with the bees in his bonnet or not."

"Do you get to publish your results?" Annja asked.

"As long as I send regular reports about my progress on areas of his interest, I'm free to pursue such other matters as I desire. Those tend to be more…interesting to the journals."

"I see." She sipped from her mug. The coffee, which she drank with a healthy dollop of milk and artificial sweetener, had gone cold. She didn't really need the concentrated caffeine blast of Middle Eastern coffee at this hour either, but she was coming down from an extreme adrenal high. She'd crash and burn soon enough despite the stimulant. "So your uncle is interested in Solomon's Jar?"

"Not at all. He'd suspect the whole legend of binding demons to build the temple smacked of black magic, actually. The particular bee in his bonnet I'm feeding now concerns demonstrating the factual existence of the Garden of Eden. Bit of a bother, really, since the location most reliably alleged is in Mesopotamia."

"That could prove inconvenient. Does your uncle expect you to do your research in a war zone?" Annja asked.

"I'm not sure the old boy's aware there's a war on," Pascoe said. "Unlike your American fundamentalists, like the ones who back Mark Peter Stern, he doesn't believe that we're living in the end times. Aside from his precious bottom line, he has trouble concentrating on anything later than Malachi 4:6."

"'And he will turn the heart of fathers to their children and the hearts of children to their fathers, lest I come and smite the land with a curse,'" Annja quoted the Old Testament's last verse. "Are you sure he's not into millenarianism?"

"He doesn't foresee the return of Elijah the prophet or the 'coming of the great and dreadful day of the Lord' anytime soon. As a matter of fact I suspect he half believes Christ himself was more than a bit of a dangerous radical."

"What's your interest in the jar, then? Care to dabble in demon binding?" She smiled as she asked, and hoped he couldn't see her eyes clearly in the gloom.

"What? Oh, that's all poppycock, of course. I do believe such a jar exists. I do believe it's been found—as, sadly, one or more far less scrupulous parties likewise appear to believe, as well."

"But you don't think King Solomon used it to bind demons?"

"As much as I believe in the Easter Bunny, Annja dear. Charming name, that—if it's really your name." He didn't wait for her reaction. "I do believe in the historical existence of Solomon, and the empire he built in the biblical story—which is itself controversial in archaeological circles these days, although don't say so aloud where any of the local savants can hear you. As you no doubt recall, since a woman who can quote the final verse of the rather obscure Book of Malachi clearly knows her Old Testament, Solomon was renowned for his wisdom, as well as for his habit of building pagan temples to gratify some of his numberless foreign wives, which quite scandalized the religious establishment, then and since.

"Now, one thing I believe our occult navel gazers and fire leapers get right is that Solomon was a highly regarded sorcerer of his time. Indeed, rather in the manner of the first speaker of the Aztec, I suspect that even though he was not of the priestly caste, he was looked to as a central spiritual leader by the Israelites of his day. Being a magician was part and parcel of being a powerful and popular king. So what could be more natural, especially in some time of unrecorded hardship such as drought or pestilence, than for the nation's chief figure, political and spiritual, to perform a public ritual of binding the evil spirits responsible for the nation's hardships in a vessel, suitably inscribed with their symbols, and then with appropriate ceremony casting it into the Red Sea?"

He sipped his coffee again and grimaced. "Cold as ice. I expect it worked, too, Solomon's public gesture. Kings whose luck runs bad at moments such as that aren't remembered for reigning record amounts of time and dying in bed, are they?"

"I suppose not. But the account you posted online claims the jar was fished out of the Mediterranean by those hapless fishermen—the news services confirmed that the deaths took place, by the way," Annja said.

"Ah, there I think vulgar legend comes to our rescue." He leaned forward and his eyes seemed to shine. "In time, the story arose that King Solomon had employed demons to build his great temple. Although that wasn't really necessary to what came next—treasure hunters, who believed that demons had the power to discover hidden treasure, and either convey it to their human masters or lead their masters to it."

"And so they fished out the jar," Annja said. "And pried it open. And then when, presumably, no treasure was forthcoming—"

"They got browned off and pitched the thing into the nearest body of water! Precisely. How it happened to be the Mediterranean is anybody's guess. But like the water in the watershed, everything that happens in the Mediterranean littoral tends inevitably to roll down to the sea. It's certainly no contradiction to the basic theory."

"I suppose not," Annja said. It's as good a theory as any, she thought. But then, I have some information he doesn't. "But why so much violence now, over a purely ceremonial bauble?"

He shrugged. "There are plenty of gits in the world who believe the fairy story about binding demons. Some of them have fortunes—speaking as the happy, or at least fortunate, beneficiary of one such git, albeit not one who'd give any yarn about Solomon trafficking with devils the time of day. They could easily pursue the jar themselves, or hire minions who may or may not believe any of the rubbish, but are quite willing to take a human life for sixpence. And, of course, such an item would be of inestimable value as an artifact, leaving aside all the mystic gibble-gabble. The world's full of pothunters. By nature they're unscrupulous—why would some of them stop short of murder, if the price were right?"

He leaned back, folded his arms and regarded her with eyes narrowed beneath a furrowed brow. "What about yourself, Ms. Annja Creed? What's *your* interest in Solomon's Jar?"

Her heart sank. She'd cleverly maneuvered him into returning to his early suspicion of her and her motives. Even if it was the last thing she wanted.

"I'm an archaeologist, too," she said, honestly.

"So I gathered." His tone was anything but friendly now.

"Like you, I have an interest in the more esoteric realms of the discipline. The jar would be more than just a part of history…."

She let her words trail away to nothing but the background murmur of traffic. Unlike the Old City, West Jerusalem seemed to thrive after dark, although there was a muted, furtive quality to its nightlife. Great, she thought. Now I sound just like Belloq talking to Indy about the Ark.

Her companion had seen that movie, too, it seemed. Scowling openly now, he tossed off the dregs of his coffee and rose. The rubber feet of his white-enameled metal chair stuttered unpleasantly on the pavement.

"My motive for seeking the jar is clear enough, in any event," Pascoe said. "I intend that it be handed over to the proper authorities. Not be stolen as so many of the world's priceless antiquities have been by immoral, money-grubbing pothunters. Or should I say, huntresses?"

He slammed the mug down on the table, making it teeter precariously. Annja winced.

"Good evening to you, Ms. Creed. I hope for both our sakes that our paths never cross again."

13

Returning to her modest West Jerusalem hotel after her less than satisfactory leave-taking from Aidan Pascoe, Annja was cautious.

Though it was late at night, a surprising amount of activity stirred in the Tower Hotel lobby. A party of Japanese tourists was checking in and some Italians were arguing theology among the potted-palm fronds in the seats by the front window. As Pascoe had predicted she aroused no interest walking through. Catching a glimpse of her reflection in a segment of mirrored wall, though, she almost lost a step.

When she drenched herself in the fountain, the blood spattered so liberally across her once-white blouse had run and faded until it looked like nothing more than pinkish orange swirls or surrealistic flower patterns. Somehow it struck her now as far more horrific than obvious bloodstains would have been. Frowning, she made it to the elevator and then her fourth-floor room before running to the bathroom and throwing up.

A shower helped her compose herself. Baths and showers tended to soothe her mind and spirit, as well as her body. Still, dressed in a fluffy white-and-blue hotel terrycloth robe with a towel wrapped around her hair, she found herself too jangled by the day's events to contemplate sleep.

Needing something to occupy her brain, and fend off random crying jags, she sat down on the bed and popped the top on her notebook computer. The hotel offered free Internet access through its wireless network. In a moment she was looking at page one of over 180,000 Google hits for Mark Peter Stern.

She made an indeterminate noise low in her throat and set the computer aside. The bedside clock-radio offered a selection of Moroccan-roll, Israeli hip-hop and bland Europop, all of which struck her ears as about equally unlistenable at her current space-time coordinates. Finally she found a classical station. Mozart was always good. Rearranging the towel around her still wet hair, she piled up pillows at the head of the bed, picked up the computer again and lay back for some serious data mining.

First she scanned news items relating to Stern and his foundation. There were thousands to choose from. She read of his cutting the ribbon to open a literacy center he had endowed in São Paulo, Brazil, with six-foot-tall blond supermodel Eliete von Hauptstark on his arm. She watched in streaming video as he trudged through an earthquake-ravaged zone in Pakistan in his shirtsleeves, even helping rescuers move rubble off a victim trapped beneath a collapsed wall. It didn't seem to be staged.

She saw pictures of him attending some Hollywood film opening, laughing with the likes of Warren Beatty and Jack Nicholson—both of whom, she was quickly able to find, openly expressed scathing opinions of him, his movement and even their celebrity friends who had fallen under his sway.

One common thread became apparent, especially paging through pictures and videos. Mark Peter Stern was seldom seen, or at least photographed, without at least one strikingly beautiful woman in his company. Most of them were famous to one degree or another, from a teenage-sex-bomb A-list actress who claimed he had rescued her from dependency on drugs and alcohol to tae kwon do black belt Hauptstark, the current rave supermodel, whose grandfather, allegedly, was a Nazi war criminal who had fled to Brazil, where he'd lived to a ripe old age. All these women wore around their gorgeous throats the braided green collar that symbolized committed Malkuth adherents.

On the sites that offered actual words concerning Stern, as opposed to strictly images, Annja found glitz, innuendo, vituperation and outright flackery.

He did profess a keen interest in biblical antiquities. Annja knew how to check on that. One thing you learned to do as an archaeology student was track down grant money like a bloodhound. The foundations and expeditions funded either by the Malkuth Foundation or Stern in person proved he backed his words abundantly with cash.

Interesting but inconclusive, she thought.

She saw three possibilities. He sought the jar for reasons she could accept as benign, in which case they might well find themselves allies. Provided, of course, he could convince her that whatever he intended was really likely to work more good than harm. That would take some doing.

Or he might want to use the jar in a way she deemed destructive—whether or not from motives he believed pure. Idealistic motives had led Sir Martin Highsmith to murder, after all, as well as to order her own execution. If, wittingly or not, Stern meant to use the jar to work evil in the world, she would find him a powerful foe. And vice versa.

Finally, he might have no interest in the jar, at which point she would cross him off the list.

Annja hadn't expected the puff pieces or the hit jobs to give her any reliable clues. After surfing various news sites, blogs and variations on the theme "markpetersternsucks.com" she took a breath and dived into the official Malkuth Foundation site.

It was professionally done, and unlike a lot of professionally designed sites, actually *well* done. It was not just visually arresting but lucid and easy to navigate, without oversize images, gimmicky hard-to-find menus or eye-itching Flash animations.

As to what it was all about…that she found somewhat less accessible.

She quickly discovered some concise and readable descriptions of the Tree of Life, the arrangement of the ten *sephiroth* and the various pathways between them, a colorful representation of which was the foundation's logo. She glossed over it, as well as a history of both the Jewish and Gentile traditions of the kabbalah. The latter read like respectable popular history, and where it impinged on Annja's expertise, such as discussing the Renaissance-age origins of modern kabbalistic study, she found it to be accurate. But neither a description of the Tree of Life nor the brief story of kabbalism was what she was after.

What she really wanted to know was what the foundation stood for that set it apart from other mystic groups.

She waded through pages of fairly standard common-sense self-improvement advice, most of it unobjectionable and probably even useful, taken in the proper perspective. And the usual peace and love to all humankind, environmental consciousness, tolerance and the like.

After two hours of diligent reading she had gained nothing but a headache. She didn't have any clearer idea of what the actual core message of Mark Peter Stern and his Malkuth Foundation might be.

Going back to her searches she was certainly able to find plenty who purported to tell her the foundation was a cult, it was sinister, it was evil, it brainwashed its acolytes.

She could find as many sites praising Stern and Malkuth to the skies. And all the sites, for and against, sported message boards wherein roared flames of such prodigious heat and volume that she reckoned Dante needed resurrecting from the dead to write up a whole new annex to Hell—a concept he, far more than Scripture, had visualized and inserted into the world's religious imagination.

When she could practically smell the brimstone she sat back and let her eyes go to soft focus. What has been learned, and what revealed? she wondered, remembering a catchphrase from an author she had gone to hear read as an undergraduate.

For all his flaws, she seemed to sense in Stern a genuine avocation, a sense of true mystic calling. It was hard for her to see at first. He was obviously a showman to a pretty unhealthy degree and, if she were any judge, a charlatan in many ways.

Is it possible, she asked herself, to be both a charlatan and the real thing? A true mystic, a true spiritual leader?

She thought of Roux. He was as fraudulent an old fart as she had ever met. But he was genuine. She had seen and heard and experienced too much to doubt he was what he said he was; if anything, there were depths to him she had yet to so much as glimpse. He *was* at least five hundred years old. He *had* witnessed the burning of St. Joan in person. He was a mystical being by virtue of his longevity; she guessed he had been, and likely still was, a sorcerer of some sort. He was also her mentor, a mighty teacher—if often by way of bad example.

That someone lied, and was caught lying, did not mean they

didn't sometimes tell the truth, she reasoned. Even truths that con-flicted with all Annja had been taught of science.

She shook her head. This is no time to get sidetracked, she told herself sternly.

None of what she had seen said anything useful about why Stern might want the jar, and whether he would prove foe or friend.

She took a deep breath, sighed it out to the sounds of a Strauss waltz. Well, that clarifies my immediate destiny, she told herself.

She was going to have to go, again, to the source.

Stern was a public figure, easily one of the hundred best-known names and faces in the current world. She reckoned that meant that each and every day a tiny but measurable percentage of all the world's population was vying for his attention.

Annja knew, even had he not been associated with controversial groups such as radical Israeli settler movements and American Chris-tian fundamentalists, he would require layers of intense security. More than physical security, he would also surround himself with phalanxes of specialists to help him run his organization and to keep people out of his well-coiffed hair.

She had to get past all that to see him. She sighed. It would be only slightly more challenging than getting access to the vaults of Fort Knox with a front-end loader and a bunch of empty crates.

She drew in another deep breath and made a disgusted face. "You know perfectly well what you need to do," she said aloud. "You're just in denial."

She sighed again. "And if I want to swim in it, it's just one country over." She began to compose an e-mail.

14

Engine off, the launch coasted into the pier on big folds of green water, their tops trickled with slightly greasy, yellowish foam. Annja took a last slurp at the straw stuck in the chilled orange juice she had been sipping at the dockside café and stood up. She wobbled slightly on her high heels. Whoa, balance, she told herself.

She started walking. It took total concentration to keep her ankles from buckling outward and making her lurch like a sailor in port after six straight weeks in high seas. She couldn't believe models could strut so confidently in such painful footwear.

Gazes followed her from the sidewalk café and among the dockside idlers. She cut a striking figure, she was willing to acknowledge to herself: her considerable height defiantly accentuated by the heels and a light yellow cotton sundress that showed off her legs in the late-morning Mediterranean heat and sunlight.

She had to work the wardrobe angle to appeal to Stern, she reckoned. She had been told often enough by eager men—young and old—that she was attractive. While she never gave her appearance much thought, she was clever enough to know how to use her natural gifts if necessary.

At the moment she felt confident the eyes following her progress toward the pier were admiring. Unless behind them their owners were snickering to themselves at the way she walked in the heels and laying odds on when she'd lose it altogether and pitch into the sea.

The launch was twenty feet long and open. A pilot sat up front with two failed-NFL-linebacker types in dark suits, and a sleek aide. On second thought Annja wondered if they were even failed; maybe they were actual players, Malkuth devotees serving their guru in the off-season. She didn't follow the game so she didn't know. They certainly looked imposing enough.

Attendants at the dock caught a line one linebacker threw and helped draw the craft into a fairly smooth landing against the big orange-and-black rubber bumpers cushioning the concrete pier. They tied it fast and the aide stepped ashore. The bodyguards stood on the boat with their hands folded in front of them. It gave them a ridiculously demure look.

The aide would have been shorter than she was even if it hadn't been for her accursed heels. He was treadmill slender, his off-white summerweight suit expensively tailored to show his form, a yarmulke not quite hiding a bald spot in his dark hair. He and the football-types all wore the green braided necklaces.

"Ms. Creed?" the aide said, approaching. "I'm Charles Sanders."

She nodded. "I'm Annja," she said. "Pleased to meet you." She extended a hand. He shook it once. To her relief his grip was as firm and dry as it was brief; she feared from the looks of him it'd be damp.

Once again her brilliant disguise was herself. She had spent the morning adding altogether too much to the burden of sorrows of her credit-card balance in a Tel Aviv boutique dressing herself in at least semifashionable mode, when constitutionally and by professional habit she was most at ease dressed in battered khakis and a boonie hat.

Sanders extended a hand to help her into the launch. Liberation be damned, she thought, and she took it and was glad. Spike heels plus rolling boat equaled unsteady Annja. She was not going to risk taking a spill and winding up in the bilge on her backside, with her legs in the air and her pretty skirt up around her waist. That would gratify the grizzled old lechers slurping their lattes at the café entirely too much. She pictured how Roux would react. Concentrate, she reminded herself.

Sanders saw her seated. The bodyguards with the pneumatic

necks cast the boat off. The pilot, a wiry little guy with a big nose and white stubble on his cheeks and no cord around his scrawny neck, backed away from the pier, then turned the boat back toward Crete and wound out the engine. The leather seat pressed against Annja's back and away they went.

Charles, as he graciously permitted her to call him, used his cell phone briefly. Then he sat down across from Annja and made small talk. She answered simply, perfectly aware that she was being vetted to make sure she was who, or at least what, she portrayed herself as being before she was admitted to the presence of the great man. Yes, the 3500-year-old Egyptian gate on Jaffa Hill was a wonder; yes, it was exciting working on *Chasing History's Monsters*. No, she had never considered becoming a model....

She looked back. Beyond wake and waterfront the town tumbled almost into the water down the Jaffa Hill headland. She saw a collection of sand-colored buildings of sundry sizes stuffed way too close together. Some of the crowding was deliberate, she was moderately sure, to enhance that old-timey Middle Eastern–village flair for the tourists. Jaffa was far older than Tel Aviv, of which it was more or less a suburb—although Tel Aviv had started as a suburb of Jaffa. It was a bit more organic and relaxed. But what you mostly saw of it now was not so old. It also struck Annja as more than a little self-consciously quaint, sort of like Santa Fe. And as in the New Mexican capital, municipal codes required buildings to *look* old, even if they went up last month. They were likely as not to hold an artist's studio, a Starbuck's with wireless Internet access or a twee boutique.

She looked forward again. The pilot threaded his way among a plentiful flock of pleasure craft, mostly riding to anchor in the easy swell. One of the world's most ancient seaports, Jaffa hadn't been a serious commercial anchorage for a century or so. Now it was mostly a tourist trap. A fair number of the tourists arrived by water, or so it appeared.

Mark Peter Stern's yacht lay out to sea beyond the common herd of the pleasure craft of the merely rich. *Zohar II* surprised Annja somewhat. A ketch with two masts, white with blue trim, fore-and-aft rigged and sails furled, showing a superstructure housing bridge and cabin above deck. At eighty feet over waterline, it was far from *modest* by any means. But it was nowhere near the ostentatious showboat Stern's flamboyant public persona had led her to expect.

So far as Annja could see, no supermodels or barely legal Hollywood actresses lounged topless on deck. That's a relief, she thought.

"IT'S HARD for most Westerners to think of 'nothing' as a positive thing—the ultimate creative force," Mark Peter Stern said, gazing out the porthole of the compartment he used as his office. Outside the sky was an almost painful blue. Cloudless. "Yet it is. From primal nothing, which is really *no-thing,* derives that which is without limits. And from there—light. Limitless light."

He turned. "From there derives our human potential, Ms. Creed. We are sprung from the light, and we know no limits. If only we let ourselves *see.*"

The office, while spacious, was surprisingly spare in furnishings. There was dark-stained oak paneling to sternum height, cream-painted bulkheads above, a large desk with a globe and a computer on it, a rendering of the Tree of Life behind it. Given Stern's notorious love affair with the camera, Annja was surprised to find no photographs at all in evidence.

Sitting on a tubular-steel-and-black-leather chair that was far more comfortable than it looked, Annja let herself smile tentatively. "I'm afraid I don't follow, Dr. Stern."

He laughed, smiled, waved a hand. "Please forgive me. I have a tendency to preach. I have so much to share with a human race that needs the truth so badly." He shook his head. "I'm sure your viewers would prefer to be spared the proselytization. Or your producers at any rate."

Thinking of boy-wonder producer Doug Morrell, who held the world's "my eyes glaze over" land-speed record, she said, "That's for sure."

She tried to remember to keep her knees closed tight. She didn't want any embarrassing moments.

Unlike her famous predecessor she was no virgin. Nor did she think of herself as a prude. But she was using her sexuality as a dodge here, as bait, and it made her feel cheap.

"You're known for your financing of archaeological researches and expeditions," Annja said.

Stern smiled. He was a handsome man who looked much younger than his forty-one years, with open features, green eyes, a shock of straw-colored hair. Indeed in person he seemed more compelling. The camera, no matter how artfully plied, could not capture the full impact of his personality.

He wore a light tan suit, cream shirt, black-and-gold silk tie. All impeccably tailored, of course; renunciation of worldly things wasn't part of his teachings—exactly. As near as Annja could tell from visiting the Malkuth Foundation's Web site, Stern's conception was that materialism was something humans had to get out of their systems before advancing upward along the spiritual path, rather like a childhood sweet tooth or adolescent acne. She wasn't clear, really.

"If you're interested, I'm always open to proposals for new digs," he said.

She smiled back. "Thank you, Doctor."

"Mark."

"Mark. Thank you. But right now I'm most interested in exploring possibilities for doing a show."

"I hope I'm not considered one of history's monsters," he said with an engaging grin. "Other than by some of my detractors, of course."

Annja laughed. She didn't have to force it. He was unquestionably likable. And something more. She remembered that the men who brutalized Aidan Pascoe in that alley wore the same green leather braids around their necks as Stern. Not that she was convinced he was complicit in the attack, but she had to keep perspective.

She was trying to channel Sabine Ehrenfeld, the German-born model who did the Overstock.com commercials. As little as Annja watched television, the model had made an impression. A woman in her forties, Ehrenfeld struck Annja as both beautiful and devastatingly sexy in a sophisticated way, without being flashy or cheap. Annja also admired the woman because she had a pilot's license and had learned how to use a handgun. Obviously, she was not afraid of her own competence.

Annja was well aware of her own sexual nature, despite wondering periodically just how it squared with her destiny as the keeper of Joan's sword. She had grown up with little by way of role models in being sexy. At least in any dignified way; plenty of the girls at the orphanage oozed overt sexuality, precisely to aggravate the nuns. Annja hadn't exactly majored in partying at college. Her studies happily obsessed her. Despite her lifelong affinity for exercise and athleticism she was at core a nerd, and knew it. So she found the most appropriate role model she could and ran with her.

"Were someone to discover an artifact such as King Solomon's fabled jar," she asked, "wouldn't that interest you?"

He raised an eyebrow at her.

"You don't think of King Solomon's Jar as monstrous in any way, surely?"

"No, no. But it is reputed that Solomon bound demons within it. That's the connection for our show. The demon aspect," Annja explained.

He studied her a moment. "If the actual jar was found, I'd be delighted, of course." He smiled warmly. "I'd like nothing better than to see it on display at the Rockefeller or the Israel Museum in Jerusalem."

Annja had the sense he was playing to an unseen audience—out of habit, perhaps, not necessarily bugs. Although she wouldn't put it past him to videotape his own interviews out of sheer vanity.

"Do you have evidence the jar has been found, Ms. Creed?" Stern asked.

"Nothing more than rumors at this point," she said. "What I wonder, from the standpoint of *Chasing History's Monsters*, is what you as a professed mystic make of the legends of the jar? They say Solomon bound the demons within it after employing them to build his temple in Jerusalem and that the jar was thrown into the Red Sea and later found by parties who released the demons to find treasure for them. What's your take on those?"

He shrugged. "I'm familiar with the legend, of course. Like much of what Christians call the Old Testament, I believe it's an allegory composed by early kabbalists. It represents Solomon's quest for spiritual mastery. It was never intended to be taken literally."

He gave her a rogue's grin. It made him look even more boyish. She felt a stirring inside, and experienced a certain epiphany as to why so many glamorous actresses and supermodels were so attracted to his teachings.

"Trust me, Ms. Creed," he said.

Whatever embers had been smoldering to life damped at once to cold embers. With Tsipporah's warning echoing in her brain, Annja bit her lip for a moment. This isn't going the way I expected at all she thought. She took a deep breath and then the plunge.

"Why was the phone number of your New York central office found on the caller ID list on the telephone of a murdered shopkeeper in Amsterdam, Mr. Stern?"

He stood looking at her in silence for a long moment. She could not truly say that his facade slipped—and regardless of guilt or innocence in this matter, she knew full well he was showing her a facade. Certainly the question, with its implicit accusation, must have been like a bucket of ice water dumped on his head.

I sure feel as if I've dived into ice water, she thought. I think I just led with my chin again. But her intuition had told her to ask the question.

"I had no idea that it had been," he said in a measured voice. "If your information is correct, it's certainly unsettling news. I hope I scarcely need to assure you that my respect for antiquities, not to mention the sorely needed international laws and treaties controlling traffic in them, tends to keep me from pursuing ancient relics in curio shops. Most likely someone in my organization has allowed commendable zeal to get the better of their judgment."

He shook his head. "It can only be coincidence in any event. No one involved with the Malkuth Foundation, with its well-known commitment to peace and justice, could conceivably have been involved in a murder over an alleged artifact."

He checked his Rolex. "If you will forgive me, I have an important phone call incoming in a few minutes. I must ask you to excuse me. You'll find it pleasant waiting on the afterdeck for the launch to take you back to shore, I trust."

She stood up. "The program—"

"Have your producer call Charles. He'll help set something up. And now, good day to you, Annja Creed."

THE GLEAMING UPPER DECK of the big white boat was deserted when
Annja emerged, blinking at more than the dazzling Mediterranean
sunlight. Not even a seagull perched on the rail.

She wandered aft from the hatchway. What went wrong? she
wondered. I totally struck out. Was it my hair? I know I'm not a
raving beauty, but I usually get more response than that. Maybe I
was playing out of my league. How could I think I could compete
with all those international sex symbols? What was I thinking?

Maybe it had been the blunt query about Trees's death. Not too
tactful, she had to admit. Yet even before she asked the question she
had sensed the conversation slipping out of control. The bold stroke,
to give it a better name than it deserved, had been an all but desperate attempt to get more out of the famed religious figure than the
same sort of cotton-candy-and-maple-syrup platitudes he exuded for
his celebrity patrons.

She walked toward the stern alongside a boom with a sail bound
to it by nylon cords. What had her totally flustered was that everything had started so well. She had expected to have to spend days if
not weeks trying to contrive a meeting with Stern. Instead she'd succeeded before she'd even properly tried.

Then she'd done a face plant into a brick wall. If that wasn't
mixing metaphors. She had never gotten quite clear on that concept.

Before she could fully comprehend what had happened a hand
seized her hair from behind and snapped her head around.

15

Annja gasped from surprise. The stinging at the back of her scalp brought unwelcome tears to the corners of her eyes. The morning sun shone on the white deck and housing like liquid incandescence, beating furnace heat against her cheeks.

Her jaw dropped. Through the dazzle she stared into a pair of angry green eyes glaring at her from a perfect face. Glaring *down* at her.

To her utter amazement she recognized the face. It belonged to up-and-coming Brazilian supermodel Eliete von Hauptstark. Her name was pronounced "Ellie-etchy," as Annja had discovered during her research about Mark Peter Stern. She was six feet tall with skin and hair like different shades of honey.

Under normal circumstances Annja would have known no more about those details than she did about the workings of a printed-circuit fabrication plant. But she'd seen much of Hauptstark online recently, as the latest addition to Stern's celebrity retinue.

Hauptstark's arm lay across Annja's shoulder. A strong hand was still wrapped in Annja's hair at the back of her head. The Brazilian woman wore a white man's shirt open over a red bikini top, pale turquoise Capri pants and white deck shoes. She looked angry.

"I beg your pardon," Annja said as politely as she could. "Please let me go. I was leaving anyway—this isn't necessary."

The supermodel let go with her right hand. Her left struck in a jab. Annja blinked furiously at the tears that sprang up in her eyes as her head snapped back. It hurt, especially since her nose had scarcely healed from her South American escapade.

She stepped back. She felt more astonishment than anger or even outrage. "What on earth do you think you're doing?" she asked.

The taller woman spun and fired a back kick into her midsection. Annja flew backward. She landed on her hip, then shoulders and slid across the smooth white deck. She stopped against something solid but slightly yielding.

Thoughts jostled for preeminence in her mind. Why is she attacking me? What the hell does she think she's doing? She got her bearings and realized she had struck a truncated cone of wrist-thick nylon rope with a grapnel-style anchor with a nasty-looking blade sticking out stacked on top of it.

Annja kicked off her shoes. Shaking her head free of the whirl of confusion, she jumped to her feet, willing her mind to clear. She drew in a deep breath to calm and center herself.

The other woman was advancing on her. Her face had now twisted with rage. Yet her eyes looked strangely blank.

"What exactly do you think you're doing?" Annja said in Portuguese, grateful for her knowledge of many languages.

If the supermodel felt surprise at being addressed in Portuguese, she showed no sign. She showed no sign of comprehension at all. Or even of being aware that Annja had spoken. She only came on, not fast, but implacably.

Annja waited with legs slightly flexed. She realized she had slid all the way to the edge of the yacht's deck. Her head was full of the smell of paint, of sun-heated synthetic and steel, even the soap with which her dark blond nemesis had bathed recently, and the slight sweat of exertion she had worked up.

She remembered that Eliete von Hauptstark was a third-degree black belt in tae kwon do. Annja herself had studied martial arts and she knew full well that formal martial arts had little to do with real fighting, but if advanced practitioners had real-world fighting experience, they could be extraordinarily formidable foes.

When she was less than ten feet away from Annja, Hauptstark did a sort of stutter step, skipping forward to launch a front kick to

Annja's sternum with a force that might have shoved the front of her rib cage right through her heart.

Annja met it with a left forearm held out at a forty-five-degree angle. It was a simple technique, powered by a turn of the hips. Had she tried to block the kick directly, her forearm would have been broken. But the beauty of the counter, along with simplicity, was that it simply added a side vector and guided the fearsome thrust past her. *A force of four ounces deflects a thousand pounds*, Annja recalled learning.

Annja felt her opponent overbalance. Using the same hip twist that powered the deflection, she drove a Phoenix-eye fist, first knuckle extended, in under the supermodel's short ribs on the left-hand side.

The tall blonde exhaled violently. It didn't slow her down, although it did take the force out of the follow-through blow, another spinning back kick, this time off the foot that had delivered the deflected front kick. The second wouldn't have landed true because she hadn't knocked Annja back with the first kick, and her opponent had closed instead. The combination attack was aborted. Hauptstark had to bend her knee to land the strike at all. She could do no more than push Annja in the small of her back with the rope sole of her deck shoe.

But it was a powerful push. Annja went flying past her in a graceless windmill of arms and legs. She felt like the coltish adolescent she had once been—not all that long ago—running out of control down a steep slope.

She regained control of her hurtling body when she accidentally ran into the side of the cabin. It knocked the breath from her. She turned, fearing a rib had cracked, as her first labored inhalation felt like a nail being driven into her side.

The taller woman was all over her like a tigress. A high kick flashing for Annja's face was a feint for a flurry of punches and elbow-strikes. Had Annja reacted by trying to block this time, instead of simply leaning her upper body back and to the side, slipping the first feigned attack like a boxer, at least one sledgehammer impact would have landed and quite possibly incapacitated her.

She stayed close to her opponent to keep her enemy's blows from having pace to gain momentum, using her forearms against the insides of the model's forearms to foul the jackhammer blows. At the same time she attempted to land short, hooking, hip-turning strikes of her own. She was still deficient in jabs, and would have to spend more time training with a Western-style boxer to master them.

If she survived.

The exchange was delivered in silence except for little cries as Hauptstark explosively expelled her breath by clenching the astonishingly well-defined muscles of her stomach at each strike. Annja slipped aside from a vicious cross and the supermodel's right fist blasted through the planking of the cabin's outer bulkhead like a harpoon. The woman seemed impervious to pain.

The hole's jagged jaws momentarily seized the supermodel's forearm like a bear trap. Annja used the opening to slam a brutal palm-heel uppercut up under Hauptstark's somewhat broad chin. The blow made her teeth clack together and lifted her slightly into the air.

Eyes literally reddened with rage, Eliete von Hauptstark uttered the first actual vocalization Annja had heard from her since the unexplained attack had begun. A furious roar, rising to a predator's unbridled scream, it was so piercing that something inside of Annja quailed. As the voice soared in pitch through better than two octaves, the Brazilian ripped her arm loose by yanking it out roundhouse, ripping a yard-long gash in the wood.

Annja gaped, stunned by violence of the move. Blood flew in scarlet strings from great furrows clawed by wood splinters in the tan satin skin of Hauptstark's forearm. An eight-inch sliver penetrated the arm like a spear. Ignoring what must have been blinding pain, Hauptstark continued the motion that had ripped her arm free into an ox-mouth blow, delivered with the back of her right wrist. It was another one of those showy traditional martial-arts moves, superpowerful but way too unwieldy to use in a real fight.

Except it came at an already off-guard opponent at bullet speed. Annja barely got both forearms up in time to save her jaw from being shattered, and likely her neck from being snapped like kindling.

The impact stunned her arms. It knocked her bodily through the air again, toward the stern. She bounced off the starboard quarter rail in lieu of tumbling over into the sea and landed in a heap on her side on the deck.

She looked up. Her opponent moved toward her with fierce deliberation. Her face, once inhumanly beautiful, was now merely inhuman, her exotic features a demon mask.

Annja leaped to her feet. Her body felt like one big bruise. She'd had enough. She concentrated her will.

SINCE SHE HAD BEEN made aware of her connection to Joan of Arc's sword, Annja had spent many odd moments trying to puzzle out under what circumstances it might rightfully be employed. Roux had so far proved of little help. His relationship to the cause of good was as puzzling as everything else about him. He tended to blend ruthlessness with an eye for the main chance that she guessed was all his own. His advice ran along the lines of quoting the words Abbot Arnaud-Amaury uttered during the Albigensian Crusade: "Slay them all! God will know his own." Or, as Roux gleefully translated it into more modern terms, "Kill 'em all and let God sort 'em out."

Killing women, children, noncombatants, the odd household pet or anything else that happened to wander into the circle of her swinging blade had little appeal to Annja's modern sensibilities. She did wonder if Roux's bloody-mindedness—which she knew from voracious childhood reading was actually British slang for extreme willfulness, nothing to do with bloodshed per se, but still doubly appropriate applied to her ancient mentor—was in part a harsh if veiled reminder that as a force for good she had to make her own moral choices and live with the consequences. Just like everyone who *didn't* have a magic sword.

She had vowed to summon the sword only in defense of herself or innocents—and only in extremis.

Eliete von Hauptstark plainly meant to kill her. It seemed likely she could, that she was about to, unless Annja did something radical.

The time had come.

ANNJA COMPOSED herself. She gave her head a slight shake. The sword gleamed in her hands.

Surprised, Hauptstark checked and recoiled slightly.

"Stay back," Annja said. "This has gone far enough. If you attack me again, I will kill you to defend myself. If you turn and walk away, we can forget this ever ha—"

With a hawk scream of fury Hauptstark launched herself.

The bull rush caught Annja unprepared. Before her reflexes could respond, Hauptstark had planted a powerful shoulder in her midriff and wrapped arms like iron bands around her upper thighs.

The air exploded out of Annja's lungs. She felt herself lifted off the deck. Then she was falling backward, seemingly in slow motion.

She collapsed herself, slightly rounding her back in hopes of taking the fall across her shoulders and not on the back of her skull.

Annja hit the deck with considerable force. Her teeth crashed together with a squeal. Had she not had the presence of mind to tuck her tongue well back against the roof of her mouth she would have bitten it in two. Her right elbow came down hard on the deck. The nerve center was struck. The arm went limp.

As she watched, the sword somersaulted out of her nerveless hand.

16

For an instant terror seized Annja. This isn't supposed to happen! she thought desperately. I've failed!

A sense of betrayal flooded her like fire. No one is supposed to be able to take it from me!

The sword had vanished.

With a flash of near manic relief Annja realized her sword had gone back to the pocket universe where it customarily awaited her summons. Then momentum slammed the back of her skull against the deck. Purple-and-scarlet lightning shot through her brain. A black fog swirled behind her eyes.

She snapped back to herself at once.

A concussion might yet be on the agenda, even a potentially lethal subdural hematoma, but she was able to focus enough to perceive that Eliete von Hauptstark sat straddling her hips, hands on her shoulders, pinning her to the deck.

The animal fury that had propelled the supermodel seemed to have subsided into systematically murderous intent. She cocked a fist.

Annja jerked her head to the right. She felt a wind of passage, then heard a terrifying crunch and felt a sting at the back of her scalp as some of her hair was driven through the deck along with Hauptstark's fist.

The power she had packed into the blow—and possibly the surprise that she had missed—made the tall woman loosen her grip on Annja's right arm. Annja moved quickly. She twisted free and drove a punch against the side of the Brazilian's jaw. Pinned as she was, she could get none of her body mass behind it; it was a pure arm punch.

Annja had very strong arms. But the model's head merely jerked to the side. Her expression didn't change as she ripped her hand free of the deck in a shower of dust and splinters.

With a convulsion of back and belly muscles Annja lifted her upper body off the deck, trying to writhe free. With her hips immobilized she had little force. Hauptstark slammed her head down into Annja's. It struck too high; they clashed forehead to forehead, instead of Annja's nose being smashed. More sparks shot through Annja's brain.

The Brazilian supermodel shook her shaggy blond mane. Annja got her feet planted and thrust upward with all the strength in her legs.

Hauptstark folded herself against Annja, wrapping her arms around her neck and shoulders. Annja heard the bestial panting behind her head, felt the woman's breath on her neck. It was like the wind from a blast furnace, hot and damp.

Momentarily freed, Annja's arms flailed. Her right hand encountered something of smooth texture but rumpled feel. She realized it was the anchor rope.

Her left arm struck her foe's forearm. She felt blood, sticky on the model's skin. Her fingers brushed sharp hardness. It was the wood splinter that had been driven through Hauptstark's forearm when she punched through the cabin wall.

Annja grabbed it and twisted as hard as she could.

Hauptstark threw back her head and howled in agony.

With the force of desperation Annja heaved her shoulders off the deck. Her right hand scrabbled like a terrified animal at the coiled rope. As the supermodel raised her free hand to chamber a hammerfist blow that would smash Annja's skull a strand of rope came loose in Annja's hand. She hauled on it for all she was worth.

She didn't know exactly what the anchor lying atop the rope coil was for. Despite having been raised within spitting distance of Lake Pontchartrain, in a town that spent a certain amount of time underwater even before Katrina brought much of the Gulf of Mexico to town for a protracted visit, Annja knew almost nothing about boats. The anchor seemed too light to make a vessel this size stay put. She figured other anchors must have been deployed.

It was still a good-sized hunk of iron. It felt as if it must have weighed eighty pounds. Under most circumstances Annja knew she would have strained to lift it one-handed.

But these weren't most circumstances. The rope snapped taut as she yanked. The anchor flew through the air, the point of its wedge blade descending like a pickax between Eliete von Hauptstark's shoulder blades.

Annja was already moving. Her right hand whipped a coil of the rope, still rippling the air, around her opponent's neck. The weight of the anchor had pushed back Hauptstark's center of mass. With a heave of the muscles of her lower back and abdomen that sent pain shooting through her belly, Annja thrust her pelvis into the air.

The supermodel was thrown bodily off her. Bleeding and weakened, Hauptstark was momentarily stunned.

Annja jackknifed. She came forward onto her own feet facing her foe. With a scream of pent-up frustration and rage of her own she skipped forward and fired a side-thrust kick into the front of Hauptstark's pelvis with all her strength.

The supermodel was long and lean, but no one could have accused her of being gaunt. Annja knew the woman was incredibly strong and still very dangerous. She also knew something more than simple jealousy was fueling her killer rage.

A voice deep inside her head was telling her what had driven the insane, and insanely powerful, attack. But she wasn't ready to listen to the voice. For all the miracles she had witnessed—had taken part in, had performed herself—there were some vestiges of her rational worldview she wasn't willing to surrender just yet.

And there were some things she didn't want to believe.

Annja turned to lean on the rail and look off across the water while she recovered her breath. She knew she had to take some decisive actions immediately. But her mind and spirit had taken as brutal a battering as her body.

The water was a lovely deep blue between the sailing vessel and the shore, with its buildings marching up Jaffa Hill. Gulls and terns wheeled and called out to each other overhead. Below them, a variety of watercraft, mostly smallish vessels, rocked gently at anchor or swooped to the impetus of sails or small engines. She gave herself over to a deliberately thought-free contemplation of the postcard prettiness of the scene.

Then, before Hauptstark could attack again, Annja climbed over the rail and jumped into the sea. She swam as hard as her tired muscles would allow. Her instincts told her to get as far from Mark Peter Stern as possible.

A sudden flash caught the corner of her eye. She turned her head to see a puff like a cotton ball, pure white, roll away from one of those pretty little watercraft, perhaps a quarter mile away across the crowded water. In the midst of it blazed a spark like a miniature blue sun. It moved. It seemed to be circling slightly, and drew behind it a corkscrew trail.

Annja dived deep.

17

Above her head a yellow glow spread like a blanket. It had a benign, almost comforting appearance.

Annja wasn't fooled by that for a nanosecond. Apparently Stern's yacht had an engine with fairly substantial fuel tanks. They had just exploded. If Annja surfaced through that deceptively gentle glow she knew she'd functionally be necklaced like a South African informer.

Having some warning about what was about to happen, she'd drawn a good deep breath. She set out swimming underwater with strong strokes of arms and legs. She may not have grown up with boats, but she'd swum like an otter since she was four years old.

She swam until the yellow glow from the surface lay well behind her. Then, lungs burning, she swam some more.

When she could no longer stand the pain, she surfaced. Behind her the *Zohar II* wallowed in the soft swell with its deck just above water. Everything from there up was a great compound billow of yellow fire, with dense, greasy black smoke roiling out of the midst of it and fouling up the sky.

She let out the deep breath she'd gasped down without volition and shook water from her nose and eyes. "Wow," she said.

For some reason the only thing she could think about for a moment was that her spike heels were still aboard the blazing yacht. "Good riddance," she said aloud.

She looked around. She was all alone in the water. If any survivors had leaped from the boat they were bobbing around on the far side of it. She turned to look toward shore. It lay perhaps half a mile off. A somewhat tedious swim, but well within her capabilities.

She heard the whine of an outboard motor. She immediately thought someone had seen her bail and had come out to finish the job. Her head and shoulders rose from the sea as she sucked down a deep breath, increasing her buoyancy, ready to dive fast and deep. She reckoned her best and probably only shot was to remain submerged until her persecutors decided she must've drowned....

"Wait! Don't be a bloody fool!" a voice called over the snarl of the approaching boat. It was a familiar voice, with a distinct educated-middle-class English accent.

She looked around. A small white powerboat slid toward her, riding a rolling crest. The driver was waving vigorously to her from behind the wheel.

"Aidan? What on earth are you doing out here?"

The engine's sound diminished as the boat approached broadside to her and stopped just a few feet away. She bobbed in the surge that rolled from it.

"I believe you Yanks have some less polite terms for it," the young man called, half standing to lean over and extend a hand to her, "but I'd call it a rescue."

He helped haul her aboard. She lay dripping puddles into what she thought might be called the scuppers. Or was it a bilge?

"The shoe is on the other foot," he said. "Or some such rubbish."

"That's fair," she said.

Annja's dress was plastered to her body revealing more skin than she would have liked. Pascoe chivalrously looked away as she tried to wrestle it back into place. He revved the engine and turned the boat around, heading into the crowd of watercraft clustered closer to shore.

"Where are we going?" she asked, sitting on the seat behind Pascoe.

"Somewhere fast," he said, "in the faint hope that we can lose ourselves. In a pinch—if the authorities nip us, say—I can claim with perfect honesty to be taking a survivor of the explosion to shore for emergency medical examination."

As he spoke she heard the warbling of electronic sirens from shore.

"You don't really need medical attention, do you?" he asked, looking concerned.

"No," she said. "You're not worried about the authorities?"

"Not half so much as I am about the lot that did in Stern and his floating pleasure palace."

Luxurious as its appointments had been, the *Zohar II* struck Annja as having been on the small side to be a "palace" of any stripe. She didn't say so. Now that survival did not require immediate action and reaction, she felt mostly stunned.

"Good point. What are you doing here, anyway?" she asked, realizing her rescuer could hardly have been nearby in any kind of coincidence.

"Keeping an eye on our friend Mark Peter Stern," Pascoe said, with a nod of his head to a big camera case that lay by Annja's feet. It sat half open, a camera with a long lens visible inside.

"Subtle," she said, watching a white-and-yellow helicopter with a shrouded tail rotor that had begun to prowl toward the blazing wreck from the shore. Her interest was abstract. Weariness descended on her like lead fog.

"But not too easy to pick up among all the other boats around unless someone was keeping a lookout specifically for such surveillance—which in Stern's case would mostly consist of paparazzi. Nobody noticed the crew on another boat setting up to fire that antitank missile, for instance."

Annja sat dripping and stared at nothing in particular. She felt numb. She knew that she needed desperately to sort out any number of things that had just happened. But somehow she couldn't muster the urgency.

Something, though, pierced her lassitude. She raised her head and looked in the direction of the smoking wreck. Other boats had begun to swarm around it in vain hopes of rescuing somebody.

"Right now! Turn hard!" she shouted.

Without hesitation Pascoe cranked the wheel hard right. A line of water spouts six feet high marched across their curving wake. Bullets would have raked the boat stem to stern had he turned a half second later.

"Bloody hell!" he shouted as the whine of the helicopter's engines and rotor chop became audible above the roar of the boat's motor. "What is it now?"

"Somebody in that helicopter flying toward the wreck is shooting at us," she called, looking back at the chopper. It hovered broadside to them now, a sleek Aerospatiale Dolphin SA-366, not twenty yards up. A man was visible in the open doorway, aiming what looked like an AK at them. "Swerve," she shouted another order.

Pascoe obligingly cranked the wheel left. Again bullets ripped the water where they would have been but for the rapid course change.

"Sod this for a game of soldiers," Pascoe shouted, barely audible above the roar of their motor. Annja didn't have the slightest notion what it meant. Their latest turn aimed them toward a variety of anchored boats. Pascoe rolled the throttle full out to put theirs among them.

"Will you check my eyes?" Annja asked suddenly.

"What? What?"

Boats flashed by to either side, rocking gently in the powerboat's wake. "My eyes. I'm afraid I've got a concussion."

"You may just be mad. They're shooting at us, woman!"

Pascoe glanced back. The chopper was approaching them slowly from behind. The gunner in the doorway seemed reluctant to fire with all the other vessels so close, just as the Briton had hoped.

Annja stood behind him, bracing herself with one hand holding the back of the seat. She flexed her legs as Pascoe turned the wheel over hard again, this time to port. They passed between a schooner-rigged catamaran and a big white power cruiser. A topless woman who had been sunbathing on the cruiser's afterdeck rose up and shook her fist after the boat whose wake had carelessly drenched her.

"Please," Annja said. "I need to know."

Pascoe's handsome face scowled ferociously. He looked intently into Annja's eyes. "Both pupils the same size. Now will you let me drive?"

"Sorry," she said. "It was important. Break left!"

Pascoe had turned them back into open water. The helicopter now prowled alongside them to their port side. The gunner raised his rifle.

The powerboat veered hard as Pascoe complied. For a moment Annja feared he turned too tightly, that inertia would have its way and break them over the berm of swell that had built up along the hull outside the turn. She feared they'd be scattered across the waves like rag dolls. If that happened they'd either be killed outright, or too hurt to do anything when the helicopter dived in close and the gunman pumped bullets into their floating bodies....

But Pascoe kept the boat on her keel. Annja was impressed at his skill. The boat passed beneath the helicopter, which turned on its axis to pursue.

"Head us straight out to sea," Annja suggested.

"What? Maybe you took too hard a crack on the head after all. That chopper's faster than we are!" Pascoe said.

But the cobwebs had cleared from Annja's brain. Perhaps it was a brand-new adrenaline dump on top of the old one. She felt much better, almost exhilarated.

"I've got it," she said.

The helicopter had spun round. A line of bullet holes appeared in the prow of the powerboat. Pascoe turned the small craft back to starboard and lit out for open water.

Annja heard the gunner's bellow of rage even above all the rotor chop and surf hiss and engine noise. Pascoe had the throttle wide open. The small boat banged across the tops of the waves, each impact like a sledgehammer to the bare soles of Annja's feet.

Suppressing a thrill of alarm that the small craft might break apart from the violence of its own passage, she crouched down in the stern. The helicopter was overtaking them rapidly. Its pilot, she guessed, was as sick of his quarry's disobliging antics as his gunner. If they did what she anticipated, the chopper would zip past them and then flare into hover mode broadside to them, so that whether they broke left, right or came straight on, they couldn't escape getting hosed down by copper-jacketed bullets.

As the Dolphin closed in, nose down to drive with its main rotor's maximum thrust, Annja stood abruptly. In her hand she held a loop of a nylon rope that lay coiled in the stern. Dangling from the end was another grapnel-style anchor. It was a much more modest anchor than the one she'd struggled with on Stern's yacht.

Well, anchors have been lucky for me today, she thought, and cast.

In a long underarm lob the anchor rose toward the oncoming rotor disk. The pilot apparently saw something flash toward his face and responded by reflex. The helicopter banked hard left. The man in the door, seemingly oblivious to anything wrong, raised his rifle to his shoulder. The chopper was close enough that Annja could see him grin beneath his dark aviator glasses.

The anchor passed between rotor blades. The trailing blade caught the rope high up near the hub.

Instantly Annja heard a change in the rotor sound. The rotor, rather than severing the tough synthetic rope, wrapped it tightly around the shaft. The anchor, brought up short, bounced upward again. This time it struck a blade.

The thin composite sandwich sheared with a crack and a screech. The face staring at Annja over the Kalashnikov's sights went pale as the helicopter rolled rapidly counterclockwise around its long axis. The pale yellow flames that leaped from the muzzle brake when the gunner's finger tightened on the trigger stabbed impotently into the sky.

The Dolphin rolled onto its back and pancaked onto the Mediterranean. Annja heard a loud crack as its backbone broke. As it began to settle in the water a yellow glow of flame began to shine from within the cockpit.

The speedboat fell away to one side, engine idling. "Bloody hell," Aidan Pascoe said. "That's impossible."

"Just dumb luck," Annja said. He stared at her, blue eyes wild.

She grabbed him by arm and shoulder and pushed him back into the driver's seat. "Drive," she said. "Or do you want to try explaining this to the Israeli port police?"

The engine snarled back to full throttle. Annja rocked back as the little craft took off across the blue-green water.

18

"Either Israeli search and rescue has some pretty harsh ideas about how to go about their business," Annja called out from the bathroom, "or we've got a new player in the game."

She dashed cold water from the tap on her face. She wanted a shower. Her dress felt like papier-mâché molded to her body, and her skin itched from dried salts and less desirable substances from the Jaffa anchorage. But there were some things to be cleared up first.

"I don't know." Aidan Pascoe sat in a chair in a corner facing the twin beds. With the curtains drawn and the light off a twilight gloom pervaded the modest hotel room. Only a buttery glow at top and bottom of the reinforced drapes showed that the sun was setting over Tel Aviv. "But I'd guess we've just had another run-in with our friends the Russian *mafiya*. It's about the right approach for brutal completists, mopping up after the way they did with the helicopter."

"You're probably right." Annja said.

The television was on with the sound muted. For about the tenth time since they'd turned it on, it showed a past-prime pop diva in London, peroxide curls awry, mascara tear-smeared, sobbing about the loss of her adored spiritual leader Mark Peter Stern as her Pakistani soccer-player husband hovered in the background looking vaguely scandalized by the proceedings.

"What does the news say?" Annja asked.

"Still blaming terrorists, of course," Pascoe replied. The screen now showed burly yarmulke-clad settlers rioting at the Temple Mount. "If it was the Russians, I suspect that terrorists will remain the official explanation, and the story won't have many legs."

"Why do you say that?"

"The *mafiya* has its influence, after all. There's been never a peep in the international media about that slight unpleasantness we were embroiled in over in Amsterdam, has there? 'Terrorism' is a useful catchword, always available to swallow inconvenient loose ends," he said.

He took a sip of the whiskey he'd bought in the hotel lobby and shook his head. "Bah. Vile stuff. Not as bad as their gin, but there you have it."

Annja splashed more tepid water on her face. It made her feel a little better. It cut the salt sting if nothing else. It didn't improve what she saw in the slightly cloudy glass, however.

"Could it have been?" she asked.

"What?"

"Terrorists?"

"Not a chance. Who'd rent a helicopter like that to a Palestinian? An expensive bit of work, that Dolphin. And also if one was positively frantic to get put under a microscope by the Israeli security service, that would be just the ticket, wouldn't it?"

"You're right." Her arms braced on the sink, Annja drew a deep sigh and considered her reflection in the mirror. She sported two black eyes and looked like a raccoon. Her cheeks were puffy and her upper lip split. Her nose had, amazingly, not been broken again.

"It's all right," Pascoe called out. "You look beautiful. Relax."

She laughed ruefully. "I look as if I just had a not very promising debut in the middleweight division."

"You should see the other guy." Pascoe joked.

She shuddered and turned away from the mirror. "Please don't say that."

"Ah. Sorry. Just trying to sound like a Yank. I wasn't thinking. Forgive me, please."

Smoothing back her hair, which felt as if it were pulling at her scalp with a thousand little hands as all the salt dried in it, she came into the main room. "It's all right," she said. "I can't hide from things I do. That way lies madness—of one kind or another."

He tipped his head and looked at her like a curious bird in the gloom. She sat on the edge of a bed.

"What was that thing that blew up Stern's yacht?" she asked. "Some kind of rocket?"

"Antitank missile. Almost certainly laser guided. It was much too big for a free-flight rocket such as an Armbrust or a Milán. And a wire-guidance system won't work over open water. Shorts out, you see."

He set his drink on the little round table by his armchair and leaned forward, knitting his hands together. For the first time she noticed they were large hands, substantial hands. They looked strong. They looked out of place with the rest of his pink-cheeked, almost juvenile appearance, although she of all people knew a working archaeologist wasn't going to have the fine, soft hands she'd somehow expected to find on the ends of the pretty young man's arms.

She put her arms straight back to either side and leaned back on them. She raised an eyebrow at him. "How come you know so much about it?"

"I was with a Javelin antitank team in Northern Ireland for a year," he said, "Royal Fusiliers. Bloody foolishness, really, since the Provos never managed to come up with any tanks."

"Was it dangerous?"

"Not for us. It was after the Provos started negotiating with Downing Street. There were a lot of nasty incidents that never made it to the telly, but they were directed almost exclusively against rival drug dealers. Lucky for me I mustered out before First Battalion got stuck into that mess over in Iraq."

"Why were you keeping watch on Stern?"

"Same reason you are," he said. "We're all looking for Solomon's Jar, aren't we?"

"What put you onto Stern in the first place?"

"You didn't think you were the only one to know about that last-call recall trick, surely? Although to be wholly candid, I merely read the telephone number over your shoulder."

She laughed. "I didn't really think about it until now. I guess I should've connected it all once I learned you were seeker23."

"You took your own sweet time coming to the Holy Land," he told her. "Did you try the Malkuth offices in New York?"

"The White Tree Lodge, in Kent," she said. "You saw the card, too, I'm sure."

"Yes. How'd that turn out?"

She felt her expression harden without intention. How much dare I tell him? she wondered.

She kept it terse. She admitted having been forced to kill to escape a death sentence in the churchyard behind Ravenwood Manor. She did skip past exactly *how* she'd fought her way free of her would-be executioners.

He leaned toward her, blue eyes intent. "We need to talk," he said.

She smiled faintly and pushed back a stray lock of hair that was tickling her forehead. She was very aware of her own stale smell of dried seawater, sweat and petroleum fractions. "I thought we were talking," she said.

He picked up his glass, looked into it. An inch of brown liquid stood at the base of a small pile of slumping ice cubes. He took the glass in both hands and, leaning forward, swirled it between his legs, elbows on thighs. The ice made tinkling music in the glass.

"Who are you?" he asked.

"I'm an archaeologist. Although I believe you once characterized me as a pothunter." She couldn't help the last coming out with some asperity; it was the ultimate insult one archaeologist could pay another.

"I think that whatever my suspicions were, they've moved well past that, Annja my dear," Aidan Pascoe said. She found she didn't mind him calling her that, even though he said it with an edge of sarcasm. "What I meant to ask was rather more along the lines of, are you human?"

She laughed. "Do you expect me to turn into some kind of reptilian alien before your eyes?"

"I'm not sure what to expect. I'd have said rubbish to all that about aliens passing as humans when I woke up this morning. That was before I saw what appears to be a very attractive and intelligent but otherwise altogether unremarkable young woman bring down an SA-366 helicopter by chucking an anchor at it."

"I told you, that was just a lucky—"

He showed her a forestalling palm. "Please. I suspect we need to trust each other. To start, I'd like to be able to trust you not to insult my intelligence. Too much has gone on, from your astonishing presence of mind, not to mention competence, during our escape in Amsterdam, to that distinctively European cross-hilted broadsword you made such short work of those bully-boys with in the Old City, which mysteriously appeared and just as mysteriously vanished. What are you, Annja?"

She sighed. "I'm afraid if I tell you the truth, you'll *really* believe I'm insulting your intelligence."

"Try me," he said.

"What would you guess, if you had to?"

"I don't believe in superheros. Although you'd look smashing in a cape and tights. Or tights, anyway. Then again, I no longer pretend to know. I accused you of being some kind of CIA agent or special-operations type, back in that canal in Amsterdam, but that doesn't answer it, either. There's not a training course in the world that could teach you to make a cast like that with the anchor. Much less summon a sword out of thin bloody air. I was never the sort to swot for the SAS. But even I know that much," he said. "So suppose you tell me, Ms. Creed."

"I'm on a mission from God."

He blinked. "You and the Blues Brothers?"

She shrugged helplessly. "Believe it or not, that's the least…silly…way I can think to put it. I'm not even formally religious. I was raised in a Catholic orphanage, mostly, but like a lot of kids who went through parochial school growing up, that tended to make me more defiant and antireligious than anything. Or at least mistrustful of organized religion."

"Very well. Go on."

She explained how she had found the medallion in the cave in France, how she had, without conscious intent, much less knowing how, spontaneously restored the broken blade with her touch. She mentioned Roux and what he had told her about her legacy as successor to Joan of Arc. She didn't see any good reason to mention Garin Braden. She wasn't sure she believed the story any more than she'd expect Pascoe would. She shrugged and looked at him.

"Good Lord!" Pascoe exclaimed when she'd finished. "You make it sound as if I've been serially rescued by Buffy the Vampire Slayer!"

"Well—not really. There hasn't been any unbroken succession of champions or anything. After they lost Joan, it basically took half a millennium for conditions to be right to appoint a new champion of good. Or anoint. Whatever."

It was not, of course, either the whole truth or nothing but the truth. But Annja felt guilty telling him even this much. He certainly didn't have a proverbial need to know more details—or even more correct ones. As it was she'd told him this edited version of the truth because she could only see worse problems arising from trying to stonewall him. He was keen and analytical enough to arrive at the truth on his own—and imaginative enough to concoct potentially disruptive theories if he missed the mark.

"That's the most preposterous thing I've ever heard," he said finally. "Then again, nothing less preposterous would begin to account for what I've experienced in your company."

He rubbed his forehead. She sat in silence in the gloom and gave him time to think. It was hard. She liked him. She felt a need to be understood by him. Yet she didn't dare give him more details than she had already. And though she didn't think of herself as particularly adroit at relations with living people, she realized at some level the best thing she could do was bite down and hold her peace, whatever it cost, and let him sort out what he'd choose to believe.

He raised his head. His eye met hers. They were large and luminous in the dim. After a moment he smiled.

"Let's get cleaned up and go for dinner," he said. "Adventuring is hungry work, I find."

"HOW DOES a self-professed agnostic get selected to be the champion of good?" Pascoe asked after they returned to the room. Once more he sat on the chair while she lay on one of the beds, propped on pillows. She'd had a tougher day than he had. They had turned on the lights by the beds. It still wasn't very bright. That seemed to suit both of them.

Dinner had passed in uncontroversial conversation. That had been by tacit agreement. Once Pascoe accepted the situation he was in, he either had a proper sense of discretion or was taking boyish delight in playing secret agent. Or, she reckoned, both.

"You aren't the first one to ask that question," she told him. "You're not the first to get an entirely unsatisfactory answer to it, either."

He looked at her a moment, then laughed. "Do you believe in Him now?"

"Well, I sort of have to. I guess. Although the impression I'm getting is that our religions don't necessarily get all the details exactly right, let's say."

"What would your illustrious predecessor say if she heard you talking like that? The angels talked to her on a regular basis, didn't they?"

"I think she may have been delusional," Annja said. "Roux never really contradicted me when I suggested that to him. Although I did feel bad about it after the fact because Joan's such a painful subject for him."

"So no angelic voices for you, eh?"

She shrugged. "If angels did try to talk to Joan, they might have had their work cut out getting a word in edgewise, if you catch my meaning. That may have been what led to her downfall—trouble sorting out the signal from the background noise and all. May the spirit of my revered predecessor forgive my saying so.

"You know, all of this isn't any easier for me to digest than it must be for you," she said.

"I suppose not," Pascoe said thoughtfully.

"In any event, no angels have spoken to me so far that I know of."

"What happens if they start?"

She smiled almost shyly. "Cross that bridge when I come to it?"

He laughed. He had a good laugh. Solid, louder and fuller than she'd expect to come out of his somewhat slight frame.

"What about you?" she asked.

He blinked. "Me? No, no angels have spoken to me, either. Not that it's ever occurred to me to listen," he said.

"No. I mean, what drives you? You seem just as determined as I am to find the jar. You'd have to be, to keep at it after all that's happened to you so far."

"Well, I do seem to have acquired my very own guardian angel, have

I not?" He smiled. "Still, I'd like to think I'd have persevered in spite of what's happened had you never intervened. Provided I *survived*, of course, which I'm realistic enough to know is far from a given."

He sat back with his chin sunk to his chest a moment, contemplating. "I could give you a load of rubbish about desire to keep a priceless artifact out of the hands of unscrupulous men but I'll spare you reciting the whole laundry list. I'm sure we both know it by heart by now."

"If we even know all the players in the game," she said.

"Lovely thought, that. It's true enough, of course. Like any responsible archaeologist I detest pothunters."

For a moment he fell quiet. Annja had closed her eyes, resting them, but she could feel his scrutiny like the glow from a heat lamp on her cheek. He still doesn't altogether trust me, she thought. Well, who could blame him?

"But I have to admit, thoroughgoing rationalist and modernist that I am, I've always harbored a hope, deep down inside, that things like the jar are *real*," he said quietly.

"I think most of us feel that way—if we're honest with ourselves," Annja said, opening her eyes. "Not many of us are brave enough to say so."

"You think? You might be right, judging from the postings on alt.archaeo.esoterica. Then again I'm sure archaeologists aren't any more prone to self-honesty than all the rest of the ruck. I frankly doubt I'd believe a word of your story if I hadn't repeatedly seen you do things which defy what I once considered rational explanation. But if I'm forced to swallow one impossibility, to say nothing of an entire set of them, others become more palatable, somehow," Pascoe said.

"All my life I've wanted to make a difference, Annja. I've always been appalled by how much ugliness I've seen in the world, how much evil. War, starvation, neglect. It's naive, I suppose, but I've never been able to see people suffering without wanting to help them."

"You're kind," she said.

He leaned forward. "Think what it would be like if the jar is *real*, Annja. That kind of power. What couldn't we do to make the world a better place?" His cheeks were flushed. His eyes glowed like beacons.

"With demons, Aidan?"

He laughed. "It sounds improbable, I know. But Solomon was a great man, a wise man. A good man, even if a lot of his contemporaries thought the worst of him for building pagan temples for his favorite wives. He didn't use the power for evil. Perhaps he even built the temple in Jerusalem using the demons, and that's a righteous thing, to be sure. It must be possible to subordinate the demons to one's will for good, as well as for wicked purposes."

Annja thought back to what Tsipporah had told her. She hadn't shared anything about the mysterious American-born kabbalist sage with Pascoe. But from the information she had provided, Annja suspected he was correct.

She felt a certain disquiet.

You're just tired, she told herself. Being silly. He's an innocent.

Pascoe had relaxed for a moment. Then his intensity returned. "What do *you* intend to do with the jar if you get your hands on it?" he asked, eyes narrowed.

She drew in a deep breath and let it out slowly. "I don't know yet."

19

"Ah." The man's teeth were brown and crooked surrounded by his short, grizzled beard. "You must mean Mad Spyros."

The quayside watering hole was not one of your quaint tourist tavernas. Nor did the clientele consist of tourists, glossy and well-scrubbed. Womb dark after the brilliant Ionian Sea sunshine outside, the tavern smelled of the same things its patrons did: fish, varnish, sweat and brutally harsh tobacco. It was a mixture nearly as potent as tear gas. Annja found it hard to keep smiling and not blink incessantly at the stinging in her eyes.

Pascoe gave her a look. His blue eyes were clear. I'm surprised they're not bloodshot, she thought.

"Spyros?" she said tentatively. "Could that be your cousin, Aidan?"

He shrugged. "Well, he's a bit on the distant side. And I've never actually met him in person, you know."

"It is short for Spyridon," their informant said helpfully. He was a short, thick man with bright black eyes shining from red cheeks, and a cloth cap mashed down on graying curls.

Annja and Pascoe had spent a sweaty, footsore day tramping the dives along the waterfront in Corfu, where the hills crowded with whitewashed buildings tumbled down almost into Mandouki Harbor. They had climbed up the Kanoni road past the archaeological museum and the old fort on its island across a causeway, along the esplanade and around the tip of the peninsula to Arseniou, then along the north shore past the container-ship fleet landing of the old port, past the late-sixteenth-century Venetian new fort toward the new fleet landing and the Hippodrome. They were posing as a pair of tourists on a genea-logical vacation, tracking down a missing relative of Aidan's. Despite the fairness of his skin, his curly black hair made it plausible he had Levantine ancestry.

To Annja's eyes he looked rather Byronic, in his white shirt with open collar and sleeves rolled up and his faded blue jeans. She knew George Gordon, the sixth Baron Byron, had come to the nearby Ionian island of Cephalonia to fight in the Greek war of indepen-dence against the Ottoman Turks. Indeed to Annja's eye her com-panion bore a slight resemblance to the infamous poet.

The man who had mentioned Mad Spyros spoke in Greek to his companions. They were a tough-looking lot, professional fishermen like the object of Annja and Aidan's search. They all laughed and nodded. Most of them were short, some wiry, some wide. One tall man with a touch of bronze to his beard loomed over Annja and rumbled something in a voice like thunder. He finished his speaking with the word "Nomiki," suggesting to Annja that was their informant's name.

"Surely it must be, as my friend Petros says," Nomiki said, jutting a thumb back over his shoulder at the big man.

"There's an appropriate name," Annja heard Aidan mutter beneath his breath. She agreed. She knew very little Greek, but she knew *petros* meant "rock."

"Spyros is our friend. But, poor man, he has taken to the drinking, to seeing bad things everywhere. He is, what you say, paranoid," Nomiki said.

He looked expectant, with his head cocked to one side. His eyes glittered like obsidian beads.

"Uh, yes," Annja said. "I think that is the word you're looking for."

"So my cousin's name is Spyridon," Pascoe said. "I don't know if I'd say he's paranoid. After all, something did kill his shipmates." The men made the sign of the cross, in the Orthodox manner that looked backward to Annja, accustomed as she was to the Catholic version.

IT WAS MURDER that had brought them to Corfu. The island was a riot of hills, intensely green with olive trees, shaped like a horse's haunch and snuggled up next to the Greek mainland in the Ionian Sea at the mouth of the Adriatic, altogether too close for comfort to the coast of turbulent Albania. Rumor had connected the discovery of King Solomon's Jar to the mysterious, violent deaths of six local fishermen reported on the wire services worldwide.

Annja and Aidan had started out that day asking about the killings. They first posed as crime tourists, what some pundits were calling the new ecotourists, people with a morbid fascination with forensic pathology from watching too many television shows.

It was not an occupation that had ever appealed to Annja. While her own profession brought her into frequent contact with human remains, like most archaeologists and physical anthropologists, she had a marked distaste for dealing with specimens that were fresh.

Not unexpectedly, the locals they questioned at first had regarded them with fascination mixed with loathing. Annja suspected that only Aidan's liberality in buying drinks for the house wherever they went—with handfuls of cash to prevent leaving plastic tracks—kept them from having to fight their way free of some places.

But gossip is a powerful force in human affairs, as Annja had discovered as a child. They soon started hearing a persistent rumor that the six crewmen who had been murdered on the boat were not the same six who had been aboard when the ancient jar was found. One member of the original crew had somehow survived.

The pair switched their focus to trying to find that lone survivor. To cover the fact they didn't know his name, Aidan claimed to be an Englishmen of Greek extraction who had heard rumors from an estranged branch of his family that a distant cousin had been involved in the horrible business of the fishing-boat murders. He told their listeners since he and his female friend had already planned a Greek holiday, he agreed to his aging mother's request to check in on Corfu and see if they could track the poor man down and bring him comfort from his displaced family in the British Isles. It was thin at best, but as far as Annja could see, it was their only option.

"WHERE MIGHT WE FIND poor cousin Spyros, then?" Pascoe asked.

Nomiki cocked his head to one side. A calculating look came into his eyes. Aidan reached for his wallet. Not quite sure why, Annja stopped him with a touch on his arm.

The Greek man spoke again to his friends. His manner was earnest. The ensuing conversation was low and intense. Annja had the impression of general disagreement, of men not accustomed to muting their emotions trying, for reasons unknown to her, to keep the argument from rising to the boisterous levels it ordinarily might. As they argued Aidan stood by smiling vaguely and humming to himself, as if oblivious to the passions being kept simmering below the surface.

Finally Nomiki turned back to the pair. "The boat was the *Athanasia*." He and his companions crossed themselves again. "It is to be found on a beach a few kilometers south of town. There you may find poor Spyros, as well. He cannot leave it behind, it seems."

Pascoe's smile widened. "Splendid! Thank you so much." Now he did dig in his pocket. "Allow me to buy a round of drinks for the house."

Nomiki leaped back as if afraid the mad young Englishman was going for a gun. "No, no!' he exclaimed, holding up callused hands with fingers twisted from being broken repeatedly hauling in water-heavy and stiffened nets.

Then he smiled. It was forced, ghastly. "It is not necessary. We do this as a favor to kinfolk of our friend Spyridon."

He spoke quickly to the others. They all seemed to draw back, then nod and smile fixedly.

Pascoe shrugged. "Well, thank you all, and good day."

He waited a moment, then turned and walked out. Annja stayed close to him. She felt a tingling sensation at the nape of her neck.

Out on the street an old man in a dark wool suit teetered past them on a bicycle. Away to the north bruise-dark storm clouds gathered above Albania. The sky was clear and achingly bright blue above them, the water a deep green inshore and a royal blue so intense it seemed almost self-luminous farther out.

"Odd," Pascoe muttered.

"What?" Annja asked.

"I've never known working men in a pub to turn down free drinks," he said.

"Maybe they felt it would be bad luck, for some reason. They were obviously still feeling the effects of the murders." Annja said.

"I can understand why." He shrugged. "Ah, well. Let's rent a car and nip down to this beach to find the boat. I don't fancy poking around a scene like that in the dark."

Annja laughed. "What? You're not superstitious, are you?"

Aidan laughed louder. He thrust his elbow out from his side.

After a moment Annja threaded her arm through his. Side by side they began the lengthy hike back to the car-rental office.

THE HILLS OF CORFU WERE a deep and beautiful green. That was the good part. Looked at more closely a note of monotony came to the fore. Most of the island's copious verdure, wild as well as cultivated, consisted of olive trees. They were the island's main, close to only crop. Export of olives to the mainland and fishing were key sources of income for the islanders, although both came well behind tourism.

Now the green, made into different hues and values by the island's vigorous relief, had begun to take on a dark uniformity as the sun declined toward the rugged mountains inland.

Gravel turned and shingle crunched beneath their feet as they made their way down the beach. At its southern extremity a boat lay beached on the shingle, heeled over onto its port side. Its bottom and screws had rusted red.

"*Athanasia,*" Aidan said, looking at the characters painted on the stern. "That's the boat we're looking for."

"You know Greek?" Annja asked, a trifle suspicious, and ready to be more than a trifle put out if for some reason he had withheld knowledge and allowed them to struggle through the whole day trying subtly to interrogate people who spoke dribs and wisps of English if any at all.

But he only laughed. "The dire consequences of a classical education," he said. "I speak a few words and understand next to nothing of the spoken tongue. But I read it fair enough. Well enough to transliterate, surely."

He walked up to the boat and rapped on the hull. It did not ring so much but echo hollowly. "Besides, this is a big craft. Maybe thirty feet long. A substantial investment, especially on a poor island such as this one. Do you see any holes in her hull? I don't. So there must be some serious reason she's moldering here on the beach with nobody trying to take her to sea."

"I guess you're right," she said. "She's a lot bigger than I thought she'd be."

"She's not even being used to dry nets," Pascoe said. Several other craft, obviously also fishing boats, bobbed at anchor not far out from the little beach. Wet nets had been spread out over upturned dinghies and stretched out on the shingle and held down with large rocks. "People are afraid of her," he stated.

Annja glanced toward the sun, which hung low and swollen above the steep green hills. "I guess we'd better take a look aboard while there's still some light," she said.

Throughout the day they had not yet found it necessary to refer to the jar itself. This was good, Annja thought. Whoever or whatever had killed those men might still be in the area, or have spies on the ground. The guilty party or parties might or might not be fooled by touristy preoccupation with the macabre, or goofy genealogical enthusiasms. But the killer's putatively pointed ears would definitely prick up if somebody turned up asking about the priceless, supernaturally powerful relic the hapless crew had pulled from the sea in its nets. Provided, of course, the murders had actually been connected to Solomon's Jar, and not some semirandom element. Such as drug smuggling gone bad, as follow-up articles said the Greek police surmised. That was the catchall of bad, lazy, or simply stymied police investigations, Annja knew full well.

Scrambling over the port rail was easy. Climbing uphill into the wheelhouse was something of a challenge, although nothing daunting to a pair as fit as Annja and her companion. Pulling herself through the open hatchway, though, she came up short.

The stench struck her like an invisible barrier.

"Ghastly," Aidan muttered. "I didn't imagine it would smell this foul after so much time."

"Neither did I," Annja said. Her cheek rode up in response to the stink, squinting her amber-green eyes. "The humid climate must keep the smell active. I guess that's why we're archaeologists instead of medical examiners."

"We're wimps," Aidan said, holding on to a stanchion right behind her. "I can live with that."

By force of will she thrust herself into the reeking dimness. Flies swarmed up to meet her. Their bodies fuzzed the air like a living haze. The sunset light shone almost directly through the cracked front port, yet it made little impression on the gloom within.

She could still see enough. More than enough.

The first impression, which did not particularly surprise her, was that someone had tossed buckets of dark paint liberally around the compartment. Copious buckets. Her stomach began a slow roll.

You've seen blood splatter like this before, she reminded herself sternly. You've even caused it. So you'd better learn to face up to the consequences of your actions, no matter how righteous.

Lest they become too easy. The voices of Roux and Tsipporah sounded in her head.

Beneath the irregular coating of dried blood the compartment was a shambles. Chair seats and backs had been ripped in parallel slashes and bled yellowed stuffing. An obvious radar screen and other navigation instruments were smashed. The chart table lay broken against the bulkhead below. Charts and logs had been torn to pieces and strewed around. The papers had mildewed and crumpled in the humidity, and some had begun to melt into the varnished wood and painted metal of the deck and bulkheads.

The sound of the flies was like an idling engine's growl.

"My God," Aidan said, coming in behind her. "A charnel house."

"Literally," Annja whispered.

He gestured around at the shambles. "Did vandals do some of this?"

"I doubt it." She pointed to a volume lying open against the juncture of deck and bulkhead. A ragged streak of blood crossed it at a violent angle. "At least some of the destruction probably happened before the murders. Or during. Anyway, as you just pointed out, nobody's tried to reclaim this vessel, despite the fact it's still probably worth the life's savings of an entire fishing crew. Who'd dare to vandalize it?"

"Not I," Pascoe said.

Her foot began to slip on the canted deck. She reached out reflexively and grabbed the back of the pilot's chair, which was fixed on a pedestal.

She felt a shock as her skin contacted the slashed leather. It was as if she had completed an electric circuit, though not unpleasant. Inside herself she seemed to perceive a hint of golden glow.

She felt a chill as if the sun had gone out instead of set. She shuddered.

"Annja!" Pascoe exclaimed, exquisitely sensitive. She felt the reassurance of his hand on her shoulder. The strength of his grip surprised her. "Are you all right?"

She shook her head as if shedding water. "Yes," in a shaky voice.

"What is it?"

"It was here."

"The jar?"

She nodded.

"That's what made you shudder like that? You looked as if you'd seen a ghost."

"Not seen, Aidan. The jar was here. I'm sure of it. But it's long gone."

He nodded. "We reckoned that."

"It's not the only thing. There was something here. Something I've sensed before. At Ravenwood Manor and the Wailing Wall. And, oh, on Mark Stern's yacht, when Eliete von Hauptstark attacked me. I just realized what it is."

"And that is…?"

"Evil." The word had force precisely because she said it quietly, with utter lack of inflection.

Pascoe looked around quickly. "Is it still here?" She could see from his frown that his trained skepticism was warring with his emotions. And losing.

"No. All I'm feeling are the traces it left behind."

"Months ago? It must have been a pretty potent evil."

Wordlessly she waved her hand around the blood-splashed cabin.

"Right," Aidan said. "Forgive my being a git."

Pupils dilated more the gloom justified, Pascoe's eyes scanned the interior, even the overhead, which was likewise liberally streaked with blood spray. "Do we need to search any further into the bloody boat?" His tone said that he fairly urgently didn't want to.

"No point," she said. "We're not crime scene investigators, thank goodness. We know what we came to learn."

Before she finished the last word he had slipped backward out the hatch. She joined him before saying, with a shaky smile, "I'm just as glad as you are."

He stood with his feet at the joining of deck and gunwale, head down with chin on clavicle and moving side to side like a bull's, drawing deep, quavering gasps of air in through his open mouth. She recognized the signs of a desperate fight against nausea.

The wind was blessedly coming in from the sea. The warm, humid air felt almost air-conditioned on Annja's face, which she realized was streaming sweat in a way the day's exertion in the sun had not been able to achieve. The moist sea breeze smelled sweet, like life itself.

Aidan clambered over the rail and jumped down to the sand. Then he reached up a hand to help Annja. She hid a smile at that. Some women she knew might have angrily spurned the gesture as chauvinistic—and it was certainly unnecessary, given that she was as strong or stronger than he was. It struck her as archaic, gallant and altogether sweet. Just the sort of thing, she thought, a well-bred and very handsome young British archaeologist ought to do. She took his hand and jumped lightly down beside him.

He withdrew it as if it were hot. "Sorry," he said, eyes down. "I think I've just been a right Charlie again."

"Not at all," she said. "I thought it was sweet."

"What now?" he asked awkwardly.

She looked to the west. The sun was almost out of sight, just a blazing white arc backlighting a rounded peak. Around them she felt the velvet mauve darkness, the cooling of the heavy air.

"Better see if we can find our friend Spyridon before he drinks himself to sleep," she said.

He touched her arm, lightly and deliberately. "Don't move," he said softly. "We may have a spot of bother."

She turned to look at him. Light and movement drew her focus beyond him, north up the beach, to where an irregular line of torches slowly approached.

They were borne by half a dozen or more shabbily dressed men. They held knives and makeshift clubs in their other hands.

20

"They've surrounded us," Aidan said through clenched teeth.

She turned to look south. A similar group approached from down the beach. Their dark, bearded faces were grim in the wavering orange light of their driftwood torches.

"Nice traditional touch, that. Torches," Pascoe said. "Pity it's not an agrarian enough setting for them to have pitchforks. Still one supposes it's the thought that counts."

Annja felt a stab of admiration for his insouciance. She felt little herself.

She recognized the approaching men weren't carrying torches to act out a classic monster-movie scene. Rather, it was because of the traditional role of fire in cleansing evil.

"If we've trespassed, we apologize," she called out to the nearer group, the one coming from the south. "We mean no harm."

Her eyes darted—her head unmoving so as not to reveal her desperation. The beach was isolated. A small scatter of shacks lay several hundred yards up the beach to the north. To the south a jutting headland walled it off. A few more little warped-plank buildings leaned in various directions across the road, a hundred yards or so inland. Help was far distant—if anyone in the vicinity would care to help them against their own neighbors.

Pebbles crunched ominously beneath boots. The torch flames were gaudy in the heavy twilight.

"You've done enough harm," called a voice. To Annja's shock it was familiar. The voice of Nomiki had coarsened to a raven's croak. "You devils killed our friends, our kin. Now the time has come for you to pay."

With a scream of jet engines, an airplane lifted off from Corfu International Airport just across the narrow mouth of the inlet. It sounded to Annja like a lost soul fleeing.

Someone cried out hoarsely. With a rush the fishermen were on them. Any doubts Annja entertained as to their seriousness were dispelled in a blink when one man took a horizontal swipe at her face with a torch. Its head blazed a meteor orange trail as she ducked back. A piece of her hair passed through the flame and she smelled the stench of it burning.

She moved quickly, tweaking the torch from its wielder's grasp and throwing it end over end to fall with a hiss and a fizz into the foam of a retreating wave. It was a small gesture, and only momentarily satisfying as more angry men crowded around.

She punched the man who had swung the torch in the face. He sat down hard with a crackle of shingle and an aggrieved outcry. "Stay behind me," she called to Pascoe without looking back.

If the fishermen felt any Old World compunctions about attacking a woman they took care not to let them show. Annja pirouetted around a clumsy knife slash, smelling a waft of alcohol breath that accounted for much of the clumsiness. She dropped its originator sprawling and gasping with an elbow at the back of the neck. Somehow she sensed it as a club swung for the back of her head. She bent forward sharply at the waist. The club swished behind her skull. She mule-kicked straight back, caught an ample abdomen with hard muscle beneath and elicited a whoosh of forced-out air as its owner was launched back several feet.

Another man rushed her, bellowing, club raised to crush her skull. She turned and charged past him, catching him with a forearm high on his chest that dumped him hard on his back and left him stunned and breathless. She stiff-armed a second attacker.

Annja moved through the crowd of attackers in a controlled

frenzy, allowing her training and reflexes free rein. Rather than block, she dodged, ducked and weaved. In preference to kicking and punching she grabbed and swung or simply pushed. She kept moving through her assailants, directing blows away from her, thrusting men into one another. Then she heard Aidan shouting angrily to the men to keep their hands off of him and she turned to glance back.

The move undid her. Strong arms thrust beneath her armpits from behind. Huge hands clasped the nape of her neck. She was lifted kicking off the ground, knowing the bronze-bearded giant, Petros, had caught her.

A man closed with her from the front, empty handed. She raised her knees and kicked him hard in the gut with both feet. He flew back, out of her sight beyond the ring of torches that had walled her in with barracuda suddenness. She became aware of various smells. Indifferently washed bodies, wool steeped in sweat, grease, sea salt and fish scales, garlic, decaying teeth, and resinous Greek wine and Albanian beer that smelled like formaldehyde, all mingled to cause a bit of sting for the eyes. She also sensed an edge of fear.

Then Nomiki himself was before her, bandy-legged and mysterious as Pan in the shifting of dark and torchlight. A snarl of hatred bared his brown and jumbled teeth. A blade protruded from his hand, with torchlight sluicing along it like the premonition of blood.

Annja kicked the knife from his hand.

Nomiki fell back with a curse as she kicked him in the face. But then her leg was seized, followed by the other, and more men piled on than she could kick away with all her strength.

She realized she had made a potentially fatal mistake. She'd been holding back when her opponents were not.

Petros's monster hands thrust her head forward, intending to snap her neck. Her neck muscles strained, popped, seemed to groan aloud as she fought his strength. She would not give in. She couldn't win, but that meant nothing to her resolve….

A voice cried, "Stop!"

It called out in English. It was a male voice, high-pitched, harsh with an accent and something more. As it penetrated Annja's fog, in which she had been aware of almost no sound since the fight began, it must have penetrated the consciousnesses of the mob swarming over her. The men actually did stop and paused in their sinister intent.

A man hobbled forward, using a broken oar as a sort of crutch. The men at the back of the mob surrounding her fell back with torches in hand like an inadvertent honor guard, producing an illuminated aisle for his approach.

Nomiki stood before Annja rubbing his jaw. He spit what looked suspiciously like a fragment of brown tooth onto the slate shingle at his feet. "Spyros?" he croaked.

At first glimpse Annja had thought the newcomer was an ancient, so hitched and painful were his movements. Now she realized the hair surrounding his head like a clumped and matted halo was dark. His naturally lean features were drawn further by pain as though stretched on a frame. His dark eyes were pits of sorrow, black in the torchlight.

Someone barked at him in Greek. He replied in a low voice, more dead than deliberately soft, it seemed to Annja.

"But Spyros," Nomiki said with a touch of whine in his voice. "They killed your mates."

"No," the lame young man answered in English. "They did not. Now go."

Petros protested. The young man's face twisted as if he had been struck. "Enough killing! Enough pain. Spare my soul more burden! Go!"

He cried out again in Greek, his tone desperate, yet angry rather than pleading. Annja felt the self-righteous energy of the mob drain away. Where they had been a pack of raging predators half a minute before, now they were just normal men, rapidly feeling themselves overtaken by shame. Like a clot of muck being washed from a deck with a hose, the erstwhile lynch mob began to come apart, and then flowed away down the beach in separating streams, as if the men were too ashamed even for one another's continued company.

Aidan knelt on the shingle by the *Athanasia*'s red hull, fists down like a sprinter's on the line, breathing heavily through his mouth. Annja knelt beside him. "You're hurt," she said.

"You oughta see the other guy," he joked through split and puffed lips. "Actually, the other guys look splendid, if you leave aside the effects of hard living and doubtful hygiene. I never laid a finger on them. Not for want of trying, though."

Despite her protests he started to rise. When his determination became obvious she helped him stand and let him lean half surreptitiously against her. His body was warm, flushed perhaps by effort and fear, against hers.

Aside from bruised cheeks and puffy eyes he didn't seem badly hurt. Apparently all that had struck him had been fists, not wood or steel. Not that fists alone couldn't do severe damage.

"You're Spyridon, then?" Aidan said to the young man who stood before them, leaning on his crutch and panting from the effects of his own passionate outburst.

"I am."

The young Englishman forced himself by visibly painful degrees to stand fully upright. Not for the first time, Annja was surprised by his toughness. He looked so boyish and—tender, perhaps, not soft exactly, she thought. But he had steel in his spine.

"We owe you our thanks," Pascoe said.

"Thank you," Annja added.

But the wild-haired head shook decisively. "You owe me nothing," Spyros said. "I do it for me. I am doomed. I hope to not be damned."

He turned and stumped off. Bats swooped overhead, taking flittering tiny insects as they followed him up the darkened beach. A gibbous moon was rising across the waves. Pollution haze or something else stained it red around the rim, like dilute blood.

They followed. "How did you know we weren't who your friends thought we were?" Pascoe called after him.

"You tourist couple, very nice," he said over his shoulder. "Who killed my crewmates—not nice."

"Might be some holes to that logic," Annja said to Aidan, quietly.

He shrugged. "Roll with it, I say."

Spyros led them to a rough shelter at the south end of the beach, masked from view by some large rocks covered in brushy arbutus and fragrant bay. Knocked together out of planks and tarpaper, it was little more than a lean-to. He lowered himself painfully to the ground, set aside his broken oar, gestured for them to sit. Annja and Aidan looked at each other, then perched side by side on a chunk of driftwood perhaps eight feet long that seemed to serve as a sort of boundary for the young man's living space.

Rummaging around in litter piled beside the shelter Spyros made a little stack of newspaper and dry twigs, broke some small bits of driftwood onto it and lit a fire from a plastic lighter. By its uneasy orange light he dug in a mound of reeking cloth Annja realized must be his bed. He came up with a bottle, upended it. She smelled the turpentine-like scent of cheap ouzo as it ran down both sides of his narrow stubbled chin.

In the firelight she studied him as he drank. He had a triangular head and hunted-fox eyes. He was wiry to the point of emaciation. His eyes were sunken deep in pits of blackness.

At last he lowered the bottle and wiped his mouth with the back of his hand. "What you want with Spyros?" he asked. He sounded sad. An undercurrent in his voice, the way he held himself, ever poised as if for flight, the way the firelight flickered from eyeballs turning restlessly this way and that spoke eloquently of a fear that nagged with ceaseless rodent teeth.

"You were part of a crew that dredged an ancient jar from the sea," Aidan said without preamble. "Is that correct?"

Spyros nodded. He looked even less happy. "King Solomon's Jar," he said.

"Why do you say that?" Annja asked.

"When it came up in our nets it look like nothing but big lump. Like lava, but green, you know? But Ioannis, my brother-in-law's cousin, he scrape some corrosion away with his knife. Beneath was yellow metal. Brass."

Next to her Annja felt Aidan shudder at such desecration of an ancient artifact. She felt some of the same thing. She couldn't muster quite the same outrage. For some reason she found herself seeing different points of view with a lot more clarity and empathy these days.

Isn't that kind of an occupational impediment for a champion of good? she wondered. It would make sense for her to start to see everything in black and white.

But that would be too easy, she thought.

"Once he clean up some, in the brass we saw drawings." Spyros said. "Engraved, very fine, but we could just see them. Almost like letters, but not like any letters I see. Not even Chinese. Not Egyptian hieroglyphs." He shook his head.

"Then Georgios, our captain, he get very excited. He had seen writing like that in some book he read once. He said it was used to write the name of spirits. He said it meant we had found jar of King Solomon himself, that he used to put spirits in.

"We laughed at him, even if he was captain. He reads too much! But he was so serious. He got angry that we laughed, so angry he threaten to heave Ioannis over the rail into the sea. Vasilios, he was our mechanic, he thought he knew too much because he lived for a time in America. He said if there were ever spirits in the jar, they were not there now, for there was no stopper. Georgios, he say that not matter. He knows someone pay much for the jar!"

For a moment the young man sat cross-legged staring into the fire. "I grew up with Vasilios," he said. "He was a year older than me, bigger. He stayed bigger when we grew. He used to catch me, rub mud in my hair, laugh and laugh. But it was just fun. He was my friend."

He looked up. "So we sailed to Haifa. A Jew met us in a launch, an Israeli. Doctor from Ministry of Antiquities. Ehud Dror his name. He was man who studies old things, a scientist, you know— what is word—?"

"An archaeologist," Pascoe said in a tight voice.

Spyros nodded. "That's right. Archaeologist. From the government. Georgios does business with him before. Sometimes we bring other things up in our nets, you know? Old things. And he paid us well, just like the captain say. American dollars."

He took another pull from his bottle. For a moment he sat staring into the small pale flames of his fire.

"Then a month ago," he said, "a lifeboat broke loose in a bad sea. It broke my ankle. I was in hospital. I have to use this—" he held up the sawed-off oar "—because the crutch the health service gave me keeps folding up. But at least they did not give me saltwater injection and call it antibiotic."

He drew a deep breath, as if nerving himself to go on. "My nephew Akakios took my place. It was his first voyage—he was sixteen. He could not believe his luck."

Emotion choked him. He tipped his head and drank again. As

he lowered the bottle, Annja saw firelight glisten in a tear track down his cheek.

"It happened just offshore," he said, "when *Athanasia* returned with the catch that evening and dropped anchor. It killed them all. Akakios, Ioannis, Vasilios, Pavlos, Stamatios, Georgios the captain. It took them all."

"It?" Aidan asked gently.

Spyros wept openly now. He shook his head as he spoke—as if denying himself hope, not denying the tragedy that had haunted his every waking thought, his every dream, since it happened. That was something he had no power to deny.

"A devil," he sobbed. "A devil killed them."

Glancing aside, Annja saw Aidan's face working in an effort to restrain his skepticism from emitting a sarcastic blurt. "Surely it was a man. Or men," he said.

"A man who did such a thing," Spyros said, "must be a devil. Or have a devil in him."

A driftwood chunk shifted, fell into the fire. Yellow sparks flew up. Aidan jumped, then cursed under his breath.

Annja leaned forward. "Why do you blame yourself, Spyridon?"

Disconsolately he shook his shaggy head. "I should have been there to meet my fate with them. Instead my nephew died in my place. And I must live knowing that I have cheated death—cheated the devil. And death and the devil, they always collect their due."

They sat a moment in silence. The night had settled in around them. Tree frogs trilled softly. The stars shone overhead.

"I have one question, Spyridon," Pascoe said. "How did word of your discovery get out? This Dr. Dror certainly made no official announcement."

"Oh, no. It was my nephew. Akakios used the Internet. He wrote about it there after some of the other crew bragged to him. I think his friends online thought he make it all up."

"But somebody took him seriously," Annja said.

Miserably, Spyridon nodded. "May the saints forgive me," he whispered brokenly. "I never believe in them. Saints. But they are all I have now."

"But what happened wasn't your fault," Annja said.

"We were cursed," the young man said almost matter-of-factly. "It was a holy artifact, but not meant to be…troubled. We did wrong to bring it up. And I did wrong by escaping punishment." His voice sounded hollow.

"And soon the devil who took my friends will find me!" He upended his bottle and emptied it with a gurgle. Then he threw it into the night. It smashed on the shingle.

Annja rose and moved toward him. He stared up at her with empty eyes. She took his hands.

"Spyros, listen to me. You can't hide from evil in a bottle. You know that, don't you?"

He looked away. "Man cannot hide from devil at all."

"But the evil has passed you by! Don't do the devil's work for him by drinking yourself to death," she said.

He looked up at her. She took his face in both hands. "Don't you see? You were spared for some purpose. You're alive. *Stay* alive. Find your purpose. Follow it. Shame the devil and honor your friends and relatives."

Sincere as she was, her words sounded lame in her own ears. Yet a strange thing happened. She felt a sense of strength, as if a golden radiance shone within her. She felt a tingling, then, in her palms, a sense of flow as from her to him.

He stared at her a moment longer. He sighed, and she had to steel herself not to grimace at the rush of breath redolent of stale wine and long uncleaned teeth. At last he began to weep, great heaving sobs. She hunkered down beside him and put her arm around his shoulder, feeling awkward.

Aidan sat across the fire from them, gazing at her, blue eyes thoughtful. She mentally dared him to say something flippant, modern, cynical and biting. But he didn't. He only watched.

At length Spyros cried himself out. Annja held him a few minutes longer as he relaxed against her. Eventually he began to snore.

She eased him down beside the fire and pulled a blanket over him. The night was still warm but she had no idea whether it would stay that way. Better a filthy blanket—the same one he used every night, anyway, it seemed—than to let him get cold. She stood and kicked the small fire apart and smothered the embers as best she could with brittle plates of shingle and some dirt she was able to scrape from beneath it. Aidan came to help. She brushed back a stray lock of hair and smiled at him.

Then they stood away from the gently snoring Spyros. "You think he'll be okay out here?" she asked.

"He's done well enough so far," Aidan said. "And anyway, would *you* want to try something with him, after what happened to us earlier? I don't doubt someone's been watching the whole time."

"Oh."

He looked up at the stars. "Do you really think it'll work?"

"What?"

"What you said to him. *Did* to him. There was something that passed between you. I felt it, but I don't know what it was. Do you think it'll help him, then?"

"I have no idea," she said. In thoughtful silence they walked back toward their rented car.

21

"Do you know," Aidan said as rain pattered down on the broad-brimmed hats he and Annja wore, "there are some most splendid Neanderthal sites in the region of Mount Carmel?"

Haifa was a somewhat gray industrial city in north Israel, tucked between the mass of Mount Carmel and busy Haifa Bay. An overcast sky occasionally spitting rain onto steaming streets may have unfairly emphasized the grayness. If the city lacked the melodrama of Jerusalem and the self-conscious quaintness of Jaffa, it felt less sterile than Tel Aviv. And it also lacked something of the tension you felt in the air like an unseasonable chill in Tel Aviv or Jerusalem, despite the city's proximity to Lebanon and the Golan Heights. Its residents, Jewish, Arab and foreign, seemed to have their minds mainly on business.

Although she knew the Old Testament used the fifteen-hundred-foot Mount Carmel as something of a standard of beauty, Annja found its gray limestone palisades a bit on the forbidding side. The green terraces of the Baha'i World Center overlooking the town were nice, though.

It was late in the morning. Wearing their usual inconspicuous garb, Aidan a blue chambray shirt and jeans, Annja a light tan cotton blouse with black-and-white streaks like Japanese brushstrokes and khaki cargo pants, they walked a little-trafficked street on the northern side of the industrial and waterfront district known as the lower city. The buildings were mostly one-story offices and shops. Though they had the low, boxy profile and dust-colored stucco of the basic adobe structures you saw at these latitudes around the world, they looked like modern cinder-block construction, with edges too raw and angles too sharp for mud brick.

"It's a little hard to believe," she said to him. "It's just, on the whole, we could be on the outskirts of Phoenix right now, if it weren't for the humidity. And come to think of it, Phoenix is pretty humid, thanks to irrigation and all those swimming pools."

"I'll take your word for it." He had a Borsalino hat or a good imitation on to protect against the weather, the brim low over his blue eyes—a pricey-looking hat, and if real, possibly one of the few affectations she'd been able to discern. His eyes lacked something of their customary glitter today, she'd noticed. He had been subdued since the campfire conference with Spyridon on Corfu.

He stopped and nodded his head. "I think we're here."

A discreet bronze plaque beside a door read Israel Antiquities Authority in English and Hebrew with a logo that looked like a stylized menorah. Annja looked over the building, which appeared no different from the others on the block, and frowned.

"I thought with all their terrorism troubles, Israeli public buildings would be well fortified," she said.

"Undoubtedly the high muckety-mucks don't think the place is worth defending," Aidan said. "You know how governments feel— archaeologists are expendable." He was making no effort to hide his bitterness.

Annja laughed because she was pleased to see him get a bit of his sparkle back. Actually, if she understood correctly, Pascoe was wrong. Israel was obsessed with archaeology. From the earliest days of its existence as a modern state some of its most prominent political and even military figures had displayed fanatic interest in antiquity, at levels ranging from impassioned amateurs to world-renowned archaeologists.

She knew Israel was also a heavily socialist country that loved its bureaucracy. And it had revered sites galore. You couldn't sink a spade in the soil without disturbing ground walked on by some notable personage from the Mideast's long and somewhat depressing history. As a consequence of all these things, a *lot* of Israel Antiquities Authority buildings dotted the landscape. But she supposed it may not have been especially useful or even affordable to defend them all like Cheyenne Mountain.

"Shall we?" Aidan asked.

They pushed in through the white-painted door. Inside it was cool and fluorescent bright. The dark-wood-and-metal desk in the reception area was unoccupied. It sported a computer, a phone and a half-full mug of coffee, showing a cartoon boy and girl leaning against each other with moonily romantic expressions. Hebrew characters were indecipherable above their heads. The air was tart with an astringent smell of dust and cleaning chemicals.

"Ah," said Aidan, sniffing. "Smells like they do archaeology here."

"Strange there's nobody here," Annja said. A door opened into a brightly lit hall behind the unoccupied desk.

"But that means there's no one to tell us not to go on back," Aidan said with a twinkle. "Easier to get forgiveness than permission, as you Yanks say."

They took off their damp hats and placed them on the desk. She walked past him through the door. The hallway beyond consisted of half walls, with glass from waist height to ceiling on either side. To the right was an office with a bookcase on the far wall stocked with books with thick, age-cracked and darkened spines.

In the larger room to the left a long table had a chunk of sandstone lying on it. An obviously ancient human rib cage and what appeared to be a curved reddish surface, apparently part of an earthenware pot or vase, had been painstaking half-liberated from a slab of sandstone. Tools—magnifying glass, steel pick like a dentist's, a cordless Makita drill with a cotton disk buffer mounted in the chuck—lay next to the slab.

Gradually Annja was becoming aware of a strange, cloying odor underlying the dust and disinfectant. At the same time she realized the tip of her left walking shoe seemed to be sticking to the floor. She looked down.

A face looked up at her from a pool of blood spilling through the doorway.

Aidan came into the anteroom door behind her and saw what she saw.

It was a head of almost stupefying normality—if you left aside the expression. And the fact it was by itself—there was that, of course. It was the head of an elderly woman, with waved gray-white hair surrounding a plumpish face, the cheeks rouged, the lips painted.

The eyes were wide in horror. The tongue, bluish, protruding from a lipstick-smeared hole of a mouth. The skin was sallow from the loss of the blood that had drained from the head to the vinyl floor.

With the pallid jowls sagging into the wide pool of blood— shockingly red with bluish undertints in the uneasy light of the over-heads—it was impossible to tell how the head had been removed from the body. *Violently* seemed a good guess.

For a moment Annja's vision—her whole existence, really—was tightly focused onto the severed head of what she presumed had been a receptionist or secretary. Drawing in a deep breath through her mouth, to avoid smelling more than necessary, she widened her vision field enough to take in the fact that visible not far beyond the head, a pair of thick, dough-pale legs protruded into view on the floor between worktable and half-window front wall. They ended in sagging wool socks and stodgy black shoes. Toes down. Annja swallowed hard at the realization that the body, presuming it belonged to the head, was pointing *away* from the door. Whatever had removed the head had carried it a short distance before depositing it near the door.

She felt a chill.

Suddenly, from the corridor's far end came a wild cry of panic. Annja focused her will. The sword came into her hand as a man burst through the door at the end of the hall, emerging from a darkness that suggested a poorly illuminated stairway. The man was tall and gaunt, with gray hair streaming in a wild nimbus to either side of a dome of olive skull. He wore a lab coat over a shirt and tie. The tie was askew. The lab coat was spattered in red.

He skidded as he broke from the doorway. He saw Annja and Aidan and called out to them in Hebrew, half-slumped against the wall as if trying to catch his breath. His eyes, already standing out of his head in terror, seemed to focus. For a moment Annja saw an expression of something like hope flicker across his face.

A growl from the stairway washed it away. He bolted toward them, arms and legs flying in a transport of panic.

A black shape shot from the doorway behind him, already waist high when it came into view, and rising. Light seemed to be sucked into it. It struck him on the left shoulder and slammed him back into the wall, pressing the side of his face into the glass. He screamed shrilly as he was dragged down to the floor.

It was a dog, huge, 120 pounds at least. Against its matte-black hide its eyes were visibly outlined in red, rolling in its big broad head. Its teeth were brilliant white.

Blood fountained around its muzzle, driven under high pressure from a severed carotid artery. The man's outcries abruptly ceased.

The dog let its prey fall to lie twitching on the speckled gray-white tiles. It raised its burning eyes to Annja. They almost seemed to widen when they saw the sword. Then they narrowed with a hatred so intelligent, so human seeming, that it struck Annja like a blow. The dog growled again.

To the depths of her being she was stricken with the most total horror she had ever known. Fear clamped like asthma on her windpipe and threatened to let go the set screws of her knees, drop her choking and weeping and crippled to the floor. She had never imagined such fear.

"Annja," Aidan said from behind her.

She made herself step forward and to her right to put herself in the middle of the corridor, squarely between the hellish creature with the gore-dripping muzzle and Aidan. "Stay back," she said without turning her head.

It seemed for a moment that she saw ghost shapes, shimmers in air above the dog's shoulders. Like a pair of shadowy wings. She did not dare even blink, but shook her head violently. The shadows vanished.

The dog darted forward. Its claws clacked on the vinyl flooring. Its snarling rose in a crescendo as it galloped toward Annja with tremendous speed, looking huge. Its upper lip was pulled back from its teeth, white swimming in red.

It was as terrifying a sight as anything Annja had seen in her life. Yet the blinding-fast attack released her from the fear that threatened to disable her. She steeled herself to face it. I've got to trust the sword, she thought. And myself, she thought.

Halfway down the hall and still a dozen feet away, the beast sprang for her. She met it with a diagonal step forward to her right and a two-handed cut that began behind her right shoulder.

She feared to strike the thing head-on. That huge sloped skull would shed a blow that didn't hit squarely, even from a preternaturally sharp blade.

Fanged jaws flew at her face, spread wide. Her stroke took the creature at the juncture of left shoulder and trunk-thick neck, angling inward toward the center of its chest.

The jaws clashed futilely beside her left ear.

Blood spurted over Annja's face. It seemed unnaturally hot. Her gut revolted. She had bared her teeth as she cut. Blood had sprayed into her mouth.

But she followed through, turning her hips, driving from her powerful legs.

She felt the sword spring free. She saw the beast strike the floor with a sodden thump.

Annja kept herself from going over backward but had to drop to a knee to do so. She held the sword raised before her.

The animal lay thrashing on the floor, one lung a deflated ruin, the other pumping its final breaths. Its other organs spilled out on the floor. Impossibly it lifted its head from the floor to stare at her. Its teeth chattered horribly in its blood-slavering jaws.

For an instant Annja had the horrific sense it was trying to *speak* to her. Then the light went out from its eyes and the head fell to the floor with a thump, the tongue lolling motionless over the teeth of the lower jaw.

She felt as if a hideous presence had vanished—and an enormous weight had lifted from her soul.

"My God," Aidan said quietly.

Slowly Annja rose. She felt the blood drying on her face, getting tacky, starting to itch. The front of her blouse and pants were sodden; she could feel the dampness against her breasts and belly and the fronts of her thighs. She became aware of a salty taste in her mouth and spit violently. It took an effort of will not to vomit.

"You killed a dog," Aidan said accusingly.

"Yes," she said. She felt a stab of remorse for the animal. "It killed that man," she said, sounding more defensive than she intended.

He shook his head. "Isn't that a bit thick?" he asked. "It was just a dog."

She drew a deep breath. He's shaken, she realized. And no surprise. It's made him irrational.

Sword in hand, she moved cautiously into the lab to the left. It was a bloody shambles. She avoided looking at the dead woman. There wasn't anything to do for her. And whatever had killed her had made a ragged job of decapitating her.

The lab was splashed liberally with blood. More surprising, notebooks had been torn and a stool and a chrome-and-leather chair had been slashed open so that stuffing swelled from them like puffy white excrescences. This scene is starting to look familiar, she thought.

Aidan stood in the hall staring in through the window at her. She backed out, moved quickly to the door across the way. "Keep an eye on that door," she suggested, nodding as she passed to the end of the hallway. "We don't know what else might come through it."

Aidan's normally pink complexion had gone ashen and green around the edges. He was breathing rapidly through his mouth. "And take deep breaths," she added. "Into the abdomen."

The office on the far side looked curiously untouched. She backed out of there and went to kneel gingerly by the side of the man who lay slumped against the corridor wall. Still keeping the sword in her right hand, she went quickly through his pockets, feeling more than a bit like a ghoul.

"It's Dror," she said, holding up a wallet unfolded to show a credit card in a plastic carrier with the archaeologist's name embossed on it.

"Hmm," Aidan grunted. His eyes weren't quite tracking. Even after all he'd been through in the past week, what he had witnessed since entering the corridor had shaken him like a fist wrapped around his spine.

He shook his head. "I'm sorry," he said, stepping around the body of the huge black dog. "I'm having trouble with the dog. I can't help it; it just seems harsh to treat an animal so, no matter what it's done. It's just a poor animal. It has no moral judgment. It can't be blamed, after all."

"You don't know the half of it," she told him, rubbing the wallet clean of fingerprints with her shirttail, or so she hoped, and slipping it back into the dead man's pocket. She straightened. "Doesn't this strike you as somehow familiar?"

He gaped at her.

"The scene on the bridge of that fishing boat in Corfu," she said. "The blood splashes. The ripping up of the furniture and the logbooks, apparently out of sheer fury." She nodded her head at the window opening onto the long lab chamber. "Same thing happened here. Not to mention two brutal murders. At least."

"You think that dog killed the crew of the *Athanasia*?" Pascoe's voice curled and cut like a whip of sarcasm. "And then what? It swam across the Mediterranean to assassinate Dror?"

"No. Not *this* dog," Annja said.

"So you suspect an outbreak of some kind of madness—mutated avian flu perhaps—that's making domestic animals run amok and rip up people and commit random acts of vandalism?"

She took a deep breath. "I agreed with you that the dog wasn't to blame," she said. "That's because the dog isn't responsible."

"But you just said—"

"But the same guiding agency did. The same entity. Do you get what I'm driving at, Aidan?"

He glared at her for a moment as if suspecting she was making fun of him. His nostrils were flared.

Then he shook himself, so violently she feared for a moment he was having a seizure. He sighed gustily. "You're speaking of demonic possession."

"I'm afraid so."

He shook his head. "It's hard to assimilate something like that."

"Yes," she agreed, "it is. Let's look around. We came here to learn some things. We need to get out of here before the authorities arrive, unless you feel like discussing demonic possession with the cops."

"Right," he said. "And perhaps we'd best discover if there are any more demonic dogs about."

"Good point," Annja said.

The room next to the office was a little storeroom filled with boxes of specimens and overstuffed filing cabinets. A door stood ajar, letting in a slice of sunlight shining down through a break in the heavy overcast. A quick glance showed it opened onto a narrow alley.

Annja caught Aidan's eye with a meaningful look. It explained how the dog had gotten inside. Or at least, it offered one explanation.

It took all her will and physical courage for Annja to grip the sword in both hands and go down the stairs through the door at hallway's end. The mere physical danger scared her, certainly. But she had faced greater danger—although the horrible savagery of the dog's attack had shaken her as few assaults from humans had. But she felt a creeping conviction that they faced a menace that was more than physical. The dread that had almost overwhelmed her when she faced the animal down clung to her like wisps of fog.

Above all she feared what she might find at the bottom of the stairs.

Her fears were realized.

The stairs turned once. The walls were cool stone and smelled of it; a relief after the abattoir upstairs. "Obviously the modern building's been built on a preexisting site," she murmured. She wasn't vastly concerned about making noise. If anything awaited them downstairs, it—or they—already knew they were coming.

"Looks nineteenth century, to hazard a guess," Pascoe said, reaching out to brush the stone with his fingertips. Though he spoke quietly, as she had, his voice was steadier, more controlled than before. In a small way she was tempted to smile. Thinking professionally was an excellent way to break the spasm of shock and horror.

But the respite was brief. The stairs emptied into a small chamber with metal shelves to either side bowing beneath the weight of the customary dusty artifacts, some wrapped in plastic, some exposed. The floor was concrete, laid when the upper structure was built, Annja guessed.

An arm lay in the middle of it. It looked male, to judge by the dark, hairy hand jutting from the blue sleeve. A heavy gold band, probably a wedding ring, encircled one finger. The other end of the sleeve was soaked in purplish blood. A raw bit of bone jutted out, yellow in the single electric bulb hanging from the ceiling.

A similar light illuminated a scene of fresh horror through the doorway. Beyond lay a storeroom with crates and boxes, many of which had been shattered or ripped open. Amid artifacts, many of shiny yellow metal, sundry body parts were strewed. By the usual mathematics—chiefly that she quickly saw two heads—she guessed at a pair of victims, including the original owner of the arm in the outer room.

"Nothing down here," Annja said. "Nothing alive." She willed the sword away.

"God," Aidan said in a choked voice. He held a handkerchief to his mouth, either in an attempt to prevent himself from vomiting or to ward off the stench in the damp basement. "Such rage."

Annja was aware of conflicting sensations, again reminiscent of what she had felt on the *Athanasia,* both a sense of intense evil and of power.

"The jar was here," she said. "I can feel it. But it's not here now. Perhaps the creature expected to find it, and was enraged by its disappointment."

"The jar itself may not be here," Aidan said, voice muffled by the handkerchief, "but there are certainly jars here. In plenty."

Preoccupied initially with assessing the casualties, Annja realized with a shock he was right. The yellow metal objects lying on the floor among the human wreckage were jars of bright brass. She knelt and picked one up that lay well away from one of the several broad pools of blood. It had the shape of a globe with a narrow funnel thrust into it from above, with two surprisingly delicate handles curving down away from the top, ending in upward-curled knobs.

"It's the same as the one I found on Sir Martin Highsmith's mantel in Kent," she said, holding it out toward Aidan. "Down to the characters engraved on it."

He slipped past her. Either he had reasserted his self-control or simply gone numb; he moved in a brisk, businesslike fashion. "They're all identical," he said.

He hunkered by a wooden crate whose lid had been pushed in. Inside stood a dozen of the jars, encased in bubble wrap. "And look at this," he said. "A shipping manifest."

22

It was raining heavily when they emerged from the front door. But the street wasn't deserted, as a quick check had indicated. As Annja and Aidan ran out, hoping anyone who saw them would believe they were sprinting from doorway to doorway in the downpour, a tall, slim figure stepped out of an alleyway and approached them. The woman was holding an umbrella above a head of long, dark hair with a white streak above the brow.

"Tsipporah?" Annja asked as she and Aidan skidded to a halt.

The older woman smiled. "You were expecting maybe Madonna?"

"Well—not a whole lot less than you," Annja said. "Didn't you tell me I wouldn't see you again?"

"Change of plans. Aren't you going to introduce me to your handsome young man?" she asked.

"Do you have someplace else we could go," Annja said, "out of the rain and out of sight? Like, right now?"

"Of course. Follow me."

She turned and walked at a businesslike pace down the street away from the Israel Antiquities Authority office. Annja and Aidan followed, crowding under her umbrella. In Annja's case, anyway, it was as much because to do otherwise would look suspicious, She was numb and pretty oblivious to getting wet. The young Englishman looked confused and more than a little suspicious, but said nothing.

At the end of the block Annja turned and looked back. Through the blinds on the front window of the building they had just left she saw a blue flash. Then with an almost dainty tinkling of glass the window blew out ahead of a billow of yellow flame.

Tsipporah stopped and turned back. "Natural-gas explosion," she said. "Accidents happen. Or do they?"

Annja looked at Aidan, then at the older woman. "No accident," she said, "as if you didn't know. They had a gas feed for Bunsen burners. It got left open. And somebody left a cigarette burning in an ashtray in the basement."

Fire was billowing upward out the front window, and smoke streamed away from the flat roof. Tsipporah nodded. "I like your style, girl."

"So Dr. Dror was involved with importing and selling fake jars of Solomon," Tsipporah said, sitting back from the card table set in the repair bay of a small garage off Chaim Weizmann Street, east of the now-destroyed antiquities authority office toward Kishon Harbor. The family that owned the garage, Tsipporah assured Annja and Aidan, was on holiday in Jaffa for a few days; no one would disturb them here.

Why exactly Tsipporah had picked the place, or how she had gained access to it—or even known about it—Annja had no clue. For that matter she didn't feel up to hazarding a guess as to why they weren't holding their discussion in the garage's business office. The fact it was small and cluttered and almost every horizontal surface was stacked with papers, work orders, receipts and God knew what else may have had something to do with it. In their brief association Annja had figured out that Tsipporah did things according to her own agenda. She probably had good reasons for them. But she was unlikely to explain. So they sat in the murky gray light filtering out of the rainy sky through windows grimy and fly specked, sipping cheap Negev wine from colorful plastic picnic cups.

"As you're probably aware, various members of the antiquities authority were implicated a couple of years ago in fabricating the fake ossuary alleged to belong to Jesus's brother, James," Aidan said.

"I had heard about that, yes," Tsipporah said with a faintly ironic smile.

"It would appear Dror and his confederates turned the scheme on

its head. Or perhaps inverted it, would be more accurate. Coming
into possession of the genuine artifact, they contrived to produce
replicas of it to sell to avid collectors, New Age aficionados and religious zealots around the world."

Annja shifted on her folding chair, not entirely comfortable in her
new lightweight cotton dress, white with little floral prints on it,
which she was quite convinced was either transparent in certain
light or would become so if she ventured into the rain in it. After
stashing her and Aidan in the garage, which smelled inexplicably of
boiled cabbage as strongly as automotive grease, Tsipporah had
nipped off to find replacements for Annja's shirt and slacks, which
were pretty liberally spattered with blood. She had come back in a
matter of minutes with the dress, presumably from a local market.

"Why not sell the real thing?" Tsipporah asked, leaning back at
ease with her hair spilling in great waves down her shoulders.

Aidan shrugged. "Perhaps a lingering respect for the genuinely
unparalleled value of the artifact to archaeology. Maybe after cashing
in as much as possible from selling the fakes, Dror intended to see
the genuine article discreetly into the possession of the antiquities
authority." He shrugged. "Or perhaps I'm giving the good doctor the
benefit of too much doubt, and he just realized he could make more
money selling fake jars a hundred times than the real one once."

"Why wouldn't he try to make use of its power himself?"
Annja wondered.

"Probably he didn't believe in its power. He could have authenticated it readily enough through metallurgy and electron spin res-
onance dating. But if he had believed, he probably wouldn't have
bothered with the counterfeiting, since if I recall correctly legend
holds that the reason the jar was dug up in the first place, and the
famous seal removed, was to use the demons to find hidden treasure."

"You're a most knowledgeable young man," Tsipporah said
with a smile.

Annja stifled a surge of irritation that the smile was returned. It
may have been that she kept seeing the older woman in softening
light, but she looked more than handsome to Annja. And Aidan
seemed more appreciative than she liked. She chided herself for
being ridiculous.

"It didn't do him much good in the end, though," Annja said.

"It most certainly did not," Tsipporah said. "It seems he encountered one of the Goetic demons. Marchosias. He's big and bad—one of the worst. But you stood up to him and won. Not everybody could do that. You've justified your role as champion, Annja Creed."

"Thanks. But it wasn't much of a fight. Not really. He—the dog he was possessing—just jumped straight at me. And I—" She shrugged. She was a little uncomfortable repeating the details, for fear of setting off the animal-loving side of Aidan again. "I would've expected him to be a cagier opponent, I guess."

"Don't underestimate either the demon or yourself. Note I don't say his name. I won't again, and I suggest you don't. They can hear their names from a long way off. What you did was confront him and stand. That's what makes you special. Pure moral and spiritual courage.

"I'd say he knew the form he was occupying stood no real chance against you, armed as you were with the sword. So he decided on an all-or-nothing assault that might get lucky—or might intimidate you into not resisting. It's not as if he had anything to lose at that point."

"Nothing to lose?" Aidan burst out. "Annja killed him."

"She killed his host, you mean," Tsipporah said. "Do you think you could hurt a demon, or even cause him serious discomfort, when he's in another's body? If he appeared in his own form as a winged wolf, the sword might do him harm—I can't say, and I'm really unwilling to speculate. It may have caused him physical pain. But only momentarily."

"And the dog?" Annja asked feeling terrible.

"There was no dog. Except the meat shell. It wasn't possessed, girl. What you encountered was a rare phenomenon the *Catholic Encyclopedia* calls demonic *obsession*. It means the original occupant's mind, will and soul have been flat-out evicted. The demon isn't sharing the space, the way it does in possession. You're dead and gone. It's easier with an animal, obviously," Tsipporah explained.

Annja shuddered. She felt a stab of pity for the poor dog, and wondered if it might linger as a ghost, after being turned out of its own body by the demon. But she felt a strange, rather silly sense of relief that she hadn't really been the one to kill the poor thing.

"Do you think someone summoned him and sent him to visit

those people?" she asked. Despite sharing Aidan's distaste for artifact forgers, she didn't share his tacit but unmistakable feeling that Dror, at least, had got what was coming to him. Not for the first time she noted that her companion, while a sweet enough young man, and definitely an innocent at heart, still possessed a not altogether attractive self-righteous streak.

"More than likely," Tsipporah said. "It wouldn't be too characteristic for a demon to act so directly on his own. But don't forget the demons have their own stake in this. I can't help wondering if the extreme violence you saw might indicate the demons' own mounting frustration at not being able to find the jar themselves."

"But the demons are supposed to be good at finding treasure," Aidan said. "Why can't they find the jar the same way?"

"The jar has ways of avoiding discovery through magical means. The demons are flying as blind as the rest of us in this." Tsipporah turned her intense dark gaze full on Annja. "You seemed to react pretty strongly to something I said, there."

"Can they do that to anyone?" Annja felt tremendous fear once again.

"Can they tempt you? That's up to you," Tsipporah said.

Annja felt her heart pounding. "But I thought—" Her voice dwindled into futile nothingness.

"You thought you'd be immune?" Laughing softly, Tsipporah patted her cheek. "You're a sweet child. But occasionally, not so bright. You have to choose between right and wrong. Every minute of every day. Just like the rest of us. Only, now, even more so. You think maybe it should be easier on you than on the average shlemiel?"

Annja could find nothing to say.

Tsipporah studied Annja a moment. "Interesting. You may have attracted some unfortunate attention, young lady.

"But believe it or not," Tsipporah said, "the reason I broke my earlier resolve and looked you up again, Annja, had nothing to do with our friends from the jar. Or only peripherally. I have some information about the human players that might prove useful to you."

"Tell me," Annja said.

"First, Sir Martin Highsmith and his White Tree Lodge. He and his little chums desire the power of the jar to remake the planet. They wish to overturn the modern world and restore all to a state of nature."

"He did seem pretty nostalgic for the Paleolithic when I spoke to him," Annja said.

"If not the Pleistocene, before there were any nasty people running around bothering the animals. Since their little plans envision overthrowing the whole order of the world, undoing all of civilization and technology and reducing the Earth's population to a few thousand happy hunter-gatherers, it's safe to assume they won't hesitate to kill anyone who gets in their way. But I guess you've had a bit of first-hand experience of that, haven't you?"

Annja nodded.

"Now, Mark Peter also wants the power to do good for everybody, whether they like it or not."

"Mark Peter?" Annja said. "You mean Stern?"

"He's dead," Aidan said. "I don't know if you follow the news, but someone blew up his yacht off Jaffa with an antitank guided missile. About two minutes after our dear Annja leaped over the rail into the sea."

"What interesting lives you young people lead these days. I do occasionally see a television news broadcast, when I can't help it. I've even been known to go on-line a time or two. As it happens I'm aware of all the things you said. And one thing more. Stern wasn't on the yacht when the *mafiya* blew it up," Tsipporah said.

Annja frowned. "But I had just finished talking to him."

"Really? Just that instant? You walked up on deck and, wham?"

"Well—not exactly." She described her encounter with Eliete von Hauptstark.

"So you might have been a bit distracted for a minute or two. Long enough for Mark Peter to grab a mask and some tanks and roll over the seaward rail, where his Russian minders wouldn't spot him. A resourceful boy, is Mark Peter. Gotta give him that. A certified scuba diver, too."

"But why would he do that?" Annja asked, shocked by the turn of events.

"Maybe because somebody tipped him off," Tsipporah said.

Aidan exhaled loudly. "I thought nobody turned on the Russian *mafiya*," he said.

"Somebody turns on everybody," Tsipporah said. "The *mafiya* have some people in it who are terrifyingly smart and some who are terrifyingly brutal, and sometimes they're the same. They have a total lack of scruples and a healthy respect for the power of terror. All true. But it *isn't* true nobody ever turns on them. That's just propaganda they spread, with plenty of help from various police agencies. The same way the Western defense establishment used to go along with the Soviet army's policy of vastly exaggerating its capabilities and combat worth. It's budget-positive behavior."

"Still, why would anyone risk crossing people like that for the sake of a man like Stern?" Aidan asked.

Tsipporah shrugged. "Why would anyone help the Russians against him, for that matter? You think the *mafiya* ran that hit on Stern's yacht without some sort of cooperation inside the Israeli government? Maybe it was just corruption, maybe it was a disagreement, let's say, with some of Stern's aims and methods—such as the covert way he's been arming radical settler groups to fight the central government. Maybe it was both. Now, I don't know, but I suspect the likeliest answer to how Stern knew to go over the side in advance of that missile was that somebody in government got wind of the plan, didn't like it and tipped him off. Maybe it was even one of his followers. Somebody outside the *mafiya* would, I grant you, have a lot less trepidation about putting a spike in their wheel than an insider."

She shrugged. "We'll never know, likely. Does it matter that much? Stern escaped, he's still in the game as much as before—and now, being officially dead and all, he's got a lot more scope for action, which would be good to keep in mind. Are the ins and outs that important?"

"Not really," Annja admitted.

Aidan was looking at the older woman with his head tipped to the side and a hard little smile. "If your mystic arts tell you all this," he said, "why don't they show you where Solomon's Jar is?"

Tsipporah laughed. "How do you know they don't, and I'm not telling you? Seriously, I can't trace the jar. It has ways of disguising itself, you might say, from spiritual detection. But the information I'm giving you now isn't quite so esoteric in origin."

"Ha! I knew it!" Aidan leaned forward. "You're intelligence. Or counterintelligence. Mossad or Shin Bet."

Tsipporah laughed again. "Whoa! Slow down, cowboy. You're riding that there horse too far, too fast. Let's just say I have my sources in this plane—and if they're a bit on the occult side, using the actual meaning of the word, well, a girl's entitled to her secrets, isn't she?"

"But you do know for a fact that Stern is still alive?" Annja asked.

"Oh, yes. And not too happy about the loss of his yacht and crew—and his Brazilian supermodel. But he probably writes them all off as sacrifices necessary for spiritual progress—his own. And the good of humanity, of course.

"He's drawn Israeli fanatics, especially among the settlers resisting evacuation of the occupied territories, to help him with promises of magically rebuilding the temple and creating a globe-spanning Israeli empire. He's also got well-heeled, rapture-happy U.S. fundamentalists bankrolling him big time with promises of kicking off Armageddon, also by restoring the temple."

Tsipporah lit a cigarette. "But he has no intention of doing so. What he wants is for the demons to make him king of the world. For the children, of course."

"Did he really do that?" Annja asked.

"Who, sweetie? You got me a bit confused."

"I'm sorry. I wasn't very clear. King Solomon. Did he really use the demons to build the temple in one night?"

For a moment Tsipporah looked at her through a cloud of smoke. "No," she said. "Not literally. The temple yarn is just a metaphor. As we've seen, the demons have a hard time acting directly in our world. Shaping and hoisting blocks of stone is a little hands-on for their capabilities."

"What about our Russian friends?" Aidan asked. "What's their interest in the jar? Or have they strayed so far from dialectic materialism that they're believing in evil spirits now, too?"

"You'd be surprised just what most Russians—including some very highly placed ones—did believe during the Soviet years. But as it happens their interests in the jar are impeccably materialistic enough to satisfy the most doctrinaire Marxist. Money. They've accepted a commission from an oligarch who's a rich and powerful collector. He's a total atheist. He basically wants to put it in his personal museum and leave it there under massive guard, so he and only he can look at it when he wants to. World without end, amen."

Aidan tossed back the last of his drink. "How selfish!" he exclaimed in disgust.

Tsipporah gave him a thoughtful look. "You might consider opening your mind to the possibility selfishness isn't quite as bad as it's cracked up to be."

"Nonsense! With all due respect. It's the root of all evil," Aidan stated.

Tsipporah chuckled. "Ah, the young. Moral certainty comes so easily to you."

23

It was twilight when the big Boeing wound down to-ward Rio de Janeiro. The city looked like a big bowl of crunchy gray urbaniza-tion poured in among a plethora of sharp hills, with green in myriad rich shades busting out through the cracks and gaps.

"It's not all favelas and Carnaval," Annja told her companion as they both leaned forward to peer out the window. "But both are im-portant in their own way."

She laughed. "How sententious is that? Listen to me. I've never even been to the place. I just read the news on-line a lot."

"We're still going to be bloody tourists," Aidan muttered. She noticed his knuckles gleaming blue-white on the back of the hand that gripped the armrest. He was a nervous flier. She had to suppress a giggle. It seemed incongruous given how calmly he had faced terrible danger and soul-wrenching horror. As usual, it seemed to be the smaller things he had trouble coping with in equanimity.

"Hardly that," she said. "Too bad, too. Although I understand Rio's like Mexico City—too big and crowded, not really representative of the country as a whole. Although it's not as big as São Paulo. Or as polluted." She shrugged. "Still, it's a city named after an imaginary river—January River, in fact. That's got to stand for something."

Having allowed Annja to take the window seat, either gallantly or because he was afraid of flying, Aidan sat in the center seat of the row. The third party was a plump, benign-looking German woman who spent the whole tedious trip across the Atlantic bobbing her gray head in response to whatever was being piped through the iPod earbuds she wore.

Annja noticed Aidan craning his head to follow the flight attendant, a willowy young woman with ebony skin, gleaming white smile and brilliant green eyes who had just spoken briefly to their seatmate in what sounded to Annja like flawless German. At the moment she was speaking very good French to a portly gentleman in a rumpled blue suit in the central seat section of the wide-body aircraft. She had several times during the flight spoken in effortless, lightly accented English to Annja and Aidan.

"She's certainly an eyeful," Annja said with more irritation than she intended.

Aidan turned his eyes forward with a shrug. "I don't mean to be impolite. But ye gods! I'm a heterosexual male, after all."

Annja nodded with what she hoped was understanding.

"Anyway, I admit I'm still trying to assimilate a Brazilian woman named Gretchen. What's up with all these German Brazilian women?" he asked.

Annja was wondering what was up not just with German Brazilians, but with women who were taller than she was. Even without the heels the attendant must have stood six feet, like the late Eliete von Hauptstark.

"Santa Catarina," she said. "A state south down the coast a ways, next door to Paraguay. It's full of Germans and Italians."

"Good Lord. Was it settled entirely by Axis fugitives fleeing World War II?" Pascoe asked.

She shrugged. "Not all of them. There are other groups, too, like the descendants of Confederate soldiers who came here after the American Civil War. I understand they enjoy reenacting antebellum Southern life."

Aidan frowned. "What in hell's that?" he asked, leaning forward and pointing out the window. "And I mean that a lot more literally than I might have a fortnight ago."

As the airplane banked toward Galeão-Antonio Carlos Jobim International Airport on Governador Island, the brown haze overlying the city and the hills beyond was underlit by an evil orange color. Scores of individual lights glowed red like gaping wounds bleeding fire.

"*Usinas,*" Annja said. "Metal foundries. They use a lot of open-furnace and crucible techniques down here that are outmoded in most Western countries, if not outlawed." At Aidan's surprised glance she smiled. "I cheated and checked on-line from the hotel in Milano. They do look like vents from hell, don't they?"

Her expression sobered. "Appropriately enough," she said, "they're our destination."

"IT'S A LITTLE BIT like a sauna, isn't it?" Annja said as they walked back from dinner at a restaurant near their hotel. Around them it was very dark. Lights shone brightly all around them and well up the hills of the affluent São Conrado neighborhood, near the southern shore peninsula that jutted into the Atlantic. It had all the subtle restraint of a black velvet painting. Around them music blared from a hundred places, nightclubs, restaurants, even the balconies of exclusive apartment complexes. A thousand beats were vying with each other and the noise of the traffic surging past. While she could make out plenty of Brazilian traditional and popular tunes, Annja was somewhat disappointed that thumping rock and hip hop seemed to be winning the volume battle.

"Too right," Aidan said. "Even after the Mediterranean the heat and humidity is a bit stunning."

"Well, it is the tropics."

"I'd think you'd be used to it, though. I thought you'd spent time down here before getting involved in all this jar madness," he said.

"That was in the high Amazon basin," she said. "Pretty much the foothills of the Andes. Higher, dryer. Cooler."

They came to a stretch of relative darkness, though the street itself was still broad, well lit and traveled. Inland a series of hills rose, their sides encrusted with lights. "Pretty," Aidan murmured.

"By night," Annja said. "That's Roçinha. The largest slum in Latin America. They call them favelas here. That term's politically incorrect now, supposedly, but as far as I can tell it's what everybody actually says."

Aidan shook his head. "I should have known," he said. "Rio's slums are legendary. Do you think we're safe? All the guidebooks are filled with masterful understatements about the risks of being out on the streets. Especially at night."

Annja grinned at him. "Do you really think we have anything to worry about?"

He sucked in his lips. "Well…they might have guns."

She continued to look at him.

"I guess you'd be a bad choice for victimization, even at that." She laughed.

"I keep forgetting you have all these abilities. You're harmless enough looking. For a strikingly beautiful young woman, that is."

"Flatterer," Annja said smiling.

He shook his head briskly. "Not so. I don't flatter."

"I'm not beautiful. I'm too tall, gangly. Plain," Annja said.

He laughed so loudly a couple of men walking by turned to stare at them. "Nonsense," he said.

"No. really. Don't make fun of me," Annja said seriously.

He looked at her with his head tipped to the side and one eyebrow raised. His eyes were so pale they seemed to glow in the shine of stars and streetlights. "Quite without vanity, are you?"

"About my looks. I guess."

"Then why do you keep fishing for compliments?" And he whooped with laughter again.

"You bastard." Annja laughed as she said it.

Ahead their hotel, the InterContinental Rio, rose from the parking lot and huge swimming pools the way Sugarloaf Mountain did from the sea off nearby Urca. All lit up by floodlights it looked to Annja like a heavily striated cut face of sandstone or limestone, one of those with the history of aeons laid out for anyone with the requisite geological knowledge to read.

She said so.

"You're such a romantic," Aidan said. "Of course, I was thinking much the same thing."

"Let's face it," Annja said. "We're archaeology dorks."

Laughing, they ran to the light blaze of the great covered entrance.

WITH GREAT RELIEF Annja sat on the foot of her bed to take off her shoes. Their room was spacious, clean and much like any fine hotel room anywhere. Not that Annja had spent much time in hotel rooms as nice as this one. She had been actively uncomfortable with the notion of staying in a five-star establishment. Also it was in the Zona Sul, the South Zone, on the other end of town from their objective of the next morning, as well as from the international airport where they'd landed and from which they'd depart.

If they survived the trip.

But Aidan had insisted. After what they'd been through, including the series of adequate but shabby rooms in Mediterranean motels and down-at-heels *pensiones* they'd shared the past few nights since he fished her out of the water off Jaffa, he said they deserved a luxury break. Besides, he paid.

He stood in his sock feet, gazing out the floor-to-ceiling window at Pepino Beach. Despite their elevation on the ninth floor there wasn't much to see beyond the bright lights of the parking lot except the tiny lights of some vessels well out on the water.

"You can go out on the balcony," Annja said.

"If I open the door it will be like being hit in the face with a wet woolen blanket," he said. "I think I'll avail myself of the wonders of modern air conditioning a while longer."

He turned and dropped into a recliner chair with a sigh. Annja lay back on the bed with her own feet, now bare, resting on the carpet. She rolled her eyes to look at him. With only the lamp between the beds lit it wasn't too bright in the room. Despite that she thought he looked troubled, in his posture if not expression.

"Something's bothering you," she said.

He shook his head. "No, no."

They had stopped off in the bar downstairs to sample the national drink, *caipirinha,* made with sugarcane liquor, called *cachaça*, mixed with lemon and ice. Unlike many of their colleagues, neither was much of a drinker. Annja felt more than a little elevated.

"Not a bit of it," Aidan said somewhat grandly.

Rather than keep her from feeling anxious about her companion's mood, her slight buzz seemed to sharpen her anxiety. She wondered at the phenomenon without knowing what to do about it.

"Come on," she said. "Please don't fence me out."

"For some reason I've been thinking about those Greek fishermen who braced us on the beach in Corfu," he said.

"What about them?"

"You didn't kill them?"

She frowned. "Would you prefer I had?"

"No. I was wondering, why not? You killed some of those men attacking me in Jerusalem."

She sat up. "They attacked me, too, if you'll recall."

"Sure. But so did the Greeks. What makes the difference, who lives, who dies?"

He frowned. "It couldn't have made any difference that those men in Jerusalem were Jewish...could it?"

Annja stood up quickly. "You can't seriously believe that about me. And don't you think charges of anti-Semitism are being tossed about just a bit too freely these days? That kind of thing is unworthy of you."

She loomed over him. She was seriously angry.

He held up defensive hands. "Sorry. Sorry, love. I don't know what made me say that. But it's a question that's...been bothering me. That's all. Some men die, some live, and you have the power to make that decision."

Annja turned away. His use of the word *love* had struck her like the jab of a baton in the belly. She knew it was casual, an English turn of phrase. No doubt it signified little more than he was slightly inebriated, enough to have disregarded the political correctness of using a word that might be deemed sexist. But still—

Nothing gets a girl worked up like reminding her how isolated she really is, she thought. She remembered Tsipporah's prediction or prophecy on taking leave of her in Jerusalem. The fact that the wise woman's other prognostication, that their paths would never cross again, hadn't panned out was small consolation right now.

Aidan was standing behind her. "Look, I know you do the best you can," he told her. "I can't really judge you, because I've no way of sharing your burden. And you saved my life twice, if memory serves. I'm a bloody ingrate and a twice-bloody fool. Please, just forget I spoke."

"No," she said. "It's true. Not that it made any difference to me that those men in Jerusalem were Jewish, if they even were—I have no way of knowing that. Not really. But what is true is that I used the sword without much hesitation and I couldn't make myself use it on those men on the beach. I *couldn't* have summoned the sword. My will was…clouded. I didn't feel in the right."

She felt him standing behind her. His breath stirred the hair at the back of her neck, where she'd tied it up to keep cooler in the muggy heat.

"I understand. I think I do. It was the intent," he said.

She shook her head. "Their intent was to kill us, those fishermen. I mean, I thought that their motives were purer—they were doing it to avenge their dead friends, and also to protect their living one. But what if the men who attacked you in the Old City thought they were doing the right thing, too? They must have, after all."

"Isn't that the burden you have to bear?" he said softly. "Trying as best you can, with imperfect knowledge and poor old human fallibility, to judge what's good and what isn't? We all have to make those decisions, I suppose. But with you there tend to be harsher consequences."

She raised her head and looked out into darkness. "You don't think I'm delusional? Some kind of psychopath, a serial killer who imagines she has a mission to cleanse the world of evil?"

"The sword is a pretty convincing delusion, Annja. And I haven't seen you execute anybody in cold blood, only defend yourself—and me. I don't pretend to understand all the moral ramifications of this mission of yours. Which I guess, now that I step back, makes me understand the pressure you're under even more."

She shook her head. "I wish *I* understood better. Sometimes I don't think I'm suited to this new life. It just sounds impossibly grandiose even to say. I don't know if anybody's up to a role like that. How can I possibly live up to it?"

Her eyes stung, filled with warm tears. Self-pity? a merciless voice reproached her in her head. Too much alcohol?

She felt his hand on her shoulder, firm, gentle. "Perhaps that's why you were chosen," he said softly. "Because you have the strength and integrity to ask questions."

She turned. Her breath seemed to catch in her chest. His eyes were fixed on hers. They seemed to glow.

She grabbed him by the head, almost roughly. She pressed her mouth to his. A frozen moment, in which her mind wheeled with fear and embarrassment. I've pushed it too far. I'll scare him off—

Then his hand was behind her neck. A quick, smooth gesture and he had plucked the long pin she used to tie up her hair. It fell in a cascade to her shoulders. Their tongues twined, their faces pressed together so hard her lips were numbed by unaccustomed pressure.

In a sudden adolescent frenzy their hands were in motion, undressing themselves, undressing each other.

By the time they had finished gracelessly hopping free of their undergarments and landed on the bed together, naked, they both were laughing.

24

"Admiral Cochrane's Forge," Annja said.

Peering through lush green underbrush, Aidan said, "The place itself is a great deal less prepossessing than the name, I have to say." He muttered a curse and swatted some kind of big green fly that had lit on his bare forearm to sink a probe.

They had parked their rented Toyota on the side of a track off the main road, crossing their fingers it wouldn't got bogged down on uncertain ground. Then they had hiked a quarter mile or so through the woods to reach the outskirts of the foundry.

Though she was in superb shape, and used to hiking cross-country, the humid heat and swarming bugs had Annja wondering if they were being paranoid in their approach. The forge, after all, had a marked blacktop road leading, they now saw, to a lot graded out of the surrounding forest. But even though the occasional dark look and scowl from her companion told her his thoughts ran down the same track she was just as glad they had taken a roundabout route. After what they'd experienced the past week or so, *too* paranoid might just prove barely paranoid enough.

The smelter was a sprawling rectangular building and seemed to be mostly metal post and rusty sheet metal in construction. Even in the bright daylight the fiery glare was visibly spilling out the front. They could feel heat on their faces a hundred yards off.

"Charming place to work," Aidan said.

"I'm sure their safety standards are as up-to-date as their equipment, too," Annja said. "Still, I guess the heat is easier to endure than starvation—even if you throw in the risk from the occasional splash of molten metal."

A few cars stood parked by the building's rust-streaked flank, several foreign sedans and a battered white Range Rover. They probably belonged to the technical staff and foremen. Annja guessed the workers probably walked.

"I don't see any sign of trouble," Aidan said. "Maybe we did hike all this way for nothing." He took off his bush hat and wiped sweat from his face with a handkerchief. He wore a light blue cotton short-sleeved shirt, now with big half moons of sweat beneath the arms, and his customary blue jeans.

Annja wore a cheap panama hat and her usual field garb of white man's shirt and khaki cargo pants. She had the sleeves rolled down for the same reason she avoided shorts in the heat—to discourage the plentiful and insolent Brazilian insect life.

"I wonder what it's like in the bloody Amazon, with all these bloody bugs they have down here," Aidan said, slapping his bare arm again. It left a smear of red against his pale skin.

"Worse in the Lower Amazon, I imagine. The Upper Amazon where I've been was not quite so bad. Close call, though," Annja said.

She studied him. She wasn't sure how she felt about the previous night. At breakfast, in one of the hotel's restaurants Aidan had been his usual self, not so much bubbling over with humor as voluble about his interests and passions with a dry backing of humor. She thought there had been an extra flush to his normally pink cheeks, but perhaps she'd imagined that. She felt as if her cheeks were a bit rosier, though. She had, however, studiously avoided letting herself think about what had happened between them. Or what it might portend.

"What do you think?" he asked. One thing you could say for him was that he seemed to have little trouble deferring to a woman in a potentially dangerous situation.

She smiled. "I say we go. Race you?"

He touched two fingers to her arm. "Won't it be less obtrusive if we just walk?"

She looked at him a moment. Then she nodded. "Good point." And that's what I get for getting cocky about my action-babe pose.

They strolled out of the brush as casually as if they came this way every day about this time. Some royal-blue-and-orange birds flew up, squalling indignantly. Annja and Aidan walked at a matter-of-fact pace toward the structure, feeling the heat on their faces grow with every step.

"Think they have surveillance cameras?" he asked.

"The place looks as if they're in there listening to an old radio with vacuum tubes," she said. "But we can't take anything for granted. Not with surveillance equipment so cheap these days. Still, does it really make a difference?"

"I suppose not."

They approached the open front of the building. From inside came a roar of noise. Ignoring a door covered in flaking green paint, they walked to the big opening. Annja leaned forward and peered around the wall.

Furnace heat and the stench of hot metal hit her in the face. Even after the heat of the tropical sunlight it was almost staggering.

"Inferno," Aidan whispered by her shoulder. He sounded truly horror-struck.

Through eyes watering from heat and the chemical smell she got an impression of a vast dark face shot through the glow of fires. Great tangled machines loomed and catwalks strung back and forth like a steel spiderweb above. Vast black cauldrons emerged from an enormous yellow furnace mouth, drooling liquid metal; streams of living flame like lava fell into molds, sparks showering and skittering on the floor as they reddened, faded, winked out. A continuous roar of noise sounded, the whoosh of gas jets, the rush of molten metal being poured, hissing and sizzling, and ruling all the ceaseless bellow of the flame.

Black men, bare to the waist, moved through the hellish tumult with almost desperate purpose, carrying long poles with hooks, and outsized tongs. Wiry torsos ran with sweat. The glare reflected and skittered over their safety helmets. The display might have stirred a favorable response inside Annja, who liked looking at well-muscled scantily-clad men as much as the next woman. Instead she found it somewhat frightening and sad.

"How can anybody work in that?" Aidan asked.

"Necessity." Annja said. "I guess if archaeology teaches us anything, it's just how much humans can learn to tolerate if they have to."

"Poor bastards," Aidan said.

"Amen. Let's get in there," Annja replied.

The brightness of the furnace seemed to make the shadows darker, defeating the lights hanging from the ceiling high overhead. There were ample hiding places, even had anyone been looking around. But no one was.

They moved toward the back, keeping close to the left wall. Exhausted crucibles, suspended from a track overhead, were conveyed out another wide opening of the far wall into daylight. Before them an enclosed space intruded onto the main floor, its lone story far below the cavernous ceiling. It appeared to contain an office with windows in its flank showing desks and computer monitors with men in shirtsleeves sitting at them. It struck Annja as being way too close for either comfort or safety to where the fuming cauldrons tipped their cargo into the waiting molds. Seven or eight yards beyond the far side of the structure yawned the mouth of the furnace itself.

Annja stopped, heart in throat.

She ducked behind some kind of great rounded gray-painted metal casing. Aidan duckwalked up next to her. "What is it?" He had to put his mouth to her ear and still practically shout to make himself heard over the tumult.

She pointed. A dozen or more men in dark suits stood confronting office workers in shirtsleeves in front of the office area. All of them wore large silver medallions on chains around their necks. One man wore a suit all of white and cream rather than dark fabric. He loomed above the others and appeared thin as a flagpole.

"It's Highsmith," she said.

"My God," Aidan said. "Those men have guns."

It was true. Sir Martin's followers, at least a dozen in view, held a variety of firearms, some handguns, some long arms—machine pistols, shotguns, assault rifles. Looking around, Annja saw more armed men moving around the work floor. The foundry workers themselves paid scant attention to them. They were probably not unaccustomed to seeing heavily armed men. Houses of the wealthy and even exclusive apartment complexes routinely sported guards carrying submachine guns in Brazil. Or maybe in comparison to the tons of two-thousand-degree liquid metal swaying over their heads and pouring out in great glaring streams like lava, the firearms just didn't seem dangerous.

"What now?" Aidan asked.

"We get in closer."

His expression told her what he thought of *that* idea. With a flip of his hand he gave her a mock-courtly "you first" gesture.

The White Tree Lodge members seemed preoccupied with keeping an eye on the foundry employees. They weren't looking around to spot people sneaking through the heavy metal machinery on the floor.

Annja and Aidan got within thirty feet of the two groups in front of the door to the office. A burly young Englishman was shouting at a short, dark man with bulging eyes, hair like Brillo pads flanking a sweat-shiny spire of skull, and his tie askew.

"Não, não," the Brazilian was saying. Annja guessed he was the foundry manager. "I do not know what the foreign gentlemen are talking about—"

"Dennis," Sir Martin said. Though he did not seem to raise his voice the name rang clearly audible above all the volcanic noise.

Without warning a short cultist with a shock of unruly dark hair shot the tall and gawky young Brazilian to the manager's left through the knee. The young man fell down howling and thrashing and clutching his leg.

Blood sprayed the immaculate ivory shins of Sir Martin's trousers. The knobbed face showed no reaction. A slight young cultist quickly knelt before his master and began dabbing at the blood spatter with a handkerchief. It only had the effect of broadening the droplets into dark smears.

Aidan tensed as if to lunge. Annja put a restraining hand on his arm.

"We can't just watch," he hissed.

"What do you suggest we do? They've got us outmanned and outgunned."

Aidan frowned furiously at her. "You've got that magical sword!"

"I can't knock bullets out of the air," she said. She looked around nervously. Though it seemed unlikely anybody could have heard their soft-voiced but intense conversation the odds against them were too high for her to take anything for granted.

"But surely you don't mean to do *nothing?*" Pascoe said.

"We'll do something," she said, wanting to keep things as simple as possible. "But we need to wait for an opportunity."

"But we can't just stand by—"

Annja grabbed him by the arm and put her finger to his lips. His eyes widened in outrage.

"Wait," she said. "The equation just changed."

She tipped her head toward the large front door. After a scowling moment his eyes followed her lead.

More men were striding in out of the brightness of the morning. They were thick-necked men, white, obviously foreigners, though their garb was mostly rough. Their posture suggested arrogance.

They too openly carried guns. Green braided leather thongs circled their thick necks.

Among them walked Mark Peter Stern in a tropical-weight tan suit, a yarmulke on his gleaming gold hair.

25

A White Tree cultist who had worked his way toward the large opening shouted and raised a handgun. One of Stern's followers fired a burst from his hip with an Uzi. The Englishman spun and fell, his weapon unfired.

Annja crouched lower, drawing Aidan down with her. She expected an instant eruption of answering gunfire. Instead the White Tree cultists seemed thunderstruck by the arrival of their rivals and the sudden death of one of their comrades.

"Sir Martin," Stern called out as he strode past Annja and Aidan's hiding place with his burly henchmen spreading out to either side of him. "What a pleasure to find you here. I wish I could say it's unexpected."

Highsmith stared at him with his dramatic white eyebrows flared in fury. "What are you doing here, you mountebank?"

"You mean your divinations didn't tell you that? Any more than it warned you to expect my visitation? Gee, it's too bad. Obviously you're too inept to possess an artifact of the power and majesty of King Solomon's Jar. Jumping naked over fires and hugging trees is more your speed, eh, wot." The last appeared to be a cartoonish attempt at parodying an English accent, and Stern had said it with a nasty sneer on his face.

"How typically American," Highsmith said. "Your feeble attempts at humor are of a kind with your so-called mystic teachings—base humbuggery fit to pull the wool over the eyes of self-besotted simpletons."

"Are they going to try to talk each other to death?" Aidan demanded. The color had dropped from his face at the murder of his countryman. His cheeks were regaining their usual hue, and his insouciance seemed to be springing back.

Annja was relieved. "I'm afraid not," she said. "I don't know if that's good or bad."

"I see your point. I deplore bloodshed. But it couldn't happen to a nicer—"

She gripped his arm and put a finger to her lips. She had begun to sense a change in the atmosphere—over the hot-metal stink and booming noise of the foundry.

Another crucible came to a stop and poured its contents in an arc of liquid fire into a mold, where it ran in rivulets into the depressions awaiting it. Now looking somewhat nervously at the invaders, with sparks cascading unnoticed around them and dancing by their feet, the workmen plied the flow with their long tools, seemingly more to make sure it behaved as expected than because they needed actively to push the process along.

By reflex Stern and his men glanced toward the fire fountain. "Take them!" Highsmith shouted.

The White Tree cultists opened fire. Two of Stern's men fell. Another backed away, firing an Uzi machine pistol from the hip. He screamed as bullets hit him but kept firing until he tripped backward over the edge of the molds and fell into the stream of molten metal cascading from the crucible. His scream rose in a crescendo, impossibly shrill. Steam gouted from his body as his flesh became fluid and sluiced from his bones. His body, half-skeletonized, sprawled across the glowing molds.

Annja ducked as random bullets cracked overhead and whined in ricochets off the machinery around them. She wished she had ducked when the shooting first began, and not seen what she had just seen. Aidan hunkered beside her, looking sick.

"What now?" he mouthed over the crackle of gunfire and shouts and screams.

"We can't just hide," she shouted back to him. "They'll find us if we do."

He nodded, swallowing spasmodically as if trying to control his emotions. Her stomach was churning. She turned away. She knew she could not afford to be incapacitated by a fit of nausea, however briefly.

Without any dignified course coming to mind, Annja crawled on all fours toward the office where it protruded onto the shop floor. Coming within ten feet of it, with what she thought might be a lathe shielding her from the interior of the building where most of the action was, and a big red toolbox on wheels between her and the office, she cautiously reared up and peered over.

Throughout the smelter, men fought furiously. Some fired at each other from behind cover. No one was having much success. Much of the equipment and even general clutter inside the vast building was steel or iron, massive enough to stop bullets. Other men whaled at each other with wrenches, metal rods, bits of scrap as far as Annja could tell. Some simply pummeled each other, wrestled, shrieked, gouged eyes and tore at throats with their teeth.

"My God," Aidan gasped from her side. "I've never seen anything like this."

They both ducked as a burst of gunfire raked across the top of the lathe table, bullets howling like lost souls as they tumbled to rip irregular holes in the thin sheet-metal wall above their heads.

"The rage and passion—they're increasing it, trying to use it to manipulate them. But at the same time all that emotion is working on them, too. They're getting themselves into a frenzy, losing control," Annja said.

A figure loomed up at the other end of the lathe. It was one of Stern's men in a torn tan shirt with epaulettes. His forehead had been cut open, turning his face to a mask of blood, making the green-dyed braid around his neck a brown-and-purplish mess. He aimed an Uzi at them, pulled the trigger.

Nothing happened. He had fired his magazine dry. Screaming with frustration, he raised the Uzi above his head as if to smash them with it. His eyes rolled in pits of blood.

From his crouch Aidan lashed out with his boot and caught the man squarely in the groin. The kick lifted the soles of the Malkuth devotee's heavy work shoes an inch off the greasy concrete floor.

Annja's close-combat instructors had warned her the famous crotch-kick did not always work. Whether he was too adrenalized for the neural overload associated with a blow to the testicles to have much effect, or just wasn't susceptible, the kick did no more than stagger the man. He came on again growling incoherently.

"Bloody stay *down,* will you?" Aidan said. He jumped up and smashed an overhand right into the man's face. Annja heard the buckling crunch as the cartilage in the man's nose broke. He went over backward with blood pulsing from his nostrils, slammed the back of his head hard on the pavement and lay moaning and moving feebly.

"Good shot," Annja said. Aidan waved his hand in the air, grimacing. "You didn't break it?" she asked.

He flexed his fingers. "No. No thanks to myself. Stupid bloody stunt to pull."

"It worked," Annja pointed out.

A violent heave of shadow caught Annja's eye in the gloom. Another figure appeared twenty feet behind them, back toward the entrance. It leveled a long-barreled weapon at them. Annja threw her arms around Aidan and half vaulted, half rolled with him over the top of the lathe. A shotgun boomed, yellow muzzle-flare blooming. Lead pellets skittered across the floor and against the lathe's metal pedestal where the two had crouched an eyeblink before.

Annja landed hard and Aidan's weight came down on top of her and squashed the breath from her body.

By force of will alone she sucked air back into her lungs with a great convulsive inhalation. She shoved Aidan aside, rolled to her feet, gathered herself and sprang.

She heard the shotgun slide being racked as she jumped over some kind of waist-high mechanism covered in black plastic and curling duct tape. She steeled herself to receive the next charge of shot at contact range. Instead she cleared the plastic-wrapped machine unopposed and the sole of her boot caught the gunman in the chest in a flying kick. He windmilled backward, the shotgun flying from his hand.

Annja did a graceless three-point landing. Pain shot from her knee where it struck the concrete floor. The impact was so savage that white lightning seemed to thread through her brain. Across the main floor someone shouted and opened up on her with an automatic weapon of some sort. To her intense relief her knee did not lock or give way when she came up on hands and feet and scrambled like a four-legged spider back to cover.

Aidan awaited her, crouched down in a narrow aisle, hair and eyes wild. With a white-knuckled hand he brandished a crescent wrench he'd found somewhere. Unfortunately the tool was no more than ten inches long and did not make a threatening weapon.

"Listen," she told him, breathing hard and massaging her right knee, which throbbed. "You just stay here until everybody's distracted. Then try to find the jar."

"What are you going to do?" Pascoe asked.

"Something showy and stupid enough to make sure everybody's looking at me," she said.

"Wait—"

She didn't. She couldn't. Bent low she scrambled several feet deeper into the foundry, back toward the office, and peered over a steel table with a shelf beneath it piled thick with rusty junk.

The fight raged unabated. She guessed both the White Tree and the Malkuth contingents had called in reinforcements. At least eight bodies were lying in her field of vision, on the floor, draped over equipment, sprawled at the base of a metal stair up to the catwalk. Meanwhile pairs and groups still shot and screamed and fought. She wasn't even sure they were paying attention to whether the person they raged and raved and struggled to destroy was on their own side or not.

Men brandishing firearms had made little impression on the foundry workers. Men *firing* firearms made quite the impression indeed. Wisely the wiry-muscled men in the hard hats had vanished. The white-collar types had retreated within the office and locked the door, leaving two of their number lying unmoving outside. One was the skinny youngster who had been shot in the knee. He had apparently bled out or been finished off somehow. Possibly he'd just stopped a stray round; it was clearly not his day, Annja thought.

Wreathed in pink ghostly flames a new crucible swung out of the furnace, white-hot metal slopping over the sides. It was an alarming sight. It would have dumped its load across the already filled mold pallet, which had not been removed out the side door along the steel track laid into the concrete floor when the last crucible had emptied itself into it. But instead of flooding the shop floor with liquid metal the vessel stopped to swing perilously midway between furnace and mold. Someone out of Annja's sight must have thrown a cutoff switch.

A man, one of Highsmith's devotees by his clothing, which looked as if it had been expensively tailored before it had been torn and yanked every which way, began hacking at the office door with a fire ax. It was a bizarre gesture. To either side the walls were mostly window and many of them had been shot out. He could have simply scrambled through with little effort. Evidently the violent frenzy had so gripped him he never even considered the possibility.

Is he possessed? Annja wondered. Maybe he's done it all himself, indulging himself in an ecstasy of pure destruction. It came to her to wonder, with a shock, whether the demons everyone spoke of were actual entities, possessed of any separate existence of their own, or were merely projections of human anger and fear and hatred.

Something possessed that poor dog in Haifa, she thought. But couldn't it have been worked into a frenzy by human rage and cruelty?

She shook herself. There was no time for metaphysical speculation—especially since the office door gave way after no more than three good whacks. The White Tree cultist charged inside, making for half a dozen office workers cowering from him. His ax was raised and an expression of mad joy twisted what otherwise might have been a handsome young face.

Annja raced forward. She jumped, easily clearing the office structure's low side wall, ducking her head so as to fit through the vacant window. Her boots skidded with a crunch on the broken glass littering the floor. She had to flex her legs deeply to keep from falling over in it.

The crazed man swung the ax at her. She jumped aside. The axhead rang on concrete, throwing up chips. With wild speed he raised it again and chopped at her.

She ducked. The axe struck a heavy wooden table littered with drawings by the wall. The blade bit deep. It stuck.

Annja shifted her balance, intending to disarm the man and then put him down, maybe dislocate his shoulder and take him out of the fight—or the fight out of him, in any case. But with mad strength he yanked the ax free in a shower of splinters, throwing it up and back over his head with such violence he almost overbalanced.

It was too much. Annja concentrated. The sword was in her hand. The man screamed and started to swing at her.

Blood gouted from his chest as she slashed horizontally through his torso, right below where his nipples must have been. He went to his knees. Blood welled up and slopped over his chin as it sprayed out to the sides from the wound. The ax fell from his hands with a clatter. His eyes rolled up and he fell forward at her feet.

From the corner of her eye she saw someone point a weapon at her. She ducked as a shot crashed. Where the bullet went she didn't know.

"Keep low," she said in Portuguese to the terrified office workers, who stared at her as if she were covered with green scales. She saw there were doors at the back of the office, apparently leading outside. "Get out of the building if you can. Lock yourselves in someplace out of sight if you can't."

It was the woman who warned her. She hadn't noticed before that there was a slender middle-aged woman in the group huddled in the office. She looked past Annja and her dark eyes went wide.

Annja spun toward the door and uncoiled from the floor like a striking rattlesnake, thrusting the sword in a long lunge.

26

The sword's tip caught a man wearing a Malkuth necklace in the center of his broad chest.

He lowered the Jericho 941 Baby Eagle handgun he had been pointing at her as if his arm was suddenly too tired to support its two-plus pounds. For a moment Annja stood face-to-face with him. He looked no older than thirty. His eyes were blue and wide. They seemed to stare through Annja without seeing her. His mouth opened but only blood came out.

His legs sagged. His jaw worked. Annja pushed him out into the cacophony of the smelter.

His body jerked as a bullet struck it. The man winced and his eyes rolled up in his head. She pushed him farther away. With the last capability of his own legs he staggered back three steps. From all around the foundry's cavernous interior the firefly lights of muzzle-flashes winked as at least twenty firearms opened up on him. The hammering noise of gunshots was like the devil's own forge, echoing within the metal walls.

As the already dying man performed his jerking dance of death Annja willed the sword back to the otherwhere. Taking a step out from the doorway, she jumped up. With hands reversed she caught the edge of the office space's low roof and pulled herself up.

The shooting suddenly stopped. As Annja had hoped, many of the gunmen had exhausted their magazines and needed to reload. She hoped to make use of the lull in the gunfight.

"Listen to me," she shouted in English. "You've got to stop this! Can't you see you're being used?"

"My, my," called an American-accented voice. Mark Peter Stern stepped into view from a side niche near the open maw of the furnace. It must have been wiltingly hot but he looked fresh, and his tropical-weight suit didn't seem to have lost a bit from the sharpness of its creases. "You're a woman of unusual talents for a TV archaeologist," he said.

"I'm a *real* archaeologist," Annja declared with a defiant toss of her head.

"You are the inconvenient young woman who came to my manor in the guise of a researcher," a voice boomed from up high. Annja raised her head. Up on the catwalk Sir Martin Highsmith stood, his own shades-of-white suit gleaming as if spotlit in the glare of the halted crucible, whose contents had only cooled to yellow from near white. Its sides glowed red. "Enlighten us, then. Used by whom?"

"Demons," she said.

The devotees of the warring sects had given off their wrestling and sniping to stare at her openmouthed. Her heart was pounding. She could see a good thirty of them still standing.

Stern laughed. "That's a good one. Demons." His followers looked at each other, then voiced an uncertain laugh of their own.

"Don't be ridiculous," Stern called out.

"You think when you get the jar you'll control them," she called. She fought to keep desperation out of her voice. She was losing them, she knew. I hope this is providing enough of a diversion for Aidan, she thought. "But you're already in mortal peril of your souls."

"Foolish young woman!" Highsmith declared in tones that rang like a great bronze bell. "Do you really think we have no means of protecting ourselves?"

She looked up at him. For a moment he seemed surrounded by a nimbus of blackness.

Suddenly she understood what was happening.

Stern and Highsmith were willing participants in creating the frenzy. Their followers truly believed they were following a righteous path. And in the quest for power everyone had been possessed by evil.

Up on the catwalk, surrounded by heat shimmer and flitting darkness, Sir Martin Highsmith began to laugh. It was a deep, rich, melodious laugh.

Mark Peter Stern joined in. His laugh was harsh and rang throughout the metal sepulcher, clearly audible above the still hungry roaring of the furnace.

One by one the men of the rival sects joined in.

Maybe I should consider switching to a career in stand-up comedy, Annja thought.

"Listen to me, please," she cried, shouting to make herself heard above the foundry sounds and the roar of laughter, now showing clear manic overtones. "We can work together. We can work things out like reasonable people."

Sir Martin's laugh cut off as if he'd been chopped across the throat. Instantly his face was suffused with blood. "You're just like all of us," he screamed, spittle flying from his mouth. "You just want the jar for yourself. Kill the meddling bitch!" he screamed.

Annja launched herself up and out as guns spoke. A great iron hook hung from the metal ceiling girders by a chain, ten feet from the lip of the office roof and about three feet above Annja's head. She grabbed the hook and swung on it.

A half-dozen rival cultists stood clumped together by the foot of the stairway up to the catwalk along the far wall. They had been brutalizing one another with fists and makeshift clubs when Annja put in her appearance. They seemed to have all been able to put their hands on firearms, though. Their aim was thrown off by Annja's unexpected—and unexpectedly swift—movement. In fact when she let go the hook and came swooping down on them they were all too startled to track and shoot at her.

It was the very response she'd been hoping for.

She came down with both feet in the well-padded midsection of a blue-collar Malkuth hardman. The man staggered and sat down hard. Suitably braked, Annja landed with both feet on the concrete in the midst of the five still standing. She had hopes of preventing more bloodshed. She strongly suspected that the high-frequency emotion of combat and the actual spilling of life force were both feeding the demons in everyone.

Taking full advantage of her skill and speed, Annja targeted two of the goons, plucking a handgun and a shotgun from surprise-slack hands before their owners could react. She pitched the weapons out into daylight through the opening yawning nearby. She kicked a second pistol from the grasp of a pasty-faced White Tree member who was pointing it at her sideways, American gangsta style. Then she spun and grabbed the flash suppressor of an FN-FAL 7.62 mm military rifle, twitched the long weapon out of its owner's hands and hit him in the jaw with it. He went down moaning and clutching his face.

That left two with guns in their hands. One man wearing a silver medallion fired a handgun. The noise and recoil so startled him that he immediately punched off a second shot on the light trigger, unintentionally to judge by the astonished look on his face. Both shots missed Annja, but one of the fat bullets hit a fellow Lodge member, one of the first pair Annja had disarmed on landing. He dropped to his knees and toppled on his face. His comrade dropped the big handgun as if it had turned red-hot.

The stout Malkuth follower Annja had used to cushion her landing had gotten his feet under him. As he raised his pistol, still hunched over and clutching his gut with his other hand, Annja did a sideways stutter-step toward him and side kicked him in the groin once more. This time she put a hip thrust into it and sent him flying right out into the sunlight.

With a wild scream a White Tree devotee cut loose from the hip with a 9 mm Franchi machine pistol, sweeping it left to right. A Malkuth enforcer and one of the gunner's lodge mates spun down in a welter of blood. Annja turned and sprinted toward the front entrance with bullets letting in daylight in a sort of irregular sine wave behind her. She dived behind a large machine and heard bullets ring off its far side like triphammer blows.

Baying like a pack of hounds, zealots of both stripes converged on her. She lay on her stomach trying to listen for footsteps. With all the noise and the echoing properties of the vast enclosed space, it wasn't easy to sort them out.

She saw a pair of oxblood shoes on the floor on the other side of a wheeled device that might have been a generator or portable power supply by her head. She prepared herself.

The White Tree fanatic spun around holding a beefy SPAS riot shotgun. Annja rolled hard, flung out a leg, caught him right on his jade tie-tack with the back of her heel. Choking and flailing, he fell, losing his grip on the weapon as it blasted noisily toward the ceiling.

Annja bounced to her feet, darted around the squat mechanism and onto the main floor as somebody else hopped out behind, spraying the oil-spotted place she'd been an instant before with bullets. Men with guns were running toward her. She summoned the sword again and charged.

She slashed left, right, left. Two men fell, screaming and spurting blood. A third stood staring in mute horror at the blood flowing freely from his numerous wounds.

Bullets snapped past her ears and cracked against the concrete by her flashing feet. She dived over a table laden with rusty parts, tucked her shoulder, rolled. She still hit hard enough to hurt and make her fear for a moment she had dislocated her left shoulder when she landed on it.

She pressed against the pedestal of a grinder. Reversing at once, she rolled back against the table she had cleared. She tried to squirm beneath the bottom shelf. A hand appeared over the table's edge, holding a Heckler & Koch MP-5K, a little stubby machine pistol with a sort of piano-leg foregrip. The gun yammered, spraying bullets at a downward angle.

The stream was directed away from her—but right against the gray-painted cast-iron pedestal of the grinder. Annja cringed and cried out as ricochets buzzed about her like angry hornets, stinging her arms and face with concrete particles as they spanged off the floor and punched holes through cans above and to either side of her.

The bullet storm stopped. Almost reluctantly she lowered her hands from her head, which she had covered in a futile attempt to protect herself from the ricochets. The compact but heavy German machine pistol bounced once on the floor next to her with a ringing sound.

She looked up. The hand lay draped over the table edge like an abandoned sock puppet. Its skin looked almost bluish white in the half light; she could see blue veins through it. She raised the sword.

Rising slightly, she found herself staring into a pair of surprised gray eyes. They showed no sign of seeing her. Nor were they likely to—they stared out from beneath an irregular hole right in the center of a high forehead, where one of the shooter's own bullets had came tumbling back and struck him.

Annja sprang to a hunched-over posture. Guns blared at her. Bent low she darted this way and that like a fox pursued by hounds, trying to throw off the aim of her multiple enemies by speed and sheer unpredictability. She knew that since few if any of them bothered to actually aim, whether or not she took a hit would pretty much be a matter of luck anyway. But moving made her *feel* better, somehow.

A pair of Malkuth goons appeared before her as she darted toward the rear of the smelter, where the furnace roared, oblivious to the doings of mere flesh. She darted right, bowling over two more men closing in from that direction, sprinted across seven yards of open floor, threw herself into a forward roll.

Another Malkuth man jumped out from behind a machine and into her path, firing a Glock. But he anticipated a target running at him upright. Annja skidded forward on her butt with bullets cracking right over her head. She thrust upward at an angle and skewered him right beneath the rib cage as she slid past to his left. He fell, sword still transfixing him, momentarily pinning her right hand to the floor.

As her feet hit the wall something made her look up and left. Sir Martin Highsmith stood at the top of the stairs with the yellow glow of the still liquid metal in the hanging crucible illuminating the right side of his body and underlighting his craggy face and mane of white hair with deceptive sunset gold. He held a 9 mm Beretta out before him like his own sword of vengeance.

"You are dead, interloper!" he declared. "You cannot reach me with that sword of yours."

He was right. As he began to trigger shots and bullets cracked around her, Annja willed the sword away. Then she yanked the Glock from the dead Malkuthian's nerveless fingers, rolled onto her back, pushing the blocky handgun out before her in a two-handed isosceles grip.

The white dot of the front sight lined up on the center of Highsmith's chest, its black post contrasting nicely with his old-ivory waistcoat. She squeezed the trigger, hoping the Glock's characteristic long pull wouldn't throw her aim off too badly. The weapon roared and bucked in her hand.

SIR MARTIN CAMDESSUS Highsmith felt a piledriver impact to the center of his chest. Instantly his gun hand ceased obeying instructions and began to drift downward. His weapon no longer fired.

He couldn't breathe. His vision blurred. He teetered.

Spirit of wild nature, who have guided me so long, he prayed, *help me now so that I might yet bring our shared vision to pass.*

But the voice in his head, which had always been so warm and honeyed, now dripped with scorn.

Useless fool, it sneered. *I have no use for failure. Die.*

Sir Martin reeled and fell backward over the rail.

He screamed as he felt the heat growing on his back like a rising sun. Screamed louder as his hair and the backs of his coat and trouser legs took fire with a huff.

And then the molten metal caught him, enfolded him and drew him into infinite agony. His shriek achieved a steam-whistle pitch and volume as intolerable agony was augmented by the moisture in his lungs boiling in an instant, searing throat, palate and tongue.

The scream died.

"WAIT," ANNJA HEARD Mark Peter Stern command. "Take the woman alive. She may know where the jar is."

Transferring the Glock to her left hand and summoning the sword back into her right, Annja leaped to her feet. With their leader gone the White Tree survivors seemed as inclined to obey the Malkuth guru as his own followers were. Annja was surrounded, a dozen men closing in on her, faces grim or gleeful over leveled weapons.

"Ah, yes," Stern said, tipping his head to one side. "That's a nifty sword you have there, Ms. Creed. If you hand it over, we might be persuaded to let you live."

Her eyes darted left and right. To surrender the sword was unthinkable. She wondered fleetingly if she willed it gone before they killed her, whether it would remain eternally sealed in its pocket universe. Probably not, she decided.

There was no possible escape for her. Even using gun and sword simultaneously she could never get through before someone put a bullet in her, or she was dragged down by sheer weight of male muscle and bone. If I go down, she thought, I go down fighting. But winded, exhausted, disoriented by the relentless attacks of the swarming demons, she hesitated for the space of half a breath.

That was all it took. Strong hands gripped her arms from right and left as two men closed with her. In despair she felt her strength and will drain from her. She was trapped.

The man to her right said, "Be a love and give us the sword, then." He was a tall, young Englishman in a dark green pin-striped suit, no tie, with curly chestnut hair. He smiled and reached for the hilt of her sword.

Then his eyes went wide and his head snapped to the side.

27

Annja's eyes widened as a cloud of pink mist and dark shreds puffed out above the left ear of the handsome young Englishman. He dropped as if he were a suit of clothes slipped from the rack.

The burly Malkuth man who had her left arm grunted. His meaty hand went slack on her arm. Turning toward him, she saw his eyes standing unnaturally out from their sockets, the skin of his face sagging.

The right side of his head was bloody ruin.

From the front of the foundry a sound erupted as if a decade's worth of hailstones were being unloaded on the corrugated metal roof at once. Out on the floor men closing in on Annja began to spin and fall with little red sprays jetting from bodies and limbs and heads.

Her head snapped toward the entrance. She gasped.

A line of men marched shoulder to shoulder into the smelter, dark forms silhouetted against the tropical morning sun. Most were firing machine-pistol-sized Kalashnikovs from the hip. They stepped aside only to walk around machines in their path. Interspersed with them was a quartet of what Annja recognized with a shock as Orthodox priests, in flowing vestments with basket-shaped hats on their heads and magnificent beards. They intoned prayers and swung smoking censers on chains before them.

In the middle of the line a smaller man was dwarfed by the burly gunners. He walked with a bandy-legged swagger of total self-assurance. He looked oddly familiar.

The man raised his hand. Flame bloomed from it—right toward Annja's face. She set her jaw and waited for the fatal impact.

Instead the bullet cracked past her head. She heard a sound similar to a bat hitting a ball. She turned back to see a Malkuth cultist toppling backward with a yard-long fixed wrench falling from his hands to ring on the concrete.

The invaders mowed down Malkuth and White Tree men with a fine lack of discrimination. Several of the well-dressed Englishmen threw down their weapons and raised their hands.

Then died.

"The Babylonians come again!" Annja heard Mark Peter Stern shout from the back of the foundry. "But I will not be taken into captivity."

All the rest of the cultists lay on the floor, dead or dying. The diminutive man with the Glock held up a hand. The shooting stopped. He halted near Annja. His men stopped at the same time, lowering their weapons but staying alert.

He was a very trim man, with receding hair cropped close to a narrow skull and piercing eyes. He wore a dark suit over a dark pullover of some sort, very well tailored to his athletic form.

It took Annja a moment to regain some composure. She looked at the man with surprise. He was the leader of the group of *mafiya* goons who had surprised her and Aidan in Amsterdam.

Mark Peter Stern's tall form suddenly appeared silhouetted against the furnace's blinding yellow maw. Blue flames jetted in like fangs from the periphery.

"I am protected by the power of the Lord of Hosts," Stern said, "'Yea, though I walk through the Valley of the Shadow of Death, I will fear no evil—'" he turned and walked into the furnace "'—for thou art with me; thy rod and thy staff, they comfort me.'"

His outline blurred as his suit took flame. He stopped. Then he turned and staggered back toward the entrance, a figure of darker flame against the furnace's brilliant fire, waving wings of fire. His hands burned like white torches.

His screaming cut through the furnace roar like a razor.

He made it three steps, then fell to his knees. A moment later and he slumped into a shapeless mound, like a wax figurine melting.

An especially tall *mafiya* man with a head like a shaved bear's and hair in his ears said something to his small and dapper leader. The smaller man shrugged.

"What's going on?" Annja asked, devastated by the carnage around her.

"We are restoring peace," the small man said. "Did you never hear 'Blessed are the peacemakers'?"

It seemed to Annja a useful distinction might be drawn between peacemaking and mass murder. However, it did not seem that it would be useful to bandy words just now.

"Why haven't you killed me yet?" she demanded.

He looked at her. No one seemed to be paying particular attention to her despite the fact she stood there with an archaic broadsword in one hand and a thoroughly modern semiautomatic pistol in the other.

"I forget my manners," the small man said. "Please forgive me. I am Valeriy Korolin, formerly captain of special-designation soldiers in armed forces of USSR. Now I work in private sector. You are Ms. Annja Creed."

She lowered her sword, which Korolin had started to examine. The big man at his shoulder crossed himself in the Orthodox manner. The constant murmur of the priests' prayer spiked briefly.

"You haven't answered my question," she said.

"You are a very courageous young woman," Korolin said, "if maybe not so prudent. But we knew that." He suddenly grinned. "We haven't killed you because you have not gotten in our way, if you will forgive my speaking candidly."

"You tried hard enough before," she said.

"Those were mistakes. In Amsterdam my men misconstrued my orders under misapprehension you might be the killers of that poor old lady shopkeeper. In Jaffa our attempt was to incinerate Dr. Stern—who seems to have escaped our efforts only to carry out our intentions by himself." He shook his head, still marveling at Stern's walking voluntarily into the blazing furnace.

"And now," Korolin said, "since it is obvious you do not have the jar, if you will excuse us—"

"She doesn't have it," a voice called from above. "But I do."

Everyone looked up. Aidan Pascoe stood on the catwalk perilously close to the crucible of still molten metal into which Highsmith had fallen. Above his head he brandished a gleaming metal jar, in the shape of a globe with a funnel thrust into it, and two oddly slender, scrolled handles.

Annja drew in a sharp breath. She could feel it. It was Solomon's Jar.

With a guilty start she realized Korolin was looking at her closely. He nodded sharply. Then he turned to look up at Pascoe.

"Mr. Pascoe," he said, "please throw down to us the jar."

"I won't," he said. "And if you shoot me, or try to take it from me by force, I'll throw it in the melt. Then no one will get it."

"What do you want it for, Mr. Pascoe?" the Russian asked.

"Tell him, Annja," Pascoe said, his voice strained.

Anna was concerned. He seemed to be standing in the midst of a dark whirlwind. She wasn't sure if she was literally seeing it with her eyes, or some other sense. But she knew what she was seeing. Aidan Pascoe was struggling with temptation.

"Why don't you tell them, Aidan," she said, trying to keep her voice neutral.

"The power to make the world a better place," he said. "That's what I've dreamed of since I was a child. What do you want it for?"

"Very simple," Korolin said. "A wealthy and well-connected collector in St. Petersburg offers a substantial sum of money for authenticated jar of King Solomon. He desires this object solely for its value as artifact of the ancient world. He is an atheist. He is merely obsessed with history."

"He wants to display it?" Annja asked.

"He wants to be able to admire it, and to show it off to favored guests, or so I presume. He is prepared to preserve it using the best modern techniques."

"What about you?" Annja asked Korolin. "What do you think about the jar?"

"I think I will receive a munificent reward for success," he said, "rather than getting shot in the back of the neck for failure, maybe."

"But the demons—"

"I myself am also atheist. I do not believe in demons," he stated with a shrug.

"Why did you bring the priests?" Annja asked.

"I do not believe in demons, but I do believe in hedging my bets, Ms. Creed. After all, if there are no demons, I have only subjected myself to smelling some incense and listening to some mumbo jumbo. And if there are demons…"

Aidan shook his head. "Selfishness. Pure selfishness. The root of all evil."

"How do you plan to make the world better, Aidan?" Annja asked.

He frowned at her. "Whose side are you on?"

"You know which side, Aidan. Ask yourself that question. Please," she said trying to quell her fear.

He looked at her, suspicion narrowing his blue eyes.

"Very well. I will put an end to human suffering—to evil, if you will—by confining the demons that were released through the selfish greed of the treasure hunters who breached the seal."

"Aidan," Annja said, as gently as she could with any hope of being heard above the furnace roar, "are you sure that would even work?"

His eyes narrowed in suspicion. "What do you mean? Of course it would do."

"Do you think all the evil went out of the world when Solomon sealed the demons in that jar, Aidan? The demons may personify human evil, abet it, but they don't cause it. Humans do that themselves. Don't they?"

Aidan was frowning. But he was also listening. Annja sensed his struggle. He had experienced so much horror. He had heard her story. He simply didn't know what to believe.

"Treasure hunters sought out the jar and released the demons back into the world because of greed. Wasn't that evil? But obviously they did it when the demons were trapped in the jar. Right?" She hoped she could reach him.

"And after you've trapped all the demons, and you find out evil hasn't left the world—what then, Aidan? When you start to feel frustrated in your very praiseworthy desire to do ultimate good—and the demons start to whisper from their captivity that they can give you the power to do the good you so want to do—what will you do then?"

He shook his head. "I don't know. But—" He raised his head. "I hear them now. Whispering to me. They're telling me not to listen to you, Annja."

She caught a breath in her throat.

He smiled. "We know what *their* advice is worth, now, don't we, Annja love? What about you? Do you want it, then?"

"No." She hoped she wasn't answering too quickly, perhaps making him think she was trying to cover uncertainty with emphasis. She wasn't. She had no interest in the relic other than to keep it from causing more harm. "It isn't for me, Aidan," she said plainly.

He glared around him as if at a flock of gnats buzzing about his head. "Should I destroy it, then?"

He held it out over the crucible. Orange light glowed on its rounded belly. The Russians raised their guns again. Korolin shouted them down.

"Do you really want to destroy such an artifact, such a part of history?" Annja called out.

He sighed and looked at Korolin. "Your principal will hire professional archaeologists to see to the jar's preservation?"

"He has already done so, Mr. Pascoe."

"And if we give you the jar, what then? What becomes of us?"

Korolin shrugged. "We walk out of here. You get on with your young lives."

"Do you trust him, Annja?"

She shrugged. "They could have shot me," she said. "I don't see we have any choice but to trust them."

He drew in a deep breath. When he sighed it out he seemed to lose an inch or two of height. "Very well," he said.

He tossed the jar to Korolin. The Russian fielded it deftly.

He gestured briskly. A man with his AKS hanging from a waist-length sling by his side brought a bulky satchel. When he opened it Annja noticed the sides were unusually thick, as if insulated. She was reminded incongruously of the packs pizza delivery stores used to keep their pies warm on their way to customers.

A man even shorter and skinnier than Korolin whom Annja had not noticed previously, in a rumpled brown suit, came forward and frowned at it through thick-rimmed and thick-lensed glasses. He nodded abruptly.

At a nod from Korolin the priest with the most grandly decorated hat and the grandest beard came up and blessed jar, satchel or both with sweeping gestures. Then Korolin carefully placed the jar in the satchel, closed it up and handed it to the bearlike man.

Korolin turned to look at Annja. "My patron, Mr. Garin Braden, thanks you," he said with a smile. Annja's blood ran cold.

He nodded and smiled. "Good day, Ms. Creed, Mr. Pascoe." And he walked with his bantam-rooster walk out the side door into the sunlight.

His men followed without a backward glance.

EpilogUE

Annja and Aidan sat at the feet of Jesus.

"You know, if there is a God, He must have a mighty sense of humor," Aidan said. "He made us, after all."

"Are you still a doubter? After what you've experienced?" Annja asked.

He angled his head to the side. "Just because I've seen some unbelievable things," he said in a quiet voice, "doesn't necessarily imply the existence of an all-powerful Creator. Nor does the existence of a living embodiment of good, actually."

She sighed. "Good point. And thanks so much for being so helpful with my own crisis of faith."

He looked at her, alarmed. Until she smiled enough to let him off the hook.

They sat at the base of the giant statue of Christ the Redeemer that gazed down upon Rio de Janeiro with arms outstretched. They watched tourists appear at the far end of the walk that led across the flattened hilltop to the statue, hot and sweaty from trudging up the 222 steps embossed in the side of the thumb-shaped granite dome called Corcovado Mountain from the road. Behind them the sun was sinking.

"Did we do the right thing, do you think?" he asked.

She didn't need to ask what thing that was. "I think that's the sort of thing that has to get left to the verdict of history," she said. "What do you think?"

He thought for a moment, then drew in a deep breath. "I think we did. Hope we did."

"I suspect that's about as much confirmation as we're ever going to get." After a pause she added, "For anything, really."

"I'm afraid you're right." He shook his head. "And I thought I could solve all the world's problems by trapping some surly spirits inside a tin pot. You must think me a right git," he said with a hapless grin.

Annja took him by the chin, turned his face to hers and kissed him. "I think you're a wonderful man, Aidan," she said when they finally broke apart.

They looked in different directions, suddenly self-conscious.

"So what's next?" he asked.

"What do you mean?" she replied, already knowing the answer.

He waved a hand. "Us—"

"What does your heart tell you?" Annja asked.

His brows lowered over his eyes, which were lighter than the tropical late-afternoon sky. "Do you answer every question with a question?"

"Do you?" she said, laughing.

"All right, then, Do you have to answer my bloody question either like Dr. Phil or a fortune cookie?"

She laughed again. "I guess it goes with the job. Or maybe I'm just rationalizing a secret desire to pontificate."

It was his turn to laugh. As always she admired his laughter in its surrender to joy.

"Hard to think of you as pontificating. Although if the church were ever to get its hooks in you, I think you'd make a smashing first female pope," Aidan said.

"Don't go there," she said, mock-serious. "There supposedly was a female pope, and she was called Joan. Controversial women of the Catholic Church by that name are something of a sore subject for me."

"I can see why."

For a moment he gazed off at Sugarloaf peak, jutting up out of the bay. He sighed again. "In my hands, just for a moment, I held—"

"Damnation," she said.

He looked sheepish. "I suppose you're right. Thank you for helping me make the right choice. Especially counterintuitive as it was."

"Don't thank me. The choice was all yours. Otherwise it wouldn't have counted."

He smiled a bit wanly. "It hurts a bit to be coming home doubly empty-handed. I don't get the girl, and I don't get the relic. Whatever am I going to tell my uncle?"

"He was expecting you to come home with a girl?" Annja said, feigning outrage.

"You know what I mean," he said.

"But you're not going back to him with nothing to show," she said. "Not unless he's so old-fashioned he doesn't watch television."

"Whatever do you mean?" Aidan asked.

"I've gotten in touch with some friends of mine who work for the Discovery channel," she said. "They'll be getting in touch to interview you. I believe they intend to devote a large part of a one-hour feature to you. And your uncle, of course, as your patron."

"To me? Because I found a jar I don't bloody *have* anymore? What am I supposed to tell them, that I handed it over to the Russian *mafiya?* Good God, woman! You'll be the ruination of me."

"No, silly. They want to make you an archaeologist superstar for your part in busting a major international relic-forgery ring that branched into multinational murder. Even if the old gent isn't satisfied with your results, you'll still have your reputation made."

He stared at her. "Whatever am I supposed to tell them?"

"Not the truth, certainly." He stared at her for a moment. Then they both laughed.

They laughed, perhaps, louder and longer than was strictly necessary. Some Japanese tourists passing by glanced at them, then quickly away. It was impolite to stare at crazy people.

"What about you?" he asked. "Did you get what you were looking for?"

She thought for a moment. "Yes," she said. "I saw a very powerful relic into safe hands."

He grinned. "I pity the zealot who tries to pry the jar out of the fortified dacha of a former KGB muckety-muck," he said. "I do believe I'd pay to see them try."

She smiled. It was in part to cover her real thoughts. She had fulfilled her true role when he made the choice to turn away from the temptation of near ultimate power the jar may have offered. She knew Garin Braden was worried about what power he might derive from the relic. She'd worry about that another time. She felt certain Garin did not present an immediate threat.

By mutual accord they stood. He held out his hands.

"It's goodbye, I suppose," he said, "and not *au revoir.*"

"It's better that way," she said. "We both know it is. What we came together to do, we've done."

"And a right lot of fun it was, too," he said, with a cockeyed leer and music-hall Cockney accent.

She smiled and kissed him. "Yes," she said quietly. "A lot of fun." She blinked her eyes rapidly to clear them of sudden moisture.

"Right, then," he said. "Goodbye, Annja love. And thanks for everything."

"Goodbye, Aidan," she said from low in her throat.

He turned and walked jauntily down the steps toward the vast and teeming city, leaving Annja standing alone in the shadow of Christ the Redeemer with his arms outstretched to the world.

THE SPIDER STONE

PROLOGUE

West Africa
1755

Under the blazing sun, Yohance's legs felt like stone, not flesh and blood. They seemed heavier than he could ever remember them being. He lacked the strength after so many miles to move them easily. In truth, he didn't think he could go much farther before he collapsed.

And what would happen then? The slavers who had destroyed his village and killed so many of his people were hard-eyed and merciless. If he fell, he knew they would kill him, too.

The chains pulled at his manacled wrists, jerking him once more into faster motion. Scabs on his wrists tore open. Blood stained his wrists, hands and forearms. Several times over the past few days, he'd prayed that the gods would take him. Although he'd always feared death, he was no longer so certain that death was frightening. Some of the other prisoners said he should welcome it.

"Come on, boy," the old man in front of Yohance snarled. He was abrupt and unkind. Judging from his behavior and the scars on his back, this wasn't the first time he'd been captured. A gray fringe surrounded his head and lined his seamed jaws. Several teeth were missing and the rest were yellowed wreckage in spotted gums. Like

Yohance, the old man went naked. None of the prisoners were permitted clothing. "You've got to keep moving."

Yohance stared at the man. He didn't know his name. The man wasn't from Yohance's tribe. Facial scars and tattooing marked him as a warrior among his own people. But the white marks against the deep ebony of his back offered mute testimony to his servitude.

"Do you hear me, boy?" the old man demanded.

Yohance nodded. He didn't try to answer. Thirst had swollen his tongue and thickened his saliva. Until these past few days, he hadn't known he could go so long without water and food.

"If you fall behind, it's not just you that will be punished." The old man yanked on the heavy chains again. The sun had heated the iron links until they almost burned Yohance's flesh.

Yohance wanted to move more quickly, but he couldn't. He was only eleven, the smallest of the men and boys he was chained to. When the slavers had taken him, there had been some debate about whether they should try to keep him or simply put him to death. In the end, his life had been saved by the flip of a coin.

The old man quickly looked away. Hoofbeats drummed against the hard-packed earth behind Yohance.

"Move faster, you heathen!" a harsh voice thundered.

Even though he'd expected it, when the whip cracked harshly across Yohance's narrow shoulders, he was shocked. Pain burst across his sunburned flesh, and the sudden agony dropped him to his knees on the trail. Sand and rock chafed against his legs, but it was hardly noticeable with the new injury assaulting him.

For a moment Yohance hoped that he would die. He remained on his knees and tucked his face against the ground. He didn't want to cry out. He bit his lip and his tears splashed against the dry ground.

"Get up," the old man ahead of Yohance whispered, tugging with weak desperation on the chain that bound them. "Get up or he will kill you."

Yohance knew that. The slavers relished seeing fear and weakness.

"Don't you just lay there, boy!" the slaver roared. "If you don't get up I'll run you down!"

The horse's hooves drummed against the ground again. Yohance felt the vibration echoing in his small, frail body. His hair hung loose in snarls, no longer bound by the ivory headband his mother had fashioned for him. If he'd been only a little older, if he'd participated in a hunting party, his hair would have been cut like a man's.

But he was only a boy. Too weak and afraid to defend himself against the aggressors who had destroyed his village and killed those of his people they didn't succeed in enslaving. The harsh crack of the slavers' rifles still sounded in his ears and had chased happiness from his dreams for three nights as they'd traveled toward the slave market at Ile de Goree.

For all his life, Yohance had heard about the slave market. The city was a rancid pool of despair and evil, filled with men who profited by selling other men. Some of those men were from Africa, but others were from England, Spain, France and beyond. All of those people trafficked in slaves, selling them or sending them to their colonies in the New World.

Yohance couldn't imagine the places some of the elders had described in the stories he'd been taught to memorize. He had sat around the campfires with his mentor and listened, still and silent as stone, as the warriors had recounted their adventures among the slavers. In every case, those men had lost someone, family or friends they would probably never again see. Sadness had stained every word, and Yohance had memorized that, too. He bore it in his heart like a boulder.

He had to do those things. He was a Keeper of the Ways of the People. Without Keepers to recount triumphs, as well as sorrows, his village would have lost its history. He and boys like him were chosen to devote their lives to remembering the history of his people. It was an honorable undertaking, an endeavor that Yohance had gladly promised his life to pursue.

According to the tales, rich men lived in wondrous cities where fire and water obeyed their every whim. In Yohance's village, women and small children tended the cook fires all day and carried buckets of water in from the stream. But, even with all those miracles at their disposal, the rich men desired slaves to work their fields.

For years, Yohance's village had remained safe. Then, before he had been born, his people had fought slavers again and again, and had finally gone into hiding, leaving their ancestral homes to climb higher in the mountainous terrain and escape the attacks. The move had brought new hardships to the Hausa people, and many times they had gone without good food. They had given up everything to avoid the slavers.

Still, the slavers had come. Three days earlier the raiders had found Yohance's village. His father believed the slavers had followed a hunting party back to them. The hunters had been trained to move carefully and to leave no trail, but they had been fortunate and had brought in enough antelope meat to feed the village for days. It had been a day of celebration. They had prepared for a feast.

The raiders had attacked in the night, rushing from the darkness and taking charge with their rough voices and fire-spitting rifles and pistols. Abed with their stomachs full for the first time in weeks, Yohance's people had been caught off guard. The raiders had taken the village without mercy, killing all who tried to oppose them and many of those who attempted to flee.

The next morning, after the slavers had gorged themselves on what food that the village had managed to put back and sated their evil lusts on the women, all the survivors had been placed in manacles and chained together for the long trek west to the coast.

For three days, the captives had walked from when the sun rose until it set in the evening. At that time, Yohance fell wherever he was permitted. The hated chains never came off. Mornings found his wounds thickly clustered with fat black flies. On each of those mornings, one or more prisoners had died in their sleep.

Such a death, Yohance had come to think by the second day, was a gentle thing.

Hafiz, Yohance's mentor and teacher in the ways of the Keeper, had died violently. As village elder, the raiders had executed him to take the courage from the village. The brutal tactic had worked. Everyone knew about the slavers. They knew if they didn't escape, if they weren't killed because they were too old or wouldn't stop fighting, they would be sent to live in far-off lands. Perhaps there they could hope to escape. Or perhaps the gods would provide a good life somewhere else.

"Get up!" the slaver snarled again. He jerked his horse to a stop only a few feet away from where Yohance lay. Two thick clods, torn from the earth by the horse's hooves, thudded against Yohance. "Do you hear me, boy?"

Yohance didn't look up. He couldn't. Looking into the eyes of the raiders was like looking into the eyes of demons.

Hafiz had told him that many of the Hausa's names came from the Arabian warriors. Their cultures had met before, in battle and tender embraces. The Hausa shared some of the blood of those fierce desert warriors. Yohance prayed for strength.

Another man rode up beside the first. They spoke in their language instead of that of the Hausa. Yohance didn't know what they said.

Part of him just wanted to stay there and die. He felt certain that would be easier. He didn't want to be torn from his home or his family. But it was already too late for that. His father was dead, one of the men who had fought, and his mother and two sisters were in chains as he was, all of them cruelly used by the raiders.

Without warning, Yohance vomited, giving in to the fear that was his constant companion. He retched and coughed. So little food and water were in his stomach. Yellow bile spilled on the ground. He felt the stone come up, and he was more fearful of that than anything else.

Hafiz had given him the stone to take care of. It represented Anansi's promise. Long ago, the trickster god had promised that Yohance's village would always stand, that his people wouldn't be scattered forever as so many peoples were.

As long as the stone existed, so too would his people.

Before the raiders had seized them, Hafiz had taken the stone from its altar and given it to Yohance. The slavers had taken the gold coins, ivory pieces and few jewels that had been on the altar, never realizing that the stone had been there, as well.

Yohance bent forward. He curled one hand around the stone before it could be seen. It was round and worn smooth from all the years that had passed since it had been created. The craftsman who had made the stone had carved Anansi's shape, a spider resting on its six hind legs with the front two lifted to attack or to defend—or, as Hafiz had said, merely to seek out the world.

Both spider and man, Anansi was the messenger to the gods. He was neither good nor evil. Instead, he was selfish and curious, like many people. Yohance had been taught to embrace Anansi's ways, to interact with the gods on behalf of his people, and to keep the records of their lives and triumphs.

"If you die and the stone is lost," Hafiz had told Yohance as the slavers' rifles blasted around them that night, "the home of our people will forever die with you. As long as this stone exists and our people have possession of it, Anansi's promise will exist."

And where is that promise now? Yohance thought bitterly. He had no doubt that Hafiz's body had by now been eaten by hyenas or leopards. Yohance knew that his father's body would be gone, as well. What the predators didn't take would be claimed by the ants and other insects. Spiders even made homes in large bodies to build web traps for bugs that feasted on rotting flesh.

Despite his anger, frustration and fear, Yohance struggled to get to his feet. His hand was grimed with a coating of bile and sand. He held the stone tightly.

One of the men spoke.

As Yohance stood, he lifted his head and gazed at them. One of the burnoose-clad men shoved away the rifle of another. Both men wore beards and carried curved knives and swords in their belts.

"You will walk?" the new arrival asked. He was older than the first.

"I will," Yohance whispered. It was the best his dry throat could manage.

"Only a little farther," the man said. "Then you will rest for a time. There will be water."

Yohance said nothing. Even the promise of water couldn't lift his spirits. Holding the hard stone in his fist, he willed himself to be as hard and emotionless. He had to have water. Without something to drink, he wouldn't be able to swallow the stone again.

Hafiz had told Yohance that was the best way to hide the stone. Once the raiders had taken his clothes, Yohance had seen the wisdom of his teacher's words. Hafiz had told Yohance that he had carried the stone in a similar manner on two earlier occasions.

Whips cracking in the air, the two slavers got the procession under way again. Slowly, with flagging strength, the line of human beings staggered into motion.

Yohance knew he wasn't the only one who was tired. A few of the stronger prisoners helped weaker ones. But they wouldn't be able to help them on the ship's journey to the New World. Disease and the stench of death filled the holds of those vessels. Yohance had been told that those who died were simply thrown overboard for the ever-present sharks to feed on.

The party crested a hill and peered down at the small watering hole against the side of a hill. Stones lined the hole's lip. Yohance's heart fell when he saw how little water the hole contained. The slavers would drink first, then their fine horses. Yohance doubted there would be any left for the prisoners.

Surprisingly, the slavers dismounted and brought out buckets and rope. As Yohance watched in amazement, the men brought up bucket after bucket of water.

"It is a wadi," the old man chained next to him said. "The Arabs build these along their trade routes. Water is often scarce. They dig deep holes, line them with rock, and the land guides the rain into them. When the water is deep enough, it will stay within the rocks rather than soak into the ground."

Yohance could only nod. Though he hadn't been out of his village before, he'd heard of such things. He waited his turn in line, then— when he wasn't being watched—he slaked his thirst from a hand-carved gourd and once more swallowed Anansi's Promise. Since they were given little food, he knew that the stone would stay within him for a time.

Harsh cracks suddenly rolled over the area. Several of the slavers fell from their mounts. They bled from catastrophic wounds and the dry earth sucked the liquid greedily down.

The prisoners dived to the ground even as other slavers toppled from their horses or dropped where they stood. In seconds, the surviving slavers took to the hills, their robes flowing in the wind as they rode for their lives.

A hush fell over the prisoners as they watched armed men walk down from the hills. All of them were black, wearing native garments and jewelry, but carrying rifles made by white men. A few also carried swords, spears and bows.

"We are saved," a man cried as he pushed himself to his feet. "They have come to free us."

The armed man closest to the speaker drew back his rifle and hit the man in the face with the brass-covered buttstock. Unconscious, the prisoner fell in a heap.

"You are *not* free!" a scarred warrior declared. "I have stolen you! Now you belong to me!"

"They are slavers," the old man whispered. "Just like the others."

The other prisoners drew quietly to one another and awaited their new fates.

"You will still go to Ile de Goree," the scarred warrior said in his thunderous voice. "You will still be sold to the New World of the white men. But if you listen and obey, you will live to do it." He glared contemptuously at everyone in the group. "Otherwise I will kill you and leave your bodies unmourned for the carrion feeders to take away in pieces."

A few of the women started crying.

Yohance sat back and prayed. He felt the weight of the stone in his stomach. Though he was still, he didn't feel rested, or even that he was gaining back any of his lost strength. He hoped only that even in foreign lands Anansi's Promise would find a way back to his home to protect his people.

But he had to wonder if the trickster's power could survive a trip to the white man's New World.

1

A mob surrounded the old warehouse in downtown Kirktown, Georgia. Many of the people carried signs and shouted angrily. Police cars and uniformed officers enforced the demarcation between the crowd and the warehouse. A news helicopter hovered overhead.

Seated in the back seat of the cab, Annja Creed stared through the morass of angry civilization. The car slowed, then finally came to a standstill as angry protesters slapped the vehicle and cursed. The action warred with the overall appearance of the city. Kirktown looked like the ideal tourist stop for anyone wanting a taste of genteel Southern manners.

We're not about manners today, Annja thought.

Kirktown was a small Georgia town that had limped through the Civil War, became a textile success during industrialization, but had struggled on into the twenty-first century. Old buildings stood with new as the town continued to grow around the industrial area, finally outliving the textile era and leaving the older buildings to rot at the center of the downtown area. Like many Georgia towns, and cities in the South in general, the population was almost equally divided between white and black families, with some Hispanic and Asian communities, as well.

And like a lot of small towns, Kirktown had kept its secrets close and its darkest secrets buried.

Annja Creed had come to help dig up at least one of those. Looking at the site and the crowd thronging it, she felt like an outsider—a familiar feeling. She'd been raised in an orphanage in New Orleans. No matter where she went in her life, most of the time she felt like a visitor.

The cabdriver, a barrel-chested Rastafarian with silver wraparound sunglasses and a gold tooth, turned to look back over the seat. "I'm sorry, miss, but this looks like it's as far as I can carry you."

"We can walk from here," Annja said.

"You can see what we're up against," Professor Noel Hallinger said. "Every time there's a race issue, the reactions are immediate and severe. I wasn't sure if the police would be able to hold the site clear long enough for me to bring you from the airport."

Annja nodded as she lifted her backpack from the seat and opened the door. Her head was already full of questions. She'd made notes in a notebook on the way. "How many bodies did you say you'd found?"

"Sixteen so far. But there may be more." Hallinger was a tall man in his early sixties. His hair had turned the yellow-white of old bone and hung over his ears and the back of his collar. His face held a deep tan that testified to long years spent outside in harsh weather. Bright blue eyes narrowed under the Chicago Cubs baseball cap. He wore jeans and a khaki shirt.

"Have you made any identifications so far?" Annja slipped her backpack over one shoulder, then wished she'd bought a newer, lighter-weight notebook computer.

"None."

"You're sure the bodies are all over a hundred years old?" Annja started for the warehouse.

"Who are you?" a tall black man demanded, stepping in front of her to block the way. He looked to be in his sixties, fierce and imposing. He wore a business suit with the tie at half-mast because of the heat. Even in November, Georgia insisted on being uncomfortably hot.

"Annja Creed." She stood five feet ten inches tall and wore a favorite pair of comfortable working jeans, a sleeveless olive Oxford shirt over a black T-shirt, and hiking boots. Her chestnut-colored hair was pulled back in a sleek ponytail. Blue-tinted aviator sunglasses protected her eyes from the midday brightness.

"Why are you here, Miss Creed?" the man boomed. His challenge had drawn a small crowd that was growing steadily. More and more heads turned toward them.

"I came to help," Annja responded.

"How?"

Beside her, Hallinger took out a cell phone and made a call.

"I'm here to help find out who those people are," Annja replied. "If we can, we're going to get them home."

"It's been 150 years or more," the man said in an accusing tone.

"That's what I've heard," Annja said.

"And you think you can find out who those poor unfortunates are?" The man glared at her with hostility.

"I'm going to try."

"Those people should be left alone," a broad woman shouted. "Just leave 'em alone. They been buried there for 150 years. Ain't no need in disturbin' they rest. All them folks what was gonna miss 'em back then, why, they in they graves, too. You got no call to be a-stirrin' up ghosts an' such."

I so did not need this, Annja thought. But she'd known what she was going to be getting into from the moment Professor Hallinger had outlined the situation in Kirktown. She'd come partly because of her curiosity, but also out of respect for the man. They'd had a sporadic connection over the Internet archaeology boards she liked to frequent, and they'd worked together for a short time on a dig outside London a few years ago.

But the oddities that had been found—which was why Hallinger had sent for her—drew her there. She knew she couldn't have stayed away from something like this. How often could an archaeologist expect to find a dig site inside the United States that might offer a glimpse into West African history?

Close to never, Annja had told herself back in her New York loft. She reminded herself of that again.

"We can't leave them there." Hallinger folded his cell phone and put it away. "That building is scheduled for demolition."

"That building's been abandoned for close to twenty years now," someone said. "It should just be shut up and left alone."

A police car moved forward through the crowd. The siren chirped intermittently in warning. Grudgingly, the crowd parted.

"Hey!" someone shouted. "I know that woman!"

Annja's stomach spasmed. She was betting there were more television watchers in the crowd than readers of *Archaeology Today* or any of the other magazines to which she occasionally contributed articles. Besides that, few of those articles featured any pictures of her. There was only one place that people might recognize her from.

"She's that woman from *Chasing History's Monsters!*"

And that was the place, Annja thought. It wasn't the first time that her part-time work on the syndicated television show had created problems for her.

Chasing History's Monsters was a weekly foray into the exploration of creatures, myths and whatever else the show's producers felt comfortable covering. Each week, at least two or three stories, legends or fables would be fleshed out and presented with a mix of facts and fiction.

For her part, Annja usually shot down the myths and debunked hauntings and demonic possession, blowing away legerdemain with research and study. Her concentration was on the history of the time, of the thinking and the people and how all of that related to what was going on in the world of today. Of course, even though she poked holes in fabrications, that didn't make true believers any less willing to believe.

"Kristie!" some young men shouted, mistaking Annja for her popular co-star. They jumped up and down, mired in the crowd, trying to get a closer look. They were pushed farther back as the police car rolled through. "Kristie! Over here!"

The tall black man turned to the police vehicle. He slammed both hands on the hood. The sudden loud noise quieted everyone.

"I've filed an injunction to stop this demolition," the man roared. "The sanctity of those graves needs to be maintained."

Two policemen stepped out of the car. The older one was black and the younger one was Hispanic. Both of them had that hard-edged look that Annja recognized. She'd seen it first on the faces of the men who patrolled New Orleans, then in the faces of men serving in the same capacity around the world.

"John," the older policeman said, "I'm going to ask you to back off once, politely. And if you don't, I'm going to arrest you."

"We have the right to assemble," the man said.

"Assemble," the officer agreed, "but not to impede. The construction company and the owners of this land have graciously allowed people to come in and make the attempt to find out who those dead folks are. They didn't have to do that. They could have just cleaned them out of there."

"Like the refuse they were treated as all those years ago?"

"I'm not here to debate, John," the policeman said. "I'm asking you to step aside and let these people get on with their jobs."

"They were murdered!" John shouted.

Murmurs came from the crowd.

"We don't know that," the policeman said. "And even if they were murdered, whoever did it is dead. We're not going to find a guilty party." He took a breath. "Now step down."

Reluctantly, the big man stepped back. A corridor opened up to the police car. Annja walked forward.

"Afternoon, miss," the police officer said. The badge on his shirt identified him as A. Marcus. He opened the squad car's rear door for Annja.

"Thank you, Officer Marcus." Annja slid into the back seat.

The younger officer put Hallinger in on the other side. They were driven to the building less than a hundred yards away. The sea of protesters, driven to a new frenzy, flowed in behind them.

"You'll have to forgive them," Marcus said. "Kirktown is usually a fine city. A place where you'd want to bring your family." He glanced up at the news helicopter circling in the sky. Sunlight splintered from the frames of his glasses. "Today…well, we're just not at our best."

"Is there a chance that any of the people located under the building are ancestors of the people here?" Annja asked.

"Probably. The Civil War and the Underground Railroad was a long time ago, but people haven't forgotten. Racial tension is something that I don't think will ever go away in this state."

"It's too easy to separate people by skin color," Annja agreed. "Then you've got money, politics and religious preference."

Marcus grinned. "Yes, ma'am. I figure that's about the size of it. Always has been."

"Before the construction workers found the bodies," Hallinger said, "protests were already working to stop the demolition. Some groups wanted to preserve the building as a historic site. Others didn't want new business coming into the area."

A large metal sign hung on the front of the four-story building. It read Weidman Brothers Construction. Future home of Lark Shopping Center.

The young officer turned around and peered at Annja. "You're not the one on *Chasing History's Monsters* who posed for *Maxim,* are you?"

"Luis," Marcus growled.

"No," Annja said. Biting her tongue, she thought, I'm the one with an actual college degree, years of training and personal integrity.

"I didn't think so." Luis looked and sounded a little disappointed. "I saw the magazine spread she did a few months ago. She looked bigger."

Since Annja was six inches taller than Kristie Chatham, she knew the young policeman wasn't talking about height.

"No offense," Luis said quickly.

Annja made considerable effort not to unload on the policeman. After all, she'd just arrived and didn't need to make a bad impression.

"Thanks for the ride," she told Marcus as he opened the door to let her out. She missed the air-conditioning inside the car as soon as the hot wind blew over her.

Hallinger joined her. "The rest of the excavation crew is inside the building," he said.

"Who do you have?"

"Kids from the university mostly," Hallinger admitted. "A retiree who has an interest in the Underground Railroad. A few people from the historical society here and from Atlanta to help with some of the heavy lifting."

Annja didn't point out that Hallinger didn't have much skilled help. The man already knew that.

"So why did you call for me?" She hadn't wanted to ask him that question until they were face-to-face.

"Because you've got some recent experience with African culture."

"With Poulson's dig?" Annja shook her head. "That shouldn't count. I was on the ground less than three weeks before the government suspended Poulson's visa." That was still a sore point with her. She'd waited years to go to Africa, then got kicked out almost as soon as she'd settled in.

"That," Hallinger told her, "is two weeks longer than I've had. You've been exposed to the Hausa culture?"

"I've read up on it. Saw a little of it while I was in Nigeria."

Hallinger smiled. "Then you're light-years ahead of my university students and volunteers."

"I couldn't have been at the top of your list," Annja said.

"No. Nineteenth, actually. I received eighteen rejections before you accepted, Miss Creed."

Okay, that stings a bit, Annja thought as she returned his smile.

"I'm just fortunate to have called you at a good time," he said graciously. "You have an outstanding reputation in the field, Miss Creed."

Hallinger was being generous. Outside of *Chasing History's Monsters,* few people knew her. She was in her midtwenties and didn't have any significant finds to her credit. But she was good at what she did and loved the work.

"Call me Annja," she told him.

"Want to go inside?" Hallinger asked. "At least the protests and the constant roar of the helicopter rotors dull a bit."

"Sure." Annja followed Hallinger. But the distinct feeling that she was being watched haunted her. It was ridiculous, of course. She was well aware she *was* being watched by the crowd of protesters and the news helicopter.

However, one set of eyes focused on her felt predatory. She *sensed* a threat. She'd never paid much attention to such unscientific evidence as *feelings* until a few months ago when she'd reassembled Joan of Arc's sword. Her sword now.

Though it was hidden away in some *otherwhere* that she could reach into to retrieve it, she could feel the plain, unadorned hilt smooth and hard against her palm. All she had to do was close her hand, will the blade to come forth and the weapon would be there.

In front of a few hundred witnesses, Annja chided herself. Not exactly the brightest thing you could do at the moment.

She stopped at the doorway and swept the crowd with her gaze. Tapping into those inner senses she was still trying to figure out how to control, still thinking some days that they were a figment of her imagination, she tried to isolate the predator.

Annja felt the pressure fade. But she was certain that someone was out there who didn't mean her any good.

"Coming?" Hallinger asked from inside the building.

"Yeah," Annja said, and she stepped into the building.

"DID SHE SEE you?"

Dack Tatum stood in the crowd outside the warehouse and looked back at the door the woman had entered through. He thought about the way she had stopped, almost as if she knew someone was watching her. A cold thrill shot up his spine.

"Dack," the voice barked through the cell phone Tatum held.

"No," Dack said. "She didn't see me."

"Are you certain?"

Dack cursed. The speaker on the phone was his younger brother Christian. Christian had always been a worrywart. Dack turned away from the crowd and signaled Vince Retter and Brian Haggle, the two spotters he'd set up in the crowd. All of them had cell phones with walkie-talkie capability.

"I'm certain, Christian. Relax, man. I got this wired. I'm rolling heavy with manpower on this op. Chances are there were just too many eyes on her. Some women feel hinky when a guy stares at her. It's no biggie."

"It is a biggie," Christian said.

Dack was a huge man, nearly six and a half feet tall. He had dark hair shaved nearly to his skull and dark eyes that looked like gun muzzles. He was in his late thirties. For ten years, he'd been an Army Ranger. Then, when he saw he wasn't going to get the promotions he wanted and saw how much money there was to be made in the civilian sector, he'd spent the past eight years as a mercenary, for sale to the highest bidder.

He didn't usually work Stateside. But everywhere outside the United States was fair game as far as he was concerned.

Dressed in shorts with cargo pockets, a T-shirt proclaiming his love for Charlie Daniels, a skull-and-crossbones bandana and mirrored sunglasses, he looked as if he'd just driven in from the trailer park to see what all the fuss was about.

"You don't know what's at stake," Christian went on.

"So why don't you tell me?" Dack entered the nearby convenience store, which was doing a booming business in beer and Icees thanks to all the protesters, police and media in the area. He grabbed a single beer from the refrigerator unit and paid for it at the counter.

"Do you remember Horace Tatum?" Christian asked.

Dack didn't. He figured it must have been the name of a family member he'd gotten introduced to at one of the reunions. Personally, he didn't remember anyone he didn't do business with. Or didn't kill. He always remembered the guys he took out. He went to sleep every night bringing their faces up in his mind's eye. It was a relaxation technique that had never failed.

"A cousin?" Dack guessed.

"No. Don't you know anything about our family?"

"You're my brother. Our parents are dead. I don't think there's anything else I need to know."

"Horace Tatum was one of our ancestors," Christian said.

Oh, one of the dead ones, Dack thought. He wasn't going to feel bad about not remembering a dead relative. Unless it was his mom or dad. But Christian had a thing about remembering dead relatives. His younger brother had become a genealogy fiend, always tracing dead relatives farther and farther back in time.

Dack felt it was better to let dead relatives lie. Christian, however, was convinced that a treasure was out there waiting to be claimed.

"So," Dack said. "Horace, relative or not, is long dead, bro."

"Yeah. But he's the one who killed those people in that building."

"So?"

"So if people find out he's the one that killed all those slaves 150 years ago, that's going to put a kink in my plans."

Christian was planning on running for the office of the state representative next term. He was one of the wealthy elite in Atlanta. Dack

knew having a murderer in the family, especially with all the attention this situation was receiving, would hurt his brother's precious
image. Christian needed his older brother to get a handle on things.

Dack walked outside the convenience store and twisted the cap off
his beer. He sipped, relishing the cool liquid against his parched throat.

"His father was Jedidiah Tatum," Christian went on.

"The guy who owned the textile mill."

"You do remember."

Actually, Dack knew that fact from one of the news pieces he'd
heard on the convenience store radio when he'd stopped in for a beer
and a package of cigarettes earlier. "Yeah," he lied.

"Jedidiah kept a journal," Christian went on.

A man's word for diary, Dack told himself disgustedly. He knew
his brother kept one, too. Two, actually. One that listed everything
Christian did, and with whom, and the other one sanitized so that it
couldn't be held against him in a court of law. Neither practice, in
Dack's view, was wise or safe. Leaving the one that listed every dirty
deed was just plain stupid. Even the sanitized one left holes that
would be questioned by anyone who could read between the lines.

"Horace knew one of the slaves in that basement," Christian said.

"Our family owned slaves?"

"Yes."

Dack felt pretty good about that. Personally, he didn't care for
blacks. Or people of color. Or African-Americans. Or whatever they
were calling themselves these days. He figured they ranged from
stupid and lazy to uppity and selfish.

"Jedidiah didn't just spin the cotton into goods," Christian said.
"He also raised the cotton. Had big fields of it around Kirktown.
Horace worked on the fields. That's how he got to know Yohance."

"Who's Yohance?" Dack took another sip of beer.

"Yohance was one of the slaves that worked on the farm. He was
the one that had the Spider Stone."

Dack's head hurt. He vaguely remembered the story. Christian
had always been fascinated by the story of the Spider Stone. When
he'd been a kid, Christian had studied the family history at their
grandfather's knee.

"What's the Spider Stone?" Dack asked.

"Horace believed it was a treasure map. Jedidiah wrote that in his journal. The night he killed all those people down in that basement, Horace looked for it, but he never found it."

"Why are you telling me this?" Dack asked.

"Because I want you to find that stone."

Dack cursed loud enough to draw the attention of a few bystanders. "I thought you wanted me to bring that building down on top of those damn busybodies," he whispered.

"I do," Christian said. "But I want the Spider Stone first."

"WE'VE GOT GENERATORS to provide power for the electric lamps we've used underground," Professor Hallinger explained as he led the way through the warehouse.

"Normally the Underground Railroad wasn't literally underground," Annja said as she followed the professor, gazing around at the history showing in every plank and joist. She loved being in old buildings that had been preserved. Stepping through their doors was almost like stepping into a time machine.

"No. It was a system of way stops used by those fleeing slavery who made their way north. Some of them went on into Canada. Usually they traveled overland through forests and swamps, off the beaten track. They used the railroad language to suit themselves. A conductor was the guide who led them out of the South along the way stops. Railroad agents were the sympathizers who hid them during the day and gave them food and supplies. But there were a few subterranean areas. Basements, root cellars, caves. This happens to be one of the latter."

"A cave?" Annja asked.

Hallinger nodded. "Beneath the building. It was used to house the furnace."

Annja surveyed the massive empty space.

The textile mills had been cavernous. Dust covered everything except the floor where pedestrians had walked it semiclean. All of the windows were boarded over, covering empty frames or remnants of glass. Empty beer cans and sleeping bags littered the floor space.

"I see the local teens didn't hesitate about claiming squatters' rights." Annja took a small digital camera from her backpack.

"No." Hallinger smiled. "A place like this must have been a godsend to preteens wanting to scare themselves with the idea of ghosts, and teenagers wanting somewhere to explore the prospects of sex, drinking and smoking."

"Not exactly a lovers' lane." Annja looked at the bird droppings that streaked the floor. Glancing up, she saw a few pigeons on the rafters.

"It was close enough," Hallinger said.

"No one found the bodies until yesterday?"

The professor shook his head as he led the way to the back of the building. "Construction workers shutting down gas mains under the building discovered a closed furnace room. I'll show you."

Annja followed him into a back room, then down a flight of stairs that led underground. Dank mustiness clogged her nose and made breathing more difficult. The only illumination came from a string of electric bulbs that led into the large basement area. Wooden shelving lined the walls and occupied the center of the room. Whatever the shelves had contained had long since vanished, either through pilfering or by decomposition.

A handful of people occupied the basement, quietly speaking among themselves as they hunkered down over ice chests with sandwiches and bottled water. They looked up at Annja and a few greeted her.

Annja responded in kind, noticing the grimy faces and casual clothing and the uneasy look most of the younger ones wore. After a brief introduction, Hallinger led Annja through a tunnel in the basement wall.

"Not exactly happy to be here, are they?" Annja asked.

"It's the bodies," Hallinger replied. "You get started in archaeology, you think your first body is going to be a mummy or a caveman."

"I know." Annja trailed the professor along the small tunnel. "My first body was less than a week old. He'd been buried at a dig site long enough to bloat and collect a number of burrowing insects."

"Where was that?"

"New Mexico. During my senior year."

"Ah, the heat. That must have made things pretty horrible."

"It was." Some nights Annja still remembered the stench.

"Who was he?"

"A grave robber. We were there helping local tribes recover artifacts, but we left the bodies intact. This guy was there collecting skulls to sell on eBay."

Hallinger scowled in disgust. "Our chosen field does attract the greedy entrepreneur looking to find shortcuts to a quick buck."

Annja agreed.

"Did you ever find out who killed your dead man?"

"No. They never even got his name. The tribal police conducted an investigation, but it didn't go anywhere."

"I'm not surprised. Desecration of grave sites won't win you any points in the Native American community."

The tunnel narrowed ahead. Timbers shored the low ceiling up in several areas. The dank smell grew stronger. Gradually, the tunnel angled upward.

"This leads to the coal furnace." Hallinger kept moving. "It was built before the basement."

"The tunnel was built to connect the new basement to the furnace?"

"I don't think so. At least, not for that reason. The furnace, the original furnace, was lost in a cave-in."

"How did that happen?"

Hallinger shook his head. "We don't know. There are signs of an explosion—soot on the walls and some blast damage. Some of the bodies were torn up in the explosion. Or maybe by people who found them later."

"If the bodies were found earlier, why wasn't something done then?"

"They haven't been found since they were buried. The entrance we came through back there had been walled over, closing off the tunnel. One of the construction workers discovered that by accident. Over the years, the mortar holding the stones together had dried out and crumbled. I don't think it was mixed well. Or perhaps the dankness of the environment contributed to the failure of the mortar. However it worked out, the team checking for gas mains discovered the tunnel. They dug it out in case there were any gas lines in there."

"Did they know what it was?"

"No. No blueprints of this building exist. It was built pre-Civil War and whatever records of the building might have been around were destroyed when General Sherman marched on Atlanta."

"Why wasn't the town razed?" Annja knew from her studies of

the war that Sherman had followed scorched-earth tactics, leaving nothing standing in his wake.

"Because it was so close to the railroad. The town became the site of a Confederate military hospital in 1863. All of the larger buildings, including this one, were used in those efforts."

"Must have made the textile mill owners happy."

"I don't think it hurt them any. Have you heard of Christian Tatum?"

"No. Should I have?" Annja asked.

"Not really. He's a businessman in Atlanta now, with subsidiaries in Charlotte and Savannah. Does a lot with government contracts. Supposed to be a big deal in military engineering. He has political aspirations. His ancestor, Jedidiah, owned this building from the time it was built until he died in the 1890s." Hallinger stopped and looked back at her. He slapped the timber across the opening. "Watch your head here."

Annja ducked down a little more and stepped through the narrow opening. When she emerged, she found herself in a large room carved out of stone and filled with the dead.

2

Annja peered around the underground room. A large furnace filled the opposite wall. A coal bin sat adjacent to it. Rotting coal filled the bin and spilled across the floor. Broad coal shovels covered in dull orange rust lay on the floor.

What caught Annja's attention most, though, were the bodies strewed across the floor. The dank subterranean environment had contributed to the growth of dark mold on the bones. The clothing had largely rotted away, leaving only scattered pieces.

Sixteen skeletons lay in disarray, spread outward from the furnace as if they'd been tossed by a big hand. All of them were burned and blackened, twisted by incredible force. Rock fragments lay among them.

"Have you moved the bodies?" Annja slid out of her backpack and took out a miniflashlight. She switched on the light. The powerful halogen beam stabbed out, penetrating the darkness more strongly than the electric bulbs.

"No, we haven't touched them yet," Hallinger said as he squatted against the wall near the opening.

Annja breathed shallowly. After 150-plus years, the bacteria that triggered decomposition had done its work. All trace of a death odor was gone. But the musty thickness of the air was still filled with particulates. She took a disposable filtered mask from her backpack and fit it over her face.

"I'm not an explosives expert." She aimed her beam at the furnace. The metal sides had been warped in the explosion.

"One of the students advanced the theory that the explosion was the result of some kind of coal-gas buildup."

Annja knew coal gas was frequently the cause of mining accidents involving explosions. It gathered in pockets, and just the slightest spark could set it off. That was one of the reasons coal miners didn't carry metal objects like rings or buttons down into a mine.

"No." Annja played the beam around.

"Why?"

"With the furnace working, coal gas couldn't build up. The flames would burn it off," she said.

"They could have shut down over the weekend. Or a long holiday."

"With the South warring with the North over the textiles market with England, I doubt the mill closed down much for holidays or weekends. Time was money. Most mill owners worked as much as they could. Even if the furnace wasn't kept fed to warm the building, it would have been banked. I don't think a buildup of gas was likely."

"Do you think it was an accident?" Hallinger asked.

Annja shook her head. "I don't."

Hallinger sighed. "Neither do I. These people were murdered."

Playing the flashlight beam over the skeletons, Annja saw some of them couldn't have been much more than children. They hadn't had a chance inside the room.

Hallinger sounded tired when he continued. "It's bad enough finding these bodies after all these years, especially with them being slaves, but having to confirm to those people out there that they were murdered is going to make things even worse."

Annja silently agreed. "Why did you ask me about the Hausa people?"

Hallinger directed his flashlight beam to a large stone lying on one side of the room. The rock was as big as two of her fists together. Someone had taken time, years probably, to smooth the rock's surface until it looked polished. Then they'd carved images with a sharp point and rubbed some kind of dye or stain into them.

Drawn by the images, Annja knelt and inspected the stone. She recognized the letters. "Hausa had its roots in the Chadic language, which is Afro-Asiatic in origin."

"I knew that much. It's also an official language of several West African countries these days."

"Have you touched this?"

"No, and it's been killing me not to." Hallinger rubbed his forehead in frustration. "Everything about this place speaks of something beyond just the Civil War."

"Why?"

"These men were carrying weapons." Hallinger raked his flashlight over the bodies.

"I saw those," Annja admitted. She studied the makeshift weapons, some of them no more than hoe handles inscribed with more Hausa writing. There were also three axes, their handles marked with more of the language. Close inspection of one of the ax heads revealed that it, too, had been marked.

"Escaping slaves didn't carry weapons." Hallinger frowned. "Getting caught with one usually meant getting hung from the nearest tree when pursuers caught up with them."

The presence of the weapons told Annja what they were looking at. "This was a war party."

"I think so, too," the professor said.

Annja put the miniflashlight between her teeth and lifted her digital camera. She focused on the rock, then on the weapons, finally taking pictures of the bodies.

Hallinger waited patiently until she was done. "Can you read the writing on the stone?"

"Some of it." Annja put the camera away. "The stone tells a story of an exodus. Of a long travel, from what I gather."

"There was a slave market not far from Dakar, Senegal."

"I know. Ile de Goree. It was one of the primary contact points of the Triangle Trade," she said.

"Slaves, rum and sugar. Those are the things that built the New World. That and the search for riches." Hallinger sighed. "People think cotton is what brought the slaves to the New World, but that was only what developed out of the slave trade."

Annja knew that was true. The early Atlantic trade had started a history of hundreds of years of pain and suffering. She pushed that out of her mind for the moment, wanting to concentrate on the dig and the unanswered questions she and the professor both had. "I'm ready to start if you are," she said grimly.

Hallinger nodded. "I'll get the crew together."

THE EXCAVATION, even though there was no digging involved, was slow work. They always were. Annja had no problem with that. She loved her chosen field. As an orphan, she'd had no real sense of connection or family. As an archaeologist, she connected not only people but also years.

In a map of the past, everyone had a place. It was just a matter of finding the proper pieces, she thought.

Like the piece of the sword she'd found in France while looking for the Beast of Gévaudan. That piece had brought a number of things together. All of the other pieces of the sword that had been sought after since Joan of Arc's death on a burning pyre over five hundred years earlier had come together. Once she'd touched those pieces, the sword had reforged itself.

Magically.

She disapproved of the term, but there was no other explanation. Annja had seen it happen. In the blink of an eye, she'd held the sword—suddenly whole—in her hand. It had never been out of her reach since.

Out of that experience, she'd begun forging new relationships. One with Roux, who claimed to have witnessed Joan's death and been charged with finding Joan's sword. Another with Garin, who had at one time been Roux's protégé but now sought to kill him and take the sword from Annja. Garin was afraid that whatever power had enabled him to remain relatively ageless for those years would fade now the sword was once more whole.

Annja still didn't know if she believed her bloodline tied her to Joan of Arc. Whatever chance she might have had of ascertaining that had been destroyed during the flooding of New Orleans. The orphanage where she'd grown up had been washed away. The nuns who raised her were dead or scattered. Most of them hadn't been concerned with the pasts of the children in their care; they'd been grooming them for the future.

But Annja believed the sword had been Joan's. Now it was hers. It had changed her life. She was still learning what all that meant.

ANNJA AND HALLINGER worked well together, directing the expertise of the retired couple who had worked dig sites before, and training the university students. Using soft rope and pitons they drove into the ground with small sledges, they laid out a grid over the recovery site. Since the bodies had been scattered by the blast, the whole floor of the furnace room was designated the recovery site.

Once the grid was laid out in twelve-inch squares, Annja and Hallinger took turns working the recovery. They moved square by square, cataloging and videotaping everything they took out. The other dig workers labeled the recovered items and packed them out.

"I'm surprised the police released this site to you." Annja searched through a pocket of a shirt fragment she took from the latest square.

"Are you kidding?" Hallinger snorted and shook his head. "They didn't want this. You saw that crowd outside. As soon as the story hit the news, people poured in from Atlanta and other nearby towns. They called the university and got in touch with me almost immediately."

"You said construction workers found the bodies."

"Yeah."

"Did they take anything?"

"I asked. For a moment I thought I was going to get thrown out. But the police chief stepped in and made it clear that my team and I were going to excavate the remains and see that they were handled with respect. The police chief reiterated my question. They said no." Hallinger shrugged. "You never know. Maybe they didn't. Most people are reluctant to touch the dead."

The pocket Annja explored yielded a folded piece of paper that had browned over the years. She didn't try to open it. That would be done under laboratory conditions to help preserve the paper and the ink.

Three coins slid from the folds of the paper. All of them were of similar design, showing a woman with braided hair under a crown surrounded by stars and a circle of wheat stalks around the words

Half Cent. United States Of America circled the wheat. The dates on the coins were 1843, 1852 and 1849.

Annja dropped them in Hallinger's waiting palm.

"Liberty braided-hair half pennies," Hallinger said as he examined them. "The full penny at the time was the size of a half dollar now."

"Those were minted between 1840 and the late 1850s," one of the students said. Brian was calm and easygoing.

Hallinger glanced at his student and smiled. "We didn't cover that in class."

Brian grinned shyly. "I've been into coin collecting since I was a kid. My dad bought me a metal detector as soon as I was big enough to carry it. We spent our weekends tramping through battle-fields all over the South."

"Your father was a treasure hunter?"

"Still is. Drives Mom crazy. But he's making serious money on eBay with the stuff he finds. Coins, jewelry, stuff like that. He's made enough from his hobby to buy an RV so he's not camping in a tent on weekends anymore. Mom's okay with that. She gets to work on her genealogy stuff."

Hallinger glanced at his watch. "Maybe we should think about taking a break. It's almost nine. We've been working for hours."

Annja nodded. She was still ready to work, but she knew she would be until she fell on her face. The idea that the group of men in the furnace room was some kind of war party wouldn't leave her thoughts. Where had they come from? Where were they going? Who had killed them? She was curious, definitely hooked on the mystery that had been dropped into Hallinger's lap.

But the professor and his crew had been on-site since early that morning.

Hallinger looked at her, and Annja knew he read what was on her mind. "Just a break. We'll be back." He turned to the students. All of them were covered in grime and sweat. They looked tired and hungry. "I'll even spring for pizza. I'm sure I can get the university to pick up the tab."

"Sure. Just let me get this." Annja reached for the large stone covered in Hausa writing. *A long journey.* She couldn't help wondering what that meant. Were they starting a long journey? Or coming back from one? Why had the men been armed when they knew it would mean death for them? Had they been on the same journey when they'd been killed?

Out in the hallway, someone yelped in pain.

"Get down!" a gruff voice roared. "Get down on the ground on your face and you won't get hurt!"

Annja put the rock aside as she stood. Unconsciously, she reached into otherwhere and felt her sword at her fingertips. She kept it ready but didn't pull it into the world with her. In two quick strides she reached the opening and peered out into the low tunnel.

THREE MEN in ski masks, maybe more, hurried along the tunnel. They all carried semiautomatic pistols sporting thick, stubby silencers. They blinded the students with high-intensity flashlights.

One of the students wheeled around and shoved a girl behind him. He reached for the lead invader. The masked man barely moved the pistol he held in close to his side. The muzzle-flash briefly flared in the tunnel, and only a slight coughing sound reached Annja's ears.

The bullet struck the student in the upper chest and forced him backward. Blood spattered the wall and coated the nearby electric bulb. The crimson liquid hissed and smoked for just a moment, then the bulb burned out and went dark.

"Sit down," the masked man ordered, "or I'll put the next bullet between your eyes."

The student was too stunned to move. In disbelief, he put a hand over his chest against the wound.

The masked man reached the student, shoving out a hand that hit the young man in the throat and knocked him off his feet. The young woman was screaming.

Annja held on to the sword hilt. It felt solid and sure in her hand. All she had to do was pull and the blade would be there in the tunnel with her.

And the big guy with the gun will shoot you. Or someone else, Annja thought. Reluctantly, she released the sword.

"You!" The masked man waved at Annja. "Get down! Now!"

Annja lay on the ground. Ahead of her, the young woman held the gunshot victim. He quivered and jerked, but Annja thought it was shock setting in. He was still breathing, so she chose to remain optimistic.

The masked man reached her. "Where's the stone?"

Annja kept her voice level, holding the fear and adrenaline that filled her at bay. "What stone?"

"Don't play games with me. The Spider Stone."

She chose not to answer. It's nine o'clock. Maybe it's dark outside, but these guys couldn't have gotten in here unseen. Someone has to have seen them, she thought.

The masked man pointed the pistol at the young woman holding the gunshot victim. She cried out in fear and tried to crawl away, but there was nowhere to go in the narrow tunnel.

"I'll ask you one more time, then I'll kill her. Where is it?"

"It's in the other room." Annja pointed.

The masked man stepped over her, following the pistol into the furnace room. Stepping into the room, tearing through the grid they'd strung so carefully, he stooped and picked up the stone in one gloved hand.

Annja waited for the police to arrive. She hoped they would, but she dreaded it, too. Police might mean gunplay, and gunplay could mean a lot of dead university students.

"No, it's here. I got it." The masked man looked at the stone. "It's covered in writing. I can't make it out. It's not in English."

For a moment, Annja thought the man was talking to himself, then she saw the outline of the cell phone earbud under the ski mask.

The masked man tossed the stone to one of his compatriots and turned to Annja. "Where are your notes?"

"I've got a microcassette recorder in my pocket," she said.

The gloved hand flicked impatiently. "Gimme."

Annja dug the device out and handed it over. She hated feeling helpless, and she was scared. But she didn't let the fear take over.

The masked man shoved the cassette recorder into a thigh pocket of his camouflage pants and sealed the Velcro tab. Seeing the military-style pant and thinking about the way the guy moved and wasn't squeamish about shooting other people, Annja thought maybe he was—or had been—military. The black boots looked like military issue, too.

The man's eyes focused on hers through the slits of his mask. "What does it say on the stone?"

"I don't know," Annja said honestly.

"The professor held up operations here till you arrived. Don't tell me you can't read the stone."

"I can. Some of it."

"What does it say?"

"I didn't get a chance to decipher all of it. It mentions something about a journey."

"To where?"

"I don't know. I wasn't the first choice for the job. I'm doing the best I can. We were working the room first. We were going to address the stone later."

Frustration glinted in the man's cold eyes. He swung his pistol toward one of the students again.

"I'm telling you the truth." Panic knotted Annja's stomach. Violence was something she still wasn't used to even though she'd been through quite a lot of it lately—since she'd acquired the sword—but she could deal with it. The possibility of watching the man shoot someone through the head to prove his point made her sick. "I could lie to you. I could tell you anything I wanted. You wouldn't know the difference."

"I'd know if you were lying to me," he said.

"Then prove it." Annja looked directly into those cold, hard eyes. She spoke slowly. "I haven't finished translating the stone yet. I don't know any more about what's written there than I've told you." When she finished, her heart was hammering inside her chest. Part of her knew that the student was about to die.

Then the masked man lifted the pistol. "All right. You don't know what it says."

Annja released her pent-up breath.

"But you can translate it."

"Maybe."

"That's why Hallinger brought you in."

"Yes."

"Fine. Let's go." The masked man caught Annja's left arm, yanked her to her feet and twisted her arm behind her.

Pain shot through Annja's arm, but she stubbornly refused to cry out. She also resisted the impulse to attempt to break free. While at the orphanage, she'd gotten involved in martial arts, then continued her studies in college and after graduation. When she was home in Brooklyn, she still took classes in various dojos and even did some boxing.

Wait, she told herself. Don't react until you have to, or until you can make a difference. She looked around at the students and hated seeing the fear in their eyes. None of them had signed on for what they were currently dealing with. She didn't want the men responsible for that to escape.

SHOVED AHEAD of the masked man, Annja hurried down the tunnel. In seconds they reached the warehouse. The plywood covering the broken windows didn't quite block out all the light. Enough remained that Annja knew at least some of the crowd still remained outside. There were probably even a few reporters waiting to do remotes for the last news shows of the evening.

The masked man shoved Annja toward a side door that had been boarded shut. A fine spray of sawdust showed on the scarred wooden floor.

One of the men opened the door, and Annja's captor shoved her through to the dark, narrow alley on the other side. In the alley, Annja heard car engines idling out front, letting her know the police hadn't deserted their posts, either.

A rope ladder dangled from the building opposite the warehouse.

"Up." The masked man pointed toward the ladder.

Annja went, moving along the ladder quickly. Too quickly as it turned out.

The man grabbed her leg. She looked down at him, one hand over the top of the two-story building. Moonlight shone against her hand, washing away all color.

"Slowly." The man held on to her and aimed the pistol at the center of her body. "Try anything and I'll drop you."

Annja waited until he released her leg, then she went up.

Another man with a rifle equipped with telescopic sights hid on the rooftop. In the distance in front of the warehouse, two police cars with spinning lights stood guard. Two men sat on the hood of one of the cars drinking from paper cups.

Annja tried not to feel angry with them. Someone had been out in front of the warehouse since the bodies had been discovered. She was certain everyone involved was getting tired of the duty.

In short order, the five men who had invaded the dig site joined Annja and the sniper on the rooftop. All of them were heavily armed.

"When do we blow the building?" one of the men asked.

"Now," the big man said.

Ice water filled Annja's veins. She couldn't wait any longer. Reaching into the otherwhere, she gripped the sword and ripped it free just as the first man started to take an electronic detonator from his chest pack. She swung at him even before the sword was completely in her reality.

"Look out!" one of the men yelled, lifting his pistol.

3

The sword appeared in Annja's hand as she swung it toward the demolitions man's chest pack. The man was caught flatfooted.

Three feet of naked double-bladed steel, honed to razor-sharp edges, whipped through the air. The sword was inelegant, a tool designed for bloody work, not a showpiece to be kept on a mantel somewhere. It was the sword of a warrior.

The sword tip sliced through the chest pack and nicked the flesh beneath. Annja could have killed the man where he stood. Instead, she whirled and caught the tumbling remote control in her free hand, folding her right leg into her chest, then driving it forward in a side kick.

The man flew backward three or four yards, landing in a heap. He didn't move again.

Annja was fairly certain she'd rendered him unconscious but hadn't killed him. She made it a point not to kill unless she had to.

She turned, too fast for any of the surprised men to stop her, though they tried. She shook off one man's hand, then swept the sword forward and blocked the sniper's attempt to shoot her. Metal grated on metal.

Professor Hallinger and the others had burst free of the warehouse. The shouting on the ground quickly escalated into mass confusion.

The man who'd taken her hostage took aim at Annja as she ran to the roof access door. She dodged, feeling a bullet scald the air close to her cheek. From the corner of her eye, she spotted the masked man taking aim again.

She dived forward, tucking the sword and the detonator in close, rolling to the side as bullets thudded into the rooftop behind her. Coming to her feet immediately, she raced for the access door and took shelter behind it just as a fusillade of bullets raked the front of the structure.

The screaming detonation of automatic fire told Annja the thieves no longer favored silence.

"Up there!" someone shouted.

Dropping to her knees, Annja glanced at the remote control and saw a panel on the back. Laying the sword aside for a moment, she opened the back and popped the batteries out. Placing the detonator on the ground, she picked up the sword and smashed the device with the hilt.

Footsteps sounded to her right.

The moon was behind the man. Evidently he hadn't noticed because his shadow stretched out before him, arriving well before he did.

Annja broke to her left. The roof's edge wasn't far away. Close enough, she thought, that she could make it. If she had to, she could probably jump to street level to escape.

But she didn't want to escape. These men had gone into the warehouse, and one of them had callously shot a student as if it were nothing.

Annja didn't intend to let them simply walk away. That hadn't been her way before she'd found the sword, and it definitely wasn't her way now.

On the other side of the roof-access structure, she could see that the other men were now in full flight. They headed north across the rooftops, away from the warehouse, leaping the distance between the close-set buildings. They'd left behind the man she'd kicked. He still lay prone on the roof.

Moving quickly, Annja vaulted on top of the access structure and scrambled forward. On the other side, the shadowy man advanced around the corner, both hands supporting his pistol as he spun to face where he believed Annja was hiding.

Her shadow, caught by the moon, shot out ahead of the structure's shadow on the rooftop. The sudden appearance must have caught the man's attention. He tried to turn and bring his weapon up, stepping back to give himself room to work.

Gripping the structure with one hand, Annja swung down, angling her body so that her left foot caught the man in the face. He went down, falling backward and losing his grip on the pistol.

Annja landed on her feet, knees bent to absorb the shock. She slid naturally into a horse stance, then swung the sword and brought the flat of the blade hard against the side of the man's head as he struggled to get to his feet. He slumped on the rooftop, unconscious.

Turning, Annja set off in pursuit of the fleeing men. Her stride was immediately long and sure, eating up the distance. She had no idea who had sent the men, but it was obvious that someone felt the stone was important.

She made the leap to the next building easily, lengthening her stride again. Ahead, the men disappeared over the side of one of the buildings. Annja ran faster.

WHEN SHE REACHED the edge of the last building, Annja peered down carefully. She caught sight of the gunman stationed below just as he fired the machine pistol he held. Annja barely yanked her head back in time to keep her face from getting shot off.

Bullets ripped through the air in front of her, then chipped into the stone side of the building as the gunner tried to correct his aim. The gunfire and whine of the bullets ricocheting from the wall rang in her ears.

Farther out, three of the men ran for a white van that skidded to a stop in front of the single police car blocking the alley from curious pedestrians. The policeman took cover behind his vehicle as he shouted on his radio. The radio squawks were overwhelmed by the sound of the gunfire.

Two gunmen slid free of the van. Both of them held fully automatic weapons that peppered the police car. The lone police officer tried to duckwalk away from his vehicle as bullets cored through the police car. Before he'd taken a half-dozen steps, he pirouetted and dropped, sprawling to the ground.

One of the gunners in the van turned his weapon on the rooftop where Annja stood. More bullets tore through brick and mortar where she took cover. Frustrated, she waited out the onslaught. She had no choice.

Rubber shrieked on the street as sirens shrilled on the other side of the warehouse.

Chancing a look down, Annja saw the white van speeding away. She also knew with the way the road curved along the warehouse district, coming back around in almost a 180-degree turn, that the thieves hadn't gotten away cleanly. She still had a chance.

She ran to the side of the building that overlooked the street where the van would have to pass along. She charged down the metal fire escape, steps banging as she made the twists and turns. She reached the final ladder, grabbed hold of it with her free hand and jumped on to ride to the ground.

Taking cover in the shadows, Annja kept her hand around the sword hilt and watched as the van came sliding around the far turn. The bright lights played over her position, then kept on moving, coming closer.

Okay, Annja told herself, this is your last chance to rethink what you're about to do. She kept picturing the innocent student the masked man had shot in cold blood. She knew that Professor Hallinger would feel responsible. She didn't want the men to get away.

Annja stepped out of the darkness into the path of the speeding van. She held the sword in both hands, up high so she could sweep the blade down.

Roux had worked with her for a time on her swordcraft, then he'd ultimately found more pleasant pursuits after spending five hundred years looking for the pieces of the shattered sword. She still practiced with the sword every day, getting to know the weapon more and more intimately as she worked.

The van's headlights fell across Annja. Shadows within the front seats moved. The passenger leaned out his window and took aim.

Annja ran toward the van, matching her speed and her stride, running toward the driver's side to make it more difficult for the gunner to track her. Bullets cracked through the air as the muzzle-flashes appeared in sporadic bursts.

At the last moment, Annja leaped, placing one foot on the van's hood and pushing off again. She arced up, twisting her body so that she flipped and landed on her feet on the van's roof. She was sure that before she'd gotten the sword she could never have accomplished such a maneuver. Now it was almost child's play.

The driver immediately took evasive action, swinging the steering wheel wildly. The van took out a line of trash cans, filling the air with the noise of tearing metal and grinding. Sparks shot out as trash cans remained stuck beneath the van.

Bullets tore through the thin metal of the van's roof. They missed Annja, who dropped to one knee and reversed the sword so that she held it point down. Using all her strength, she plunged the sword down through the roof.

Annja missed the driver by inches. The sudden appearance of the sword slicing through the van's top startled the driver. He pulled hard to the right, slamming the van into a wall in an effort to dislodge Annja.

Grimly, she hung on to the front of the van. She didn't want to let the men escape, not only for wounding the college student, but also because she wanted to know the reasons for the attack in the first place. Why was the stone so important?

Sparks cascaded along the van's side, coming in a deluge as the vehicle left scarred building walls in its wake. The grinding sound erased all but the shrill cries of the police sirens. The van gained speed.

Annja didn't know if the men could manage to escape from the police. They seemed well organized, but she didn't want to take any chances. Bullets ripped along the van's rooftop, missing her by inches.

Moving quickly, she vaulted forward and landed on the hood in a crouch. On the other side of the cracked windshield, the driver and the passenger looked incredulous. The passenger finished reloading his machine pistol and leveled the weapon.

Annja struck first, shoving the sword's point toward the driver and shattering the glass. The driver ducked, pulling hard on the steering wheel.

Already off balance from the impacts against the wall, the van slid to the left, then came up on two wheels in a slow roll. Annja jumped clear, hurling herself from the path of the sudden explosion of bullets.

Annja landed in a crouch, allowing her legs to absorb the shock of the landing. Surprise filled her for just a moment. Then she accepted what she'd just done by instinct. Having the sword or simply reforging the sword had changed her. She still wasn't sure of everything that had occurred or would continue to occur. But it no longer shocked her or scared her.

The van careened over on its side and skidded along the street. Even before it slammed to a stop against one of the buildings, the rear cargo doors opened and three men rolled free. Annja ran toward them, catching up with the first one before he got to his feet. She swung the sword and brought the hilt down on the man's head, knocking him unconscious with the blow.

Ducking the second man's attempt to pull up his machine pistol, she swept his legs from beneath him with her own, then grabbed his hair through the mask and slammed his head against the street. He went limp and the gun clattered to the ground.

The third man snarled curses at her as he pointed his pistol. Before he could fire, Annja rolled and came to her feet. She swung the sword and knocked away the pistol. The bullet missed her by inches as the weapon went flying.

Recovering almost immediately, the man launched himself at her, punching and kicking. Annja recognized him at once as she stepped clear of his attack. He was the leader, the one who'd so coldly shot the college student.

Tossing her sword to the side, Annja felt its absence as it phased back into the otherwhere. Taking another quick step back, she set herself, left forearm raised in front of her and right hand clenched at her hip. She blocked the man's attacks in rapid succession, turning aside a punch with her forearm, two kicks with her lead leg, then stepped in low to deliver a kidney blow as he tried to set himself.

He cried out in pain.

Savage satisfaction lit through Annja as she heard him. Still in motion, slipping to the man's right, she reverse kicked, bringing her foot high enough to collide with the man's face. Incredibly, he remained standing.

Okay, Annja thought, that's not good. She bounced back on her toes, setting up with her right leg forward this time, changing strong sides so he'd have to adapt.

The man spit blood.

"That's DNA evidence," Annja taunted. "Even if you got away, which you won't, the police would be able to track you down."

He snarled, "You won't know how that ends up." He curled his hands and tucked them in close to the sides of his face, elbows out to block. "I'm going to kill you," he said. Then he attacked.

Annja gave ground, knowing his weight was an advantage that she couldn't meet head-on. Her hands and feet flew, blocking, parrying, turning. Despite her skill, the impacts would leave bruises.

She escalated her defense, still giving ground but circling now. Then the rhythm changed. His breath started coming faster, his lungs sounded like stressed bellows pumps. For every three punches or kicks he threw, she threw one back, each one placed with telling accuracy, thudding into his face, his chest or his legs. She patiently allowed him to exhaust himself.

When she saw his strength was flagging, she stepped in close and swept his legs. As he fell, Annja hammered him twice in the face. He tried to get up, but she grabbed the back of his head with her hands and kneed him in the face.

His nose broke with an audible crunch. Unconscious, he rolled over on his back.

Police sirens screamed as they closed in.

Annja didn't want to be caught there. The police would have too many questions about how she had overcome a van full of armed men. She turned and ran into the night.

ANNJA LOOKED UP from the stone she'd been working on since the Kirktown Police Department had shut down all activity at the warehouse and brought everyone to the police station. Annja was seated at a borrowed desk in the detectives' bullpen.

The man standing beside the desk looked as though he was in his early thirties, with curly brown hair, dark green eyes and a square face. He wore jeans and a white snap-button Western shirt, cowboy boots and a tan corduroy blazer with leather elbow patches. He dropped a black cowboy hat onto the desk beside the stone covered in Hausa writing.

"I'm Detective Andrew McIntosh." He extended his hand.

Annja took it, feeling his flesh hot against hers in the semicooled office space. "You don't look like a detective," she said.

McIntosh reached into his back pocket and brought out a badge case. He flipped it open to reveal the badge and ID.

Annja kept her eyes on his face, studying him, but she read the ID from the corner of her eye. "It says you're from Atlanta. Not Kirktown."

McIntosh smiled. "Most people don't see past the badge."

"I do," Annja said.

"Kirktown doesn't usually find murder victims 150 years old. Or have running gun battles with terrorist weapons in their streets. Since both happened more or less on the same day and appear to be connected, the captain of detectives here in Kirktown asked for some help on this one. I volunteered."

"Are things that boring in Atlanta?" Annja was responding to the cocky smoothness the man demonstrated. The overconfidence rankled her.

He smiled, and she could see the mischievous little boy he'd probably been twenty-something years ago. His cheeks dimpled.

"Actually, that's a funny story. I'm on administrative leave." McIntosh pointed to a chair beside the desk. "Mind if I sit?"

"The police station would seem to belong more to you than to me," she said coolly.

"This is Georgia, Ms. Creed. Some of us still have manners. My momma always said it was impolite to sit with a lady without asking."

He was a charmer, Annja was amused to discover. She wondered if the down-home good-ol'-boy routine was an act. If it is, it's a good one. She was intrigued. She turned a hand toward the chair. "Please."

McIntosh sat.

Around the bullpen, several of the students and Professor Hallinger sat with detectives while giving statements.

Annja waited until he was settled. "Why am I being interviewed again?"

"You've been interviewed before?" McIntosh seemed surprised by that.

"I have been. And you know that. I just saw you talking to the detective who interviewed me."

McIntosh grinned like a kid who'd been caught with his hand in the cookie jar. "I could have sworn you were totally involved in that rock."

"I am. I could be more involved if I wasn't trying to translate it while sitting in a police station filled with people."

Leaning forward, McIntosh looked at the lettering and the pictographs. "You can read that?"

"That's what I'm trying to figure out."

McIntosh glanced at the notebook Annja had been working in.

Annja shifted just enough to shield the notebook.

Smiling easily, McIntosh leaned back in the chair. "You're an interesting woman, Ms. Creed."

"Thank you. But you didn't answer my question."

"Actually, I did. I was asked to interview you again because you're so interesting."

"How interesting?"

"Well, it's interesting that Professor Hallinger decided to call you in—"

"Because I have a little familiarity with the Hausa language," Annja said.

McIntosh nodded. "It's also interesting that the men tried to swipe that stone shortly after you arrived."

"They waited till after it got dark. Otherwise the police officers would have spotted them entering the warehouse," Annja said.

"Maybe."

Annja arched an eyebrow. "Or maybe I arranged for them to be here?"

"Someone did."

"It wasn't me."

McIntosh smiled at her. "I hope that's true. You're a good-looking woman, Ms. Creed. But you were also the one they decided to take with them when they fled the scene."

"Because I could read some of what's written on this stone."

"How did they know that?"

"While they were taking us prisoner, they asked."

McIntosh raised his eyebrows innocently. "So you just told them you could?"

"Like you, they saw my notes," Annja said, no longer conceal-
ing her irritation.

McIntosh grinned. "See? That's interesting, too."

"I escaped from those men, Detective McIntosh."

"That's what I was told."

"Then what do we have to talk about?"

"Let's see if we can come up with something," he said. Reaching
into his jacket pocket, McIntosh took out a small bound notebook
and a half-dozen pens held together with a rubber band.

"Why are you on administrative leave?" Annja took a sip from
the cup of coffee she'd been given. It had gotten cold, but long hours
at her work had accustomed her to that.

"What?"

"You said you were on administrative leave."

"I am."

Placing her elbows on the desk, Annja leaned forward and looked
into his eyes. "Tell me why."

McIntosh sighed. "Are you really going to make me tell this story?"

"Yes."

"It's embarrassing."

"I like stories. Otherwise I'm going to call a lawyer in and have
him ask you and the Kirktown Police Department why my time is
being wasted. Not only that, but I'm going to return my producer's
phone call. Maybe I can help increase the media attention you're
getting here."

McIntosh feigned a frown, but Annja knew he was a natural-born
storyteller. As an archaeologist, she'd learned to recognize people like
that. Sometimes they helped on a dig site and sometimes they hindered.
She needed to know what McIntosh was—a help or a hindrance.

"I was on stakeout," McIntosh said. "My partner and I were
working a serial burglar downtown. Guy was working hotels. For a
city with a lot of tourists that come in, that's not a good thing."

"I can see that," Annja said, sitting back.

"In addition to stealing valuables, the guy also had a pantie
fetish." McIntosh paused. "I don't want to offend you."

"Hey. I live in New York. Talking about underwear isn't going to
offend me."

McIntosh appeared to relax. "I'm gonna remember you said that. Anyway, I got the idea to use a bloodhound to track the guy. The chief has one of the best at tracking men, but the dog is one of his favorites. I kind of borrowed him without telling the chief. I guessed that maybe the thief was someone staying at the hotel. Thunder—that's the name of the chief's dog—hit on a scent almost immediately."

Annja grinned, enjoying the laconic way the detective spun the tale. The experience was even more amusing because she knew he was lying, probably making it up on the spot.

"Well, Thunder lit out. I did my best to keep up. But you have to imagine the scene. We're talking a five-star hotel here. Thunder is racing down the hallway, hits the stairwell, and down we go. He's baying to beat the band. You ever heard a bloodhound working a trail?"

Annja nodded, grinning wider now.

"I'm talking about those long, loud, *mournful* howls. If you don't know what it is, you might think somebody was getting killed. Or maybe it was some kind of monster loose in the hotel. Well now, there were a lot of people in that hotel who hadn't heard a bloodhound baying before."

"Must have really gotten a lot of attention," Annja said.

"We did. Way more than I ever wanted to. The chase ended up in the hotel lobby. The guy was there checking out when Thunder hit him. His bag popped open when it hit the floor. Jewelry, cash and panties scattered everywhere. The thief pulled a gun and shot Thunder before I had a chance to clear leather with my pistol."

"Poor dog."

"Nah. Thunder's all right. Just grazed his scalp. But it was enough to leave him scarred and gun shy. The chief wasn't happy about that." McIntosh shrugged. "So that's how I ended up on administrative leave."

"And you were the first person the Kirktown Police Department thought to call when things got out of hand here." Annja smiled in mock wonder. She started clapping, drawing the attention of everyone in the room.

McIntosh had the decency to look embarrassed. Maybe he really was, she thought. He reached over and took Annja's hands, stopping her from clapping.

Annja twisted her hands from his and leaned back, crossing her arms over her breasts. "That's the most creative load of BS I've seen someone come up with on the spot in a long time."

"What are you talking about?" McIntosh looked mystified.

"You're a Fed, McIntosh. You're using the Atlanta PD as a cover. No one around here would know you."

Some of the easygoing demeanor dropped from McIntosh's face. His features took on a distant hardness. "You *are* an interesting woman, Ms. Creed."

"One that has a job to do, and I can't do it here. So either cut to the chase or let me call my attorney."

"I'm with Homeland Security. We have power you haven't even seen. The attorney happens when I say it happens," McIntosh said firmly.

"Great. There's nothing more I like than being threatened by my own government. I get enough of government meddling when I'm on digs overseas." Annja took a deep breath. "I've been on the phone with the producer of the television show I work for every thirty minutes since I've been here." She wondered if her pseudo-celebrity status could actually be useful.

"I'm aware of your television presence," McIntosh said, sounding unimpressed.

"I've talked him out of hiring a crew out of Atlanta to cover this." Annja paused for dramatic effect. "So far. But one missed phone call, you can bet he's going to send someone in."

McIntosh reflected on the situation for a moment. "You get more interesting the more I know you."

"You should see me in action with an attorney and a camera crew, then."

"Have you had dinner, Ms. Creed?"

A glance at her watch told Annja it was almost two in the morning. "No."

"Let's get out of here and get something to eat. And I'll tell you why Homeland Security is interested in this."

"Can I bring the stone?" she asked.

McIntosh hesitated for just a second. "Sure."

4

The Clover Bee Truck Stop lay west of Kirktown along the highway that connected the city to Atlanta. The diner glowed against the darkness. Several 18-wheelers sat parked for the night in the lots outside.

"Not exactly haute cuisine," McIntosh apologized as he parked the car. He reached into the back for a slim metal briefcase. "But at two o'clock in the morning, you're not going to get much to choose from in Kirktown."

Annja slung her backpack over one arm and picked up the cloth bag holding the stone. Professor Hallinger had looked at her in surprise as she'd left with the artifact, but he hadn't asked any questions.

"Trust me. An all-night diner is great compared to having to eat powdered eggs out of a cup while holding your hand over it and hoping the dust doesn't completely wipe out the flavor. You swallow the eggs without chewing so you won't have to hear the grit grinding," Annja said.

McIntosh held open the door.

Inside the building, the convenience-store area occupied the left side, filled with spinner racks containing DVDs, books, audio books and maps. Phone-card vending machines shared space with video games and packaged, single-serving traveler's aids. Shelves in the center of the store contained everything from snacks to phone accessories to DVD players.

The restaurant area was rustic, made of large timbers and bathed in the golden glow of lamps mounted in wagon wheels. Glass tops covered red-and-white-checked tablecloths.

"Well," McIntosh said, "it's better than I'd hoped."

A short, heavyset woman led them to a booth. Even though it was dark, Annja wanted to sit by the window after having been cooped up down in the warehouse's furnace room and the police department.

McIntosh sat across from her. He put the briefcase on the bench seat beside him.

"Bowling ball?" the woman asked when Annja put the cloth bag on the table.

Annja smiled. "Paperweight."

The woman shrugged. "Must be for a big stack of papers. Do you know what you want to drink?"

"Diet Coke. Do you have breakfast?" Annja asked.

"Twenty-four hours a day, hon."

"The cook any good?"

"I eat here."

"Good enough for me. I'm ready to order." Annja's stomach rumbled as she looked at McIntosh.

"Me, too. Start and I'll catch up." McIntosh gave the menu a cursory glance.

Annja stuck with breakfast, ordering eggs over easy, hash browns with onions and cheese and jalapeños, toast, biscuits and gravy, sides of sausage and bacon and a pecan waffle. She also asked for milk and orange juice.

The server glanced at her in surprise.

"She's not shy, is she?" McIntosh asked.

"I was going to ask how you afford to keep her." The server took McIntosh's order, collected the menus and retreated.

Annja took her notebook computer from her backpack, placed it on the table and powered it up. "You're buying," she said.

"Why?"

"Because I'm down here as a freebie, and Homeland Security has deep pockets these days. Otherwise, we don't talk."

"As long as we talk, then." McIntosh looked at the computer screen.

The screensaver showed a crude drawing of a female warrior holding a spear while standing atop a wall. She wore a gold crown and was adorned with gold bracelets and a necklace of cat's teeth, either leopard or lion. Annja had never found out which.

McIntosh pointed at the screen. "Who's that?"

"Queen Amina. Or Aminatu, depending on your source material. She was queen of Zazzau during the last part of the sixteenth century. She led her troops in battle and negotiated—at the business end of a spear—safe passage for all her trade caravans."

"I've never heard of her. Or Zazzau."

"I hadn't, either, until I went to Nigeria."

"So as an archaeologist, you don't know about all of history?"

"Do you know about every murder that took place in Atlanta? Last year?"

"I suppose that is a lot to know."

"I've got an ongoing education. It's better to accept that and move forward."

"What were you doing in Nigeria?"

"The same kind of work I'm doing here." Annja frowned. "But what I was studying wasn't the same. While I was there, I was studying the culture of a fierce, dynamic people who dominated parts of the trans-Atlantic trade routes. Here, I'm helping Professor Hallinger find out who those murder victims were."

"I thought they were slaves trying to flee along the Underground Railroad."

"They were. But they were also Hausa."

McIntosh nodded toward the stone. "That's what the stone tells you?"

"Partly. Also the signs on their weapons and some of the copper bracelets they wore. They were slaves. I don't know how long they had been in the United States. But they kept the Hausa ways in spite of their circumstances."

"How old is that stone?" McIntosh asked.

"I'll have to do some tests on it, but I think it was around a hundred years old when it went into that furnace room."

"That makes it between two and three hundred years old."

Annja nodded.

"What is the stone? Some kind of religious icon?"

"No. It's more like a—" Annja hesitated. "A book," she said.

"I guess they didn't believe in light reading material."

McIntosh's quick, offhand dismissal of what the people in that furnace room had accomplished offended Annja. She pinned him with her gaze. "Do you know much about what a slave's life was like during those years?"

"Only what they teach you in high school," he said.

"Have you ever seen slavery? Been in countries where it still exists to this day?"

"No."

"Then don't act like this is a joke. Generations of people lived hard, small lives filled with fear, oppression and abuse."

McIntosh looked at her. "Hey, I can tell I touched a nerve here. I apologize. I didn't mean to do that."

Annja forced herself to take a deep breath. "It's not you. It was being down there with those bodies today. Not all slaves were treated harshly, but those people were. Most of those bodies in the furnace room showed fracture lines where their arms and legs had been broken. Several of them were missing fingers. The smallest skeleton down there, a boy maybe twelve or thirteen, was missing half a foot. The cut through the bone was clean."

"An accident?"

"No. Slaves who ran off usually got hobbled in some way. One of those ways was to chop off half a foot or the whole foot. I'd bet that's what happened to him."

McIntosh grimaced. "Not exactly breakfast conversation."

"You didn't bring me here for breakfast conversation." Annja didn't feel sorry for having said what she did. "I didn't come here for breakfast conversation."

The server returned with their drinks.

"What I'm trying to point out is the incredible risks those men— or whoever was responsible—took in hiding this stone." Annja reached into her backpack and brought out her digital camera. She quickly hooked the camera up to the notebook computer through a USB connection.

"What are you doing?" McIntosh asked.

"I'm going to post a few of the pictures I took today on a few of the newsgroups I'm a member of."

A troubled look tightened McIntosh's face. "I don't know if I should allow that."

Annja focused on him, unsheathing some of the anger that roiled through her. "Do you know what this record represents?"

McIntosh let out a breath. "No."

"Neither do I. Posting pictures on these newsgroups is one of the avenues I have open to me. Evidently this stone is interesting to you and Homeland Security or you wouldn't be here."

"I'm sure we have experts who could look at that stone and decipher it," he said.

"If you had someone who could do that, or one of your supervisors thought it was necessary, you'd have already taken the stone," Annja said.

McIntosh said nothing.

"You're not here because of the stone, are you?"

After a brief pause, McIntosh shook his head.

Annja studied him. "If it wasn't the stone, it must have been the men. They moved like military men. Soldiers." She let that last thought hang.

McIntosh didn't go for the bait.

"You know who they are. But you don't know what brought them here," she said, trying another approach.

Shifting uncomfortably, McIntosh folded his arms and leaned back. "You're way too good at this."

"It's just a process of elimination. I'm in a field where I have to make educated guesses about things that happened hundreds and thousands of years ago. By comparison to millions of years of history, the present-day political atmosphere is a piece of cake. Something about those men made you—or Homeland Security—paranoid. If you want to know what I know, we need to talk."

"This is a sensitive issue," McIntosh said.

"One of the students was shot tonight." Thankfully, Annja had been told he would recover. "I'd say that was pretty serious."

"Have you ever heard of a man named Tafari?" McIntosh asked.

Annja started to say no, but then a vague whisper of memory tugged at her. "I heard the name while I was in Nigeria. He's into black market goods and drugs, I think."

"How do you know that?" McIntosh's eyebrows knitted.

"Look," Annja said, "you can ask me questions with the hope of getting information or of confirming your paranoia. But you can't do both. If you want information, it's going to be a two-way street. If you're just interested in making yourself paranoid, I'm just going to eat breakfast."

"All right. Information, then." McIntosh put his elbows on the table and pressed his hands together. His eyes never stopped roving, but they never neglected Annja, either. "Tafari isn't just a guy into black market goods and drugs. That's actually the tip of the iceberg. He's a warlord. One of the most feared in the area."

The title *warlord* wasn't just thrown around in Africa. Even before she'd gone there, Annja had known that parts of the continent were torn apart by the existence of what were basically feudal rulers. They were hard men driven by their own desires and needs.

"You're familiar with this kind of man?"

Annja shook her head. "I've never met one of them. But I've heard stories."

"Whatever you've heard, it's worse." McIntosh turned to the briefcase, flipped through the combination lock and took a thick file from inside. He opened the file on the table, using one side to block all other views.

Annja stared at the cruel face featured in the top picture. It was a waist-up shot of a powerful-looking African with beads and shells in his hair. He held an unfiltered cigarette to his lips. Blue-black tribal tattooing marked his skin, as did scars from past wounds. He wore a khaki BDU festooned with grenades and knives.

"Tafari?" Annja asked.

"Yeah." McIntosh's eyes never moved from the man's face. "This guy is a stone killer. If he decided that he didn't like you, if there was a buck to be made in the deal, he'd kill you in a heartbeat."

Annja watched as the Homeland Security agent flipped through other photographs. All of them were graphic and in full color.

"We want him for crimes against Americans." McIntosh tapped

a picture that showed three dead men lying at the side of a dirt road. "Tafari has killed tourists, as well as relief workers. England wants him for the same thing. Even the United Nations wants him taken off the board."

As Annja watched, more pictures of gruesome murders were quietly turned over, building a stack in no time. "I get that he's a killer. But what does that have to do with me?" she asked.

"Not you." McIntosh flipped through the photographs and pulled one out. The photo was obviously a police mug shot, showing the man full face and in profile. "Recognize him?"

"No."

"His name is Nwankwo Ehigiator. He was one of the men in Dack Tatum's group."

"The men who invaded the dig site?"

"That's right."

Annja shook her head. "I don't know him. I don't know Dack Tatum, either." But there was something about the name that sounded familiar.

"Dack Tatum is Christian Tatum's brother."

The name struck a chord. "Christian Tatum owned the warehouse where the bodies were found," Annja said.

"At one time. From what I got from Ehigiator, Dack was here because of his brother. Until tonight, Christian had evidently been entertaining dreams of political office. Unfortunately, the Atlanta police have taken him into custody at this point and he's being charged with conspiracy to commit murder."

"Christian Tatum sent his brother to blow up the warehouse?" Annja couldn't believe it.

"Yeah."

"Why?"

"The arresting officer who took Tatum from his home said that he was there with a journal. They're going over it now. It belonged to one of the Tatum ancestors."

"Jedidiah?" Annja asked. "Jedidiah Tatum built and owned the textile mill."

"Horace," McIntosh said. He flipped through his notebook. Annja noticed the pages were covered with a strong, neat hand. "He was Jedidiah's son. The old man beat the kid and made him work with the slaves in the fields. As a result, the kid hated the slaves. He found the group in the furnace under the textile mill and dynamited them. His father nearly killed him because it destroyed the old furnace and caused a cave-in. But by that time the new system had already been built. Jedidiah decided to leave the furnace room buried to cover up his son's crime."

The cold-blooded act shocked Annja even though she'd seen the blasted remnants in the room. "Why did Horace do it?"

"To get back at the escaped slaves."

"For escaping? That doesn't make sense. He could have told his father."

McIntosh shrugged. "I don't know the particulars. Horace was eleven. You find a kid that age who's homicidal, generally they don't think much past the next thing on their list. If they have a list."

"Can I see that journal?" Annja asked.

The federal agent hesitated.

"It might help me identify the people in that furnace room."

"I'll see if I can make that happen," he said.

"You still want the translation from the stone. I can make *that* happen," Annja said.

McIntosh smiled. "Done. I'll have the book here by morning."

The waitress arrived with platters of food and quickly served it. Annja and McIntosh forgot about conversation for a moment while they dealt with the meal.

"CHRISTIAN TATUM WANTED to blow up the building in case any evidence about his ancestor's murder still existed," McIntosh said as he pushed his empty plate away. "The building was sold during the Depression. I don't think anyone thought much about it after it was boarded up in the 1970s. Then the bodies were found. So Christian Tatum called his brother."

Annja sat back in the booth. Her eyes kept straying to the stone covered in Hausa writing. Her brain picked at words here and there. She wanted to go back to her hotel room and work.

"Homeland Security got interested in what was happening here because of the other man you identified. Ehigiator. Who is he?" Annja asked.

"Ehigiator is a mercenary, like Dack Tatum. Professional soldier for hire. He's been linked to Tafari on several occasions."

"You think Tafari sent him to join Tatum's group of mercenaries?"

"No. Ehigiator has been with Dack Tatum's group for the past year and a half. During that time, Ehigiator has worked several solo assignments for Tafari. Assassinations of police and political figures who have pursued him or who have gone into the bush in an effort to get the villages he preys on to stand against him. We know Tafari was interested in something at the site because one of the snitches we use brought us that information."

"But you don't know what it was?"

"Not precisely, no. However, we do know that Tafari is interested in West African artifacts. The snitch who contacted us told us that Ehigiator had been offered a bonus by Tafari if he could recover the Spider Stone."

"Was Dack Tatum working with him?"

"No. Christian Tatum also wanted the stone."

"Do Christian Tatum and Tafari know each other?" Annja asked.

"We don't think so."

"Dack Tatum came after the stone. Otherwise he'd have blown that building apart." With us in it, Annja thought. She shivered a little when she realized how close the dig personnel had come to getting killed.

"We think he wanted it for his brother. Christian Tatum's notes in his ancestor's journals alluded to a treasure that's connected with the stone."

Annja thought about that. Many maps and artifacts came with legends and stories attached to them that suggested treasures could be found if the secret could be unlocked. Most if not all of those myths and legends were false. In fact, there were a number of artifacts said to exist that probably were as ephemeral as the stories themselves.

"Tafari wants the Spider Stone for the treasure?" she asked.

"We don't know why Tafari wants it," McIntosh admitted. "It's enough that he does. All of his life, Tafari has been interested in ways of consolidating his power base. He achieves part of that by using supernatural objects to terrorize the villagers. Hexes. Voodoo. That kind of crap."

"You can't just dismiss voodoo," Annja said quickly.

McIntosh chuckled and shook his head. "Don't tell me you believe in that stuff?"

"I maintain a healthy respect for voodoo. It's a belief system with roots deep in several religions. For those reasons alone, voodoo has power."

"Yeah, well, you can have it. My agency wants a shot at Tafari. If we can use this—" McIntosh glanced over at the stone "—to bring Tafari out into the open, we might be interested."

"Where is Tafari now?"

"In Senegal. He's never left that country. And he hasn't been caught by authorities since he was a kid. He escaped an execution squad somehow." McIntosh finished the rest of his coffee and covered a yawn. "But if he wants that stone, he'll find a way to get to it."

Despite the quiet of the restaurant, Annja again felt as if someone was watching her. She glanced out the window, but the pump area was largely empty. Only a couple of cars were gassing up.

"Something wrong?" McIntosh asked.

"Long day." Annja pushed out of the booth. "Thanks for breakfast, but if I'm going to figure out anything about this artifact, I've got to get back to my hotel and get to work."

McIntosh took out a business card and wrote on the back. "That's my cell number on the back. If you need anything, let me know."

"The journal," Annja replied. "As quick as you can."

He nodded.

Annja reached out for the heavy stone. As soon as she touched it, she felt an electric tingle. And the sensation of being watched grew even stronger.

5

The man's frightened breath could be heard if a person was patient and knew what to listen for.

Tafari practiced patience and did know. He knelt, secluded in the tall grass under a copse of twenty-foot-tall trees. Night covered the land all around him, but the moon was full and bright. And he had a hunter's eyes, trained not to look directly at something, but to look for movement or a void in otherwise natural surroundings.

He listened to the short gasps and plaintive cries as the man called on his gods to protect him. Tafari smiled. There would be no protection. There was no mercy in him tonight. He would not even grant the man a quick death. He wanted to feel the man's terror and smell the stink of it on him.

Slowly, Tafari drew the long knife from the sheath at his waist without a sound. He rose silent as a shadow and stayed low as he stalked the man through the brush and grass, tracking his prey by sound. It was a game he'd played before, with men, as well as animals.

Short and stocky, Tafari had always had a powerful build. Now he wore only a leather loincloth and the knife. His bare feet moved easily across the hard ground, protected by years of calluses. Many of the young men in his group liked European clothing and shoes. They wore those things when they were in the big cities, but Tafari didn't allow them when they were in the brush.

He had only been to Dakar once. His father had taken him when he'd finally given up trying to survive in the brush and had decided to get a job in the city. Three weeks later, his father had been killed, knifed by a stranger in an alley for the coins he carried in his pockets.

Tafari had returned to the jungle where he had been born. Only ten years old, he'd survived by hunting and stealing chickens from the villagers because no one wanted the extra burden of raising another child. Especially one who wasn't their own.

In spite of his hardships and the lack of help, Tafari had flourished. At sixteen, he had joined a Yoruba warlord named Foday who preyed on the villagers and attacked and harassed the white men who came to Senegal to hunt. They'd killed some of them outright, but others they had held for ransom for a time before killing them.

Six years ago, when Tafari had been twenty-seven, a group of British mercenaries had come to Senegal looking for Foday. They found him. They'd been hired by a family who had bought back a corpse. When the mercenaries were finished, so was Foday. They'd killed the warlord and decapitated him, taking his head as proof of his death.

Tafari had gone down in the battle, taking two rounds through the abdomen. The mercenaries had left him for dead. He'd almost died before he was able to stanch the bleeding.

But he had lived. And he'd gotten the group back together, proclaiming himself as leader. He'd only had to kill two other men who had wanted to challenge him. After that, the men realized that he was going to lead them to heights that Foday hadn't taken them. Now the group lived better than they ever had, with their pick of women and anything the villages had to offer.

Over the years, Tafari had taken in three times as many men as Foday had been willing to recruit. Keeping them fed and happy required aggressive planning. That had necessitated having more and better weapons so he could in turn control larger groups.

As a result, he had helped hide al-Qaeda terrorists, when the United States government had invaded Iraq, in exchange for assault weapons. That had earned him eternal enmity from the Americans. Occasionally mercenaries entered the brush seeking the bounty on Tafari's head.

The man he hunted now had been one of them.

Tafari's warriors had allowed the mercenary unit to get deep within the brush, then they'd taken them in the night, killing the guard and stealing the Land Rover the men had driven. On foot, the men had tried to make their way back to civilization.

For the past four nights, Tafari had hunted them, taking them down one at a time. Each night for the previous three nights, he had killed one man.

Tonight he would kill the last one.

Movement broke to his left.

Like a predator, Tafari went immediately still. Action attracted his eye and lifted images out of the darkness. He held the long knife down by his leg.

The man was white, pale against the night. He'd tried to rub mud over his features, but he hadn't been able to conceal himself well. Big and hulking, doubtless made so by working out and the drugs that made men's muscles balloon, he looked like a monster in the darkness. Tafari had deliberately saved the largest man for last. The man wore a camouflage shirt and pants and boots that hadn't been off his feet in three days because the first night Tafari had taken one man's boots and they'd had to travel much more slowly.

Less than fifteen feet away, Tafari could smell the stink of fear on the man. The man had had no rest. Last night, he and the other man had tried to walk through the dark hours. They couldn't. At a cold camp, they'd tried to stay awake all night. Tafari had slept only a few feet away. Then he roused before dawn, walked into the camp, and slit the other man's throat, leaving him dead for the survivor to find.

The man out in the brush had awoken lying next to a dead man. He had run through most of the day, trying to use the sun as his guide because his compass and other equipment had been taken. As a result, he'd gone in a large semicircle and had exhausted himself and what little water he'd carried.

During the day, Tafari had slept and rested, looking forward to his final night of hunting. Taking a fresh grip on the knife, he moved stealthily after the man. He came up on him from behind, levering an arm across the man's forehead and yanking his head back to expose his throat.

"You are dead," Tafari told the man in English. He'd learned the language piecemeal over the years, from other warriors, as well as the Europeans he did business with. In West Africa, English was the chosen language of drug dealers, traffickers in human slavery and the black market.

"No!" the man shouted. He struggled to get free, but Tafari wrapped his legs around the man and rode him like a beast.

"You came here," Tafari said, "to my place. To take *my* life. That is unforgivable. Now you will pay for that with your life."

"Don't! You can't do—!"

Tafari rested the edge of his blade against the man's throat. "I can. You can't stop me."

Squealing in horror, the man tried to run, aiming himself toward a tree.

Taking gleeful pride in the man's fear, Tafari rode him, hanging on despite the man's efforts to pry free the arm around his head. The man's teeth gnashed as he tried to bite his tormentor. He grabbed for the knife. Tafari raked the sharp edge across the man's palm, slicing it to the bone. Blood sprayed everywhere, slung off by the man's exertions.

The man howled again and rammed Tafari into the tree. The impact hurt, but Tafari only drew himself more tightly to the man and laughed in his ear.

"Now," Tafari snarled, "you will die." He clamped his teeth on to the man's ear, tasting the man's blood. When his victim reared his head back to try to tear away from the teeth, Tafari slit his throat and felt hot blood cascade over his hand and arm.

Tafari rode the man to the ground as he died, never once letting him forget who had killed him. When it was over, he stood and hacked the dead man's head from his shoulders.

Holding the man's head by the hair, Tafari stood and presented his offering to the dark gods he worshipped, telling them this was a sacrifice he had made in their honor. If a man had to sacrifice to the gods, Tafari believed it had to be in blood. There was nothing else so precious.

At that moment, a large pharaoh-eagle owl glided across the round face of the silver moon. The bird's tawny, white-and-black feathers gleamed in the light. A dead mouse hung from its talons.

"Both of us were successful hunters tonight, brother," Tafari told the owl. He felt certain the bird's presence was an omen, a promise of good things to come.

The winged predator made no response and quickly disappeared from sight.

Kneeling, Tafari wiped his knife clean on the dead man's clothes, then stood and gave a loud whistle. In the distance, an engine started and headlights sprang to life. He walked toward them, holding on to the head.

The driver pulled the jeep to a stop in front of Tafari. Three other men, all young and armed with assault rifles, sat in the back. Most of them wore tribal tattoos and necklaces of gold and ivory. They flaunted their wealth, because in West Africa wealth meant power.

"You've finished your hunt," Zifa stated. He was young and hard, a man not to be trifled with, though most didn't realize that until too late. Scars covered his arms and there were a few on his handsome face. When he had been younger, in his teens, he had fought with knives for prize money in Dakar. To lose was to die. He had never lost, but he had been cut several times.

"I have." Tafari plopped the dead man's head on the front of the truck. The other heads he'd taken were already tied there, all of them bloated and turning black from the heat. When he was done with them, he intended to have them returned to the man who had hired them.

One of the men in back clambered out with elastic ties. He quickly secured the head to the jeep's hood, then stood back and admired his handiwork.

Tafari waved the man into the jeep. He pulled himself into the passenger seat. "Have you heard from Ehigiator?" he asked the driver.

They had communications equipment at their base. Some of the younger recruits had been to college and had learned about such things. Tafari prided himself on being able to use the knowledge they had for his own agenda.

"No." Zifa put the jeep into gear and pulled around in a tight turn. Then he was following his headlights, using the vehicle's bumper to chop through the brush. There were few roads in northwestern Senegal. Most of the ones off the main thoroughfares were trails villagers used to get from one market to another.

"Perhaps it is too early." Tafari studied the landscape.

"Perhaps." Zifa drove easily, at home with the vehicle as it crashed through the brush. "There is another matter."

"What?"

"The Hausa village to the north."

Tafari knew of the village. Over the past few weeks, the people living there had become a thorn in his paw. "What about them?" he asked.

"They continue their rebellion."

Tafari thought about that. In the overall scheme of things, the village wasn't much. It was like a raindrop in a monsoon. But it had the chance of becoming something much bigger if those who lived there persisted in their defiance of him.

"Why haven't you dealt with this?" Tafari demanded.

Zifa didn't react to the anger in his voice. He focused on his driving, and that angered Tafari further. He had placed Zifa second in command, had killed a man who had been with him longer but didn't have the cunning Zifa did. Failure in that position wasn't an option.

"Jaineba is there," Zifa said. "You said you wanted to deal with her."

Tafari cursed and spit. He didn't want to deal with the old woman. Nor did he want anyone else to deal with her until he knew for certain how he was going to handle her.

"She is there now?"

Zifa nodded.

A trickle of fear seeped through Tafari's bowels. He still didn't know what to do about the old woman, but he couldn't put it off. He glanced at the line of heads bouncing on the jeep's hood. He'd made his offering to Ogun, chief among the *orisha*—the sky gods—and appealed to that god's sense of vengeance, praying that all of his enemies might be struck down in the days to come.

Still, Jaineba was a person of power. Ancient and withered, the old woman was tied to Africa in ways that Tafari still didn't understand.

But he couldn't put off dealing with her if she was getting in his way.

"Take me there," he commanded.

Zifa brought the jeep around, churning dirt as the wheels chewed into the earth.

Reaching back over the seat, Tafari took the Chinese assault rifle one of the men on the rear deck handed him. If he had his choice and the situation demanded it, he would rather kill the old woman with the knife. But she commanded magic. He wasn't too proud to use the rifle if it came to that.

His thoughts strayed to the Spider Stone, wondering if Ehigiator had been successful in wresting it from the Americans and the police. The Spider Stone was important. Especially if all the myths about it were true.

THE PHONE RANG.

Seated in bed at the hotel Professor Hallinger had arranged for her, Annja grabbed the phone by reflex. She pressed the talk button and put it to her ear.

"Hey, Annja."

She recognized Doug Morrell's voice at once. Her producer at *Chasing History's Monsters* had a distinctive New York accent. "Doug." She glanced at the hotel clock. It was almost 4:00 a.m. "You're up late or early," she said.

"Both," Morrell replied. "I'm sneaking home after picking up a girl at Dark Realms."

Annja knew Dark Realms was a Goth bar in Manhattan that her producer liked to frequent. In the nightclub, he was a count and high in the pecking order of wannabe vampires. Although he wouldn't admit it, Doug liked playing a vampire and hanging with the night crowd.

The bar was owned by Baron Riddle, a mysterious millionaire who'd gotten rich with the five Goth clubs he'd built around the United States. There was a waiting list for memberships.

"Sneaking home isn't exactly the gallant thing to do after a tryst," Annja pointed out.

"It wasn't a tryst," he protested. "More like an exchange of fantasies. We did the biting thing. A little playacting with ropes and interrogation—"

"Stop." Annja sat up straighter in bed, trying to work out the kinks she'd developed while working on the translation of the stone.

"What?"

"Too much information. I really don't need to know all the details of your little fang fest. You called at this hour for a reason?" she asked wearily.

"I just heard about you on CNN. The thing down in Atlanta. So I thought I'd give you a call and see if there's anything in it for us."

Annja answered immediately. "No."

"Aw, come on," Doug whined. "This could be big."

"You just want to jump on the coattails of the CNN coverage." Annja couldn't believe the story had made national news. Must be a slow news night. Or maybe they were wanting something off the beaten track, she figured.

"It is an opportunity," Doug replied. "Ratings matter."

"There's nothing for you here. No monsters. Those people were killed 150 years ago by a kid with a grudge and a racial issue."

"We could work with that. Any chance that the warehouse is haunted?"

"I thought you hated ghost stories," Annja said. Every time she had advanced the idea of pursuing a story and had to cite spectral manifestations as the only lure, Doug had shot it down.

"I do hate ghost stories. We're not *Ghosthunters*. We chase monsters."

"No monsters here," Annja said.

"Are you sure about that?"

She reached for the cup of coffee on the nightstand. "I'm sure," she said.

"I'll take a ghost if I have to," Doug said. "Maybe we can parlay it into something else."

"This is legitimate archaeological work." Annja said that slowly, willing it to sink in. Ever since she'd picked up the job at *Chasing History's Monsters* so she could have travel expenses paid for trips to places that she couldn't get to on her own, she'd worked hard to keep her real work separate from the sensationalism the television show demanded. "It's not television fare."

"CNN seems to be running with it. They're even playing you up in the piece. Professor Annja Creed. Don't tell me you haven't seen it."

Annja glanced at the armoire on the other side of the room. She hadn't even opened it. "Haven't even turned the television set on."

"You should."

"It's been a busy night. Maybe you missed the part about us almost getting blown up."

"You almost got blown up?"

Annja sighed. Doug had a tendency to hear only what he wanted to hear. "I guess you didn't call to see how I was doing," she said.

"How are you doing?" Doug asked.

"I'm fine. But I've got a lot of work to do."

"What work?"

"Translating the stone we found."

"What stone?" He sounded excited.

Annja had to smile. Doug Morrell truly had the most one-track mind of anyone she'd ever met. "I need to get back to it. I'll talk to you later."

"I should have asked how you were first, huh?"

"It would have been nice, but it wouldn't have been you."

"I do care that you're all right."

"I know."

"Friends?"

"Friends."

"So if you find out the warehouse was haunted…?"

"Good night, Doug." Annja closed her cell phone. Reluctantly, she got up from the bed and walked to the window. From there she could see the top of the warehouse. The lights of the police car whirled in the darkness.

She walked to her notebook computer and logged on to the hotel's WiFi link. Once she was on the Internet, she opened up the archaeology newsgroups she favored. She'd placed pictures of the Spider Stone and some of the history of the site in the forums under Spider Stone less than an hour earlier. She hadn't expected much, but there were already three responses.

She opened up the first one and began to read.

6

Caught the story on CNN tonight. You're one hot-looking babe. Married? Looking for a cheap fling with a guy who can talk three languages?

Great, Annja thought. And you probably sound just as charming and irresistible in all three languages. She hoped the other postings weren't as juvenile. She skipped the rest of the entry and moved on to the next one.

I blew up the pictures of the stone, hausaboy@africanskys.org wrote. The digital camera you're using is freaking awesome. Wish I could afford one.

That looks like the Hausa language, unless I'm way off base here. Saw the story on CNN and got intrigued.

From what I've been able to translate so far, the stone describes a journey from the author's homeland to America back in 1755.

Okay, Annja thought, I'm evidently dealing with someone who's better versed in the Hausa language than I am. She checked the writer's e-mail and saved it off to a working file.

The date caught her attention. If the stone was dated as being from

1755, it had been one hundred years old before it ended up in the warehouse furnace.

Wait, she chided herself. You're tired. The story might have a date in it, but that doesn't mean that's when the stone was inscribed.

The post continued.

Have you translated the writing? If not, I might be able to assist. I'm Nigerian. Currently going to school at USC. Majoring in computer arts but have an archaeology jones I just can't shake.
If you can shoot the rest of the writing in sequential order, I'd be happy to help.

Even though archaeology relied on discipline, skill and exposure, Annja knew that luck couldn't be beaten. She got her camera out and shot the stone again, overlapping the pictures so the writing could be viewed continuously.

Once she had them finished, she posted them to a Web site she maintained as a clearinghouse for projects. She created a page just for the Spider Stone images.

Then she wrote a note to hausaboy@africanskys.org.

Here are the pics. Thanks for your time! Would love to compare notes when you get something ready.

The third posting was from mythhunter@worldoflegends.net.

Just caught the pics you posted. Can't help you with the language, but maybe with some of the myth behind the stone. Are you familiar with Anansi? He was an African god. A trickster. His legend crossed to North America when slaves were brought over. He's still a major folklore presence in the Caribbean.
Don't know if the rock you're looking at has anything to do with Anansi, but the spider pic is totally cool.

Annja was familiar with Anansi. As a trickster god, Anansi had been a neutral figure, working always for his own ends as much as for the gods or men. According to legend, Anansi was the son of Nyame, the sky god, and taught mankind the skills of agriculture. He also negotiated rain, which put out wildfires that ravaged the countryside. One of his chief duties was acting as intermediary for mankind with other gods.

From what Annja had managed to translate from the stone, Anansi was praised as being an intermediary for whoever had told the tale.

She wrote a quick thank-you note and closed out of the newsgroup.

She stood, took a deep breath and went through a few tai chi forms to loosen up. Go to bed, she told herself. Get some sleep. You've got a full day tomorrow.

She retreated to the shower long enough to soak for a few minutes and clear her head. When she returned, feeling refreshed and more tired at the same time, her cell phone rang.

She scooped it up from the bed, checked the caller ID—thinking it might be Doug Morrell with a new angle and plea—and saw that it was Bart McGilley. She answered.

"Annja?" Bart was a homicide detective in New York. He was also a good friend and resource. He was always there when she needed a date to go to a function in New York. She sometimes reciprocated for him at police functions, allowing both of them to mix and mingle without getting hit on. Annja realized his recent engagement put an end to that part of their relationship.

"Hey," Annja said.

Despite what was going on in his life or the lateness of the hour, Bart McGilley always sounded positive. If Annja didn't know him so well, didn't know that that was just how Bart was, she would have been instantly suspicious. In fact, when she'd first gotten to know him, she had been suspicious. No one could be that well adjusted. Especially not in New York.

"You called," Bart pointed out.

"I did."

"You said the time didn't matter."

"It doesn't," Annja said.

"So what's up?" For Bart, he sounded tired.

"I take it you haven't been watching CNN," Annja said. The story was already cooling off on the news network, but it was still being given a quick mention in the roundup.

"No. Got called in on a multiple homicide between rival gang members. There are some new players in town who haven't learned that they can't lean on Russian *mafiya* territory. Have to tread easy with this one—otherwise the media will play it up and we'll have terrorist stories on everybody's radar again."

"Oh." Annja didn't know what to say. Their professional worlds were like oil and water until she needed background information on someone shady or until Bart had a case that involved art or collectors of artifacts.

"You didn't call to find out about my day," Bart prompted.

Quickly, Annja outlined her situation. As always, Bart was a good listener, never asking questions until she'd finished.

"What can I help you with?" Bart asked.

"I just want to make sure McIntosh is who he says he is." Working as an archaeologist meant double-checking every scrap of information that turned up. She'd learned in the early years that she couldn't always trust people. Some lied intentionally, but others assumed they knew the truth or tended to say what they wanted others to hear or hoped to pull someone into line with their thinking.

"I can do that." Bart paused. "But what you're involved in could be dangerous. Any time you throw the race issue into a volatile environment, it doesn't take much to set things off."

"I know. You should try working a dig site when you've got a couple countries interested in whatever you find. Getting torn between the British government and the Roman Catholic Church is no picnic." That had happened while she'd been working near Hadrian's Wall in England, causing days of delays. The find had turned out to be mildly exotic, the grave of a celebrated Roman general who'd disappeared into history and was at first believed to be the source of the legend of King Arthur. That hadn't turned out to be true, but it had been exciting at the time.

"Yeah, but at least they aren't trying to kill you," Bart pointed out.

They talked for a little while, enjoying the easy camaraderie of their friendship. After making tentative arrangements to meet when she got back to New York, they hung up.

Worn out, Annja glanced at the clock. It was almost 5:00 a.m. She set the alarm for eight o'clock and turned out the light. She slept well, but a spider kept weaving webs throughout her dreams, trying to trap her. Thankfully, she had her sword and managed to cut her way free.

ANNJA WOKE before her alarm sounded. That wasn't unusual. When she was on a dig she never slept for long. She was ready to go again.

She dressed in casual clothes and took a look outside the hotel window. The protesters had returned to the warehouse. There was no sign of the media yet.

She checked the archaeology message boards. There were several new messages. Most of them addressed the mythological nature of Anansi. Annja wasn't too interested in that aspect of the puzzle yet. At best, myths and legends only told part of the story.

But there was a new e-mail from hausaboy@africanskys.org dated only a few minutes earlier.

This isn't the stone you should be looking for. According to the writing on the stone you currently have in your possession, there is another. It is the more important stone. It has a map or something on it. This one is just a record and a false lead, IMHO.

In my humble opinion. Annja decided she would take that. The part of the text and pictographs she had deciphered had alluded to something like what hausaboy was describing.

Looking at the time on the e-mail, she decided to take a chance that he might still be online. She quickly drafted an e-mail to him and sent it.

Are you still on-line?

After a few seconds, an offer to go to instant messaging popped up on her screen. Annja accepted immediately.

Good morning, hausaboy wrote.

I was hoping you would still be on, Annja typed.

I've got class in a few minutes, but I'm cool for now, he replied.

I don't want you to be late.

No sweat. I'm setting the curve in the class.

Annja smiled at that. There was nothing wrong with getting a brainiac for a resource.

Good for you! Let me know when you need to go.

Okay. I looked you up on the Internet, too.

Annja didn't know how to respond to that so she didn't. She never paid attention to what was written about her. She had contributed several articles to different Web sites about archaeology. She wondered if he'd read some of them.

Found out about *Chasing History's Monsters*. That surprised me.

Not my best work. *CHM* allows me to go places I want to go without paying for it, Annja typed.

That's cool. Checked out a few of your articles. You know your stuff. If I'd thought you were just out looking for freebie research, I'd have taken a pass.

Thanks. Archaeology is what I do. *CHM* is part of what it takes to get to do it more.

I can respect that. Anyway, what I've translated so far is that there are at least two stones. The one you sent me pictures of and another one.

The smaller one you mentioned, Annja wrote.

Yeah. I think it's the key to this stone or something else.

Annja was intrigued. Why do you think that?

Because of some of the symbols copied to the large stone. It's like whoever inscribed the large stone knew someone else would expect them to be there. They're on there out of context.

Explains why I was having problems with the translation.

LOL. Probably. Bunch of gobbledygook the way it's written now. You kind of have to read between the lines.

Thinking of the war party that had accompanied the Spider Stone, Annja wrote, Do you know who might have been looking for the stones?

No. The text just mentions the enemies of the people.

The people?

The tribe the stones belonged to, hausaboy explained.

According to what I was able to translate, this Spider Stone was a gift of the gods, Annja typed.

Right. A gift from Anansi. You're familiar with him?

Spider god. Trickster. The myths about Anansi got integrated with a lot of cultures in North and South America.

Exactly. Anyway, this smaller stone was supposed to have been given to this tribe by Anansi. It was a promise.

A promise about what? Annja asked.

That they would always exist. That they wouldn't be destroyed.

That thought settled uneasily in Annja's head. It was a big promise, and one that hadn't been kept. For the stone to have come to the United States meant that at some point that village had been invaded by slavers who had stolen the people away to sell on the slave blocks. It made her sad, but slavery had centuries of sadness tied to it.

Have you ever heard of a stone like this? she typed.

No. But I did a search for it last night. You probably did, too, her translator wrote.

Annja felt chagrined.

No, I didn't. I had to deal with the police last night. Never even thought about it.

She hadn't thought about it. The idea that other people knew about it had never occurred to her.

Look at this Web link, hausaboy wrote.

Annja clicked on it and another page opened up. The header immediately identified the Web site as a collector's market specializing in West African artifacts.

Several pictures showed statues of warriors, gods and animals from different cultures like a four-hundred-year-old wooden Igbo maiden mask, a two-thousand-year-old Nok ceramic sculpture of a lion, colorful *djembe* and *dunan* drums, a Benin copper funerary mask almost eight hundred years old and several ivory carvings, as well as wooden ones.

Annja looked for the stone but couldn't find it.

I don't see the stone, she typed.

No pic. Look under Searching For.

Halfway down the page, Annja found a listing for art pieces that collectors were searching for. The entry read:

Looking for Anansi Stone. Hausa design. The stone has an image of a spider (Anansi) on it. Some refer to it as Anansi's Promise. Information leading to the piece will be rewarded.
Contact Yousou Toure
(yousou.toure@artforms.senegal)

The instant-messaging box beeped for attention as a new message cycled into it.

Did you find it?

Yes. Just looking at it. The stone's been buried for over 150 years. That means someone has been looking for it for at least that long.

Some families get it into their heads to collect stuff their ancestors were looking for. This could be a case of that.

Annja silently agreed.

Anyway, I thought you might be interested, hausaboy wrote.

I am. Thank you.

Okay, gotta go. I'll keep working on these pics.

Do that. If something comes to fruition out of this, I'll hook you up for a finder's fee, Annja typed.

You don't have to do that, but if you want to, feel free. Tuition isn't getting any cheaper.

Thanks! Annja shut down the instant-message block, then closed her computer.

ANNJA'S PHONE RANG when she was in the hotel lobby. She paused, shifted her backpack and retrieved the device from a side pocket. "Annja Creed."

"Did I wake you?" Professor Hallinger's voice sounded chipper and alert.

"No, I've been up for most of an hour."

"So have I. I couldn't sleep anymore, so I finally gave up and came to the dig. Where are you?"

"Leaving the hotel. You'll see me in a few minutes."

"Have you had breakfast?"

"Not yet."

"If you'll stop at Wally's, the small café across the street from the hotel and pick up two breakfasts, I'll buy."

Annja smiled. "You've got a deal, Professor."

"It's the least I can do after everything I've gotten you involved with," he said.

"Are you kidding? I live for this kind of thing."

"Still." Hallinger cleared his throat. "I've got something to show you when you get here."

"Taunt me like that and you may not get breakfast. I may come straight over. Curiosity often gets the better of me."

"You'll want breakfast. *I* want breakfast. We may work straight through lunch."

"All right. I just finished swapping e-mail with a guy at USC, a student, who knows the Hausa language."

"He's studying it?"

"No. He's from Nigeria and he has an interest in history."

"How fortunate," the professor said.

"Not fortunate," Annja said because she'd seen other information come by way of the newsgroups. "That's just the World Wide Web at work."

Hallinger sighed. "I step into the cyberworld with extreme reluctance. Sometimes I wonder what archaeologists a thousand years from now are going to think of our culture."

"We've got more written for them to study than at any time in history. Just the personal information on MySpace.com and other places would more than fill the library at Alexandria. Much of what we know about life in Restoration England during the seventeenth century comes from the diaries of Samuel Pepys. He covered what happened during the plague as well as the Great Fire of London."

"Yes, but what if an electromagnetic pulse were to strike the earth?" Hallinger asked. "Either from a solar flare or from a smart bomb? All those computer records could be wiped out in the blink of an eye. Everything would be lost. To that future archaeologist, it would appear that we were a culture of wastrels, producing diapers and plastic bottles that will last a thousand years."

"Let's concentrate on what we have here now," Annja suggested.

"You're right, of course." Hallinger sounded embarrassed. "What did your cyber colleague tell you?"

"I'll tell you when I get there." Annja folded the phone and put it away. But before she'd reached the door, she heard someone call her name.

"Miss Creed."

Turning, Annja discovered an old woman sitting in one of the chairs in the hotel lobby.

She was black and looked to be seventy or eighty years old. Dressed in a yellow print dress and wearing thick glasses, she reminded Annja of the nuns who'd raised her at the orphanage. She held a thick bound book against her chest, arms crossed over it protectively.

"Yes?" Annja stepped toward the woman.

"I wanted to talk to you," the woman said. "About the people found in the basement of that building." She paused. "I think I know who they were."

7

Jaineba sat cross-legged in the small hut and breathed in the smoke of the white *ubulawu* coming from the small brazier hanging from the iron chain connected to the spit over the fire. She wore a loose-fitting grand *bubu,* a big dress popular in Senegal, and a scarf that held her cotton-white hair back from her face. The acrid smoke burned her nasal passages for a short time, then it came easier.

White *ubulawu* was also called the dream root. A botanist Jaineba had once guided through the savanna had told her the root was called *silene capensis.* Jaineba had no need for the names educated men gave things. She practiced her magic as her grandmother had taught her. Too many things changed in the world, and it had been that way since she'd been a little girl.

Sometimes when the young children of the villages saw her for the first time—that they remembered, anyway—they tried to guess how old she was. Even Jaineba was no longer certain. No one had marked the year of her birth. They only remembered who had been around when she'd been born. She guessed that she was eighty or ninety. An old woman by anyone's standards.

But her job was not yet done. Sadly, she had no granddaughter to pass her craft to. Some days she found great sadness in that. But the gods were good to her. No matter the sadness, every day she found something to rejoice in. Even after all that she had seen, wondrous and miraculous things like a child being born or a lion passing by her without offering any threat or a desert transforming into a beautiful flower garden during the rainy season, there was always something new. Or she could borrow the new eyes of the young and exult in the discoveries children made.

She breathed in the smoke and chanted. She wanted to slip into the dreamworld. That seemed easier these days, as if that world paralleled hers now instead of meeting occasionally like forbidden lovers.

The white *ubulawu* aided her in her visits to the dreamworld. The smoke's magic also held at bay the evil spirits that feasted on the unwary.

She hunted for the dreams she'd been having, hoping to see more this time. Still, they eluded her.

You're being too selfish, she chided herself. Only seldom do the gods allow you to peek into what they have planned for the world. You can't demand more than they are willing to give.

Footsteps sounded in the doorway.

Jaineba breathed out, releasing her hunt for the dreamworld. She opened her eyes and blinked at the rectangle of harsh morning light. It framed the woman standing there. But she was not the woman Jaineba had seen in her dreams.

This woman was black. The one in the dreams was white.

Her visitor was tall, several inches taller than Jaineba's own five feet, and young, probably no more than thirty. She had clear brown eyes and wore her hair cut short. Her face was slender and strong, an easy face to get to know, and one that turned the heads of men when she passed by. She had a woman's full body, though Jaineba felt the woman was on the thin side. She wore jeans, hiking boots and a white pullover that contrasted sharply with her dark skin.

She was British, speaking in that clipped and rapid accent and having only a few words of the Hausa tongue. Jaineba knew her name was Tanisha Diouf. She was an engineer working for the Childress Corporation exploring for oil.

"Little mother," Tanisha said quietly. "Am I interrupting?"

The young woman's formal manners had surprised Jaineba. Most European, Arab and American people who spoke to her had a habit of dismissing her out of turn because she was old or because they'd heard that she practiced magic.

"No." Jaineba waved her into the hut. "Come. Come."

Hesitant, Tanisha entered the hut.

Jaineba waved to an area on the other side of the fire.

Tanisha sat and quietly waited.

That was another quality that Jaineba liked. The young woman knew how to offer respect.

"Are you well?" Jaineba asked.

"I am. And you?"

"The gods watch over me, child. You need not concern yourself over my welfare."

"I know. But I do." Tanisha smiled. "Without you, I could not get the things done that I need to do."

"You are blessed. I have told you that."

Tanisha smiled. "I know. But some days I don't feel so blessed."

"How are your children?"

The woman had two sons, healthy sons, which would make her a wealthy woman in most villages. They were six and eight, and boys in the truest sense because they were unafraid of exploring their new environment. When their mother wasn't around, which wasn't often, the boys talked of hunting lions with the other boys of the villages. Jaineba knew their mother would panic if she only knew.

"They're fine. I didn't bring them with me this morning," Tanisha said.

"That's too bad. I would have enjoyed seeing them." Jaineba fanned the embers of the dream root. They burned quickly, putting another small cloud of smoke into the hut.

"They won't be happy when I tell them that I saw you without them. They enjoy your stories."

"Of course they do. All children enjoy my stories." Jaineba looked at the younger woman. "The stories belong to them, too."

Tanisha didn't respond to the statement.

Jaineba was used to that. The mother doesn't feel the kinship with the land that her children do. She was all right with that, and she understood it. Children's senses were so much more alive than an untrained adult's.

Since they had met, Jaineba had told Tanisha that her home was here, in Africa. Not in England. Despite her own denial, Tanisha Diouf was one of the Hausa people, one of those whose ancestors had been sold on the slave auction block.

"Why did you come here?" Jaineba asked.

"To see you."

"Have you eaten?"

"Yes."

"You can eat again. You are too skinny." Jaineba stood, grabbing hold of her gnarled walking staff and pulling herself to her feet. She shuffled to the door of the hut and looked out.

Tanisha's Land Rover had caused a stir in the village. Children stood around it in fascination, admiring and touching the vehicle with hesitant but curious fingers. Most of them had never seen anything like it up close. The village was normally a place travelers passed by. No one ever stayed there.

Jaineba called to one of the women and told her to bring food. Then she turned back to her guest. "Why did you come to see me?"

Tanisha frowned. "Last night someone tampered with the trucks and the equipment at the camp."

"It was no one at this place." Jaineba settled herself on the pile of furs the village women had given her to rest her bones.

"I didn't think so. But I need to find out who it was, and I need to find a way to get them to stop."

"There are many who don't want to see the white man's machines tear through our lands."

"The refinery that Childress is going to build will provide jobs," Tanisha said.

Jaineba heard the timbre in the other woman's words. Tanisha Diouf believed what she was saying. "Those who oppose you don't feel they need jobs," the old woman said.

"They may say they don't want the jobs, but they'll make a big difference to the people who live here," Tanisha said.

"Working for the outsiders changes everyone's life. Change is not always something people want. Often it's not even good."

"This could be good. It could mean health benefits for families. There would be more food. No one would have to go to bed hungry."

Jaineba looked at the foreign woman for a time. She liked her. Tanisha Diouf was a strong-willed woman who made her way in a man's world. Jaineba understood that. With her magic and her ability to heal, she walked in a man's world, as well, taking up the mantle of leadership. Too few women did that.

"I hear what you are saying, child," Jaineba replied in a calm voice.

"It would help if you would talk to these people."

"Not everyone wants to listen to an old woman."

"You could make them listen," Tanisha implored. "They do listen to you."

"Perhaps," Jaineba said. "But let me ask you a few questions."

Tanisha waited. A sense of urgency burned in her eyes.

"Does everyone in your country get enough to eat? Do all the children have full bellies before they go to bed?"

Uncertainty made Tanisha's face heavy. "No. But the opportunity is there. It's just that not everyone takes advantage of the programs that are available."

"Does everyone have a job?"

"All the people that want one have a job," Tanisha said.

Jaineba felt compassion for the younger woman as she made excuses for her country and her way of life. "Does everyone who has a job have the job they wish?"

Tanisha sighed. "That would be too much to ask."

"Is it?"

"The opportunity is there."

"But the opportunity for servitude at a job or a corporation also exists. Even the men who work for Childress Corporation are not all happy working here. They would rather be somewhere else. Yet they are here. Away from their families and the way of life they're familiar with."

Tanisha fell silent.

"What you offer, what your employer offers, is not a bad thing." Jaineba felt compassion for the younger woman. So young, and so certain she had all the right answers. "But the changes they would make in our land would be permanent."

"It's progress."

"Africa," Jaineba stated quietly, "is familiar with progress. We have had it since the Europeans first began trading with our country. In the north and in the south. *Progress* is forced on us at every turn. Our people have died as a result of the diseases they have unleashed there. I have seen whole countries abandoned by the Europeans and Americans when it suited them. They took away the jobs and all the money they brought into those countries. But they left their sicknesses, their vendors selling products families could no longer truly afford, and the feeling that nothing Africa had to offer was good enough. Do you know what it's like to live without hope?"

Sadness darkened Tanisha's eyes. "No. Not to that degree."

"Women in this village have buried their children," Jaineba said quietly. "They have seen their husbands and sons lured away to big cities like Dakar. They have seen their friends and daughters taken by the warlords, to be used, then cast aside or killed." She was silent for a moment. "And all of this has come about because of *progress.*"

"It doesn't have to be that way," Tanisha said.

"Africa," Jaineba said, "has its own pace. We are the cradle of life. Most scientists believe humankind began here. We had, until all the genetically modified crops were pushed on our farmers, more plant diversification than any other place in the world. Did you know that?"

"Yes."

The woman whom Jaineba had sent for breakfast stopped in the doorway. She held bowls of *uji,* a thin gruel made from cassava. Her daughter held pieces of a fresh mango.

Jaineba nodded.

The woman and her daughter entered the hut respectfully and served the breakfast. Tanisha was polite and made certain to thank both, meeting their eyes with her own.

The little girl, no more than six or seven, smiled shyly. Jaineba thought perhaps Tanisha was the first foreigner the little girl had ever seen.

The mother scolded her daughter for staring, then apologized to Tanisha in her own language. Of course, Tanisha didn't understand. That was one reason she'd sought Jaineba. She needed an interpreter.

"What's she saying?" Tanisha asked.

"She wants you to forgive her daughter," Jaineba explained.

"For what?"

"For staring and being impolite."

Tanisha smiled reassuringly at the mother and daughter. "Please tell them that I took no offense, and that her daughter should be curious."

Jaineba did.

Reaching into her pocket, Tanisha took out a small vial of lip gloss. She applied it to her lips, then offered it to the little girl.

The little girl hesitated, looking up at her mother. The mother looked at Jaineba. The old woman nodded. With her mother's permission, the little girl took the lip gloss and awkwardly put it on her lips, looking pleased with herself.

Tanisha laughed, and the sound within the hut was infectious. "I love my sons," she said as the mother and child departed, "but I would have loved to have a daughter."

"It's not too late," Jaineba pointed out. "You are still young."

"No way." Tanisha used the wooden spoon to eat the *uji*. "I have a career. I don't have time to have another child."

"So you're trading a dream of yours for your own personal progress?"

"Two boys are almost more than I can keep up with," Tanisha said. She frowned. "In fact, I often feel torn between them and my job. I was fortunate Mr. Childress was generous enough to allow them to come with me."

"If they had not come, where would they be?"

"At my mother's."

Jaineba knew from past conversations that Tanisha's husband had been a soldier and had been killed three years earlier.

Tanisha popped a piece of mango into her mouth, chewed and swallowed. "The problem with the attacks on the equipment remains."

Jaineba finished her *uji* and set the bowl to one side. "You must be patient."

"I can't afford to be patient. If I don't find some way to stop the attacks, the security teams are going to start taking more punitive action."

"What will they do?"

"Mr. Childress hires mercenaries," Tanisha said. "Not all of them are good men. In fact, I'd say most of them aren't good men." She shook her head. "I don't know what they'll do, but I know they won't sit back quietly. Mr. Childress isn't paying them to do that."

"What are you afraid these men will do?" Jaineba asked.

"Go into the bush after the men who are damaging the equipment."

"That will be dangerous for them."

"They know that. I think several of them are looking forward to it."

Jaineba breathed in deeply. Some of the smoke from the dream root remained. She closed her eyes for a moment and reached for the woman in her dreams. For just a moment, Jaineba sensed the woman. She's close, she told herself. She already has the trail. She will be here soon.

"Did you hear me?" Tanisha asked.

"Yes." Jaineba opened her eyes. "Things will work out, child. You must believe that."

"Someone is going to get hurt if this keeps up. I can't sit by and do nothing."

"There is nothing you can do. These men will clash, and some will be hurt. Possibly even killed. Surely you knew that when you took this job."

"No." Tanisha spoke quietly. "No, I didn't. Or maybe I didn't want to believe it."

"You are coming to a crossroads, and you will have to make a choice. I'm sorry. I wish that your way could be easier, but it isn't. This is the path the gods have put you on."

"I can't accept that there's nothing I can do," Tanisha said.

"You're not responsible for this."

"I'm working as lead on the engineering team. I have to assume some responsibility."

"What about Childress? Shouldn't he share some of the responsibility, as well?"

"Mr. Childress is responsible to the shareholders in the corporation. He has to regard their interests first."

"He will do nothing when fighting breaks out," Jaineba stated.

"I don't know. He's put a lot of his own money into this venture. He wants to see the oil refinery turn a profit."

Jaineba nodded, knowing she shouldn't take any of this on but unwilling to leave Tanisha alone with her distress. "I will see if there is anything that can be done," she said quietly.

"Thank you. I hoped you would say that."

"I can't promise anything."

"I know."

The roars of straining engines sounded outside.

"Was anyone with you?" Jaineba asked.

Tanisha shook her head.

Reluctantly, dreading what she felt certain she would find, Jaineba pulled herself up along her staff. Her bones felt weak and fragile. She swept a hand over her dress, smoothing out the wrinkles. She walked outside as the engines growled a final time and died.

A military-style jeep sat alongside Tanisha's Land Rover, which proudly proclaimed Childress Construction, Inc. on its sides. The English vehicle was a rolling billboard for the corporation.

Several warriors of the village gathered. They stood in pants and shirts, most of them barefoot. Some of them had weapons, mostly machetes they had brought with them from the farms where they worked, but a few of them had pistols and old single-shot Enfield rifles. None of them stepped forward to challenge the intruders.

The women sent the young children to the huts. The village was built on the eastern side of the hill. Most people coming from Dakar along the old trade roads didn't know the village was there unless they were already aware of its existence. As soon as the children were inside the thatched huts, they stuck their faces to doors and windows.

The man in the passenger seat of the jeep climbed down. He was in his late thirties. The sun and elements had weathered and darkened his skin. Tattooing and scars marred his face. Even without the additions, he wasn't a handsome man. He looked brutish, like something only half-made. Gold hoops dangled in his ears. The leather loincloth hung from a leather tie around his hips to a few inches above his knees. A silver headband inlaid with garnets and ivory glinted in the sun.

A long knife, almost a machete, hung in a scabbard at his side. A bandolier containing extra magazines draped his chest. He carried an AK-47 in one hand with the muzzle pointed at the ground.

"Who is he?" Tanisha asked.

"His name is Tafari," Jaineba answered. Too late, she realized that she should have had the Englishwoman remain inside the hut. Already Tafari's hot gaze had locked on to her. "He is a very bad man."

8

"My name is Mildred. Mildred Teasdale."

Annja held her hand out to the old woman. "It's a pleasure meeting you, Ms. Teasdale."

"Thank you." The woman's grip was solid and sure, but dry and papery. Her palms were lined with calluses, marking her as a woman who had worked hard all her life.

"You said you thought you knew who the men were in the furnace room?"

Mildred nodded. "Because of an ancestor of mine. A man named Franklin Dickerson."

"I'm sorry, but we haven't identified any of the men in that building," Annja admitted.

"Franklin wasn't one of those men, Miss Creed. But his younger brother, Moses, was. My family's been wondering what happened to young Mose ever since he disappeared all those years ago."

Annja was intrigued. "How do you know your ancestor was one of those men?"

"Because we kept a family history." Mildred's hands tightened on the book she held. "Franklin Dickerson was one of the slaves who learned to read and write. He took his life in his hands by doing that. If his masters had found out, they'd probably have killed him. Black men weren't supposed to learn how to read back in those days."

"I know," Annja said.

"Some of them learned anyway," Mildred went on. "In secret. They prepared themselves for the day they could steal away north on the Underground Railroad. They'd heard a black man who could read and write could get himself a good job in the North."

Mildred nodded. "I come from Augusta, Georgia," she said. "None of my family ever really escaped to go north. We thought Mose might have been the only one. But we knew something must have happened to him because he would never have stayed away from Franklin. Those brothers were close in everything but their politics. The rest of the family stayed here through the worst of everything. But Franklin Dickerson kept his precious journal. In the beginning, that record wasn't anything more than a collection of tattered papers."

Annja didn't mean to look impatient. In fact, she hoped that she didn't look that way. But she felt it. She searched for the best way to excuse herself.

"I know you have things to do, Miss Creed," Mildred said, "and I know there are a lot of people waiting to hear what you people find out today. I'm just trying to help make it easier. And to get some sense of closure for my family. I think I can help you identify those men."

Annja thought of the crowd of protesters standing out in front of the warehouse. Anything that shows some forward movement is going to win everyone over, she thought.

"Can we sit?" Mildred asked. "So I can show you this book? I promise I won't take any more time than you can give me. If you don't think I have anything useful, I'll just go on my way."

Annja agreed.

Mildred led the way to the chairs and found two side by side. She waved Annja to one of them, then sat in the other. She opened the big book.

Neatly arranged printing filled the first page: "A Slave Dreams of Freedom. By Franklin Dickerson."

"Not exactly the most original title someone could come up with," Mildred said, "but Franklin had poetry in his soul. If you took time to read the book, you'd see that."

"I'm an archaeologist, Mrs. Teasdale. Most of the documents I study aren't perfect. Reading the journals of Lewis and Clark as they explored the Louisiana Purchase taught me that knowledge of the language isn't a prerequisite for intelligence."

"My father was a fisherman," Mildred said. "He always said that a man who tried to make a living wasn't any better than the net he could cast. He wasn't a man of letters, either, but he was a storyteller. He knew his way around a metaphor. In keeping with that, Franklin's net had a lot of holes in it, but it was big. He captured a lot of the slave's experience in his writing."

The television in the lobby was tuned to CNN. A quick update on the situation in Kirktown flashed on. Looking at the screen, Annja realized that more protesters had gathered at the warehouse and that the media had returned.

"Franklin could only print," Mildred said with a note of embarrassment in her voice. "That was one of his regrets. He liked the flowing hand that some journal keepers had."

Annja understood that. She kept journals herself, and her handwriting and illustrations were points of pride for her.

"This book was rewritten from the texts that Franklin Dickerson wrote," Mildred continued. "I've got most of the original papers, but some of them have faded over the years. This book wasn't prepared until just before Franklin's death in 1886. He was buried on five acres of ground that he managed to buy and raise a family on." She smiled. "I've had offers from universities that want this book."

"I can imagine. It's quite an impressive document," Annja said.

"It's about my family. That's why I'm not giving it up. But I've allowed copies to be made. They tell me it's not the same as having the original."

"It's not," Annja replied. "There's a lot you can read from the original document that a copy just won't reproduce."

"Anyway, let me show you the parts I wanted you to see." Mildred thumbed through the book. On page thirty-two, neatly numbered in the upper right-hand corner, she stopped.

An illustration in the center of the page drew Annja's attention immediately. The drawing showed a stone with a spider on it. Unconsciously, Annja reached for the drawing, tracing the spider with her finger as her mind jerked into high gear. The paper felt thick and grainy and had yellowed considerably with age.

"Is this it, then? Is this the stone the rumors say you found?" Mildred's voice tightened in excitement.

Annja studied the stone, noticing only then that it rested in someone's palm in the illustration. Judging from the comparison she was able to make, the Spider Stone was about the size of her thumb.

"Is that the stone you found?" Mildred repeated.

"No," Annja said, thinking of hausaboy's announcement that the stone she'd asked about was a copy of another stone. "It was much bigger than this one."

"This was the original stone, according to Franklin," the older woman said. "The second stone, the larger one that you found, is a copy of the true stone."

Annja didn't let her excitement betray her. She knew that sometimes when archaeologists interacted with someone who had a story to tell, that person would elaborate or guess at what the listener wanted to hear. The storyteller wouldn't knowingly lie, but could embellish or twist the truth. "Why was the stone copied?" she asked calmly.

"Because people had heard of it. Once people started talking about the Spider Stone, a second one had to be created. In the early days, no one knew. But as Yohance started to pull others to his side and give them their histories, more people knew about the Spider Stone."

"Do you know what the Spider Stone is?" Annja asked.

Mildred looked at her. "In this book, Franklin says that the Spider Stone has magic. An old magic given to the Hausa people by an African god."

"Anansi."

Mildred nodded and smiled. "The spider god. Now, I don't believe in such foolishness myself. I'm a Christian. I go to the Baptist church right down the street from my house in Augusta. But I'm reminded that sometimes God works in mysterious ways. I believe that He could have revealed Himself to Yohance's people in another way. And God has been making promises since the Ark of the Covenant."

"Was there anything specific the Spider Stone was supposed to do?" Annja asked.

"It was supposed to protect the Hausa village that it was given to. Not protect them from the things that happened to them, but make sure that village would never die. Not as long as the stone existed. That's what Yohance told Franklin."

"Who was Yohance?"

"Well, now," Mildred said, "that's a story."

TAFARI STRODE toward the old witch woman. Some called her a healer and a seer, and believed she did only good things with her powers. A thrill of fear wormed up his spine. He stopped fifteen feet away when he'd intended to walk up close to her and make her back away fearfully.

Jaineba didn't move.

In fact, Tafari's approach also caused the woman standing beside the old witch to step forward. He stopped and grinned, lifting the assault rifle meaningfully.

Most of the villagers drew back at the gesture, but a few of the men stood their ground and held their weapons. A handful of others took a step forward.

"Stupid woman," Tafari spit. "You tempt the gods with your foolishness. My trouble isn't with you. I've no wish to kill you." But he wouldn't hesitate to kill her if it became necessary.

The younger woman said nothing, but her eyes remained focused on him. She was afraid. Tafari saw that in her. She was afraid but she didn't give in to her fear.

"She doesn't understand you." Jaineba's voice was calm and held no hint of trepidation.

Tafari took in her clothing. "She's a foreigner." His words dripped with disgust.

"She's my friend," Jaineba declared.

Those words, Tafari knew, were intended as a warning.

"As my friend, she is also under my protection." The old woman fixed him with her fierce gaze.

Tafari held up a hand. In response, the gunner in the back of the jeep aimed the light machine gun mounted on a tripod at the two women.

The handful of men who'd found the courage to act moved forward again and started objecting to Tafari's presence. The machine gunner swept his weapon toward them and fired a line of bullets into the ground at their feet. Tafari had specified that no one was to be hurt unless he ordered it or they were attacked. He wasn't afraid of the men of the village, but he was afraid of the witch.

The foreign woman caught the witch's arm and tried to drag her back. With surprising strength, Jaineba resisted. The woman looked confused.

"You can't stay here," Tanisha said.

"I will." Jaineba never took her eyes from Tafari. "He will not hurt me. And he will hurt no one in this village, either."

Tafari smiled. "You're too sure of yourself, witch."

"I know how to treat a carrion feeder."

Anger stirred inside Tafari, but he made himself stand steady when he itched to curl his finger around the assault rifle's trigger and blow the witch's head from her shoulders.

Only he couldn't be sure that even that would kill her.

All his life Tafari had heard stories about Jaineba's powers, how she had made the dead live, though not in the same fashion as the *bokors* who practiced voodoo and made the living dead walk. Jaineba's grandmother, the one she had learned her skills from, had risen from the dead three times after drowning, being shot by a white man and being struck by lightning. She hadn't died until she'd decided her granddaughter was fully trained.

"You're an American," Tafari told the woman in her own tongue.

"I'm not. I'm English."

"I am Tafari." He was smug about himself, trusting that the name would leave an impression on her. He wasn't disappointed. Fear glinted a little more sharply in her eyes.

"What are you doing here?" the woman demanded.

"Tanisha," the witch said, "let me handle this. He is here to see me." Jaineba locked eyes with Tafari. "Aren't you?"

Tanisha. Tafari committed the woman's name to memory. She was a beautiful woman. He had left beautiful women dead and dying behind him.

"I am," Tafari agreed. "You're involving yourself where you're not wanted."

"I do what I want," Jaineba declared in an imperious voice. "No man may ever tell me what to do."

"Maybe you're protected by the gods, witch," Tafari said in his own language so the people of the village would understand, "but the people you're turning against me aren't."

"They are protected by me."

"Even when you're not there?"

Jaineba stepped forward, leaning on her staff.

Tafari resisted the impulse to raise the assault rifle and fire. His second impulse was to step back from the woman. He stood his ground, but he was aware that he leaned back from her.

"Harm any person under my protection and I will place a curse on you, Tafari. By the bones of my grandmother, I promise you that. You will never know peace. You will never know a time when you are not in fear for your life." Jaineba drew a calm breath and never blinked. "Do you understand me?"

Everything in Tafari screamed at him to break eye contact and look away from the old woman. She had powers that he could only guess at. He believed that. She had the power to curse a person.

An ivory poacher she had crossed paths with a few years ago had laughed in her face and shot a young warrior who had tried to avenge the disrespect. As Jaineba held the dying warrior, she cursed the poacher. Three days later, the poacher was killed by a leopard in an area where the big cats hadn't been seen in years. Leopards didn't usually attack men. It was later found and killed, but by all accounts it was far north of its usual hunting grounds.

Even before that had happened, people who knew Jaineba told several stories about the powers the witch wielded.

"You can't save everyone, witch," Tafari said.

"That remains to be seen," Jaineba snarled. "Don't presume to threaten me. I won't permit it."

Tafari searched her for fear. He couldn't see any, couldn't hear it in her voice and couldn't smell it on her the way he could with so many men who feared him.

"Your time is almost up," Tafari said. "You're old. You never had children of your own. Your last apprentice died from a sickness you failed to cure in time." He shook his head and smiled. "After you, there is no one to carry on your traditions." He smiled again, wider this time. "Perhaps I can wait."

She had no reply to make.

Leaving her standing there, Tafari walked back to the jeep that had brought him, pulled himself into the passenger seat and sat with his assault rifle across his knees. He was still afraid of the witch, but he felt certain that would soon pass. When it did, he would kill her.

He told Zifa to get them out of there. As Zifa turned the jeep around, Tafari looked at the Land Rover. It was nearly new, an expensive piece of equipment. He couldn't read the lettering on the side, but was familiar with it from past experience. Childress Construction, Inc. seemed to be everywhere these days.

But now he knew where to find the woman, if he ever wanted her. Sharp hunger rose up in him as he glanced back at her.

Like the other villagers, the woman couldn't stay under the witch's protection forever.

"The boy who brought the Spider Stone to America was named Yohance," Mildred said.

"I thought you said the boy your ancestor talked to was named Yohance." Annja took notes in her hardbound notebook. It was five inches wide and ten inches tall, fitting comfortably in her hand. That was important because often when she was out in the field at a dig she didn't have a desk or even a flat surface to write on.

In her loft, she had scores of notebooks. Most of them had been scanned onto disks and placed into storage. Even then, she hadn't been able to get rid of the original notebooks. They represented her work, her time and her love of what she explored.

The book she worked in now was new, but already she'd filled up several pages with notes, questions and illustrations. Several of the pages had tabs stuck to them, marking areas where she'd devoted a large amount of time to wrapping her brain around something.

"Franklin knew a Yohance," Mildred explained. "But all of the Keepers were named Yohance, even when that hadn't been the birth name their mothers had given them. They changed their names when they became the Keepers."

"Who were the Keepers?"

"The Keepers of the Spider Stone, of course. It's covered here in

Franklin's book." Mildred turned the page and found a drawing of a young boy in chains. He looked scared but determined.

"Franklin was quite an artist," Annja said.

"You should see the pictures he's drawn in here." Mildred's eyes gleamed with pride. "This book, it's the most precious thing I own."

"This Yohance was a slave?"

"He wasn't born into slavery like the rest of the Keepers were." Mildred gazed at the small boy. "The first Yohance came from West Africa. His village was destroyed by Arab raiders."

"When did that happen?"

Mildred shook her head. "I don't know. It's not written in this book. I don't think Franklin knew."

Annja wrote, "First Yohance?" then added, "Check slave rolls." Over the years, databases had been created that listed some of the slaves who were brought over on the slave ships. There was a chance the boy might be listed there. Of course, she was well-aware there was also the chance that the ship's captain had simply renamed the boy when he'd sold him.

"The Keeper was supposed to protect the Spider Stone," Mildred went on.

"Slaves weren't allowed possessions except those given to them by their masters," Annja said.

"Yohance hid the Spider Stone."

"How?"

"He swallowed it. The Spider Stone was small enough to permit that. When he excreted it, he would clean it and swallow it again." Mildred looked at Annja. "Can you imagine what that must have been like?"

"No," Annja answered. She honestly couldn't.

"When the first Yohance realized that he wasn't going to live long enough to escape, he groomed another boy to be the next Keeper."

"Any boy?"

"It had to be a Hausa boy," Mildred replied. "Franklin wrote that the first Yohance kept track of bloodlines. He tried to keep the stone in the hands of the purest Hausa he could find, someone who had a link to his village. Otherwise the Spider Stone's power would be lost, you see."

Annja nodded, fascinated with the story.

"As I said, Franklin and Mose were close. They were lucky enough to be kept on the same plantation not far from this town. Farther to the south. I've been out that way and walked over the fields they used to farm when they were boys." Mildred smiled and shook her head. "It made me feel closer to them, made me feel like I almost knew those two boys. Like I could just reach out and touch them. But I'm sure that was just my imagination."

"I don't know," Annja said. "Sometimes when I'm at a site, I can close my eyes and almost hear the people who once lived there. That could be a thousand years ago."

"Maybe we just both have overactive imaginations," Mildred said.

"And maybe we're just sensitive to things other people miss," Annja replied. Since the sword had come into her possession, she'd discovered that sometimes those feelings within her were even stronger.

"It was Yohance who separated Franklin and Mose when nothing else would do it," Mildred said.

"What happened?"

"Franklin sought Yohance out. By this time, Yohance—the Yohance Franklin and Mose came to know—had gathered men to his side."

"Who were the men?"

"Other slaves. But they were all of the Hausa bloodline. As were Franklin and Mose."

"You're of Hausa blood?"

Mildred nodded. "I didn't know that till my daddy read Franklin's book to me when I was a little girl. It wasn't until I was in college that I was even able to look up the Hausa people and find out who they were."

"They were traders," Annja said. "During their time they were fierce, noble and intelligent."

"I know. I take a lot of pride in coming from people like that. But it doesn't matter to my kids. I tried to introduce them to the history of the Hausa people, but they didn't care. They told me they had to live in this world, and it wasn't such a good place." Mildred shook her head. "None of them live around here anymore. I guess they all finally followed the North Star out of here."

"How did Yohance separate Franklin and Mose?" Annja asked.

"Yohance and his bodyguards—"

"Bodyguards?" Annja was startled.

"Franklin called them Yohance's protectors in his book. Yohance had another name for them, but Franklin didn't even try to spell it. He used protectors, and you can tell it was a young man trying to show off his vocabulary. Anyway, they had decided that they were going to try to escape the plantation. This was in 1861."

"The Civil War was starting," Annja said.

Mildred nodded. "It was. Franklin had kept up his reading. He'd read several abolitionist papers that said the North would have an easy victory over the South. Franklin believed that. Yohance believed that the early months of the war would provide the most confusion and they could take advantage of that to slip away."

"They were on a plantation owned by Jedidiah Tatum," Annja said.

Mildred looked surprised. "How did you know that?"

"The textile mill where the bodies were found," Annja explained, "was once owned by Jedidiah Tatum."

"I didn't know that."

Annja decided not to tell the woman that Horace Tatum had dynamited the men in the underground furnace. Eventually that news would come out, but the longer that was kept out of the news, the less complicated things at the dig would be.

"Yohance wanted to escape," Annja prompted.

"He did. He believed that they could reach Canada, and from there they could join a ship bound for West Africa."

"Why would he want to go there?"

"Because of Anansi's promise. Yohance had been told by the Yohance before him, and so the story had been told, that their village would rise again if the stone found its way home."

"By magic?" Annja asked.

"Well," Mildred said, "there was some talk of a treasure, as well."

9

"I thought you weren't coming."

Annja handed one of the takeout food containers to Professor Hallinger. She was later than she'd wanted to be. She felt as if most of the morning had escaped her, but the conversation with Mildred Teasdale had left her with excitement thrumming in her veins.

"I hear we have quite a crowd out there again." Hallinger sliced into a thick stack of pancakes.

"We do." The darkness in the furnace room was complete. Only the lanterns strung along the wall allowed the dig crew to work.

"You'd think the possibility of getting shot would have scared some of them out of it," the professor said.

"Not necessarily," Amber, one of the college students, said. "It brings out the gawker gene."

Hallinger looked at her and smiled in confusion. "What?"

Amber shrugged. "Call it the stupid factor if you want. It's the same thing that happens when there's a car wreck or a really bad tornado or fire. People just naturally wander out to see what's going on, never realizing that they could get swept up in it."

"The gawker gene," Hallinger repeated. "I like that."

"Do I get an A?"

"No."

"Bummer." Amber frowned theatrically and went back to helping restring the grid. Most of it had already been replaced.

Annja looked around. "We lost some students."

"The one who was shot, naturally. And three others. Their parents arrived in the night to claim them and take them home from the police station."

"I missed that," Annja said.

"I'd heard you were out having breakfast with the dashing young detective from Atlanta."

Annja glanced at the professor.

Hallinger held his hands up as best as he could while laden with the breakfast container. "Don't shoot the messenger. People talk."

"Kind of goes along with the gawker gene," Amber said. "They gawk. They talk. So how was breakfast? That guy looked totally hot."

"For one, he's not a detective. He's Homeland Security." Annja didn't want to hold back any of the information she'd discovered. They all deserved to know as much as she did so they could make informed decisions.

"Why would Homeland Security be interested in our dig site?" Hallinger asked.

"They're not. They're interested in the mercenaries. One of them turned out to be connected to a West African warlord who's interested in the Spider Stone."

Hallinger frowned. "That puts a different spin on things, doesn't it? I don't want my students in the line of fire," he said.

"I don't think we're going to have any more problems," Annja said. "Besides that, we've got Homeland Security peering over our shoulder now."

"Still—" Hallinger looked uncomfortable.

"Professor," one of the other students said, "there are more cops out there today than there were yesterday. I think they imported." He looked around at the other students. "I don't know about anyone else, but I got into this field for the opportunities to get a better look at the past. Maybe this isn't digging up a pyramid in the Valley of the Kings, but this is as close as I'm going to get right now. I'm not going to leave unless somebody orders me out."

"I could do exactly that," Hallinger threatened.

Annja said nothing. They needed the help, but Hallinger was in charge.

None of the students looked as if they were going to go without a fight.

They're drawn to the potential danger as much as the mystery of who these people are, Annja realized. She knew the feeling. When she'd found the thief's corpse out in New Mexico, that same mixture of feelings had been a siren call to her. They still called out to her whenever she worked a dig.

"All right," Hallinger relented. "You can stay. But we leave the site tonight before it gets dark."

The students had no problem with that.

"I know who these people are," Annja said. She quickly relayed the story she'd been given by Mildred Teasdale.

When she was finished, one of the students said, "If that woman has all the names of the slaves that were caught down here by Horace Tatum, we don't need to do anything else." He sounded disappointed.

"That's not true," Annja said. "Most archaeologists approach a dig with expectations they believe will be met. Mysteries come along, but they're usually small ones. What we're going to do here is verify the story I was told this morning."

"How?" a student asked.

"By examining the artifacts they left behind," Hallinger answered. "That's what archaeologists do. That's what we'll do."

"We're ahead of the game," Annja said. "We've got an actual record to match up against." She pulled out her notebook. "Besides names, I've got descriptions that will help in most instances." She returned the notebook to her backpack. "But to spice it up a little, so we'll literally leave no stone unturned, I'm going to tell you this. We're looking for another Spider Stone. This one will be about the size of the ball of your thumb."

"What's so important about it?" one of the students asked.

Annja grinned, knowing the answer was going to spark another round of excitement. "It's a treasure map," she said.

For a moment, silence reigned in the basement furnace cave, as if everyone present had taken a collective breath and was now holding it.

"Totally freaking cool," Amber whispered, grinning.

"Yeah," Annja admitted. "It is." Archaeologists were only about a step removed from fortune hunters.

THE BASE OF OPERATIONS Tafari had established was in a collection of hide tents that blended with the surrounding brush and trees. Even if a helicopter searched for them, either from Dakar or from one of the American or European corporations, he was sure they wouldn't be found.

Zifa pulled the jeep under a net that had been woven into the surroundings. A live carpet of greenery covered the net.

A man walked from the tent that held the communications gear. Even though they'd muffled the generator that powered the satellite uplink and computers as much as they could, the sound remained steady and constant. Tafari hated it but could do nothing about it.

"I have some bad news." The man was young, one of those Tafari had enticed away from Dakar. He knew how to use computers. His name was Azikiwe. He wore brightly colored shorts and an NBA tank top. He spoke French—the official language of Senegal—better than he spoke the Yoruba dialect.

Tafari couldn't remember what the NBA was. It was an American or European thing that he had no interest in.

"I'm in no mood for bad news," Tafari warned, choosing to speak in Yoruba.

Taking heed, Azikiwe switched languages. "The man you sent to get the Spider Stone is in jail. His lawyer called to let you know."

"Tell the lawyer to get him out."

"He's trying, but that doesn't seem likely."

"Why not?"

"There are other outstanding charges against him."

Remembering that was true, Tafari reconsidered his options. "Did the lawyer say if the Spider Stone was there?"

"Yes. Ehigiator saw it himself. For a moment, he had his hands on it."

That irked Tafari. He had been so close to his prize. "Where is the Spider Stone now?"

"The archaeologists have it."

"Where?"

"I don't know."

Tafari walked past Azikiwe and into the tent. It was much cooler inside than outside because a large window air-conditioning unit sat on crates. The young men who knew computers claimed they needed it to keep their machines cool and operational. Tafari suspected they wanted it to keep themselves cool.

Rubber sheets that didn't conduct static electricity covered the ground. Three workstations containing the computers that connected the outpost with the rest of the world were spaced around the area inside the big tent. Each workstation also had a small television.

Azikiwe hurried forward and shut off the television on his desk. Seeing the mostly black men running up and down the floor while bouncing or throwing a ball reminded Tafari what the NBA was.

Azikiwe tapped the keys on his computer, then pointed at the screen. "That woman is the one who found the Spider Stone," he said.

"You're sure?" Tafari asked.

"Yeah." Azikiwe plopped down into the chair in front of the computer. "I downloaded the CNN footage of her. The stuff that was aired last night, as well as other files I found. I even got a couple of episodes of *Chasing History's Monsters*."

"What is that?"

"A television show."

Tafari had never understood how so many people could simply sit and watch television.

But he understood the draw of electronics. People everywhere wanted electronics. His black market operations kept trading in electronics, mostly things he didn't even know the nature of. It was enough that others were willing to trade for them because he could use the artifacts and ivory they traded to sell in Europe and America.

"The woman is supposed to be very smart," Azikiwe said. "Her name is Annja Creed."

"Smart?" Tafari asked.

"She's an archaeologist."

"Another bone rattler," Tafari said, thinking of Jaineba. "I've had my fill of them today."

The television screen filled with images of the woman walking through a cavernous vault.

"She's walking through a German mausoleum," Azikiwe said. "She was searching for some mad Nazi doctor who was rumored to still be alive and be behind a rash of killings."

"Was he?"

Azikiwe shrugged. "Annja Creed never found him. She went through the records of several homeless people and those needing psychiatric care, but she never found any proof. The thing that saved this particular episode was her knowledge of German history. She had fascinating stories about gargoyles that were built."

"What is her interest in the Spider Stone?" Tafari asked.

"I don't think she intended to find it." Azikiwe rested his elbows on the arms of the chair and steepled his fingers. "According to the news story, she was called there to help identify the corpses found under the building."

"What bodies?" Tafari hadn't been told about the bodies. Ehigiator had only mentioned the presence of the Spider Stone. That had been one of the items he'd told all his people to look for. Ehigiator was one of the go-betweens the warlord used to ferry around the black market artifacts he shipped to America.

"Slaves," Azikiwe replied. "They've been there for 150 years or more."

That explained why the Spider Stone dropped from sight. Tafari watched the news footage until it showed the Spider Stone.

"Stop it there," Tafari ordered.

The screen locked on to an image of the Spider Stone. A policeman held it and explained in English that they weren't sure what it was, but he knew it had been found in the furnace area under the building, and that the mercenary team had wanted it.

"The men Ehigiator was with wanted the Spider Stone?" Tafari asked.

"Yes." Azikiwe nodded.

"But this," Tafari said, "isn't the Spider Stone."

"What do you mean?" the young computer tech asked.

"I mean that there is another Spider Stone. This one is only similar. It's far too large." Tafari peered more closely at the screen. "No, this was made as a decoy, or perhaps to honor the original Spider Stone." He looked at the tech. "Get my nephew on the phone. He is in Atlanta. I will talk to him."

ANNJA WORKED slowly and carefully. It was the only way to work in archaeology. So much could be—and had been—lost by those who hurried through a site.

In the early years, when the fortune hunters had plundered the Egyptian tombs seeking only gold and jewels, a number of clay tablets containing invaluable records, histories and insights into science and religion had been lost. Greed had plunged men through shelves, returning those tablets to the dust from which they'd come.

"You're smiling."

Annja looked up at Hallinger. "I shouldn't be," she admitted.

The professor handed her a bottle of water. "Tell me. Anything that can make you smile while we're down in this dungeon has got to be worth a moment's diversion."

Annja took the bottle and twisted off the cap. The water wasn't cold or even cool, but it was wet and she felt parched. Her shirt and pants were drenched with perspiration, and grime crusted her exposed skin and had managed to slide down inside her clothing. She was uncomfortable physically, but mentally she was on her game. They were making good, if slow, progress.

"I was thinking about your comment earlier, about the fragile nature of the digital information storage we now have."

"Yes?"

"I was thinking of the clay tablets the Egyptians, Babylonians and other cultures used. How they were destroyed by tomb robbers, earthquakes and floods. If Atlantis truly existed and wasn't just something Plato made up, then it sits somewhere at the bottom of an ocean and probably most of those records are destroyed, as well."

Hallinger grimaced. "You haven't exactly been thinking happy thoughts."

"What I'm saying is that each culture that cares to make records does the best it can with what it has. Think about the oral historians used by the Native Americans along the northwest coast of the United States and Canada. They didn't have a written language. Oral historians were inviolate and had to be at every peace conference and war that took place. If one of them was inadvertently killed by another tribe, the offending tribe had to give one of their young boys to be trained as an oral historian by the tribe that suffered the loss."

Hallinger slipped his glasses back on. "I see your point."

"We do what we can. Right now, the digital format is better than anything we've ever had," Annja said.

"I know." Hallinger sighed. "I also know how much we've possibly lost over time."

"Professor Hallinger!" Excitement rang in the student's voice. "Over here! I think we found it!"

Annja tossed her empty water bottle into the trash bag they'd set up to handle refuse so it wouldn't get mixed up with what they were handling. She stood, feeling the painful burn in her thighs and calves from squatting for so long. Carefully, she stepped through the grids.

The team had cleared over half of the room, taking the skeletons from the site one bone at a time when they had to. Most of them had been identified by descriptions of personal effects and old injuries Franklin Dickerson had recorded in his memoir. Only two of the skeletons hadn't been identified, and with all the names given in the book, that probably wouldn't be too difficult.

Everyone had crowded around the find, but they pulled back long enough to allow Annja and Hallinger to close in. The student who had made the find directed a flashlight beam at a small stone, plucking the object from the dank shadows under the skeleton's thin hipbones.

Even lying on one side as it was, Annja could still see the distinctive spider design that had been carved into it. They'd found the real stone.

10

The stone was about the size of the ball of Annja's thumb. It was striated, with differing layers of sedimentary formation that showed brown and gold with threads of red.

"A tiger's eye?" Hallinger asked.

Annja asked for her camera and it was quickly handed over. "Maybe." She took pictures from different angles, catching the stone from the best views possible before it was moved. Covered by dust as it was, the stone was difficult to see. But once seen, the spider carved into it was unmistakable.

"Anybody know what tiger's eye is?" Hallinger asked. "Any geology minors in the room?"

"Me," a student replied. "Tiger's eye is a chatoyant gemstone."

"Oh, that really helps," someone said.

Despite her excitement at the find, Annja smiled and paused. Even though one of their number was still in the hospital, the students had remained enthusiastic.

"Chatoyancy refers to the reflective ability of the stone," the student went on. "If the stone has a fibrous structure or fibrous imperfections, it's called chatoyant. It's a lot like single-crystal quartz."

"Is it from Africa?"

"It could be. But tiger's eye is found in a lot of places, including the United States and Canada. This rock could have been mined or found right around here."

Handing off the camera, Anna reached through the skeleton's bony pelvis and plucked the stone from the ground. She turned it over, holding a mini-Maglite on it.

A scarlet spider showed up instantly.

Utter quiet fell over the group. Only the buzz of the electric lanterns was audible.

"That's the Spider Stone," someone whispered.

"Yeah," Annja whispered. "It is." She rolled the stone over her palm, taking in the smooth chill it held.

"I guess this is Yohance," another student said.

Annja flicked the light over the necklace the skeleton wore. She checked the image of the river splitting the mountains against the image she'd copied into her notebook. "This is Yohance," she said.

"I thought he was a boy."

"The first Yohance supposedly came over to America as a boy," Annja corrected. "The Yohance in Franklin Dickerson's narrative was in his late teens or early twenties. The same age as most of you."

"We could have checked out at the same age he was last night," someone said.

"We didn't," someone else said.

"Did he just drop the stone there?" a student asked. "I don't see a purse or pocket he was carrying it in."

"He wasn't carrying it in a purse or pocket," Annja said. "He carried it internally."

"What do you mean?"

"He swallowed it, then defecated it and swallowed it again."

"Eww," Amber said. "That's just gross." She wrinkled her nose in displeasure.

"I'm sure he washed it in between," one of the students said.

"That's how all the Yohances carried the Spider Stone," Annja said.

"And that doesn't gross you out?" Amber asked.

"No," Annja said. "It's just the way it was." She shone the mini-Maglite on the tiger's eye. "After the flesh rotted away, the stone was left behind."

"It sank through the body?"

"Unless it was released when he voided himself after dying. That could have happened, too."

Despite the situation, Annja couldn't help taking a little perverse enjoyment in the discomfiture of the students. You people have a lot to learn about the field of archaeology, she thought.

"What's wrong with the skeleton's ribs?" someone asked.

Handing the stone to Hallinger, Annja studied the skeleton. Something *was* wrong with the ribs. They looked as if they'd been cracked, but she knew that wasn't the case because the fractures weren't spaced as they would have been from a blow, or even several blows.

She reached out and felt the cracks, realizing at her touch that they were notches. Upon closer inspection, she saw that they were of different depths. "Those were caused by a knife." Annja shone the light around and found a rusting knife near the hand of a skeleton sitting up against the wall. The knife had a heavy blade, one that had been made by a skilled craftsman. "There," she said.

"That looks like a bowie knife," someone said.

"It's a fighting knife," one of the male retirees said. "It looks like whoever that is spent some time gutting Yohance."

Annja silently agreed. "Maybe the explosion didn't kill them all at once. Whoever that was may have tried to cut the Spider Stone out of Yohance. But either he couldn't find it in the darkness or the stone had already entered the intestines."

"He tried to do that in the darkness?"

"We didn't find a lantern that seemed to survive the explosion." Annja directed her beam at one of the nearby lanterns they'd found in the room. The glass was shattered and the frame was bent. "I think he tried to do it in the dark. By feel."

Someone made gagging noises.

"Committed," Hallinger commented.

"Very," Annja agreed. She glanced at the Spider Stone again. What secrets do you hold? She took a deep breath and forced herself to relax. "Okay, we've got a few more hours before it gets dark. We found one of the things we came down here for, but there's still more we need to do. Let's get it done."

More quietly than before, and maybe a little enthusiastic about their find, the group started sifting through the rubble.

"What about the treasure?" one of the students asked.

"That story is hundreds of years old. I doubt it's still there," Annja said. But she realized that didn't mean everyone else who knew the legend of the Spider Stone felt the same way.

11

"You don't look like an African prince."

Icepick leaned across the table in the club and smiled at the young blond woman seated across from him. "And what does an African prince look like?" he asked.

The blonde gave him a cool look, as if she were merely humoring him. "Like Eddie Murphy."

Icepick grinned. The young woman had a sense of humor. He liked women with a sense of humor. When he scared it out of them, they were more docile than women who worked out of anger.

"I am an African prince," he told her. "I promise."

He thought he could have been a prince, too. He was tall and well built, with a shaved head and tribal tattooing that marked his arms, the back of his neck and his shoulders. He wore black jeans and a turquoise T-shirt that fit him like a second skin. A black leather jacket hid the SIG-Sauer semiautomatic pistol he had snugged into a shoulder rig. A gold Rolex watch, gold chains and a gold cap on a tooth completed the ensemble. His dark skin was flawless except for the tattoos.

The blonde looked like a professional, an executive or a lawyer. She looked sleek and beautiful in her business suit.

At another time, Icepick would have been more willing to chase her. But he was at the club on business. He glanced around, taking his eyes from the woman for the moment partly to make sure his men were paying attention and partly to remind the woman that she wasn't the only female in the room.

Terrence and Pigg sat at another table nearby, flirting with women. All of them looked as if they had money, so attracting women was no problem. Terrence, tall and rakish, would have attracted attention anyway. Pigg was a solid, blocky mass of a man with a vicious underbite that had helped give him his name.

The club was small but successful, a new business growing red-hot by word of mouth in Atlanta. It was called Nocturne which had something to do with night, Terrence had told Icepick. Terrence had been to college.

Icepick was part owner of the club. He'd been a silent investor when it had opened. He didn't invest because he'd expected it to be successful, but because it was a good place to sell drugs—his main business. He'd hoped to create a market where he could deal directly with a younger crowd and so he could move his operations off street corners. He hadn't expected the club to become successful and start drawing some of the new money in Atlanta.

Then Lyle, whom Icepick had met on the streets, looked at how much money he'd started making at a legitimate business without selling the drugs he'd helped sell for the past five years on street corners. Now he seemed to think he was too good for that business.

Icepick was there to remind Lyle that he had a past and a commitment that wouldn't go away.

"You don't seem like royalty," the blonde told him.

"What do I look like?" Icepick asked.

She considered him for a moment. "A drug dealer," she said.

Icepick put a hand over his heart and grinned. "You wound me."

"Or maybe a government assassin."

"Is that a step up? Or a step back?" Icepick loved playing the game with women who thought they held all the cards.

"Sorry. I just call them as I see them."

"What would it take to convince you I'm an African prince?"

"A crown."

"My father doesn't let me take it out at night," Icepick joked.

The blonde thought. "Maybe a royal bodyguard."

Icepick pointed to his men.

"They look like thugs," she said.

"And how is it a royal bodyguard should look?"

"I don't know. Royal?"

Icepick knew the woman was rounding the corner from humor to sarcasm. "I'll show you something." He waved to Hamid, one of his bodyguards.

Hamid came over at once, carrying a sleek briefcase that was chained to his wrist.

"Put it on the table and open it." Icepick didn't glance at the briefcase. He knew what it contained. He'd put it there.

Producing a key, Hamid opened the briefcase. Inside, in specially cut foam inserts, lay a mask made of gold and crusted with rubies, topaz and diamonds.

The jewels caught the woman's eyes at once. She reached for the mask, then pulled her hand away. "Did you steal that?"

"No." That was the truth. The mask was going to be a bribe for another deal he was working on.

"What is that?"

"A funerary mask."

"What's a funerary mask? Like something made after a person's dead?"

"Yes."

"That's a really ugly mask."

Icepick knew the woman was lying. She'd been captivated by the jewels and the gold. And now that he knew he had her hooked, he also knew he could trump her with guilt. "It was my grandfather's." Of course, that was another lie.

"Oh, I'm sorry." She looked embarrassed and shocked.

Both of those emotions were weaknesses, as far as Icepick was concerned. "You couldn't know. After all, you don't believe I'm an African prince." Icepick waved Hamid away.

The man closed the case and returned to his seat just a short distance away.

"What are you doing with your grandfather's death mask?"

"I'm taking it back to my country. It was loaned to the Jimmy Carter Library and Museum in Atlanta. It was part of the exhibit 'The

African-American Presidents: The Founding Fathers of Liberia, 1848–1904.' It was released back into my custody this afternoon. Now I'm flying back home in two days. But first I wanted to see more of this city. I've only been here a few times. I'm visiting family on my mother's side."

Icepick had lived in Atlanta for many years, though he had been born in Senegal. His mother had never left that country.

"I'm really sorry," the woman said.

"It's all right."

She shrugged. "It's just that, you know, I'm a woman here by myself. I get hit on a lot when I go to a bar by myself."

"That's totally understandable. If I were so inclined, I would hit on you."

"You're not?" she asked.

"At first, I just thought I would get to know you. Now…" Icepick shrugged. "Of course, if you find my interest in you unwelcome, all you have to do is say so."

"No. That's all right."

"I'm glad."

"So," the blonde said, "what country are you prince of?"

Returning his attention to the young woman, Icepick said, "Nigeria. West Africa," Icepick told her. "Right on the coast of the Atlantic."

She nodded and sipped at her drink, but Icepick thought that was just to let him know it was empty again.

Icepick waved a server over and ordered another round.

"You're a prince of Nigeria?" the blonde asked.

It would have been easy to simply say yes, but Icepick had learned to be elaborate with his lies. People believed an elaborate lie wrapped around a hint of truth more often than a simple lie.

"No," Icepick said. "Nigeria is made up of what used to be several African empires. Have you heard of the Yoruba people?"

She shook her head.

At that moment, Terrence stood and attracted Icepick's attention. He nodded toward Lyle, who was walking through the club with a couple of his own bodyguards in tow.

Lyle was tall and dapper, in his early thirties. The dark blue suit he wore looked expensive. Icepick had good suits back home in his closets. Despite the darkness filling the club, Lyle wore sunglasses and looked like a young Ray Charles.

Irritated with Lyle's timing, Icepick stroked the back of the blonde's hand. "The Yoruba are a proud people," he said.

"How long did you say you were going to be in town?" the woman asked.

"A few more days."

The blonde smiled. "Maybe we could get together. I could show you around."

Icepick smiled. "I'd like that."

"Do you have a card?"

Icepick hesitated.

Then the woman shook her head. "That was stupid. You're not from here. Why would you have a card?" She rummaged in her tiny purse and produced a business card. "That's me. Sandra Thompson."

"It says attorney-at-law."

"That's right. I specialize in corporate law. Mergers. Tax shelters. That kind of thing."

"You must be very smart to do something like that."

"I like my job and I'm good at it."

Lyle walked into his office, never looking around. He was totally secure in his environment.

Icepick was about to change that. "If you'll forgive me, I've got something I need to attend to," he said.

"Sure." The woman glanced at her watch. "Actually, I'm about to turn into a pumpkin. I've got to go." She swept her purse from the table and flashed him a smile. "You have my card. Call me." Then she was gone, and the heads of several men turned in her direction as she crossed the bar.

Icepick watched her all the way to the door. Then he got up and walked toward the office. Terrence, Pigg, Hamid and three other men fell into step with him. By the time they reached the office door, all of them had suppressor-equipped pistols in their hands.

Nodding to Terrence as they stopped at the door, Icepick stepped to one side. Terrence lifted his pistol and fired into the locking mechanism. The muzzle-flashes were lost in the light show, and the sound of the bullets crunching through the lock was covered by the music.

Icepick kicked the door open and shoved his head and shoulders through.

The office was small and filled with electronics. Monitors showed pictures from a dozen different angles inside the club, and each of those rotated through still other cameras.

Lyle sat at the big desk in front of the monitors. His two bodyguards occupied chairs on either side of the desk. Both of them were on their feet and trying to draw their weapons, no doubt alerted by the monitor system.

Icepick shot the first man through the head twice. Before the corpse had time to topple backward, Terrence shot the second guard through the chest and neck. The second man took a little longer to die, but he was dead within seconds.

Lyle stood, throwing his hands high. "Don't shoot! Please! Don't shoot!"

Crossing the room, Icepick grabbed Lyle's suit coat and shoved him back into the chair. Terror widened Lyle's eyes. Then Icepick closed them when he pistol-whipped the man across the face with his gun. Without a word, he pressed the pistol barrel into Lyle's throat, pinning him against the chair.

"Move and I will kill you." Icepick ripped Lyle's sunglasses from his face. The man's pupils were pinpricks, advertising the drugs in his system.

"Don't kill me," Lyle whispered. "Please don't kill me."

"You've been cheating me," Icepick said.

"No!" Lyle shook his head desperately. "No! I haven't been cheating you! I swear!"

"I've got someone in the club. You've been skimming."

"That's a lie!"

"It's not a lie." Icepick slapped Lyle with the gun butt again.

Lyle's cheek opened up and blood ran down his face. He whimpered and tears spilled from his pinprick eyes. "I'm sorry! I'm sorry! I'll pay you back!"

"Put your hands on the table, Lyle."

"No." Lyle's refusal came out as a whimper.

"Put your hands on the desk or I'm going to blow your head off."

Reluctantly, Lyle put his hands on the desk.

Reaching into his jacket, Icepick took out an ice pick.

"Don't," Lyle pleaded. "Please. Please don't."

Without a word, without mercy, Icepick plunged the ice pick through Lyle's right hand and impaled it on the desk.

Lyle cried out in pain.

Icepick plucked the handkerchief from Lyle's jacket pocket and shoved it into his mouth.

Still sobbing, Lyle fell forward when Icepick released him. He reached for the ice pick. The handkerchief in his mouth muffled whatever sound he was making.

"Don't touch that," Icepick ordered. "You try to pull that out and I'll kill you."

Lying on the desk, staring in agony at his maimed hand, Lyle cried.

"I helped you get where you are today, Lyle," Icepick said. "I talked to my uncle for you. He agreed to set us up in business. He fronted the money you spent on this place. He expects a return on his investment. Not to be ripped off. Do you understand?"

Lyle nodded.

"If we have to have this discussion again," Icepick promised, "I'm going to ship your head to my uncle."

"It won't," Lyle gasped, "happen…again."

"Good." Icepick released the club owner and stood. He looked around the office. "Get this place cleaned up. Quietly. I don't want any of this rolling back on me. If my ankles get covered from now on, I'm going to bury you in whatever I'm looking at during that moment."

Turning on his heel, Icepick walked to the door. He shoved the SIG-Sauer back into the shoulder leather. Pigg opened the door without a word.

As he left the club, Icepick's cell phone rang. He fished it out of his jacket pocket and flipped it on. "Yeah."

"Nephew," Tafari said in the Yoruban language, "I need you to do a task for me."

"Of course. All you've ever needed to do is ask."

"There is something I want in a small town outside Atlanta," Tafari said.

"Anything," Icepick answered, but he was thinking about his uncle. Tafari was a hard man. He wouldn't have let Lyle live. But somebody had to get rid of the bodies, Icepick reasoned.

Almost twelve years ago, Tafari had sent his sister's only son to Atlanta to start managing some of the illegal trade in African artifacts that brought in so much money. Icepick had shown resourcefulness and an understanding of the criminal economy that his uncle had been pleased to discover. Icepick had negotiated a small drug-dealing business, then shipped the drugs to Tafari. Once the drugs reached Senegal, Tafari sold them to merchant ships in Dakar. The crews in turn took the drugs to other ports of call.

Everybody made a profit. It remained a constant source of revenue for them.

"The Spider Stone has been found," Tafari said.

Outside Nocturne, Icepick froze, caught in the glare of the neon signs. Cars passed in the street, but he hardly noticed them. The whole time he'd been growing up out in the savannas, his uncle had talked of many things. Legends and myths, and tales of gods. But one of the most repeated legends had been the one of the Spider Stone. The Hausa village that had possessed it had been said to have been blessed in trade. Supposedly, there was a treasure trove awaiting anyone clever enough to find it.

"Where is it?" Icepick asked.

"In a small city outside Atlanta. A place called Kirktown. Can you get there?"

"Of course," Icepick replied. "I can be there before morning."

"Do that. It would be best to work under the cover of night."

It would, Icepick thought. Ever since he'd left Africa, then changed his name to his current one, he'd been aware of the magic in the night. Predators thrived there.

And he was one of the best predators his warlord uncle had ever reared.

12

"What have you gotten yourself involved in?"

Bleary-eyed and tired, Annja really wasn't in the mood for any remonstrations. Especially not from the man currently connected to her by cell phone.

Roux was the only name she had for the old man. At least she thought "Roux" really was his name. He sometimes used others and "Roux" might have been just as false.

"Nothing." Annja straightened her back, stiff from being in a cramped, bent-over position for hours. She and Hallinger were working together in a small warehouse not far from the old textile mill. Other units in the warehouse were rented out as garages and paint-and-body shops, and the stink of the chemicals filled her nose.

The university had hired a small security service from Atlanta. The men sat around the archaeologists drinking coffee, reading gun magazines and reliving past postings with each other.

Having the men there didn't make Annja feel particularly safe. She felt more invaded than anything else.

Body bags containing the remains of the slaves who had been killed in the furnace room lay on the floor. Hallinger and Annja had commandeered tables for use in studying the various artifacts they'd recovered.

There were a few artifacts, most of them related to the Civil War.

But the thing that caught their attention now that the slaves had been identified was the Spider Stone.

Roux snorted.

Annja sighed. Despite having spent months around the man, she truly didn't feel that she knew Roux any better than she had when she'd first met him. There was so much that he hadn't told about himself, and probably most of it he would never tell.

How could you live five hundred years and not have left traces of yourself everywhere? she wondered. How could you keep all those stories bottled up?

None of that made sense to her.

Garin—who also went under other names these days—was easier to understand. He was a self-motivated person, and all she could truly count on him to do was look after his own interests. Garin had tried to kill her shortly after he'd found out that she had the reassembled sword. He was convinced that he was going to start aging at any time now that the sword was whole and in Annja's hands.

She didn't know what was going to happen. She was very aware that she had been changed by the sword's power, but she didn't know if those changes had been completed. She had no idea if they'd affected whatever spell or force or cosmic happening that had allowed Roux and Garin to live for five hundred years.

"Getting yourself killed isn't an optimum career choice," Roux groused.

"That didn't happen," Annja argued. She knew he was only worried about what might happen to the sword. *If something happened to the sword—or to me—are you afraid you'll be held accountable again?* It was a question that always hummed in the back of her mind whenever she talked to Roux.

"According to what I saw on CNN a few minutes ago, getting killed was a near thing," Roux said.

"That was yesterday."

"So today is better? You're safe?"

Annja looked around at the bored security guards. "Yeah. I'm safe."

"Good. I don't want worrying about you throwing off my game."

You're worried about me? That thought warmed Annja for just a moment, then she reined in those feelings. They were just the remnants of being raised in an orphanage.

Roux wasn't exactly a fatherly figure, but there was something demanding and dependable about his presence. If they were on the same side in something, she knew he would never abandon her. He'd proved that when she'd first found the sword and had to fight to keep it. But he'd let her go her own way after that.

Still, the sword somehow bound them and she was distinctly aware that both of them knew it. Neither of them was happy about it, but it was interesting.

"I doubt you'd worry too much about me," Annja replied.

Roux snorted again. "All of this is over people who've been dead for the last 150 years?" he asked.

"Not completely," Annja admitted. "Do you know much about the Hausa people?" She knew that Roux had a vast knowledge of many subjects. She always learned something new whenever she talked to him.

"Which empire?"

"What do you mean?"

"There were several empires. Come, come. You're supposed to be the archaeologist. I'm just a dabbler with an interest in old things."

With five hundred years' experience, Annja thought. No archaeologist I know is going to be able to put together that kind of résumé.

"I don't know which empire yet." Annja knew there had been several Hausa trading empires.

"Then what are you dealing with?"

Annja gazed at the tiger's eye stone that Hallinger was observing under a computer-assisted magnifying glass they'd borrowed from the university. From time to time, the professor took digital captures of the stone's surface. They were slowly mapping the intricate Hausa language written on the surface.

"A stone," Annja answered.

"Doesn't sound interesting to me."

"It's supposed to be a treasure map."

Roux laughed. "Treasure maps litter history. Even those a hundred or two hundred years old usually turn out to have been part of some con man's game."

Someone called in the background. The voice was soft and young.

That irked Annja a little, though she knew it shouldn't have. She knew Roux had a fondness for young women. Every time Annja had visited the old man at his rambling mansion outside Paris, he'd always had a woman with him. None of them ever stayed long.

"I'm going to have to go," Roux said. "Someone requires my attention."

Randy old goat, Annja thought. But she said, "Sure."

"You may send me a few pictures of your latest hobby. If you wish. Perhaps I could help."

"Are you sure I won't be taking up too much of your time," Annja said.

Roux huffed. "There's no reason to be persnickety, Annja."

"I'm not being *persnickety*," she argued.

Hallinger looked over his shoulder at her, then quickly returned his attention to the Spider Stone.

"You sound it to me," Roux said.

"Maybe you should have your hearing checked."

"Why? Everything else seems to be functioning well. I don't get any complaints," Roux said.

Now that's an image I don't need, Annja thought.

The soft voice called again, sounding more needy this time.

"Send me the pictures if you've a mind," Roux invited.

"Maybe." Annja was unwilling to commit to anything.

"On that note," Roux said, "I'll say goodbye. Stay well, Annja. I wouldn't want anything to happen to you."

He hung up while Annja was still trying to figure out how to react. Roux cared about her. Somewhere inside, she knew that, but caring about her exposed him to a lot of hurt. For five hundred years, he'd watched anyone he'd grown close to grow old and die. If they managed to grow old.

Except for Garin. During most of that time, Roux's ex-apprentice had tried to kill him whenever they were around each other. Finding Annja and the sword had brought them together briefly. She knew their relationship was complicated.

Annja put her cell phone in her pocket. Roux cared about her.

Maybe it's hard for you to accept that, she told herself. She'd walled herself off from most people. She had some friends, good ones. And even a few who tried to mother her, the way that Maria Ruiz, the owner and chef of Tito's, her favorite Cuban restaurant in Brooklyn, did.

But there had never been anyone like Roux in her life.

"You okay?" Hallinger asked.

"Yes." Annja stepped over to the coffeepot in the corner and poured another cup.

"Your dad?"

Annja frowned and shook her head. "Definitely not."

"Sorry. Sounded like you were talking to your dad."

"He's just…just a guy I know."

"Oh." Hallinger looked away, clearly feeling awkward.

Annja suspected the professor thought she'd been talking to someone she felt romantic about. "It's not like that," she said.

"It's really not any of my business."

"No," Annja said, feeling flustered, "I mean it. It's not like that."

"I believe you."

Get a grip, Annja told herself. But she couldn't let it go. She suspected maybe it was because she was tired. "He's a…mentor."

"A professor?"

And didn't that just bring up the lovely subject of star students crushing on professors? Annja let out a breath. "You know, I just don't want to talk about it."

"Okay." Hallinger didn't look at her.

Maybe it would have helped if he had. Then she could have known what he was thinking, and maybe he would have been thinking that nothing she said was any of his business and that would have been the end of it.

But he didn't look up.

"He's just this guy. A really *old* guy." Annja described Roux that way because that fact seemed important. "He knows a lot about history."

"A historian?" Hallinger asked.

"More or less."

"That's a good field. I've always been interested in history myself." Hallinger shrugged. "I guess it's a natural spin-off from archaeology. Reading other people's interpretations of an event or a person."

"He just called to check on me."

"That was thoughtful."

"He's not really that thoughtful."

Hallinger continued working.

"He knows a lot that I would like to know," Annja said. "Except he won't tell me. He says I need to find out some things for myself."

"My dad used to tell me the same thing," Hallinger said. "He was an archaeologist, too."

"The guy I was talking to isn't my dad."

"You said that already."

Annja sighed and gave up. There was no explaining Roux. She couldn't even explain the man to herself. Whatever tied them together wasn't going away, and she didn't know whether to feel glad or threatened by that.

Hallinger glanced at her. "Are you really all right?"

"Yes," Annja replied, folding her arms and sealing off the confusion of emotions that ran through her. *No.* She really needed a good night's sleep.

"Ready to work?" he asked. "I think I've found a map."

"YOU THINK they got enough Five-O there?"

Icepick gazed from the shadows of the alley across the street from where the woman archaeologist was supposed to be holed up with whatever she had found. Three police cars sat out in front of the building.

He looked at Terrence. "We don't have a choice about this. My uncle sent me to get this thing."

Terrence nodded. He knew Tafari, and he knew the warlord would not allow them to back off just because of the police.

The men were pumped on speed, tense and wired up, ready to take action. Dressed all in black, the members of the small army held assault weapons and were connected by walkie-talkie headsets.

"What we need is a distraction," Icepick said. "Send Pigg and a couple of others to the bank we passed on the way into town. Have them plant some of the explosives we brought, like someone's trying to break into the bank, then wait for my signal. That's far enough away to buy us time to take down the warehouse, get the stone and hit it. By the time everything gets sorted out, we'll be gone."

Terrence nodded and turned to make things happen.

Crouched with his back against the wall, Icepick took out a small vial of cocaine. His uncle didn't like him using the hard drugs, but Icepick kept his use to a minimum. They were just for times when he needed an edge.

He shook some of the cocaine onto the back of his hand, then snorted it. He licked the back of his hand and felt his tongue grow numb. The cocaine was good, expertly cut.

New energy blossomed within Icepick. He forced himself to wait although his nerves jangled for him to be up and moving.

He reached under his leather duster and took out the Glock 18C machine pistol. The weapon looked like a normal semiautomatic handgun, but it was configured to fire through a 17-round or 33-round magazine in a single pull of the trigger.

The pistols were usually employed by American law-enforcement agencies, but Icepick had negotiated the purchase of a few dozen. The weapon had been featured in one of the *Matrix* films and *Terminator 3*. After seeing the Glock there, Icepick had decided he had to have one.

Several 33-round magazines filled the deep pockets of the duster he'd had specially made. It was like something Neo from the *Matrix* movies would wear, too. He also wore a Kevlar vest. It was bullet resistant and would stop most rounds. He'd take a vicious beating from the blunt trauma, but a few bruises were a small price to pay. But he didn't plan on getting shot at all.

Icepick inserted one of the 33-round magazines. High capacity meant that his team didn't have to be accurate. They just had to be careful not to shoot each other.

Pigg and the two men Terrence had chosen drifted away into the night.

Crouching, zinging inside, Icepick whistled tunelessly while he waited.

HALLINGER *HAD* FOUND a map.

Annja shifted through the images the professor had taken and fed into the computer. The digital images could be dramatically blown up.

"Do you see it?" Hallinger asked.

"I do." Annja manipulated the image. "The map's unmistakable."

"But we have no reference points." Hallinger sounded tired. "It could be anywhere in Africa."

"West Africa," Annja said. "We know that because of the Hausa language."

"The Hausa were once scattered across a far larger part of Africa than they are now," Hallinger pointed out. "Where this map is depends a lot on how old this stone is."

"Not the stone," Annja said. "The carving."

"Agreed." Hallinger leaned a hip against the table and looked disgusted.

"The carving is exquisite work." Annja studied the lines. "There's not a misplaced line in the map."

"The Hausa worked in stone."

"But whoever made this was a gifted craftsman. That's going to narrow the field a bit."

"I shouldn't allow myself to be disappointed," Hallinger said. "It's not like we're going to get to go look for the treasure."

Annja looked at him and smiled. "Is it the treasure you want?"

"If the Hausa put gold and ivory away for a rainy day, you can bet they put away more than that. That place, wherever it is, could also be a library containing records, histories and a real look into the Hausa culture during those days. Some of the oldest empires of civilization are in those areas." Hallinger rubbed his jaw. "I wouldn't mind being remembered as the guy who found something like that."

Neither would I, Annja thought. She turned and leaned against the table, too. She was aware that some of the security guards were watching and listening to their conversation even though they were trying to be subtle.

"Maybe we can get a shot at doing that," Annja said.

Hallinger stared at her.

"My producer on *Chasing History's Monsters* has wanted in on this," Annja said. "So far I've kept him out of it. The last thing we needed was a film crew leaning over us."

"Agreed. But you think he might be interested in this?"

Annja smiled. "An ancient map to a lost treasure of a people protected by a spider god? He'd go for it in a heartbeat. There's only one catch."

Hallinger lifted an inquisitive eyebrow.

"We'll need a monster. Or a legend of a monster."

"We haven't found any monsters yet that weren't of the human variety," Hallinger pointed out.

"We could play up the Anansi angle. Anansi wasn't always a good god. He's believed to have come from the Ashanti people. Maybe there's something there."

"If you're talking about Africa, and especially West Africa, you're talking about *voudoun* and zombies."

"I think my producer may finally be as sick of doing stories about zombies as I am." Annja thought about it. "Maybe we could work with the cult aspect of the *bokors*. They lean toward the dark side of *voudoun*."

"They create the zombies."

"Without getting into the whole zombie litany," Annja said.

"With the Islamic influence, we also have the jinni."

"Weak." Then Annja reconsidered. "Actually, we haven't done anything with jinni that I know of."

"Several of the African cultures also believe in lycanthropes," Hallinger said.

"But we don't have a specific monster. Or person who was thought to be a monster. A general story about werewolves wouldn't fly."

"That makes a difference?"

"Can you believe it?"

"I have to admit," Hallinger said, "I've seen the show. I wouldn't have thought there was much criteria for acceptable monsters."

"There is," Annja said.

They both fell silent for a moment.

"What about vampires?" one of the security guards volunteered.

"Vampires," Hallinger said.

Annja shrugged. "My producer loves vampires. He hangs out at vampire clubs and plays a count."

"Terrific," the professor said dryly. "You know, this is a sad statement on our profession that we even have to sit around discussing such subjects."

"It's all about acquiring funding," Annja replied. "You have to get creative when you're going after funding."

"In 2002 and 2003," the security guard said, "they had a bunch of vampire attacks in some country. Killed a governor and a bunch of other people. Started a riot."

"Malawi," Annja said.

The guard snapped his fingers and pointed at her. "That's it."

"Only one person was killed during the riot. Four other people, including the governor, were stoned but lived. The citizens thought the governor was in league with vampires." Annja had been offered the story at the time. She'd passed. Kristie Chatham had accepted the story, negotiated a fat bonus for the travel, then proceeded to run screaming through the streets of Blantyre, Malawi.

No vampires had ever put in an appearance. There was no mention of the hominid remains and stone tools that dated back more than a million years. The episode had still gotten one of the highest ratings in the history of the show.

"Maybe we just need to sleep on this," Hallinger suggested. "By morning, we could have a new take on what we're doing."

Before Annja could say anything, a loud explosion sounded outside.

"What the hell was that?" one of the guards shouted.

No one had an answer. They all stood and put their hands on their weapons.

Apprehension triggered Annja's personal early-warning system. She put her hand out and touched the sword but didn't draw it from the otherwhere. There were too many people around. But she had the definite sense that something very wrong was happening.

13

Icepick cursed. The sound of the explosion at the Executive National Bank could be heard throughout all of Kirktown.

"Done." Pigg's voice over the earpiece sounded distant.

"How much of that damn plastic explosive did you use, Pigg?" Icepick demanded.

"Enough, man. That bank's front door is in splinters. There's alarms going off everywhere."

There was no arguing that. Even where Icepick was, with the echo of the explosion bouncing around inside his skull, the strident wailing of the alarms screamed through the streets.

"We're haulin' ass," Pigg advised.

"Get clear." Icepick took a fresh grip on his pistol as the three police cars in front of the warehouse burned rubber getting into motion. He supposed that every cop dreamed of catching a bank robber.

In seconds, the police cars had disappeared, roaring toward the other side of Kirktown.

"All right," Icepick said, "let's move." He led the way across the street, closing in quickly on the warehouse door they'd figured was closest to the area where the archaeologists were working.

Annja Creed. He rolled the woman's name in his mind, enjoying the sound of it. She was a good-looking woman, and his uncle hadn't said he had to keep his hands off of her. It was always better to ask forgiveness than to ask permission, he thought.

Terrence came up behind him and took the other side of the door. One of the other men came forward with a shaped charge. Icepick took care to surround himself with capable people when it came to killing. The killing itself could be learned on the spot, but getting into areas rapidly took special skills.

"Back," the man said. He'd once been part of a special-forces unit, trained by the military to do exactly what they were doing now. Urban assault, he called it. "Fire in the hole."

In the next instant, the door lock exploded and was driven into the room beyond. The door bounced in the frame, letting Icepick know that it was free.

He grabbed the door with a gloved hand, feeling the incredible heat the detonation had left, and yanked it open. Embers spilled out in an arc.

Icepick went into the room with the Glock held before him. A lot of television shows had military and law-enforcement personnel holding their side arms in two-handed grips. Icepick had never done that. He'd learned his gun skills on video games, and the lessons had translated easily to real guns on the street.

A small lobby equipped with a desk and a phone led into the large work area behind it. The lobby door opened and a heavy-set security guard stepped through.

Squeezing the trigger, Icepick put the first two rounds through the man's belt buckle, then felt the gun rise through the next six. The security guard's shirtfront turned red, and he fell backward into the next room.

Icepick went after the man, moving into alignment with the doorway the same way he would in Halo or any of the James Bond video games. Another guard lifted his weapon and fired from ten feet away. At that range, missing Icepick was almost impossible.

Two rounds struck the Kevlar vest, slamming into Icepick's chest and causing him to stumble back. He cursed but brought the Glock up anyway, triggering a spray of bullets that caught the guard at the ankles and stitched their way to the top of his head.

Terrence was beside him as he ejected the empty magazine and slammed another one home. Terrence took aim, but two security guards fired first. Their bullets went wide of Icepick but took out three of the men crowding into the doorway. At least one of them was dead, hit between the eyes.

Then Terrence opened up and dropped both security guards. He wasn't pretty when he shot, but the reflexes were there.

Looking across the room, Icepick saw the archaeologists running toward the back door. He grinned. They weren't getting away—they were running straight for the rest of Icepick's group.

ANNJA HELD on to Hallinger's arm and ran toward the back door. She had no idea who the black-clad men were, but she knew that hanging around to ask questions was a bad idea.

Bullets whipped along behind her, smashing into the body bags lying on the floor. A light exploded overhead, then dropped free of its moorings and smashed against the concrete floor in a shower of glass.

The back door started to open, alerting Annja to the fact that someone was entering from the alley. She slammed against Hallinger, catching him midstride and knocking him into the wall. The air went out of him in a rush and he dropped to his knees just as bullets chopped into the wall. He ducked all the way down.

Annja went airborne as she neared the door, then crashed into it in a flying kick. The impact slammed the door hard. Two men tumbled to the ground, but four more pushed the door open in a split second.

Annja knew she couldn't run. There wasn't enough time. She pushed herself to her feet, sprang forward and grabbed the first man's arm as he took aim. Controlling the arm, using the limb as a lever and her body as a fulcrum, she wheeled and hip tossed him. The man flew across the alley and slammed awkwardly into the wall.

The man's neck snapped on impact. The brittle, crunching sound reached Annja's ears even over the sound of gunfire coming from inside the warehouse.

Annja hadn't intended to kill the man, but for the moment she was just grateful to be alive. She threw herself to the left of the next man as he fired. The flaming muzzle tore away the darkness in the alley for a moment. Bullets cut through the space where Annja had been standing. If she hadn't moved, she'd have been dead.

Holding her curled fists beside her face in a defensive position, Annja swung her right leg around in a roundhouse kick. Time seemed to have slowed down slightly as it sometimes did when adrenaline spiked her system. She knew she was really moving fast. The surprised looks on the faces of the men gave that away.

The man she kicked went down as if he'd been hit by a truck. His pistol skidded from his hand.

"Now you gonna die!" another man yelled.

Annja didn't try to figure out who spoke. Both of the remaining men were dangerous, and Professor Hallinger was still inside the building.

She took two steps and vaulted up onto a Dumpster behind the warehouse. The men turned toward her, chasing her with their bullets, knocking pieces of broken brick from the wall.

Still on the move, Annja leaped up and somersaulted in the air. She reached for the sword and the weapon filled her hand. She swung the blade at one man's pistol, knocking it from his hand in a shower of sparks.

Then she landed behind the second man. Desperate, alarm stamped on his face, the second man tracked her, firing along the warehouse wall and up into the air. His pistol emptied before he could bring it back down, but he swung it at Annja's head.

Blocking the blow with her left forearm, Annja snapkicked the man in the groin and took the fight out of him. While he struggled to remain standing, she brought the sword hilt crashing into his forehead. He fell to the ground.

Annja turned and surveyed the alley. All of the men were down. More shots sounded from inside the warehouse.

She released the sword, dropping it back into that unknown space, then scooped up two of the pistols from the ground. Both of them had extended magazines that made them look slightly cartoonish.

Annja had taken gun-safety courses on revolvers, semiautomatic pistols and rifles. She was good with firearms but preferred not to use them. Bullets didn't recognize friend from foe, and she didn't have control over them like she did the sword once they were unleashed.

Stepping back into the doorway, she peered around the corner. Professor Hallinger had his hands lifted over his head and was slowly getting to his feet.

The African-American with the shaved skull who appeared to be the leader was talking, one hand pressed to an ear.

Radio communication, Annja realized. She knew he'd be aware that he had lost the team outside.

Two other men approached Hallinger, trailed by a third.

"Get your hands up!" the third man ordered. "Keep them up where I can see them!"

Obviously shaken, Hallinger stood his ground and kept his hands raised.

The two men closed on him. Annja let them, wanting them close enough that there could be no mistake.

"What's your name?" the man asked.

"Hallinger," the professor responded.

"Do you have the Spider Stone?"

Annja was surprised, although she couldn't think of any other reason for the men to raid the building.

"No," Hallinger replied.

Annja felt the weight of the stone in her shirt pocket. She'd grabbed it instinctively, remembering the times when dig sites she'd been on had been raided by bandits or fortune hunters.

"Where is it?" the man asked.

"I have it," Annja said as she swung around the doorway and dropped the pistols into position.

All three men tried to respond to the threat, but they were too late and they knew it.

Willing herself to be cold, remembering how the invaders had shot the security guards without warning, Annja squeezed the triggers. The pistols erupted in her hands like live things trying to escape traps. They climbed steadily as bullets tore into the three men, driving them backward in quick stutter steps. The final bullets tore into the lights, knocking two of them down in crashing heaps.

The man with the shaved head dived to the ground, followed by the two other men who remained of his attack group.

Throwing down the empty pistols, Annja caught Hallinger's arm and got him moving.

"You killed them," the professor said incredulously.

"They didn't give me a choice." Annja pushed Hallinger through the door just ahead of the fusillade of bullets that slammed into the wall after them.

In the alley, Hallinger froze for just a moment, looking down at the men Annja had left in disarray. He looked up at her. "*You* did this?"

"Those men are coming after us." Annja shoved him toward the street. *"Go."*

Hallinger lurched into a run, then put his heart into it. His feet slapped against the pavement.

Annja reached for the sword and it was in her hand. She took up position behind the Dumpster, crouching so she couldn't be seen. Her heart thudded in her chest.

At the end of the alley, Hallinger had reached the street and was running for his life. He turned and was out of sight just as their pursuers rushed from the doorway.

Annja watched from the shadows, letting the first man pass her by. Then she lunged to catch the second man, hoping it would be the man with the shaved head. If she could get her hands on the leader, maybe the other two could be controlled.

It wasn't him. Annja caught the man's jacket with her left hand and slammed into him hard with her left forearm. The air left his lungs in a rush and he doubled over. Annja pushed him backward into the leader, sending them both down in a heap.

Twisting, knowing how precarious her position was, Annja went for the first man. He was only a few feet away, already firing at her. Quick enough to dance between lightning strikes, Annja dodged to the side. She brought the sword up in both hands with blinding speed, slapping the flat of the blade against the man's temple. Out on his feet, the man slumped to the ground.

Annja turned quickly, moving toward the last man.

He pointed his pistol at her as he got to his feet. "You're finished," he growled.

Without a word, Annja brought the sword down in a glittering arc. The keen blade smashed the pistol's body. The weapon fired, but the bullet struck the sword blade and ricocheted into the warehouse wall.

The man cursed in disbelief, staring at the ruined barrel. He tried to fire again, but the pistol had jammed. He suddenly remembered the pistol in his other hand and drew it up.

Annja gripped the sword and spun, bringing her foot arcing down on the man's wrist. Bone broke and the man cried out in pain as the gun flew from his fingers. Before he could move, Annja swept the sword around, slicing neatly through his Kevlar vest as if it were cheese.

The man looked down at the gaping cut as if expecting to see his intestines come tumbling out. They didn't. Annja knew she'd missed his body by less than an inch. She'd intended to.

"Now," she said, "would be the time to surrender."

Moving with surprising speed, the man turned and ran toward the other end of the alley. He got just enough of a jump that Annja didn't catch him until he'd reached the corner.

"Come get me! Come get me!" the man yelled.

Annja knew he was communicating with the rest of his team. As she reached the corner, she saw a big dark luxury sedan hurtling down the street. The lights pinned the fleeing man and the driver stepped on the brakes. Rubber shrieked and the vehicle slewed sideways as the driver tried to control it.

The man slowed, anticipating catching a ride.

Annja never broke stride. Her quarry turned at the last moment, his hand on the car's front fender. His eyes widened as he saw her.

She leaped, letting the sword slip away, and crashed into the man, driving him back across the hood of the oncoming car. They slid across the hood and smashed against the windshield, turning it into a frosted glaze of cracks. They rebounded and tumbled over the side.

For a moment, Annja was stunned. She wasn't strong enough to body block moving vehicles. But her quarry had fared worse. His face was a bloody mess and his right arm was bent unnaturally behind his back.

He wasn't trying to get up.

Annja struggled to get to her feet as the driver got out of the car with a pistol in his fist.

"Icepick! Man, I couldn't stop, dawg!"

"Shoot her!" Icepick ordered hoarsely.

The big man took aim.

Annja dodged, leaving the street just as the bullet scarred the pavement.

Three gunshots rang out in quick succession. The big man jerked backward. Puzzled, he glanced down, seeing the blood pouring from his mutilated neck. At least one of the rounds had torn out his throat. He slumped to his knees and fell forward.

A harsh voice boomed out, "Homeland Security! Drop your weapons! Now!"

A flashlight beam blazed out of the darkness and splashed over the car. The two men inside threw their weapons out the window.

"Ms. Creed, are you all right?"

Annja recognized McIntosh's voice then. "I am. What about Professor Hallinger?" she asked.

"He's safe. We've got him."

McIntosh closed in with three other men who were dressed in street clothes. Swiftly, they took the men into custody.

"Do you normally tackle guys into cars?" McIntosh asked.

"Kind of seemed like the thing to do at the time," Annja said. "They killed the security guards in the warehouse." She looked down at the man at her feet. "I couldn't let them get away with that."

McIntosh looked at her silently for a short time. "No. I suppose you couldn't."

FOR THE SECOND NIGHT in a row, Annja sat in the Kirktown Police Department. She sat in one of the straight-backed chairs with eyes closed.

"Hey," a soft voice said beside her.

Blearily, Annja glanced up.

A gray-haired detective with his tie at half-mast looked down at her and held out a cup of coffee. "I would have let you sleep, but McIntosh asked me to make sure you were awake. I think he's going to want to talk to you in a little while."

Annja took the coffee and gazed out the window. Full morning had dawned. Puffy clouds floated by in the blue sky outside.

"Thanks," she said.

"You're getting to be quite a celebrity," the detective said. "The guys around here are thinking about giving you an honorary police commission. You've collared more violent criminals in the last two nights than most of them have their whole careers."

"Not exactly what I'd intended to do here."

"The Homeland Security team says you tackled that guy Icepick. Put him up against a moving car."

"Who?" Annja looked at the man.

"Icepick." The detective frowned. "You didn't get his name?"

"There wasn't a lot of time for introductions."

The detective smiled. "Lady, you're about as tough as I've seen them."

"Thanks." Annja sipped her coffee and found it hot and bitter. "I think."

"It was meant as a compliment," he assured her.

"You called him Icepick."

"That's his street tag. His real name is Gani Abiola."

After a moment of reflection, Annja shook her head. "I don't recognize the name."

"He usually hangs in Atlanta," the detective said.

"What's he doing here?"

"He hasn't said. McIntosh has been with him since we brought him in. The guy lawyered up almost immediately, but he's in the system. We're not starting from scratch on this one. We'll get answers. Guys like that can't run and hide for long."

Looking across the room, Annja saw Hallinger asleep at a desk. As archaeologists, both of them had learned to sleep anywhere and any time they had the chance.

"The prof's doing okay," the detective said.

"Good. We both got lucky. But the security guards didn't."

"Looks like two of them are going to pull through," the detective said.

Part of the acidic knot in Annja's stomach came undone. "I thought they were all dead."

"So did the EMTs and our guys when they first arrived on the scene. But they weren't. That's a good thing. You learn to take those when they come." The detective looked toward the back of the room. "Here comes McIntosh."

Turning in the chair, Annja looked back and saw the detective making his way toward them. McIntosh looked frayed. He carried his cowboy hat and jacket in one hand. His pistol stood out prominently on his hip.

"Hey," he said when he reached Annja.

"Hey."

"Want to get out of here?"

Feeling more claustrophobic in the detectives' bullpen than she had down in the furnace room, Annja stood. "I do."

"Let's collect the professor. I've got a deal for the two of you."

Suspicion filled Annja. McIntosh started toward Hallinger at once.

"What kind of deal?" Annja asked.

"The two of you are really interested in that treasure map you found on that stone, right?"

"Are you interested now, too?"

"Me?" McIntosh smiled and shook his head. "Not me. I don't believe in fairies or treasure maps."

"The map is real," Annja said.

"I believe you believe that, but from what you've said, you don't even know where to find that area on that rock."

"Not yet. But that doesn't mean we couldn't."

"That's what I told my boss." McIntosh stopped at Hallinger's side and gently shook him awake. Hallinger sat up slowly, reached for his glasses and put them on.

"Why would you tell your boss that?"

"Because he needed to know that you guys could probably find it."

"Why did he need to believe that?"

"So he could appropriate the money to send us there."

Annja stared at McIntosh.

"Your boss is sending us where?" Hallinger asked.

"To West Africa," McIntosh said. "Wherever you want to go." He looked at Annja. "If you're interested."

14

"Let me get this right," Doug Morrell said. "You're going to West Africa to go chasing after this Spider Stone?"

"I really can't talk about it." Annja pulled on her backpack and grabbed her suitcase. She'd packed light to come to Atlanta. Now she was paying for it because she didn't have everything she wanted from her Brooklyn loft.

"You can't talk about it," Doug repeated.

"That's right." Annja took a last look around the hotel room, then stepped through the door.

"Annja," Doug whined, "this is me. You can't hold out on me."

"I can. I am."

"That goes against everything our relationship stands for."

"We don't have a relationship." Annja stopped in front of the elevators. "We have an arrangement."

"That's cruel," Doug said.

The elevator doors opened and Annja entered. She hoped she'd lose the phone signal, but she didn't. "You had first dibs on sending me to West Africa," she stated.

"West Africa is big," Doug said. "Where are you going in West Africa?"

"You're not thinking of sending Kristie there." Annja wanted to scream because she knew that was *exactly* what Doug Morrell would be thinking.

"Hey, there's a story here," Doug insisted.

"No monsters."

"It's Africa. There's gotta be zombies."

"I thought you said zombie stories are out with the show."

"We got zombies and an ancient treasure map in this," Doug said. "That's really cool."

The elevator opened and Annja stepped out into the lobby. McIntosh stood near the checkout desk with four men in plainclothes. They looked like an NFL offensive line.

"Annja, you gotta let me in on this," Doug whined. "You're all over the news. CNN. Fox News. MSNBC. I've even heard Larry King is trying to get hold of you."

"Larry King?" That stopped Annja for a moment. She liked watching Larry King, but she couldn't ever imagine meeting the man, much less being interviewed by him.

"That's what I was told. You're major news right now."

Those were the magic words. *Right now.* Annja knew several archaeologists who had enjoyed momentary fame during unusual finds or when some popular legend or myth caught the attention of the public. It never lasted.

"You can't buy this kind of advertising," Doug said.

Annja knew that, but she was thankful for it, too. She liked living her life out from under the microscope. Obscurity was a good thing. She didn't care for the limelight despite the pieces she did for *Chasing History's Monsters.* Those were a means to an end, and she felt they gave her the opportunity to at least teach a little about what she knew and loved.

"Did you hear me?" Doug asked.

"I did." Annja walked to the checkout desk.

"I already took care of the paperwork," McIntosh said, taking her suitcase and handing it to one of his agents. "We're ready to roll. Finish your call."

"I don't think you're seeing the opportunity that you have here," Doug said. "This is freaking huge."

"Is that the television producer?" McIntosh asked.

Annja nodded.

"Let me have the phone." McIntosh radiated impatience. He held out his hand.

Pushing aside the immediate resentment she felt, Annja handed over the phone.

"Doug Morrell," McIntosh said in a voice that crackled with authority. "This is Special Agent McIntosh of Homeland Security. This conversation is over." He shut the cell phone and handed it back to Annja. "Let's go. We're going to have to hurry if we're going to make the flight out of Atlanta to Paris."

Annja was about to put the phone away when it rang. McIntosh shot her an irritated look. She answered the phone because of the look more than anything else. She wanted the relationship with McIntosh clarified. *I'm here because I want to be.*

"Hello."

"Is that guy really a special agent from Homeland Security?" Doug asked.

"Yes."

"Man, that is so awesome! Annja, seriously, you can't just shut me—"

Annja ended the call and turned the phone off.

McIntosh took the lead. As soon as they walked through the hotel's front door, they stepped out into a crowd of reporters. Annja stopped for just a moment, staring out in disbelief.

Hallinger stepped up beside her. "McIntosh kept the media out of the hotel," he said.

Voices filled the immediate area as television reporters began their spiels. A phalanx of Kirktown police parted the crowd. McIntosh took Annja by the elbow and led her to the second dark sedan in a five-car convoy of similar vehicles.

"Is it true you're going to find a lost treasure?" a female reporter asked.

"No comment," Annja answered automatically. *You've been watching too many movies,* she told herself.

McIntosh stopped for just a moment and turned toward the reporter. "Where did you get that information?"

The reporter immediately responded with another question. "What are you going to do with the treasure when you find it?"

"No comment," McIntosh responded.

Annja slid a pair of sunglasses from her backpack and looked at McIntosh. What are you up to? she wondered.

One of the special agents opened the car door and McIntosh folded her inside, sliding in to join her. She was sandwiched between McIntosh and another Homeland Security agent. Hallinger was put into the front passenger seat. The reporters and other members of the crowd pressed in against the windows.

Annja placed her backpack on the floorboard between her feet. She unzipped one of the pockets, took out a sheet of paper and handed it to McIntosh.

"What's this?" McIntosh asked.

"A list of books I'm going to need."

"Books?"

"Reference books. History books. Maps."

"Is this going to be expensive?"

"Probably. Most of those are textbooks. They're not cheap. I already have most of them in my loft, but you'll have to have someone purchase those for us along the way."

Hallinger reached into his pocket and came out with a folded piece of paper. "I made a list, too."

Reluctantly, McIntosh took the professor's list, as well.

"If there are any duplicates," Hallinger said, "just cross them off."

"Actually, make sure we get two of each," Annja said. "It would be better if we had our own books to search through."

"Well," Hallinger said, "that is true. What with notes and possibly needing to consult the same book at the same time."

"Didn't you learn anything while you were getting your degrees?" McIntosh asked.

"Archaeology isn't like law enforcement," Annja said pointedly. "We don't get an updated list every day of who the bad guys are and what steps to take when we find them. There are thousands of years of human habitation to learn about, and millions of years before that. A lot of archaeologists specialize. But some of us, like Professor Hallinger and myself, understand that archaeology and the study of civilization is a lifelong pursuit. Even your doctor hands you off to a specialist when things get to be unfamiliar. That specialist is just like us. He or she will open a book, get on the Internet or call a colleague to get more information."

McIntosh held up his hands. "Point taken." He handed the lists to the agent on the other side of Annja. "Call it in."

The agent made the call, told whomever he was talking to that the books needed to be delivered to Charles de Gaulle Airport in Paris and started reading off the book titles.

Annja focused on McIntosh. "Do you want to tell us now why Homeland Security has agreed to fly us to West Africa?"

McIntosh grinned at her. "For the treasure hunt, of course."

Annja just looked at him.

"I thought a little humor might help," McIntosh said.

"Two security guards died last night," Annja said. "I'm not in the mood for humor."

McIntosh sobered.

Despite his devil-may-care attitude, Annja could see that he was tired, too.

"Actually," McIntosh said in a more subdued tone, "you're going to be bait."

"GANI ABIOLA, the guy from last night that you came to know as Icepick," McIntosh said, "is the nephew of Tafari."

"The West African warlord you mentioned," Hallinger said.

Annja sat at the table in the small security room McIntosh had arranged at the Hartsfield-Jackson Atlanta International Airport. She picked at the breakfast tray the security personnel had delivered right after they'd arrived.

"Right," McIntosh agreed. "Tafari has become a person of interest to Homeland Security."

"You mentioned that he had ties to al-Qaeda," Annja said. "That he'd provided training camps for them."

McIntosh nodded and tapped a button on the notebook computer that had been delivered with the meal. Someone had put together the file he was now using. "The department has reason to believe that Tafari's exposure to al-Qaeda goes deeper than that."

Pictures scrolled across the computer screen. Several of them showed scenes in the African savanna lands, filled with short trees and scruffy brush. They were obviously surveillance shots taken with long-range lenses.

"Intelligence suggests that Tafari has been part of a biological-weapons research effort on behalf of al-Qaeda," McIntosh went on.

"What makes them think that?" Annja asked.

"That's classified information, Ms. Creed."

"You said we're being used as bait."

"To draw Tafari out. Not al-Qaeda."

"And if we just happen across a biological-weapons research center while we're out in the bush?" Annja asked.

McIntosh shook his head and looked very confident. "You won't be anywhere near al-Qaeda."

"You can guarantee that?" Hallinger asked.

"I feel very confident about that," McIntosh replied.

"That's reassuring," Annja said.

"Look," McIntosh said, "I understand the sarcasm. I really do. Personally, I didn't want to put you people in the field." His eyes turned harder. "You're civilians. You're not trained for this. If I was in charge of this expedition, neither one of you would be going. We've got other people that we have access to that have some training. Enough to save themselves." He looked at Hallinger. "You've got no experience at all when it comes to this."

"I'm not going to argue with you," the professor responded.

"And you." McIntosh looked at Annja and took a deep breath.

Annja returned his challenging gaze full measure.

"You tackle guys in the path of oncoming cars," McIntosh grated. "Not exactly the brightest thing I've ever seen. There's a certain lack of subtlety in something like that."

Annja resisted the impulse to fire a rejoinder.

"Whether you go with us or without us," McIntosh said, "you know that Tafari is interested in that Spider Stone you found. Going over there by yourselves—if you could find someone to pick up the tab—isn't a good idea, either. No matter what you do, you're going to be dealing with him. You're better off letting us deal with him. That's what we're trained to do."

Silence hung in the room for a moment.

"You know," Hallinger said quietly, "Special Agent McIntosh has a valid point."

Reluctantly, Annja agreed.

Someone knocked on the door.

"Enter," McIntosh said.

One of the agents posted outside opened the door and stepped inside. He held up a hand. "Five minutes until we board."

McIntosh nodded.

The agent stepped back into the hall.

"Okay," McIntosh said, looking back at Annja and Hallinger, "it's show time. Are you in or out?"

ANNJA WOKE on the plane. It was dark. For a moment she didn't remember where she was and she knew she was very tired. She traveled a lot, but there was something about flying at night that she found unnerving. A heavy book rested on her lap, and she shifted it to a more comfortable position.

"I could put it in the overhead compartment."

McIntosh sat on her left. He held out a hand.

Annja memorized the page number and passed the book over to him. He stood long enough to put the book away.

"Pillow or blanket?" he asked.

"No. Thanks."

McIntosh dropped into his seat. "You okay?"

"Yeah."

"Looked like you were sleeping okay."

"I shouldn't have slept," Annja said. "There's a lot I should be doing."

"You're tired." McIntosh shifted in his seat until he was comfortable. "When you're tired, you're supposed to sleep."

"I slept a little in Paris." They'd had an eight-hour layover in the City of Lights. Everything was hurry-up-and-wait.

While they were in Paris, Annja had thought about Roux. She'd almost given in to the temptation to call him, but she didn't know what she'd have said. Trying to figure out where Roux fit in her life was confusing.

"You slept maybe three hours in Paris," McIntosh commented.

"I've slept less."

"The night before was no picnic, either. It catches up to you after a while. You're not going to do yourself any good if you're dead on your feet when we get to Dakar."

"I'll be fine by the time we get there." Annja lifted the window cover.

A silver quarter moon hung over a bed of fluffy white clouds. The sky was indigo above the clouds but quickly deepened to black.

"How far out are we?" Annja asked. She'd been immersed in one of the books containing topographical maps that had been delivered to de Gaulle and hadn't noted the time.

McIntosh glanced at his watch. "About two hours. You still have time for a nap."

They were scheduled to land in Dakar at 8:15 p.m. local time.

Annja closed the window cover. "You've got a fixation on naps, Special Agent McIntosh."

"I just wish I could sleep. I never can on an airplane," he said.

"Why?"

McIntosh shrugged. "I never have been able to."

Annja looked over her shoulder, spotting Hallinger and the other Homeland Security agents. McIntosh had assured her that most of the men with them had come out of the CIA and had previous experience in West Africa. Most of them, Annja had noted, were also African-American. They looked like grim, competent men.

"Nobody else seems to be having a problem." Annja resettled in her seat.

"Yeah, well, I wish I wasn't."

"You're not quite living up to the big, bad special-agent image, McIntosh."

"This isn't exactly what I set out to do."

"You didn't want to be a spy guy?"

McIntosh's lips curled into a smile. "I wanted the babes. Don't get me wrong there. I grew up on James Bond movies. But after you reach a certain point in your life, you realize those are just movies."

Annja smiled back. She liked that McIntosh could be honest, and that he'd seen the world differently as a boy. Some men never grew up.

"Then how did you get to be a spy?" she asked.

"I'm not a spy. I'm a federal agent."

"There's a difference?"

"I think so. I chase threats to our country. It's an important job.

My dad was a cop. I was, too. He did Vietnam. I did the first Gulf War. After that, cop work made sense. I was good at what I did. Made detective in Atlanta pretty quick. I liked the work. Putting bad guys behind bars. I thought that's what I'd do until I retired, then maybe join my dad's security agency. He started that up when he pulled the pin."

"Then why the change to Homeland Security?"

McIntosh was quiet for a moment. His eyes didn't meet hers. "My mom and dad had never been to New York City. They'd always talked about going. My mom more than my dad."

Dread knotted Annja's stomach. She was certain she knew what was coming, but she couldn't stop it. She'd elicited this by trying to question McIntosh's motivations.

"They went to New York," McIntosh went on in a voice that was devoid of emotion. "They were inside the World Trade Center the morning it came down. We were on the phone, Dad giving me grief about something. Just like usual. Then…they weren't there anymore." He was silent for a moment. "After that, when the Department of Homeland Security was formed, it made perfect sense to me that I be part of it. So I've been working out of the Atlanta PD ever since."

Without a word, Annja reached over and took his hand. She felt the calluses under her fingertips. "This isn't the hand of a guy who just rides a desk."

"No." McIntosh squeezed her hand gently, accepting the support she offered. "I have a small ranch. I do a lot of the work myself." He looked at her. "You know, I've been partnered with a lot of guys who would tackle a perp onto the hood of a moving car, but I wouldn't want them holding my hand."

Annja laughed, and in that, with the return of the humor, the melancholy was put in abeyance. At least for the moment. She was sure it returned regularly.

"So tell me," Annja said.

"What?"

"Why are you scared of sleeping on planes?"

McIntosh smiled. "I was on a plane that went down, barely survived the crash."

She looked into his eyes. "You're lying."

"I have episodes of missing time on airplane flights."

"Fear of alien abduction?" That was an urban myth made popular by *The X-Files*. Annja shook her head and rolled her eyes.

"Don't believe that one, either?" he asked.

"I'll know the truth when I hear it."

McIntosh took a deep breath. "You ever watch *The Twilight Zone?*"

"Sometimes. The Rod Serling version or the later one?"

"The classic episode with William Shatner."

"The gremlin on the wing?" Annja laughed, and it felt good to do that. For the moment, they were thirty-five thousand feet in the air and Kirktown's violence and the danger coming with their arrival in Dakar seemed a million miles away.

"Hey," he protested. "That's not funny."

"Yeah, it is."

Then McIntosh's eyes crinkled as he smiled, too. "Yeah, I suppose maybe it is." He was quiet for a moment. "In all seriousness, Tafari is a dangerous man."

"I kind of got that the first time he almost killed us. I learned clue-gathering from watching Scooby-Doo as a little girl."

McIntosh shook his head. "I can't imagine you as a little girl."

"I was. Once."

"Where did you grow up?"

"New Orleans."

McIntosh grimaced. "Not a lot of good things have happened there lately."

"No."

"But you live in Brooklyn now."

"I see somebody did a background check," she said.

"I did an Internet search, too. You beat Kristie Chatham hands down when it comes to archaeology."

Annja cocked an eyebrow, waiting for the rest of it. McIntosh didn't say anything more. She kept looking at him.

"What?" he asked finally.

"That's all you're going to say?"

"If I said anything else, I think I'd be in trouble. No matter what

I said. And I really don't want to jeopardize the hand-holding because it kind of helps on the whole gremlin thing."

Smiling, Annja leaned back in her chair. "Wise move, Special Agent McIntosh." She closed her eyes and slept.

15

Annja stood as the plane door was opened and the passengers were allowed to start filing out. McIntosh handed down her book, then grabbed his own kit and waited.

"We'll let everyone else deplane first," he said. "Then we'll move as a group."

"Doesn't that mean they'll get us all in one concentrated burst?" Annja asked.

McIntosh frowned at her, but his eyes still held a twinkle. "You've got a demented mind."

"Ever wonder why Scooby and the gang separated every episode?"

"I'd always thought it was so they could get confused over who was who under the sheets. If it had been an armed engagement, somebody would have gotten killed."

"Okay, that takes the fun out of it," Annja said.

"I just want us to stay safe."

Annja took out her cell phone and turned it on. There were nineteen missed calls. Eighteen of them were from Doug Morrell. The other was from a number that surprised her.

Annja punched in the number and waited.

"The producer?" McIntosh asked.

Annja shook her head, but she didn't bother to explain.

"Ah, Annja, you decided to return my call." Garin Braden's voice was deep and guttural, reflecting his German heritage. The voice fit the man. Garin stood six feet four inches tall and had broad shoulders and a powerful build. His long dark hair matched his magnetic black eyes. A goatee usually framed his mouth and gave his face a roguish cast.

"I did," she replied.

"And what would Roux say if he knew?"

"To stay away from you and not trust you, I imagine," Annja replied easily.

McIntosh looked at her.

Annja shook her head and listened to Garin roaring with laughter.

"You do amuse me. I appreciate that."

"What did you need?"

"Nothing. I just happened to see the footage of you in that small town in Georgia—"

"Kirktown."

"Whatever it's called. Anyway, I saw it and I thought I'd give you a call and see how you were faring."

The plane was emptying slowly, but most of the passengers were now off.

"I don't have a lot of time," Annja said.

"I won't take up much of it, then. Are you well?"

"Yes."

"Good."

"Were you worried?" Annja asked, immediately suspicious.

"Not really," Garin admitted. "You've always shown yourself to be a woman who could handle herself." For a moment, an awkward silence stretched between them.

"Was there anything besides checking on my health that was on your mind?" Annja asked.

"A warning, perhaps. I take it Roux hasn't been forthcoming with everything you can expect now that you have the sword in your possession."

For just an instant, Annja felt the sword hilt press against her palm. She didn't know if the sword felt threatened or she did. Maybe it was both.

"I get the feeling there's a lot he hasn't told me," Annja said.

"The news reports mentioned a Spider Stone. According to the legend behind it, the stone was supposed to be some kind of gift from a god."

"Anansi."

"Ah," Garin said. "The spider god. There's a lot of power in an entity like that."

Entity? Annja thought. Not mythical being?

"Dealing with something like that, if the stone truly was given by Anansi to the person who carried it, could prove decidedly dangerous."

"I'll keep that in mind," Annja said.

"Do so. There will be powerful men after an item such as that."

"Do any particular names come to mind?" Annja asked.

"No, but I do know there are evil men in the world. I don't want you to come to any harm until we meet again."

Because you want to harm me? Annja wondered. A chill ghosted up Annja's spine. She remembered how Garin had attacked her in her loft. Then they'd turned around and had breakfast with Roux, who'd also come calling, and then he'd loaned them his private jet while she finished up the bloody business relating to the Beast of Gévaudan.

Like Roux, Garin Braden was a confusing man.

"I would like to see you again, Annja," Garin said. "Call me. We'll do lunch anywhere in the world that you want to."

"Sure," she answered casually. She wanted to see him again, too. Not because he was good-looking and rich, though that would have been enough for most women. But because he might talk and reveal some of what he'd seen and done during the past five hundred years.

Roux would never do that.

"Be safe, Annja," Garin said. "If you need anything, call me."

While Annja was trying to figure out how to respond to that, Garin broke the connection.

"THE CITY'S DIFFERENT than I thought it would be," McIntosh said.

"How?" Annja studied the Dakar sights through the tinted window of the rental sedan the Homeland Security team had secured.

"It's bigger. A lot bigger. And modern."

Annja smiled. "Don't tell me you were expecting grass huts."

"No, but I just didn't expect *this*. It seems like any city in the United States. Except for all the French advertising."

"French is the national language," Annja said.

Neon lights splashed over the car's windows. The downtown area was still throbbing and active. Pedestrians filled the streets as they walked from bars and taverns. The Atlantic Ocean was only a short distance away to the west.

"Over two million people live in Dakar," Annja went on. "A lot more come into the city to work at service jobs in hotels, bars, tourist areas. The architecture of the newer sections of the city looks like any other large city. But if you see the older sections, like the Kermel Market, you'll see colonial houses that date back to the mid-nineteenth century. The big market, Sandaga, is located in a neo-Sudanese building that is absolutely wonderful to walk through."

"Fond memories?" McIntosh asked.

"I read it in the travel guide," Annja said, laughing.

"Probably won't be a lot of time for sight-seeing," McIntosh informed her.

"I know."

"Who are we meeting here?"

"Jozua Ganesvoort," Annja said.

"He's an archaeologist?"

"No. He owns an import-export business that's been in Dakar for over two hundred years."

"Why are we meeting him?"

"Because he's an armchair historian who has access to ships' logs that date back to the early years of the slave trade."

"And you need the ships' logs?"

Annja looked at him. "Yes."

"Why?"

"To see if we can find a reference to Yohance. The first Yohance. The one whose village was razed and who was taken into captivity and sold as a slave. If we find him listed, there may be some mention of where he was from. Once we get close enough, the map carved on the stone should be enough to get us the rest of the way."

"You don't have to do that," McIntosh said.

Annja felt slightly irritated. "Yes, we do. That's what Professor Hallinger and I came here to do."

"You're going to be exposed if you start traipsing around all over this city."

Her irritation grew. "Hallinger and I didn't come here to sit around as bait."

"We can't guarantee your safety unless you follow procedure."

The car stopped at a light. Shadows bumped and moved across the windows. McIntosh reached for his pistol under his jacket.

Annja looked at the men and women, young and old, lurching at the car. Many of them were maimed, missing fingers and hands and eyes, their faces horribly scarred. Their skin was mottled with leprosy or ashen-gray with illness.

"Calm down," Annja said. "They're just beggars. The city is full of them."

The beggars pleaded in a number of languages, all of it sounding sad and hopeless.

Annja reached into her pocket for some money. Quickly, she pressed money into the hands before her.

When the light changed, the beggars backed off.

"It's not a good idea to give them money," the driver said. "Once they find out you'll do it, they'll stay after you."

"You've been here before?" Annja asked.

"A few times." The man looked at her in the rearview mirror as he pulled through the intersection.

"Then you know that those people can't do anything else but beg," Annja said. "They live outside the city in cardboard huts and sleep three and four to a room. They have to get water from a standpipe every day and sometimes stand in line for hours to do that. Then they have to walk or crawl or drag themselves into this city every day in hopes of begging for just enough money to do it all again the next day."

The driver looked away.

Annja leaned back in the seat and settled into the shadows. Neon colors continued to slash across the windows.

"Sorry," McIntosh said. "I guess I overreacted. For a minute there I could have sworn we'd been overrun by zombies."

"They're just poor and sick," Annja said. "They can't fix that.

Someone has to help them. That's one of the things I hate about traveling. No one seems to care about the poor. Governments don't want to deal with the issue because it's too expensive. And tourists feel like their vacations are getting interrupted." She took a deep breath. "There's so much history in these places, but all the resources have been tapped out, or they haven't been able to compete in world markets." Annja sighed.

They rode the rest of the way to the hotel in strained silence.

Annja felt guilty about that, too. She wasn't being fair. McIntosh and the other agents hadn't known what they were getting into.

She'd overreacted because she'd almost allowed herself to forget.

ALONE AT LAST, Annja stripped off her clothing and stepped into the deep bathtub in her hotel room at the Novotel Dakar. The hotel was located near the business district. Her room was at the front of the building, facing the Atlantic Ocean and the Ile de Goree.

The scented bath smelled divine, and she could already feel the heat from the water penetrating her muscles. Lying back, she luxuriated in the bath, letting it soothe away the aches and abrasions from the fights she'd had. In Atlanta, she'd only taken showers, always in a hurry.

Tonight it was comfort time.

She loved baths. She'd had a large tub installed in her loft when she'd signed her first contract with *Chasing History's Monsters.* In the beginning, she'd thought the show—and she—would only last a season. She wasn't an actress and the show—in her opinion—wasn't very promising. So she'd splurged on the tub and tried not to feel guilty.

Taking a deep breath, she submerged, sliding under the water and letting the heat soak into her. She closed her eyes, feeling almost weightless in the water.

Don't go to sleep, she warned herself. More than once she'd woken in cold water, undoing all the good the hot bath had done.

In an effort to stay awake, she thought about McIntosh.

She was certain that he'd put her in the big suite on purpose, and she doubted that Hallinger or any of the Homeland Security agents had matching accommodations.

The room's a peace offering, she realized. She wondered if she needed to apologize for the episode in the car on the way over. After that, her mind wandered to other thoughts of McIntosh that were entirely healthy and not exactly conducive to relaxation. She decided to push all of that out of her mind and concentrate on the puzzle of the Spider Stone. That's what you're here to do, she reminded herself. You're not some kind of bounty hunter for terrorists.

Unable to hold her breath any longer, she regretfully surfaced. The knots of tension that had tightened her back and shoulders had, for the most part, disappeared.

Reaching over the side of the tub, Annja dried her hands and arms on a towel and reached into her backpack where she'd placed it on a small folding table. Working in the tub wasn't new to her. Her mind was too busy to properly soak if she didn't occupy it. She took the Spider Stone from one of the pockets and held it up to the light.

Amber gleamed like cold fire along the striations.

Hallinger had enlarged photos of the stone in his room, claiming that he'd rather work with them. Since he didn't know the language, he was working with topographical maps of Senegal, trying to overlay the map on the stone onto the country.

While she'd been on the plane, Annja had worked through most of the message, but she wanted to check her findings. There was only one place to do that.

She got out of the bath, wrapped herself in a bathrobe and set up her computer. When she was online, she logged onto the message boards.

There were several messages. Evidently the people on the board had figured out who she was. She usually logged in with a different name on each project and sent private messages to people she'd worked with in the past who had proved reliable.

Most of the messages were from teens with out-of-control hormones, or men who were old enough to know better. Interestingly enough, there were also overtures from females, which was really different from the normal responses.

She scrolled through a number of propositions and jokes looking for anything that might be useful. Finally she came across a private message from hausaboy. Annja opened it.

Hey, Annja. I got most of the message translated. Cool stuff. Lotta work. Here's the story, and I say "story," even though Hausa believers might consider that term sacrilegious, because that's how this tale comes across to me.

Sometime years ago, one of the earliest ancestors of this particular Hausa village—think the name translates into "Falson's Egg"—was under attack from fierce enemies. He prayed to Anansi, who was the chosen god of his people, and asked that his village might be spared.

Unfortunately, that was one of Anansi's less responsible days. He was off on his own pursuits and ignored the pleas of the villagers he'd chosen to adopt as his own people. That happened sometimes with any of the gods of whatever mythology you want to ascribe to.

The village was destroyed by fire or lightning—I can't be sure of the translation. Something like that.

Annja had struggled with the same translation. Fire and lightning were interchangeable in some instances.

When Anansi returned to the village, he was sad. He promised the people who had survived that they would be safe from that point on. The villagers had to travel far away. Anansi had to find them, but he did.

Anansi gave the medicine man the stone. The location of the new village was drawn on the stone's surface, as was Anansi's likeness. It was his promise that they would be taken care of. As you know, Anansi wasn't around the night the slavers ransacked the village.

There's also some mention of a curse against anyone not of the village who might come into possession of the stone.

Great, Annja thought. All I need is to be cursed.

Thought you might want to know that last part. Personally, I don't believe in curses.

Annja quickly typed out a response.

Hey, hausaboy, thanks for all your help. I'd come up with pretty much the same thing. If there's anything I can ever do for you, please let me know.

After she sent the e-mail, Annja went back to her bath. The water had chilled slightly while she'd been busy. She turned on the hot water and opened the drain at the same time. Almost immediately, the water began to warm.

She thought about the possibility of a curse as she studied the Spider Stone. Curses were old. They depended on local belief systems and chance. If enough people believed in a curse, it didn't take much coincidence to make believers out of everyone around. As a result, curses were generally the first line of defense for grave sites.

Reaching for her backpack, she rooted for the topographical maps of Senegal she'd had McIntosh arrange for her. She'd been over them before, during the layover in Paris and while on the plane. Maybe now that she was relaxed, something might jump out at her.

She froze when she heard a noise in the bedroom.

It wasn't repeated.

Annja stood in the bathtub. She reached for the flannel shorts and Brooklyn Dodgers jersey she liked to sleep in when she was traveling.

She pulled on the clothing as quickly and silently as she could. Surreptitious noises came from the outer room again, and this time there was no mistake.

Someone's in the room! The thought crawled across Annja's mind and sent a shiver up her spine.

16

The bathroom was a dead end. There was nowhere to go, no real room to fight even with the spacious accommodations.

Annja summoned the sword to her hand, wrapping her fingers around the hilt as she took a firm grip. She took in a deep, quiet breath, then let it out as she slowed her heart and forced herself to be calm.

The only choice was whether to stay in the room until whoever was out there came in after her or charge out to meet them. Frugal or foolhardy.

Annja decided to set her own destiny. That had always been her preferred path. Gripping the door handle, she twisted it and pulled the door open.

Four young and hard-eyed men stood inside her room, lit by the bedside lamp. All of them were dressed in American-style warm-ups and basketball jerseys, as if they'd just stepped off the court of an NBA game. Except these men were carrying suppressed pistols and machetes. Two of them stood guard near the bathroom door while the other two went through Annja's suitcases and books.

They didn't expect her to come out of the bathroom. Evidently they felt confident enough to try to search the room before any violence broke out.

Definitely not random burglars, Annja thought. They're here for the stone. She was conscious of the slight weight of it in her pocket even as she drew back the sword and launched herself at the first man.

The man lifted the pistol and fired. The bullets cut the air by Annja's head. She didn't hold back, couldn't hold back.

Months of practice with the sword had made it more a part of her than it had been when the pieces had re-formed. Annja sliced into the man's forearm. Before the shock or the pain had time to register on him, before his pistol had time to hit the floor, Annja swept the sword across his body.

She darted behind the man, taking brief refuge there. Bullets slapped into the stunned man.

Annja whirled, the world slowing down around her, and turned to face the second man by the bathroom door. He was only then registering surprise that he'd shot his compatriot instead of Annja. Or maybe he was surprised about the sword she wielded with such deadly skill.

Either way, his surprise didn't last long.

Annja lunged with the sword, bringing it up as she ducked beneath the man's outstretched arm. She heard the pistol cough twice before the sword pierced the man's chest.

The man sagged immediately. He dropped his machete and grabbed Annja's wrists. Dying, he tried to bring the pistol in line with her head.

Annja kicked her attacker backward. Still transfixed by the sword, he stumbled toward the other two men. The remaining invaders abandoned their search of the suitcases and reached for their weapons.

The suite was large, providing some room to maneuver.

Annja ran toward the only light on in the room. Jumping up, she delivered a high kick to the lamp, shattering the lightbulb in a shower of sparks.

She landed in a crouch, one hand on the floor to maintain her balance. Pistols coughed behind her, and muzzle-flashes marked the locations of the two men. They had remained close together.

The darkness inside the room was almost complete. Only a sliver of moonlight penetrated the heavy drapes and fell across the floor.

Annja gripped the sword and rose, standing straight and making for the wall, working from memory. Her bare feet made no sound as she moved.

The two men spoke in nervous voices. They spoke a dialect Annja didn't understand, but their anxiety and anger were easy to read.

Annja knew she could have headed for the door, but she couldn't be sure they hadn't locked it behind them. And fumbling with the lock in the darkness, making all that noise, would draw a hail of bullets.

The second bedside lamp winked on, unleashing a pool of dim yellow light. The man who had turned it on was squatted down behind the bed, on the other side from Annja. His partner was across the room.

Both men started firing, but Annja had already leaped forward, the sword in both hands. She brought the blade down, splitting the gunman's head and turning the sheets crimson. As she vaulted over the dead man, she kicked the light, plunging the room into darkness again.

For a moment she held her position, listening intently. The traffic noises in the street reached her ears.

"Stay back!" the man warned in heavily accented English. "Stay back or I will kill you!"

Annja tracked the man's voice, realizing he was making his way toward the door. Moonlight fell across his back for just a moment, outlining his upper body and blinking against the gun.

"Who sent you?" Annja asked, and moved to the side immediately.

Muzzle-flashes tore holes in the darkness.

"Did Tafari send you for the Spider Stone?" Annja whipped back to the other side of the room and advanced in long strides.

The man fired again, and this time the pistol blew back empty, the sound sharp and distinct. He turned and fled, his feet slapping against the floor.

Annja pursued, knowing that none of the other men were alive. She wanted at least one witness who could talk.

The door opened and the light from the hallway hurt Annja's eyes. She blinked but never broke stride, managing to grab the door before it closed.

The man broke to the right, running hard. He still carried his machete in his left hand.

Annja ran after him, driving her legs like pistons, quickly closing in on the man. Ahead, a young couple turned the corner from the bank of elevators. They saw the man with the machete and froze like deer in headlights.

The man lifted his machete, his intent clear.

Releasing the sword, Annja felt it fade away as she threw herself forward in a feet-first baseball slide. The carpet bit into her skin, promising abrasions and burns, but she collided with the back of the man's legs before he could bring down the machete.

As the man buckled under her onslaught, Annja reached up and caught his arm, controlling the machete. The young man managed to get the woman out of the way as Annja and her prey skidded into the wall.

Off balance, Annja hit the wall hard enough to drive the wind from her lungs. Dazed for a second, she held on to the man's arm, then struggled to her knees as her opponent tried to fight his way free. Annja closed her free hand into a fist and hit the man in the jaw. His eyes rolled back and he slumped over.

Breathing raggedly, her breath just coming back to her, Annja looked up at the young couple. "Do you speak English?"

"That," the young man whispered hoarsely, "was incredible! I thought he was going to kill us!"

"Yes," the young woman at his side said. "We speak English."

Annja thought she detected a German accent but wasn't certain. "Do you have a cell phone?"

"He just came out of nowhere!" the man said. "I felt like I was in one of those American slasher movies!"

Great, Annja thought, feeling the aches and pains seeping into her again and wrecking all that the bath had accomplished.

"I have a cell phone." The young woman held it up.

"Please call the hotel and ask for security." Annja started going through the unconscious man's pockets, looking for identification. "Tell them what happened."

"I saw my life flash before my eyes!" the man said. Then he held his head. "I've got to sit down. I'm going to be sick." He swayed unsteadily and sat against the opposite wall. He stared at the unconscious man. "He really was going to kill us, wasn't he?"

Annja didn't answer. The young man was going into shock. But the woman with him was clear and concise as she dealt with the hotel staff.

A shadow fell across Annja. Startled because she'd sensed no approach, she reached for the machete lying nearby. She had the wooden hilt in her hand when she saw the old woman standing before her.

The woman wore a dark red dress that almost reached the ground. A scarf of a similar color held her cotton-white hair back from her lined face. Annja guessed that the woman was seventy, with a lot of hard years behind her, but she could have been even older. She carried a gnarled wooden staff in one hand.

"You have finally come," the old woman said in accented English. "I knew that you would. My prophecies are never wrong."

Prophecies? Annja stared at the old woman.

Then hotel security arrived in force and things really got crazy.

TAFARI WALKED into the village with impunity. He carried pistols in each hand. They were the Glocks that his nephew had sent him, with extended magazines and fully automatic function. He used them to cut down two Hausa warriors who challenged him.

Neither of the men carried firearms. One had a tribal spear that was probably more heirloom than weapon, and the other had an ax used for chopping firewood. The bullets smashed into them and drove them backward.

The cries of women and children pierced the chatter of automatic weapons. Those silenced, one by one, as the raiders cut them down.

Tafari had given orders that there were to be no survivors. He kept walking, picking out targets as they appeared, changing magazines in the pistols as he needed to.

"I am Tafari!" he yelled at the villagers. "I am the death-bringer!"

He knew he looked the part. Naked except for a loincloth, his body was covered in painted tribal markings. White paint lifted his face out of the darkness and made it a skull.

His men flared around him, many of them dressed and marked as he was. Two of them carried military flamethrowers and sent streams of liquid fire rolling into the thatched huts. The wood caught instantly and burned incredibly fast.

Gray smoke poured across the sky, giving the illusion of chasing back the night.

Four jeeps circled the village deep in the savanna. Machine

gunners on the rear decks executed anyone who tried to escape the slaughter at the village.

"I am Tafari!" he howled. "Beloved of the gods! I speak the words of the gods! You chose to ignore my warnings! You chose to disobey me! Now you will all die!"

In only a few minutes, the village was filled with the dead and the dying. The stink of burned flesh mixed with the acrid smoke.

His weapons recharged, Tafari led the hunt for the survivors. They killed them where they lay one by one.

When they were finished, Tafari gave orders to bring the chief and his grandson to him. Tafari stood waiting in the center of the village. He had sent men into the village to capture the two before they had begun the killing.

The chief and his grandson, a boy of nine or ten, were forced to their knees in front of Tafari. Fear strained the old man's gray-stubbled face though he tried not to show it.

"You are an abomination," the chief declared. His voice was hoarse with emotion and from the smoke. Tears leaked down his withered cheeks.

Tafari struck the old man with one of his pistols, breaking the teeth down to yellow stumps. The chief cried out in pain and collapsed to the ground. Blood pooled from his split lips.

The boy cried out and reached for his grandfather, hugging him around the waist.

Holstering his pistols, Tafari reached over his shoulder for the machete in the leather sheath and drew the weapon clear. Firelight gleamed along the blade's keen edge.

The old man looked up as Tafari swung the machete. He barely had time to get a hand up and whisper, "No!"

Then the blade sliced through the old man's hand, dropping his fingers to the ground, and cut deeply into his neck. Blood spattered Tafari's face and chest at the impact. It took Tafari two more swings to hack the head free of the skinny body.

The boy screamed in fear and backed away from the corpse. He tried to get up and run, but Zifa backhanded him to the ground.

"Don't kill him," Tafari ordered. "Someone has to carry the message."

Zifa nodded. Instead, he stepped on the boy's shin and broke the bone with a snap. The boy wept almost silently, wrapping his arms tightly around himself.

Grabbing the old man's head, Tafari squatted and held it in the terrified boy's face.

The boy closed his eyes, shivering in fear.

Tafari relished the fear. Fear was indelible. Once someone was marked by fear, that emotion left permanent scars. He reached out and slapped the boy's face. "Open your eyes," he screamed.

The boy tried to turn his head away. Zifa caught his head and forced it against the ground.

Slapping the boy again, Tafari said, "Open your eyes or I will kill you like I killed your grandfather."

The boy opened his eyes, almost convulsing in fright.

"I am Tafari. Tell everyone who did this to your grandfather. To your people. And to your village. Do you understand?"

The boy nodded.

"Say my name."

"Tafari."

"Good. Tell all that you talk to that they will not listen to Jaineba anymore. Tell them that they will not attack the refinery trucks and equipment anymore. Those things are now under my protection. Tell me that you understand."

"I understand."

"Then you may live." Tafari stood and nodded at Zifa.

Stepping back, Zifa yanked the boy to his feet. He stood awkwardly on his broken leg, lip trembling and eyes watering.

"Go," Tafari said. "Before I change my mind."

Limping, the boy made his way through the burning remnants of the village. He disappeared into the night.

"He might not live to see morning," Zifa said. "There are many creatures in the night."

Tafari caught movement from the corner of his eye. When he glanced up, he saw the pharaoh-eagle owl gliding above the treetops, skirting the flames that licked at the huts. He took heart in the omen of good fortune.

"If he does not," Tafari said, "the message will still be sent. These people will obey me."

Scanning the immediate area, Tafari found a pole about four feet long and used his machete to sharpen both ends. He thrust one end into the ground, then shoved the chief's head on top of the other end. The pole wavered for a moment, but held up under the weight.

Tafari stood back and admired his handiwork. Even if the boy died somewhere in the night, daybreak would still see his message written for all to see.

The sound of a roaring engine drew near.

Sheathing his machete, Tafari again drew the pistols. He stood waiting.

Four men rode in the jeep. They were from the communications camp and had been instructed to bring him word of the capture of the Spider Stone.

"The team failed," a slim warrior with an eye patch told Tafari.

"How?"

"They went after the woman. They thought she would be the easiest to capture. Instead, she killed three of them."

Tafari digested that. It wasn't easy. He hadn't expected the woman to be much of a problem. The way his nephew had explained what had happened in Georgia was that the police had intercepted them.

"She killed three men?" Tafari asked.

"Yes."

That put things in a different light. "What about the other archaeologist?"

"They never got to him."

Tafari waved the man away. Turning, he looked at the head mounted on the pole. It was a temporary setback. Nothing more. He wouldn't let it be anything more.

"Send more men," he told Zifa. "Tell them to kill the woman if they have to. I want the Spider Stone."

"It will be done."

Tafari gazed out across the carnage that remained of the village. The flames leaped high into the night sky, illuminating the face of the village chief. His adversaries didn't know whom they were dealing with, but he would show them.

17

"They killed *themselves?*"

Seated on a chair outside her hotel room, Annja returned the Dakar police inspector's gaze. "Yes," she replied, keeping a straight face.

The inspector's name was Oumar Mbaye. Short and stout, he wore the khaki uniform and red beret of the local police. He was in his early forties and had served on the Senegalese police department for twenty of those years. He'd expressed that to Annja in an effort to keep her calm, and maybe to intimidate her a little.

Annja was calm, but she wasn't intimidated. The only thing that had unnerved her was the old woman who stood just down the hallway.

Lurked down the hallway, Annja thought irritably. That's definitely a lurk. She glanced at the woman standing there so patiently and calmly, as if she had all night. It was beginning to look as if Mbaye's investigation was going to take all night.

"They killed each other with knives?" Mbaye's eyebrows were raised in disbelief.

"Machetes," Annja corrected. "Those were machetes that I saw. Guns and machetes. If they had knives, I didn't see them."

"But they had guns!" Mbaye almost spluttered.

"I know they had guns. They shot at me with them."

"And they *missed.*"

Annja thought about that for a moment. "Perhaps that's why they brought the machetes."

"Because they were such terrible shots with the guns?"

Annja gave him a winning smile. "That sounds good, don't you think?"

Mbaye frowned at her. "No, I don't think that sounds good. Not good at all."

"Do you have another explanation?"

Pointing a finger at her, Mbaye said, "*You* killed them."

"Why would I do that?"

"Because they were in your room."

"Just for clarification, we are in agreement that the hotel room those men are lying in is mine?"

Mbaye huffed.

"And the lock was tampered with?"

"Yes, yes, yes. All of that is true. But you can't go around killing people in Dakar, Miss Creed, no matter what the provocation."

Annja agreed. "But I didn't kill anybody," she said.

Mbaye sighed.

"What's he saying?" McIntosh stood at Annja's side. He didn't speak French so he was locked out of the conversation. "He's not happy. I can tell just from looking that he's not happy."

"He's not happy," Annja agreed.

"Why isn't he happy? Are you telling him something you shouldn't be?" McIntosh had sent for a French interpreter from the embassy but no one had arrived yet.

"He has three dead men in my hotel room to explain," Annja replied. "That's a lot of explaining to do, even in Dakar."

The city was known as a crime capital and had a lot of trouble with student demonstrations. The American Embassy had issued warnings to American tourists not to gather near protesting students or in dangerous parts of the city.

"Are you cooperating?" McIntosh asked.

"He wants me to admit to killing those men."

McIntosh considered that. "Well, don't cooperate that much. I mean, if you killed those guys, don't tell him that."

"Thanks for the vote of confidence."

"It's not like this would be your first time to kill somebody. You killed those guys back in Georgia."

Mbaye smiled broadly. Then he reached inside a pocket and brought out a cigarette pack and a lighter. He lit up and smiled again.

McIntosh leaned back against the wall with a look of helpless frustration. "He understands English, doesn't he?"

"Yes," Annja said.

McIntosh cursed.

"Well, now," Mbaye said in English, "it seems we're all in agreement that Miss Creed killed the men in her room."

"He speaks English pretty well, too, don't you think?" Annja asked McIntosh.

"Why didn't you tell him you only spoke English?" McIntosh griped.

"Because the police officer who first arrived on the scene couldn't speak English. He could only speak French and an African dialect that I couldn't speak. I didn't want to get shot, so I spoke to him in French."

"It's a shame for an educated person to hide the fact that he or she has an education," Mbaye observed. "We are living in enlightened times."

"Enlightened times don't include letting hired killers go after a hotel guest," McIntosh replied.

"Americans have made a lot of enemies overseas of late." Mbaye breathed smoke out. "We can't be held accountable for the enemies your country makes."

"This doesn't look like something my country is responsible for."

"Really?" Mbaye lifted his eyebrows. "Then what does this look like?"

Annja folded her arms and waited to see if McIntosh would mention Tafari. If he did, they were going to be shuttled out of Senegal just as quickly as they'd arrived. The Senegalese government wasn't going to condone American espionage activity on their soil.

"I'll let you talk to the American Embassy," McIntosh replied.

And that would be a mistake, too, Annja thought. Once the embassy staff got involved, they'd want to be part of everything. Soon there would be a whole parade of people trekking around.

She looked at Mbaye. "How much?" she asked.

Mbaye smiled. "Ah, you've been to our country before."

"What?" McIntosh asked. "How much for what?"

Annja switched to French. "Let's speak in this language."

"Of course." Mbaye waved away a lungful of smoke.

"How much to conduct the investigation?"

"Three would-be rapists, murderers or thieves?" Mbaye shrugged. "What seems fair to you?"

"They're already caught," Annja pointed out. "It's not like you're going to have to go looking for them."

Mbaye grinned.

"What's going on?" McIntosh asked. He tried to step between them, but two of the khaki-clad policemen moved forward and blocked him from their superior.

"The fourth man says you attacked them with a sword," Mbaye said. "He claims that you killed all three of them."

"One of them was shot."

"Only after he'd been cut badly by a large blade."

"Did you find a sword?" Annja asked.

Frowning, Mbaye shook his head. "We haven't given up looking."

"Everyone needs a hobby," Annja said with a shrug.

"Perhaps you used one of their machetes."

"If I took one of their weapons away and used it to save myself, would I be found guilty of anything other than self-defense?"

"No. Of course not," the police inspector said.

"Then how much do you need to do the investigation and bring charges against the fourth man?"

Mbaye hesitated. "Two thousand dollars."

"I'll give you a thousand."

"That's robbery."

"To file a report? I don't think so," Annja said.

"I could put you in jail."

Annja remained calm. "The American Embassy would get me right out again."

"We are at an impasse," Mbaye stated.

"Not if you want a thousand dollars."

"She's being generous," a man said, also in French. "I wouldn't give you a thousand dollars to carry away the bodies of those three dead villains."

Annja turned in the direction of the voice.

A man approached from the hallway. He was blond and fair-skinned, somewhere in his fifties, Annja guessed. His blue eyes stood out like sapphires. An expensive suit draped his lean frame, and the jacket he wore could have paid for a small car.

"Mr. Ganesvoort." Mbaye inclined his head in an abbreviated bow.

The man extended a hand to Annja and took hers in his warmly. "Good evening, Ms. Creed. I'm Jozua Ganesvoort."

"Mr. Ganesvoort," Annja said.

"Please. Call me Jozua." Ganesvoort smiled.

Jozua Ganesvoort was a businessman whose family had moved from the Netherlands to Senegal 250 years ago. He was also the man Professor Hallinger had arranged to see concerning the origins of Yohance and the Spider Stone.

"This isn't any business of yours, Mr. Ganesvoort," Mbaye said.

"I disagree. Ms. Creed and Professor Hallinger are scheduled to be my guests in the morning. I would be remiss if I didn't make an effort to ensure that they made it to my home safely."

Mbaye turned to Annja. "One thousand dollars will do nicely."

Turning to McIntosh, Annja said in English, "Give him a thousand dollars."

"Why?" the Homeland Security agent asked.

"To close the case and cut us loose."

"That's bribery."

"No," Annja said quietly, before Mbaye could take offense, "that's how things are done here. The Dakar police department is undermanned and underfunded. They supplement their incomes by charging for police services."

"That's not how we do it in Atlanta."

"We're not in Atlanta," Annja reminded him.

Scowling, McIntosh shifted his attention to Mbaye. "Do you take traveler's checks?"

"Of course."

"What brought you here?" Annja asked Ganesvoort, in English so McIntosh would understand.

"A phone call, actually." Ganesvoort looked around curiously. "From a woman. She sounded rather old, but I didn't recognize the voice. She knew me, though. And she knew that you were going to be my guest tomorrow morning."

Annja searched the hallway, but there was no sign of the old woman.

I knew you'd come, she'd said.

But who was she? And how had she known?

"YOU'VE FOUND the Spider Stone, I see."

Seated beside Ganesvoort in the limousine that had pulled up in front of the hotel then swept her and Hallinger away, Annja nodded. They'd left McIntosh behind, which hadn't set well with him. McIntosh hadn't wanted Annja to leave, but he was unable to stop her. The trip to Dakar had already been paid for. She enjoyed being able to slip McIntosh's chains. It put them on more equal footing. They were in her world now, not his.

"May I see it?" the historian asked.

Annja hesitated only a second and hoped her indecision hadn't been noticed by their host. She handed him the stone.

The tiger's eye gleamed honey-gold as he turned the stone in his fingers. "Beautiful."

"What do you know about the Spider Stone?" she asked.

"Only that it could lead someone to a fabled treasure left by a ruined Hausa village. And that it was presumed lost. Most people thought the Arab raiders made off with it when they attacked the village." Ganesvoort returned the stone and looked at her with those bright blue eyes. "I presume the Spider Stone made it to the New World by way of one of the slaves?"

"Yes," Hallinger said, looking flustered. "From the accounts we've had access to, a young slave named Yohance brought the Spider Stone to the fledgling United States before there was even a United States."

"Fascinating." Ganesvoort rubbed at his chin. "I'd heard the stone had disappeared almost three hundred years ago. Before my family set up shop on Ile de Goree. Of course, I'd always believed the Spider Stone to be one more myth. Africa is a land filled with stories of vengeful gods and wondrous things. Even though we've pierced so many of her mysteries, so many yet remain." He smiled. "Of course, you already know that. That's why you do what it is you do." He spread his hands. "Now, why do you want to see my collection of ships' logs?"

"We're trying to find what ship Yohance went out on," Annja answered. "And we're hoping the captain made some notation of where he was captured."

"They didn't all make notes," Ganesvoort warned.

"I know," Hallinger said. "But several of the ships' captains were extremely detailed."

"And you had nowhere else to go." Ganesvoort grinned.

Annja returned the grin, caught up in the excitement of the hunt. "And we had nowhere else to go."

"I have a large collection of logs."

"The precise reason I called you," Hallinger said.

"With over three hundred years of slavery open to you, you're talking about a lot of searching."

"We had to figure out the time frame from how many Yohances there had been," Annja said. "We figured a median age of around twenty-five or thirty for each Yohance. Some died younger than that and some lived longer."

The car sped in silent smoothness toward the harbor. Silver-gray smog hung over the dark green water. Ships and pleasure craft lined the harbor.

"The Yohance we found went missing in 1861," Annja said.

"And what number Yohance was he?"

"The fourth."

"Then by your own criteria, the first Yohance had to have arrived in the colonies 100 to 120 years before that."

"Your family trafficked in slaves," Annja said. There's no polite way to put that, she thought.

"They did," Ganesvoort replied. "At the time, slavery was the largest commerce Ile de Goree had to offer." He gestured out the window at the city around them. "Everything else grew up around slavery. Dakar didn't really get built and come into its own until after the slave trade was outlawed. The European need for slaves as a product benefited from the fact that there were so many cultures living here. No one owed any allegiance to anyone else. Every person was fair game as someone else's prize. If the different tribes hadn't preyed on each other, not nearly as many slaves would have been captured."

"Can you imagine what it must have been like?" Annja asked. "Captured, marched in chains down to Ile de Goree and sold like a loaf of bread?" It was hard to contemplate. Slavery had always been abhorrent to her. The most horrifying thing was that some nations still practiced it, and there were hidden flesh traders who trafficked in sex slaves. Annja knew nearly forty thousand women a year went missing, most of them thought to have been taken for the sex trade.

"It had to have been horrible," Hallinger said.

"The transatlantic slave trade took root here in 1513, only eleven years after the first slave was sold, and lasted until the mid-eighteenth century," Ganesvoort went on. "Some scholars contend that fully twenty-four million people were displaced as a result in those three-hundred-plus years. Twenty percent of them died in the slave ships during the journey. They weren't fed or watered or cared for. The dead were thrown overboard to prevent the healthy from getting sick."

"Scientists who study sharks will tell you that shark migratory patterns still follow the old transatlantic slave-trade routes," Hallinger said. "They got used to feeding along those shipping lines."

The limousine arrived at the harbor and they got out. Men dressed in ship's whites and carrying pistols in shoulder holsters transferred Annja's and Hallinger's bags to a long yacht.

With the breeze in her hair and powering over the rollers in the bay, Annja relaxed a little as she stood at the bow.

"Do you like boats, Ms. Creed?" Ganesvoort asked.

"Call me 'Annja.'"

The man nodded.

"I do like boats," Annja admitted. "There's something very calm and peaceful about the ocean."

"Until you get astride her during a tropical storm. Then anything can happen." Ganesvoort studied her. "Do you know who the men were that attacked you?"

Annja shook her head.

"They belong to a man named Tafari. You've heard of him?"

Annja brushed her hair out of her face. That didn't take long. "Yes. I've heard of him."

"He's a very dangerous man, and a murderer several times over."

"There's something you should know," Annja told him.

Ganesvoort smiled. "That Tafari seeks the Spider Stone? I already know that. The man believes in myths and legends and half-buried secrets. He intends to become a legend himself. He'll kill anyone who stands in his way." He looked at Hallinger, then at Annja. "You, my old friend and my new friend, need to always keep that in mind."

18

"So this is how the rich live."

Looking up from the ship's log she was currently perusing, Annja smiled at McIntosh. The Homeland Security agent had arrived by ferry the following morning. Ganesvoort had arranged transportation, a horse-drawn carriage, to his manor house on the north end of the small island.

"Yes," Annja agreed. "It is. Some of them. Of course, Ganesvoort could have opted for the Howard Hughes lifestyle there at the end."

The manor house had been built up over the years. It had begun life as a Portuguese villa, then had been taken over by Ganesvoort's ancestors and enlarged to a sprawling fifteen-thousand-square-foot residence. Annja didn't know how many bedrooms and bathrooms the house contained, but there were many. There were a handful of dining rooms and two grand ballrooms. As a result, the rooms weren't all built on the same level, but the various architects—including the French, who'd had the last opportunity to give the structure a facelift—had managed to pull it all together with unforgettable elegance.

The manor house had a state-of-the art surveillance system and a small army of armed guards.

The room she was using was a reading room on the second floor. The north wall was nearly all glass, with a beautiful balcony that overlooked the ocean. In the distance, sailboats and fishing boats plied the waters.

"I don't like the windows," McIntosh growled.

"I love the windows," Annja replied. "It's the north light. The most even light of the day. Painters usually prefer the north light when they're working on a canvas."

"A sniper," McIntosh pointed out at the sea, "on one of those boats could cause a problem."

"Put there by Tafari, I suppose?"

"Yes." McIntosh frowned at her. "You're not taking this very seriously."

Stretching to relieve her back for a moment, Annja decided to deal with the issue head-on. "If Tafari wanted me dead, this would be a dangerous place for me to be."

"He does want you dead. Those guys last night tried to kill you."

"They would have killed me as long as they could get the Spider Stone. They planned to get the Spider Stone, then kill me. Shooting me from a ship out at sea isn't going to get Tafari the Spider Stone, is it?"

McIntosh didn't answer.

Turning her attention back to the ship's log, she said, "Think of me sitting here as being that enticing bait you wanted me to be when we got here." She smirked a little at McIntosh's frustration with her. "I sit here and he can't have me. What better bait could you possibly hope for? It's got to be driving Tafari crazy."

"That's not what I meant."

"It *is* what you meant. Your best hope is that Tafari gets as tired of waiting as you do and makes a move against us so you can nab him."

McIntosh appeared to give that some thought. "What do you think the chances are of him doing that?"

"*I* wouldn't do it," Annja said. "I'd wait until I left the house and probably this island."

"That's you. You're probably smarter than Tafari."

"Thank you. I am definitely smarter than Tafari. On any day of the week that ends in *Y.*"

"Don't get cocky."

"I'm not. You see, I know I have a weakness," Annja said.

McIntosh looked at her, not understanding.

"When I figure out where Yohance came from and I know where the map shows, I'm going to go there. I'll bet Tafari knows that. That's when he'll get his opportunity to get the treasure and kill me, too."

That possibility turned McIntosh's frown even deeper.

Annja sat at a French provincial desk that had probably seen service in one of Louis XIV's courts. The chair, of course, was modern although built in a style that accented the desk. Comfort, when working for hours leaning over old documents and maps, was paramount.

"I still don't think you're taking this seriously enough," McIntosh said.

"On the contrary. I'm taking this very seriously. That's why I'm working as hard as I am."

"You don't normally risk your life doing your job."

Annja lifted an arched brow. "Really? You don't call exploring almost forgotten ruins—where cave-ins can occur and diseases run rampant—risky? Going to remote dig sites where a hospital is two days or more away? Falling from a cliff or through a trap some ancient dead man set to keep thieves from his remains? And that doesn't take into account bandits, robbers, slavers, mercenaries or drug traffickers that you can run into who think you have something they want or that they can use you in some fashion to get past the next checkpoint."

McIntosh tried to interrupt.

Annja didn't let him. "Do you know that most countries still distrust archaeologists? Well, they do. Want to know why? Because archaeologists have a long history of being spies for the United States and British governments. A lot of governments see us as a necessary evil. We bring in money to help them extract a past they might never see without outside funding." She paused. "Archaeology isn't as bland as you seem to make it out to be."

"Not the way you do it," McIntosh grumbled.

"What does that mean?"

"It means that you seem to attract trouble."

Annja couldn't argue with that, so she didn't. Instead, she turned back to her work. Almost five minutes passed in silence.

"How long is this going to take?" McIntosh asked.

Only slightly irritated because she'd been expecting the question from the moment McIntosh had arrived and started pacing, Annja said, "As long as it takes."

"You're reading books." McIntosh approached her and took the top book off the stack.

"That's what archaeologists do."

"I thought you broke into graves, found cities that had been buried in lava, looked for dinosaur bones and located shipwrecks."

"We do that, too."

McIntosh hefted the book. "If you were getting paid by the pound, you'd make a fortune."

Annja looked at McIntosh pointedly.

"What?" he asked.

"You're talking. It's hard to read when you're talking. I mean, I can do it, but then I'd be ignoring you. So I'm giving you warning, I'm going to work until lunch. If you talk to me before the lunch bell rings, I'm going to ignore you." Annja turned back to the book.

And she ignored him.

HOURS LATER, seated at the beautiful table in one of the dining rooms, Annja piled her plate high with food. Plates of suckling pig and pheasant, fresh fruit, a half-dozen salads and several desserts, including three different sorbets, covered the table.

"This is wonderful," she said.

"I see you're ambitious," Ganesvoort observed.

Annja felt only a little self-conscious. She'd always been a healthy eater, and the past few days she hadn't exactly been meal conscious. "I haven't eaten this well in a long time. Thank you very much. I'll be embarrassed later."

Ganesvoort smiled. "Don't be embarrassed. It's my pleasure. My cook thanks you, too. It's not often that she gets to go all out. My tastes are simple and don't challenge her. I throw the occasional party simply to keep her from turning in her resignation out of boredom. But she tells me that party preparations are not as personal as cooking for overnight guests."

"I'm glad she likes cooking for guests. We may be here for a few days." Annja sipped her wine.

McIntosh looked up from his plate. "Days?"

"Or weeks." Hallinger used his knife and fork industriously, throwing himself into the meal, as well. Annja had noted the color in his face, as well as his energy.

"Why weeks?" McIntosh asked. "I thought this was a simple research job."

"Because there are a lot of logs to go through," Annja replied.

"We don't even know if the information we're looking for is here," Hallinger added.

"Aren't those logs alphabetized?" McIntosh asked.

"Some of them are, Agent McIntosh," Ganesvoort said. "However, I must apologize. My collection has merely been a hobby, a sweet passion, not something I felt I had to pursue every day. I've only cataloged about two-thirds of the journals and logs that I've bought over the years. I've read and am familiar with far less of them."

"Isn't someone in charge of cataloging things like that?" McIntosh asked.

"Like what?" Annja asked.

McIntosh shrugged. "*Historical* things."

"Who's to say what a historical thing is?" Hallinger asked.

McIntosh thought about that for a moment. "I don't know."

"Nor does anyone else."

"But there are historical preservation societies. I worked a murder case that involved a group like that in Atlanta."

"Those societies," Ganesvoort said, "are just as self-serving as my own interests. They choose houses or other landmarks for preservation because they want something to champion. I enjoyed reading ships' logs and imagining what a maritime life might have been like back in those days. When I sit down with one of those old books, it's like I'm taking that voyage myself. The story, the men, the problems, they all come alive around me. Even in the unskilled writings of the captains, first mates and officers of the watch."

"I'm that way about open and unsolved cases," McIntosh said.

Ganesvoort nodded. "I see. In its own way, an open case is very much a historical document, dealing with murders that happened years ago."

Annja hadn't thought about a police investigation like that.

"Right," McIntosh said. "When you start looking through an

unsolved case, you have to put your mind back in the time that the murder took place. Figure out what the people were doing, what they were thinking."

"And what their world was like on a day-to-day basis," Annja said.

"Yeah."

"That's what an archaeologist does," Annja said. "We take artifacts—things left behind by others—"

"Clues and evidence, as well as hunches based on case data that lead to profiling, to use your terminology," Hallinger said.

"—and we attempt to reconstruct the world those people lived in. What they struggled for and what they dreamed of," Annja finished. "In the end, though, we know we've only been able to deliver our best guess. Eventually, someone will come along to challenge or refute what you said. Like when Michael Crichton postulated in *Jurassic Park* that dinosaurs were fleet and warm-blooded like fowl rather than ponderous and slow-moving like lizards. That turned the science community on its collective ear, even though the conjecture had been out there for a long time. Crichton made the theory popular and put it into the public eye. Laymen started asking questions, and scientists—wanting funding and attention—acted on it."

"History," Hallinger said, "in the end is subjective. People never know what to throw away or what to keep. These days, we try to keep most everything. But even recent things, things that touch our daily lives, get recycled as junk. Did you ever read comic books or collect baseball cards when you were a kid?"

"I did," McIntosh admitted. "I still have the baseball cards, but I sold the comics when I started getting into girls. Comics and girls don't mix."

"Depends on the girl," Annja said. "I still read comics these days and graphic novels, too. Picture storytelling has been around since the first cave painting."

McIntosh smiled. "I would never have guessed that you read comics."

"There's a lot," Annja said, "that you don't know about me."

For a moment, McIntosh held her gaze, then he nodded and dropped his eyes.

Annja forced her attention back to her own plate.

FOUR DAYS LATER, they got a break.

Hallinger sprinted into the room where Annja was working. McIntosh had taken to looking through the English ships' logs for the name Yohance. He was a quick reader, but bored easily. Still, it kept him quiet most of the time.

"I found him!" the professor exclaimed as he burst into the room carrying a large ship's log.

After days of looking at them, Annja knew that ships' logs came in different sizes and degrees of craftsmanship. Some of them had been made by abbeys or by printing shops. But just as many had been handmade.

The people who had kept them were just as varied as the logs. Educated and uneducated men assembled their thoughts on the pages as best as they were able. Ships' captains, first mates, quartermasters, officers of the watch, common sailors and even cabin boys— those who had become somewhat literate—had all left their marks.

Despite the pressure to solve the riddle of the Spider Stone, Annja had found herself entranced on more than one occasion. Understanding Ganesvoort's hobby of choice was easy. Whole worlds opened up in those pages.

"You found Yohance?" Annja whispered the name, afraid to say it too loudly.

"Yes." Hallinger marched into the room like a commanding general. "The time frame is right. It says here that the slaves were brought aboard in July of 1755." He plopped the log down in front of Annja.

"'Yohance' is a common name," she said, striving to keep her hopes in check and to play the devil's advocate.

"I know, but it appears that our Yohance's arrival on the ship garnered attention from the captain and ship's crew. Actually caused a bit of a furor."

"What kind of furor?" Annja asked.

"Several of the ship's crew thought the boy was cursed. Or marked by the gods. Most of the sailors at that time were very superstitious. There was even some discussion of heaving the boy overboard at one point."

Annja turned the log so she could better see it. The writing was French, put there in a fine, strong hand by Captain Henri LaForge of *Cornucopia*.

"Where's Yohance's name?" McIntosh leaned over Annja's shoulder, squinting at the cursive writing.

Annja was conscious of him there, of the heat from his body and the scent of his cologne. But the possibility of discovery took precedence over whatever feelings his proximity stirred up.

"Here." Annja placed her finger on the first mention of Yohance's name.

"I see the name," McIntosh growled, "but I can't read the rest of it."

"That's because it's in French."

McIntosh shot her a look of impatience. "Maybe you could translate."

Before Annja could begin reading, Ganesvoort entered the room. Lights danced in his eyes. "You found him?" their host asked.

Smiling, Hallinger looked up at him. "I did."

Ganesvoort clapped the professor on the back. "So it is true?"

"At least this much of the story. It remains to be seen if the treasure is real."

"My little hobby has turned out to be worth something after all."

"It has," Hallinger said.

Ganesvoort flopped in one of the nearby comfortable chairs. "Thank God. I was beginning to feel that this one had slipped by us."

"Well," McIntosh said, "it didn't."

"The chances of such a thing being mentioned are so small," Ganesvoort stated. "Twenty-four million slaves passed through this island. God knows how many ships and ships' captains. With this kind of luck, we could go to Monaco and become fabulously wealthy."

"I thought you already were," McIntosh said.

"I am. But you know what I mean." Ganesvoort turned his attention to Annja. "Does the listing show where Yohance was from? Usually you don't get much information."

"This is more than a listing." Annja held the book up for him to see. "There appear to be a number of entries."

Ganesvoort leaned forward like an enthusiastic child awaiting a favorite bedtime story. "Come on, then. Let's have the story."

Annja sipped from her bottle of water and began to read aloud, translating the French to English effortlessly.

19

July 14, 1755
Henri LaForge, Captain of Cornucopia
Afternoon
Prevailing Winds, Easterly
Weather, Good
Our arrival in Ile de Goree was met with relief by my crew. After the tropical storm that very nearly laid waste to us in the Atlantic, we were all very happy to be alive.

We've spent the last six days partaking of the island's delights. I myself spent some time with my good friend Andrew Wiley, captain of *Bess,* which he named after his beautiful bride. We talked and ate, told of our troubles and our travels. Then we went to the auction block and both bought slaves to fill our holds.

Everything proceeded without incident until we arrived back at the ship with our goods.

"Goods?" McIntosh interrupted. "He's referring to the slaves?"

"Yes," Annja answered.

"They were considered nothing more than cargo," Ganesvoort added. "I don't think anyone truly realizes how inhumanly these people were treated, despite everything that's been written."

Annja continued reading.

I feel very confident of the lot I bargained for. They were
newly arrived to Ile de Goree. I learned that they were taken
by fellow tribesmen, which is all to the good, I think. Although I've been involved in a number of engagements with
pirates and am accustomed to living my life through quick
wits, a musket and a good length of steel, I don't think I'd like
to tempt the fates by leading expeditions into the interior to
gather slaves.

Most of the men are in good shape. They should give several years of labor wherever they end up, once they are gen-
tled. A few of them are belligerent and think they are cunning.
I'll have that beaten or starved out of them by voyage's end.

The women are young and healthy, and no few of them are
comely enough for what they are. They will make good do-
mestics and breeding stock.

A few of them are already with child. If they survive the
voyage, they will fetch an extra penny on the auction block.
Wiley said he's heard of some captains who keep the more
comely looking women aboard ship and let the men have at
them, ensuring a pregnancy and more money when they sell
them by adding calving and proving they're fertile.

There was a strange incident which has got my crew talking, though. There is a young boy, perhaps ten or twelve, about
the same age as my Georges, who has caused consternation.
His name is Yohance, I have discovered, and he is rumored to
be a medicine man or something like that. Since my crew
tends to be more superstitious than God-fearing, they put great
stock in stories of curses and the other black arts that seem so
prevalent among this species.

This situation will bear closer scrutiny because several of
the other slaves we have on board treat this boy with a defer-
ence that I can't for the life of me understand. He's not even
attained a man's growth.

"Obviously several of Yohance's fellow tribesmen were bought
at the same time," Ganesvoort said.

"Yes," Hallinger said. "That fits with what we were able to find out from Franklin Dickerson's journal back in Georgia."

Annja took another sip of water and continued with the next entry.

July 17, 1755

We are at present three days' journey out of Ile de Goree. Thus far, the wind has proved capricious at best. We've not been able to hold a strong heading and have had to shift constantly.

Several of the crew have reported rumors that we have been cursed for taking the boy Yohance from his homeland.

I have not yet ascertained who started this rumor, but I intend to have none of it. Rumors fester like boils aboard ship, without a proper way of dealing with them. Once I find out who is behind it, I will have the skin off that man's back.

"With that in the log," Hallinger said, "Captain LaForge was evidently putting his crew on notice. But it didn't do any good."

July 19, 1755

The situation has worsened. Today Colbert, a gunnery mate, fell upon Yohance and demanded that he lift whatever curse is suspected of being placed on the ship. We've been two more days with the fickle wind, and a storm is brewing in the west, showing signs of giving chase to us. The men are mortally afraid of going through such a blow again.

In response to the attack on Yohance, two of the slaves rose up and pulled Colbert down, beating him unmercifully. Jacques de Mornay, my first mate, had to shoot one of the slaves before order was returned to the hold.

The slave died. There was no saving him. I ordered the body thrown overboard to the ever-present sharks. I also informed Colbert that I was taking the price of the slave out of his wages. However, I fear dissension is rapidly spreading through my crew.

Annja studied the next entry and was surprised. "This is written in Latin." She looked up at Hallinger.

The professor agreed. "I looked back through the ship's log. Whenever Captain LaForge wished to remain circumspect in his musings, he used Latin."

"He was a highly educated man," Ganesvoort said. "How did he end up doing something as dangerous and hard as being a ship's captain?"

"From the earlier entries I read," Hallinger said, "LaForge was born to a wealthy family. His father was a highly successful merchant, and his mother was linked to nobility. But Henri LaForge chose not to be the merchant his father wanted him to be. He went to sea instead, taking over one of his father's ships so that he could see more of the world that he'd read about."

Annja understood that choice. She'd felt the same way while growing up in the orphanage. Her one touchstone throughout her youth had been her martial-arts classes. Sister Mary Annabelle, eighty years old and irrepressible, had taken part in the *tai chi* classes where Annja had started out.

Before and after classes, Annja had talked to the instructors whenever she could. Many of them had been from Japan or Korea. Those conversations had whet the appetite to travel that staying cooped up in the orphanage under the supervision of nuns and reading histories had already inspired.

"Do you read Latin?" McIntosh asked.

"Yes," Annja replied, and she continued with the narrative.

July 22, 1755

My first mate has had some experience with slaves in the wild, and he understands some of their language. He learned from some of the other slaves that Yohance is a medicine man among his people, and that he is believed to have great power.

What concerns me is that I think Jacques, who normally has a good head about him, might believe some of these stories that we might be under some curse from an African god. I reminded him that we are both men of strong faith, and that none of the magic practiced in those dark lands will ever be proof against God.

I worry that he might be succumbing to the same fears that plague the other crew members. We met in my cabin and shared a bottle of good port that I normally keep for the end of a successful voyage, but I don't think either of us felt entirely satisfied when we parted.

July 24, 1755

The storm overran us last night. We caught only the outer fringes of it, but it was enough to thoroughly unnerve my crew.

Cariou and I were hard-pressed to keep control of the situation. The storm hit just after dusk, during the dark hours of early evening while we were sitting down to dine.

The ship reacted violently in the blow. Several yardarms snapped off, which are being replaced today, though the storm conditions persist and I fear we're mired within the storm, always bumping into the violence of it. It feels as though we are caught in some grand trap and are doomed.

To make matters worse, the slaves began wailing and calling on their deities to save them. Their moans and fearful cries further took the strength from my men. Cariou and I had to arm ourselves and threaten to shoot any man that abandoned his post.

Even then I feared that someone would.

In the worst of the gale, the boy, Yohance, somehow quieted the slaves. I think that he knew we would kill one of them to make an example for the others if they did not quiet. Instead, he sang some song, something that I never discovered the nature of. After a time, the storm eased and we were once more in control of our course instead of being tossed about like a child's toy.

However, the crew now treat Yohance differently. We've still got a long voyage ahead of us, so I have to take steps to end this. He is not some magical being as the slaves would have us believe. I refuse to entertain that notion even for a moment.

"That sounds as if he's having his doubts," McIntosh commented dryly.

"If a man gets out on the sea long enough," Ganesvoort stated quietly, "he can convince himself of nearly anything."

"The stuff you've read about the Spider Stone," McIntosh said, "doesn't mention anything about this, does it?"

"It does mention a curse." Annja sipped her water again.

"A curse?" Uncertainty darted in McIntosh's eyes. "Neither of you mentioned anything about a curse."

"I thought you wouldn't believe in something like a curse," Hallinger said.

Maybe you're beginning to have a few doubts yourself, Annja thought. "Still believe archaeologists lead laidback lives?" She wasn't able to resist taunting. Just a little.

"Curses don't exist," McIntosh replied.

But Annja knew the mood had altered as she read the entries. There are still any number of things out in the world that we can't explain, she thought.

"Do you carry a lucky charm, Special Agent McIntosh?" Hallinger asked.

McIntosh looked self-conscious. "A pocket angel. A lot of the guys I know carry one. Or something like it."

"Because you believe it will help protect you?"

"As a precaution. When my dad was on the job, he carried one, too. It's like crossing your fingers. Doesn't really mean anything."

"Actually," Annja said, "crossing your fingers is a throwback to England's belief in witches. Crossing your fingers would ward off witches. Basically making the sign of the cross with your fingers. If you encountered a witch, making the sign of the cross would send her on her way."

"Belief in magic is an ingrained trait," Hallinger said. "You won't find a culture anywhere that didn't or doesn't believe in some sort of sorcery or magic."

Annja returned to the ship's log, still on the Latin entry.

I had Yohance brought to me tonight. I wanted to put an end to all this foolishness. Since I didn't speak his dialect and the boy had no English, I had de Mornay in attendance because he could speak the boy's savage tongue. I swore the man to secrecy, made him give me his gravest oath that he would not let slip anything that we discussed in my quarters.

The boy, Yohance, was afraid. I could see it in him. That vulnerability again reminded me of my own son, Georges, and how he might fare under these harsh conditions. But Yohance kept himself composed despite being outnumbered and outgunned.

I had my first mate ask the boy his story, how he came to be in Ile de Goree.

The boy told us of his village near the confluence of the Semefé and Bafing Rivers.

Annja stopped reading and looked at Hallinger. "Did you read this?"

The professor nodded. "I wanted to wait until you were up to speed before we began searching. There's still a lot of area to cover. And that's if Captain LaForge and his first mate actually got everything right."

"Doesn't that map on the Spider Stone show two rivers joining?" McIntosh asked. "That seems like it would be hard to miss."

"No," Annja said. "The problem we've had so far is that there aren't large numbers of Hausa living in Senegal. If they're not here now—"

"Then chances are good that they weren't here then," Hallinger finished. "The Hausa people date back to 500 A.D., and their ancestral lands in Nigeria have been occupied by civilized peoples since prehistoric times. Between 500 and 700 A.D., the Hausa began consolidating, developing seven city-states that were believed to have been founded by Bayajidda, a hero of their people who supposedly had a magic knife fashioned for him. He used the knife to fight his enemies and rescued the queen of Daura and her people from a giant snake."

"The queen married Bayajidda," Annja said, taking up the tale, "and they had seven sons. By the thirteenth century, the Hausa controlled most of the trade in those areas. They also mixed with the Fulani people, whose roots are Muslim. After a series of jihads in

the early nineteenth century, the Fulani took over, forming the
Sokoto Caliphate, which became the Fulani Empire."

"Wars generally ruin records and documents," Ganesvoort put in.
"They also tend to scatter people. For Yohance's people to be where
they were—"

"Somewhere near Kidira from the sound of it," Annja said,
looking at a map she had on the desk.

"—they had to have gone far from their homelands," Ganesvoort said.

"Not necessarily," Hallinger said. "Yohance's people may have
already been scattered."

"There are pockets of Hausa scattered all across West Africa,"
Annja added. "According to the words on the Spider Stone,
Yohance's people had already fled from invaders."

"Probably the Yoruba." Hallinger stroked his chin. "They'd been
an aggressive people until the Fulani. Empire put them out of
business."

"So what happened to Yohance?" McIntosh asked.

Annja smiled. That's the thing about history, she thought. Everybody thinks it's a boring subject until they learn it's really about people.

Annja returned to translating the captain's writing.

The boy was reluctant to say anything more, but I knew I
had to get to the bottom of the medicine-man myth. When I
asked him about it, he refused to answer.

I've dealt with reluctant men before, and I'm not leery of
employing tactics that some would deem harsh or cruel. A man
has to know what a man has to know.

After growing frustrated with questioning the boy, I took
out a knife and cut off his left ear. After all, a slave doesn't use
an ear to work, and the amputation didn't make him deaf.

Yohance cried and became very afraid.

I told him I would cut the throat of one of the other boys if
he didn't tell me what I wished to know. Looking at his own
ear lying there before him, he believed me. And that was good
because I don't make idle threats.

He told an incredible tale. I believe it was a complete fabrication, but I knew he hadn't created the tale. It had been handed down through his people.

His people hold to the savage belief that their gods are some kind of animal. Or gods can be found in animals. Heresy, all of it, and spread by the Devil himself to undermine the faith of good Christians.

According to Yohance, the spider god of his people, gave them a vast treasure after he allowed their village to be destroyed. He also gave them a weapon, a curse that they could visit on any enemy.

I didn't believe any of it, but I could tell that de Mornay did. I remonstrated the boy, told him the error of his ways regarding how he was causing the other slaves to act, and I told him that I would hold him responsible for their actions. If anything further happened, I swore to him that I would tie a bag of cannonballs around his neck and hurl him into the Atlantic. Then I sent him back to the hold.

I have every confidence that I have seen the end of this matter.

When she finished reading the entry, Annja felt slightly sick. She had a strong stomach and she'd read about and even seen much worse in her own work, but the thought of the boy being so harshly treated at the hands of uncaring men touched her.

"That's it?" McIntosh asked.

"There's one other important entry," Hallinger said. "Just a few days later. It's written by Captain LaForge's lieutenant."

Annja read the entry.

August 2, 1755
Maurice Cariou, Lieutenant of Cornucopia
Evening
Prevailing Winds, Northerly
Weather, Poor
It is with a heavy heart that I take up the pen to finish the work begun by my captain, the good Henri LaForge. I pray that he is with Our Lord, and that his name will always be remembered with favor.

The storm that has constantly dogged our tracks on this voyage caught up with us once again last night. I've never seen such a determined effort on part of something that is without purpose, human or divine, that acted so cold-heartedly.

While we were lashed about, Captain LaForge took the deck and gave his courage and strength to our crew. During the worst of the storm, a sail came loose and whipped across our rear deck, malevolently wrapping the captain in the ropes and dragging him overboard. He was gone, vanished into the sea before we could do a thing about it.

I shall be glad when this voyage is over. Ever since we have taken on the boy Yohance, luck and fortune have been against us. I struggle not to be a superstitious man because I don't want to affront God, but in these circumstances I find myself hard-pressed not to at least wonder.

"Interestingly enough," Hallinger said, "if you read the entries before that one, you'll see that the storm never once let up. It stayed on the ship's tail. Many of the ship's crew grew increasingly agitated. Captain LaForge had to take more and more aggressive means to keep the situation under control. After he cut off Yohance's ear, the crew turned against him, believing that he was responsible for the storm's continued fury."

"What you're saying is that you don't think LaForge's death went exactly the way his second-in-command said it did," McIntosh said.

"You're the expert in our midst when it comes to murder," Hallinger said. "What do you think?"

"I think it's awfully convenient that a whole ship's sail could come loose in a major storm and only take out one guy."

Annja agreed. Then she turned her thoughts to the puzzle of the Spider Stone again. They had a direction. They almost had a location. All they had to do was get there.

Looking at Ganesvoort, Annja asked, "What's the quickest way to Kidira?"

20

Looking up from the train seat, Annja saw the smiling face of one of the two young boys in front of her. As it turned out, the fastest way to Kidira was on the Dakar-Niger Railway. Going hundreds of miles overland by car would have taken nearly twice as long, even factoring in the five-hour delay in leaving Dakar. Punctuality wasn't one of the railway's strong suits.

Nor was comfort. The train generally concerned itself with cargo first and passengers second. Or third or fourth or fifth, Annja was quick to realize. Cargo was the big ticket for the railway, moving goods in from the coast to the interior.

She was jammed into a narrow seat with little room. There was no dining car, so meals had to be packed on. Fortunately, Ganesvoort's chef put together an excellent picnic basket.

McIntosh slept only a few seats over, lulled by the slow sway of the train. The CIA agents accompanying them occupied other seats. Three rows up, Hallinger and Ganesvoort conferred, going over topographical maps on Hallinger's computer just as Annja was doing, comparing the pictures they'd taken from the Spider Stone to the physical features of the land.

The two boys and their mother had sat in the seats in front of Annja. The mother had looked tired and frazzled. She'd stayed on her cell phone nearly the whole trip, evidently stressing over the conversation. Something somewhere wasn't going right.

"Hi," Annja said to the small boy.

The boy leaned over the back of his seat and peered at Annja's notebook computer. "Playing video games?" His English accent was unmistakable.

"Not exactly." Annja grinned at the boy's curiosity. She guessed that he was five or six, dressed in a red T-shirt, denim shorts and high-top basketball shoes.

"My brother plays games on his computer."

"He does?"

The little boy nodded. "Yeah. All the time. He gets in trouble with my mom because he doesn't know when to quit."

"I see." Glancing over the top of the seat, Annja saw the little boy's older brother by maybe three or four years was sound asleep. The mother had walked to the other end of the train car, evidently seeking a better connection for the phone.

"My name's Bashir." The boy stuck out his hand.

Annja took the hand and shook it. "Nice to meet you, Bashir. I'm Annja."

"You have a pretty name."

Chuckling, Annja said, "Thank you."

The boy waited maybe a heartbeat, then looked at her in exaggerated annoyance, as if she'd missed something she should have automatically known. "Don't I have a pretty name?" he asked.

With the prompting, Annja immediately understood what she'd done wrong. "Yes, you do. I was trying to think if I've ever heard that name before, and I don't think I have. You have an unusual name, too."

Bashir smiled then. "My mom says my name means 'bringer of good news.' What does your name mean?"

"I don't know."

Bashir looked puzzled for just a moment. "Didn't your mom tell you what your name means?"

"No," Annja said truthfully, feeling just the smallest twinge of pain stab at her for a moment. "She didn't."

"Oh. My brother's name is Kamil. It means 'perfect.'" Bashir leaned in and cupped his hands around his mouth. His whisper was still loud. "Only he's not perfect—he's a slob."

Annja laughed. "I see."

Bashir looked at her curiously. "Are you an African?"

"No."

"I had to ask 'cause I found out there's white Africans, too. I didn't know that till I came here with my mom."

"I'm an American," Annja said.

"Our ancestors were Americans, too. But we're English now. Before we came here, we lived in London. My mom says our ancestors went to England after President Lincoln freed the slaves." Bashir thought some more. "Can I see your marble?"

"My marble?"

"Yeah." He pressed his hands together and smiled, revealing a gap where his two front teeth had been. "The pretty yellow one."

He meant the Spider Stone. Annja had had it out earlier, looking at it again and trying to get a deeper feel for it.

"Do you promise to take good care of it?" she asked.

"Sure."

Annja took the Spider Stone from her pocket and gave it to the boy.

He turned it around and around in his hands, studying it with complete fascination.

Bashir handed the Spider Stone back to Annja. "Why does it have a spider on it?"

"That spider represents Anansi. Do you know who Anansi is?" Annja asked.

Bashir's forehead wrinkled. "Some kind of hero?"

That's close enough, Annja thought. "Right. He's a hero. Anansi is a spider who lives here in West Africa."

"A spider?"

"Well, sometimes he can turn into a human."

Bashir grinned. "Brilliant. Do you know any stories about him?"

"I do." Annja put the computer aside and gave Bashir her full attention. "Anansi is one of those guys who seems to always get into trouble. Because he's always doing something or because he's after something he wants. And he wants a lot."

Outside the train windows, the countryside whipped by. Most of it was savanna, dry and covered with scrub brush and stunted trees.

"One day Anansi decided he wanted to be the king of all stories," Annja began. "So he went to his father, Nyame, who was the sky god."

"Anansi's dad is a god?"

"It's just a story."

Bashir looked at Annja as if she were a simpleton. "I know that. I'm not a baby."

"Sorry," Annja said.

At that moment, the mother arrived. She looked embarrassed. "I really must apologize," she said. "I asked him not to bother anyone."

"It wasn't a bother," Annja said. "It was kind of nice to take a break. And you have a terrific kid."

Bashir beamed. "She was telling me about Anansi. He's a spider god who can be a spider or a human, and he's supposed to live right here in West Africa, only he's really just make-believe."

"I hope you don't mind," Annja said.

The woman sat down, turned so that she could face Annja and smiled. "No, but I should warn you that you're dealing with an over-active imagination that requires constant feeding and attention." She offered her hand. "I'm Tanisha Diouf."

"Annja Creed. Nice to meet you." Annja shook her hand.

"How far are you going?"

"Kidira," Annja said.

"We are, too."

"With the kids along, it looks like vacation, but with all the phone time involved, it looks more like work," Annja said.

"Work. Definitely. I'm an engineer for Childress Construction."

"Is that part of Childress Corporation?"

Tanisha grimaced. "I see you've heard of us."

"Only this morning while waiting in the train station. I scanned the newspaper and saw Childress mentioned."

"Not a lot of people here like us," Tanisha said.

"Because of the oil refinery that's being built?"

"Exactly. Childress Corporation is the parent. The construction arm is one of the subsidiaries. I happen to be the engineer in charge of the project."

"Sounds like a big job."

"It is. Some days, like today, I think it's too big. Being a single mom is hard enough without being a single mom out of the country. But the opportunity and the pay is great. When I finish this, I can put both my boys through college on the bonus money I'll earn." Tanisha glanced at the topographical maps Annja had been studying. "What do you do?"

"I'm an archaeologist."

"Now, *that* sounds interesting."

"Some days are more interesting than others," Annja replied.

"May I?" Tanisha gestured toward one of the maps.

"Be my guest."

The woman picked up the map, then another one. "I don't think this is far from where we're putting the refinery in, actually."

That got Annja's attention immediately. "Really?"

"Really. What are you out here looking for?"

"A Hausa village that was destroyed in 1755."

"The sad thing is, you'll probably find lots of those. There's a lot of unrest in the savanna even now. Our work sites keep getting attacked by tribes that don't want us there. At least, they have been getting attacked. The last few days have been pretty quiet. You'll want to be careful out there."

"I will," Annja said.

Tanisha handed the maps back. "You're not traveling alone, are you?"

"I'm with a small expedition."

"Let me make a phone call. If it looks like we're heading in the same direction, maybe I can get you in with us when you have to go overland. If that's all right."

"I'd appreciate that." There is safety in numbers, Annja thought. But she feared it might also mean that she might endanger Tanisha Diouf and her children.

ALMOST TWO HOURS LATER, Annja stood on the small platform outside the passenger car. The train's wheels rumbled over the tracks in steady monotony. Darkness filled the savanna on either side of the railroad line, but the silver moon lit the sky.

She sipped from a bottle of water and ate pineapple chunks from a small plastic container Ganesvoort's cook had supplied. Fatigue ate at her, but she knew it was from spending the past few days doing nothing physical. She'd been active all her life. Inactivity seemed to take more out of her than physical exertion did.

Standing, breathing rhythmically, feeling warm despite the chill of the wind pulling at her clothing, Annja stared into the darkness around the train. She felt at peace, and a sense of belonging. There was a power in the land around her, and she sensed it in a way that she never had before. She soaked up the sensation, reveling in it, and her heart lifted.

Then she realized she wasn't alone. Someone was watching her.

"Here."

Annja spun, facing into the train car.

The African woman from the hotel stood before her, leaning on her staff. She wore a black grand *bubu,* and the extra material belled around her.

"You feel it, don't you?" the old woman asked. "You feel the pull of this land on you." She waved at the savanna. "This is where the world began, where humanity took root and spread across the world. We all belong to Africa. So many have forgotten that."

Annja was silent.

The old woman smiled. "It's just me, daughter. You have nothing to fear from me."

"What do you want?" Annja asked.

"Nothing that you can't give."

"Don't talk to me in riddles."

"I'm not. I'm telling you the truth," the woman said.

"Why are you following me?"

"I'm not following you. At this time, we happen to be traveling in the same direction. You pursue the answer to the Spider Stone. But you're not the one to solve that."

"I've already solved it," Annja said. "All I have to do is find the cave where Anansi put the treasure."

"You're not here for the treasure."

No, Annja admitted to herself. I want to see what's there. I want to read the books that were left. I want to know what those people knew. I want to look back through that window in time to another world. Even if only for a little while.

The old woman shook her head. "That is not your path. You are here only to go so far, Annja Creed."

"How do you know who I am?" Trepidation jangled inside Annja. She knows you from the hotel, she reasoned. All she had to do was talk to the police or the hotel staff. What was more mystifying was how the woman knew Annja was at the hotel to begin with.

"You have finally come." Annja remembered the woman's first words to her.

"I know who you are because I've been trained and blessed by the gods to know these things," the woman said. "And I know you by that sword you carry."

Annja wondered how much of the fight in the hotel the woman had seen. Only Annja, Roux and Garin knew about Joan's sword. *My sword.*

"You're a warrior," the woman said. "You have been blessed—or cursed, depending on how you wish to view it—to affect changes in the lives of people who hang in the balance."

Annja shook her head in disbelief. So much of what the old woman was saying reminded her of the talk she'd had with Roux in her loft all those months ago. If she didn't sound so much like Roux right now, I'd swear she was crazy. Then again, maybe both of them are crazy.

She might have believed that if she hadn't seen the sword become whole again, if she couldn't pluck it out of thin air whenever she wished.

"I came here tonight to warn you," the old woman said.

"Warn me about what?"

"Your enemies are close."

"By design," Annja said. "I meant to draw Tafari out. I can take care of myself."

The old woman nodded. "I know. But you must take care of others, too."

Annja resisted the impulse to ask whom she was supposed to protect.

"Tanisha Diouf has a part to play in this," the old woman said. "She and her two children must be protected. They are going to be in the eye of the storm." She pointed toward the front of the train. "Now look. Your enemies have gathered."

Unwilling to look, thinking that it was some kind of trick, Annja hesitated. Then the train's brakes locked up and the metal wheels shrilled across the steel tracks.

Off balance, distracted, Annja fell, tumbling toward the edge of the platform.

21

Annja flailed for the railing around the platform. Her left hand caught, but the right hand missed. Around her, sparks shot out for yards, showering the ground and the brush. Small fires had already started in the wake of the train. The squeal of metal on metal as the wheels skidded along the tracks sounded like the howl of a gigantic beast.

She regained her balance as her right hand took hold.

An explosion of light struck the locomotive. The sound of the detonation followed.

The train whipsawed like a snake. Train cars flipped from the tracks onto their sides. Bedlam filled the night.

Annja looked for the old woman. She was nowhere in sight.

The train car shuddered as it slammed to a full stop. Then it reared up like some rebellious beast. A roar of incredible clanging and shredding metal filled Annja's ears. At the front of the train, the lights of several vehicles suddenly flared to life.

Trap! Annja thought. Either the attackers had used an anti-tank weapon of some kind or they'd mined the tracks.

She leaped from the train, landing in a crouch. Covering her mouth to keep from choking on the huge cloud of dust the wreck had created, Annja scanned the landscape. The vehicles—jeeps and motorcycles—closed in rapidly.

She darted behind a tree as a motorcycle rider spotted her and lifted a pistol in his left hand. The rider was African, dressed in Kevlar armor, his face painted like a skeleton. Bullets smashed into the tree, tearing bark free in chunks.

The rider leathered the pistol and gunned his machine after Annja. Other shots echoed over the broken terrain as she ran.

Abruptly, knowing the man was on the verge of running her down, Annja stepped aside and wheeled to face her attacker. She timed her move, trusted her strength and resiliency, and swung her left arm out, clotheslining the man and knocking him from the motorcycle.

The man landed at Annja's feet. The impact had knocked the air from his lungs. She kicked him in the face, rendering him unconscious.

Kneeling, she stripped an assault rifle from the man, took the bandolier of extra magazines, and the pistol and holster, as well. She buckled the belt around her waist, reloaded the pistol with one of the extra magazines on the belt and stood with the assault rifle in hand.

She wasn't sure what kind of rifle she was holding—she guessed a Russian or Chinese weapon—but she knew how to use it. At the moment, that was enough.

Armed, she ran back toward the train. Whoever the attackers were, and she was pretty sure whom they belonged to, she didn't think they were going to take any unnecessary prisoners.

TANISHA DIOUF MADE herself stand. Dazed, she looked around for Bashir and Kamil. Her children were the center of her life. They were all that she had left of the dreams she and Kevin had had when they married.

"Mom! Mom!" Bashir yelled, tears streaming down his face. "The train wrecked!"

Kneeling, Tanisha helped her youngest up from the clutter of baggage that had tumbled from the overhead compartments. "Easy, Bashir. I've got you." She put her arms around him, felt him shaking and shivering in his fear.

He held on to her tightly.

Gently, Tanisha disengaged from him and took one of his hands in hers. Panic welled up inside her, threatening to spill out of control. Where's Kamil? Please! Please don't let anything have happened to my baby! She looked around, but the car had plunged into total darkness.

A light flared to her left. Someone had a flashlight.

In the glow of the beam, Tanisha saw that it was Jaineba. The old woman stepped through the wreckage of the train car as calmly as though she were out for a Sunday walk.

"Jaineba," Tanisha called.

"I hear you, daughter," the old woman said. "You're going to be all right. You've just got to keep your wits about you."

"My son," Tanisha said. "Kamil is missing."

Pausing, Jaineba braced her staff against her shoulder and reached down into the debris. She grabbed Kamil's hand and pulled him free. Kamil stood, but he had a cut above his left eye that bled terribly.

"Kamil!" Tanisha let go of Bashir's hand and grabbed Kamil's head in her hands. She turned his face toward the light to better see the cut. It was deep and would require stitches, but it wasn't life-threatening.

"I'm all right," Kamil protested. "What happened?"

"I don't know." Tanisha gazed around.

The men who had been with Annja Creed had weapons in their fists. Some of them were taking still more weapons from luggage cases.

Seeing the men with guns didn't surprise Tanisha. They'd seemed to her to be the type of men who would carry weapons. They moved calmly and efficiently.

"Where's Annja?" one of the men asked.

"She was just here, Agent McIntosh," one of the other men said.

Agent? Tanisha was surprised about that. She'd guessed that the men were bodyguards for the archaeologist, hired to protect the expedition she was directing.

"She went outside," Tanisha said.

McIntosh directed his flashlight on her. "Who are you?"

"Tanisha Diouf. Annja and I were talking earlier. I saw her go out the back of the car."

The American agent cursed and started for the back door.

"What happened?" someone else asked.

"The train's under attack," the agent said.

Tanisha realized why the train had been attacked. A large part of the cargo was equipment—bulldozers and other earth-moving equipment—to replace the machines that had been destroyed by the tribesmen fighting against encroachment onto what they claimed were their lands. She was sure the Childress Corporation was their target.

"Come on," Jaineba said, waving to her. "We must get the children out of this place. It's very dangerous."

Tanisha nodded and started to follow the old woman to the back of the car. She was disoriented because the car lay on its side.

A shadow fell over her. Looking up instinctively, Tanisha saw a man—not a man, she corrected herself, a skeleton—squatting next to the shattered window. He had a rifle in his hands.

All of the memories of the voodoo ceremonies she'd seen in and around Dakar came back to Tanisha in a flood. She'd never believed in any of it, not the zombies, not the *loas* riding willing hosts who gyrated to the savage beat of drums and bit the heads off chickens for tourists.

None of that is real, she told herself.

But she was certain she was staring into the face of death. She tried to open her mouth in warning, but she knew she would never get the words out in time.

ANNJA RAN to the overturned train car she'd been riding in. From thirty feet away, she saw one of the attackers clambering along the side. The skeleton-faced man stopped and took aim with his rifle.

Raising the assault rifle to her shoulder, Annja squeezed off a burst. The man jerked as the bullets struck him, but she hadn't hit any mortal areas. Spinning, the attacker lifted his weapon and took aim.

Before he could fire, before Annja could move, the window at his feet exploded in a hail of shattered glass. Gunshots rolled from inside the train car, and the skeleton-faced man jerked like a marionette in the hands of an unskilled puppet master. Then the dead man collapsed.

A moment later, McIntosh came through the door at the back of the train car. He held his pistol in both hands and moved well enough that Annja knew he wasn't hurt.

A jeep roared along beside the train. A man in skeleton makeup hung on to a light machine gun mounted on the rear deck.

"McIntosh," Annja yelled in warning. "Look out!"

McIntosh went to ground at once, taking cover behind the

platform beside him just as the jeep's searchlight swept over him and the machine gun chattered.

Using the tree beside her to steady the assault rifle, Annja opened fire. Her bullets raked the side of the jeep, missing the driver, as well as the gunner. Okay, so you're not Annie Oakley, Annja thought, adrenaline surging.

McIntosh fired from cover, a carefully measured 2-round punch that caught the driver in the face. The jeep swerved out of control and slammed into a tree. The gunner flew out of the vehicle and landed in a heap. Before he could get up, McIntosh shot him, as well.

"Who are they?" McIntosh asked.

"They didn't exactly introduce themselves," Annja replied.

McIntosh jogged over to the jeep and helped himself to the dead men's weapons. Other agents did the same. McIntosh also helped himself to one of the bloody Kevlar vests and tossed the other one to Annja.

"Put that on," he growled.

Two other motorcyclists closed on their position. McIntosh and three of the agents took aim and cleared the seats.

"What do you suppose the chances are that the brakeman had a chance to call in the attack?" one of the agents asked.

"Even if they had a radio and were in contact with someone at the railroad," another agent said, "it's going to be hours before anyone comes looking for us."

"The jeep might still be drivable," one of the men said.

"See if you can get it started," McIntosh said. "We need to get the women and children out of here."

Annja started to respond to that, thinking McIntosh was being sarcastic and referring to her. Then she saw Tanisha Diouf and her two sons. The old woman, Jaineba, was right behind them.

Tanisha was hunkered down beside the train, holding Bashir in one arm while she held Kamil's hand with her free hand. She looked frightened.

The jeep roared to life. The agents quickly hustled Tanisha, her sons and Jaineba into the vehicle. One of the agents manned the deck-mounted light machine gun.

"Clear the battle zone, then take cover," McIntosh ordered. "Keep the civilians safe and healthy. We're going to see if we can keep the opposition distracted and whittle the odds down."

The agent wished them luck and pulled out, keeping his lights out so he wouldn't be noticeable immediately.

McIntosh pulled the team together, organizing them into two groups. "We go forward," he told his troops. "Slowly. Take out anybody who isn't us and isn't a civilian."

"With those skull faces they're wearing, there won't be much worry about who's who," one of the agents said.

They went forward slowly, and they killed everyone who was wearing a skull face. They also added to their armament and ammunition with every encounter. Annja immediately saw that McIntosh's agents were far more skilled at this kind of warfare than their attackers.

"When we left Dakar earlier today," Annja said to McIntosh while they regrouped, "you were upset because you thought we might lose Tafari."

McIntosh grunted sourly and looked down at the dead man at his feet.

"I think maybe we have his attention," Annja said.

TAFARI CURSED the ineptitude of his men as they lost battle after battle. He watched through night-vision binoculars, only catching glimpses of the woman and the men who protected her.

"They're too skilled," Zifa said. "Our people haven't ever been up against men like this. Our warriors have had an easy time of it killing ill-equipped tribesmen."

Gazing through the binoculars, Tafari watched as one of his jeeps suddenly swerved and overturned. A jeep with a flamethrower mounted in the back suddenly burst into flames and became a ground comet as bullets tore through the fuel tanks. Burning quickly, the jeep slammed into one of the train cars, came to an abrupt stop and sagged as the tires melted and blew.

"All we're going to do tonight is lose more men," Zifa reasoned.

Tafari knew Zifa was right. There were still plenty of warriors he could use, but the ones who survived the night would tell the others if he used them so coldly.

Besides, he had access to other men, trained mercenaries, who could track and kill Annja Creed and the Americans. He hadn't expected the resistance they'd had tonight. There'd been no way of knowing what those men were like.

He had expected the train wreck to have caused more damage than it had. No one else had recovered as quickly as Annja Creed and her bodyguards had.

"All right," Tafari grated. "Call them off." But he promised himself there would be another opportunity. Soon. And when that opportunity came and the American archaeologist was within his grasp, she would die a very slow, painful death that people would remember for years.

More than that, the treasure that Anansi had given the Hausa people would be his.

"THEY'RE PULLING UP stakes and leaving," McIntosh said.

Beside him, hunkered down behind one of the train cars, Annja watched as the skull-faced warriors withdrew from the battle.

"Do you think it's a trick?" she asked.

"No," McIntosh said. "I think they've had all they could stand. But we're going to stay put until we know for certain." He glanced at his watch. "It'll be dawn in a couple more hours. We'll see how things look then."

"We need supplies," Annja said. "If they return in the morning, with more men, we don't want to get caught out here without water." She nodded at the overturned train. "We also need to find out if anyone in there needs medical attention."

"You're not a doctor," McIntosh said.

"I'm trained in first aid," Annja said. "I've stitched myself up when I had to."

McIntosh stared at her. "You've stitched yourself up?"

"And a few other people when we were too far from civilization or didn't have access to medical care."

"The lady's right, McIntosh," one of the agents said. "If there's people in that train who've been hurt and there's something we can do for them, I think we need to get it done."

McIntosh nodded. "All right. But we operate in two-man teams and stay in constant radio communication." He and the other agents wore walkie-talkies with earbuds and pencil mikes that lay along their jaws. "Annja, you're with me."

22

Annja jogged to the nearest passenger car and heaved herself inside. There were only three passenger cars. The rest were all cargo cars. They'd go through them, too, looking for railway personnel and supplies—water, food and first-aid kits, but there was less chance of anyone being inside those cars.

McIntosh wasn't happy about her decision to be on one of the search teams. He'd wanted her to stay put. But as she'd informed him, she was highly capable when it came to field medicine.

The car was dark inside.

Annja wanted to use her flashlight, but McIntosh had forbidden their use and she understood the reasoning. A flashlight would attract sniper fire if their attackers had only drawn back to a safe range instead of leaving the area completely.

Nine people were inside the car. All of them were frightened. Thankfully, all of them spoke French so Annja was able to calm them down and allay their fears that they were the attackers.

One of the men had a compound fracture of his left leg. With the slight glow of the moon in the car, Annja could see where the white bone had pushed through the dark flesh of his thigh. The femur was jagged and uneven. He'd bled heavily at first, but most of that appeared to have stopped.

McIntosh cursed.

The man's eyes widened and he clutched at the hand of the woman cradling his head in her lap.

"Stop," Annja told McIntosh, kneeling beside the wounded man.

He was in his early sixties, white-haired and clearly frightened. His eyes rolled and his breath came in short gasps. The woman who cradled his head in her lap looked as though she was his wife. Three small children, probably grandchildren, sat nearby.

"This man is scared enough," Annja went on in a calm voice. She smiled reassuringly at the man. "If you get upset, he's going to panic."

"If that wound doesn't get closed up, it's going to get infected. This train isn't the most hygienic environment."

"I know."

"If infection sets in, he could lose that leg."

Annja forced herself to draw a deep breath. She knew that, too.

"Have you ever dealt with an open fracture before?" McIntosh asked.

"No," Annja admitted. "But I know how to handle it. I need a med kit and some kind of anesthetic."

McIntosh talked briefly over the radio. Within a few minutes, one of the agents showed up with a medical kit they'd salvaged from the locomotive.

"The engineer and the brakeman are both dead," the agent said. "Took a direct hit up there. They probably died instantly."

Annja didn't let the news touch her. It was too depressing. So far they knew of seven people who had died in the attack. One of them had been a child.

You'll grieve later, she told herself. Do what you can for the others now.

She opened the med kit and found ampoules of morphine. In a calm voice, she told the man that she was going to give him something to take some of the pain away, and she told him there would be pain involved in her fixing his leg.

Grimly, face ashen in the darkness, the man nodded. "Thank you for everything you're doing, miss."

"You're welcome. Now just lie back and try to take it easy." Annja used an alcohol swab on the inside of his right elbow. She gave him the morphine and waited.

Gradually, the old man's eyes glazed and his breathing slowed and deepened.

Annja turned to McIntosh. "I can't do this in the dark."

McIntosh sighed. "I know. Give me a hand and we'll cover the windows as best as we can."

Together, they scrounged for something to use to cover the windows and found bolts of cloth in one of the cargo cars. They cut the material into squares with pocketknives and used strapping tape they'd found there to hold the cloth in place.

By that time, the old man was deeply under the influence of the morphine.

"I'm going to need you to help me do this," Annja said. "If I knew he'd get medical attention within the next two hours, I'd just immobilize the leg. I'm going to have to assume that it's going to be longer than that. We've got to align the break."

"Tell me what to do." McIntosh put his rifle down nearby. Following Annja's directions, he gripped the man's upper thigh.

The man groaned a little.

"I'm hurting him," McIntosh said.

"It's going to hurt," Annja replied. "If I could put him out, I would."

"You've got more morphine there."

"I could give him too much. I've given him all I think I safely can. Just hold on to his thigh. When I start realigning the bone, I'm going to pull it back into the flesh. If that jagged end slips around too much, it could cut the femoral artery and he'll bleed out in minutes and there's not a thing we can do about it." Annja looked at McIntosh. "Are you ready?"

He gave a tight nod.

Working carefully, Annja stripped the man's shoe off and gripped his foot by the heel and by the top. She pulled steadily, ignoring the man's cries of pain and his wife's plaintive cries to stop what they were doing.

Finally, after a lot of hard work, the broken femur oozed back through the hole in the flesh with a slight sucking noise and disappeared. Annja kept on working, feeling the ends of the bone grate together until she judged she had the best fit possible.

Annja then fashioned a splint for the man's leg using materials she salvaged from the train.

After she'd finished, the man quietly went to sleep.

"Watch him," she told the woman. "Keep him still. If there's any problem, come get me."

"Of course," the woman said. "Bless you for all that you have done."

Annja smiled at the woman. "He's going to be fine. You'll just have to take care of him for a little while after the doctors finish with him."

"Always," the woman said proudly. "I always take care of him."

A FEW MINUTES LATER, Annja stood outside again. The wind felt cool after being inside the train car. McIntosh put a bottle of water in her hand. She opened it and drank gratefully.

McIntosh nodded toward the train car. "What you did back there, most archaeologists don't do that, do they?"

"Not unless they have to take care of someone who's been hurt. Most of us have taken first aid."

"How many times have you done this?"

"Counting this time?"

McIntosh nodded.

"Once."

DAWN STREAKED the eastern sky purple and gold. As night swiftly disappeared, so did some of the fear that had hung over them since the attack.

If it hadn't been for the skull-faced corpses littering the ground, and the fact that another passenger had succumbed to his injuries, the morning might almost have seemed normal.

Annja sat on the ground with her back to a tree and felt the world warm up around her. She wanted a long bath and a comfortable bed, but her mind kept buzzing with thoughts of the Spider Stone. They were close to the area where Yohance had come from. She felt certain about that.

She took the stone from her pocket and studied it again. Her backpack lay nearby. One of McIntosh's agents had recovered it and brought it to her. A brief examination of the computer revealed that it was still in working order.

Footsteps drew close to her. She looked up and saw McIntosh approaching.

Professor Hallinger and Jozua Ganesvoort slept on sleeping bags that had been taken from the cargo cars. Both had spent the night tending to the injured passengers.

She waited for McIntosh to speak.

"We still haven't made contact with Kidira," he said. McIntosh definitely looked worse for wear after being up all night. His clothing was bloody and dirty. He carried the assault rifle in his hand, as if it were a growth that had sprung up overnight.

"They'll send someone," she said.

"We've got enough jeeps to get everyone out of here."

"That would mean crossing a lot of open space, though," Annja said without disguising her concern.

McIntosh sighed. "I know. I've been thinking about that, too." His radio squawked for attention. "McIntosh."

"We have a problem," a man said. "One of the two sons of the lady engineer has a laceration above his eye. We haven't been able to get the bleeding stopped. She wants to know if Ms. Creed could take a look at it."

McIntosh looked at Annja.

Annja nodded.

"Sure," McIntosh said. "We'll be right up." He offered his hand and helped Annja to her feet.

She hoisted the backpack over one shoulder and bent down to retrieve the med kit. Most of the supplies had been exhausted.

"Last night," McIntosh said as they walked toward one of the jeeps they'd commandeered, "that woman said you'd gone outside the car."

"I did," Annja said.

"Why?"

"I needed some air."

McIntosh snorted as he started the engine. "You're lucky you weren't killed."

Looking at the wrecked train, Annja said, "We all are."

"CAN YOU CLOSE the wound?"

Annja pushed the two edges of the laceration above Kamil's eye together. The edges met perfectly, offering mute testimony that it had been a slice and not a tear. Blood wept slowly down the side of the boy's face.

"I can," Annja said, "but I'm not a doctor."

Tanisha stood behind Annja, looking over her shoulder. "I know," Tanisha said. "But the wound needs to be closed. Kamil says he's feeling light-headed. I'm afraid he's lost too much blood."

"Light-headedness could be from lack of sleep or a concussion," Annja said.

"The size of his pupils match. If it was a bad concussion, the pupils wouldn't match and he'd have a horrendous headache."

Tanisha was anxious about her son's condition. Annja felt the tension coming off the other woman in waves. It's not just the wound. It's about being out here, as well. Not knowing what's going to happen or if her kids are going to be safe, she thought.

"I don't have a headache," Kamil said.

Tanisha and her boys sat away from the train with the other civilians. The precaution was in case Tafari's men returned, hoping to catch them unawares. They had food and water and shade, but Annja could tell they were all worried.

Maybe McIntosh is right, she thought. Maybe we should take our chances about going cross-country.

But they were more than an hour away from Kidira by train. Traveling by jeep over the rough terrain would certainly add to that time.

"I need to sit down," Kamil said. "I feel sick."

"Okay," Annja said. "Have a seat." She held on to the boy's arm and helped him sit. Then she looked at Tanisha. "I can close the wound, but I'm not a professional. If the hospital has a plastic surgeon on call, Kamil won't have much of a scar. If I close the wound, I don't know what it'll look like."

"If the cut stays open and gets infected," Tanisha said, "it won't matter if a plastic surgeon is on call at the hospital. The hospital is hours away, and there's no telling how long the wait will be once we get there. I don't want to risk an infection."

"Do you want to do this, Kamil?" Annja asked. During childhood in the orphanage, she hadn't had much control over her life. She'd gone to doctors and dentists when and where she'd been told. She'd resented the impersonal actions. She didn't want to treat Kamil that way.

"Not really," the boy answered.

"We're going to do this," his mother replied, her voice firm. Then it softened. "I don't want you to get worse, Kamil. If this wasn't necessary, I promise you I wouldn't have it done like this."

"Okay." Kamil didn't sound very happy, but he reached out to take his mother's hand.

Annja prepped the wound, cleaning it out with antiseptic and applying topical antibiotics. "Close your eyes, please."

Kamil did, and sat tense as a board.

"Ooh, Kamil," Bashir whispered, eyes wide. "Annja's got a needle. A *big* needle."

Kamil groaned unhappily.

"Hey, Bashir," Annja chided. "I thought your name meant you brought *good* news."

The younger boy clapped his hands over his mouth. "Sorry," he said quietly.

Working quickly, Annja injected local anesthetic around and into the wound to numb it. She used the smallest curved needle in the med kit and put six close-set stitches above Kamil's wound. The smaller and closer the stitches, the smaller the scar.

When she was finished, Annja washed the blood away, put more topical antibiotic on the closure and bandaged the wound.

Once done, Annja had a moment to relax. She suddenly realized she hadn't been alone when the train was attacked. She looked for the old woman, Jaineba.

"Looking for someone?" Tanisha asked.

"I saw an old woman last night," Annja said. "You were with her when you came out of the passenger car."

"Jaineba?"

Annja remembered the name and nodded.

Looking around, Tanisha shook her head. "She was here earlier, but I don't see her now. In fact, I don't know how long it's been since I saw her."

"Is she a friend?" Annja asked.

"Maybe," Tanisha answered. "I think she believes she is. She's a Hausa wisewoman. She lives up in the hills around here."

"Here?" Annja asked. "Not around Dakar?" Excitement flared in her as she thought about the few Hausa villages that were in the area. Most of the Hausa in West Africa lived in Nigeria, not Senegal.

"I don't know if she's ever been to Dakar."

"She's been to Dakar. She was there last night," Annja said.

Tanisha looked at Annja doubtfully. "I don't mean to sound as though I doubt your word, but are you certain it was Jaineba you saw? Some old people tend to look alike."

Annja nodded. "It was Jaineba. She knew me."

"Had you met before?"

"Never."

"Then how did she know you."

"I have no idea."

"That's strange," Tanisha said.

Taking a bottle of water from the box of supplies they'd gathered from the train, Annja silently agreed. Then again, strange things had started happening to her the day she'd found that piece of the sword in France. Strange things had continued happening ever since.

THE SAVANNA FILLED with people an hour later. Tribesmen in loincloths or T-shirts and shorts came with their wives and children from all directions and descended upon the train like carrion feeders.

McIntosh stood, his rifle at the ready.

"Don't shoot," Annja said. "They don't mean us any harm. They're just here for the cargo." She didn't know how she knew that, only that she sensed no menace.

"Hold your fire," McIntosh called over the radio.

All around them, his men held their weapons up.

The tribesmen smiled and waved and yelled out greetings in English and French. Most of them were empty-handed.

They didn't leave empty-handed, though. Crawling through the cargo, the men, women and children made their selections—as much as they could possibly carry—and returned to the trees and grasslands, disappearing almost at once. Within the hour, there was no sign that they'd ever been there.

"Shopping day," McIntosh commented. Then he sat down in the shade.

Annja joined him. "Someone let them know the train had been derailed," she said. "If they know, other people have to know, too."

"I'm going to give the railway another hour," McIntosh said, "then we're going to caravan out of here. If we'd left this morning, we'd already be in Kidira. I don't want to be out here when it gets dark again."

Me neither, Annja thought. The idea of being trapped in the open by Tafari's men again wasn't a happy one.

FORTY-THREE MINUTES LATER, a train from Kidira chugged into view. The people who'd been stranded by the attack gave voice to a small cheer.

Gendarmes, the military law-enforcement body outside the metropolitan areas of Senegal, occupied the train in force. Dressed in green fatigues and blue berets, they stepped off the train armed to the teeth and took control of the area without hesitation.

The passengers and their luggage were loaded onto the new train. Work crews and security guards wearing black uniforms with Childress Security Division stamped on them stayed behind to begin salvaging what they could.

ANNJA, HALLINGER, Ganesvoort and McIntosh took one of the private salons in the new train and sat down to figure out how they were going to proceed with their treasure hunt.

"I think we should turn back," McIntosh said.

"Turn back?" Annja asked in disbelief. "It was your idea to come."

"It was," McIntosh admitted. "But I was thinking that Tafari would be easier to handle than he is. I thought we could get him off to himself long enough to lock him down. According to our intelligence, his troops were scattered. After last night, we know that's not true." He leaned back in his seat. "Much as I hate to admit it, we're outgunned."

"Just because you're giving up on the possibility of getting Tafari doesn't mean we should back off finding the treasure that Anansi left the Hausa," Hallinger said.

McIntosh shook his head. "Listen to yourself, Professor. You're talking about chasing after an unknown treasure left by an African spider god. It's a story. Make-believe. Nothing more."

Hallinger held up his thumb and forefinger a fraction of an inch apart. "We're this close to finding Anansi's treasure trove."

"You don't know that," McIntosh said.

Anger mixed with Hallinger's words. "We didn't come this far just to give up."

"If you keep this up," McIntosh said, "you're going to get killed. It could have happened last night. I knew it was a mistake to leave Dakar. I should have put my foot down then. We're not set up to deal with something like this. We should have been able to grab Tafari somewhere along the way. That was the plan."

"That was *your* plan," Hallinger replied brusquely. "Annja and I came to find out the truth about the Spider Stone. Just because your plan isn't going to work out doesn't mean ours won't."

"I'll pull the funding on this operation," McIntosh said.

"And I'll underwrite it," Ganesvoort stated quietly. He looked at Hallinger. "If you'll permit me. I've never been part of something like this, and I have to admit that it holds a certain allure."

"You're on Tafari's turf out here." McIntosh sounded exasperated. "Are you people not listening?"

Annja ignored the conversation, concentrating on the topographical maps she'd taken from her backpack. You're not going to see anything you haven't seen before, she told herself. It was hopeless. The map on the Spider Stone didn't match up with anything she could see on paper.

McIntosh was right. They'd come to the end of the chase. The puzzle couldn't be solved. She didn't have enough pieces to make it work.

Worn and tired, not knowing her next move, Annja looked out the window. High in the sky, she saw a lone falcon riding the wind currents. The bird dropped like a stone, plummeting to earth and scooping up a small hare.

She felt as powerless as the hare, and she didn't like it.

23

Seated in a jeep with the canvas canopy up, Tafari waited outside Kidira at an abandoned warehouse and watched the train roll toward the railway station. The building was just outside the city's border so none of the guards would bother him. Outside the city limits, the country turned immediately hostile and dangerous.

Tafari knew the woman archaeologist would be on the train and that vexed him. The night's events had not happened the way he'd imagined them.

Furthermore, the destruction of the train had caused an unplanned rift with his partner. That partnership was a lucrative one, and it promised to be even more so in the future.

"Here he comes," Zifa said.

Zifa's comment was unnecessary. Parked out by one of the truck loading docks, there was no traffic. The luxury Mercedes couldn't have been missed.

Tafari stepped from the jeep. For the meeting, he'd put on one of his camouflage khaki uniforms. It was what all of his men wore when he wanted people to recognize them and know he had sent them there.

The Mercedes pulled up and sat idling. The rear window rolled down.

"Ah, General Tafari," a suave voice called from the back seat. "Join me."

"I'm fine out here," Tafari replied. "I prefer the night air to the air-conditioning inside the car." He wore body armor under his jacket. In addition to the pistols on his hip and under his left arm, he also wore one snugged against his back. With his hands clasped behind him, it was within easy reach.

Tafari viewed the partnership as one of convenience and not trust.

"Then I'll join you." The man got out of the car. Tall and elegant, with black hair and blue eyes, and wearing a tuxedo, Victor Childress was CEO and chief stockholder of Childress Corporation. If he had a pistol under his jacket, it didn't show.

"The train was a mistake," Tafari said. That was as close as he would come to an apology.

"A very costly one," Childress agreed. "Some of that equipment is going to take weeks to replace. And I'd already spent weeks getting those units."

Tafari said nothing. What had been destroyed had been destroyed. His pride and his purpose would remain resolute.

"Why did you do it?" Childress took out a gold cigarette case, selected two cigarettes and offered one to Tafari.

Tafari took the cigarette and leaned in for a quick light. The cigarettes were a personal blend, far superior to anything he could ever get his hands on. He blew out the smoke and let the wind carry it away.

"The woman archaeologist was on the train," Tafari said. "She eluded me in Dakar. She's traveling with a group of killers that I think belong to the CIA or an American military detachment. I also believe they were sent here after me."

"Not for the purpose of protecting the woman?"

"The woman is a lure to get me out of hiding. When my nephew was arrested in the United States, his connection to me would have become known to the American government."

"Then blowing up the train was a good idea," Childress said.

"Last night it was."

"It's just unfortunate that I had so much equipment on that train. And that they're still alive. It's going to be weeks before the Canadians put up the money to fix the train."

That didn't concern Tafari. He never used the train. Even after the Canadians had bought the railway and improved the traveling conditions and timeliness, the train offered too many opportunities for his enemies to get to him.

Childress looked at the city in the distance. Lights lit Kidira, but it was dwarfed by Diboli, the city just across the Senegal River that made up the border between Senegal and Mali.

"Do you really believe this treasure exists?" Childress asked finally.

"Yes."

"What do you think is there?"

Tafari shrugged, not wanting to make his partner greedy. He'd seen greed dissolve a great number of partnerships, especially those that were made out of convenience rather than passion or a shared belief.

"Gold. Ivory. Gems. Perhaps some art pieces museums or collectors might pay handsomely for. Senegal has a long history of trade empires. Even before the slave trade took root here, the Hausa and my people, the Yoruba, pushed vast fortunes throughout the trans-Saharan trade routes."

"Someone could have found this treasure and stolen it away a long time ago," Childress said.

"If that had been the case," Tafari said, "someone would have heard of it. The legend would not have persisted."

"It could be a myth, nothing more."

Tafari dropped his cigarette to the ground and crushed it underfoot. "The Spider Stone is real. My people have seen it. If one is real, then I will believe the other is real, as well. Until I find out differently."

"You need a partner in this endeavor."

"No," Tafari said, "I don't." He had already partnered with Childress in the oil-refinery business. Jaineba encouraged the tribesmen to attack the equipment when they could, but Childress had cut Tafari in to make object lessons of those tribesmen who interfered. Once the Kenyan oil was being refined in the Childress refinery, Tafari would become a rich man.

Childress turned to the warlord and smiled. "Yes, you do. Especially one who can deliver the woman to you."

"You can do that?"

"I can. One of my employees, Tanisha Diouf, called me to ask if we could accompany the archaeologist group into the savanna. Evidently the location of the treasure is somewhere near where we're building the refinery." Childress shrugged, his hair blowing in the wind. "She'd asked me that *before* you blew up the train. All I have to do is say yes."

"A partner like that," Tafari said, "would be good to have."

"I'm glad you see it that way," Childress said. "I thought you would."

Tafari also thought that if Childress became too much of a problem, it would be just as easy to bury him with the rest of them.

AT THE POLICE CHECKPOINT in Kidira, Annja had to show her ID and allow officers to go through her luggage and computer. She'd traveled enough and gone through the process enough that having her panties and bras put on public display was no longer embarrassing.

When the security check was finished, she shoved everything back into her suitcases, shouldered her backpack and walked out with Hallinger.

"This isn't turning out the way we'd planned, is it?" Hallinger asked.

"No."

"Jozua meant what he said about underwriting whatever we want to do."

Annja glanced at Ganesvoort. The man was already arranging taxis for the group to take them to their hotel. She wasn't even sure if they had a hotel, but watching Ganesvoort in action, she was willing to bet he'd arranged one.

"I know," she said. "But at this point, until we can refine our search area or beef up our protection, I don't think wandering around the savanna is such a smart thing to do."

Hallinger looked disappointed. "Let's at least sleep on it before we make a decision."

Annja agreed. She didn't like giving up on anything.

There's a way around this. I'm just too tired to think of it at the moment, she told herself. She remained hopeful, to a degree, but the effort was hard.

THE HOTEL WAS a dump. Even with all the money he had, it was the best Ganesvoort could do.

Annja sat on the bed in her underwear and a T-shirt, sweltering in the heat. There was no air-conditioning, and hardly any wind blew through the solitary window that opened up onto an alley. A tall building next door blocked whatever wind might have been out there.

Loneliness and disappointment filled her. She couldn't talk to McIntosh because he was still upset that they hadn't agreed with him about leaving. Hallinger and Ganesvoort had been down in the lobby poring over maps and pictures when she'd left them.

She wanted to talk to someone. She'd tried Bart McGilley's number but all she got was his answering machine. It was the same with the three numbers she had for Roux. Wherever he was, he was choosing to be unavailable. She'd drawn the line at calling Doug Morrell because she'd been avoiding his phone calls for days and really didn't want to deal with a backlog of guilt.

Feeling dejected and slightly overwhelmed, she sat on the bed with her back against the wall and her computer on her thighs. Slowly, carefully she scrolled through everything she had, glancing frequently at the Spider Stone until, finally, she couldn't keep her eyes open anymore.

A CELL PHONE CHIRPED for attention and a man answered. Waking with a jolt, Annja realized someone was in her room and that she was sleeping on top of the bedclothes. Her back was to the door and to whoever was watching her.

She focused on the sword. All she had to do was close her hand around the hilt and it was in bed with her.

"You're awake," a familiar gruff voice said. "Don't pretend that you aren't. I saw the change in your breathing. And don't come up swinging because I didn't come here to—"

Angry, Annja twisted and threw herself from the bed. She brought the sword up between her and her uninvited visitor.

Garin Braden sat in a straight-backed chair that looked entirely too small for his stature. His magnetic black eyes glinted with amusement as he held empty hands up at his sides. Long black hair framed his ruggedly handsome face. A goatee covered his chin but not the sardonic smile. His suit was elegant, carefully tailored.

"What are you doing in my room?" Annja demanded.

Garin held the cell phone close to his ear just long enough to say "I'll get back to you," then he closed the device and dropped it into his pocket. "I came to see you, of course."

"How did you find me?"

"Magic," Garin answered. "I looked in my crystal ball and—*poof!*—there you were." He paused. "Why don't you put the sword down?"

"Because I like the sword," Annja replied. She also liked the fact that Garin was afraid of the sword. After he'd lived fearlessly for the past five hundred years, it calmed Annja a little to know that he was afraid of her. "And the last time you and I were alone together, you tried to kill me."

That had been in her loft in Brooklyn. She'd surprised him and ended up with the sword at his throat, ready to kill him in a split second if he hadn't backed off. Roux had arrived about then and kept her from doing it.

"If I wanted to kill you," Garin said, "I could have done it while you were sleeping."

Annja didn't know if that was true or not. When it came to Garin, she had no idea what to believe. She might choose to get along with him, but she'd never trust him if she didn't have to.

"Look," Garin said in a calm voice, "I came here to help."

"Me?"

He made a show of looking around. "I don't see anyone else here. Which is a sad thing, because I was told Special Agent McIntosh is a rather good-looking man."

"Let's get back to how you found me," Annja said.

"Boring," Garin told her.

"Tell me and I won't split your nose with my sword and let you bleed all over that expensive suit."

"Fine. Credit cards."

"Credit cards? I haven't used any credit cards."

"No, but Special Agent McIntosh has. They're all on Homeland Security accounts. Hacking into their system and finding that out caused some consternation, I tell you. I tracked the credit-card usage from Georgia to Dakar to here."

"McIntosh didn't pay for my room."

"No, but Ganesvoort did, and I knew he was traveling with you."

Annja thought about that, searching for Garin's angle. He had one, she was certain. The man always had one.

"Trust me," Garin said.

"No." Her answer was flat and immediate.

"You should."

"Why?"

"Because I know something about Anansi's treasure that you don't. In fact, I think I know where it is."

"Then why aren't you claiming it yourself?" Annja asked.

Garin sighed. "I'm rich several times over. Even if I were to live forever, which I hope to, I could maintain my lifestyle of extravagance on just the interest my investments and companies make." He smiled. "I wanted to do the treasure hunting with you. To vicariously enjoy your success."

That's not the whole truth, Annja told herself, but it's close. She still didn't lower the sword.

"Annja," Garin said softly, "you're a beautiful woman. I have to tell you, I could probably spend the day staring at you in that T-shirt and panties." He ran his eyes over her.

Annja suddenly felt exposed. She held her aplomb with difficulty.

"But they're not going to let you eat breakfast downstairs in the restaurant like that," Garin went on. He smiled again, flashing white teeth. "Of course, we could order room service and stay in."

"You are a filthy, disgusting pig," Annja said, irritated because she didn't know what to do. Curiosity wouldn't permit her to throw Garin out of the room without hearing everything he had to say, and she wasn't quite ready to kill him.

Yet.

She willed the sword away and it vanished. Then she took a pair of jeans, clean underwear and bra and a cotton top from her suitcase. She strode toward the bathroom, away from Garin.

"Hey, Annja," he called.

She stopped at the door. "What?"

Smiling, he said, "Could you come back here and walk there one more time? I've never really noticed how your—"

Annja stepped into the bathroom and slammed the door, cutting him off. She was frustrated by Garin's crude nature, but part of her was glad to see him and she didn't understand that at all.

"WE REALLY SHOULD have gone somewhere else." Garin stared at the menu with no enthusiasm. The plastic protecting the typed sheets was stained. "Surely they've got a better restaurant than this."

"This isn't a date," Annja pointed out.

The restaurant was small, more like an afterthought to the hotel than anything else. The menu was extremely limited, but the food smelled good enough to make Annja's stomach rumble in anticipation.

"Maybe I'll just have a coffee," Garin said.

"Eat something," Annja urged.

He peered at her over the menu with interest. "Why? Are you worried that I'm going to starve?"

"I'm hoping you'll choke." Actually, she didn't want to eat alone. She could, and often did, but not when there was an alternative. Maybe Garin was a cold-blooded killer, a thief and a cheat, but he could also be breakfast company.

"Now, there's a cheery thought. And after I've flown so far to see you," he said.

"It's not that far from Germany to Senegal," Annja replied. "And it's not like you actually came to see me. You've got an ulterior motive."

"You've got such a bad impression of me."

"People who try to kill me generally leave a bad impression."

"I'm surprised you came to breakfast with me at all, in that case."

Annja glared at him. "Me. You. Small talk." She shook her head. "It's not going to happen. Get around to whatever brought you here and let's deal with it."

A server came to the table. She was short and plump, in her middle sixties and missing her front teeth. She smiled at them and said good-morning.

Garin ordered for them both, in the native dialect, and in a manner that got a bigger smile out of the tired server.

"You ordered for me," Annja said when he turned back to her.

"I'm sorry," Garin said. "It's a habit I sometimes forget about. When I was a young man, ordering for a woman was both an expectation of the woman and an art for the man. I didn't mean to offend you."

Surprisingly, Annja believed him. "No. Actually, I thought it was kind of charming."

He smiled and looked pleased with himself, erasing some of the charm.

"Seriously, though," Annja said, "we need to talk about why you're here." She glanced at her watch. "You've got fifteen seconds."

"A challenge then."

"Thirteen."

"I think that if you're not careful when you enter Anansi's treasure vault, you're going to unleash a plague that could destroy most of western and northern Africa."

Annja stared at him.

"How am I doing so far?" Garin asked.

24

After the unexpected announcement, it took Annja a moment to find her voice. "You're lying."

Garin laughed at her. "I'm lying? That's the best you can come up with after I tell you that a plague is waiting to be released?" He sipped his coffee. "Why would I lie?"

"To get my attention."

Garin gestured expansively. "I already have your attention. Despite my slight indiscretion—"

"Trying to kill me isn't a slight indiscretion."

"A momentary lapse in judgment."

Annja started to protest again.

Garin held up a hand and looked irritated. "*Whatever* you wish to call it." He took a breath. "Despite that, you talk to me whenever I wish because you're willing to do whatever it takes to get knowledge out of me that you wouldn't otherwise have."

Folding her arms across her breasts, Annja said, "You're not the only man I know who's lived more than five hundred years. In fact, I'm not at all sure how long Roux has been around."

"Nor am I," Garin admitted. "But I am sure of one thing. You won't be able to make casual conversation with Roux and have him trot out his past to be picked over like a buffet line. The only time he tells you anything is when he has his own motivations for doing so. Believe me. I've tried."

"He's trained you well."

Garin grimaced. "I'm not at all like that old fool."

"Maybe you are, more than you like to admit." In fact, upon observing the two of them together, Annja had the distinct opinion that the two acted very much like father and son.

Five hundred years of failed expectation and rebelliousness. Man, that'll leave a mark, she thought.

Garin cursed and shook his head. "We've never seen eye to eye. Roux continues to insist that good will triumph over evil."

"I guess you can't afford to think that way."

"Because you think I'm evil?" Garin asked, sneering.

"Yes."

"I'm not evil. I'm merely a man after my own pursuits."

"You've killed and stolen to get them," Annja said.

"So have you."

Annja gasped. She *had* killed. No more than thirty-six hours ago.

"You killed people to save your life, or to save the lives of others," Garin said. "So you excuse yourself for it. I don't have a problem with that. I excuse myself for the same reasons."

"*You* tried to kill me."

"Will you get over that already?" Garin breathed impatiently. "You threatened me."

"How?"

"The sword. Everything that I am, everything that I have gone through, is because of that sword. Now it is in your hands. When that happened, when I first realized that you had it, can you imagine how I felt?"

Annja couldn't.

"After five hundred years, I'd begun believing that it would never return. Then you came along. And it did. After it had been shattered into pieces. I was afraid. When I attacked you, I wasn't in my right mind. You can't just label people so conveniently," Garin said. "Do you honestly believe Roux is a pure force of good?"

Annja didn't know. She wanted to believe the best of Roux, but he had bailed on her when she had so many questions about the sword and what she was supposed to do. He'd just given her some pop-psychology answers and left her to deal with it. He'd made it clear he didn't see any need to be further involved.

But he'd also told her that she could affect the balance between good and evil. Did she believe that?

Garin scowled. "Roux has filled your head with that crap about the destiny of the sword, hasn't he? And you've really bought into it."

Annja didn't care for the demeaning tone of Garin's words.

"He told me the same thing, once upon a time," Garin said. "Do you know what we did?"

Annja shook her head.

"Roux chased women and gambled across Europe and Asia," Garin said. "Then Roux became intoxicated with the idea of Joan."

"Why? What drew him to her?" Annja asked.

"Probably the same things that draw him to you. She was young—younger than you—and independent. A woman who wouldn't give herself easily to any man."

Annja knew that Roux liked young women. He was rarely without their company at home and abroad from what she had seen.

Frustrated with the conversation, and not liking how it was making her feel, Annja said, "We're not here to talk about Roux."

"I only wanted to put him in perspective so you could better see me," Garin said. "You paint me as a villain, yet I'm the one who showed up here to help you."

Annja restrained from asking him why. "Why do you think the treasure of Anansi has a plague in it?" she asked instead.

As GARIN SPOKE, he studied Annja. He knew that she didn't trust him. He didn't care. She didn't have to trust him, but only had to let him into the expedition. That was all that he wanted.

But he couldn't get the image of her sleeping atop the bedcovers out of his mind. She was a tall woman, and full-bodied, equipped with warm curves over muscle. Strength sheathed in beauty. That was what she was.

Before he was able to truly launch into the story, the server arrived with their breakfast. Despite his complaining about the probable condition of the food, it looked and smelled good.

They ate while he talked, moving through the mango, bananas and *uji,* sorghum bread and beef strips. He'd ordered as much for her as he had for himself. He'd seen Annja eat before and had been impressed.

The hunger to know what he knew showed in her eyes. She wanted to ask him about what he'd seen, what he'd done, and he knew that, as well.

"I was here in West Africa during the slave trade," Garin went on. "In fact, I knew Jozua Ganesvoort's ancestors. For a time I did business in Ile de Goree."

"Selling slaves?" she asked. The accusation was soft in her words, but it was still there.

"No," he lied. "I sold goods and managed a banking operation." That was the truth. He'd dabbled in many things.

Annja continued eating and listening.

"There's more to the legend of the Spider Stone," Garin told her. "In the Old Testament, God smote the pharaoh and his people with plagues."

"Ten in all," Annja said. "I'm familiar with the story. There's been some conjecture that the plagues may have been the result of activity in the Thera volcano 650 miles away. The Nile could have been polluted by the volcano stirring up the silt and rendering the water undrinkable. That would have accounted for the dead fish, as well. It might even have been red algae, a blood tide. With the water gone bad, the frogs would have abandoned the river and allowed the insect population to grow. Disease-carrying insects could have infected livestock and given the people boils. Plagues of locusts happen even without any of these other events, and enough of them can even make the sky dark. With the volcano involved, perhaps it was ash floating in the air. As for the firstborn dying, if the food was ruined they may have died from the diseases it carried."

"And what does the field of archaeology say?" Garin asked.

"When it comes to the Bible, archaeologists are divided," Annja admitted. "Some treat it as a historical document, and others believe it's a work of fiction."

"Designed to keep the believers in line."

"Perhaps."

Garin smiled. "What if I told you that those Biblical citizens weren't that far removed from people today? That there existed within their ranks men who would use whatever means necessary to achieve their ends."

"That's mankind in action," Annja said. "No surprise there."

"True. However, research I've done indicates that some of the people scattered after the pharaoh figured out that the disease that ran through his city wasn't all due to the Hebrew god. The pharaoh's men discovered that some of the diseases had been deliberately started by men."

"Where did you get this information?" Annja asked.

Garin reached into his pocket and took out a USB flash drive. "I have copies of the document."

Annja pushed her empty plates away and put her computer on the table.

Watching her become absorbed in the task, Garin felt a glow of success.

WORKING QUICKLY, Annja opened the flash drive. There was only one file on the device. She copied it to her computer—she couldn't risk Garin snatching it away whenever he wanted—and opened the file. There were several folders tucked inside the main file. Most of them were jpegs.

"They're photographs of tablets recovered from a Hausa village about a hundred years or so after they were written," Garin said. "Evidently the author couldn't live his life in anonymity. That's probably how the pharaoh found out about his culpability in the plagues."

Annja studied the first photograph of a clay tablet. It appeared to be similar in nature to those used in Egypt at the same time period.

"I can't read them. Can you?" Garin asked.

"No," Annja replied.

"Select the next jpeg and you'll see a translation."

The next file had a picture of the same tablet with a translation overlaid on it in white letters. Annja read the story.

While I lived among the dark men and feared Pharaoh's revenge, I had cause to once more use the potion I had concocted to ravage Pharaoh's army.

My adopted village was approached by a young man, no more than a boy, who said that his own village was beset by enemies.

I was touched by the boy's story of how Anansi, the spider god of his people, directed him to me in a dream. I knew that he probably came to me because I have solved many problems for this village where I have chosen to stay.

He appealed to my vanity, praising me as one who has been chosen to be spoken through by his gods. Since his people do trade as much as they do and carry news of many countries, I thought it would be best if I maintained their friendship.

I gave him a pot of the potion and told him to spread it in the water of his enemies. I told him that only a small amount would be necessary, for it was very powerful and water in these lands is a precious commodity, just as it is in Egypt.

Annja launched into the second set of tablets. Excitement stirred within her, along with fear.

I saw the boy again today. He told me that the men who attacked his village are now dead. The potion has always performed well.

When I asked him what he did with the rest of the potion, he told me that Anansi directed him to put it in the place of treasures so that it might be used again if needed.

He gave me a small bag of emeralds and rubies. Before he left, he also showed me a small stone he's inscribing that will tell the history of Anansi's promise to protect his people. On one side, the stone bears the image of an atrocious spider. The other holds the language of his people.

Finished with the translations, Annja stared at Garin. "Is this true?" she asked.

He nodded. "You're hunting something that could kill you and a lot of other people."

"And you're here because you care about people?"

"No," Garin said. "I'm here because I care about you."

Annja didn't believe him. There was more. She waited.

Garin cocked an eyebrow and grinned. "But there's more, Annja. For five hundred years, only Roux and I have shared the mystery of the sword. I'd given up on it. But you came along and made that mystery new again. Made it attainable once more. Or at least clothed it in that illusion. And you've turned our two-sided war into a three-way battle. I've never gotten the best of Roux. With you at my side, I think that balance of power could change."

"Why would I ever help you?" Annja asked.

"Because one day, you may not have a choice. Roux is not your benefactor. If you get in his way—and you might—he'll step on you."

A chill threaded down through Annja's spine as she faced the possibility that Garin might be speaking honestly.

"Well," Garin asked, "do we have a deal? Or did we just have breakfast?"

25

Annja made the introductions, giving Garin's name as Gar Lambert, a professional treasure hunter she'd bumped into while in town.

Hallinger and Ganesvoort seemed pleased by the possibility that someone familiar with the area—and someone who had armed men at his disposal—could join the expedition.

McIntosh and his entourage weren't so easy to convince. They sat together at the back of the room Garin had reserved for the meeting.

"It's amazing how you just happened to come along," McIntosh said.

"Not so amazing," Garin replied. He'd changed clothes, dropping the suit and slipping into jeans and a khaki shirt. He also affected an American accent. The skill of weaving different accents and behaviors was something Annja had noticed in both Roux and Garin. Both men were as skilled as trained actors. "I've been watching the news. I knew Annja was in West Africa. We've already been here for weeks."

The dozen men who followed Garin were hard-eyed and silent. Most of them looked as if they'd fit right in with the Kidira citizens. Except that most of the Senegalese didn't look like killers.

"When we ran into each other earlier," Annja said, "I explained what we were doing." She looked at McIntosh. "I also told him we were short on manpower."

Garin smiled. "Naturally, I couldn't let Annja go trekking around the wilds of the savanna unprotected. Especially not with Tafari gunning for her."

"Naturally," McIntosh said sarcastically.

Annja didn't say anything, although the expression on McIntosh's face made it tempting. She kept quiet, and after a few minutes, everyone began discussing how they were going to get the expedition under way.

"How WELL do you know this guy?"

Annja glanced at McIntosh as they walked along the sidewalk.

Garin and his crew of mercenary cutthroats had set out to finalize the vehicles and armament they were taking.

"I trust him," Annja said.

"With your life?"

"Yes."

"What about the lives of the rest of us?"

Annja stopped and wheeled on McIntosh so fiercely that he backed up a step. "I trust him with the lives of other people as much as I trust you with them, Agent McIntosh."

Passersby started going around them, giving them a wide berth.

"Furthermore," Annja said, "you and your men don't have to take this trip if you don't want to."

McIntosh got his feet under him and leaned into her. "I came this far with you. I'm not going to turn tail now."

"We're not on your turf anymore," Annja said, feeling a little concerned for him. "This isn't Atlanta. That wilderness out there isn't like anything you've ever dealt with. This is my game now."

"Except for your buddy. Looks like it's his game, too."

"He's been around this kind of thing longer than I have," she said.

"Tafari is still out there somewhere, Annja."

"I know," she said. "That'll give you the chance to capture him like you wanted. You should be glad."

"Well, I'm not." McIntosh was breathing hard.

Annja got the impression he was about to do something stupid, like try to kiss her. That's the last thing I need right now, she told herself.

McIntosh cursed and walked away.

"SOMEBODY'S COMING."

Annja looked up from her computer and stared down the trail that cut through the savanna. Kidira was hours behind them, and the western sky was starting to turn purple with the dimming of the day. They were making their way toward a distant hill to the west. Locals, Annja had discovered when she'd asked, had called the place Brothers of Water. Given that the Spider Stone showed a suggestion of waterways in the map—at least, she *hoped* it was a suggestion of waterways—Anansi's treasure was likely to be hidden somewhere near there.

Garin rode in the lead Land Rover. His driver halted. The other drivers behind him fanned out, all of them parking in a formation that allowed for defensive moves.

"I need you to stay put, Ms. Creed," Annja's driver said. He rolled the vehicle to a stop, then closed a big hand around the assault rifle between the seats.

Annja put her computer away. She wore a .45-caliber semiautomatic on her hip. Her T-shirt and cargo pants were soaked through from the heat. She wore a New York Yankees baseball cap and wraparound sunglasses.

All of Garin's crew had drawn their weapons. McIntosh and his people had, too. The possibility of an outside threat seemed to unify the two forces.

The approaching Land Rover halted a few feet in front of Garin's vehicle. Tanisha Diouf slid out of the passenger side. She was dressed in khakis, a green T-shirt tucked into her pants. Stopping, she called out, "Annja Creed."

Annja stepped out of the vehicle and onto the trail. "Tanisha."

The woman's face split into a wide, generous smile. "You've been invited to join us."

"Us?" Annja echoed.

Tanisha pointed to the side of her Land Rover. Childress Corporation was emblazoned on the side. "I talked to Mr. Childress. He agreed to help you get as far into the savanna as safely as you can. If you're interested."

"I am," Annja said.

Tanisha walked over to her. "I was hoping you would say that. My boys have been worried about you. They thought maybe something had happened to you after you left us."

Annja grinned. "I'm glad nothing's happened to you."

"Mr. Childress believes the train was attacked by bandits hoping to steal some of the cargo," Tanisha said. "The next time he has a shipment coming in, it'll be protected."

Annja nodded.

"Mind if I ride with you?" Tanisha asked. "We can talk along the way."

"Sure."

Garin's men repositioned themselves, making room for Tanisha.

"Follow that vehicle," Tanisha instructed the driver. "We've got a base camp not far from here."

Tanisha looked at Annja. "Do you have those maps you had on the train? Let me have a peek and maybe I can get you closer to where you need to go."

"ARE YOU an investor, then?" Victor Childress peered at Garin.

"Yes," Garin replied. "Well, not really investing so much. That's a little rich for my blood. But I do speculate. If something catches my eye."

Annja sat at the folding table their host had provided. Everyone was relaxing after a generous meal.

Bashir sat on her lap and kept distracting Annja with whispered comments despite his mother's admonitions. Kamil had allowed Annja to take a look at his cut, even though it interfered with his manly acting. She'd been pleased to find the wound was healing well.

"Oil is where the money is," Childress said. "If you have it, you make money. But do you know who else makes money?"

Annja knew Childress had consumed a fair bit of wine with the meal.

"Who?" Garin asked as if he was intensely interested. For all Annja knew, maybe he was.

"The people who transport it and sell it at the pump, of course," Childress said. "And the corporations that refine oil."

"I guess that's true enough," Garin said.

McIntosh was ignoring the conversation for the most part. His attention was directed at the dark savanna outside the ring of lights that lit the camp.

"Did you know that Nigeria, not that far from here, actually," Childress said, "is the largest African producer of oil?"

"No," Garin replied.

"Well, they are. Unfortunately, that country is being torn apart by American oil interests and a corrupt government. Hobbled as they are, battered between gangsters and native militias, they can't enter a competitive market. Also nearby, Mauritania's army ousted their president and are looking to do business. In the past, they've had to go through American companies. Childress Corporation is here to change that."

From the short time she'd been around the man, Annja could see that Childress had a high opinion of himself. With McIntosh and Garin already butting heads over who was the alpha male of the expedition, there was too much testosterone in the air.

"I contracted with the Senegalese government to set up a refinery out here," Childress said. "We're in the process of building it now. At the same time, another facet of Childress Corporation is also laying pipe from Mauritania to Senegal. When everything's finished, we'll pump the oil across from Mauritania and refine it here. We hope we'll pick up some business from Nigeria, as well."

ANNJA WORKED in the small dome tent she'd set up for the night.

A shadow darkened the door and Garin's deep voice said, "Knock, knock."

"Come in." Annja sat cross-legged on the floor of the tent. The computer was plugged into an electrical outlet maintained by one of the camp's generator trucks.

Garin entered the tent, having to hunker low. He scowled, then spoke in Latin. "Speak this language. I don't want to be understood by the guards posted nearby, or by the bugs."

"What bugs?" Annja asked in Latin.

"Our host is spying on us."

"Why?"

Garin grinned. "Because he's not a good guy. All that talk he had of setting up a refinery to do fair business with Mauritania and Nigeria? Do you know what he's really banking on?"

"No."

"Bandits. Oil thieves. They've got them all over those countries. As Mauritania was getting ready to enter the oil market, the army pushed out the president, broke off relations with the Americans and went into business with an Australian firm. Nigeria has been conducting sporadic warfare over oil for years. Tanker trucks are stolen from those fields all the time."

"That's going on in the Middle East, too," Annja said.

"Everyone's watching the Middle East," Garin said. He shook his head. "Childress is setting himself up well. He can deal with the bandits in all those countries to subsidize his legitimate business, and have an oil refinery that can sell gasoline right back to the locals, as well as ship it out to the rest of Africa and even Europe. It's a sweet setup. But do you know what he needs?"

Annja didn't like where her mind automatically went because it left Tanisha and her children exposed. "A local warlord to handle all the strong-arm work," she said.

"You know," Garin said, "you don't think like an archaeologist."

"To the contrary," Annja said, "if you study history, you'll see that every culture, nation or people that existed or exists was influenced by what they had or what they wanted or needed. If they had something, they lived a life of other people trying to take it away from them. If they wanted or needed something, they lived a life struggling to get it." She sighed.

She looked at Garin. "So we can't trust Childress."

"No." Garin grinned. "But we let him think we do."

"You think he's going to sell us out to Tafari?"

"I think he already has. Once you find Anansi's treasure, the jaws of the trap will close."

"Then it makes no sense to try to find it," Annja said.

"Now you disappoint me. If we try to leave, deviate from our mission of trying to find the treasure, the jaws of the trap will close anyway. We'll have to fight and maybe lose a lot of people. But if we find the treasure, Tafari and Childress should at least be distracted. Then we'll act to do what we can."

"We could try to slip away. Choose the path of least resistance." Annja didn't want to chance getting McIntosh, Hallinger or Ganesvoort hurt. It was her fault that they'd come this far.

"What about the woman? The engineer and her kids? The other

innocent people who are part of this operation? Do you want to just leave them out here?" Garin asked.

Annja knew she was tired because she hadn't thought far enough. She'd been using all her energy to try to find a match on the maps. She shook her head.

"I'd be willing to bet that Tafari or Childress will use your connection to them against you," Garin continued. "After you had the little boy on your knee for most of the night, you've left yourself— and them—open to that." He paused. "If it was me, I would use them against you."

Annja knew he told her that honestly, even though it would remind her of the reasons not to like or trust him. But he knows I don't have a choice now, she thought. I have to trust him. And maybe, if he wants to find Anansi's treasure, he has to trust me.

She took a deep breath and let it out. "What do we do?"

In the darkness of the tent, Garin's lips curled back in a wolfish smile. "When the time is right, we'll act."

Annja nodded.

"I'm going to have to come see you more often, little angel," Garin said in a light tone. "You do lead an interesting life." He turned and crawled back through the tent flaps. "I just hope the cursed luck of that sword doesn't get you killed." He tossed her a smile over his shoulder as he disappeared into the night lying in wait outside.

THE CARAVAN STARTED out early the next morning. In spite of all he'd drunk and the lateness of his evening, Victor Childress was one of the first to be ready. He wore safari clothes and carried a big-game hunting rifle slung over his shoulder.

"Since I seem to be having trouble with the local toughs," he said, "what with the equipment sabotage and the train wreck, I thought I'd get better equipped."

Annja looked at him, wondering if what Garin had told her the previous night was really true. Childress seemed amiable and harmless, actually enthusiastic about helping. But she couldn't shake the feeling that Garin was right.

It takes a villain to know a villain, she told herself. She wondered again about Garin's own motivations, and whether he was the villain she'd thought him to be. Here he was, laying his life on the line. But for what?

"You don't have to come," Annja told Childress. "I think we've got enough people to handle everything."

"Nonsense." Childress sipped gourmet coffee from a stainless-steel mug. "If you and your group hadn't run off those sods that ambushed the train, they might well have made off with all of my equipment. I'm certain that's what they were after."

Annja wondered if he was attempting to allay any suspicions about Tafari.

"While we're waiting on replacement equipment," Childress said, "I can spare Tanisha and a few of my men to help you out for a few days. Once the new equipment gets here, we'll have to tend to our own kettle of fish."

Annja made herself smile and thank him.

The group set out across the savanna, following the course she'd developed from the map on the Spider Stone.

BY MIDDAY, everyone was hot and tired. They followed trails made by wagons and carts when they could, picked up fragments of foot-paths and game trails when they couldn't and blazed new paths when they couldn't do anything else. One of the Land Rovers went down with a flat tire, bringing the caravan to a halt.

Annja stood in the shade of the vehicle she rode in and compared the terrain to what she understood from the Spider Stone. Either it's starting to look familiar because I've been looking at it too long, or we're getting close.

As she opened a bottle of water, McIntosh joined her. His shirt was dark with sweat and a film of dust that stuck to the moisture. She tossed him a bottle of water from the cooler in the back of the Land Rover. His men and Garin's had set up a defensive perimeter around the vehicles.

"I keep getting this feeling we're being followed," McIntosh said as he opened the water and drank.

"We are." Annja nodded upward at the large birds that floated gracefully in the still sky. They were two feet long with a wingspan nearly three times that. Brown feathers covered their plump, ungainly bodies, and their heads were a pinkish bald knob.

McIntosh shaded his eyes and looked up. "What are those?"

"Hooded vultures. You'll find them in the wild, as well as around towns."

"I thought I saw some like them in Kidira."

Annja nodded. "They feed near slaughterhouses more often than they feed out in the wilderness. They're the smallest of the African vultures, but the swiftest. Generally they're the first to find a carcass, but they're so much weaker that everything else drives them away."

"They've spotted us and think we're going to croak, huh?" McIntosh said.

Despite her misgivings, Annja smiled. "I hope not."

McIntosh spoke without looking at her. "I think you're right about Childress."

She'd gone to McIntosh's tent after Garin had left hers, and told him what Garin suspected. McIntosh had said he doubted that Garin knew what he was talking about.

"Why the change of heart?" Annja asked.

"Do you know many millionaires who figure they have time in their day to intentionally go out and try to get themselves killed?"

"What are you talking about?"

McIntosh looked at her. "I don't think Childress would be out here beating the bush with us unless he thought he had a lock on things." He nodded toward the man, who was conferring with some of his own men. "Whatever's going on in his mind, he thinks he has a free pass."

Annja agreed.

"I think we need to drop this," McIntosh went on. "Just tell Childress that you were wrong, that Anansi's treasure is a big hoax—"

"He's not going to believe that if Tafari doesn't believe that."

"Tell him the treasure isn't located anywhere around here."

Annja was quiet for a moment. The men had finished replacing the tire on the Land Rover, and everyone was preparing to continue.

"It is, though," Annja said. "And I'll bet Tafari knows it is, too." She took out the Spider Stone and looked at the map etched on its surface. She knew every line of it by now. "Leaving isn't the answer. We're too deep into it now. The only way out is to go through with this."

26

"You haven't asked me why."

Looking up from the maps they were studying as they ate, Annja studied Tanisha Diouf. "Asked you why what?"

"Why I'm out here."

Annja didn't understand.

"In the savanna," Tanisha said. "When I could be home in London with my kids." She glanced at Kamil and Bashir. The boys played in the nearby scrub, going deeper and deeper into the wilderness as they got braver. "To hear my mother tell it, where I should be with my kids." She sighed. "There's nothing worse than a mom call."

Annja had seen Tanisha talking on the satellite phone earlier.

"Does your mom call to give you grief over what you do?" Tanisha asked.

"I kind of missed out on that," Annja said.

"You lost your mom?" Tanisha looked stricken. "I'm sorry. I didn't mean to bring up anything that would—"

"Actually, I was raised in an orphanage."

"I've seen you on that show—"

"*Chasing History's Monsters,*" Annja said.

"—and no one ever mentioned it."

"Not exactly something you want advertised on a television show like that," Annja said. She waited a beat. "So why are you?"

"Why am I what?" Tanisha asked.

"Out here. In the wilds of West Africa. With your boys."

"I was working for Childress in London. Operating some of the drilling platforms he's working in the North Sea. I had a deal set up with him where I was two weeks on-site and two weeks home with my kids. Still available for calls, though." Tanisha ate another peach slice. "Then he approached me about this." She waved her fork around to take in the savanna.

"Was the offer too good to turn down?"

"It was good. Don't get me wrong there. But it was something else that made me come here."

Annja waited.

"I grew up in London," Tanisha said. "But my grandparents grew up in the United States. In Georgia. Near Atlanta. Before that, according to my father and grandfather, my people were here."

"West Africa?"

Tanisha nodded. "They were from the Hausa." She looked at Annja. "The same people who made that Spider Stone." She shrugged. "So, in a way, taking this job meant that I could see my homeland. I didn't know if it would make a difference."

"Does it?"

Tanisha hesitated. "I don't know. The job and the boys have been keeping me frantic. The sabotage and destruction of the equipment has been the worst. That always causes a drain on time and energy." She took a deep breath and let it out. "But sometimes, when I'm alone or it's really late at night, or when I'm talking to Jaineba, this place just feels like home." Shaking her head, she looked at Annja. "Isn't that weird?"

Annja thought about the sword she carried, the one Joan had carried into battle. I've seen stuff a lot weirder than that, she thought.

AN HOUR LATER, they came to a rise and Annja looked down into the slight valley below. A small stream, nothing like the Senegal River or any of the other three that fed the country, wound through the valley and—for a time, just as the Spider Stone map showed—became two streams.

There was something about the land that drew Annja's attention.

Pieces of the Spider Stone's map and the topography files she'd been studying fit together inside her head.

She had the driver stop and she got out at the top of the hill.

Garin, noticing that she had stopped, ordered his vehicle to a halt also. He clambered out with his assault rifle in hand.

"What is it?" he asked.

"We're here," Annja said, controlling the excitement that filled her. "This is the Brothers of Water."

Garin looked around at the area. "You're sure?"

Annja nodded. She saw the landmarks she'd been searching for— the hills that formed a bowl-shaped depression and the two streams that made a wishbone only a little to the right of her position. There, like the Senegal River was formed by the mixing of the Semefé and Bafing Rivers, the two streams came from one, then pooled into a depression at the bottom of the valley.

"It's here," she said. "Or it doesn't exist at all."

THEY BEGAN in the center of the valley. Annja marked off sections by natural landforms. The hunt kicked off in earnest.

"What are we looking for exactly?" McIntosh asked.

"A door," Annja said. "At least, that's what I think it is. On the map on the Spider Stone, it shows a rectangle that I think is a door."

"But you might be wrong," he said.

"Archaeology isn't as exact a science as mathematics or physics," Annja said. "There's a lot of guesswork involved, conclusions that you draw that may never be proved."

"The rectangle could just as easily be an unmarked grave," he said.

Annja replied grudgingly, "Yes. But that's not what the stone says."

TAFARI WATCHED the woman search the valley. Hours passed and the sun settled over the western horizon. Still, she didn't give up.

Nor did he.

He lay on his chest on another hill and held a pair of binoculars to his eyes as the woman continued her quest. Eventually, some of those hunting in the area were pulled off the search to set up camp.

Zifa crawled up to him and handed him a satellite phone. "Childress," Zifa said.

Taking the phone, Tafari cradled it to his face and said, "Yes?"

"I think this is a waste of time," Childress complained. "Whatever she thinks she has, whatever you think she has, she doesn't have it."

Tafari said nothing. He kept watch through the binoculars. Below, the searchers were starting to use flashlights, not even giving up to the night.

"Did you hear me?" Childress demanded.

"I did," Tafari replied.

"What are you going to do?"

"Be patient."

"It's just a superstition," Childress argued. "If there was anything to find here, it would have been found by now."

"Sometimes," Tafari said, "secrets don't come out so easily. What you're talking about in this place, the gods have hidden."

"In the morning," Childress said, "I'm leaving. This has ceased to be amusing."

"You would never make a good hunter," Tafari told the man. "And if you leave now, you can consider our partnership in the matter of this treasure at an end."

"Why?"

"If you're not here to labor for the fruits, you won't be allowed to partake in the banquet."

Childress sounded upset. "I did my part. I delivered the woman."

"But now you've become a part of it. If you leave this expedition early, that could warn her. She already senses that she's being followed."

"If she does, I haven't seen any sign of it," Childress said.

"You're a civilized predator," Tafari said. "You don't know what to look for out here. The woman does. If you leave tomorrow, you will end our agreement because your departure will jeopardize my effectiveness in trailing her."

"All right," Childress grumbled. "I'll be here for a few more days. No more than that." He broke the connection.

Tafari handed the phone back to Zifa.

"There is a problem if the woman continues in the direction she's headed," Zifa said.

"What?"

"The village we destroyed a few days ago lies less than two miles farther in the direction she's going."

Tafari had almost forgotten about the Hausa village they'd eliminated. "Maybe it would be good if she and her friends see that place," he told Zifa. "That way she'll know what I'm capable of."

FRUSTRATION CHAFED at Annja as she stared through the darkness. But the feeling that she was at the edge of discovery wouldn't go away.

Moving slowly through the brush, her eyes burning, she searched for anything that might suggest a hidden place. Graves could often be found by earth that sank in after them. So could collapsed buildings and remnants of cities. Refuse built up over time, and she had no way of knowing how long ago Anansi's treasure had been hidden.

"Annja."

She ignored McIntosh's call, knowing he would only want to try to talk her into giving up the search for the night.

"Hey." McIntosh caught up to her, flashlight bobbing through the scrub brush. He took her by the elbow.

"Let go," she said.

He took his hand back. "I'm not asking you to give up," he said. "Just to wait. It's dark out here. Somebody's going to get hurt. Come eat. Get some rest. Then start again in the morning when it's light. Everything will look different then."

He's right, she thought. She forced herself to take a deep breath. One of the most important things she'd learned while on digs was that the expectations of the leader tempered those of the people working the site. Pour on the expectation too early, keep them working too long and too hard, and there would be less to work with.

"You're right," she said.

"ANNJA," Tanisha called.

Groggy from being sound asleep, her dreams filled with spiders, maps and murderous men, Annja blinked her eyes and focused on Tanisha Diouf as the woman unzipped the tent and climbed in.

"What's wrong?" Annja asked.

"Bashir's missing," Tanisha replied. "I looked for him, but I can't find him anywhere."

Fear tightened Annja's stomach, and she felt a chill against the back of her neck. Rain slapped against the tent, and from the sound of it she knew the ground outside was soaked.

"How long has he been missing?" Annja dressed quickly.

"Five, maybe ten minutes. I went looking for him, but I couldn't find him." Panic ate at the edges of Tanisha's words.

Annja pulled on her hiking boots and laced them up. A glance at her watch showed her it was just after 6:00 a.m. It didn't sound as though anyone else was up. "We'll find him. Are Garin and his men up?"

"The sentries are."

"None of them saw Bashir?"

"They saw him walk into the brush. They didn't see him walk back out."

Annja grabbed the pistol and slung the assault rifle. Reaching down, she grabbed her backpack. It contained medical supplies, rope and extra gear.

"Why did Bashir go into the brush?" Annja asked.

"To use the bathroom. He's shy about that. Kamil knows he's supposed to go with him, but he said he couldn't wake up." Tanisha shook her head. "I didn't even know he was gone until I woke up a few minutes ago and he wasn't there."

Garin was up when Annja left her tent. So was McIntosh.

"What's going on?" Garin asked.

"Bashir is missing," Tanisha cried.

Garin looked over to one of the hard-eyed sentries.

The man shook his head, then spoke German. Annja listened.

"Did you see the boy?" Garin asked.

"The boy went into the brush," the man said. "He does that. Likes to be by himself. Shy kidneys. I didn't think anything of it."

"Has anyone been around?"

"No."

Garin held the assault rifle, barked orders to his men and looked at Annja. He spoke in English. "Let's find the boy."

FOLLOWING Bashir's trail across the muddy ground was easy at first. The rain had softened the surface enough that his footprints sank into the ground. However, that same rain also threatened to wash them away.

Annja moved quickly. Mud clung to her hiking boots and made her feet heavy. Sucking noises sounded every time she lifted the boots clear of the muck.

Bashir had managed a circuitous route through the brush. From the way he stopped and his feet turned around, it was evident he was tracking something. A short distance on, Annja found the tracks of a hare.

"A rabbit," McIntosh said, dropping to one knee to examine the tracks.

"Bashir saw them all day yesterday," Tanisha said. "He wanted to make a pet out of one of them."

A short distance ahead, Annja saw where a sinkhole had opened up in the earth, leaving a gaping maw almost four feet across. Her heart trip-hammered in her chest. She'd suspected that Anansi's chamber was underground, but there was no way of knowing how large it was.

"Oh, my god," Tanisha gasped. She jerked into a run.

27

Annja caught Tanisha around the waist and held her back from the sinkhole.

"Let me go!" Tanisha struggled, but Annja was able to hold her. Garin moved in to help.

"Bashir may have fallen into that hole!" Tanisha said. Her tears mixed with the rain.

"I know," Annja said as calmly as she could. "If he's in there, we'll get him. But we won't be able to help him by losing our heads." She stared into Tanisha's eyes. "Do you hear me? Don't waste time."

Tanisha nodded.

Annja passed the woman off to McIntosh, then shrugged out of her backpack and took out a coil of rope. She tied the rope around a tree in a quick, practiced flip.

"I've got you," Garin told Annja, taking hold of the rope.

Annja nodded at him, then knotted the rope around her waist and went as quickly as she dared to the edge of the sinkhole. She focused on saving Bashir, not finding the little boy drowned in a huge pool of mud.

She eased over the edge of the hole, taking heart in the fact that the sinkhole hadn't crumbled any farther and that the mud pile at the bottom of the hole wasn't large enough to cover even a small child.

Annja spotted muddy footprints on the stone floor of the tunnel. Crouched down at the bottom of the drop, some ten or twelve feet below the ground, she realized that she was standing in a passageway.

"Annja," Garin called.

"I'm all right. Bashir's not in the mud." Annja knelt and examined the stone flooring. Flat stones made up the bottom of the passageway. More stones supported the sides. A quick check over her head, dragging her fingers along the tunnel's ceiling, told her that stones had been used there, as well.

Thin streaks made from small fingers stained the walls. As Annja studied them, the mud began to run.

"Bashir was here, though," she called up. "The sinkhole leads to a tunnel." A puddle of water came halfway up her boots. He got scared he was going to drown, she thought. Or that no one was going to find him.

"Where is he now?" Tanisha asked.

Annja peered into the darkness. "I don't know. Get some flashlights and get down here."

TAFARI ROUSED the instant Zifa touched him. "What?" he asked.

"Childress called," Zifa said. "It appears that Annja Creed has found a tunnel to an underground structure."

"Get the others," Tafari ordered. "Let's go see what the woman found." He strapped on his guns over his loincloth, then opened the tin containing the paint he used to mark himself as a warrior of his people. He started putting on the skull face by touch.

"BASHIR." Annja called the boy's name as she went forward through the passageway. The floor tilted, heading deeper into the earth. Her voice echoed ahead of her, letting her know that she'd barely seen any of the underground space that existed. *Bashir.*

"Annja?" The boy's voice came out of the darkness. In the next moment he was stepping into her flashlight beam. He was covered in mud. "Annja!"

She knelt, holding on to the boy as he desperately wrapped his arms around her. Then he was sobbing, shaking against her, knotting his fists in her shirt.

Annja didn't say a word, just held him and let him know she was there. She rubbed his back.

"I was lost," he said.

"I know," Annja replied.

"I was chasing after a rabbit. I didn't know it was leading me into a trap."

Annja smiled. "I really don't think the rabbit built this, do you?"

Bashir pulled his head off her shoulder and sniffled. "No. Bugs Bunny would never live in a place like this." He looked around.

"That's probably true," Annja agreed. "Are you all right?"

He nodded.

Annja made him step back so she could survey him from head to toe. Muddy and teary-eyed, Bashir didn't seem to be any worse for the wear.

Holding on to his hand, Annja walked him back to the sinkhole. McIntosh, Garin, Tanisha and Childress had gathered around the opening. They lowered a rope and pulled Bashir up. Mother and son had a tearful reunion.

"Is it down there?" Childress asked, more animated than ever. "Anansi's treasure?"

"I don't know," Annja said. "I didn't reach the end of the passageway. It goes on for a while."

Lightning flickered against the cottony-gray sky of early morning. Thunder pealed like a cannon, drowning out the constant hiss of the falling rain for a time.

"With the sinkhole opened up like that," McIntosh said, "the rain could flood the passageway."

"We could try to close it up," Childress said.

"No," a woman said.

They all turned and found Jaineba standing at the edge of the savanna. She wore a brown grand *bubu* and leaned on her staff.

"This is the time to seek out Anansi's treasure," Jaineba said. She strode from the tree line and stopped in front of Tanisha. "This is why you were brought back to our people, daughter. Blood of your blood was sworn to protect this place and these secrets."

Blood of your blood? Annja thought.

"Me?" Tanisha asked.

"I have seen you in my dreams," Jaineba said. "And this one, too." She nodded at Annja. "Your coming was foretold to me months ago. It was time for this place to be found." The old woman put her hand on Bashir's head, then on Kamil's. "These two are of the warrior blood of the Hausa who once lived in these lands. Those people were friends to my people. Their medicine man was charged with preserving the secrets of Anansi that were given to his people. But he was taken from these lands by slavers after his people were destroyed."

Annja listened, not knowing how much of the old woman's story to believe.

"You are Yohance's descendant, daughter," Jaineba declared. "I see his blood in you."

Tanisha shook her head.

"It is true," the old woman said. "Just as Yohance was charged with caring for the Spider Stone and the secrets it contained, so are you now charged with bringing forth the secrets Anansi left in this place."

"But that can't be true." Tanisha's voice was hollow.

"Search yourself, daughter," Jaineba encouraged. "You have told me before that you feel tied to this place in ways that you don't understand. Now it is time to see that your spirit longs to be here so that it can join the spirits of your people."

"My mother and father have never wanted to come to Africa."

"Not everyone who is gone from this place will feel the pull." Jaineba stared into Tanisha's eyes. "But you feel it strongly."

Tanisha said nothing.

Thunder boomed.

Kamil and Bashir pulled in closer to their mother.

"Which is it to be, daughter?" Jaineba asked. "Do you turn your back on your true past? Or do you seize your destiny?"

Destiny. The word hit Annja with a jolt. When she'd picked up the sword fragment, she'd set her foot upon her own destiny. And it had led her here.

"I'm going down there," Garin stated gruffly. "Even if it's only to get out of this rain." He looked at Annja.

Annja knew it was Tanisha's decision to make. She looked at the woman.

"This is your passion, your love, isn't it?" Tanisha asked. "To see old things. Relics and artifacts. It's not about the gold or silver for you."

"No," Annja answered honestly. "It's about touching the past." She made herself smile. "For all we know, that passageway goes nowhere. Or to a flooded room. Anything that might have been in there could have been taken long ago." She couldn't help thinking about the plague that Garin had insisted still remained within the chamber below.

Tanisha was quiet for a moment. "All right," she said in a soft voice. "Let's go see what there is."

THEY CAME to the end of the passageway. A large wall of stone blocked the path.

"A dead end?" Childress said, playing his light over the craggy stone surface. "That's what we came down here to see? A dead end?"

Annja handed her flashlight to McIntosh, then went forward to examine the wall. Tanisha joined her.

"Do you think we're dealing with a counterbalanced wall?" Tanisha asked.

Turning to McIntosh, Annja said, "Play the flashlight beam along the bottom of the wall."

McIntosh did.

"Watch the silt in the rainwater," Annja said.

As they watched, the murky sand and mud slid quietly under the edge of the rock. The two surfaces had been fit together so smoothly that the delineation between them wasn't readily apparent.

"The Egyptians did a lot with counterbalanced walls," Annja said. "Since we're not so far away from that culture, and the Hausa who built this wanted to remain secretive, maybe they mimicked some of the engineering feats the Egyptians used."

"Found it," Tanisha said, her hand resting at a point midway down the wall to the right side. "Everybody step back. I don't know which way this is going to turn."

After everyone was clear, Tanisha triggered the release mechanism. A four-foot section of the wall swiveled. Rock chips and pebbles ground audibly under the massive weight of the hidden door.

Taking her flashlight back from McIntosh, Annja stepped through the door on one side while Tanisha slid through on the other. Their flashlight beams hit the treasure waiting on the other side at the same time.

Childress cursed in stunned surprise.

The room was huge, at least 150 feet across. Several fortunes in gold and silver, ivory and gems, occupied stone shelves made of carefully placed rock. The riches immediately pulled the attention of Garin and his men. Likewise, McIntosh and his group of CIA agents were drawn in.

Hallinger and Ganesvoort seized on the same thing that caught Annja's attention. Clay tablets sat in neat piles.

Mesmerized, everyone moved forward.

"Can you read it?" Hallinger whispered to Annja as she carefully lifted a tablet.

She looked at the row of characters. "I can pick out some words here and there, but this is even older writing than what's on the Spider Stone."

"Do you know what we have here?" Hallinger asked. Then he answered his own question before she could make the attempt. "This is the history of a people. Probably a history that isn't even known today."

Annja knew. This was the kind of find all archaeologists dreamed about. This was the kind of event that made careers.

It was also the kind of thing that allowed them to be caught off guard.

Assault rifles on full-auto opened fire. A hail of bullets struck Garin's mercenaries, chopping many of them down where they stood with their hands filled with gold coins or jewels. Some of them managed to pull their own weapons and start firing back.

It was enough to break the line of skeleton-faced men into confusion as several of their number pitched over dead. Annja could tell by the surprise on their faces that they hadn't expected to get routed—even if only momentarily. She was certain the attackers were Tafari's men.

"This way!" Tanisha yelled, throwing herself toward the back wall.

Garin and McIntosh had their assault rifles up, opening fire and spraying bullets at the warriors in the other doorway. Half of their men were down and probably dead.

Return fire from Tafari's men hammered piles of treasure. The room plunged into relative darkness as many of the flashlights winked out and the ones that survived were extinguished so they wouldn't draw fire.

Tanisha kept her light on. She ran toward the back wall without hesitation, seeking something on the wall. Annja was surprised when that section of the wall spun out to reveal another tunnel.

The survivors raced through the second door, hurling themselves from the death room as Tafari's men launched a new fusillade of bullets.

On the other side of the door, Tanisha reached up and adjusted the hidden mechanism. The massive door shut again. The gunfire became muffled.

Garin leaned against a wall and changed magazines in his assault rifle. "How did you know about the other door?" he asked.

"That end of the room was the same size as the other one," Tanisha answered. "And I couldn't imagine anyone only building one way into that room, knowing they could be trapped by a collapsed passageway."

"If you'd guessed wrong," Hallinger gasped, holding a hand to a bloody wound in his side, "we'd all be dead."

"We were almost dead anyway," Garin said. "That was a stupid mistake." He grimaced in displeasure. Blood wept from cuts on his cheek and forehead. Either he'd been grazed by bullets or splinters of flying rock.

"That means this tunnel has to lead to the surface somewhere," McIntosh said. He took a flashlight from his pocket and shone it around.

"Unfortunately, we don't know how far away that might be," Garin said. "And the whole time we're looking for another way out of here, Tafari is loading up as much of the treasure as he can. Including, possibly, the plague."

"My boys," Tanisha said. "My boys are still out there."

Her words, the desperation and the fear, filled the passageway with silence.

Annja took stock of them. Other than Garin, McIntosh, Hallinger and Ganesvoort, who had a wound in his thigh that needed tending, only three other men had survived the attack. Sporadic gunfire from the treasure room let them know no one else would live.

Without a word, Tanisha took off, running toward the end of the new passageway.

Annja ran after her. She knew if Tafari found the boys, he would kill them.

They ran through the darkness, sometimes stumbling and falling, but getting up again and going on.

Behind them, Annja heard the massive door open, followed by a brief volley of gunfire, and knew that they were being pursued.

TAFARI POINTED his assault rifle at the open door of the treasure room. "Hold your fire," he ordered his men.

They'd already fired into the darkness. It had taken them a while to figure out the mechanism of the door. Too much time, he now saw.

"They got away," Childress said.

"I see that," Tafari said angrily. He quickly divided his men and sent a group of them down the throat of the passageway after those who had escaped.

"They can't get away to tell someone," Childress protested. He gestured at all the gold and silver. "It'll take days, maybe weeks, to get all of this transported out of here. The rain will make that even harder. Carrying this much weight, trucks will get stuck." He reached out and picked up a small fired-clay pot that caught his eye.

The pot was white, covered in gold filigree and sealed with wax. It was an oddity against the other treasures.

Tafari glanced around the room. It was more than he'd ever thought might be there. He reloaded his weapon. "They won't get away," he said. Lifting the assault rifle, he pointed it at Childress. "And I don't need a partner anymore." He pulled the trigger and unleashed a 3-round burst.

Childress dropped like a rock, a look of surprise frozen on his face.

Tafari plucked the pot from the dead man's hand and ran down the passageway. He had the engineer's children. That gave him an advantage no one yet knew about.

28

The tunnel came to an abrupt end.

Annja swung her flashlight up and examined the ceiling. There was no hint of a door. Whatever had been there all those years ago had filled in with silt and debris.

"Move," Garin ordered, slinging his assault rifle and reaching into the combat vest he wore. He extracted a grayish lump of what looked like modeling clay. "Plastic explosive. There's going to be a lot of noise. Cover your ears and get back."

Annja grabbed Tanisha's arm and pulled her back. Hallinger had one of Ganesvoort's arms slung over his shoulders and was supporting the man's weight. Both of them were breathing hard, almost to the point of exhaustion. She knew they couldn't go on much farther.

Garin prepared the charge.

When the plastic explosive detonated, a thousand pounds or more of mud was blown outward. A lot of the mud came down, splattering all of them.

Even with her ears covered and her mouth open to equalize pressure, Annja was temporarily deafened by the blast. The concussive force had knocked everyone to the ground.

But when the chaos ended, the hole was open and passable.

Annja recovered quickest. She pushed herself to her feet and climbed up the pile of muddy earth, emerging into the rain on a slope overlooking the valley. Getting her bearings, she looked around and spotted the camp. She could see a group of men guarding Kamil and Bashir.

The two boys sat on the rear deck of a jeep, looking wet and frightened. Their hands were bound.

The explosion had alerted the guards. One of them manned the .50-caliber machine gun mounted on the rear deck and he opened fire immediately.

Garin was just climbing out of the hole.

"Down!" Annja shouted. She couldn't really hear herself so she wasn't sure if he heard her. She ran toward Garin, leaping up and hitting him squarely in the chest with both feet.

Caught by surprise and hit hard, Garin tumbled back into the hole.

Annja hit the ground and rolled down the incline. The machine gun rattled, the rounds tearing chunks out of the ground as the gunner closed the range. She realized that somewhere in the chaos she'd lost the assault rifle and the pistol. All she had now was her sword.

That's all I need, she told herself grimly. She leaped, throwing herself forward in a swan dive down a particularly steep section of the hill. Hitting hard, she rolled and slid behind a copse of baobob trees. The extraordinarily thick trunks of the trees provided good cover.

Annja stayed in motion, though, circling the trees to the left. Bullets hammered the trees, shearing through some of the smaller branches and dropping them to the ground.

Once in the tree line near the camp, there was plenty of cover. She used it, closing in on the guards.

Almost on top of them, Annja spotted Jaineba stretched out on the ground. The old woman's chest was soaked with blood.

Horror and anger shot through Annja, forming a powerful concoction of emotions. She summoned the sword to her right hand and ran.

The men were busily engaged exchanging shots with someone on the hill. She thought it might be Garin or McIntosh, or perhaps both. They were having a hard time because Kamil and Bashir were too close.

The three guards suddenly turned to face her, bringing their weapons to bear.

Annja willed herself to go dead inside. There was no option to be merciful. Whatever chance the boys had depended on her.

She ran straight at the men, plunging the sword through the heart of the first man, then stopping her forward momentum and pivoting on her right foot, yanking the sword free as she came around. Still holding on to the sword with both hands, she whirled, cutting the second man as she sliced through his ribs under his right arm and through his heart.

Lifting a foot, she kicked the dying man free of the sword and turned to engage the third man, who was aiming the machine gun toward her. The heavy-caliber rounds tore through the ground and the brush and poked holes in some of the tents and one of the Land Rovers.

Annja threw the sword, stepping into the effort with all the grace of a baseball pitcher delivering a fastball. The sword sailed straight and true, piercing the man through the solar plexus and knocking him back from the machine gun.

Vaulting up onto the jeep, Annja grabbed the sword and willed it away. She tore at the ropes that bound the boys, then tucked them into the back seats of the jeep.

She ran to Jaineba and saw that her chest rose and fell in a shallow rhythm. Annja carried the woman and belted her into the passenger seat. Jaineba groaned in pain and Annja chose to view that as a good sign.

Bullets were cutting leaves from the trees, coming from the group of men boiling from the sinkhole. Tafari led them.

Luck was with her. The jeep didn't require keys. All it had was a starter button. Annja hit the button and got the engine turning over.

"Hang on!" she shouted to the boys, then let out the clutch. All four tires screamed for traction on the wet ground. After they'd chewed through the top layer of mud, they grabbed hold and sent the jeep screaming forward.

Driving wildly, in skips and jumps, Annja brought the jeep to a stop in front of Hallinger and Ganesvoort. She got out while McIntosh, Garin and three other men provided covering fire.

After helping Hallinger put Ganesvoort into the back of the jeep, Annja turned to Tanisha and said, "Get them out of here."

Tanisha didn't hesitate to slide quickly behind the wheel. She took off and bullets chased the jeep up the hillside.

Garin tossed Annja one of the assault rifles he was carrying. "I picked that up where you dropped it. You'll need to reload."

Annja did, taking a magazine from the bandolier across her chest.

From a prone position, Garin fired spaced shots that took down targets among Tafari's skull-faced warriors.

"According to the map," Annja said, "there's a rope suspension bridge over a hundred-foot chasm only a few miles to the west. If we can get another vehicle, and if we can beat Tafari there, we might be able to stage a strategic retreat."

"I hate retreats," Garin said. "Just means you have to fight someone again. I'd rather finish this."

"We're severely outnumbered here," Annja pointed out.

"Yeah," McIntosh said, firing deliberately, "but the numbers are getting less and less all the time."

A growling-engine noise arrived about two seconds before the jeep did. It screamed up the hill on the blind side, airborne and almost coming down on top of them.

Annja threw herself to one side, waited till the jeep landed, then sped in pursuit. If it had kept going, she would never have caught it, but the driver cut the wheels to come around in a tight turn. Still running, Annja ripped bursts through the driver and his two passengers before they recognized her as a threat.

The jeep stalled out.

Annja grabbed the dead men's clothes and hauled them out. She crawled behind the wheel. She pulled the vehicle around and headed back to the others.

"Let's go!" she shouted over the gunfire.

Tafari and his men were loading into vehicles. It wouldn't be long before their position on the hillside was overrun.

As soon as the last man was aboard the jeep, Annja released the clutch and sped off in the direction Tanisha had driven. She hoped Tanisha had remembered the bridge. As Annja topped the rise, she saw that the bridge was closer than she'd thought, just at the bottom of the hill. Tanisha was already headed across it.

Annja drove as fast as she dared, closing in on Tanisha. The jeep slewed wildly as she overdrove the control. She had to downshift to recover, and lost speed doing so.

But they were closing on the suspension bridge. Tanisha was already halfway across.

"Get ready," McIntosh called from the back. "They're coming. Start evasive maneuvers."

Annja rolled the steering wheel back and forth, feeling the soft earth peeling away under the tires. Worse than that, the gearbox was picking up mud. She feared it might fail at any moment.

"Incoming!" McIntosh yelled. "Bear right! Bear right!"

Annja pulled hard right, almost flipping the jeep. Beside her, Garin cursed.

The grenade landed just ahead of them to the left. Mud rained down on them and a yawning crater opened up. It was close enough that Annja's left tires both dipped sickeningly into the hole and threw her out of control again.

McIntosh brought up his rifle and fired steadily.

Glancing at the cracked rearview mirror, Annja saw one of the men fall from the lead pursuit jeep then get run over by one of the others.

At least three vehicles followed them. Annja knew even if they made it across the bridge, they'd never be able to escape. And they were being followed too closely to stop and somehow destroy the bridge.

If we stop, Tafari will put one of those grenades right into us, she thought. The best Annja could hope was that the blast would destroy the bridge and Tanisha and her sons would go free.

She turned to Garin. "Take the wheel."

He stared at her. "What?"

"Take the wheel!" When Garin did, Annja squeezed out onto the running board and let him take her seat.

"What are you doing?" McIntosh yelled.

"A true act of desperation," Annja replied. She knew she'd be pushing her strength and speed to the limits—if she pulled off what she was thinking of. And there was a good chance that she wouldn't.

But it was all that she had left.

"Incoming!" McIntosh yelled again.

"Hold on!" Garin warned, then he yanked the wheel.

This time they almost drove straight through the explosion. The concussion nearly tore Annja from the jeep. Smoke and mud filled the air and nearly overcame her.

When she looked forward, she saw they were at the bridge. The tires rumbled over the wooden planks, and the vehicle swung and swayed enough that Annja felt certain they'd never make it across.

A rocket from another jeep shot past them, then impacted on the opposite chasm wall. The sound of the explosion echoed in the hundred-foot drop.

Garin cursed.

Tafari abandoned his rocket launcher and took up his assault rifle. Standing in his seat, he shot at Annja.

Annja held tight. Tafari's jeep had gained the bridge. She waited for the right moment, then released her hold on the jeep and leaped. She grabbed hold of the bridge's rope support and somehow managed not to be torn free. She spun around and touched down on her feet. Reaching over her shoulder, she took a deep breath and summoned the sword.

Realizing what the madwoman intended to do, Tafari shouted at the driver, "Run her down! Run her down *now* or we are dead men!"

The jeep wobbled dangerously.

"Keep it on the bridge!" Tafari howled. "Keep it on the bridge or I'll kill you!" He pointed the assault rifle at the driver's head.

Annja raised the sword and prepared to cut the ropes.

It's too soon! Tafari realized, watching the jeeps on the other side. The first vehicle was clear of the bridge, but the second vehicle would be lost if she cut the ropes too soon.

Everything slowed down in Annja's mind. She saw Tafari's jeep bearing down on her. She cut one rope and swung out over the gorge. The maneuver took her out of the path of the bullets and bought a little time. It had to be enough.

Annja swept the sword through the bridge supports on the left side. Garin had made it safely across the gorge. Ahead of her, Tafari stood up in the jeep and tried to swing his rifle around.

Too late, Annja thought, feeling the bridge tilt sickeningly.

The bridge twisted. Tafari kept his finger on the trigger, firing the whole way through. Bullets cut the air beside Annja, coming within inches.

Swinging wildly, she saw a white clay pot spill from a pack in the rear of Tafari's jeep.

The plague!

She made a grab but the jar slid over the edge of the failing bridge. The remaining ropes gave way, and Tafari's jeep flew out over the gorge. When it hit the ground, it exploded into an orange fireball.

Breathing hard, hardly believing she was still alive, Annja clung to the shredded ropes as Tafari's surviving warriors lined up at the gorge's edge and brought their weapons to bear.

Twisting, Annja swung through the air away from her enemies. She turned to meet the gorge wall with bended legs.

For a moment, sporadic fire hammered the gorge face around her. Then she heard rifles from above and knew that Garin and McIntosh were returning fire. Tafari's remaining men quickly lost interest in being a private shooting gallery and backed away from the gorge.

Annja held on to the rope, caught her breath and made the long climb to the top.

EPILOGUE

"When are you coming back home?" Doug Morrell asked.

Annja held the satellite phone to her ear and grinned as she watched Kamil and Bashir playing with the baby elephant in the middle of the Hausa village.

"Soon," she told him.

"The reason I'm asking," Doug said, "is because I'm getting some heat from the network. You've been in the news a lot lately, but you haven't done a piece for the show."

"Haven't found any monsters the show would be interested in," Annja said.

Tafari was dead. She, Garin and McIntosh had climbed down to the bottom of the gorge and made certain of that.

"Well, I may have one for you," Doug offered.

"Some place cool, I hope," Annja said. She'd had enough of the sun and the heat for a while. In Brooklyn, people were already starting to feel the first bite of winter. She was ready to see snow.

"Ever heard of the *wendigo?*" Doug asked.

"There's no such thing as a *wendigo,*" Annja said. "That's just a myth created by Native Americans who turned cannibal either by circumstance or by choice."

"My people think the show's fans want to see a *wendigo.* There's one in Canada," Doug insisted.

"Send Kristie."

"Nope. The last time we sent Kristie, she got frostbite. She wasn't happy. Her fans don't like it when she has to cover up in a parka. Her ratings took a definite dip. I got called on the carpet over the whole thing."

"Look, I'll give you a call in a couple days," Annja said. "When I've got a better handle on things here." She broke the connection before he could argue.

Annja walked through the village. Even though she didn't know the language she felt comfortable there. Not as if it was home, but it was a good place to stay.

The baby elephant was frustrated with all the children around it. Dipping its trunk into the gallon water bucket, it drained the bucket nearly dry. Kamil, Bashir and nearly every other child in the village held their breath expectantly.

The elephant unleashed a deluge of protest. The kids ran squealing, laughing and spluttering.

Stepping into the hut where Jaineba was being cared for, Annja saw the old woman was awake.

"You are still here?" Jaineba asked.

Annja frowned. "Why does everybody keep asking me that? It's like I'm not welcome."

The old woman smiled. "Come. Sit." She patted the ground beside her. Despite her age, she was recovering well from the gunshot wound to her shoulder.

Annja sat.

"Don't you worry. You're welcome. You'll always be welcome in this place. Everyone keeps asking you because everyone else has already gone," Jaineba said.

It was true. Garin had left almost immediately, taking a share of Anansi's treasure with him, of course. The plague pot hadn't been recovered, but an environmental team found no evidence of any contamination of any kind. Annja didn't know if the plague threat was ever real. She also didn't know what Garin was up to but she decided to let that thought go for now.

McIntosh had returned to Atlanta, riding high on commendations from the Department of Homeland Security. He'd invited her to visit his ranch some time. Annja thought she might really enjoy that. However, she didn't know if she would ever take him up on it.

Professor Hallinger had to report back to the university, and Jozua Ganesvoort had returned to Ile de Goree to see if he could plunder any more legends from his collections of captains' logs.

"I've got a lot to do with the Hausa tablets," Annja said. Most of them had been destroyed during Tafari's attack in the treasure room, but enough remained to add to some of the knowledge of trade in the area.

"Do you like that kind of work?" Jaineba asked. "Working all day in a room by yourself?"

"It's what I trained to do," Annja said.

"But it's not what you want to do now. Not entirely. You're a champion. You're going to meet people and help them with their problems. Help them have clearer eyes. Like you did with Tanisha."

"I didn't do anything with Tanisha," Annja protested. "She decided to stay here all on her own." Her part of the treasure would allow her to do that.

"That's not true," the old woman said. "If you hadn't come here seeking answers to your own puzzle, she'd have never found her true way."

Annja didn't argue. It didn't do any good to argue with Jaineba. She would either win or insist at a later date that she had.

The old woman dropped her hand to cover Annja's. "You're changing, child. Growing new eyes and seeing new things. You'll be more than you ever thought you could be, but you can't go back to being what you once were. That isn't what being a champion is about."

"How do you know all this?"

Jaineba smiled. "Because I've known champions before, and I know how they live." Her face saddened. "I know how they die, too. So you be careful out there, Annja Creed, while you're finding your way through your new life. Given the chance, I'd like to meet you again when you get back this way."

The sound of children's laughter invaded the hut and brought a smile to the old woman's face. Then she turned back to Annja.

"Your life is going to be hard at times," the old woman said. "Filled with some hard choices to make and hard things to see."

"I kind of get that, but I don't know what I'm supposed to do about it," Annja said.

"Well, child, what you should do is take time to wash the elephants."

Puzzled, Annja smiled and shook her head. "Take time to wash the elephants?"

"That's right."

Bashir parted the cloth covering the door and stuck his head into the room. "Hey, Annja."

"Hey, Bashir," Annja replied.

"Want to help wash the baby elephant?"

Annja looked at the old woman in surprise.

Jaineba nodded solemnly and shooed her away with one hand.

"Sure," Annja said.

"Great!" Bashir trotted over and extended his hand.

Annja let the boy help her up. Then she held Bashir's hand, enjoying the boy's excitement, and went out into the bright sunlight to wash the elephant.

Look for
THE SOUL STEALER
by AleX Archer

Annja Creed jumps at the chance to find a relic buried in the long undisturbed soil of Russia's frozen terrain. But the residents of the town claim they are being hunted by the ghost of a fallen goddess said to ingest souls. When Annja seeks to destroy the apparition, she discovers a horrifying truth—possibly leading her to a dead end....

Available May 2008 wherever you buy books.

Fearing the unknown can be scary. Facing the unknown can be deadly.

ROGUE Angel
AleX Archer
THE SOUL STEALER

GOLD EAGLE ®

GRA12TR